Skinny Lizzie

●

Second Chance

ELIZABETH WAITE
OMNIBUS

Skinny Lizzie

•

Second Chance

LITTLE, BROWN AND COMPANY

A Little, Brown Book
This edition first published in Great Britain by Little, Brown in 2000
The Elizabeth Waite Omnibus Copyright © Elizabeth Waite 2000

Previously published separately:
Skinny Lizzie first published in Great Britain in 1997 by Warner Books
Copyright © Elizabeth Waite 1993
Second Chance first published in Great Britain in 1995 by Warner Books
Copyright © Elizabeth Waite 1995

The moral right of the author has been asserted.

A CIP catalogue record for this book
is available from the British Library.

ISBN 0 316 85520 0

Printed and bound in Spain

Little, Brown and Company (UK)
Brettenham House
Lancaster Place
London WC2E 7EN

Skinny Lizzie

Chapter One

1932, London

'Aw, COME ON, Mum, if we don't get a move on we'll be late for the concert.'

'Oh, do shut up and stop fidgeting. It's no good us going out this early.'

Ten-year-old Lizzie Collins, thin as a whippet and just as quick, shook her long fair hair and accepted her mother's scolding with goodwill and cheerfulness. All the week she was able to take life as it came, but this was Saturday and Saturday evenings were different. They were the highlight of her life.

The Collins family lived in a typical back street in south-west London. Aunt Daisy took on the role of head of the family because each day her mother would be up early and off to her job at the Dawsons. Lizzie hated the Dawsons. They always seemed to come first with her mother. Half a crown a morning they paid her mum, and for that she did every menial task asked of her, even down to scrubbing the doorsteps.

Even Christmas morning was the same. Ever since Lizzie could remember, she and her younger brother Syd had walked to Balham with their mother. Down the back area steps they would troop

– into the kitchen, which was always a scene of great activity, women coming and going in all directions, calling Christmas greetings to their mother, not pausing long enough for an answer. Hanging her own and their coats on the hook behind the door and donning her flowered, wrap-around overall, their mother would hand tea cloths to Lizzie and Syd and then start work. Plates piled high, vegetable dishes and soup tureens, gravy boats and stands, platters so large that they needed two hands to lift them, glasses, cups and saucers.

She would fill the deep sink with hot water, adding soap flakes and a handful of common soda from the large brown earthenware jar which stood on the window sill, and then the washing-up would begin. With her arms in soapy water up to her elbows, her back and shoulders stooped low, she barely stopped to take a breath, let alone have a rest. She worked away until the stacks grew smaller, Lizzie and her brother hardly able to keep up with the drying.

The last stage was the worst. Every glass had to sparkle. Taking three dry glass cloths from a line strung beneath the shelf which was high above the kitchen range, Nellie Collins would help her two children. Each glass had to be held up to the light, checked that there were no smears or finger marks.

There was one thing in the Dawson's favour though. Mr Dawson always drove them home in his car, probably because he knew they were all too tired to walk.

Once home, Lizzie stopped envying the Dawson children their huge Christmas tree and toys and got ready to enjoy herself. All preparations for the Collinses' Christmas meal had been done days in advance and Aunt Daisy always had the cooking well under way. Lizzie loved Aunt Daisy, who was like a second mother to her. Daisy was her father's unmarried sister, and since he died Mum always said that if it hadn't been for Daisy they would have fared a lot worse.

Lizzie didn't miss her dad. He had hardly ever been at home anyway. Besides, there was always Leslie and Connie to turn to.

There were eleven years between her mother's first two children and Lizzie and only eighteen months between Lizzie and young Syd. Having Leslie for an older brother made up for the loss of her father. He adored Lizzie and she knew it, and Connie was the best of sisters. In fact, Lizzie felt so secure within the love of her mother, Aunt Daisy and her brothers and sister that it never entered her head that she should feel deprived.

Nellie Collins had been born within the sound of Bow Bells, making her a true cockney. Her actual place of birth had been The Cut or, to the uninformed, The Lambeth Walk, and she passionately loved London and its people. She had come to live in Tooting when she married Albert Collins, for better or worse as she had vowed – over the years it had turned out to be a bit of each. She was in her early forties now, with a tiny face to match her stature. She was still a good-looking, slim woman after having had four children and not exactly an easy life. Early on in her days in service to the upper classes, Nellie had formed a set of high principles. But, as time passed and circumstances worsened, she had tempered them with down-to-earth common sense. She loved her children and lived for them, though Lizzie worried her more than the other three put together. Lizzie was skinny, far too skinny.

Not that she was undernourished, far from it. Maybe they didn't always have the best of everything, but Daisy, who did all the cooking, was a marvellous cook and no one in the house ever went hungry. Daisy would say, 'Our Lizzie has hollow legs.'

'Wiry, that's what our Lizzie is,' Nellie would proudly tell folk. The truth was, she was never still for two minutes at a time. She had reckless energy and was brainy with it. Her teachers at school wrote glowing reports of her work at the end of each term, but still Nellie worried about her. She was far too strong-willed for her own good. She wanted the moon and the stars to go with it and God alone knows what else.

An atmosphere of excitement always hung over the house on Saturdays. The nearby Fairlight Hall, which was run by the Shaftesbury Association, was known far and wide. Church services, Sunday school, prayer meetings, mothers' meetings, Girls'

Brigade, Boys' Brigade, magic lantern shows, all were weekly events at Fairlight Hall, but the Saturday concerts were the favourites. These were mixed entertainments with singers, dancers, comics and magicians. Short sketches always seemed to include a rich old gentleman with a heavily bandaged, gouty foot which the maid would accidentally trip over, and although this sketch in various forms would be performed each week, the feigned extreme pain on the face of the old man and his blasphemous curses never failed to bring roars of laughter and loud hooting from the audience. An entrance charge was made for these shows; sixpence for seats at the front of the hall and threepence for seats at the back. The Collins family couldn't always afford to go – until, that is, Mother got her job when Toc H decided to sell refreshments during the intervals.

Although Toc H was started as a club for soldiers during the 1914–18 war, it continued to do good works after the war, particularly in poor city areas. So, when a local member had approached Nellie Collins with the offer of an evening's work each week for the princely wage of three half-crowns, Nellie gasped in surprise and pleasure and accepted at once.

By this time Leslie had joined the Army, and Connie was 'walking out' with her boyfriend. So at about eight o'clock, Aunt Daisy, Mum, Syd and Lizzie would set off for Fairlight Hall. Their first job was to set out rows and rows of cups and saucers, for it was a very large hall, packed every week with eager audiences. Then, as the lights were dimmed and the opening musical number began, an official of Toc H would find them empty seats in the house. Often Syd and Lizzie ended up sitting on the floor between the gangways, but they didn't care; they got to see the concert for nothing. During the interval, it would be Aunt Daisy with her arms deep in soapy water at the sink doing the washing-up, while Syd and Lizzie dried. Nellie thought she had the easiest job, collecting the dirty crocks on large tin trays, making numerous trips from hall to kitchen and back again. All four of them were given a free drink, with iced or Chelsea buns for the two children. As a bonus, any refreshments which remained unsold were given to Nellie free of charge, plus those precious three silver half-crowns. Imagine! It took her three whole mornings to earn that amount at the Dawsons!

When saying her prayers on a Saturday night, Lizzie never forgot to say, 'God bless the Toc H.'

Between having their midday meal and getting ready to go to the concert, the shopping had to be done. It was always Lizzie who accompanied her mother on these expeditions to Tooting market. There were times when Lizzie found the bargaining that went on a great source of amusement, but on Saturdays she felt irritable and hoped her mother wouldn't take too long deciding just what she was going to buy.

It was a busy scene that confronted Nellie and her daughter on this particular evening, much as it was every Saturday evening. The open-fronted shops, the street traders and barrow boys, all plying their different trades, shouting their wares, each a keen competitor for customers. Shopping for food amongst the working class was undertaken on a daily basis, mainly because their income was earned and paid daily. The prosperity promised in 1918 at the signing of the Armistice had never come about. It was 1932 now and still men walked long distances in search of employment. One-day odd-jobs found eager takers; even one good day's work and pay made life look a little rosier.

'Are we going to the market first, Mum?' Lizzie wanted to know.

Her mother shook her head, 'We'll try the Mitcham Road first. Meat's the most important, we can get our vegetables on the way back.'

Late-night shopping at the butchers, of which there were at least four in the Mitcham Road, had become a battle of wits. Those well enough off to be choosy about their weekend joints would have shopped earlier in the day, but at this time of night it was a different matter. It was essential that the butcher sold off all his perishable items by the time he pulled down the shutters that night. Anything left would definitely not be in an edible state come Monday morning. Better to sell it off cheaply; a blessing in disguise for the poor.

Nellie had stopped at two butchers, hesitating while Lizzie impatiently scuffed her feet. She put a loving arm about her daughter as they walked on.

'Don't worry, love, they'll start auctioning the joints off soon, then we won't be long. We shan't be late for the concert, I promise.'

True enough, further along the road, a crowd of women had assembled on the pavement in front of the next butcher's shop. The proprietor was deliberately keeping them waiting, allowing the tension to build. The laid-out enamel trays were still full of meat, although the fresh parsley, arranged so neatly between the rows at the start of trading early that morning, was now visibly wilting. The men working at the blocks still wore their blue and white striped aprons, so clean and fresh at the day's start, now stained and bloody. The master butcher had donned a straw boater before coming out, setting it at a jaunty angle on his head. To his upper lip he had attached a false waxed moustache. This always made Lizzie laugh as it did all the other children in the crowd.

The November evening had turned bitterly cold, having rained heavily earlier on in the day. The pavement on which the women now stood was not only wet but had begun to harden into ice. Hardly any one amongst them was wearing boots or shoes that were weather-proof; their toes and fingers were stiff with cold; their winter coats far too thin to keep out the biting wind. Cold, tired, with hardly more than a few shillings in their purse each would be hoping for – no, praying for – the chance to pick up a bargain. In her mind's eye each woman was already seeing a joint roasting in the oven for tomorrow's dinner, big enough to feed the whole family and, with any luck, enough left over to be served up with bubble and squeak for Monday's meal.

That's the dream they had. It was often not the reality. Many a woman went home with her shopping-bag holding little more than odds and ends: a scrag of mutton, a piece of leg of beef (fit only for stewing), or a bit of belly of pork. Still, these working-class women were marvellous cooks, producing meals of great nourishment, roughened toil-worn hands making the lightest of pastry for a pie.

Finally, the master butcher came to the forefront, placed a large wooden crate dead centre to the waiting women, climbed up on to it and raised his megaphone to his mouth. The megaphone made his voice audible even at the back of the crowd where Lizzie stood with her mother. His patter started; a few bawdy jokes which were lost on those cold women, who were after food, not comedy: 'Git your money ready, ladies, I'm gonna give you all a treat tonight. Move in closer, there will be bargains for everyone.' Two assistants now took up their places on either side of the crate on which the butcher was perched, armed and ready with a stack of brown paper bags. When a price had been agreed and a buyer found, the meat would be tipped into a carrier bag, held up by one of the assistants. No effort was made to wrap each item separately, this being deemed an unnecessary luxury for the poor.

'Look 'ere me darlings, Sunday joint, sausages for the ol' man's breakfast and dripping to put hairs on yer chest.' Loud and rough, his voice droned on. Most in the crowd had heard it all before; it was the meat on offer that they were interested in, not his commentary. Still he kept trying to gain their good-will, working hard to induce amusement, even hoping for a laugh, but only provoking the odd half-suppressed giggle. He gave up. With an exaggerated sigh he shouted, 'Right, now to the serious business . . .'

He picked up an empty enamel dish. Silently he turned to the display of meat in front of which he was perched. Taking down a rib of beef, he held it aloft for a moment before placing it into the dish; two breasts of lamb were added with great cere-mony, a thin end of belly of pork, two long strings of sausages, and to top the lot a wax packet contain-ing beef dripping. Lowering the dish to the eye level of the women at the front of the crowd, brandishing the contents in front of them, he quietly said, 'Eight bob.' No response. Straightening himself upright, he yelled, 'First hand up gets the lot for seven and six.' Again no response. Everyone knew it didn't pay to rush. 'Six shillings,' his voice boomed out even without the use of his megaphone. No one in the crowd uttered a word. Leaning forward, the butcher focused his stare on a fat woman. 'Look luv, didn't you hear what I said?' Raising his voice even higher, 'Six bob the lot.' The woman shifted uncomfortably, saying nothing, averting her eyes away from his stare. 'Well, I'll to go hell and back. You lot can walk up and down this street till midnight, you won't find a better bargain.' He spoke quickly, 'Tell yer what I'll do. Do yer like offal? Yer should do, it's bloody good for yer.' Lowering the dish he scooped up a large handful of liver from a tin pail which stood on a bench to the left of him. Into the dish it went, slithering and slipping over the strings of sausages, now entwined amongst the red meat. 'Wait for it. I'm not finished yet.' A whole shoulder of lamb was quickly placed on top of the now overful dish. 'That's the lot.' This decided, there was a long pause before the butcher, his endurance now pushed to the limit, shouted, 'Now it's got to be worth three half-crowns of anybody's money.' Setting his feet more widely apart, he drew a deep breath. Again he threw out the challenge. 'Seven and sixpence.' Self-consciously, the women looked at each other. There wasn't one amongst them who wouldn't have dearly loved to call out, 'I'll have it,' but three to four shillings at most was their mark. Frustrated to the point of anger, the butcher lost his temper; as yet he had not made one sale since starting his auctioneering. 'Right, who'll take the bloody lot for nothing!'

'My Mum will. My Mum will.'

Lizzie's voice rang out sharp and clear. Nellie put her arm out to restrain this impetuous daughter of hers but Lizzie had gone through the crowd like lightning, not slowing down until she cleared the ring of pushing women. Then the audacity of what she had done dawned on her. Lizzie's heart was racing. 'Dear Jesus, let the ground open and swallow me up,' she prayed.

Nervously, she looked up at the great hulk of the butcher towering above her, still holding that dratted dish of meat between his hands. Hastily she dropped her eyes and hung her head. The silence which followed seemed to last forever.

Then the mumbling from the crowd began. 'Gawd bless the poor little mite,' one woman called out. Then the fat woman, who had been made to feel a fool earlier on, decided to put her twopenny worth in.

'Gawd bless her my arse. Cheeky little cow. Bloody good 'iding is what she needs.'

Normally Lizzie would have rounded on the woman, quick to repay in kind. Not now, though. She felt sick. Bending his knees but keeping his back perfectly straight, the butcher brought his face down almost level with Lizzie's. Her nostrils filled with the smell of dried blood coming from his stained apron and she felt even more sick.

Speaking gently, with a soft, quiet voice, the big man said, 'For your cheek, love, it's all yours.'

Straightening himself up, he turned to an assistant. 'Hold open a carrier,' he ordered. Slowly, deliberately, he tipped the whole contents of that enamel dish into the paper carrier-bag; liver clung to the sides of the dish, he removed it pushing with the flat of his hand. Now, for the first time, he stepped down from the crate, folding over the top of the brown paper bag. Not trusting the handles, he held it out towards Lizzie. Using both of her arms, she clutched it to her chest but found she couldn't move. She remained rooted to the spot, staring at the man.

'Off you go missy, you ain't as daft as you look,' and with that he laughed out loud.

This comical remark suddenly made Lizzie relax. She turned and walked back towards her mother. The women parted to make a path for her, and she stared insolently at the lot of them.

'You little bugger showing me up like that!' One of her mother's hands grabbed her, the other raised in anger to strike. Instinctively, Lizzie ducked. Still the blow caught the side of her head, leaving the ear stinging and the tears burning at the back of her eyes.

Rebellion seethed in her as her mother pushed and shoved her along the pavement. Hiccuping, trying to stifle her sobs, Lizzie asked herself angrily what had she done wrong? The butcher had offered the meat free and surely you had to be out of your mind not to accept an offer like that. Why was her mum so mad at her? She forced the tears back. She was not going to cry; she would not let her mother see how much she had hurt her. 'I'm never gonna come with her again to get the rotten shopping,' she vowed. Still holding the carrier-bag tightly to her chest but trying to think how she could get rid of it, they turned the corner of the street into the darkness of a side road.

'Lizzie, I'm sorry. I'm sorry,' Lizzie heard the sob

in her mother's voice and realized that she, too, was crying.

This sudden change of attitude not only baffled Lizzie but also set her off crying again.

'Can we go 'ome now,' she snivelled.

'Don't cry, don't cry,' her mother implored her. 'I didn't mean to hit you, truly I didn't.'

She relieved Lizzie of the dreaded carrier bag, totally ignoring the wet stain on the front of her coat caused by Lizzie having clutched it too closely, allowing the blood to soak through from its unwrapped contents, and dropped it whole into her large patchwork shopping-bag. Before moving, Nellie drew her young daughter into her arms and hugged her so tightly Lizzie rocked on her feet. Lizzie decided she would never understand adults, they seemed to have their emotions well and truly mixed up.

Walking quickly now, Lizzie's hand was clutching tightly to her mother's free one. Back in the brightly lit Mitcham Road, the gutter was packed with barrows. Barrows piled high with fruit; barrows offering vegetables, salad, flowers, even shell fish; the barrow boys had it all.

Nellie ignored them all, making a beeline for the cooked-meat shop. Pungent, delicious smells filled the air yards before they actually reached the shop. What a layout! Pigs' trotters, faggots in hot gravy, rissoles, shiny fat sausages, pease pudding, meat pies in all shapes and sizes, even pigs' heads split in half and roasted – the choice was endless. Lizzie's mouth was watering; suddenly she felt very, very hungry.

'What would you like, love?'

Lizzie couldn't believe her ears. Sometimes on a Saturday evening while shopping, her mum would buy a tuppenny pie and they'd have half each, eating it walking along. But it didn't often happen. Usually they passed this shop; her mother's finances didn't stretch to shop-bought cooked meats. Now she was being offered a choice. What a decision! Inside the shop nothing mattered at that moment but the fact that they were going to have something hot and tasty to eat.

Behind the counter an imposing lady with a fat red face smiled broadly at them as she asked, 'What's it to be, missus?'

Nellie had only a moment of indecision. 'Four meat pies, please.'

'Mince or steak and kidney?'

'Oh, steak and kidney, please.'

'Blimey,' the word came quietly from Lizzie's lips, they were the dearest and Mum was buying four!

Wrapping the hot pies in two large sheets of white paper the woman beamed as she handed the parcel to Nellie.

'They're nice. You'll enjoy them,' she said.

Nellie smiled and nodded as she bent to place the pies most carefully on the top of her shopping-bag. Then, opening her purse, she paused and impulsively said, 'And one hot saveloy for us to eat now, please. Oh, and would you mind cutting it in half?'

' 'Course, I will, luv.'

Taking a long, black-handled knife from the bench behind her, the woman easily sliced the large, red, spicy sausage into two equal parts, then, tearing off a strip of white paper, she wrapped each uncut end of the saveloy, leaving the hot, steaming end protruding.

Handing one half to Nellie and the other half to Lizzie, she asked, 'What 'ave you done my darling to deserve this treat?'

Lizzie smiled but didn't answer; she was impatient to get her teeth into the fleshy sausage.

'Well now, that'll be one and a penny, four pies at threepence each and one saveloy a penny.'

Nellie counted out the money and said, 'Thanks a lot.'

'You're welcome,' said the woman. 'Tat-ta lovey, 'ope to see you again.'

Lizzie, her mouth filled with hot sausage, grinned. Then, as chirpy as any sparrow, she called back over her shoulder, 'I hope so too. 'Bye for now.'

Nellie, having finished eating her half saveloy, hoisted her heavy shopping bag up into her arms and mother and daughter quickened their pace as they rounded the Broadway and made for the covered-in market.

Lizzie knew the routine off by heart. Passing Emanuel's and their beautiful layout of imported fruit and vegetables, 'Far too expensive,' her mother muttered.

'Hello, Jack,' she called as she propped her shopping-bag against the front of Smith's stall, where the sheet of imitation green grass hung down. 'Got an empty box for me?'

'Sure, Nellie, help yourself,' swarthy looking Jack Smith called in answer as he came towards them.

Nellie went behind the stall into the depths of the area at the back used for storing empty crates and unpacking them at the start of each day. She appeared a moment later, holding a light-weight wooden box; the bottom was firm but the sides were only slates of wood. Jack Smith bent low and lined the bottom with a thick wad of newspapers.

'Potatoes, Nellie?'

'Yes please, Jack, five pounds, and a pound of carrots and onions mixed.'

These items having been weighed and tipped into the box, Nellie added, 'One swede, two parsnips and a cabbage. That's the lot, thanks,' she said, opening her purse to pay.

'No fruit this week, Nellie?'

'I dunno,' she was slow to decide.

Reaching for a large orange as a specimen, Jack told her, 'These are as sweet as a nut. Penny each, but ter you, seven for a tanner.' Before Nellie even had time to agree, he crouched down and from beneath the stall produced a cardboard box. 'There's some specky apples here and a few loose bananas. Want the lot for tuppence?'

'Go on then, I'll have the oranges as well.' There was a wide grin on Lizzie's face as the fruit was added to the rapidly filling box.

'Right, that's one and ninepence the lot.'

Nellie took a florin from her purse and, as she passed it over to Jack, she exclaimed, 'Oh God, I've forgotten the celery.' Aunt Daisy would have been upset. Sunday tea was not complete without a stick of celery.

'Penny more to pay then, Nell. Fourpence a head it is,' he said as he totted it up.

Wrapped in newspaper, the great bunch of celery topped the vegetables and fruit, its green leaves, looking bright and fresh, sticking out from the rolled newspaper.

'Can we go home now, Mum?' Lizzie pleaded.

Opening her purse again, Nellie said, 'Just run up to Eggee's for me, there's a good girl. Get two pennyworth of pieces a bacon and that will be our lot.' Seeing the desperation in Lizzie's eyes, her mother added gently, 'It won't take you two minutes. We'll be home with plenty of time to eat our pies before we set off for the concert. Go on, love, I'll wait here with all the shopping.'

Lizzie took the threepenny piece from her mother's outstretched hand and ran off. She didn't mind going to Eggee's stall because it fascinated her. As the name implied, Eggee sold eggs. It was an extra large stall, divided into two halves. On the egg side was a grading machine, its many lights giving off warmth as brown, white and speckled eggs gently came down in a continuous line, to be sent off in different directions according to their weight and size. Mid-week her mother often sent her here with a basin to buy cracked eggs. She always came willingly, knowing that there would then be scrambled eggs for their tea. Besides she and Syd had great fun making the toast; kneeling in front of the bars of the grate, red hot from the range fire, they would use the long-handled, three-pronged toasting forks, daring each other to get closer all the time until the slices of bread ended up with burnt stripes. Making the toast was always a good laugh. No – it wasn't that she minded running the errand; she just didn't want to be late for the concert.

It was to the opposite side of the stall that Lizzie needed to go now. Every variety of cheese you could think of was sold here, plus bacon. Lizzie liked Mr Eggee. She was repeatedly scolded by her mother for not calling him by his proper name which was Mr Goldberg, but to her he was Mr Eggee and there was no disrespect in calling him that. He was a heavy-set Jewish man with black hair and bright dark eyes which now had a gleam of amusement in them behind his rimless spectacles as he watched Lizzie approach.

His voice was friendly as he called, 'Hallo, Skinny Lizzie.'

'Hallo, Mr Eggee,' she returned.

'Is it bacon you were wanting?'

'Yes, please. Mummy said, may she have twopennyworth of pieces?'

'Your mamma certainly may. Pieces, we have plenty. 'Tis a good time you choose to come.' Turning, he tore down a large greaseproof paper bag from a string of them hanging on a steel rail. Walking to the slicing machine, he began to fill the bag from a white enamel tray which lay beneath the cutters. Too small to be sold as rashers, he regularly sold these pieces quite cheaply.

'There you are then, young Lizzie. Now be sure my regards you give to your mother.'

Reaching up, she was given the bag of bacon pieces plus one penny change from the threepenny bit. 'I will, Mr Eggee. 'Bye, thank you.'

Her mother was right, Mr Goldberg was a kindly, generous man, and Lizzie liked him because he was always so friendly. There were not many she would allow to call her Skinny Lizzie, not without giving tit for tat. But with Mr Eggee Lizzie knew that it was said affectionately.

Aunt Daisy always maintained that these pieces of bacon were the best value to be found this side of heaven. Firstly, she would sort out all the lean pieces which provided a good breakfast for them all. Next, the thick ends would have onions and sage added, rolled in a suet crust and boiled in a pudding cloth to create a good dinner. Lastly, the real fat lumps were rendered down in the slow oven at the side of the kitchen range to supply dripping for their toast.

Still waiting by Smith's greengrocery stall, Nellie looked rather woebegone. 'What's the matter, Mum?' asked Lizzie.

'Nothing, love, a bit weary, that's all.'

Making a space amongst the vegetables, Lizzie placed the bacon in the box. Now, how were they going to get this lot home?

'Come this side of me Lizzie.' Balancing the shopping-bag in the crook of her right arm, Nellie placed four fingers of her free hand underneath the first row of slats on the side of the wooden box, leaving her thumb on top. With a nod of her head she made a gesture for Lizzie to do likewise. 'Lift,' she instructed. Walking with the box between them required bodily effort. Nellie, although only five feet four inches tall, was a good deal taller than Lizzie. Unevenly balanced and looking peculiar to say the least, they made their way out of the market.

Outside, the weather had turned decidedly worse; the harsh wind was bitter, threatening a severe storm. They had to wait for their chance to cross the main road which was still busy with traffic. Trams rumbling, clanging and swaying, travelled in both directions. Lorries, cars, push-bikes, everyone seemed hell-bent on greater speed. At last there came a break in the traffic and they stepped forward, walking awkwardly, and, more by luck than judgment, they reached the far pavement in safety. They stopped a moment and drew a deep breath.

In Selkirk Road, the jellied eel shop was now open. Nellie called a halt.

'Put the box down, love.'

'We're not gonna have eels as well, are we?' Lizzie wanted to know.

'No, we're not.' Taking two pennies from the pocket of her coat, Nellie held them out to her daughter. 'Just go in and ask Beccy to put twopennyworth of mash in a bag.'

Of all the shops, the eel shop was Lizzie's favourite. Fish and chips was all right, even good sometimes, but pie and mash was better, and eels and mash with its green liquor was the best treat of all. The liquor (or gravy) was supposedly parsley sauce, but, as Aunt Daisy said, no parsley ever made her sauce as green. It was a well-guarded secret of the Harrington family who owned the business. On the rare occasions that Syd and Lizzie were given a penny each at suppertime, Syd would opt for a pennyworth of chips, while Lizzie would go for a penny basin every time. All the basin contained was mashed potato and the green liquor for a penny. Eels were three pence a portion. At the rear of the shop, there were many marble-topped tables with high-backed benches for seating; each table had its own huge tin pepper and salt pots and, best of all, chilli vinegar. Chilli vinegar was not like the vinegar they had at home; small red strips of cayenne pepper floated, clearly visible through the glass bottle. Seated at one such table, in the noisy, steamy atmosphere, greedily spooning the liquor, lavished with pepper and the hot, spicy vinegar, into her mouth, always hoping that an odd piece of eel had slipped in, was a treat indeed to Lizzie.

'Lizzie, come down here,' Beccy Harrington, the daughter of the shop owner, had spotted her in the crowded shop. Blousy, very fat, common even, but with a heart of gold was a good description of Rebecca. She and her parents lived directly opposite the Collins family. 'What-cha want, ducks?' Beccy asked as she bent low towards Lizzie.

'Would yer put twopennyworth of mash in a bag for me mum, please?'

'No bother, luv, wait there.'

Within two minutes, Beccy was back, handing Lizzie a parcel that was not only heavy, but very, very hot. Taking the two pennies, she bent and planted a smacking kiss on Lizzie's cheek.

'Off to the concert, are you?' Without waiting for a reply, Beccy pushed Lizzie in the direction of the shop doorway. 'Night, night Lizzie. See yer in the morning. God bless,' Beccy called affectionately.

'Night, Beccy. Thanks ever so much.'

Turning at last into Graveney Road where they lived, they found it deserted. Not teeming with children as was normal. No clanging of meat hooks against steel hoops, no girls skipping, chanting their timeless rhymes, no tops being slashed down the centre of the road by means of home-made whips. The cold weather brought a change of character to the street, giving it a desolate air. For once, the youngsters had obeyed their parents, staying indoors in the warmth of the family kitchen. Lizzie and her mother stooped and placed the wooden box on the pavement. Lizzie unlatched the front garden gate, took the shopping-bag from her mother's arm, and went ahead up the path to the front door. Using her knee to lever the box waist high, Nellie held it in front of her stomach, one hand on each side. Pushing with her hip and bottom, she got the front door open and called out, 'Daisy, come an' give us a hand, will you?'

The kitchen door opened, the lights from the gas mantles in the room beyond streamed out, lighting up the passage. Daisy's bulky frame filled the doorway. A few steps forward and Daisy stopped dead in her tracks.

'God above,' she exclaimed, 'whatcha do, rob a bank?' Nellie leaned against the wall, suddenly helpless with laughter, while tears streamed down her face. It took her a couple of minutes to collect herself and to be able to speak, during which time Daisy stood watching her dumbfoundedly.

'Help us get it all in,' Nellie managed to say, and then, speaking as if to herself, she added, 'you're never gonna believe it.'

Young Syd, hearing all the commotion, put down the comic he had been reading and came into the hallway. He was feeling irritable, his mum seemed to have been out for ages, and he was sure that Lizzie would goad him. 'I've had half a hot meat pie,' she would tease, 'it was ever so good.' Well, if she had, he hoped it choked her.

'I'm starving, Mum,' he whined.

'All right, son, give me a minute and we'll all eat.'

Grudgingly, he helped his auntie drag the box

down the passage and into the kitchen. Nellie worked as she talked. Four plates were placed in the oven at the side of the kitchen range. Daisy and she began to take the meat, piece by piece, from the sodden, bloody carrier-bag as Nellie told her tale, right down to the last detail. Lizzie, sitting on the fire box at the end of the fender warming her feet and holding her hands out to the red glowing coals, was tired of listening to them. Endless questions and answers.

'She never did,' said Aunt Daisy for the umpteenth time.

'She did, brazen as you like.'

'Mum. You've bin all through it a dozen times. Can we 'ave our pies?'

'Yeah, pie and mash,' Syd added, glinting at his sister as he sat up to the table. At last. No one was talking. The pies were good, much better than the twopenny minced meat ones, Lizzie decided. The pastry was fluffy, flaky, the inside piping hot, with a generous amount of meat and thick rich gravy. Definitely worth the extra penny if you could afford it.

Her plate now empty, Lizzie sat back and smiled to herself. It was because of her that her mum was able to buy those pies; it couldn't have been such a bad thing she'd done. No. 'I'd do it again an' all,' she promised herself, but she was level-headed enough to fathom that chances like that don't come twice in a lifetime.

*

Eventually they were ready. Aunt Daisy, as ever looking as neat as a pin, used her long hat-pin to secure her navy blue felt hat securely to her head. Mum had her best coat on, a hand-me-down from the Dawsons which secretly Lizzie admitted looked very nice, the fur collar framing her mother's lovely face and keeping her ears warm. Syd and Lizzie brought up the rear, each warmly clothed, long scarves wound around their necks. They all set off for Fairlight Hall and their Saturday concert.

Chapter Two

THE NEXT DAY was Sunday. Grandma's day. Grandma Collins was a small, weather-beaten woman only just turned sixty, but years in the open air selling flowers from her stall at the Broadway had dried up her skin so that she looked older than she was. Her shiny silver hair swept up on top of her head and her firm mouth reminded Lizzie of Queen Mary.

Harriet Collins had rarely, if ever, shown either of her two children the affection they deserved. Widowed while still young, she had become hard and bitter. Yet somehow Daisy had grown into a cheerful loving woman, despite the fact she had never married, and Albert had grown into a jolly, outgoing man, charming all the women with whom he came into contact. Half the time his affairs were no more than infatuation, but for Nellie, his wife, each new affair was disastrous. Disastrous because she truly loved him and suffered terrible rejection and humiliation.

Seeing Nellie's distress had brought anguish to her mother-in-law and she had often prayed that Nellie would come to terms with the inescapable facts of life about her son. When, however, Albert Collins was involved in a fatal accident, Harriet had

reflected bitterly that maybe she could be held somewhat responsible for her son's attitude to life. Yet,
even at the funeral, she had not felt able to voice her
feelings. Warmth and sentiment were lost to her.
Much as she admired her daughter-in-law, even
loved her, and longed to relieve her own pent-up
emotion, she could not get the words out. 'Perhaps,'
she told herself wearily, 'I've left it too late.'

Only Lizzie was the exception. 'Mischievous little
monkey,' her gran was often heard to mutter, but
those cold eyes would soften at she gazed at her
youngest granddaughter. Only Lizzie, with her
exasperating ways, was able to penetrate the invisible barrier and somehow manage to get her gran to
show her feelings.

Harriet Collins came in from the scullery, carrying
a scuttle of coal, as Lizzie opened the front door of
her grandma's cottage.

'Hallo, Gran. Mum says dinner will be on the
table for one o'clock and we've not ter be late.'

'She did, did she?' Harriet dumped three big
lumps of coal on to the glowing fire and then
upended the colander into the centre. The fire hissed
and steam rose as the wet vegetable peelings and
stale tealeaves banked down the heat. 'An' what 'ave
you been up to this week, Lizzie?' Gran asked as she
twisted round from the hearth and got to her feet.

Lizzie raised her eyebrows and put her hand over
her mouth. 'Eh, I don't think I better tell you. Wait

till you see what we've got for dinner today. Aunt Daisy said we can 'ave a choice.'

'A choice? What of – a stew or a pie, I suppose.'

'No, Gran, real roast. Honest. You'll see. Me, Mum and Aunt Daisy will tell you all about it. So come on, get yer hat and coat on.'

You bet they'll tell Gran the whole story and it'll take them for ever, Lizzie told herself. She was getting a bit sick and tired of her aunt's probing of every little detail and Syd's quizzing of the affair.

While Gran was getting herself ready, Lizzie had a good old poke around. To her, Gran's cottage appeared like something out of a story book. Silverdore Terrace has just five cottages, set beside Blunt's market and almost opposite the central hall in Mitcham Road. It was just a few minutes' walk from Tooting Broadway, and yet to anyone discovering these dwellings for the first time, it was as if time had passed by this tiny corner of South London. Outmoded, ignored, but loved by their elderly occupants, each cottage boasted a hundred-foot-long front garden. There was nothing at the back except a small yard, an outside lavatory and a cold-water tap. The front of the dwellings made up for this. A joy to behold at any season of the year, flower beds, flowering shrubs, and tall hollyhocks were tended with love and efficiency. In spring, flowers in abundance would nod their heads in the pale sunshine, while in summer, rose bushes bore blooms of every conceivable colour – pale pink, dark pink, white, yellow, peach, orange and every shade of red, all seemed to bloom for ever. There were lavender bushes and hydrangeas with flowers as big as dinner plates. Gran even had a holly bush in her garden and as Lizzie looked this cold Sunday morning at the bright red berries with which it was covered, she mulled over in her mind once again the difference between Silverdore Terrace and the street of back-to-back houses where she lived. It was only a two-up-and-two-down dwelling and the front door opened directly into the living room, but to Lizzie the garden alone made it a special place.

When they got to Graveney Road it was half-past twelve and Gran followed her usual procedure. She went upstairs and locked herself in the bathroom where she used the toilet and washed her hands, then went on up the extra five stairs into Nellie's big front bedroom and laid her hat and coat on the bed. This ritual took about ten minutes. Afterwards, she came downstairs and went straight through into the kitchen. Outside in the scullery, Daisy would grin at Nellie and under their breath, in unison, they would murmur, 'Inspection over.'

Connie had already laid the table for seven; Bill, her young man, having been invited to Sunday dinner this week.

'Sit up, all of you,' Nellie inclined her head towards Grandma and at the same time opened the kitchen door and called up the passage, 'Come on, Syd, and you, Lizzie, sit up at the table.'

As they took their places, Daisy brought the vegetable dishes in from the scullery, and set them down in the centre of the table. Nellie, her face red and wisps of hair escaping from her usually immaculate coiled plaits pinned each side of her face, entered, carrying a huge willow-patterned meat dish on which lay the now roasted rib of beef and the shoulder of lamb which she set down in front of Bill.

'Would you do the honours please, Bill?' Nellie quietly asked. 'I always feel a man carves meat much better than us women do.'

Bill Baldwin was grateful to Nellie; he had felt a bit out of place amongst all these ladies but she had set him at ease. 'I'd be honoured,' he told her as he picked up the carving knife and bone-handled steel which Nellie had set down beside the dish. With an exaggerated flourish he criss-crossed the blade of the knife back and forth against the hardened rolled steel, winking at young Syd as he did so. Satisfied that the knife was sharp enough, he asked, 'Now, Mrs Collins senior, what is it to be, beef or lamb?'

Nothing had been missed out today. Nellie had chopped the dried mint which hung in bags above the copper, adding a liberal amount of sugar before pouring on the hot vinegar; Daisy had dug up a root of horseradish from the backyard and had persevered with the grater, even though the strong herb had brought tears to her eyes. Daisy handed the plates around and soon there was a heaped plate set before each of them and they all began to eat.

The conversation was noisy until Aunt Daisy

pleaded, 'Let's eat up while it's all hot. You can all ask questions and get your answers,' she said, looking directly at her mother, 'when we get to pudding.'

The kitchen was warm, the fire burnt brightly as they continued to sit around the table. Apple pie and custard had been consumed by each of them, despite the huge first course, and now the tea tray with its large brown earthenware teapot stood centre of the table and a Sunday-best cup and saucer stood in front of each person. Daisy removed the woollen tea-cosy and began to fill the cups, having first poured in the milk. Explanations were over. Gran had gasped as Nellie had, for the hundredth time according to Lizzie, gone through the whole story. Connie and Bill thought it was hilarious.

Lizzie had had enough of being made to feel a fool. 'Well, Gran, what would you 'ave done?' she asked in a loud voice. 'There was this bloke propped up on a wooden box looking right comical an' all I can tell yer, what with his false moustache an' daft straw hat, doing his best to sell a load of meat. What 'appened? He got carried away. Nobody could afford all what he put in that dish and he ended up losing his temper. T'was his own daft fault. Showing off he were. "Who'll 'ave the bloody lot for nothing",' Lizzie mimicked. 'What yer supposed ter do? Stand there all posh an' quiet like, pretend you 'aven't heard him. Only a half-wit would do that. Anyway, I noticed you all enjoyed your dinner. Free or not, it never worried any of you.' Lizzie's tirade came to an end. It had to; she had run out of breath. Everyone glanced at each other.

Nellie finally broke the silence, 'Oh Lizzie love, we didn't mean to upset you.'

Then Daisy's voice held a note of pleading as she said, 'Of course we didn't, come on now, give us a smile.'

Lizzie's temper had burned itself out; slowly a smile came to her lips and quickly became a great grin as she felt Syd kick her leg beneath the table.

'Oh Lizzie! Lizzie!' Gran moved her face until it was touching Lizzie's and then pressed her lips against her granddaughter's cheek.

Dumbly Lizzie raised her hand and felt the place where her Gran had planted a kiss. Suddenly, everything was wonderful. Great. She began to laugh. The laughter was infectious, and soon everyone was laughing fit to bust. As Harriet Collins wiped her face, she cast her glance ceilingwards. It didn't do to have a favourite but how could she help it? One in a million was this harum-scarum granddaughter of hers. If she could hold on to that temper of hers she'd go far. Got a sensible head on her shoulders, our Lizzie has, if only life would give her a few breaks. One thing was for sure, no one could ever say that Lizzie was backward in coming forward. Harriet was surprised to find herself admitting that she loved her youngest granddaughter with all of her heart.

It was nearly dark when Lizzie got home from

school on Friday afternoon to find Syd sitting on the doorstep.

'What are you doing out here?' she asked.

He didn't answer and she tutted as she pushed by him. Opening the letterbox she slipped her hand in and pulled on the length of string which hung down with the key inside the door.

She unlocked the door and pushed it open with her knee. 'Come on Syd, you go first and light the gas mantle and as soon as I've got me coat off I'll make us a drink.'

Syd was on his feet now, but he hung back and hesitated. It dawned on Lizzie that Syd was afraid of the dark. Mum and Aunt Daisy were away at their mothers' meeting. They went every Friday afternoon to the Central Hall and didn't get home until about five-thirty. It was still only half-past four. If Lizzie hadn't come straight home, what would Syd have done? Stayed sitting on the cold flagstones? He knew the front door key was on the string. She wanted to hug him, but Syd wouldn't stand for being mollycoddled.

'I'll go first,' she said softly. 'What would you like, a cup of tea or Oxo?'

'I'd rather have Oxo, an' Lizzie, I'm starving. 'Ave we got to wait till Mum comes home before we get our tea?'

Lizzie laughed out loud. 'We'll find something,' she assured him.

Ten minutes later, after Lizzie had put the poker into the banked-down fire, the two of them sat on the hearth rug, each with a thick slice of bread and dripping, smothered with pepper and salt and a mug of scalding-hot Oxo.

'Wonder what we got for tea,' Syd said as he sniffed hungrily at the appetizing smell that was coming from the side oven.

'Smells like hot-pot,' Lizzie told him. They both liked that, plenty of vegetables, dumplings and gravy.

'Hope we've finished our tea before Tim and Joey come round,' Syd muttered to himself, while staring into the fire.

'Oh no!' Lizzie exclaimed, very annoyed. 'It's not bath night for the Hurleys tonight, is it?'

'So Tim said when I left him. "See you later for our bath", that's what he said.'

'I wonder why Polly never mentioned it,' Lizzie mulled this over in her mind.

The Hurleys lived in Selkirk Road, and their house stood back to back with number thirty Graveney Road which was where the Collins lived. John and Kate Hurley were warm, friendly people. John Hurley was a fortunate man in as much as he had a regular job; storeman up at the Co-op. Kate, his wife, was everyone's friend, a hard-working woman, whose hair had once been a lovely blonde colour, now turned grey. A lovely smile was always on her face, showing exceptionally good white teeth, and it lit up her merry blue eyes. There was a saying Kate Hurley was fond of: 'Never bother

trouble till trouble bothers you', and by that she
seemed to set great store. The Hurleys had three
children, two boys, Tim aged eleven, Joey just nine,
and Polly, who was older than Lizzie by just four
days. Lizzie couldn't remember, or even imagine,
life without Polly. They were best friends, always
had been.

The bath routine was a palaver Lizzie could have
done without tonight. She had wanted to go round
to Polly's house and discuss what Miss Roberts had
been talking about so earnestly before she dismissed
class – the dreaded scholarship exams. Still, never
mind, these bath occasions often turned out to be
quite jolly gatherings and she'd still get to see Polly.

There weren't many houses in the district that
could boast a bathroom. Indeed, Nellie would tell it
that when Albert Collins brought her from Lambeth
to Tooting as his bride, there were three things that
immediately made her take to the house. One, bay
windows upstairs and down. Two, Venetian blinds.
Three, a bathroom with an indoor lavatory. Once,
the great cast-iron bath had stood gleaming white
against the wall, now its under-belly and huge claw
feet had turned rusty. Dust had collected beneath it
in far unreachable corners. There was no running
hot water – there never had been. Just the solitary
brass tap which gave out only cold water. Two years
ago, the landlord had made life somewhat easier.
His workmen had removed the big old copper from
the scullery and filled the space with a gas cooker
and a gas copper. No longer did a fire have to be lit

beneath the grey hearthstoned beast in order to heat the water. All that was needed now was a supply of pennies to feed the slot-meter and just one match with which to light the jets, which were set underneath the bottom of the copper.

Having this new-fangled copper did not eliminate all problems. A water supply was not connected to it. Cold water still had to be drawn from the tap above the scullery sink which stood at least six feet away on the opposite wall. Bucket after bucket needed to be filled and carried across to the copper. When boiling, there was a tap placed low down from which the water could be drawn out. Then the fun would begin. From the scullery, through the kitchen, along the passageway, and up the stairs into the bathroom, buckets had to be lifted almost chest high in order to tip the boiling water into the bath.

At seven o'clock, Nellie was trying hard to get cleared up. The copper was nigh on boiling and condensation was running down the scullery walls. 'Move your books,' she said to Lizzie, as she threw the dark red chenille cloth over the scrubbed table top, she didn't want Kate to see the place in a mess.

Daisy was laying sheets of newspaper over the linoleum up the passage, which would soak up some of the water that would inevitably get slopped in the process of reaching the bathroom.

John Hurley preceded his family, taking off his coat as he came into the kitchen. He was a short, stocky man, with strong brawny arms. Kate fol-

lowed, wearing her Sunday coat and hat. Tim, the
eldest boy, had a sly look about him, in Aunt
Daisy's opinion, while young Joey, with huge
brown eyes and a mop of dark curly hair was everyone's favourite.

'Right, out the way kids,' John Hurley ordered,
'we'll soon have the bath filled.'

Lizzie looked at Polly and a nod of her head suggested that they made themselves scarce in the front
room.

An hour later, John Hurley had taken himself off
to Wimbledon dog track. Using the long, hooked
poker, Daisy had removed the top plate of the hob,
leaving the fire open. The flames, now exposed to
all the draughts, were leaping and flickering, giving
out extra warmth. Tim and Joey, wrapped now in
towels, glowing and clean, their well-scrubbed faces
a shiny red, sat giggling and laughing, playing mar-
bles with Syd. Polly, who had bathed first, was
dressed; her hair now straggled round her face in
damp tendrils. Nellie came in from the scullery
carrying a wooden tray; three cups and saucers holding strong, sweet tea were set down for the women
and five tin mugs of cocoa were handed out to the
children.

All eyes were turned to Daisy and dribble came
from young Joey's lips as she asked, 'Who wants a
lump of bread pudding?' Rich and dark, full of fruit
and peel, the top heavily dredged with sugar, its
spicy smell filled the kitchen.

'I do,' five voices called while heads nodded in eager agreement.

Time for bed. Lizzie and Polly clung together. 'See you in the morning,' Lizzie called after her friend.

'Yeah, night. God bless you,' Polly answered.

'Thanks, Nellie, you too, Daisy. It's bin a real treat,' Kate hugged them both.

'You're more than welcome any time,' they told her.

Closing the front door behind the Hurleys, Daisy grinned at Nellie as she gathered up the sodden newspaper. 'Only don't make it too often,' she muttered.

Pouring another cup of tea for themselves, Nellie and Daisy marvelled at the rigmarole they went through every time they or their neighbours wanted to use the bathroom.

'I'd just as soon sit in the old tin bath in front of the fire,' Daisy exclaimed.

Nellie gave her sister-in-law a lopsided grin and then both of them burst out laughing. Each was fully aware that that was exactly what Daisy did whenever she had the house to herself.

Christmas that year was marred for Lizzie by two things. Leslie was now stationed in Malta. Without Les, things couldn't be the same. Lizzie adored him, he was a father to her as well as a brother. The second thing really narked Lizzie. Her mother insisted she still had to go to work for the Dawsons on Christmas morning.

But there were some compensations. Snow was forecast and that meant great fun out in the street with all the other kids or even up on the common if Mum felt up to the walk, and Connie was getting engaged to Bill. Bill Baldwin was like one of the family already. He was a big husky lad with light brown hair, not a bit shy now he had got to know them all. Bill was devoted to Connie; he loved her with all his heart, and had known she was the one for him from the moment he'd set eyes on her. Since there was only him and his widowed mother, Nellie had invited them to join the family for Christmas dinner.

A week before Christmas, Bill came upon Syd arguing with Lizzie in the backyard. 'What's up, kids?' he wanted to know.

Syd confided in him, 'We've only got four bob in our money box and the present we want ter buy for Mum and Aunt Daisy costs five bob.'

Bill looked at them thoughtfully. 'That's a lot of money to spend on one present.'

'We know that,' said Lizzie, 'but it's what they want. We heard them talking.'

Bill worked in Billingsgate Fish Market. The hours were long and the work hard but he made good money working on commission. It was a problem how he could give these two nice children a shilling without hurting their pride. A penny from him every Saturday had become quite acceptable but a shilling was a lot of money. He was too wise to offer it outright.

'Tell yer what. I haven't got round to cleaning my bike for more than two weeks now. The front lamp is so dirty it's a wonder a policeman hasn't stopped me, and the rear light is not much better. Just 'aven't had the time.' He drew in a deep breath and pretended to be considering the matter. 'If I give you two sixpences each, you wouldn't clean me bike for me, would you?'

A great grin spread on Syd's face while a flash of hope lit up Lizzie's blue eyes. ' 'Course we will,' they chorused. Rags and a tin of Bluebell metal polish were produced and they set to with a will.

Once inside the china shop, Lizzie gazed fondly at the twenty-one-piece tea services set out on a stand behind the counter.

'Which one do you like best, Syd?' she said.

He pointed to a blue willow-patterned set. 'What d'you think of that one?'

'Oh, no. Gran's got that pattern, so has Mrs Hurley; let's buy Mum and Aunt Daisy something different.'

Twice the blonde assistant with the red-painted fingernails asked if she could help them.

'No, we won't be a minute,' they told her – but they were. At least twenty minutes had passed before they settled on a cream-coloured set with a honeysuckle design.

Handing over their shillings, sixpences and pennies, Syd nudged his sister, 'Go on Lizzie, ask her.'

The assistant smiled, 'Ask me what?'

'Please . . .' still Lizzie hesitated.

'. . . Deliver it to our house.' Syd got it out in a rush. 'It says goods costing five shillings or more will be delivered free of charge.'

'That's quite right, young man,' the assistant told him, as she reached for a pink form.

And so, on Christmas Eve, a puzzled Aunt Daisy signed for and accepted a large wooden box.

Lizzie and Syd clutched at each other's hands, squeezing every now and again as they watched their mother and their aunt discard the straw on to the kitchen floor and extract six cups, six saucers, six tea plates, a milk jug and sugar basin, and, lastly, the large bread and butter plates. Nellie's face was wet with tears, and Daisy, her eyes brimming, stared in amazement at the china and the straw now scattered widely.

'Come here, ducks, and give your old aunt a kiss,' Daisy said as she drew Lizzie to her.

Even Syd was smiling as he brushed at his cheek with his fist to remove the dampness where his mother has planted several kisses.

Christmas was good. Mrs Baldwin had proved to be a jolly sort, joining in games and giving a solo of 'Silent Night' whilst Nellie played for her on their upright piano. And on Boxing Day it did snow. Waking to a stillness that only comes with snow, Lizzie ran to look out of the window. A pure white, unblemished blanket covered everything except the tips of the chimney pots. The only sound was from a few sparrows visible in the yard, twittering away near the back door asking to be fed.

'Come on, Syd, wake up!' Lizzie shouted as she ran to the small box-room which Syd had as a bedroom all to himself. 'It's bin snowing.'

As she pulled the covers from his bed, Lizzie looked around the small space. Syd had a bookcase, which Leslie had made for him; it was full of comics and paperback books. He also had a small table and one chair, ideal for doing his homework, except that Syd never bothered to do any.

A thought came to Lizzie, as she tickled her brother's toes and he gave her a brutal kick. If, in the new year, Connie was to marry her Bill, she would then have a bedroom of her own. In her mind's eye, Lizzie was already seeing the room she now shared with her sister set out as she would like it, if only she could wheedle her mother round to her way of thinking. That should be easy, she told herself, and if her mum wasn't forthcoming, there was always Gran. Gran had some lovely pieces of furniture, much more than she needed. Yes, Lizzie was confident the new year would see her settled very nicely into a room of her own.

Chapter Three

As ALWAYS, JANUARY was bleak, with short hours of daylight, and dark, bitter-cold evenings. One day, as Lizzie came through the school gates, she heard her younger brother yelling coarsely, 'Wait for me, Liz. You'll never guess what,' he panted as he drew near. 'Our teacher says we can 'ave all the tar blocks we want so long as we've got something to carry them 'ome in.'

'You're barmy,' Lizzie retorted. 'What would we want with a load of messy old tar blocks?'

'Bet Mum would be glad to 'ave some. Save her coal, wouldn't it?'

Lizzie pondered on this. Syd was a likeable little dare-devil with his friendly and carefree approach to life, and at times he could be very thoughtful, even loving.

'If I mend the wheel on me barrow, will you come up the High Street and 'elp me get some on Saturday? Will yer?' he pleaded. 'All the other boys are gonna get some.'

Lizzie nodded; her eyes were merry and her lips smiling as she took hold of his hand.

During the short walk home, Syd chatted away very excitedly, telling her what his teacher had told the class. The Ministry of Transport had com-

manded that all the tram tracks in the centre of main
roads had to be renewed. Removal of the old tracks
meant the discarding of wooden blocks embedded
on either side.

As it turned out, the whole district was on to a
good thing once work started. Men were taken on
as labourers, digging out the existing rails, thrilled
at the prospect of a few weeks' steady employment.
There wasn't a kid who didn't enjoy the excitement
of it all as they lined the gutter and stared in amazement. Pick-axes were vigorously swung, by tough,
weather-beaten young men, in a repeated rhythm.
The piles of old tar-sodden blocks grew larger as
heap after heap was tossed aside. Great cauldrons of
hot tar stood on the edge of the pavement, each with
a fire glowing brightly beneath, and filled with thick
jet-black steaming liquid with a pungent smell so
strong it took one's breath away.

'Breathe deep,' mothers were admonishing their
children. 'It'll do yer chest a power of good.'

If it didn't burst your lungs first, Lizzie thought,
as she and Syd joined the scrambling, pushing, shoving mob to fill their barrow once more.

The whole show moved with great speed. All too
soon the length of High Street from Trinity Road at
Tooting Bec, right through to Tooting Broadway
was completed. Four lanes of shiny steel rails were
set centre to the road and the gangers moved on
towards Colliers Wood and south Wimbledon.

Nellie went back and forth from the pavement,
where Syd and Lizzie had tipped their load, to the

backyard, transporting six to eight blocks at a time in her shopping bag. Daisy toiled away, stacking the rough, dirty blocks of wood as high as they would go in the garden shed.

'Don't sit on them chairs,' Nellie called out as Syd and Lizzie came in through the back door, 'and both of you get them dirty boots off.' She glanced across at Daisy, 'Look at them, right filthy the pair of them!'

In no time Nellie had stripped them of their outdoor clothes, made sure that they had washed their faces and that their hands were thoroughly clean. By now, Daisy had the table laid with a sumptuous feast of sausage and mash, with jam roly poly and custard to follow.

The tar blocks proved to be a godsend. The next few weeks were bitter. Snow lingered and turned into dirty, mushy heaps, ice formed in the gutters and no water came from the scullery tap. All the outside pipes were frozen.

Inside, the kitchen was warm and cosy. The fire roared away all day and was well banked down at night, never allowed to go out. It spurted and crackled dangerously as the children sat doing their homework while Nellie knitted and Aunt Daisy sewed. The tar blocks were pitted with gravel and as the tar melted the tiny stones were shot out, making sounds like pellets being shot through the air as they hit the hearth. Lizzie and Syd would laugh aloud and protest as their mother placed the fireguard in position.

'The only person not showing a profit from all of this is the local coalman,' commented Nellie.

'You can say that again,' Daisy retorted. 'Thanks to our two kids, those blocks will help eke out the coal for many a long day.'

Nellie nodded her agreement. 'And you know what, Daisy, there shouldn't be half the children bad with chest ailments this winter. You've only ter open the front door to realize that.' For there was hardly a family who hadn't amassed a store of tar blocks and everywhere the air was acrid with the fumes of burning tar.

As winter at last gave way, the pale early spring sunshine brought out the women to gossip over the back fences once more. Then there was another upheaval in the district – hard to believe, but true. Electricity was coming to Tooting. Arguments ranged back and forth as to the merits of this wonder. The municipality was undertaking to provide this service free of charge for a limited number of points in each house. Any additional sockets would have to be paid for.

Upheaval came to the back streets this time. Pathways and roadways were dug up and wide open trenches were laid bare during the laying of the cables. Boisterous kids harassed the workmen. Floorboards were taken up in downstairs passages and women fought a losing battle against the dust and dirt. When completion was almost reached, the inevitable official in his bowler hat appeared. Holding his clipboard firmly, pencil poised, he raised his eyes to the top of the front door.

'Ah, yes. Number thirty, Mrs Collins, right? How many extra points will you be wanting?' he enquired in his posh accent.

Daisy and Nellie answered in unison, 'None, thank you.'

'You do realize our free instalment offer only covers the ground floor?'

Nellie wrinkled her brow but said quietly, 'Never mind, we'll just have ter make do.'

'My dear lady,' he replied, 'you will have no light or power points in the upper regions of this house.'

Daisy scowled at the man, 'We've got by with gas all these years and it won't kill us now not to have electricity in the bedrooms.'

He smiled sardonically, turned away, then hesitantly said over his shoulder, 'If you change your mind over the next three days, the same offer will stand.'

They didn't change their minds, no more than many other occupants of the road did. In fact, it was a long time before the electric light which had been installed in the downstairs rooms was put to full use.

'Switch it off, switch it off,' Nellie screamed at Syd, who had demanded the honour of being the first to flick the brass switch.

Nellie was in a state of panic, 'It makes the place look so dirty,' she sadly remarked.

'Indeed, it does,' agreed Daisy.

The ceilings were smoke-blackened from the con-

stantly burning kitchen range, and the gas jet fixed
above the mantle shelf which gave out heat as well
as providing light had left a filthy stain on the wall.
The new light with just a bare bulb illuminated the
room so brightly that it clearly showed the grime
which had previously been ignored.

Lizzie was glad her bedroom still only boasted a
gas bracket. At times, to save money, even this was
not lit. She and Syd would be given a candle, placed
in a saucer of water, to light up their rooms while
they got into bed. Lizzie even liked to lie and watch
the weird patterns on the walls and ceiling made by
the flickering flame, but she hated the smell which
lingered when her mother snuffed out the light
between licked finger and thumb.

Tomorrow would be Good Friday and school had
broken up at midday. There would be two whole
weeks' holiday. Lizzie was spreading dripping on a
slice of toast but her thoughts were elsewhere – on
the fact that she had sat her scholarship exams.

After tea that evening, Lizzie walked round to
Polly's house. She was longing to ask Polly what
she had thought of the exam questions. The light
was on in the kitchen and the fire glow showed
clearly through the back window, so she knocked
on the door and opened it, as she always did, and
called out, 'It's all right, it's only me, Lizzie.'

The kitchen was deserted, but someone was
moving about upstairs. Surprised to see neither Mr

nor Mrs Hurley, she went to the bottom of the stairs and called up.

Polly answered, 'I'll be down in a minute.' She clattered down the linoleum-covered stairs, and came into the kitchen, grinning at Lizzie and pointing to a chair. 'Pull it up to the fire,' she ordered, and threw herself into another chair opposite.

Lizzie sat down and Tibbles, the Hurley's tabby cat, hugged against her legs. 'Where's your mum?'

'Gone to the pub with dad. Won't see them before closing time.'

Lizzie laughed, 'I'm glad they've gone out, I was going to ask you about the exam. How d'you think you got on?'

Polly frowned, 'Wouldn't like to say, really. How about you?'

Lizzie shook her head. 'Dunno. Glad it's over, though. Don't suppose I got many questions right.'

Polly protested, 'Oh, come on, Lizzie, they weren't that difficult, were they?'

Lizzie forced herself to agree. Now that she had found out what she wanted to know, she wished that they could just forget the whole matter. It would be weeks before they got the results. 'I hope we both pass,' she said listlessly.

'Well, worrying won't make it so. Will it?' Polly laughingly answered, as she suddenly stood up. 'Come on, let's go round to the Selkirk Pub. If we call through the door, me dad's sure to buy us a ginger beer and a Darby biscuit.'

Together they ran down the road, quickening

their steps as they neared the pub, taking the front steps two at a time. Polly saw her dad as soon as they opened the door, slumped in a chair near the dart board, a frothy pint in his hand.

'You've got a cheek, the pair of yer,' he told them, but his cheerful face was creased with laughter as he turned towards the bar.

Side by side, the two friends sat on the steps, glass in one hand, large round biscuit in the other. Easter would begin tomorrow. On Holiday Monday they would probably all go to Mitcham Fair. The scholarship suddenly didn't matter so much.

'Glad we came out, aren't you?' Polly asked.

'Yeah. Your dad's great,' said Lizzie. All the worry and agony of sitting the exam seemed remote and dim now. 'Want to come with me ter see me gran tomorrow?' she asked.

'Love to,' said Polly.

The lovely month of June came again. For the past weeks, there had been great excitement in the Collinses' house. Nellie had baked rich dark cakes which the local baker had promised to ice. Aunt Daisy had sewed a white silk dress for the bride and a pink dress for the only bridesmaid. Connie was to marry her Bill and Lizzie was to be her only attendant. Disregarding the cost, tradition was adhered to. Nearly all the neighbours were inside the church and everyone held their breath as Connie came down the aisle on John Hurley's arm.

Lizzie had always thought of her sister as plain,

even straitlaced, but nothing was further from the truth today. A crown of orange blossom with a froth of white veiling framed her face. She carried a small posy of pink roses and the colour matched her rosy cheeks. Lizzie stood shyly behind her sister and offered up a silent prayer that when the time came for her, too, to be married, she might look as beautiful as Connie did today.

Once outside, the crowd began throwing confetti and yelling good wishes. Syd was wearing his first pair of long trousers and Lizzie could scarcely believe that this clean, tidy, blond, curly-haired boy was her young brother.

The reception was a cold salad meal laid out in the function room of the Selkirk Pub. At six o'clock, when the public bars opened, spontaneous gaiety broke out and a good time was had by all.

Connie's departure from the house was not such a wrench. She and Bill had rented the top half of Dolly Whitlock's house, which stood at the far end of Graveney Road and meant that Connie would still be a daily visitor.

The wedding was over but excitement was still in the air. The summer horse-race meeting at Epsom was due and on the second day the most famous race of all would take place – the Derby. The Fountain Public House in Garratt Lane was running an outing, with four bus loads of people. The whole Collins family, with the exception of Gran, was going to Epsom for the day. Six-thirty in the morning and the pub was packed as folk filed through and out of the back door to board the buses.

'Can we go upstairs?' Polly yelled at her parents.

Mr Hurley set down the crate of booze he was helping his mates to load on board, wiped his sweaty forehead with his forearm and grinned at his only daughter, 'Yes, all right, but sit still. See the boys don't run about till yer mum and me get there.'

Five children made a dash for the stairs. Polly and Lizzie grabbed a seat together, while Syd, Tim and Joey squashed up on a double bench. Finally, to loud cheers, they were off! As they left London behind and entered the green Surrey countryside, they joined the already jam-packed main road to Epsom: open-top buses, hackney carriages, motor cycles with side cars, charabancs, all their seats filled to capacity.

Pearly kings and queens, regally seated in their horse-drawn carts, rubbed shoulders for the day with true royalty. Bumper-to-bumper with cars and commercial vans were Daimlers and Rolls Royce limousines, their occupants smiling and waving just as enthusiastically as everyone else.

They finally arrived at the course and were directed by policemen into a special parking area reserved for buses. Shopping bags and boxes were unpacked and food in plenty was set out on the grass. Serious drinking began for the adults. And the kids had all the pop they wanted. Spread out wide, away from the course, was the fairground. Coffee stalls, beer tents, tipsters, gypsies, fortune tellers and racketeers, all contrived and schemed to earn a few quid from the day's racing.

It was a brilliant day and the sun shone with a vengeance on the thousands who had turned up to chance their luck on the horses.

'They're off,' the cry went up as the first horses left the stalls.

'Quick,' Lizzie grabbed Polly's arm, causing her to drop the long iced bun she was munching. 'Let's get to the rails.'

They elbowed their way through the crowd, the shouting and cheering so loud it was enough to burst the eardrums. The two friends held on to each other tightly as the horses came into sight, their hooves pounding the track as they thundered past between the rails.

Later that afternoon the mums gathered the children together and took them over to the fair. Toffee apples, candy floss, humbugs and bags of hot chips combined with rides on the roundabouts and the big dipper.

All too soon it was time to go home, but the fun wasn't over by any means. Crowds lined the pavements, dozens of children to the forefront.

'Chuck out yer mouldies,' they bawled. By now ninety per cent of the racegoers were tipsy and they responded willingly. Handfuls of farthings, half-pennies and pennies were chucked over the sides of carts, out of the windows of cars, buses and the charabancs into the road. Dodging the traffic, evading the horses hooves, pushing, shoving, struggling with each other to reach the coins first, the children swarmed, unaware of the dangers, enjoying the rough and tumble and laughing gleefully as the toffs in the big cars raised their top hats to them.

Dirty and bedraggled they alighted from the buses in Garratt Lane. 'You go on 'ome with the kids,' John Hurley slurred as he and his mates tried to rouse one man who was paralytic with drink, unable to move from the pavement where he sat.

Wearily, the four women and five children set off for home. At the gate of number thirty, all good-nights having been said, Daisy almost as an after-thought asked, 'How much did you win, Kate?'

With a humorous grin on her face, Kate answered, 'Five pounds one shilling – not bad, eh? You and Nellie aren't out of pocket on the day, are you?'

Daisy looked at her sister-in-law and they both laughed. 'No,' they both answered, and Nellie added, 'We made a bob or two.'

Chapter Four

THE LETTER ARRIVED on a Saturday morning. Lizzie
picked it up from the mat and stared at the envelope
for a long time. Franked London County Council,
she knew exactly what it contained and dallied with
the idea of throwing it into the fire unopened. 'Oh,
Jesus!' she whispered in an agony of frustration.
'What am I going to do?'

Lizzie lay in bed that evening and thought confus-
edly about her day and in particular about the examination for the scholarship. She had passed and that
was something she had not really imagined would
happen, although she had allowed herself to dream
that it might.

Her delight was tinged with guilt. Why should
she be privileged when her brothers and her sister
hadn't been? To go to the High School would cost
money. Maybe she would be entitled to a grant, but
it certainly would not cover the cost of uniforms,
books, travel to and from school and many more
untold items.

Her mother's delight as she read the letter had
been a joy to see. Tenderly she had hugged Lizzie
to her, murmuring, 'Well done. Good girl.' Aunt
Daisy's congratulations had been more hearty. She

had grabbed Lizzie, sweeping her off her feet, and was triumphantly swinging her round and round when the kitchen door opened and Gran stood there.

'Our Lizzie's passed her scholarship,' Daisy quickly told her mother.

'I'm not a bit surprised; ever since she could toddle, she's had her nose stuck in a book,' the old lady retorted dryly.

'Oh, say you're pleased, Gran,' Lizzie pleaded.

'Of course I'm pleased,' she said quietly. And she was.

To Harriet, this little girl was everything. She wanted to pet and cuddle her but she was not used to showing affection. Silently, she vowed that nothing, if she had her way, would stand in the way of her favourite grandchild being granted the chance of a good education.

In the scullery, Lizzie was putting on the kettle when she heard her elders in the kitchen discussing finances. She wanted to put her hands over her ears as she heard her mother sadly say, 'I only hope we can afford it.' Whichever way she looked at it, Lizzie knew the cost would be far more than her mother could manage.

Double delight: Polly had also passed.

'How did your dad take the news?' Lizzie asked, as she cut two lumps from the cold bread pudding.

'He was very pleased,' Polly assured her, smiling at the memory. 'Mum said afterwards, it knocked him all of a heap. He wouldn't believe it at first, kept saying brains didn't run in the family. He said he is coming round to talk to yer mum about money, and how they are going to manage.'

During the whole of the summer, endless opinions were exchanged and ideas debated. Leslie wrote from Malta that his blonde whippet of a sister was a genius and for his mother to buy Lizzie a bicycle on the never-never and he would give her an extra sixpence a day to pay for the instalments.

John Hurley voted this a good idea for the pair of them. 'I'll see what Nick Shephard can do,' he told Nellie.

She grimaced. Nick was their insurance man whom Nellie never quite trusted. Black hair smarmed down with grease, blue eyes and a pencil-slim moustache and always smartly dressed in the up-to-date fashion, he was a hit with most women, though not with Nellie.

Every Saturday morning he called for the weekly payments on their Britannia insurance policies. 'Royal Britannia, two tanners make a bob, three make eighteen pence and four make two bob,' the kids in the street would chant as he did his rounds.

Nick Shephard had a sideline. He sold things on the weekly. Towels, sheets, boots, shoes, you name it, he would do his best to get it. Where from was a closely guarded secret.

'Two bicycles?' His brow puckered then suddenly he was grinning. 'Leave it ter me. I'll have them for you by next Saturday.'

He shook hands with John Hurley but Daisy

blocked his way as he made to leave their kitchen. 'These are for two young girls. We don't want no rubbish nor yer stolen bikes. Do you understand me?' She looked sternly into his eyes.

'Trust me, Miss Collins,' he entreated. 'As if I would do anything to jeopardize the good relationship I've had with this family for years now.'

But her next words were menacing. 'Just remember what I've said.'

The evening before school started found Polly and Lizzie in the big warm kitchen of the Collinses' house. Nellie and Aunt Daisy had taken themselves off to the Selkirk for a glass of stout and a singsong, and Syd had gone to his Boys' Brigade meeting. The two girls sat one each side of the kitchen table, labelling their books and sportswear.

'All finished,' Lizzie said as she put her plimsoles on top of her books and shut the lid of the small case.

John Hurley had bought Polly's uniform from Morley's, the official school outfitters, but Lizzie's had been lovingly and expertly made at home by Aunt Daisy. The regulation cloth and colours had been available from Smith's in the Mitcham Road. Both girls had been taken by their mothers to the Royal Co-operative Society. There, by means of mutuality cheques, navy-blue knickers, black stockings, shoes and plimsoles plus vests and blouses had been bought.

Mutuality cheques were a godsend and repayments were strictly weekly. If you had a Co-op representative call, one shilling in every pound had to be paid extra as interest. However, if you took your weekly payments to the Co-op bank (and this entailed climbing a flight of forty steps) for twenty consecutive weeks without fail, no interest was charged. Come rain or hail, Nellie went to the bank religiously each week. Using mutuality cheques, she and Daisy could buy while prices were at their lowest.

'So,' Polly concluded, 'tomorrow is the big day.'

Lizzie grinned, 'And about time too. Wonder how we'll get on, it still seems too good to be true. You and me going to the Elliott High School in Southfields.' She nudged Polly and they both giggled. 'Hope the other girls in our class are not stuck up.'

'Who cares if they are,' Polly looked lovingly at her friend as she squeezed past the new Raleigh bicycle which stood propped against the wall of the passage. 'We'll have each other. We'll get by,' she declared.

' 'Course we will,' agreed Lizzie.

Chapter Five

IT WAS NEARLY Christmas once more, the third since Lizzie had been at the Elliott School. Alone in the house, Lizzie, not yet dressed, sat in the old armchair by the fire. There was only one person outside her family who she had bought a present for, and that was Polly.

Lizzie disliked her classmates more than she dared to admit, and the very thought of Miss Dawlish, her headmistress, filled her with a forlorn air of defeat. Without the company of the happy-go-lucky Polly, she would really have hated school.

Miss Dawlish was a snob. There were no two ways about it. 'It is a privilege that should never be taken lightly,' she would intone from her high dais each morning as she gazed over her pupils at assembly. 'You are members of my school at the expense of the ratepayers,' she would insist. 'You owe it to them to prove that you are the cream of the cream.' Lizzie had never worked out the meaning of that statement.

Miss Dawlish failed to accept the fact that she had pupils from an impoverished background. A great charity worker, she would regularly urge her girls to bring donations for the relief of the poor.

Lizzie's contributions were small; more often than

not only what Gran gave her. She knew only too well how her mother struggled to provide the elementary necessities for her to attend the Elliott, and so she rarely made a difficult situation worse by asking.

'Old bitch,' Lizzie would mutter to herself when Miss Dawlish smiled sweetly as better-off class-mates ingratiated themselves.

'Boot-lickers,' Polly would mumble. She agreed whole-heartedly with Lizzie about Miss Dawlish, and certainly there was no love lost between her and her condescending classmates.

However, she didn't fare as badly as Lizzie. She had a father in full-time employment and was able to acquire such things as her own sports equipment. Although she willingly shared with Lizzie, it still left Lizzie vulnerable to their sick jokes.

The highlight of the past year had been their street party. Polly had let the cat out of the bag at school. 'A street party! How disgusting,' the tall, freckled-faced teacher's pet Marion had mimicked.

All south London had street parties in 1935. King George V and Queen Mary had been on the throne for twenty-five years and their Silver Jubilee was a grand excuse for a celebration. For weeks ahead, men had collected pennies up and down both sides of the street every Sunday morning. 'It's to give the kids a good time. God bless yer,' they would say at each house, as coppers were pushed into their collecting tins.

The men were as good as their word. The great day had been declared a public holiday. From the pub, stacks of trestles were brought forth and set up in the centre of the road from one end to the other. Large planks of wood formed table tops, red, white and blue paper cloths were laid, and endless rows of benches provided the seating.

High above, lines stretched from upstairs windows were joined to their neighbours on the other side of the street. Banners and flags made out of old cloths dyed in tin baths to all shades of red, white and blue, showed how patriotic the Londoners could be.

Children were seated near to their own front doors and were waited on by the adults. There were jam, fish-paste and cheese sandwiches, lemonade and ginger beer, fancy cakes and chocolate biscuits, with jelly, blancmange and ice-cream to round it all off. 'Smashing,' was the unanimous verdict.

When darkness came, children sat along the kerb stones, watching the antics of the adults. Tunes were pounded out on old upright pianos, and accordions took over when the piano players had a rest for a few pints. 'Knees Up Mother Brown', 'The Lambeth Walk', 'Knock 'em in the Old Kent Road', 'My Old Man Said Follow the Van', 'My Young Man is Up in the Gallery' – these and many more well-loved songs were sung lustily, if not tunefully, as neighbours weaved their way back and forth across the street. In the morning, there were empty bottles by the dozen, beer bottles, pints and quarts, cider bottles, lemonade bottles all stacked up along the pavement.

'Wonder if we could nick a few, get the money back on the empties,' Syd considered as he went to call for the Hurley boys.

'Tell you what. It wasn't only the kids that had a good time,' Daisy declared as she swept the front path and Nellie retrieved more empty bottles from the front garden.

Lizzie found herself laughing at the memory as she told herself to get cracking and get dressed. Blow the Elliott, Miss Dawlish, and all those posh girls, who thought they were much better than anyone else.

The bells sang the arrival of 1936. Neighbours came out into the roadway to sing 'Auld Lang Syne' and to kiss and hug each other. Only one person was missing; that was Leslie. Lizzie missed her big brother. She wrote him a regular weekly letter, telling of her progress at school, which was surprisingly good, and skilfully she outlined her grievances. His replies never failed to make her laugh. 'Don't stand for no argy bargy from them. Give as good as you get, Lizzie,' was his advice.

The year had scarcely begun and the whole country was in mourning. King George V was dead. Connie said she didn't want to go to see the King's lying-in-state.

'I do,' Lizzie said. 'Please, Bill,' she implored her brother-in-law, 'will you take me?'

' 'Course I will, love, if your mum says it's all right.'

They came out of the underground tube station to find everyone else in London had decided to pay their respects; mounted police were controlling the crowds. They queued for well over an hour on a bleak January day made worse by a keen wind that was blowing off the River Thames. At last they entered Westminster Hall. It was difficult to see anything at first as they slowly shuffled forward in step with everyone else. Gradually their eyes became accustomed to the dusk interior.

A solitary wreath lay on the coffin and tall, beautiful floral tributes nearby made the air sweet and heavy with perfume. Women and children wept. Men looked solemn. Lizzie was afraid to look, attracted far more by the soldiers and their uniforms as they stood guarding the body – heads down, perfectly still like statues. As they passed out at the other end of the hall, Bill squeezed Lizzie's hand; she had never let go of his since entering the hall.

'There, Lizzie,' he said, 'you'll never forget the death of King George V, will you?'

'No, I won't,' Lizzie solemnly agreed.

Plans for the coronation of Edward VIII were going ahead, but all the time Mrs Simpson was on the scene. She became the main topic of conversation everywhere, discussed in shops, on buses, in the streets and pubs – not always discreetly. Boys and girls alike sang saucy songs about her, ridiculing her for having designs on England's future King. Opinion was divided. Many thought he would be a good King because he had shown a keen interest in social problems. Others were opposed to a marriage because she was a divorced woman and an American. Preparation for the ceremony of crowning the sovereign continued. Edward would be crowned King in Westminster Abbey, but would Mrs Simpson be his Queen Consort?

At last, in the following December, Edward VIII finally announced that he would abdicate. 'Good riddance to bad rubbish,' declared Harriet Collins. But the repercussions of his action were colossal. Souvenirs that had been made in their thousands for the coronation were now utterly worthless. There would be no coronation, and traders sustained great losses. No one escaped. From the largest stores down to fairground traders and barrow boys, all were left with coronation mugs, cups and saucers, wall plaques, bowls and teaspoons on their hands. Now they couldn't give them away, let alone sell them. Edward VIII's renunciation of the throne had been disastrous in more ways than one. Folk looked back over the past twelve months as 1936 drew to a close and shook their heads.

Lizzie wrote an essay as part of her English exam and for once won congratulations from Miss Dawlish. 'The past year has to be one of the most important years in the history of the Royal Family,' she wrote. 'Three different Kings had each sat on the throne of England in such a short space of time.'

The following year, 1937, was relatively uneventful in England, although there were disturbing rumblings from Germany, where Adolf Hitler was initiating a large re-armament programme.

'He won't stop till he dominates the world,' declared Fred Johnson, the milkman for the whole street.

'Rubbish,' declared Jackie Jordon, Nellie's next-door neighbour. 'We've sat on them once, you don't think we're daft enough to let 'im drag the Germans into another war?'

'We'll have to see, won't we?' Gran put her two pennyworth in, as she opened the front gate.

Actually, she wanted to get Nellie and her daughter inside, off the doorstep. She had more personal worries to discuss. She had lived through enough wars and wasn't about to get upset over something that might never happen. She'd bigger problems to worry about just now. Compulsory purchase of her house and the ground it stood on, that's what the letter had said. Well, she'd see about that!

''Allo, Gran, who's upset you?' Lizzie cheekily asked as her grandmother pushed past the knot of people on the doorstep and made her way down the passage and into the kitchen.

'Never you mind, just put the kettle on,' she snapped. Her eyes were blazing and her cheeks flamed as she savagely removed her hat-pin and hung her hat behind the door. It was not a bit like Gran to

be so short-tempered, least of all with her beloved
Lizzie.

By suppertime, the whole street knew that Silverdore Terrace was to be pulled down. The very
thought of Gran's lovely home disappearing made
Lizzie feel sick and she burst into tears and threw
her arms about her Gran's neck.

'Stop it! Crying won't help. I'm going to the solicitors first thing tomorrow; I'm also going to make
sure the newspapers hear about this.' Gran, pale and
very angry, snatched her letter up from the table and
shoved it into her bag. 'They'll 'ave ter do more
than just send a letter if they want my house. Lived
in Silverdore since I were married at seventeen –
that's coming up for fifty-four years. Try chucking
me out! Just let them try!' Gran yelled threateningly.

The young lady in the solicitor's office was brisk
and efficient as she ushered Daisy and Harriet into
the main office. Mr Martin came from behind his
desk to shake their hands. Tall and neatly dressed in
a navy-blue suit, striped shirt with a stiff white
collar, he epitomized his profession.

Having read through the letter, he cleared his
throat and with one finger eased the stiff collar about
his Adam's apple. 'I'm afraid this is watertight,' he
said. He was all sympathy. 'It's an odd business, I
don't like it one bit,' he told them. 'Legally, though,
there is not much I can do about it.'

With a melancholy nod of her head, Harriet Collins made to rise.

'Wait,' Mr Martin himself rose. 'Perhaps it would be better if you let me explain the situation fully,' he suggested. Harriet sat down again and nodded dumbly.

Mr Martin carefully weighed his words. 'Your ownership of the cottage is not in dispute. It is the land on which it was built. The freeholder, as he is known, owns the land for ever and he has fairly wide powers to do with the land as he wishes. These cottages were built in 1816 when a lease on the ground was granted for a fixed period only. Over the years, all owner-occupants, including yourself, Mrs Collins, have paid ground rent to the freeholder and observed the terms of the lease granted by the original freeholder. That fixed period came to an end twenty years ago. Clearly, then, the freeholder has been lenient and is now well within his rights to ask that the land be given back. There is nothing we can legally do to restrict the freeholder from having use of his land.'

Daisy felt utterly inadequate. Her mother sat still, eyes cast down, her body slumped; a sad sight indeed. Until two days ago, Harriet Collins had thought of herself as a house owner. Apparently she had been deluding herself. Ownership had been meaningless.

'No one will be harassed,' Mr Martin assured them as he saw them to the door. 'Indeed the company involved are being quite generous. They are offering compensation to all owners although the amounts will be relatively small.'

Harriet had a determined air about her in the days that followed and everyone was careful not to ask what her plans were come the day when she would have to leave Silverdore.

'She'll tell us when she's ready,' Aunt Daisy told Lizzie, but Lizzie still regarded her Gran with caution.

Then one day Lizzie called in unexpectedly and found her Gran crying. It almost broke her heart. 'You must come and live with us, Gran. We'll take care of you,' she said.

Gran nodded and held her arms out wide. Hugging Lizzie close, she pressed her lips to the top of her granddaughter's head. 'Oh, I'm just a silly old woman clinging to the past. I'm fine now that you have come to see me.'

They had tea together and Harriet sat watching Lizzie as she ate, with the light from the fire dancing on her long, silky hair and her young, unlined face.

'I'll never see her grown into a woman,' Harriet sadly told herself.

Sunday was a lovely spring day, really warm and with just enough breeze to stir the leaves on the trees. The sky was cloudless and the birds were singing as Lizzie set off to bring Gran back to spend the day. Turning the Broadway, she broke into a trot. Gran always had a treat ready for her every Sunday morning: a brandy snap, a fairy cake hot from the oven, or even treacle toffee.

'Your Gran's sleeping late, not like 'er,' old Mr

Thompson told Lizzie, his gnarled fingers clutching his walking stick as he leant heavily against his front gate.

'No. She'll be out the back,' Lizzie reassured him.

'I'm here, Gran,' she called as she opened the front door.

There was no answer. Lizzie didn't move for a long time, but stood looking at the cold ashes in the grate. No matter what time of the year, Gran always had a fire. A lump rose in her throat and tears stung the back of her eyes and she couldn't move.

She wanted the comfort and happiness of seeing her Gran. She wanted to be hugged and kissed. Intuition told her to be afraid. Her Gran had said no developer would get her out of this house alive. Lizzie's glance took in the orderly state of the room. The furniture shone, antimacassars on the chair backs were set dead straight and the brass firearms and fender gleamed. The room was perfect except for the dead ashes in the grate, and the total silence.

Slowly, Lizzie climbed the stairs.

Her grandmother lay still in her bed. She must be dead, Lizzie thought, trying to stay calm as she watched the sunlight playing on her grey hair. Around her Gran's lips, a slight sweet smile lingered such as there had never been in life. Such sadness swelled up inside Lizzie that she didn't know what to do, so she just stood there for an endless time beside the bed, her eyes never leaving the face of this grandmother she had loved so much. Then the tears came and she raged, 'You can't be dead, Gran. It's Sunday. I've come to take you to our house. I can't bear this. What will I do without you, Gran? Please, don't be dead.'

Lizzie only vaguely remembered walking home. First her mother, then Aunt Daisy held her and stroked her hair and wept with her.

The funeral was on Friday and Lizzie was surprised at the number of people who crowded into their front room. She was pleased, though, at the numerous funeral tributes which lay on the pavement outside their house. Going to the lavatory was the only excuse she could think of to escape when the black hearse, drawn by sleek grey horses, turned into the road.

She couldn't stay and watch the flowers being placed around the coffin which held her Gran's body. Relief was all that Lizzie felt when finally it was all over. Aunt Daisy was grey-looking and tired, and Nellie had cried so much she was unable to speak.

Lizzie did her best to console them and later it was she who coaxed her mother and her aunt to eat. When night came, Lizzie went wearily to bed, wondering if the terrible aching and longing for her Gran would ever ease. Saying her prayers, she still said, 'And please, God, bless Gran.'

Weeks had gone by when the letter from the solicitors arrived. No one, except Lizzie herself, was surprised to learn that Harriet Collins had left her house and all her worldly goods to her granddaughter, Elizabeth Louise Collins.

The special pieces of Gran's furniture John Hurley offered to store in his large shed. Wrapping the legs of chairs, tables and bureaux with sacking, he carefully stacked and covered it all. The rest was sold.

Once all the legal transactions of Lizzie's legacy were settled, there had been two hundred and forty-one pounds left to her, plus the settlement the developers had promised to pay when demolition of Silverdore took place. Her mother and her aunt persuaded Lizzie to put the whole amount into a Royal Arsenal Savings Account and forget about it until she was older.

By September, several things had happened in Tooting, all tied up together, changing the Broadway for ever.

A new market opened and Silverdore Terrace was destroyed completely. Once the clearance scheme started, it made great progress. The developers' intention was to build a cinema on the site. The surrounding ground would be a car park.

Lizzie went back only once more to see her little bit of countryside set back from the busy Mitcham Road. It'll be gone soon, she thought, and she felt angry at God for letting it happen and even more angry that He had seen fit to take her Gran. It was just a peaceful row of five white cottages, each with its own extremely long front garden full of flowers, but there simply wasn't anywhere else like this peaceful haven. Not in Tooting there wasn't.

Chapter Six

IT WAS BITTERLY cold out of doors and not much better within. The wind roared and found every nook and cranny. Windows rattled and curtains moved and the draught beneath the doors was enough to cut your feet off. Ice formed on the inside of the bedroom windows and still the snow didn't fall.

'Would be a damn sight warmer if it did snow,' Aunt Daisy said as if she were a weather expert.

The year of 1938 was only two weeks old and it had brought nothing but misery. Lizzie and Polly couldn't ride their bikes to school, not in this weather. The tram fare was a penny return but wherever they got off the tram, they still had a long walk. Southfields was such an awkward place to get to.

Polly stood with her hands spread to the kitchen range which, despite all Nellie's efforts this morning, was refusing to burn properly. A sudden gust of wind brought smoke swirling out into the kitchen. Usually, Lizzie was ready and waiting when Polly called for her, now she came into the room, flinging her woollen scarf twice around her neck.

'Oh, it's perishing upstairs,' she said, blowing on her fingers, putting on her gloves. ''Bye Mum, 'bye Aunt Daisy,' she called as the two of them went up the passage. It was a quarter to eight and it was still dark as they let themselves out into the street. It would be dark again by the time they reached home tonight.

Daisy wondered just how long her loving niece with the soft blue eyes and long fair hair would be able to stand the pace. She worked so hard, persevering at her homework every night, determined to be at least within the top ten girls in her class. As she had remarked to Nellie over the Christmas holidays, their Lizzie was far too thin. Her arms were so frail and her legs were like sticks, and just lately she had developed a dry cough.

Lizzie wasn't looking forward to going back to school. She had earned the respect of her teachers with her academic achievements and admiration from her classmates for the way in which she excelled on the sports field. Only Miss Dawlish remained a thorn in her flesh.

At first her mother had been reluctant to attend the school nativity play, in which Lizzie had been cast as an angel. On numerous previous such occasions, Nellie had been only too aware of the headmistress's condescending attitude and had been hurt by it. The audience had loved the show, jumping to their feet and applauding loudly as the whole cast took the last curtain call. It should have been such an enjoyable evening and Lizzie knew how proud her mother was feeling. She had, however, watched with dismay as Miss Dawlish approached her mother, manoeuvring her into a corner of the hall with great skill – expert that she was! Lizzie was fuming, knowing there was nothing she could do. By now, she was used to her headmistress's ruthlessness – but her mother was not.

Kind and compassionate herself, Nellie was nonplussed, not understanding this educated woman's self-assurance and worldly attitude.

'The old bitch,' Lizzie muttered aloud, 'she certainly picks her time.' But it was typical of the woman – the bigger the occasion, the more important Miss Dawlish felt. Lizzie was trembling as her headmistress turned away and her mother came towards her.

There was an uneasy look on Nellie's face, but she forced herself to smile and took hold of Lizzie's hand. No reference was made as to what had taken place, yet Lizzie could see that her mum was confused and had been thoroughly embarrassed by whatever Miss Dawlish had chosen to say. Unforgivable. That was Lizzie's reaction.

One day, she vowed. That woman will get her come-uppance – arrogant old cow!

All went smoothly that first day back at school. Lizzie hadn't been singled out at assembly by one of Miss Dawlish's barbs although she had fully expected to be. And her form mistress showed great kindness and concern about her.

At break time, Polly and Lizzie had decided to stay in the classroom. Lizzie shivered as she held her handkerchief over her mouth, trying to quell a fit of coughing. Miss Lemkuler looked into her pupil's face and felt pity and admiration. It was a shame that this girl came from such a poor home, but in spite of this she worked hard and was determined to make something of her life. To some extent she understood Miss Dawlish's attitude; so many girls from working-class families had been forced to leave the school without completing their education. Places in good schools should only be allocated to pupils whose parents could afford to keep them there until they were at least sixteen years old. Education, according to Miss Dawlish, was wasted on the poor of this world, and it was not in her nature to make an exception.

'You shouldn't have come to school this morning, Lizzie, if you are unwell,' said Miss Lemkuler, as she placed her hand on Lizzie's forehead.

'I'm all right,' said Lizzie abruptly. Then, involuntarily, she let out a cry as a pain shot through her side.

Miss Lemkuler calmed Lizzie down and sent Polly to the cloakroom to fetch her outdoor clothes. 'You are to go home and go straight to bed,' she said.

It was more than an hour later that Lizzie, dragging her feet, came down the front garden path. Aunt Daisy met her at the door, asking no questions. She flung her arms around Lizzie and led her into the kitchen. Within minutes, Lizzie had her face bent over a steaming bowl of boiling water to which Daisy had added Friar's Balsam, with a Turkish towel covering her head, and soon Lizzie was sweating profusely.

By the time Nellie arrived home from work, Lizzie was seated in a chair in front of a roaring fire. She was pale and silent, all her pains eased for the moment. A wad of thermogene wool had been placed on her chest by Aunt Daisy, kept in place by two strips of red flannel.

Two bricks, heated in the oven, and a stone hot-water bottle were carried upstairs and placed in Lizzie's bed. Nellie made her a cup of Oxo and told her to stay by the fire and give the bed a chance to get warm.

Three days later, and still Lizzie did not feel well.

'I think you should take her to see the doctor,' Daisy said as she and Nellie stood gazing at the sleeping Lizzie.

Nellie tucked the bedclothes tightly about Lizzie and sat beside her. 'If only she'd eat,' she whispered.

'Come on now, let's go to bed and make up your mind to get her to that doctor tomorrow. She'll be fine, you'll see,' but Daisy spoke without conviction.

The waiting-room was depressing. The lower half of the windows were crudely painted with dark green paint, keeping out almost all available daylight. A single gas bracket set on the wall to the left of the black iron fireplace struggled to burn brightly but only succeeded in casting gloomy shadows.

The buzzer sounded for the third time. 'Come on, dear, it's our turn,' said Nellie. Two old men moved their feet and one woman sneezed and shook her head as they walked by.

'Do we have to go in?' whispered Lizzie furtively. She was scared of doctors.

The surgery was more brightly lit and infinitely warmer. Doctor Pike did not bother to stand up, just raised his head from the book in which he was writing, and silently motioned Nellie to sit in the only available chair. It took only minutes for him to examine Lizzie. Blushing, feeling awkward, she stood before him in her vest, knickers and black woolly stockings.

'Deep breath . . . breathe out . . . say ninety-nine. All right, get dressed.' Turning to Nellie, he almost recited, 'Not enough sleep. Not the right diet. You might try her on cod-liver oil and malt; she needs building up.'

Washing his hands at the small sink in the corner of the room, Doctor Pike half turned and added, almost as an after-thought, 'Perhaps you should take her to St James's. I'll write a letter; it won't take me a minute.' Licking the flap, he sealed the envelope and passed it over to Nellie, saying, 'Outpatients, tomorrow morning, eleven o'clock.'

The consultation and advice cost two shillings.

Coal and food were expensive and money was short, so it fell to Daisy to take Lizzie to the hospital, whilst

Nellie was away doing her morning stint at the Dawsons.

That awful smell of carbolic! The long draughty corridors, loud footsteps ringing out on the stone-tiled floors, people in white coats hurrying in all directions. Shunted from one cubicle to another, Lizzie was weary. She had coughed so much, her chest was sore and her very bones ached. Lying now on a high metal couch, covered by a red blanket, she just wanted to sleep. Aunt Daisy pulled aside the curtain that divided one cubicle from the next, bent over and smiled lovingly at her niece. Lizzie stared at her with penetrating blue eyes, 'What's happening? Are we going home now?'

Daisy hesitated, her own eyes glistening with tears. 'They want to keep you in, Lizzie.'

'What?'

'Sh!' said Daisy. 'You mustn't get excited.'

Lizzie was shaking visibly and her big eyes looked at her aunt full of pleading, wanting to be taken home.

A sister in-charge came. 'Now then,' she said, 'we'll put you into a chair and get you up to the ward.' Her voice was soft, but unwavering.

The kitchen was crowded. People seldom popped in and out of Nellie Collins's house. She didn't encourage them. Now Jackie Jordon and his wife Doreen stood by the fireplace, Mrs Beasley from number nineteen with her youngest baby cradled in her arms, Alfie Brown, the street bookmaker and his runner, Tommo, all were there. All had come to commiserate because young Lizzie had tuberculosis.

'Christ, that's infectious, that is,' wailed Nora Beasley, "as it affected both her lungs?'

Neighbours and friends were all very well, but Nellie wished they'd go home. She appreciated their kindness but – but what? She hadn't really taken in what Daisy had so patiently explained.

All she knew, her Lizzie had been kept in hospital. Dare-devil, tomboy Lizzie had consumption. She'd seen it coming and shut her eyes to it.

'It's all my fault,' she reproached herself. 'I could see her getting thinner every day, and what did I do about it? Nothing! Oh, it's not fair, it's awful.' She backed away as Doreen Jordon tried to console her, took refuge in the scullery and gave way to a flood of tears.

Lizzie remained in St James's for six weeks. Her mother visited daily, and Aunt Daisy came with Kate Hurley when visiting times were allowed. John Hurley came up some evenings bringing Polly and young Syd with him, but they were only allowed to see Lizzie and wave to her through the window. No children were allowed in wards where patients had infectious diseases. Even adults had to don white masks which covered the lower half of their faces.

One day, two doctors endeavoured to explain to Lizzie why she couldn't go home. Instead, she was being transferred to a sanatorium.

Pinewood Sanatorium was at Wokingham in

Surrey, but as far as Lizzie was concerned it might just as well have been hundreds of miles from London. She had never seen anywhere remotely like it. She was settled into a room with just four beds, white walls and ceiling and white-and-black tiled floor. The curtains and bedspread and draw-around screens, all matching, were made from a flowery material so pretty as to delight the patients, and seeming to bring the garden into the room.

It was not a bit like the many-bedded ward she had just left. Through the wide-open windows, Lizzie could see a view that was unbelievable. As far as the eye could see there were trees, tall, stately, dark green pine trees. She had hidden her head beneath the bedclothes last night and cried herself to sleep. She didn't want to go to no rotten sanatorium, miles away from London, with no visitors – not even her mum.

A fresh-faced, smiling young lady gently placed a tray on the table which straddled Lizzie's legs and propped her up against a great mound of pillows. The smell of the cooked lunch was good and suddenly Lizzie realized she felt hungry.

It wasn't going to be so bad here after all, she told herself as she picked up her knife and fork.

Chapter Seven

AFTER WHAT, TO Lizzie, seemed endless exami-
nations and tests, she was back in her bed. 'I feel
sick,' she moaned. A nurse ran forward, grabbing a
dish from the shelf; she held Lizzie's head whilst she
vomited into the bowl. Then she wiped her mouth
and laid her back on to the pillows.

Lizzie began to cry. She felt frightened and lonely.
Had she been abandoned by her family, sent to this
place out of the way? It wasn't fair. It wasn't her
fault she'd got tuberculosis. Why, if she had to be
ill, did it have to be something that was catching. In
despair, she began to thrash about. The nurse came
back over to her; gently she sat on the bed and drew
Lizzie's head to her breast.

'There, there now, darling,' she said. 'Susan's
here. I'll stay with you.' She rocked Lizzie to and
fro and stayed with her until she sank into a natural
sleep.

The next morning, after breakfast, the nurse
Lizzie now knew as Susan draped Lizzie's dressing-
gown around her shoulders. 'You look beautiful,'
she told her, adding, 'and that's good, because
Doctor Bennett is coming to see you.'

Lizzie looked startled. 'I haven't got to have more
things done to me today, have I?' she asked.

Before Nurse Susan had time to reply, a jovial-looking young man approached the bed. He towered above Lizzie, smiling broadly, his hands in the pockets of his white coat, a blue striped shirt open at the neck.

Lizzie snuggled deep into her pillows, fear showing in her eyes. 'What are you going to do with me now?' she demanded to know.

'Tell you my name first,' he said, drawing a chair up close and taking hold of Lizzie's hand. 'You had a rotten day yesterday, didn't you?' Lizzie made no reply.

'Well, never mind. My name is Stephen Bennett. I know yours is Lizzie Collins and I am going to be looking after you.' Still Lizzie made no comment. She wasn't in a chatty mood this morning.

After a moment of tension, he nudged her with his elbow, leant forward and winked. 'Tell you a secret. I've only been here three days longer than you have. I don't know anyone and Nurse Susan doesn't cuddle me to sleep like she did with you.' Susan blushed scarlet and Lizzie stared at him in astonishment, dumbfounded as to how he knew about that.

'Come on, Lizzie,' he said casually, 'be my friend.'

'Well,' Lizzie appeared to be considering it, 'not till you tell me what else you're going to do ter me.'

The doctor stared at her and she stared back. Then he grinned. 'It's a deal,' he said, holding out his hand which Lizzie solemnly shook. 'Usually, when people are ill with tuberculosis, we have to give one of their lungs a rest. So, we do an operation which cuts the cord holding the lung up and it collapses. To keep the lung rested and to enable the patient to breathe, we pump air into it. Artificially we do the work the poor old lung would be doing if it wasn't so poorly.'

Lizzie's eyes had never left his face while he had been relating these details. Now she moved away warily. 'Well, you ain't gonna do that ter me,' she said.

'Let me finish, Lizzie,' he pleaded. 'All that business we put you through yesterday told us you don't need an operation.'

'Thank God for that,' Lizzie exclaimed defiantly. 'So can I go home now?'

Across her head, the nurse looked at the young doctor and they smiled at each other and he said, 'We've got ourselves a real bright spark here.' To Lizzie he begged, 'Be patient, there's a good girl.' Then, with a gentle expression on his face, he told her, 'You have fluid on your right lung and you need to stay with us for quite a while. Still, we shall get you into a healthy routine and you'll find out that those of us who work here are not such a bad lot. You might even come to like us.'

His lips were smiling as he finished and his eyes had a mischievous glint in them.

After several days had passed, Lizzie was well aware of the routine, though she was astounded to learn that she would still have to spend at least six more weeks lying in bed. At eleven o'clock each morning either Susan or Linda (Linda being the other nurse assigned to Lizzie's room) would stand over her as she swallowed a raw egg. Even beaten up in a glass with milk added, Lizzie found it revolting.

To follow was a section of a fresh orange on to which halibut liver oil had been dripped. Lunch was at one o'clock. By two o'clock, complete silence. 'Break it if you dare,' the red-headed freckled-faced Linda had warned Lizzie, though a smile had lingered about her lips as she spoke. Not a soul moved anywhere until four o'clock.

At bedtime, one of the nurses would command, 'Open wide', and two spoonfuls of Gee's Linctus would be poured into her mouth. Never did she have to settle down to sleep without a good-night kiss.

The two nurses liked her and Lizzie liked them. They giggled with her and made fun of Sister Cartwright, who bustled in and out of the ward, her eyes taking in everything, but who really was a nice old softie. They told her humorous stories about the doctors and they showed her affection. It didn't stop Lizzie missing her mum and Aunt Daisy or Polly, and as for her brother Syd, who was more often than not a little devil, she missed him like hell; but when Susan and Linda were around, she didn't feel quite so lonely.

Visitors were allowed once a fortnight on Sundays. When Nellie Collins had received the visitor's pass she had sighed deeply and sought advice from Daisy.

'I could just about scrape the coach fare together but that would mean going empty 'anded,' she dolefully told her sister-in-law.

' 'Lotter good that would do our Lizzie,' said Daisy, ever the practical one. 'No. Get together the things we know she likes, some embroidery or knitting to keep her occupied and fer Christ's sake don't forget her books. Toc H will let yer 'ave as many books as yer want.'

'Then what will we do with them? Cost a fortune to post a parcel like that,' Nellie's voice almost broke. She was very upset.

'We'll take 'em up to the Elephant and Castle on the tram. Stop worrying. It'll be all right. You'll see.'

Come Sunday morning they were up and ready early. Syd was sent to spend the day with Connie and Bill.

'Wind's still cold,' Daisy warned, 'we'd both better put a scarf on.' Then they were off to catch the tram from the Broadway, each carrying a heavy parcel.

An inspector at the bus station pointed out the coach. 'Runs right into Pinewood grounds it does, missus,' he told them. 'Fare's four and six each.'

Nellie couldn't bring herself to make the request, but Daisy was not to be put off. 'That's what we come 'ere for,' she muttered to herself as she

approached a group of drivers. 'Excuse me,' she
called, 'which one of you drives the coach going to
Wokingham?'

'I does, as it 'appens,' said one of them, separating
himself from his mates. 'What can I do fer yer, luv?'

Daisy hesitated. He was a big, red-faced man,
smartly dressed in his uniform overcoat, a white silk
scarf knotted at his throat.

'You wouldn't oblige me, would yer?' she got out
at last. 'Take a parcel for me niece? She's down there
in the Sanatorium.'

'Don't yer want ter make the trip, lady?' He could
have bitten off his tongue as soon as the question left
his lips. Nellie had come to stand alongside Daisy.

Two more forlorn-looking long faces, Ted Baker
told himself, he hadn't seen in many a long day. Yer
silly sod, he chastized himself, they ain't got the
money for the fare. God, he wished it was up to
him. He'd have them on that coach all right, and
bugger whether or not they could pay. 'I'll take it
fer yer with pleasure,' he said.

'There's two parcels,' Nellie spoke quietly.

'All the better, luv. What's the young lady's
name?'

'Lizzie Collins,' they answered in unison.

'Well, if yer Lizzie comes ter meet me coach, I'll
tell 'er you both send yer luv, shall I?'

'She's confined to bed,' Nellie said with a sob in
her voice.

'Well, never mind. This is me regular run. Nurses
are used ter me 'anging around fer two hours every

other Sunday, give me a cup of tea, regular as clock-work they do. They'll see your Lizzie gets her par-cels all right.'

'Mister, you're a good sport,' Daisy said.

'No trouble at all, darlings, and if yer want ter make it a regular thing, yer know every other Sunday I'd be more than happy ter oblige.'

'Please, have this for your trouble,' Nellie said, holding out a sixpence.

Ted Baker told his mates afterwards that a lump the size of a billiard ball filled his throat then. His big hand gently closed round Nellie's, curling her fingers inward over the coin. Kindly he whispered, 'Put it away, missus. I might need someone ter do me a good turn some day.'

They lingered long enough to watch the coach pull out from the bus station, a sad-looking pair. Daisy, a healthy buxom woman at least four inches taller than her sister-in-law, looked neat and tidy in a well-fitting brown costume with a lace-collared cream blouse. She worried about Nellie and wished that she had been able to afford to pay her coach fare.

'I miss Lizzie so much,' Nellie said, as she groped in her bag for a handkerchief for she was blinded by tears.

'I know yer do, luv, but she's in the best place. We'll have her home soon, you'll see.' And as she uttered the words, Daisy silently prayed that they were the truth.

Lizzie was thrilled. Fruit, boiled sweets, a new face flannel and lovely scented soap were in one parcel, and in the other were wool, knitting needles and a nice slip-over pattern, which had been cut out from *Woman's Own*, and there were lots of books as well!

'Look at all the letters you got,' cried Nurse Susan, as she tidied Lizzie's bed. 'Well, I'm off for my tea now, I won't be long. Don't go getting too excited.'

When she had gone, Lizzie began reading. One letter was from Mr and Mrs Hurley, who now signed themselves, Aunt Kate and Uncle John. That was nice. One was signed by several of the neighbours, and enclosed were four stamps. One was from Connie and Bill with a postal order for two shillings.

Tears trickled down her cheeks as she read the next one. 'Be good now, whippet. Eat all your food and take your medicine because I want to see you fat with rosy cheeks when I come home.' Oh Leslie, so far away in Malta.

She was slightly put out as she read one her mother had received from Miss Dawlish. 'We do wish Lizzie well, her classmates miss her, as does the entire staff. Such a bright pupil of whom I have great hopes.' Had she misjudged her headmistress all these years? Lizzie doubted it!

The longest letter was from Polly. 'Soppy old thing you, Lizzie, getting ill like that,' was how she started it. 'You'll never guess; I've got a boyfriend.

Fred Holt is his name.' Lizzie brightened up a bit as she scanned the pages. A good laugh was Polly, and a good friend. She read on, 'The Granada is open, you'll have to come when you get home. Expensive, though. Costs ninepence downstairs. Fred took me upstairs. You have to walk through a hall of mirrors. Costs one and threepence. Reginald Dixon was playing the organ in the interval. You know, we've heard him on the wireless. He plays in Blackpool Tower. Oh yeah, and everyone going into the pictures that week got a free stick of Blackpool rock. Want a lick? – HA, HA! Seemed funny though, Lizzie, going to the cinema built on the place where your Gran's house used to be.' Not funny, thought Lizzie, as she folded up the letter, real sad.

Lizzie had had a bad week. It started on Monday. Nurse Susan and Sister Cartwright had pulled the curtains around her bed, sat her up and removed her nightdress.

'Knees up my lovely,' said Sister Cartwright, 'lean forward, head down.' Her voice was kindly, but the determination was there.

Two older doctors talked *about* her, but not *to* her and Lizzie didn't like that. Doctor Bennett appeared, smiling broadly, his fair hair tousled, in need of combing; he winked at Lizzie as she raised her head. Tap, tap, the doctor's fingers beat along her ribs.

'Ah, there it is. Just a little prick, Lizzie,' he said casually. It wasn't. It hurt like hell and Lizzie cried out. Both Nurse and Sister held her hands.

'Be brave,' Susan whispered, 'it won't be long.'

It seemed to take hours and Lizzie got hot and flustered. One tall doctor loomed over her. 'All over, child,' he said. 'Look, we struck gold.' He held aloft a large syringe, the tube of which was filled with a murky yellow fluid. He patted her head and moved away with his colleague.

'Please, Nurse, may I have a drink?' Lizzie pleaded.

'Of course you may, pet,' said the motherly Sister Cartwright, pulling Lizzie's head towards her ample bosom. 'You've been a good, brave girl. You will get better now that the doctors have got that nasty fluid off your lung.'

Sister was right. Two weeks later and Lizzie was up and about. She was weak as a kitten at first, and the nurses laughed at her first attempt to stand. Her legs buckled beneath her. Dressed in a navy-blue skirt and neat white blouse, with shoes on her feet for the first time in weeks, Lizzie was ready to leave the main building. She was going to the camp.

Long rows of wooden huts, partitioned off to give each patient a single room, set in the heart of sweet-smelling green pine trees. All through the woods tracks had been cut and laid over with cinders. Each room had a large window in the outside wall, but no pane of glass. Whatever the weather, there were no shutters. If it rained too heavily, beds were covered by a tarpaulin.

Exercise, rest, and good food was now the order

of the day. Walking the cinder tracks between the tall pine trees was a morning routine. Each week the distance was extended. The afternoon two-hour bed rest was still obligatory. Twice a week, patients listened through headphones to a recorded message. 'Your illness probably started with a common cold,' the voice droned on, 'built up to bronchitis, developed into pleurisy, thus causing tuberculosis. The remedy is to eat fat. FAT builds up bodily resistance. It is good for you; you must eat it.' Lizzie vowed that she would.

The rooms on either side of Lizzie were occupied by young girls, for which Lizzie was grateful. In the main building, her room had held, besides herself, three older, very sick ladies. Nice enough, but not very companionable. Twenty-five-year-old Mary Gibson had a fresh, healthy face and didn't look at all ill. 'Blimey, she's young,' had been her first words when introduced to Lizzie. A proper cockney lass, was Mary. Do I speak like she does? Lizzie wondered after a day or two, and promised herself she'd try to do better.

Anne Caxton was almost twenty. Just the opposite from Mary, slightly frosty at first. Her eyes were deep brown and framed by long, stiff black lashes. Her expression was discouraging, as she eyed Lizzie up and down. Happily, she thawed as the days passed and Lizzie was pleased to have two friends.

Lizzie, arriving at the gate to pick up her weekly parcel from the coach driver, stopped to listen to what the older patients were saying.

'There is going to be a war,' said a tall, educated-sounding lady.

'Yes, you can bet on it now,' said another.

'We shall all be sent home,' a third patient told the group, as if she were privileged to prior information. Lizzie liked the sound of that. The thought of the country going to war didn't particulary worry her.

The coach turned in at the gates and came to a halt with a squeak of brakes. Ted Baker and Lizzie had become friends and, as the door of the coach opened, he grinned down at her and gave her the thumbs-up sign, nodding his head backwards. She looked in the direction he indicated and was flabbergasted. Her brother Syd was kneeling up on a seat, his nose pressed flat against the window. His eyes were wide and he was grinning like a Cheshire cat. In the gangway, crushed with passengers, was her mum. Further down was Aunt Daisy. Lizzie was overjoyed. She jigged up and down on the spot. She couldn't believe it, she had visitors.

Nothing could spoil that day. They had a picnic in the woods, Lizzie showed them her room and took them to the main building to meet Nurse Susan and Nurse Linda. The time went all too quickly. Suddenly the bell went, summoning them back to the coach.

'Don't forget to say thank you to Ted Baker, will you Lizzie,' her mother said. 'Heart of gold that

man's got, his mates too. It was them that helped
us out with the fare.'

Ted Baker brushed aside Lizzie's thanks. 'See you
in two weeks,' he called, as the coach door closed.
Lizzie ran alongside waving until her arm ached.

'Crikey,' Mary said, 'you've got real nice folk,
ain't yer?'

'Yes I have,' Lizzie agreed.

The patients didn't get sent home and England
didn't go to war. Prime Minister Neville Chamberlain went to Germany to talk to Adolf Hitler. He
was sincere in his efforts, and came back waving a
piece of paper, saying, 'Peace in our time'.

At first Lizzie was disappointed not to be going
home, but not for long. November came and Lizzie
was much better. Now she could go home!

The ambulance came to a halt in Graveney Road,
and when the doors had been opened it seemed to
Lizzie that the whole street had turned out to welcome her home. Tears choked her. What a home-
coming, what a surprise! The strong, tanned arms
that lifted her down belonged to her eldest brother
Leslie. His service of seven years in the Army was
over. He had been given his discharge. Lizzie was
happy, so happy! What a wonderful Christmas this
will be, she told herself.

And it was.

Chapter Eight

ANOTHER NEW YEAR. 1939.

The papers were full of dire predictions and most people hoped they were exaggerating. Many others knew war was only a matter of time.

Leslie Collins was amongst those who were not lulled into a false sense of security by the words of Neville Chamberlain. Council offices were offering Anderson Air Raid Shelters free of charge and Leslie collected one. The erecting of this caused so much interest amongst the neighbours that the local paper sent a reporter to investigate. Come Friday, Leslie's picture was in the local paper. With Syd beside him, their shirt-sleeves rolled high above their elbows, they stood beside this ugly, weird monstrosity which now stood deep in the backyard. Both brothers had blond, almost white hair, masses of tight curls which hugged their heads and which they both hated. Their teeth were also alike. The top rows were white and even, the lower ones showing gaps.

'Lucky that is;' said Nellie, 'if you can put a six-pence between your teeth' (and both of her sons could) 'you were born lucky,' she insisted. They differed only in height. Syd, at fifteen years old, was already almost as tall as Leslie.

'Like his father,' Daisy remarked, 'gonna top six foot, you see if I'm not right.'

'Hope so,' said Syd. He badly wanted to get into the Army. If war did come and he was really tall, he could put his age up and get away with it, he told his mother. Nellie shuddered at the thought.

Lizzie didn't go back to school; she got a job.

Spring came and the trees on the Common were loaded with blossoms. On Whit Monday Leslie took them all to Hampstead Heath. Folk loved the Heath on a bank holiday because of the fair. Lizzie was breathless as she enthusiastically threw her last wooden ball at the elevated coconuts.

'Hopeless you are,' Syd told her, pushing her aside. Syd threw each ball with grim determination. He struck with his third attempt and Lizzie shrieked with delight as the coconut fell to the ground. Syd ran to retrieve his prize.

The stallholder put in a replacement. 'You're good you are, sonny,' he said, as he patted Syd's head.

'Yeah, bowl for England he might one day,' yelled an admiring onlooker.

Leslie and Bill treated them to rides and Lizzie found the swing-boats exciting. 'Pull harder,' Syd ordered, as the swing began to soar. Boys were hooting with laughter as they watched from the ground. Girls' dresses were billowing high, giving glimpses of petticoats and legs in silk stockings.

Mum and Aunt Daisy found them and said it was

time to eat. Families were flocking to the grass areas
for picnics. Hard-boiled eggs, ripe tomatoes, cheese
sandwiches, Swiss jam roll and fruit cake – everyone
tucked in; Daisy poured tea from two vacuum flasks
and there was lemonade for those who wanted it.

As they left the Heath, music still blared out from
the merry-go-rounds. Shrieks and squeals still mingled with loud shouts of laughter. London families
were still enjoying their bank holiday.

No gloom and doom talk of war. It had been a
smashing day.

The sun had shone for weeks on end as if to defy
the bad news. 'We definitely will have a war,' said
John Hurley as he passed the official letter back to
Leslie.

It was the beginning of August, only eight
months since Leslie had been demobbed. He was
to report to Aldershot. He was on the first-reserve
register.

Seven days later, and again the local paper carried
a photograph of Sergeant Collins who was receiving
new recruits, known as militiamen, into Aldershot
Barracks. Two weeks after that he was home again,
this time on a forty-eight-hour pass.

'Remember, sleep in that shelter,' he repeatedly
told Nellie, 'don't take chances.'

'Oh, they won't bomb London,' cried Aunt
Daisy, wanting to evade the subject altogether.

When Leslie went back to barracks the goodbyes
and hugs were emotional. Daisy had lost a fiancé in

the last war and memories flooded back. Nellie's heart was full of fear as she held her first born. Syd made a joke, 'Have a uniform ready for me,' but Connie wiped away a tear and Lizzie locked herself in the bathroom. She didn't want Leslie to go away again and couldn't help herself. She had to cry.

Sunday morning, 3rd of September.

Folk were out on their doorsteps and all front doors were flung wide open. Those fortunate enough to own a wireless set had the volume turned full up, blaring out for all to hear. Big Ben chimed, then struck eleven o'clock. There was a silent air of expectancy throughout the whole street.

'It is with regret that I have to inform you a state of war now exists between ourselves and Germany.' Neville Chamberlain's voice came over the air with a feeling of finality.

The silence remained in the air for a full minute. Maurice Smith from the other side of the road broke it. 'What the 'ell did we go through the last bleeding lot for?' he stormed aloud. Everyone glanced at the pinned-up left sleeve of his jacket. It was twenty-two years ago that he had lost his arm in the First World War. His next-door neighbour let out a strangled yell of rage and then everyone began talking at once.

'Oh, the poor kids,' wailed Doreen Jordon, 'they'll all have to be evacuated.'

'I'll join up, soon as I can,' vowed Syd.

'Oh Christ, my Bill will 'ave to go,' Connie said, brushing away tears.

'What the 'ell is that?' The question came from several mouths as the air was rent by the wailing of the sirens.

'Bloody eerie, ain't it?' said one old woman.

Nellie gathered her family together and took them back inside the house. 'Let's hope it's only practice,' she said as she filled the kettle and got down the flask in readiness for the air-raid shelter.

But it was a false alarm, and soon the moaning, long drawn-out, all-clear sounded.

'We're all right now,' Daisy said calmly.

Nellie offered up a silent prayer and made the tea.

Children up and down the street were saying their goodbyes. Labels hung round their necks stating their names and addresses. Carrier bags held their sandwiches and gas masks in cardboard boxes hung over their shoulders. Women threw their aprons over their heads so that their tears wouldn't be noticed as teachers marshalled groups down the road. The street seemed different after that. Abandoned, clean and tidy, and far too quiet.

To top the lot, council workmen came with lorries to take down the iron railings which had adorned low garden walls, and dismantle the chains which had hung for years between posts. Wrought-iron ornamental gates were wrenched from their hinges and all were carted away.

'What the 'ell is going on?' residents wanted to know.

'It's to help the war effort,' was the only explanation the elderly council men could give.

Weeks turned into months and all the young men were getting called up. Connie's Bill went into the Navy and Leslie was back with his regiment in Malta. The new year came and wartime in London became a reality. Food was rationed, coal was short, fresh meat and fish were hard to get and corned beef was a handy substitute. Every single thing was rationed. The Ministry of Food dealt with the issuing of ration books. Fawn coloured books for adults, green coloured for children under five years of age.

Rationing made life hard for wives and mothers and rows brewed up in shops.

'Whatcha mean, I've had me tea ration?' they would shout.

'I dunno what the world's a coming to,' grumbled another. 'Not a bit of sugar in the 'ouse an' she says I can't 'ave any for another four weeks. A bloody month, mind you!'

Life was tedious. Stockings were hard to come by. Sally Silverman's stall in the market looked dull, dusty and empty.

'Only got lisle ones ter offer you gals,' Sally miserably told them.

'Not even fully fashioned, are they?' Polly asked.

'No, love, fully fashioned they ain't. Turn them inside out, cut the edges from round the heel why don't cher? That way they don't look so bad.'

'They don't look so good either,' grumbled Polly.

Silk stockings from Sally had cost one shilling a pair since God knows when, and they'd been fully fashioned. Now she wanted one and ninepence for lisle ones. They hated this boring old war; they hated the blackout and were already sick to death with shortages.

The last few days of May 1940 were like a nightmare. Rumours were unbelievable. France had fallen to Germany. British troops were stranded on the beaches of Dunkirk. German planes bombarded the helpless men. The sea lay in front of them, German troops behind them.

Old men stood in the Selkirk Pub and cried openly in frustration as they listened to the news on the wireless. The obscenities they yelled did little to relieve their anger.

Boats of all shapes and sizes were put to sea. Men who hadn't navigated a vessel for years volunteered. The Navy did their bit, under horrific conditions thousands of men, not only British soldiers, but French and Belgian also, were plucked from those beaches. Trip after trip was made and men still cried. Some were speechless with shock. A mass of dead bodies covered the beaches, with more floating gently in the sea. Yet it had been a miracle, the evacuation of Dunkirk.

Britain now stood alone.

Not long afterwards the bombing of London began. Night after night the sirens wailed the warning. Deep shelters in parks and on commons were filled with families. Hundreds more made for the Underground stations, sleeping on the platforms. Young and old alike endured the hardship, too nervous to be above ground where bombs were falling and the noise of anti-aircraft guns was deafening.

Lizzie got home later each evening. She had landed a good job as a ledger clerk with A. T. Hart, the quality butchers. With the outbreak of war, she, along with all the clerical staff, had had to leave the comfort of her office and come out into the shop, serving customers, wrapping meat, marking ration books and taking money. Because of a shortage of staff she sometimes had to work in different shops. For three weeks now she'd been in the Chapel Street shop. It was near the London docks, an area that was a prime target for the German bombers.

Sure enough, they came over early one evening. It was the roughest raid so far. Incendiary bombs rained down and flames shot high into the air; clouds of dust rose up and the acrid smell was choking. Lizzie walked over London Bridge, coughing and spluttering, her eyes were red and sore. Air-raid wardens and policemen were everywhere.

'Where yer making for?' someone asked her.

'Tooting,' Lizzie managed to mutter.

'Come along, this way,' a hand guided her.

'Buses are few and far between, but you might be lucky. Tube stations are all closed,' volunteered the warden.

'Thank you,' Lizzie blubbered, just wanting to get home.

The next morning, Lizzie awoke with a headache and sore throat. She staggered downstairs into the kitchen and gratefully sipped the tea that her mother had made for her.

'You'd better stay home today,' Nellie insisted.

'All right,' Lizzie croaked.

She pushed aside the plate of toast Aunt Daisy offered, but held out her hand as her aunt said, 'There's a letter for you.'

At that moment Polly pushed open the door and burst into the room, waving a buff-coloured envelope. 'Snap!' said Lizzie, waving her identical one. She tore open the envelope and a long whistle escaped from her lips.

'You too?' Polly asked. Their letters were the same. Call-up interview, Thursday, two p.m., in the Central Hall.

In just two weeks' time, they would both be eighteen.

Smiling slightly, the woman on the other side of the table agreed to interview them together. 'Stay calm,' Lizzie told herself. There was no way she was going to go into the Forces.

'How about munitions?' the posh voice asked.

'Oh no!' Polly looked at Lizzie and they both shuddered at the thought.

'Work in a factory?' was the next suggestion.

'Never!' they both agreed.

'How about the ATS? At a later date, of course,' the genteel lady offered.

'Me dad says it will be all over come Christmas,' said Polly defiantly. 'We ain't gonna go in no army.'

'We shall see,' the woman sighed. 'Meanwhile, these forms have to be completed.'

The interview wasn't going at all well. The lady took off her spectacles and rubbed the bridge of her nose. 'Land Army?'

They both gagged at the thought.

'The trams or the buses?' she put forward in desperation.

The two girls giggled. 'Don't fancy the trams,' said Lizzie, 'buses might be all right.'

'Yeah. Nice uniform they have on the buses,' said Polly.

Relief flooded through the interviewer. She was anxious to be on her way. London in the blackout was no place to be.

'So, I'll state your preference for war work with London Passenger Transport,' she said, writing on the forms, not waiting for an answer.

They contained themselves until they were at the bottom of the stairs, then the pair of them fell about laughing. Boisterously, they punched each other, 'We're gonna be clippies.' The very thought brought forth more laughter which echoed loudly against the tiled walls. Swiftly they ran out into the Mitcham Road. Who'd have believed it? They were

going to help the war effort, they were going to
work on the buses.

Chapter Nine

THREE WEEKS' TRAINING at Chiswick, on full pay, had gone remarkably well – except for one incident.

Alan Cooke, a retired driver, having served twenty-four years at Shepherd's Bush Garage, was in charge of the class. Twelve girls in all, Lizzie and Polly going to Merton Garage, the others to various depots.

What Alan Cooke didn't know about schedules wasn't worth knowing. Tall, good-looking in a rakish kind of way, he fancied he was God's gift to all women – even at his age. At break-time, Lizzie was unusually quiet.

'What's the matter?' Polly asked, as she set two large mugs of tea down.

'I can't stand that man. He's 'orrible,' said Lizzie.

'Why? What's he done now?'

'He pinched me nipple.'

'You're joking!' Polly couldn't help it, she laughed out loud.

'So you think it's funny, do yer? Well I 'ope he does it to you.'

'I'll bloody kill 'im if he tries,' said Polly, her temper rising.

During the afternoon session, Polly kept her eyes on Mr Cooke. He approached Lizzie, coming up from behind. Leaning forward, he placed his two arms over her shoulders, supposedly to check what she was writing. Quick as a flash, Polly was out of her seat. Between thumb and fingernail, she pinched a lump of his backside, giving it a good, hard nip.

He sprang backwards and let out a cry of pain. His instinct told him it was Lizzie's mate who had attacked him, but he couldn't prove it.

'He won't try his tricks on you again in a hurry,' Polly said with a satisfied smirk on her face as they walked to the bus stop.

'You're a bitch, Polly,' Lizzie laughed as she spoke. 'Did you notice he didn't sit down all the afternoon?'

They ran up the road, giggling as they went.

They left Chiswick the proud owners of a full uniform. A leather shoulder bag with two compartments, and a wooden ticket rack completed their issue. How neat they looked – Lizzie, small-boned, fair complexion, her long hair tucked into a snood; Polly, tall and slim, her dark hair cut to shoulder-length and worn with a fringe. Their only complaint was that the serge trousers were itchy.

Six weeks later, and they had taken to their wartime job like ducks to water. Both girls were on the same shift, but not the same route. Lizzie loved the job, she liked meeting people, but she did get tired.

The grimness of each day seemed to get worse. The air raids were becoming a habit, a fact of life accepted as an inconvenient annoyance but no more than that. Even the stories of bombed factories, direct hits on shelters and folk losing their homes didn't shock people as it had at the beginning of the war.

Lizzie, and many like her, began to think that it was safer to be in the open during a raid, rather than huddled up below ground. It was bad enough coming home by tube late at night. At Tooting Broadway, the whole platform seemed to be a tangled mass of humanity, huddled together, no room to turn, let alone move about. The stench of bodies was awful. Once clear of the arms and legs, Lizzie would run like a wild hare. At midnight, steel floodgates would slam shut and folk sheltering below were then entombed until the next morning. Lizzie couldn't bear the thought.

Finally, she decided she had had enough of their Anderson shelter. If she had to spend one more night sleeping against the damp wall, listening to Aunt Daisy snore, her mother sucking boiled sweets and old Mrs Ticehurst, whom Nellie had taken under her wing, cluck away at her loose false teeth, not to mention the lapping of water under the floorboarding and that horrid musty earthy smell, she'd go mad.

When she got home, she went straight upstairs to bed. Nellie objected, then pleaded. 'You'll be killed,' she wailed.

At least I'll die in comfort, thought Lizzie as she snuggled down in her clean, comfortable bed. She ignored the gunfire, the searchlights, which criss-crossed the sky and lit up her room, even the bombs, and had her first good night's sleep for months.

'About time we saw a bit of life. Never go anywhere now do we?' Polly sounded right fed up.

'Two toast and cheese,' Elsie called from behind the canteen counter. Lizzie rose and went to fetch her snack.

'You were a long time. What were yer talking to Elsie about?' Polly wanted to know.

'A night out for us, actually,' Lizzie said, wrapping up the large piece of cheese and putting it in the pocket of her overcoat. Her mum and Aunt Daisy looked forward to the bits and pieces she smuggled out from the canteen.

'A night out where? The last one didn't turn out so well,' grumbled Polly.

They had been on early shift, so one evening they had gone up to Rainbow Corner at Piccadilly. Talk about the League of Nations! Yanks, Canadians, Australians, Poles. The dancing was all right, they certainly didn't lack partners; it was the close clinches that bothered them.

'Elsie said troops are moving on to Garratt Green.'

'So?'

'Whatcha mean, so?'

'Well, what difference will it make ter us?' Polly grunted through a mouthful of rissole.

'Fairlight Hall is putting on a dance Saturday night, you know, to welcome them.'

'Only be a gramophone. Bet yer life they won't have a band.'

'Oh, for Christ's sake, what's the matter with yer, Polly?' Lizzie asked in desperation.

'Sorry, Lizzie,' Polly said apologetically. 'Don't mind me, I'm just having one of those days.'

On Saturday night, they fished out their high-heeled shoes and long skirts, made up their faces and curled the ends of their hair with hot tongs and went off to this sevenpenny hop at Fairlight Hall.

Lizzie looked across the hall at a dark-skinned, blue-eyed, wavy-haired lance corporal and fell head over heels in love. She felt good in her long black skirt and pretty pink chiffon blouse as she danced close to her new-found friend, whose name was Charlie Wilson.

Polly was getting on well with his tall, lanky friend, who was called Frank. So well, in fact, that when 'In The Mood' came blaring from the gramophone the two of them gave an exhibition.

Their bodies were as one as they matched their steps to everyone's favourite quick-step. Partners fell back, leaving Polly and Frank a clear floor. The record came to an end and they hugged each other, hot and sweaty as they were. A burst of clapping showed admiration and Polly blushed.

'Who's Taking You Home Tonight', was the last record to be played and couples dreamily danced the waltz with the lights dimmed. Charlie sang, his lips close to Lizzie's hair, "I'm pleading, please let it be me."

The four of them left the hall together Polly and Frank lingered in Garratt Lane, and Lizzie yelled back, 'We're going on, Polly. I'm on at a quarter-past five in the morning.'

'All right,' came Polly's reply, 'see you tomorrow'.

Charlie left her at the gate. He hadn't attempted to kiss her and Lizzie was disappointed.

'We'll be here for a while. I shall see you soon,' he promised, and Lizzie hoped it was a promise that he would keep.

On Wednesday when Lizzie finished her shift at one-forty-five at Tooting Bec, Charlie was there waiting for her. He bent down and gave her a swift kiss.

'Okay, Lizzie?' he asked as natural as you like, as if they had known each other for years.

His uniform was well pressed and you could see your face in the toe-caps of his boots. Lizzie gave him a lovely smile and he smiled back.

Catching her in his arms, he swung her in the air. 'Oh, I haven't been able to get you out of my mind, Lizzie. I want to spend every spare minute I get with you.'

Lizzie laughed; she liked his authoritative tone. He went back to the garage with her, waiting while she paid in her day's takings, then they walked all the way home to Tooting, talking non-stop.

Her mother and her aunt warned her to be careful. 'Take things slowly, please,' Nellie pleaded. 'Couples rush to get married in wartime and live to regret it,' she wisely told Lizzie. Their words were wasted.

Eight wonderful weeks and she had been with him wherever possible. Now, as the leaves on the trees began to turn beautiful shades of red and brown and the evenings drew in, Charlie came to say goodbye. His battalion of the Royal Artillery Corps was moving on. On the doorstep Lizzie snuggled close and Charlie covered her lips in a long kiss. It was wonderful. It was different from all the others kisses, long and passionate.

'You will write to me, won't you?' Charlie begged.

'Of course I will, darling,' Lizzie promised.

'If I get a long leave, will you marry me?' he asked.

'Yes, oh yes,' she answered, her eyes wet with tears.

''Allo, Lizzie. Long time no see.'

Lizzie's face broke into a smile as she punched the threea'penny ticket and handed it to Sadie Braffman. 'How's yer mum?' she asked.

'She's better. Misses me dad a lot though.'

'Yeah,' Lizzie muttered thoughtfully. 'A lot of people do.'

Bernie Braffman had been a great character and had had two stalls in the market for years. Lizzie had stood at the corner of Blackshaw Road and watched his funeral procession pass.

One bystander had uttered a statement that had struck in Lizzie's mind. 'In this life, you're as rich as the number of friends you got. Well, Bernie Braffman was a rich man.' What better epitaph could a man have?

'You finishing now?' Sadie asked as she watched Lizzie pick up her ticket box from underneath the stairs.

'Yep. Thank God. Not a bad duty, this one though. Six-three out of the garage in the morning, finished now at Tooting Bec twelve-forty-five. Two journeys to Shepherd's Bush, only one up to Crystal Palace.'

'Come and 'ave a cuppa coffee with me?' Sadie suggested hopefully.

' 'Course I will, can't stay long, though. Gotta pay in at the garage.'

They sat facing each other across the oil-cloth covered table in the steamy cafe, while Lizzie sipped her coffee and Sadie poured out her troubles.

'It's no joke 'aving to cope with two stalls,' she complained, staring fixedly at Lizzie, her stout body pushed tight into a grey costume which emphasized her ample bosom. Her jet black hair and olive skin were lovely, her best features really, thought Lizzie, who found herself feeling sorry for Sadie without really knowing why.

Lizzie listened attentively and made noises of encouragement. 'What's ter do, I don't know,' Sadie went on. 'Since my brother David got called up and me dad's gone, I 'aven't opened the bedding stall.

It's not worth it. Coupons for this, dockets for that, queues at the warehouses and what for? Nothing. You wouldn't believe it.'

Sadie paused for breath, 'I have to keep the grocery stall going, don't I? 'Asn't been too bad so far, but now, staff I can't get. Not a soul. I tell`yer, Lizzie, a man I wish I was. Off ter the war I'd be.' Then she shot a question at Lizzie out of the blue, 'Have you finished for the day?'

'Yes, I told you already.'

'Same time all the week?' asked Sadie.

'Till Friday,' Lizzie told her. 'Saturday and Sunday rosters are different.'

'Oh, Lizzie,' Sadie practically shrieked, 'you could help me out no end.'

'Me? How?' But already Lizzie suspected what was coming.

'Do a few afternoons on the stall with me, and what about when you're on late turns, a few mornings, eh? You'll do a few mornings maybe, then?' The worried look on Sadie's face tore at Lizzie's heart.

'Well, I'll give it a try. Nothing definite, you know. See how it goes.'

'Oh, d'yer mean it?' Sadie said and, to Lizzie's embarrassment, she flung her arms round Lizzie's neck and kissed her noisily.

So now Lizzie had two jobs.

It was pouring with rain when Lizzie came out of the garage. Wearing a long mac, with her hair covered by a scarf, she looked tired and dejected. All she really wanted to do was to go home and get into bed. Instead, she was doing a stint up at the market this afternoon.

She shouldn't grumble, she told herself. In the couple of months that she had worked for Sadie, she had done pretty well. Sadie was grateful, kind and generous, and what's more, they had a good laugh most of the time, especially when Polly was able to do a turn on the stall as well.

Lizzie was pleased to see her sister Connie in the scullery when she pushed open the back door. Short and sturdy, bursting with energy, she wore a smart, long dress. Being pregnant suited Connie.

'Hallo, love,' she smiled and greeted Lizzie warmly. 'Mum told me what time you'd be home. I've boiled some potatoes and I've got a tin of pilchards. You 'aven't eaten in the garage, 'ave you?'

'No,' Lizzie answered, 'I wasn't gonna bother.'

'I really wanted ter tell you about our Syd,' Connie said as she vigorously beat at the potatoes in the saucepan with a fork.

'Why? What's up with Syd?' Lizzie sounded angry.

'All right, all right,' said Connie, trying to calm her.

A few weeks before, the police had been round. Syd and his mates had stolen a bike. Since Bill had been called up, Syd had lived with Connie. It was better than being on her own, Nellie had decided.

''As he been a nuisance or 'as he been pinching again?'

'Nothing like that, 'onest Lizzie. Give me a chance. The fact is,' Connie hesitated, 'he's run off. Gone to join up.'

'What?' roared Lizzie. 'He's too bloody young.'

Connie plopped a spoonful of mash on to the plates, which each held two pilchards, then spooned the tomato sauce from the tin over the fish. Lizzie felt afraid; Syd could be a right little sod, but he was their young brother, the baby of the family. Trouble was, he looked so angelic. He could lie through his teeth, smiling all the time and folk believed him.

She ate her lunch without really enjoying it and was grateful when Connie cleared away their plates.

'Well now, what's Sadie got to sell that's special today?' Connie asked, as Lizzie pulled her trousers off and stepped into a brown tweed skirt.

'Dunno till I get there. Might be Camp coffee,' she suggested.

'Well, whatever, don't you go overdoing it, love,' Connie said kindly, 'and don't start worrying about Syd. What's done is done, and there is nothing we can do about it now.'

'Does mum know?' asked Lizzie.

'Yes, she does, and she didn't take it too bad.'

Lizzie wrinkled up her face. 'Poor old Syd,' she said. 'He's not so bad, you know; I hope he's got a guardian angel.'

There was a lively atmosphere in the market that

afternoon. Most of the stalls were open and each seemed to have something to offer because queues had formed everywhere.

'Marvellous, ain't it?' one woman remarked to Lizzie as she counted out her change. 'Now there's plenty of work about and we've gotta bit of money, the things ain't around to buy any more.'

Tommy Clarke's stall had oranges today and young women with babes in their arms, toddlers in push-chairs and prams waited patiently. Old Tommy served them from an open wooden crate only if they had green ration books. Oranges were only for the under fives. Probably the first time some kiddies had ever seen one.

Mrs Scott, seventy if she was a day, resolutely kept her son's hardware stall going. Today she had a few Axminster rugs but the supply would run out long before the queue had dwindled.

Sadie's voice was persuasive as she walked the length of the line of women who clutched their canvas and paper bags. 'Custard powder, matches, some bottled coffee, Daddie's Sauce, even a few Chivers' Jellies we've got today. So, spend some ration points with us, please.' It was only by taking coupons and bundles of points to the Ministry of Food that traders were able to obtain dockets which enabled them to replenish their stock from the warehouse.

Lizzie had just finished serving old Maggie Watson. She was a good customer, with a houseful of daughters and children, and she had at least a dozen ration books. Women gazed in envy as she packed jars of jam, packets of sugar and tea into her bag.

Sadie smiled sweetly and, turning to Lizzie, said, 'Let Mrs Watson 'ave another coupla jellies. A lot of children she's got to feed.'

'Fanks, Sadie, yer a sport,' said Maggie Watson, handing over the extra coppers to Lizzie.

'Next, please,' Lizzie called, after having paused to blow her nose. Her mum stood in front of her.

Nellie passed a dog-eared fawn-coloured ration book over to her daughter, saying, 'I'll 'ave all that's going and a tin of spam, please, don't think there's enough points left for anything else.'

Lizzie placed a packet of Foster Clarke's custard powder, a large bottle of Camp coffee, Scott's porridge oats, one jelly and one box of matches on the counter. 'Sorry, mum,' she said, 'all the Daddie's Sauce has gone. I want twelve points for the spam, please.'

With scissors in hand, Lizzie bent her knees and cut the strip of points marked C from the ration book and let them fall into the already overflowing tin, which was on a shelf beneath the counter. Flicking through the pages, Lizzie found what she already knew, no tea coupons, no sugar allowance, no soap docket. She hesitated. Then, with grim determination, she straightened her back and got up on to her feet. Boldly, she took two quarter-pound packets of tea down from the shelf, a two-pound bag of sugar, two tins of spam and a tablet of Lux toilet soap. Setting the lot down, Lizzie quickly totalled up the amount. 'Five and tenpence ha'penny, please, Mum,' she said, handing back the ration book, and reaching for her mum's shopping-bag in which to pack the goods.

'See yer later,' she said cheerfully to her mother, getting in return only a nod and a frosty stare. The queue moved up and Lizzie worked on.

Lizzie felt done in as she opened the front door. Hardly had she got inside the house when Nellie started.

'What d'yer think yer up to? Eh? You knew we didn't 'ave coupons for those things,' stormed Nellie.

'So I gave you a few extras, that's all.'

'That's all!' her mother yelled. 'Yer could go ter prison, so could I, so could Sadie!'

'She never meant no harm,' cried Aunt Daisy.

'Don't you side with 'er,' Nellie turned on her sister-in-law. 'You weren't there. Bloody awkward I felt.'

'You took it all though, didn't you?' Lizzie retaliated.

She regretted this remark immediately. Her mother went berserk.

Lizzie had had enough. 'Right,' she screamed, as she let her fist come down so hard on the table that the cups jumped. 'Put it all in a box and I'll take it back to Sadie in the morning. I'll tell 'er what I did. All right. That satisfy you?'

Silence. Silence so great you could cut it with a knife.

'Well?' Lizzie yelled so loudly that her mother and her aunt backed away. 'Well?' Lizzie repeated as she watched her mother shake her head and wring her hands.

'She can't,' Aunt Daisy said quietly.

'She can't what?' demanded Lizzie.

'Give it all back. Yer mum's given some of it away.'

Nellie put out a hand. 'Don't be cross, Lizzie,' she implored.

'Jesus Christ,' Lizzie muttered, gazing at her mother with perplexity. 'One minute you're gonna kill me, next yer tell me not to be cross. I don't believe this. So go on, tell me.'

'Well we didn't need the coffee. Not now we've got the tea. So I let Mrs Gregory have it.'

'And?' Lizzie asked loudly.

'Well, old Mrs Durrel's only got one ration book, living on 'er own. I gave her a tin of the spam.'

Lizzie looked across at her aunt. Daisy was having a helluva job controlling her amusement. She winked at Lizzie. That did it.

Lizzie suddenly saw how comical it all was. It was like a slapstick scene from the Saturday concert. Her hands flew to her mouth, but it was no good, laughter bubbled out and Aunt Daisy joined in.

The relief was apparent in Nellie's voice as she said, 'How about a nice hot cup of tea?' It was too much. The last straw. There hadn't been any tea in the house for the last three days, and wouldn't be now if it wasn't for this afternoon's do!

Chapter Ten

THE JUNGLE OF London's back streets now showed signs of being war-torn. Where once panes of glass had let the daylight into houses, now there was darkness. Windows shattered by bomb blasts weren't replaced, merely boarded over.

The raids tended to be lighter now and mostly on the coastal towns. People became complacent and none more so than Lizzie – until one night the droning of the incoming bombers throbbed menacingly once again. Bombs streamed down from the sky, one landing with a thud which shook the houses but did not explode.

Lizzie didn't realize just how near it had fallen until she left the house just after four o'clock the next morning. She found a scene of activity. In the darkness, torches flashed, voices came from all directions.

'Hoi! Don't go down there,' shouted an air-raid warden but his voice only panicked Lizzie into hurrying faster. Reaching the corner of the road, she came to an abrupt halt, trembling and unable to move she stood rooted to the spot.

The unexploded bomb had torn into the end wall of the first house. Its nose was embedded, its fin tail protruding at least two feet. Voices yelled at her from the darkness.

'Move. Come on, yer silly cow, move yerself,' a cockney voice boomed out.

'Cross over to the other pavement and walk towards me, slowly,' instructed a voice firm with authority.

Lizzie did move slowly, praying as she went, 'Please don't let it go off.'

Safely round the corner she wanted to be sick. Nothing had prepared her for this. Half of Selkirk Road had gone. Just a pile of rubble remained. Lizzie stared, speechless with shock, terrified for Polly and the Hurley family.

By some miracle, their side of the road had only caught the blast. 'Thank God,' she murmured; and again, 'thank you, God,' as Aunt Kate and Uncle John came towards her, dusty and battered, but otherwise unhurt. Now Lizzie began to cry, her legs were trembling. 'Where's Polly?' she whispered.

'It's all right,' Aunt Kate told her, 'she's been taken to hospital. She was cut a bit by the flying glass.'

Hardly had the mobile canteens moved off and the firemen rolled up their hoses, having hosed down the blackened framework and steaming bricks, than the sirens were wailing again.

At ten minutes to eight, the Bendon Valley Laundry suffered a direct bit. Only those who were late for work that morning escaped. Over seventy women, including Mrs Baldwin, Connie's mother-in-law, were killed in that raid.

Later the same day, the Bomb Disposal team safely defused the unexploded monster and carted it away on an army lorry. The gaping hole in the side wall of the house was crudely repaired.

A sad silence settled over the district for several days but life went on.

London became fairly quiet after that, as the air raids became far less frequent.

Connie gave birth to a seven pound boy, whom she named William after his father, and everyone was sad that Bill's mother had not lived to see her grandson.

Lizzie was doing very nicely financially. She drew her wages from Sadie and put them into her Post Office Savings Account. There were weeks when she was also able to save a substantial amount from her bus wages. This was because of spreadovers.

Crews took the buses out from the garage very early in the morning, carrying office cleaners and factory shift workers. The next couple of trips would be for the office workers. Then, to save petrol, the buses would be parked in the City, and the driver and conductors travelled home by tube train. They had four to five hours' free time before going back to collect their bus and doing the homeward runs. For these split duties, wages were paid from signing on to signing off – as much as thirteen hours for some duties. Lizzie was surprised at just how much she had managed to put away.

She was also surprised at the speed with which Polly decided to get married.

Polly had been badly shaken when Selkirk Road had been hit by bombs and had been allowed to leave her job on medical grounds. She had become good friends with Arthur Scott, who had lived in the same road all his life, and whom she knew quite well. It wasn't until Arthur was invalided out of the Army that Polly and he became interested in each other. He was a strongly built young man, aged about twenty-two, with broad shoulders and thick forearms. His reputation had always been tough and there was a rawness about him that made Lizzie feel apprehensive, but he and Polly seemed to suit each other well enough.

They had found a house to rent in Wilton Road, Colliers Wood, and had set the wedding date. The fact that Polly was pregnant probably brought the date forward.

The preparations for Polly's wedding made Lizzie feel quite envious. Charlie wrote regularly, but it wasn't the same.

There were sandbags piled up each side of the doorway at Wandsworth Town Hall, which slightly put the dampers on the wedding guests, but Polly looked lovely, her dark hair gleaming beneath the pale blue wisp of a hat she wore, and her bright eyes sparkling with happiness. The coupons for her cream-coloured two-piece had been begged and bor-rowed, but the outcome was worth it.

Arthur Scott looked quite presentable dressed in a suit, with white shirt and dark tie. He stood grin-ning as the registrar pronounced them man and wife. Suddenly Polly Hurley was Mrs Scott.

Wilton Road was only ten minutes' walk from Merton Bus Garage and Lizzie became a frequent visitor there. The house Arthur had found to rent was large and comfortably furnished. Lizzie loved it from the moment she walked through the door, even though most of its windows were boarded up. In the front room there was an open-ended sofa and two big armchairs, drawn up beside a blazing coal fire.

'Crikey,' said Lizzie, 'ain't you lucky? How long have you got it for?'

'Till the war ends, I suppose,' said Polly, shrug-ging her shoulders, 'but come on upstairs, I want to show you something.'

Polly flung a door open on the first landing, 'What about that then?' she cried.

Lizzie stared in amazement. 'A modern bathroom with a geyser an' all, oh, ain't you lucky!' she said again.

Seven months later, Polly gave birth to a tiny scrap of a girl. Strange how big, strapping Arthur was so gentle with the baby, and so proud of Polly. They named the baby Lucy, after his mother.

*

Lizzie picked her way carefully through the garage. She'd been on middle shift, having just paid in her takings. It was a quarter-past eight, no one was about and the great depot was eerie. Pitch dark. Because of the blackout, what few lights there were were covered by black tin shades with small slits to let through just a faint glimmer. Buses were shunted into position, ready for the morning, the concrete floor was smeared with petrol and diesel and the air smelt foul.

A man stepped forward, blocking her way, and for a moment Lizzie was petrified. The smell of the uniform told her it was a soldier. An arm stretched out and a familiar voice said, 'Hallo, Lizzie, my darling.'

'Charlie?' she asked with some apprehension.

'Who else meets yer from work and calls yer darling?' he answered and she knew he was smiling down at her.

'Oh Charlie,' she whispered, before his lips covered hers.

Holding her close, he said, 'I've got four days' leave before we take off again. I've been ter your 'ouse, yer mum said I can stay there.'

Four whole days, it seemed too good to be true. They clung to each other in silence until Lizzie said, 'Polly's is nearest, let's go and 'ave a cuppa with 'er and Arthur.'

Lizzie couldn't take her eyes off him as Polly busied herself making the tea. His mop of dark hair grew thick and curly at the nape of his neck and she longed to run her fingers through it.

Lizzie telephoned the garage and was granted leave. The next few days were bliss, every minute they spent together. At night, with Charlie lying so near in what was Syd's room, her longing for him grew. If only there had been enough time, they might have been married. If only . . .

Lizzie tried to take everything in her stride, but when Charlie left again, she felt very low. It seemed this war was lasting for ever.

They only got occasional letters from Leslie. The wireless told how the island of Malta was being bombed day and night. And young Syd was in Germany; they received a few airmail letters from him with many words crossed out by the censor.

Connie had left London, she and baby William were down in Plymouth. That way, whenever Bill got shore leave, he and Connie could be together. Like many other families, theirs was totally split up.

Lizzie's heart missed a beat when one lunchtime she got home and found not one letter from Charlie, but two. Aunt Daisy was away, doing her bit for the war effort (every afternoon she manned the mobile canteen on Balham Station), and her mum was busy ironing. Nellie took up another flat iron from the range, held it to her cheek, then spat on it, finally wiping it with a clean white cloth. 'Don't sit there musing over yer letters, Lizzie, open them, for Christ's sake!'

'I'll make us a cup of tea first,' Lizzie answered, playing for time.

Setting a cup down on the dresser, Lizzie said, 'Drink it while it's hot, Mum. I'm gonna take mine upstairs.'

Nellie sighed. Lizzie was such a good-hearted girl, a worker an' all. She proved that, but she didn't seem to have much luck. Life hadn't been that good to her so far, and Nellie hoped against hope that this Charlie was the right one.

Upstairs it was dark, chilly and drab in her bedroom. With the window boarded over for so long, she'd forgotten what it was like to be able to look out of the window, and with the wallpaper peeling from the walls it wasn't exactly the most pleasant of places to be. Lizzie lit the gas, lay on the bed and tucked the eiderdown tightly round herself.

The first letter was ordinary, saying how much he had enjoyed seeing her, thanking her mother and her aunt for putting him up. Only the last paragraph made Lizzie shiver with fear. 'God only knows when I'll see you again, Lizzie,' he wrote, 'we have been issued with tropical kit.'

The second letter was oh, so different. 'I love you, Lizzie,' was how it began. She could feel her heart thumping. The words were so sincere. A glorious feeling came over her; she closed her eyes and hugged her pillow.

They seemed to have had such a short while together and it was only from previous letters that Lizzie had heard about Charlie's earlier life. His mother had come to London from Scotland to be in service. She had died only days after he was born. No one had ever told him of his father and he had been brought up in a Shaftesbury Home for orphans near Blackfriars Bridge.

Now Charlie had opened up his heart to her and poured out his true feelings. He had been so moved by the sight of Polly and Arthur in their nice, clean, warm house and baby Lucy had been the icing on the cake for him. 'I've never had a family. Come to that, I've never had a home, not even a room of my own.' The words of his letter blurred as Lizzie's eyes filled with tears. 'Will it ever be our luck, Lizzie?' he asked. Sadness gushed through her. This rotten war, the loneliness, the longing, it seemed as if it was lasting a lifetime. 'Oh Charlie,' she cried, turning face down in her bed to muffle her sobs.

Later, she rinsed her face and hands under the cold tap in the bathroom and went downstairs to have her evening meal with her mother and Aunt Daisy. But her thoughts were miles away with Charlie. Come the end of the war, she'd have a home ready for him. A place that would be theirs, and they would have a family. She'd make it up to him for all those long lonely years.

By the time the day was over, she had made a firm decision.

She was going to buy a house.

Chapter Eleven

1943 CAME IN bitterly cold. Every single thing seemed to get worse, except for the fact that they no longer had to endure the Blitz.

All the STL registration buses disappeared from Merton Garage and were replaced by Daimlers. No longer were the passenger seats padded and upholstered. Rows of plain wooden benches had to suffice.

Lizzie, used to digging her knees into the sides of the seats in order to keep her balance when collecting fares, now found it much harder in more ways than one. After only one week, her shins were black and blue with bruises. 'Look on 'em as yer war wounds,' Polly laughingly told her.

Lizzie's bus route had also been changed as had her driver. She was now on the 118 which ran through Streatham Vale to Clapham Common. The route was mostly through nice suburban districts but in the Vale there were quite a few factories. Now her passengers were mostly young factory girls and women, her kind of folk and she liked the change a lot.

The Smith meters factory was on war work and the girls told Lizzie it was all very hush hush. And Payne's firework factory now made rockets and varicoloured lights for the Merchant and Royal Navy.

Pascall's sweet factory gave Lizzie the greatest laugh. 'God knows what their wartime turn out is,' she remarked to her mother one evening as she told of her day's work.

'But 'ow about this, Mum. One girl told me, if you go there on a Friday morning and take two pounds of sugar, yer can get a pound of boiled sweets or toffees in exchange.'

'Really!' Aunt Daisy butted in. 'But where does the sugar come from?'

'That's exactly what I asked her, Aunt Daisy. Who the hell's got two pound of sugar to spare? Seems some folk have, this girl told me. Big families mostly, I suppose. Still, she's promised ter bring me some off-cuts. Broken bits of sweets they are. They don't get many, but she said she'll try.'

'Cor, that would be nice,' said Nellie. The sweet ration was eight ounces every four weeks which didn't go far.

Also in Streatham Vale was the big cemetery and at its gates was a new double-fronted florist shop. Lizzie's new driver, Bill, jumped down from his cab and came round the bus to talk to Lizzie.

'I'm just gonna see if I can order any flowers from Mary. It's the wife's birthday next Monday. Ain't many flowers about anywhere, but old Mary seems to get hold of a good supply.'

Lizzie nodded and stood watching the queue of people board the bus and Bill walk over to the shop.

He was, or had been, a very tall man, but his shoulders now stooped and his uniform hung loosely on his lean frame. He should be enjoying his retirement really, Lizzie thought, even his eyesight wasn't all that good. Many a corner he turned with two wheels of the bus hitting the kerb.

Bill came out of the shop and Mary Chapman came with him, pausing only to lock the shop door.

''Allo Lizzie, my love,' Mary said as she heaved her great bulk up on to the platform. 'Christ,' she said, eyeing Lizzie from top to toe. 'This job ain't done you any 'arm 'as it gal. You look marvellous.' And she was right.

Despite the cold weather, Lizzie bloomed with health. Her skin glowed, her fine cheek bones had more flesh covering them and her long fair hair tucked into a lacy black snood shone through like golden corn.

'And rationing ain't made you any thinner, Mary,' Lizzie laughed as she pushed her towards a seat just inside the bus. Lizzie collected her fares and plonked herself down on the long seat next to Mary.

''Ere love, yer don't want a couple of days extra work, do yer?' Mary asked.

'Aw, gor blimey,' cried Lizzie, ''ow many more? I've got two jobs already.'

'Shame,' Mary muttered, 'I could do with someone like you. Knows hows ter keep her mouth shut.'

'I'm not with you,' Lizzie said, 'what's so secretive about your trade?'

'It's the shortages, ain't it? Funerals are like processions now. Sad, but a fact of life. Can't get any decent blooms and as fer the frames fer the wreaths, like bloody gold dust they are.'

'So, what can you do about that?' Lizzie wanted to know.

'Bribe the grave diggers of course,' Mary said. Lizzie looked startled. 'Don't hurt no one, you know. The dead can't see the wreaths, nor smell the flowers. They're only a comfort for the living. Soon as the relatives have gone, the old men pass the floral tributes through me kitchen window and I re-use the frames, even some of the flowers and most of the moss. God won't take umbrage over that, I'm sure.'

The look Mary gave Lizzie defied her to say otherwise. In spite of her misgivings Lizzie had to smile. Mary's sense of self-preservation was quite exceptional. Blame the war, she told herself yet again.

The bitter cold weather continued and the nightly black-outs made trips for pleasure almost impossible. It was weeks since Lizzie had heard from Charlie and she felt depressed. There didn't seem to be any bright spots left in her life.

She was awoken one morning by a piercing scream, a scream that she admitted afterwards she would remember for the rest of her life. She jumped out of bed and ran out to the landing.

Leaning over the banister, she took it all in at a glance and she felt her heart stop. The dreaded yellow telegram lay open on the linoleum. Her mother lay prone on the floor and Aunt Daisy was sitting on the stairs, silently rocking herself back and forth.

She didn't have to give a thought as to whom it was. Lizzie knew. She went bare-footed down the stairs, stepped over her aunt and picked up the flimsy paper. LESLIE COLLINS the words jumped forth. Killed in Sicily. What the bleeding hell was he doing in Sicily! Wasn't Malta bad enough? The lump was so large in her throat that Lizzie almost choked. Her chest felt as if an iron band encircled it, drawing tighter every minute. Her eyes and nose ran, and her ears ached.

Slowly, she went back upstairs, ignoring both her mother and her aunt. She couldn't console either one of them; her own pain was too severe. She loved Leslie so much and she would never see him again.

Then came one of the worst periods of the war. Hitler sent his doodle-bugs to England. Flying bombs without pilots – a mysterious danger droning their way through the sky, flames shooting out from their tails. Londoners raised their weary faces and stared in disbelief. Quite suddenly the engine would cut out, but it would not fall at once. On it would glide for breath-taking seconds before hitting the ground. Everyone held their breath, you could feel the unnatural silence. Lips moved and everyone prayed the same prayer, 'Please God, don't let it fall on us.' It fell elsewhere and people were safe – until the next time.

Aerial bombing had never been like this. The bomp-bomp, thud-thud of British anti-aircraft guns told people that their side was fighting back. Men and women had become defiant, cursed the Germans and got on with their wartime jobs. Now, with these buzz-bombs, they felt defenceless.

It was Sunday lunchtime and all three of them were at home. The sound of a single engine was suddenly immediately overhead. They froze. The heavy droning stopped. 'Down, quick, get down!' Nellie ordered, almost dragging Lizzie beneath the kitchen table. Seconds later, the kitchen door burst open, their last intact window blew in and dust and glass showered down into the passageway.

'Bloody Hitler,' yelled Daisy, forced out of her complacency for once.

They went out into the street. Black smoke and flames shot high above the rooftops of the houses opposite. The doodle-bug had dropped just two streets away. So near and yet, thank God, so far.

Lizzie would be twenty-one years old in August, and Nellie prayed that they would all live to see the day.

Summer came early. The lovely May days were really warm. Lizzie got compassionate leave from her job; she needed a break. *Gone With The Wind* was showing at the Mayfair Cinema and long queues formed to see it. Lizzie paid three and six

each for three reserved seats and took her mother
and her aunt.

Another evening Arthur's mother minded baby
Lucy and he took Polly and Lizzie dancing at the
Streatham Lyceum. Lizzie didn't really enjoy herself; she felt lonely. But returning home with these
happy friends, she spied a 'For Sale' notice posted
up on the front door of a house opposite. All her
determination returned.

Wilton Road was a short cul-de-sac with a dozen
semi-detached houses on the side where Polly now
lived and only six large detached houses on the
opposite side of the road. Colliers Wood was a very
nice surburban district and Lizzie decided that she
could do a lot worse.

The very next morning Lizzie took the tram to
Wimbledon. William Fox & Sons estate agents obviously catered for opulent clients. The only sign of
war was the scrim, glued tightly to the plate-glass
windows and which obscured the comfortable office
from the stares of passers-by. A portly, middle-aged
man turned to greet her as she opened the door. A
smile lit his face, a mass of fuzzy grey hair topped
his head. 'Mr Brownlow,' he said, offering his hand.

Lizzie gave her name and explained that she was
interested in the Wilton Road property.

'Ah!' he exclaimed. 'Come into my inner office,
if you please, Miss Collins.'

Lizzie obeyed reluctantly, staring at him curiously
as she walked slowly after him.

'Be seated, be seated,' he waved his arms towards

an armchair, then he turned his back on her and
shuffled several papers from a cabinet. 'Are you in
business, Miss Collins?' he unexpectedly asked.

'No,' she answered. Today, she wore an old, but
still smart, pin-striped grey suit with a dusty pink
tailored blouse. Her long hair hung loose, secured
only on the side with two tortoiseshell combs. She
wasn't about to tell this stranger that she was a
clippie.

'Ah, ah,' he repeated in a low voice. 'Very wise
decision,' he went on, 'to buy property at this point
in time. Risky, but worth the gamble. Boys will be
coming home. Whole streets of houses demolished.
Thousands married in haste, nowhere to live.' He
thumbed through the piles of leaflets now lying on
his desk, his head bent low, his voice only a
murmur. He might have been talking to himself.
'Terrible, terrible housing shortage come the end of
this war,' he paused, raised his eyes to Lizzie, 'you
mark my words.'

He sounded so kind, so reassuring, that Lizzie
relaxed. 'Three properties in Wilton Road,' Mr
Brownlow said as he held out the details. 'One, an
executive sale. Number nineteen, owner in a nursing home, number twelve, family evacuated,
decided to stay in Devonshire. Would you like an
escort or shall I entrust you with the keys?'

When Lizzie felt she could get a word in edgeways
and that Mr Brownlow was listening to her, she
assured him she would be able to view the properties
quite safely on her own. 'I'll bring the three sets of

keys back to this office this afternoon,' she promised.

'How kind, how kind,' he repeated in his low voice as he handed Lizzie the labelled front door keys.

The first house, a few doors away from Polly, was nice and Lizzie was tempted. It was very similar to Polly and Arthur's but, being unoccupied, it looked dusty and wretched. The second one she dismissed straight away; there was too much structural damage.

The third one was on the opposite side of the road. Detached, with a large front garden and a circular drive, this looked like a rich man's house. Lizzie consulted her estate agent's list. Work had been started with the purpose of turning the building into flats, then abandoned.

She used the key and opened the front door. The hall was very long, with black and white ceramic floor tiles. The first room was enormous, with bay windows reaching from floor to ceiling and a huge fireplace with marble surroundings.

At the end of the hall, there was a wood-panelled dining room and, beyond that, a white-tiled kitchen. What she thought was a cupboard turned out to be a modern bathroom. That was wonderful!

The first floor had four rooms and an old-fashioned bathroom, complete with a copper geyser on the wall. The top of the house was a complete surprise. A door at the head of the stairs opened into a self-contained flat, just one large room, a small kitchenette and an alcove that held a toilet and a deep porcelain sink.

From up here, the windows looked down over a neglected garden where several shrubs still fought for survival. It also gave Lizzie a good view of the district and the River Wandle as it snaked its way through grassy banks. What couldn't I do with this place! I could make it pay, Lizzie told herself.

All the way back to Wimbledon, Lizzie was doing her sums. She found the offices of William Fox & Sons closed for the day. She slipped all three keys through the letterbox, glad to have time to ponder on things and make up her mind.

Indoors, Lizzie rushed upstairs and took off her coat. Excited now, she wanted to tell her mother all the news and sound her out over the ideas that were forming in her head.

Nellie was slumped in the chair, staring into space. A quiet 'Hallo' was all the greeting she gave Lizzie. In her lap lay a photograph of Leslie, and she sounded so depressed that Lizzie was alarmed for her.

'I'll tell you what,' she coaxed, 'come and sit nearer the fire while I make us a cup of tea, then I'll brush your hair for you. You always like that, don't you?'

Perched on a foot-stool behind her, Lizzie took out the many hair pins which held her mother's plaited hair in circles on each side of her face.

Then she unbraided it and began to brush her

mother's hair with long, firm strokes. Nellie sighed
and closed her eyes and Lizzie's heart ached for her.
Now was not the time to discuss buying a house
with her mother. She would have to make her own
decisions.

June came in wet and windy, a disappointment after
the warm month of May. It was three days later
when Lizzie, well wrapped up in her bus overcoat
and with her hat pulled well down over her ears,
braved the biting winds and went over to Wimbledon again. She shook hands with Mr Brownlow,
who was obviously pleased to see her and made no
reference to the fact that she was wearing the bus
uniform.

By the time Lizzie had finished telling Mr Brownlow that if mortgages could be arranged she would
like to buy number nineteen Wilton Road in her
brother Sydney's name and number twelve in her
own name, he was smiling at her with a drowsy,
gloriously happy expression. Not much property
was being bought. Not with this wretched war
going on.

'Leave everything to me, Miss Collins,' Mr
Brownlow said. 'First we should talk finances.
Number twelve's asking price is £950. I don't think
we can get the vendor to come down on that. Nineteen is a different matter.' He shuffled through his
papers. 'Ah yes, ah yes,' he was repeating himself
again, '£650. Too ambitious. We will make an offer
of £500.

'Now, about deposits?' he asked.

Lizzie brought out her notebook and read from it, 'I could pay £250 on number twelve and £120 on nineteen.'

'Good, good,' he mumbled, as he wrote.

'Also,' Lizzie said, 'I would like to pay one year's mortgage on each property in advance.'

This statement did surprise Mr Brownlow, and he raised his eyebrows in question. 'I have quite enough money,' Lizzie assured him, 'and who knows, the war may well be over by then.'

'Indeed. Let us pray that it is, Miss Collins,' he answered, thinking to himself what an astute young lady he was dealing with.

Lizzie went to the same firm of solicitors that had dealt with her grandmother's affairs. They agreed she was perfectly entitled to use the amount the developers of Silverdore had paid over.

Within eight weeks she had signed contracts so that she and her brother Sydney were, in conjunction with the Abbey National Building Society, owners of two houses in Wilton Road, Colliers Wood.

Chapter Twelve

THERE WAS TO be more tragedy for the Collins family before the year of 1944 was out, for Hitler had one last surprise up his sleeve for the suffering Londoners. Deadly rockets, packed with explosives, were launched over the Channel. Because they were supersonic they gave their victims no warning whatsoever – no sound of engines, no rush of air, just the devastating explosions!

Lizzie was in Smith's the drapers in Mitcham Road when one landed on Tooting Bec Common. Luckily, she was only slightly hurt when falling masonry knocked her to the floor.

'What yer doing down there?' two air-raid wardens joked, as they shifted broken sandbags and helped Lizzie over the pile of debris.

'Well, me name wasn't on that one, was it?' she told them as she wiped the dust from her eyes.

But just a week later a rocket hit Balham Station. Aunt Daisy was killed outright.

Lizzie stood in the passage hugging her mother. Both of them were sobbing. 'Oh God!' Nellie cried. 'How much more can we take? I give up. I really do. I just want to die myself.'

Of course she didn't give up, but she raged in her

heart against the cruelty of this war, and her own suffering.

She and Lizzie, like everyone else, lived day by day, month by month, giving each what comfort they could.

The Allied troops had landed in France in June 1944, giving everyone hope that the war would soon be over. But the advance to Paris and beyond was painfully slow, with fierce fighting all the way. Many sons and husbands were lost and many tears were shed. Christmas came and went; it was 1945, and still the war dragged on.

One morning the alarm clock rang loudly and Lizzie, still muzzy with sleep, reached out and only managed to knock the clock to the floor.

'Damn and blast,' she said as she groped around in the darkness. 'Christ, it's only ten minutes past three.'

Still not fully awake she went downstairs and put the kettle on, lighting the gas beneath it. 'Damn,' she said again, as she held the empty tea tin. 'Oh well, if I sign on early enough, I can go into the cafe next door to sort out my ticket box and have a large tea and two slices of dripping toast at the same time.' She had a wash at the scullery sink and struggled into her uniform.

It was the first week in May 1945, still dark at that time in the morning, and still quite nippy, Lizzie decided, as she closed the front door behind her.

Rounding the corner she stood stock still. She was like a rabbit trapped in the headlights of a car.

She just could not move.

Not one, but two trams were standing at the Broadway. Both were ablaze with lights. From stem to stern, every window was unblacked. It could not be true. It had to be a vision.

'Run!' a voice yelled at her to get out of the way of the tram.

'Yeah, come on, run,' other voices chorused.

'The war's over', a deep-sounding response echoed again and again.

The war was over.

Germany had unconditionally surrendered to the western Allies, and the festivities began and continued for days. No one went to bed, street parties were the order of the day. Pianos were pushed out into the roads and were never short of a pianist.

Lizzie persuaded her driver to abandon their regular route and drive the bus to Graveney Road. He sat on an upturned wooden box outside number thirty, a glass of beer in his hand. Their bus, now parked by the kerb, was swarming with kids. They clambered over the wooden seats, they tore up and down the stairs, hung out of the windows and rang the bell non-stop.

And Lizzie did not give a damn.

Bonfires burnt all night; time had no meaning. For the first time in six years, folk felt free to laugh, sing, shout and to cry with relief. Many mourned their lost ones, others thanked God that their menfolk had been spared and would be coming home. For Nellie in particular, the deaths of Leslie and Aunt Daisy had left an unbearable sorrow and no amount of celebration could raise her spirits or comfort her heart.

Patching up the houses began. Boarding was taken down from the window frames and sandbags were removed. Holes in ceilings and walls had to be ignored for the time being. Some returned home, to sleep in their own beds for the first time in years.

But Japan still hadn't surrendered and the awful decision was made that brought about a swift and total end to the war. The first atomic bomb was dropped on Hiroshima on August 6th and, a few days later, a second bomb was dropped over Nagasaki.

'Jesus, Holy Mary,' whispered Nellie as she turned the knob to silence the wireless. 'It's beyond belief what man does to man in the name of war.' She turned ashen-faced to Lizzie, who was sitting silently, staring into the fire, tears running unheeded down her cheeks.

Charlie was coming home.

Lizzie flew about in a fever of anticipation. She had a bath and washed her hair and, wearing her favourite sage green dress, she paced the floor of the front room like a caged lion. She saw him through the window when he was halfway down the road – his cap on the back of his head, his kit-bag perched

on one shoulder, his face deeply tanned. She opened
the door and ran. The moment she reached him, he
dropped his kit-bag and his strong muscular arms
went around her.

'Oh, Lizzie, Lizzie,' he murmured.

Regardless of women on the doorsteps, children
staring and the milkman in the middle of the road
grinning broadly, they stood clinging to each other,
lost in a world all of their own on the pavement of
war-battered Graveney Road.

Clutching his arm tightly, they eventually went
up the road and into the house. Once inside, they
literally locked themselves together, their arms
about each other, their bodies pressed close. 'Oh,
God, I've prayed for this moment,' Charlie whispered.

When at last he released her, Lizzie was trembling
violently. Nothing had changed. Charlie still had
this extraordinary effect on her. 'I still can't believe
it,' she cried as she put out a hand and touched the
lean lines of his face and then ran her fingers through
the dark hair which still clung in waves to the back
of his neck. 'You really are home, Charlie!' she
whispered.

Emotions ran away with them; they forgot about
everyone except themselves. A discreet cough from
Nellie brought them back down to earth.

'Welcome home, Charlie,' Nellie said with a sob
in her voice. She was thinking of her eldest son who
would never now come through that door.

Charlie walked forward and clasped her in a great bear hug. 'Thanks, Mum,' he said.

They were married five weeks later.

What a rush!

Sadly, Lizzie thought of Aunt Daisy, who undoubtedly would have made her wedding dress. Leslie, too, was uppermost in her mind, for it should have been him who walked her down the aisle.

In the end, it was Sadie Braffman who attained the unattainable – a wedding dress and veil for Lizzie, a cream linen suit for Nellie and a peach-coloured, floor-length dress for Polly who was to be matron of honour. Uncle John, gave her away. St Nicholas's Church was hushed as Lizzie at last became Charlie's wife. The guests were happy and Lizzie prayed that the dear ghosts whom she felt were truly present, were also happy.

Syd was coming home at last and, impossible as it seemed, he was already married! After days of waiting, the couple arrived.

Everyone stared open-mouthed at the slim, rather flashily dressed young lady with peroxide-blonde hair. She wore a bright red suit and a large black picture hat. A brilliant diamanté necklace hung at her throat.

Nellie's disappointment showed on her face as Syd introduced Doris as his wife. She was twenty-four years old, two years older than Syd, very shy and quiet despite her appearance and the fact that she had served five years in the R.A.F.

Lizzie liked Doris instantly. Syd had grown, now six foot two inches tall, but his gappy smile hadn't changed and his blond hair was even lighter. Syd had always been a bit of a devil; more than likely he had chosen Doris's outfit in order to shock. Lizzie understood him so well. Even now she could read him like a book and still she adored him. Doris's front teeth protruded slightly, but because of the frankness of her expression and the sparkle in her eyes, she exuded a bubbling attractiveness that Lizzie warmed to immediately.

Doris obviously liked Lizzie in return, for she said, 'It's nice to meet you; I've heard such a lot about you.'

Lizzie looked across at Syd. 'Don't believe all he tells you,' she said with a grin, 'we can be friends in spite of him.'

And they were.

Chapter Thirteen

AMIDST MANY PROBLEMS, they all moved into Wilton Road and Lizzie carried on with her job on the buses just the same.

Syd and Doris were fairly lucky. Number nineteen had had the carpets (such as they were) left intact, together with several odd items of furniture, so at least they had the basic necessities; and with the dockets and coupons that they were allowed, they set up a comfortable home.

Syd used his demob money to buy an open-backed truck. He was down at the railway sidings each morning before it was light, loading up with hundredweight bags of coal. Touring the back streets, he would sell the coal door to door, sometimes making two or three more trips when the weather was cold.

Polly and Arthur had now bought number seven as sitting tenants, thus securing what had already become a much-loved house with good furniture. Arthur had been promoted and now had a good job in the offices of a brewery firm at Morden.

Things were not so straightforward for Lizzie and Charlie. The rooms at number twelve were vast, the windows enormous. A utility bedroom suite, obtained by docket, looked lost in the bedroom. It was banished to the top flat, while Gran's lovely old pieces of furniture were brought out from Uncle John's shed and thoroughly cleaned. The elaborately carved side table looked well in the hall and two bedside cabinets went one in each of two bedrooms on the first floor. A hand-carved dresser fitted exactly into a corner of the top flat. Lizzie wished she'd saved more.

Beg, borrow, even steal if Charlie had his way, became the order of the day. Second-hand shops, junk yards and markets, everyone foraged for Lizzie. Syd threw thirty bobs' worth of lino off the back of the coal truck one morning. It was a godsend. Charlie cut and shaped it, fitting it into three ground floor rooms.

After a time spent cleaning and decorating number twelve, Charlie took a job on the buses at Merton Garage. He hated it. He hated the hours, the traffic, and most of all the uniform. But he loved the social side of bus life, especially the darts.

A buff-coloured envelope brought another setback. Inside was a document stating that number twelve Wilton Road had to be registered under the Town and Country Planning Act. A visit to Somerset House was needed.

'No sweat,' said Charlie, 'a day up in town will be great. Go to a show, shall we, Lizzie?' he asked and she readily agreed.

Finding the registrar's department in Somerset House was something of a problem. Everyone in the building seemed hell-bent on rushing somewhere. At last, a kind, elderly gentleman with a thin face and rimless spectacles explained things. The Act had only come into being since the war and it only affected property costing more than seven hundred pounds.

Stamp duty now had to be paid according to a scale, which in the opinion of this legal-looking gentleman was not excessive.

A few moments later, he produced a seal with which he made an impression over wax on three sets of documents and indicated where Lizzie should sign. He looked up and said, 'The duty payable is ninety-six pounds exactly.' The bottom dropped out of Lizzie's world.

They didn't go to a show and Lizzie was very subdued all the way home. Her capital wasn't going anywhere near as far as she had hoped.

At least they had a double bed, which looked ridiculous standing in the centre of their enormous bedroom. All they had to hang their clothes on were nails knocked into the walls and Lizzie now felt these would have to suffice for some time to come.

She had let two bed-sitting rooms on the first floor. One to Paddy Betts, a tall, red-faced Irishman, and the other to a city-slicker type who travelled daily to Whitehall, a Mr Joseph by name.

The top flat had looked so homely and comfortable when finished that Lizzie had been tempted to move up there herself. Instead, she chose as tenants Hilda and Wally Saint, both of whom also worked on the buses out of Merton Garage.

'Oh, well,' Lizzie told herself, 'I will just have to keep our bedroom door locked so that the lodgers don't see we haven't got any furniture.'

Charlie didn't care two hoots either way. 'We have our bed,' he said with a wicked leer, 'what more can any man ask?'

What more indeed? Lizzie often asked herself.

She and Charlie had a relationship that was rewarding, full of warmth and certainly never dull. They had fun together, they argued and shouted at each other, they made love, and Lizzie counted her blessings.

One evening Nellie came in the back door, her face was red and her eyes excited.

'Hallo, Mum,' Lizzie called from the dining room, which only held a folding table and two wooden kitchen chairs, 'bring a cup through with you, I've only just made this pot of tea.'

Charlie stretched out on the hearth rug giving his chair to his mother-in-law. 'Had a win on the dogs, have yer, Mum?' he asked, winking at Nellie.

'No, I haven't,' she answered quickly. 'But I have found you a beautiful wardrobe for two pounds.'

'Two pounds! Crikey that's cheap,' exclaimed Lizzie.

'Well, that's what Mrs Dawson said you can 'ave it for.' Lizzie's hackles rose. The Dawsons again. Still her mother bowed and scraped to them.

'Must be rotten with woodworm if they're letting it go for two quid,' Lizzie said spitefully.

'Never mind her,' Charlie said, acting the peace-maker. He had heard all about the Dawsons and in a way he didn't blame Lizzie. Her mother did work hard for this family, had done for years, and Lizzie resented the fact.

They went to Balham in Syd's truck. Nellie and Lizzie squeezed into the cab with Syd. Charlie rode on the open back.

The Dawsons hadn't changed. They were just as Lizzie remembered them. Mrs Dawson, plump, big, towering over everyone, with hands that were podgy with gold rings on almost every finger. He, dressed in a dark suit, gold watch and chain stretched across his waistcoat, was as pompous as ever.

One glance at the wardrobe and Lizzie bit her tongue and kept quiet. She wanted it, very badly. Charlie paid the two pound notes and Mr Dawson helped Syd to dismantle this huge piece of furniture into three separate parts. Lizzie didn't believe what she was seeing and avoided looking at her mother who was smiling smugly.

Next morning, Lizzie had a rest day. She, Polly, Doris and Hilda Saint sat on the floor of Lizzie's bedroom. They were all seized with fits of the giggles. Each had taken a turn with a tin of Ronuck furniture polish and a yellow duster. The monster occupied the whole of one wall and was shining like a new dollar.

It was never meant for use in a modest home like Lizzie's. Each end section was a separate wardrobe with hanging space and footwear rails. The centre part had a full-length mirrored door, behind which lay glass-fronted drawers. Each drawer, and there were ten, held a slot-in label kept in place by brass fittings. Into the drawer marked 'Socks', Doris very solemnly placed four pairs belonging to Charlie. Polly then made a great ceremony of laying Lizzie's underwear into the space labelled 'Lingerie'. This set them off again, tears of laughter running down their cheeks.

'Well, you must admit,' Polly chortled to the others, 'it is a magnificent piece of furniture. Probably came from Harrods,' she added with a supposedly posh accent.

'One thing's for sure,' Lizzie piped in, 'I'll have ter work all me rest days if I ever hope to fill it.'

Within forty-eight hours Lizzie had added another great object to her room. She had swapped duties with another girl, just for the one day. Now on the 93 route there was a bus stop just outside a newly built parade of shops. A long queue of people moved slowly and Lizzie stepped down from the platform and idly looked at the window displays. A splendid sideboard caught her eye. 'Taken in part exchange', stated the Times Furnishing Company ticket.

Without regard for her passengers, Lizzie was in that shop before she could change her mind. 'How much?' she gasped to the astonished salesman. He must be dim-witted, Lizzie thought to herself, as he stared blankly at her.

She plucked at his sleeve and pointed at the side-board. 'How much?' she repeated.

'Er, five pounds,' he stammered.

Lizzie thrust a ten-shilling note at the now totally bewildered young man and fled, shouting back over her shoulder, 'Keep it for me, please. I'll be back about four.'

Lizzie's temporary driver wasn't too pleased with her, but she didn't care. They were late, the bus was overloaded with passengers and the one behind was half-empty. Lizzie collected fares, hummed to herself and pictured her new sideboard with its great ornate overmantle in her dining-room.

All she had to do now was to persuade Charlie to buy a couple of decent armchairs, or better still, a three-piece suite. Well, tonight would be the best time for that!

Time passed quickly and Lizzie wondered cautiously why she was so lucky. There wasn't a day that she didn't feel totally happy.

Doris and Syd were expecting their first baby. Polly's little Lucy had just started school. They spent evenings in each others' houses, playing cards or just talking.

Syd bought a television set. Well, he would! He would never alter – live for today was his motto, why bother to save, tomorrow could take care of itself. Doris was still a bit of a mystery to them all. Sometimes Lizzie thought she saw a scared expression in those lovely blue eyes.

'If Syd ever gets on ter yer, Doris, you let me know,' Lizzie repeatedly told her.

'No, I'm all right, really I am,' Doris would assure her. 'Syd is real good ter me.' That Doris loved Syd was only too obvious. In fact, what Lizzie feared was true, she was bewitched by him and even sometimes afraid of him.

Hilda and Wally Saint usually joined in their get-togethers and all eight of them would go off to other bus depots to watch two teams play darts. Charlie was the champion of Merton with Wally running a close second. When the game was over the fun began for the women, the home garage would supply food for a buffet, drinks would flow freely and, with any luck, the men could be persuaded to dance with them.

It was a good job that they went by a bus on loan to the darts team; the men were often too legless to walk to a bus stop.

Christmas was fantastic. All four families, friends and relations ate their Christmas dinner at Lizzie's. All, that is, except Doris. She was in hospital after having given birth to a bonny eight-pound boy. Lizzie went to the hospital on Christmas afternoon, armed with a bagful of soft cuddly toys for her new nephew, Raymond, and an expensive lacy nightdress for the sister-in-law that she had come to love so dearly.

The whole party had assembled in Polly's house by the time Lizzie got back and it was there that

Polly's parents and Lizzie's mum dropped their bombshell. They were going to Newquay in Cornwall to run an hotel.

At the end of the war, Connie and Bill had chosen to stay in Plymouth and they had only seen them and little William once since then. Lizzie felt like panicking. Was her whole family to be split up and scattered?

A distant cousin of John Hurley's had, before the war, bought a small hotel in Newquay, but she'd lost her husband in the war, had a bad stroke herself and was selling up. John and Kate had jumped at the opportunity and had talked Nellie into going with them.

'Don't worry, love,' said Nellie kindly, when all explanations had been given. 'I'm not giving up me house. I'm only going to help get the place ready, though I suppose I might stay for the first season.'

A smile crossed Lizzie's face, 'I can't see you, Mum, in a short black dress and frilly apron.'

'Don't be so cheeky. You want to save up and come down there for a holiday. Maybe next September, eh, Lizzie?'

'Yes, maybe,' Lizzie answered, 'but you haven't gone yet.'

Three weeks later, on a bitterly cold, frosty morning, Lizzie stood on the railway platform with Polly and waved until the train was out of sight.

'How d'you think they'll do?' asked Lizzie.

Polly screwed up her face, 'Dunno, bit old aren't they?'

Down the platform came a mobile canteen selling hot drinks and Lizzie immediately thought of her Aunt Daisy; she'd lost her, and now her mum had taken herself off to the back of beyond.

Still in a depressed mood, she suggested to Polly, 'Let's go and have a drink.'

Nearly an hour later they came out of the railway bar, Polly had drunk two gin and tonics and Lizzie had had two whiskys with dry ginger. Both girls were smiling now.

'Good luck to them,' Lizzie muttered.

'Yeah, that's it. If that's what they want, good on them for 'aving a go,' said Polly.

The next few weeks the weather didn't let up. Every day was bitterly cold. Already they had had snow, which hadn't cleared and the gutters were full of dirty brown slush. Nellie wrote each week, giving full details of how they were preparing Bay View Hotel for the coming season. She seemed determined that, come September, Lizzie and Charlie would be taking a holiday in Newquay.

At the end of February, Lizzie stood staring into their bathroom mirror, a satisfied grin spread over her face. A knock came on her kitchen door and she called out, 'Come in.'

'I thought I heard you being sick,' Hilda Saint said.

'I'm all right now,' said Lizzie in a clear, decisive voice, coming out of the bathroom.

'You haven't got the 'flu, have you?' Hilda asked.

Lizzie burst out laughing. 'Nothing could be further from the truth,' she protested. 'I'm on top of the world.'

Hilda stared at her and the truth dawned. 'You're pregnant!' she exclaimed.

'Yes, yes, yes,' cried Lizzie as she did a little jig around the kitchen, 'two months almost to the day'.

'How can you know that?' Hilda asked.

Lizzie smiled knowingly. That was a secret she was only going to share with Charlie.

In bed that night, Lizzie cuddled up to Charlie and reminded him. 'Charlie,' she whispered in the darkness, 'remember when you did a day's work on the 118s and we 'ad a row?'

Charlie had other things on his mind as he ran his hands up her smooth legs. 'We always have a row when we work together,' he said.

'Yeah, I know, but that was different. Oh, leave off, Charlie!' she protested as he tried to silence her by placing a hand over her mouth.

'Oh, all right then.' He gave in and half sat up, resting back on his elbows. 'Get to the point,' he insisted.

Lizzie switched the bedside table-lamp on, nestled close and kissed his rough, whiskery face. 'You need a shave.'

'For Christ's sake, Lizzie!' Charlie exploded.

'All right, all right,' she answered calmly and almost dreamily. She went on, 'We had stopped outside St Leonard's Church and among the people waiting to board the bus were a young couple with a young baby. I stowed their fold-up pram under the stairs for them.'

Charlie sighed and put his arms around Lizzie, pulling her head down on to his hairy chest. He hadn't a clue what she was talking about.

'I stood gazing at that baby, watching as the mother loosened the shawl. Next thing I heard was the cab door slam and seconds later you came around the back of the bus, jumped on to the platform and grabbed me.'

Recollection came back to Charlie. 'Hey,' he roared, 'I told you to stop day-dreaming and ring the bloody bell, and all you went on about was what a lovely baby it was.'

'That's right, go on, what else did yer say?'

'Nothing.'

'Not much you didn't, Charlie! You told the whole damn bus you were quite capable of making your own.'

'Get on,' he said through his wide grin.

'Yes, and that wasn't all,' Lizzie told him, disentangling herself from his grasp. 'You kissed me, and when I told you all the passengers were looking, you said, "Good, let 'em look." Everyone ended up laughing at me.'

'Ah, poor Lizzie,' he mocked, 'but what's made you bring all that up now, for God's sake?'

'Because I am going to leave the job.'

'What! After all this time you're gonna leave the job because I kissed you when passengers were looking?'

'No. Because that night you made me pregnant.'

Charlie sat bolt upright in the bed; he looked absolutely bowled over. Quietly he said, 'Why you sly old thing.'

'Not so much of the old,' she laughed.

'Oh Lizzie, Lizzie, Lizzie,' he murmured and there was deep affection in his voice.

Then suddenly he punched the bedclothes and let out a roar which must have woken up half the street. 'Now,' he said with a wicked gleam in his eye, 'if you've finished talking about the past, can we get back to the present?'

When spring eventually came round again, life seemed to Lizzie to be almost too good to be true. The girls worked hard in their houses during the morning, and then took themselves out for the rest of the day. They went to parks, up on to the Common, even took bus rides to Box Hill, where they lay on the grass, ate sandwiches, drank lemonade and watched Lucy play with Raymond. Weekends they walked to Tooting, bought their fruit and vegetables in the market and haggled with the butcher.

Charlie often said it was a wonder that the girls hadn't worn a triangular-shaped track in Wilton

Road as they went continuously from one house to the other.

Hilda was slightly the outsider, mainly because she still went out to work, but Lizzie knew she was happy enough. She never used make-up, her hair was always sleek and shiny but dead straight, and she adored her Wally. Lizzie thought it was a case of an attraction of opposites. Hilda was big-boned, fair and tended to be a bit overweight, while Wally was slender, dark-haired, dark-skinned, with a pencil slim moustache and eyes that were almost black. They were both good company, especially on the private outings.

These outings had become a regular thing, running every Sunday from each bus garage throughout the fleet to spend the day at the coast. Drivers were mainly volunteers. The cost was four shillings for adults return, and a half a crown for children. Lizzie, Polly and Doris would wash and set each others' hair, paint their fingernails and try on each others' dresses before Sunday came around. Polly was the tallest of the three, still slim, dark and with lovely soft skin that tanned easily. Doris and Lizzie could have easily passed for sisters. Same height, same slim build, same blue eyes and fair hair, though Doris still used peroxide which Lizzie thought was a pity. In all the time Lizzie had known her, she had never heard Doris raise her voice in anger. She seemed so demure and unobtrusive. Kind acts and deeds which she accomplished for elderly neighbours she did without thought of reward or recognition.

It was on one such outing to Bognor that they discovered what a truly lovely voice Doris had. The day had been grand; the girls had hardly left the sands. At lunch time, the men had taken themselves to the pub where they drank a considerable number of pints between them. They came back when the pub closed, sank down into deckchairs, put handkerchiefs over their faces and fell asleep.

The girls didn't mind; they were used to it, they told each other, as they played about at the edge of the sea, their dresses tucked into their knickers.

Everyone sat still and silent on the homeward coach until it was time again for the pubs to open.

'Pull up, driver, nice big coach park at the Wheatsheaf,' shouted Syd, whilst dozens of male voices backed him up.

Soon, Charlie was seated at the piano inside the bar, while Wally, Arthur and Syd belted out the words to the all-time favourites he was playing.

It began low-pitched. Lizzie and Polly turned and looked in amazement. Doris was singing. Gently the words of 'Charmayne' came from her lips; she looked utterly at peace. The whole busy bar became hushed, listening to Doris's soft crooning voice. There was a moment's complete silence as the last notes faded away, then thunderous applause came from everywhere.

Doris blushed and hung her head.

'You're gorgeous,' Lizzie whispered to Raymond,

who was asleep on her lap. She bent and kissed his warm forehead. 'And, young Raymond, there's a helluva lot for you to learn about your mum!'

It was late in August. Lizzie had been feeling rotten for two days when Doris resolutely took her by taxi to the Wilson Hospital.

'Her frame is very small,' the doctors stated, 'we shall transfer her to Hammersmith Hospital.'

Charlie was frantic when he came home and found Lizzie missing. But he was full of pride when, the very next day, she had the baby – a boy of almost eight pounds, with a shock of dark hair and those blue eyes so very much like his own.

Everyone had argued about the baby's name. If it was a boy, Nellie had said, call it Brian. Brian! Never in her life. That was the name of the eldest Dawson boy.

Phillip, Syd wanted. Or Frederick, suggested Polly.

Only hours after he was born, the registrar came around the ward. He peeped at the half-asleep Lizzie, and whispered, 'I won't bother you.'

'Please,' her hand stayed him, 'Robert Leslie Wilson,' she stated firmly, having sought no one's advice, not even Charlie's.

When Lizzie arrived home, they had acquired another addition to the family – an Old English sheepdog puppy. Charlie's conductor had been living in a Nissen hut and, when granted a council house, was told no pets.

'Couldn't let him be put down, could I, love?'
asked Charlie.

'No, of course not, he is lovely,' Lizzie quickly
assured him. 'What's his name?'

'Bob,' said Charlie.

'Yeah, Bob-Bob,' said Raymond, his big eyes
pleading with his auntie to let the dog stay. Stay he
did and became everyone's friend.

When the baby was just three weeks old, Polly came
across the road waving a telegram from her parents.
Doris had tagged in behind and they all laughed in
disbelief as Polly read aloud, "Come on holiday
now. All eight welcome. Don't forget the children.
Love you. Mum and Dad."

They couldn't refuse. They didn't want to.

So it was all arranged. The train fare was very
expensive but an overnight coach left Victoria at
ten p.m. three evenings each week.

Their tickets cost four pounds return for each
adult, two pounds each for Lucy and Raymond and
the baby went free. Hilda and Wally Saint were thrilled to be included in the invitation and Arthur Scott
assured them that Polly's parents were kind and generous folk and that the season was probably all over
and the bedrooms would be empty. Paddy Betts and
Joe Frost promised faithfully to take good care of
Bob-Bob.

It was barely daylight when the coach driver pulled

into the Newquay terminal, but Nellie, Kate and John Hurley were there waiting.

Utter confusion followed; everyone wanted to hug everyone else, the two little ones were irritable after a long weary journey and wouldn't go to their grandmas, and Baby Robert started to cry.

Arthur took charge. The hotel was only a few yards from the harbour coach park and soon everyone was seated in the basement kitchen, around a huge circular table which had a well-scrubbed top.

Blue and white mugs filled with scalding tea were set in front of each of them. The two toddlers and the baby were already fast asleep and tucked up safely.

Quietly Lizzie took stock. Then she glanced at Polly and they each blinked to take away the tears.

Their parents looked awful! John Hurley had aged ten years in the past ten months; his hair had receded, leaving a shiny bald patch, his eyes looked sunk in their sockets and the amount of weight he had lost was considerable. Kate looked very pale and tired and Nellie was hobbling. She had tripped going up the uncarpeted stairs from the basement to the entrance hall, knocking her shin badly. A lump had formed, which the doctor now said was thrombosis.

Hotel life hadn't proved to be easy.

'Eighteen hours a day, seven days a week,' John Hurley told them quietly. 'We hadn't reckoned on being at the visitors' beck and call every minute, day and night.'

'Never mind,' Kate said, 'season's over and done with now and we'll see you all have a grand holiday. By Christ, we've missed you, ain't we, Nellie?'

'More than you know,' Nellie agreed as she gazed at the group of young friends, which included her son and daughter.

'Now, let's see about breakfast,' ordered Kate as she stood up and prepared to tie an apron around her waist.

'Oh no you don't!' Everyone turned to look at Doris as she spoke. 'We can get the breakfast.' She spoke quietly but with weight behind her words. 'Get your mum and your aunt and uncle upstairs to bed. Then you men can take all the suitcases to the rooms and by that time we'll be ready for you to lay the table.'

The men had been standing open-mouthed. No one had seen Doris in charge before, let alone heard her issue orders.

The gardens at the back of the hotel were beautiful. Lush lawns sloped directly down to Newquay's famous beach.

As a big family they did everything: took boat rides, swam and paddled in the sea, collected shells and picnicked on the golden sand. Everyone looked and felt better as the sun continued to shine down each and every day through that September.

Two days only were left of their fortnight's holiday and all was quiet and peaceful as they sat sipping coffee on the top lawn.

The bell in the reception hall sang, shattering the silence.

'Leave it, Polly,' her father said as she rose to go and answer it. Persistently it rang again, longer this time.

'I don't mind,' Polly said, 'I won't be a minute.'

She wasn't. Almost immediately she came across the grass, her long brown legs showing to advantage beneath her very short shorts. 'Eight people for bed and breakfast,' she called, 'they want four double bedrooms for two nights.'

'Tell them no. We're closed up for the winter,' John Hurley was emphatic in his refusal.

Polly didn't argue. Minutes later she rejoined the group, started to collect the cups and saucers on to a tray and said, 'Move yourselves, the beach is calling.' The matter was forgotten and everyone enjoyed another lovely day.

Except Charlie. It had turned eleven o'clock when they put the cards and the cribbage board away and everyone said a tired but happy good-night.

Lizzie reached over to put the light out when Charlie caught hold of her arm. 'Lizzie, how much does Uncle John charge for bed and breakfast?' he asked.

'Whatever are you on about?' Lizzie stifled a yawn. 'If you're worried about what he's gonna charge us, don't be. Mum has worked for next ter nothing. We won't have to pay him much.'

'No, it's not that. Listen, Lizzie, please. How much do you reckon he charges, have a guess?'

'Well,' Lizzie considered, 'twelve and six a night, maybe fifteen shillings.'

'Yeah, that's about what I thought. So even at twelve and sixpence, eight people for two nights comes to ten pounds.'

'Oh, I get it,' Lizzie cried, 'you're on about those people Uncle John turned away this morning, aren't you?'

'Well, yes I am,' he said thoughtfully. 'I push a bus around the streets of London for six days and all I get is five pounds eight shillings. Don't make sense, does it?'

'Oh forget it and let's get some sleep, Charlie,' she pleaded. 'It's our last day here tomorrow and we want to make the most of it.'

They did go to sleep, but Charlie didn't forget the matter at all.

Chapter Fourteen

BACK HOME IN London, Charlie promptly bought a copy of Daltons Weekly and eagerly scanned the pages which had hotels and guesthouses for sale. He wrote in answer to a few of the advertisements and received prompt replies.

Lizzie listened as Charlie read out the details, showing an interest she did not feel, never dreaming anything definite would come of this pipe-dream.

Two weeks later, a second letter arrived from the proprietor of a guesthouse at Woolacombe Bay in North Devon.

'As you have shown interest in my property, perhaps you would care to view, stay a couple of days,' the letter said. Enclosed were two return railway tickets to Ilfracombe.

'Well, he's keen,' Lizzie cried, as she and Charlie re-read the letter. 'You're not going, are you?'

'Why not?' Charlie asked. 'It's not going to cost us anything and I have got Tuesday and Wednesday rest days next week.'

During lunch, Charlie was very quiet and as Lizzie made a start on the washing-up he called out, 'I won't be long, I'm going to the phonebox.'

As he came back into the kitchen, grinning from

ear to ear, Charlie declared, 'All settled. That Frank Fleming seems a decent bloke.'

Lizzie had to smile; despite her misgivings she could see that Charlie already had a vision of himself as an hotelier.

Oh, what the hell, going to view a place didn't commit them to anything and it would keep Charlie happy. Woolacombe Bay, near Ilfracombe, she muttered to herself as she searched for the previous letter, which contained a brochure. She had never heard of either place.

At six o'clock on Tuesday morning, a taxi came to take them to Paddington. Robert had been left with Doris and Syd. A lot of persuasion had been needed to get Lizzie to agree to leave the baby behind, but in the end she saw the sense of it and it was only for two days.

For the first part of the journey, Lizzie slept and when she woke up the countryside had changed considerably. Through the carriage windows, she watched as the train rattled through tiny villages which had low-built farm houses, tall barns and green fields. Trees and hedges were decked out in all the glorious colours of autumn. She felt much more optimistic.

The train finally came to a halt. There were no tracks left. 'The back of beyond,' Lizzie said to herself, and all her doubts returned. It was raining, fine rain – half-rain and half-mist. Frank Fleming had no difficulty in identifying them for they were the only passengers to come through the barrier. Having shaken hands, he helped Lizzie into the back seat of his car while Charlie took the front seat beside him.

The journey to the hotel took about thirty minutes, during which time Lizzie clutched the seat as the car negotiated hills so steep that she wondered just what kind of a place they had come to. Mrs Fleming waited in the doorway to greet them, but as they climbed the front steps, the wind blew with gale force and the fine rain whipped their faces.

It was not a good beginning.

A hot meal was ready for them in the dining-room and as they ate Lizzie studied their hosts. Mr Fleming was not at all as she had imagined him. He was a good-looking gentleman in every sense. Nicely tanned, with a well-cut suit, a full head of bushy hair, dark but streaked with grey gave him a distinguished look, which was emphasized by thick horn-rimmed glasses. An egg-head type, Lizzie decided, not knowing herself exactly what she meant by that.

Lizzie settled in her mind that Mrs Fleming was about forty years old, tall and elegant. Wavy brown hair framed her oval face and when she smiled her mouth revealed lovely white teeth. Her manner was friendly enough.

They finished eating and went into the adjacent lounge. Mrs Fleming brought coffee for each of them, but made her excuses, saying she had to attend a meeting. Mr Fleming suggested that he and Charlie got down to brass tacks. 'Got a lot to accomplish in this short time,' he said.

Lizzie almost retorted, 'Don't mind me, I'm only here to make the numbers up,' as they began their tour of the guesthouse. There were two rooms they had not seen on the ground floor: one was a double bedroom and the other was the kitchen, which was spacious, clean and with more equipment than Lizzie had imagined.

The basement, a small, cosy sitting-room and just one bedroom, formed the Flemings' private quarters. There were three more floors above ground level, each having large landings and long corridors, four bedrooms and one bathroom on each floor.

All were nicely furnished.

Back downstairs, seated in deep armchairs, drinks were served and a fellow guesthouse owner from nearby joined the group. 'Bill Rush,' Mr Fleming said with a wave of his hand, 'meet Mr and Mrs Wilson.'

Bill Rush was a jovial, outgoing man with a big beer-belly and it was soon obvious, at least to Lizzie, that he was not impartial at this meeting.

Lizzie moved her seat backwards, letting the three men group themselves in a semi-circle. She had decided to be a listener to their conversation rather than a participant. Both Frank Fleming and Bill Rush extolled the virtues of the hotel trade. Besides the high profit on capital outlay, one enjoyed a marvellous way of life. According to them.

Mr Fleming was waging a battle he was determined to win, as he worked on Charlie and ignored Lizzie. He trotted out smooth, plausible reasons why Charlie should lose no time in going ahead with the purchase of this guesthouse.

'Do you mind if I go to bed,' Lizzie interrupted, 'it has been a long day.'

Much later, Lizzie feigned sleep as Charlie crept into the bedroom. She wanted no more discussion tonight. The mood she was in she might say something that she would be sorry for.

After breakfast next morning, they went for a walk. Just Lizzie and Charlie on their own. The beach was breathtakingly beautiful. Sheer golden sand stretched as far as the eye could see, banked by green cliffs and dunes. Hardly a word was spoken as they walked at the sea's edge, each deep in their own thoughts.

Mr and Mrs Fleming were ready to take them into Ilfracombe by the time they got back to the house. 'I've telephoned my bank manager. He will be more than pleased to see you,' Frank Fleming spoke directly to Charlie.

'Bank manager!' Lizzie hissed at Charlie as they went out to the car.

'Leave it out, will you, Lizzie?' he whispered aggressively. 'It's better to sort things out while we're on the spot.'

'What bloody things?' she demanded to know, her temper rising.

There was no time for Charlie to answer; Mr Fleming was holding open the door of the car for her. Perhaps it was just as well; Lizzie was getting a bit tired of being given the cold shoulder and was rapidly reaching the point where she would explode and a blazing row would be inevitable.

Charlie and Frank Fleming went off together; it had been half-heartedly suggested that Lizzie accompany them but she had refused. Mrs Fleming had business of her own to attend to, so Lizzie walked down Market Street to the seafront.

Horrible, was her first impression. Bleak, rugged and desolate. She had never encountered such a place before. Steep, steep hills, huge granite rocks at the base with the angry sea swirling and crashing over them, sending showers of spray high into the air.

'Oh, all I want is to go home,' she mumbled to herself. She missed Polly and Doris, but most of all she felt lost without her baby. This place felt lonely, not a soul was about. No, definitely not for me, she determined; I need folk around me. Give me good old London any time.

They were well on the way home when Charlie came over to where Lizzie was stretched out on the seat.

They had the carriage to themselves, just as they had on the journey down. He lifted her legs and sat down, letting her legs lie across his knees. 'Never seen you so angry, Lizzie, want to talk about it?' he asked.

'What's the point?' she argued. 'They've hooked you good and proper.'

'Oh, don't talk rubbish,' Charlie cried – but that was like a red rag to a bull.

'It's you that's been listening to all that rubbish. Rubbing his hands is Mr Fleming; thinks he's got a right bleedin' daft one in you.'

Charlie's hand flew up, but he stopped short. God, he thought, I almost whacked her one. He sighed deeply and went back and sat across from Lizzie.

'You don't believe it's a good business proposition, then?' he asked quietly. She didn't answer. 'Come on, Lizzie,' he urged, 'get it off yer chest; why are you so dead against the idea?'

Lizzie felt too upset to talk sensibly.

'They're taking you for a ride. I never heard no mention of any work. Do their guests take care of themselves? Who does the cleaning? Who makes the beds? Who prepares and cooks the meals? And, where do yer get the shopping from? I never saw no bloody shops.'

Charlie couldn't help it, he had to laugh.

'And no bloody market either,' Lizzie added for good measure, as she herself began to laugh.

The weeks raced towards Christmas, and although Lizzie was fully aware that Charlie was still negotiating with Frank Fleming she chose to ignore the fact.

An uneasy truce existed between her and Charlie. The parents all stayed down in Newquay but everyone crowded into a telephone box to talk to them on Christmas morning. Doris and Syd hosted the festivities at home and, with the children and an added baby, nothing was left to chance. Chocolate figures adorned the tree and dozens of gaily wrapped presents lay on the floor around its base.

Charlie did make one attempt to bring North Devon and the hotel trade into the conversation, but it was Doris who tactfully and quietly changed the subject. Lizzie had long since come to the conclusion that her sister-in-law was a rare person indeed.

With the coming of January, the pressure from Mr Fleming increased and Lizzie and Charlie rowed openly now. One very bitter argument ended by Charlie shouting, 'Do as yer like, I don't care, but I'm going to Woolacombe if I have to walk there.'

'Well, walk there then, damn you,' muttered Lizzie, but either Charlie never heard or he was past caring what she thought.

Every problem that arose, Frank Fleming found a way around it.

'He's got us an eighty per cent mortgage,' Charlie announced one morning as he read yet another letter. 'And we don't have to worry about the twenty per cent. He's willing to wait for that till we sell this house.'

'I bet he is,' Lizzie said over her shoulder as she left the room.

Lizzie thought she had heard it all until one day when Charlie came home jubilant.

'I've signed the contracts,' he cried. 'Completion day is 15th of February.'

Lizzie felt her heart miss a beat. Until this very moment she had never truly believed that Charlie would do this to her. Not go this far without really sitting down and discussing it with her.

Charlie watched as the tears filled Lizzie's eyes and ran unheeded down her cheeks, and the sight of her affected him so much that he almost cried himself.

'Please, Lizzie,' he began, 'it will be a wonderful life, truly it will. Think about our Robert, growing up down there by the sea, he'll be so healthy.'

'And London would kill him?' Lizzie asked sarcastically.

As usual it was Doris with her gentle, placid ways who became the arbitrator. 'You don't have much choice, do you?' she wisely pointed out to Lizzie. 'Not if you love Charlie and I know that you do. The only alternative is for you to stay here and then, as sure as eggs are eggs, you two will end up getting a divorce. Why don't you give it a try?' she beseeched Lizzie.

To Charlie she spoke outright. 'You've gotten away with murder, you have, Charlie Wilson! Just you remember this was all your idea and watch out for our Lizzie.'

Charlie at least had the good grace to look crestfallen and to keep his mouth shut.

An air of despondency settled over the house as it became obvious that Charlie was to have his way. Everyone made their own arrangements. Hilda and

Wally decided to leave London; a new bus garage was to be opened at Stevenage in Hertfordshire, and to every crew that volunteered, a brand new council house was on offer.

Joe Frost decided to marry a widow lady he had been seeing for the past ten years, and Paddy Betts was going home to his wife Oaife and his two children – he had found out that the streets of London were not paved with gold.

Moving day! Charlie had left with the removal van early in the morning and now it was time for Lizzie to depart. She had deliberately made herself look smart. She dressed in a well-cut suit and a pale blue blouse, her camel swagger coat on top, and her hair was tucked up in a cloche hat that would keep her ears warm.

It was a bright sunny morning and Doris told her that was a good omen. Doris got into the taxi that would take them to the station, while Lizzie gave Polly a final hug.

On the railway platform, the two girls clung to each other, oblivious to the hustle and bustle all around them, the shunting, hissing, steaming trains, the clanging of the wheel-tappers' hammers, the pigeons in their hundreds flying high up into the great glass roof. Taxis, porters, trolleys piled high with mailbags, people of all nationalities, the overriding smell of soot, dirt and grime – this was the dear old City of London that Lizzie was leaving behind.

Reluctantly, Lizzie took her seat in the carriage, unhooked the lead from the dog and placed it in the bag that held napkins, baby food and sandwiches. Doris kissed the baby one last time and hesitantly held him out for Lizzie to take, then she stretched out her arm and patted Bob-Bob who lay on the floor between the two bench-seats.

'Bye, Bob-Bob,' she whispered and, as if in answer, he twitched his nose and gazed up at her with his soulful brown eyes.

'Stand back, mam,' a porter ordered as he slammed the door of the carriage. To Lizzie the sound had a ring of finality about it.

Hardly out of London, the sunshine disappeared and the weather turned horrible. High winds and sleet. Passing through the countryside, the sleet changed to snow, pure and white, the flakes splashing against the window panes of the fast-moving train. The scene was pretty; hills and fields lay as if beneath a huge white blanket.

Lizzie fed the baby and cuddled him tightly.

There was no one to meet her this time. Lizzie struggled to get everything out of the carriage and on to the platform. The solitary ticket collector offered to fetch the baby's pram from the guard's van. Suddenly a taxi driver appeared and took charge.

At least Charlie had remembered to send a taxi. The removal men had unloaded and gone and Charlie had been busy. The house was warm and the lounge and dining-room were set out, though Lizzie thought that their few bits and pieces looked ridiculous in such large rooms. The basement flat was cosy. The bedroom looked nice and Charlie had even made up the bed and placed Robert's cot close. The sitting-room had rugs on the floor, two armchairs, Gran's carved dresser and their wireless set.

'Welcome home,' Charlie said as he kissed Lizzie.

She didn't answer. A lot of water would flow under the bridge before she regarded this place as home.

They ate a good meal in the basement and Lizzie suggested that, before they settled down for the evening, they should have a walk around upstairs. Charlie seemed reluctant, but Lizzie went ahead.

She felt like screaming, but what good would that do, she asked herself as she slammed yet another bedroom door and ungraciously pushed past Charlie and went back downstairs.

Twelve rooms upstairs, and not a curtain at the windows, not a carpet on the floors and not a stick of furniture to be seen anywhere!

Passing the green baize-covered noticeboard in the hall, Lizzie tore down a handwritten account. Headed Mr and Mrs Wilson, it read: Items not paid for. Stair carpet £75.00, stair rods £10.00, television aerial £10.00, £95.00 to pay.

Now, she did scream.

'We haven't even got a bloody television,' she yelled.

There was worse to come! The kitchen had been

stripped. Only the gas cooker remained. Refrigerator, free-standing cupboards, kitchen utensils, even the china, all had gone!

'Calm down, please, Lizzie,' Charlie implored, as he pushed her down into an armchair and got down on his knees. He held her hands tightly as he explained, 'Frank Fleming is taking me to Bideford tomorrow morning where I will be able to order every single item needed to stock out this guesthouse. He has promised me that no deposit will be necessary. It's the way they do things down here. Everyone makes the total payment at the end of the season.'

Lizzie only gazed silently at him. What she felt at that moment for Charlie was utter contempt. What had he done? That he had been conned was as plain as the nose on his face, but what were they going to do about it? She just did not know.

'Let's go to bed,' she said quietly, and Charlie sighed with relief.

Mr Fleming kept his word and took Charlie to Bideford. Lizzie kept out of his way.

That evening she and Charlie together looked through the order forms. Lizzie gasped as she entered each item into an exercise book. Twelve bedroom suites, ten double beds, six single beds, blankets, sheets, pillows and pillowcases, bedspreads, towels, tablecloths and serviettes.

The total cost appalled her; they were getting deeper and deeper into debt.

She couldn't resist saying to Charlie, 'Let's hope we live long enough to pay it all off.'

Another thought struck her. 'What about chairs and tables for the dining-room?' she cried. 'And utensils for the kitchen, not to mention a bloody fridge!'

'Don't start again,' Charlie begged her. 'Frank said you can get most of those things at the auction sales.'

'Oh, it's Frank now, is it?' she said cynically. 'Well, you go with him and see how you get on.'

'I can't; I'm going home tomorrow.'

'Oh, you bastard,' she screamed, full of frustration, and tears welling in her eyes.

'We agreed, Lizzie,' he appealed, 'I'd stay on the buses at least until Easter. We need the money to live on.'

'Need the money, do we?' she said sarcastically. 'You're a bit late in the day to give that a thought, Charlie Wilson, and what's with this going home bit? You said welcome home when I got here – thought this was home now.'

'Oh, you know what I mean, Lizzie.'

She cut him short. 'Oh yes, I know what you mean only too well, Charlie. You go home, live with my brother and Doris, go to work, play your bloody darts and there's me stuck down here with the baby, no friends, no family, no money and no bleedin' furniture. Well, you want to tread carefully, Mr Bigshot, I might just decide to come home as well!'

Lizzie cried herself to sleep that night but she didn't resist when Charlie drew her into his arms and held her close.

'You needn't come to the station to see me off,' said Charlie. 'It only means more expense, bringing you back again.'

What you're afraid of, Charlie, me darling, Lizzie thought to herself, is that I might just get on the train with you. The taxi moved off and Lizzie closed the heavy front door. She paused a moment; the silence was deafening. She really was all on her own now, just her, the baby and the dog. No Doris and Polly just across the road. No Hilda upstairs. No trips to Tooting Market and a cuppa in the cafe. No dark-haired Lucy demanding a story, no chubby Raymond to throw his little arms around her neck. Slowly, she went to the basement and sat down. She was aware that her head ached and her throat felt so tight she could hardly breathe.

She buried her face in her hands and she began to cry as though her heart would break.

She hadn't felt so lonely before, not in the whole of her life.

Chapter Fifteen

THE BED WAS too large, the reading lamp too low,
Lizzie missed Charlie and she hardly slept at all that
first week.

The quiet, endless, lonely days stretched into even
longer lonely nights.

'What in God's name am I doing here?' Lizzie
asked herself a dozen times each day.

The weather did nothing to lift her spirits. It was
raining really heavily; torrents of water slashing
against the windows. She watched from the lounge
windows, the sea showing signs of great turbulence,
the high winds droning and whining, not a living
soul in sight.

The front garden, which only the previous day
had been so pretty, all the shrubs coated with fine
snow, was now bare, flattened by the force of the
gale.

She shuddered with dismay. There would be no
going out today, not even for a walk. Bob-Bob
would have to make do with the back garden.

Before leaving London, Lizzie had used the reference section of the local library, searching out which
areas of the country had their wake weeks at different periods during the summer. She had placed small

advertisements in local papers in such places as Manchester, Blackburn, Bolton, Liverpool, Derby and Birmingham, offering room and full-board for six guineas each person per week with big reductions for children.

One morning, she heard the letterbox click and was up the basement steps in a flash. Loads of letters were lying spread out on the mat.

Without waiting to get dressed, she read each one. For the first time in days her spirits lifted. She couldn't wait to get pen and paper and start to answer these enquiries.

'Dear Mr and Mrs Brown, with pleasure we can offer you a really nice room which looks out over the sea.' That was how she began each letter.

The trouble was, she had to run up and down the stairs, often with the baby in her arms, and always with Bob-Bob at her heels, trying to familiarize herself with the locality and number of each room and visualize whether just a double bed or maybe a double and a single bed for a child would fit into a particular room.

Not easy when every room was bare.

Lizzie was delighted as the deposits started to roll in, and she made a wallchart setting out the weeks from Saturday to Saturday, from Easter until October. As she filled in the definite bookings, it became apparent that she was only fully booked for the four peak weeks. Nothing at all for Easter and very little for May, June or September.

One morning, the post was all answered and Lizzie decided to give herself a break. It was a dry day, cold but bright. With the baby in the pram and the dog bounding along ahead, she took the winding path upwards away from the beach, climbing steadily.

Pushing the pram was no mean feat and Lizzie was thankful that she had worn flat-heeled shoes.

Finally, she reached the top of the cliffs. The view out over the Bristol Channel was glorious. She found a sheltered spot and sat down. Apart from the postman and the lady in the general stores, which served as the post office as well, Lizzie hadn't spoken to a living soul all week.

Not likely to find anyone to natter to up here, she told herself as she listened to the cry of the seagulls and the gentle noise from the sea far below.

It was much later when she set off in the direction of home, reaching the house just in time. As she put her key into the lock of the front door, there was a loud clap of thunder, the light seemed to fade, and an eerie greyness settled over everything, obliterating the cliffs.

'Good job we went out early,' she said to the baby, and to Bob-Bob. 'Do you think we're going to have a storm?' Neither one of them answered her.

At times, the only links she now had with reality were the Saturday night phone calls she received from Charlie. As she listened to him and longed to see him, she wondered why he was working in

London. Coin after coin she would hear drop into the telephone box as he prolonged those precious moments.

The new furniture arrived. Now Lizzie had plenty of jobs to do which would use up her pent-up energy.

She dusted furniture, unpacked bed linen and made up beds. She was a frequent visitor to auction sale rooms, and became quite good at catching the eye of the auctioneer, and soon crockery, cutlery, tables and chairs had all been purchased. Curtains remained a problem. Measurements had been sent to Doris, who purchased material as cheaply as possible from the markets. Charlie gave her the money, but his wages were being stretched to breaking point. He still had the mortgage on number twelve to pay and some weeks he had nothing left to send to Lizzie.

The stream of deposits was now drying up; the main four peak weeks being fully booked.

The day came when Lizzie had no money in the house. There was enough food in the cupboard to keep her going, but she had to have milk for young Robert.

With the baby in the pram, she walked to the clinic. After much hesitation, she swallowed her pride and entered.

The rosy cheeked, plumpish woman seemed nice enough.

'Please,' Lizzie began, 'would you allow me to

have a tin of dried milk and pay you next time I'm passing?'

'Of course we will, mi dear,' the kindly soul said cheerfully as she reached for the large tin. 'Is there anything else you'm be wanting?'

'No, thank you,' Lizzie said gratefully. The cost of the tin was one and tenpence-hapenny and Lizzie was almost in tears as she walked back to the guest-house. 'Jesus only knows how I came to be in this state,' she said to herself. 'One minute I had a big house, rents coming in regularly from three lots of tenants, and Charlie in a good job. Now I ain't even got two bob to me name. Fancy! Having to ask for milk on tick before I could make the baby his bottle!'

Aunt Daisy's old sewing machine came into its own. Evening after evening, when Robert was asleep, Lizzie slaved away on it until she had curtains, of a sort, ready for every room.

Saturday night came again and the telephone rang. 'Hallo, Charlie,' Lizzie said brightly after she picked up the receiver.

'That's where you're wrong, my love, it's me, not Charlie.' Nellie's voice was loud and clear, and Lizzie was so excited.

'Mum, how are you? Oh, it's so lovely to hear your voice. How's Aunt Kate and Uncle John? I'm sorry I haven't got round to answering your letters. Without your letters and those from Doris and Polly I think I would go off my rocker stuck down here.'

'Lizzie, Lizzie, stop it,' Nellie called down the

line, when at last Lizzie had paused to take a breath. 'We're all fine, stop worrying. How is baby Robert?'

'He's been a bit rough all day, wheezy-like, got a croaky cough an' all. What d'yer reckon, Mum, should I call a doctor in?'

'Without delay,' Nellie said and went on, 'I really rang to say I was coming to see you. Could you put up with me for a coupla weeks?'

'Oh, Mum, do you mean it? Really? When?'

'There you go again; like a bull in a china shop you are. It won't be for about ten days, when I've booked my ticket. I'll let you know. I'll be coming by coach.'

'All right, Mum. Make it soon as you can. I love you.'

'I love you too, Lizzie. Watch out fer the baby. Get the doctor to him. Night love. God bless you.' Nellie hung up and Lizzie replaced the receiver and hugged herself.

She hadn't seen her mum since last September and now she was coming to stay.

Lizzie spent the night tramping back and forth across the bedroom floor. Each time she looked into the cot the baby seemed worse, she had tried nursing him but he was so fretful. At last it was daylight and she telephoned the doctor.

'You must be very careful with him, Mrs Wilson,' the young doctor said when he arrived. 'Keep him in one room, constantly warm, no draughts and as much liquid as you can get him to take.'

'Is he going to die?' Lizzie asked with fear apparent in her voice.

'Oh, come now, Mrs Wilson,' the doctor protested. 'Your baby has bronchitis and he does need careful watching, but there is no need for such a pessimistic attitude.' Lizzie shuddered, and the doctor felt remorse. 'You look as if you could do with a rest, Mrs Wilson, have you anyone who will stay with the baby a while?'

'No, no one,' she answered sadly.

'Well, I'll get the prescription for you and you'll see, in a few days' time your baby will be well on the road to recovery.'

Charlie telephoned each night and Lizzie's first reaction was resentment. If she hadn't been stuck down here miles from everyone she knew and loved, in an unfurnished house, Robert never would have caught a cold in the first place.

The days were long and the nights even worse.

She listened to the wireless just to hear somebody's voice and on this particular morning she wasn't paying much attention to what the announcer was saying until the words 'Festival of Britain' made her sit up sharply.

Of course! It was 1951. Immediately all her longing for London returned. How many times had she been the conductor on a number 49 bus travelling from Shepherd's Bush to Crystal Palace! The bus would travel down Kensington High Street, turning right at the Albert Hall and into Gloucester Road,

down Onslow Place on into Sydney Street, stopping
outside the dear old Chelsea Palace. That had been
a real treat that had, being taken by Mum and Aunt
Daisy to see music hall at the Palace. On down
Oakley Street and into Cheyne Walk. That was the
lovely bit, a view of the Thames and, to the left,
Albert Bridge. From here the bus turned right and
continued   on   over   Battersea   Bridge . . .
Battersea . . . Battersea Park – that's where it would
all happen. For months and months plans had been
under way in London ready for this Festival of Britain, and the main base of operations was to be on
the South Bank of the Thames, overflowing into
Battersea Park.

'Christ!' Lizzie muttered out loud. 'I've leant out
from the back of the bus many a time and watched
that entrance on the far side of Albert Bridge go up.'

She listened to the voice of the announcer forecast-
ing how many visitors from all over the world were
expected to visit Battersea when the Festival was
opened by the King and Queen. Londoners in their
thousands were certain to flock to the fairgrounds
and exhibitions. 'Well here's one Londoner that
won't be able to go,' said Lizzie who was now feeling very sorry for herself. It was bad enough being
stuck down here in the back of beyond with a sick
baby without having to be reminded of all that was
going on back home in London.

She got up from her chair and went downstairs
to her basement bedroom and tiptoed in to look at
Robert. He was sleeping now, although his little

face showed that he was still burning up. Quietly, she went back up the stairs and into the kitchen.

It wasn't fair, her being here. No family, friends, or even neighbours. The silence and the loneliness was driving her mad. What if Robert should get worse? What if he died? She couldn't wrap him in a blanket here and run with him through the park to The Nelson Hospital. She didn't even know where the nearest hospital was. There were buses, she knew that. About three a day. Maybe more on a Friday going to Barnstaple on market day. Market day! I miss the market every bloody day, she thought.

Here she didn't have a soul to say good morning to. For the umpteenth time she asked herself, 'How did I let it happen?'

It was Charlie who had thought himself the clever one but look who had ended up being conned rotten; it was her who has been turfed out of house and home to cope with this so-called gold-mine, with him still living in Wilton Road with her friends and family to see that he wants for nothing. If she stayed here much longer she'd forget what the sound of her own voice was like, never mind about other people's. 'I'll tell yer this, Charlie Wilson,' she said, 'if our marriage survives this, it'll be a bloody miracle. The way I feel right now I don't know whether to hit the bottle or cut me throat.'

On the third day, she bathed Robert for the second time that day, not immersing him in the water, merely sponging his hot little body and changing his damp night clothes. The doorbell rang just as she was laying the baby back down into his cot.

The doctor had shown compassion, calling in to see Robert each day, but he had already called at nine o'clock that morning and she wondered who her caller could be as she came up into the front hall.

She opened the door and then flung it wide as she stared in amazement. Doris and young Raymond were standing on the doorstep.

'I don't believe it!' Lizzie cried as she swept Raymond up into her arms and nuzzled her face into his hair. Doris flung her arms around Lizzie and they clung together for a long time.

Eventually Doris asked, 'May we come in?'

Lizzie laughed. 'Oh, sorry, come on in.'

'Well, I should hope so after all the miles we've travelled,' Doris said. 'And where is that nephew of mine?' Then, much more sombrely, she asked, 'Is he any better, Lizzie?'

Lizzie still couldn't take it in. She busied herself putting the kettle on, talking all the while, assuring Doris that she felt sure that the critical stage had passed.

'He's not nearly so fretful now. He's sleeping better, but his chest is still tight and that horrible cough seems to rack his little body.'

Lizzie couldn't put her finger on it but something was wrong. Doris seemed drained of energy. Surely the train journey couldn't have been that tiring. No, there was something else, Lizzie was sure of it. She

settled Raymond with milk and chocolate biscuits
and brought tea for Doris and herself to the table.

'Now,' she said, 'let's have it, Doris. Whatever it
is that is wrong with you, you're gonna have to tell
me.'

'I know,' Doris said, and she looked so sad that
Lizzie felt her heart miss a beat as intuition warned
her of trouble.

'Well?' Lizzie whispered.

'It's your mum, Lizzie. She died on Tuesday.'

For a long moment neither of them spoke, then
Lizzie stood up and moved to the window.

'Tell me it isn't true,' she pleaded, but she
expected no answer and Doris gave none.

'Peacefully. There was no warning. She had a
heart attack.'

'I only spoke to her on Saturday. She said she
was coming here to stay with me.' Her voice broke
suddenly as tears spilled down her face, while Doris
watched helplessly.

The funeral was to be in Newquay on the following
Monday. Lizzie couldn't take the baby and she
wouldn't go without him.

'That's why I'm here, love,' Doris said. 'No one
expects you to go. Syd and Charlie are going with
Polly and Arthur.'

'Oh,' was all Lizzie managed as an answer.

At two o'clock on Monday, when Nellie Collins
was being buried in Newquay, Lizzie sat alone in a

church in North Devon. She wasn't at all sure what she was doing there; she couldn't even bring herself to pray.

She did, however, talk to her mother.

'Sorry, Mum, that I am not there. You wouldn't want me to leave Robert would you? I love you, Mum, love you, love you,' she repeated over and over again.

Syd and Charlie arrived late on Monday night. It was not such a happy reunion as it should have been.

The two men did several jobs, such as stretching and laying carpet that Lizzie had acquired as a job lot.

Alone one morning, Syd told Lizzie all the details of the funeral. 'Aunt Kate and Uncle John were really upset,' he told her. 'It was such a shock. Polly and Arthur are staying on with them for a while. They're thinking of selling the hotel and moving back to London.'

'Wish some bugger would buy this place,' Lizzie muttered beneath her breath as Charlie came into the kitchen.

Saturday afternoon, and Lizzie stood forlornly watching the taxi disappear into the distance. They had all gone again, on their way home to London. 'Par for the course,' she said to the dog as she made a bottle for the baby.

Chapter Sixteen

SLEEP EVADED LIZZIE again that night, but rising next morning, looking and feeling like hell, she came to a decision. She was going to pull herself together. Charlie hadn't really forced her to come here. True, he had made it very difficult for her to say no, but all that was in the past and she could hardly back out now.

'So, stop wallowing in self-pity,' she said firmly to herself. 'Who knows, Charlie might just be on to a winner with this place.' If only she could be certain of that, she thought as she came up the stairs and opened the kitchen door.

Bob-Bob came leaping across the room to say good morning, licking her hand with his long pink tongue, his tail wagging furiously. Lizzie was all smiles as she patted him.

'You don't mind living in Devon, do you?' she laughingly asked as she unlocked the back door to let him out. She watched as he bounded off up the garden. 'He's happy enough,' she said aloud, and the thought crossed her mind that perhaps, if she stopped yearning for London, accepted the situation, maybe even started to count her blessings, then life for her would begin to look a lot rosier too.

'Right,' Lizzie decided, having bathed and fed the

baby, 'we'll put you in your pram and push it out into the garden this morning.'

She was wearing slacks, with a pale blue round-necked jumper, but as she looked in the mirror, she wrinkled her nose in disgust. Her hair was a mess. So, she spent a good ten minutes brushing it hard and then she tied it back from her face with a piece of black velvet ribbon. 'Now, how about some make-up?' Her expression was thoughtful as she did her eyes and eyebrows. For too long she had let herself go and she had to admit that she already felt much better for having made the effort. 'Definitely better,' she muttered after having applied lipstick.

Perched halfway up a pair of steps, Lizzie was happily humming to herself as she endeavoured to hang curtains at the lounge windows. She heard a sudden slight movement out in the hall and she almost toppled over, as Frank Fleming appeared in the doorway.

'Good morning, Mrs Wilson,' he said cheerfully as he removed his trilby hat.

'Good morning,' Lizzie replied, not feeling in the least bit pleased to see him. How dare he walk straight into the house without knocking! He must have come down the lane and in through the open back door. Daft old Bob-Bob hadn't even barked.

He came straight to the point. Looking up at Lizzie, for she hadn't bothered to step down, he asked, 'Has the sale of your London house been finalized?'

'Not that I've heard,' Lizzie said.

'Well,' Mr Fleming continued, 'there is the little matter of nine hundred pounds owing to me. Eight hundred to complete the sale of the house and one hundred for goods I left behind.'

Lizzie surveyed him in stony silence.

Mr Fleming's eyes narrowed. 'Time is going on, and I would like the matter settled. Your husband indicated to me that there would be no problem with him finding a purchaser. I, too, have commitments on the hotel that I am buying.'

Not wanting to lose her temper, Lizzie only said, 'I know that.'

'Well,' just the one word Mr Fleming uttered, but his voice had suddenly become much harder.

Lizzie's face went pale and she drew in her breath as she slowly came down the steps.

Now she was at a disadvantage for Mr Fleming was a good deal taller than her. Her temper was rising, but she held it in check as she said, 'You urged my husband to buy this property, you got him a mortgage, you said you'd wait for the balance. I don't recall any time being set for him to pay you the rest of the money.'

Mr Fleming's eyes blazed, 'Dammit, I did everything I could to help your husband. I understand the position you're in, but I have liabilities too. I need that money; I can't afford to wait for it.'

'Bit late now, isn't it? You should have thought about that when you were pushing my Charlie,' she fired back and watched the expression on his face turn to real anger.

Abruptly, Mr Fleming turned to go, then stopped dead in his tracks. 'One week today I'll be back, and let's hope we can sort things out more satisfactorily then than we have today.'

'I'll be here,' Lizzie said stubbornly.

Strangely, Lizzie didn't feel a bit nervous as she watched him storm off down the garden. At least she had stood her ground with Mr Bloody Fleming; she hadn't let him walk all over her.

After dinner that night, Lizzie didn't put Robert down in his cot; she sat nursing him. Bob-Bob settled himself in his usual place at her feet, his head raised to lie against her shins.

She was considering her options.

Suddenly she sat up very straight and Bob-Bob looked at her reproachfully with his doleful eyes, cross at having been disturbed.

Bank managers! That was what they were for, to give advice. She had opened an account at Barclays when the deposits had started to come in and had been given a cheque book. Well, now she was going to make an appointment to see the manager.

Next morning, Lizzie telephoned as soon as the bank was open. At two p.m. sharp she presented herself, together with the baby in the pram.

Graham Blackhurst, attired exactly as she had imagined in a charcoal grey suit, white shirt and striped tie, stood smiling in the doorway of his office.

Lizzie hesitated, her nervousness obvious.

'It's all right, Mrs Wilson, please bring the pram in with you,' he said reassuringly. Seated opposite him, Lizzie unbuttoned the jacket of her navy blue suit and decided that Mr Blackhurst was no more than forty years old, despite the fact that his fair hair was receding.

'Now, Mrs Wilson, how can I be of help to you?' he asked, and his voice was not only soft, but kind as well.

In a barely audible whisper, Lizzie said, 'I would like the bank to lend me nine hundred pounds.'

If Mr Blackhurst had burst out laughing, Lizzie would not have been at all surprised; her request spoken out loud sounded comical even to her. But he didn't laugh, he leant towards her and courteously said, 'Why don't you tell me what you need the money for.'

Lizzie sighed, wondering if she really did have to tell this stranger all the ins and outs as to how she came to be in such dire need.

'Take your time, Mrs Wilson,' he encouraged her.

Slowly, to begin with, Lizzie told the bank manager that she needed the money in order to pay Mr Fleming. Then her hesitation gave way to resolution. No longer were her words faltering; she held nothing back. It was as if she needed to talk. She had bottled things up inside her for so long, only able to speak out loud to herself or to the dog. Now she had the opportunity to unburden herself to another human being, someone who was a good, attentive listener.

She suddenly realized that she had been talking non-stop for a very long time. Not once had Mr Blackhurst interrupted her. Almost in mid-sentence, Lizzie paused and raised her head to meet the eyes of this quiet gentleman. The eyes she now looked into were an unusual shade of grey and Lizzie felt that they were smiling at her.

Very gently, Mr Blackhurst put a question to her, 'Do you have any collateral?'

Lizzie didn't even know the meaning of the word. He sensed her discomfort.

'Additional security?' Still Lizzie made no reply. 'Shares, jewellery or property? Anything of that nature, Mrs Wilson. I am not being inquisitive, I do need to know.'

Lizzie twisted her hands in her lap and bit her tongue, saying angrily beneath her breath, 'If I had all those things, I wouldn't be here asking you for money.'

'Sorry, Mrs Wilson, I didn't hear you.'

'No, nothing,' Lizzie said indignantly. Then, as an afterthought, she added, 'Only my London house.'

Graham Blackhurst straightened himself up in his chair. Already, he had a lot of respect for this young, slim woman who had come into his office, looking so very despondent. He had read her file, only a few pounds in a recently opened current account. It seemed that her resources were stretched to the limit and beyond. Then there was this matter of Mr Fleming. Everyone in the village knew Frank Fleming –

many to their cost. A good businessman, without a
doubt, but God help anyone who crossed him.

'Tell me about your London house, Mrs Wilson,
is it in both your husband's and your names?' He
awaited her reply with interest.

'No, Mr Blackhurst.' Cautiously Lizzie considered the question before she continued. 'I bought
number twelve and number nineteen Wilton Road
in Colliers Wood during the war, or rather, I paid
the deposits and got the rest of the asking price on
mortgage.'

More and more, Graham Blackhurst was becoming convinced that this young lady from London
had a great deal of common sense. He also suspected
that, given half a chance, she could very well
become a shrewd businesswoman.

'So, are both properties registered in your name?'

'Oh, no, I bought number nineteen for my
brother.'

'And number twelve, is that jointly owned with
your husband?' He was fully aware that he had asked
this question previously but he wanted to be absolutely clear in his mind on this very important point.

'I wasn't even married then, Mr Blackhurst, my
Charlie and I weren't married until the war was
over.'

'I see,' he said, and his grey eyes twinkled at her.
'And you've never altered the registration?'

Lizzie was baffled again. Why the hell did he keep
on and on about Wilton Road. 'I did have to go to

Somerset House once,' she shot at him. His hopes dropped drastically.

'Do you remember why?'

'Yes, the property had to be registered under the Town and Country Planning Act.' His hopes rose again.

'Did you have any legal papers to sign?' and he emphasized the word YOU.

Lizzie's thoughts went back and, without thinking where she was and to whom she was talking, she burst out, 'Yeah, and I had to pay bloody ninety-six pounds for stamp duty.'

The tension was gone. Graham Blackhurst threw his head back and burst out laughing. Would that all his customers were so straightforward!

Lizzie felt her cheeks flame and her hand flew up to cover her mouth.

She waited a few seconds and then she apologized.

'Not at all, Mrs Wilson,' he said, still grinning broadly, 'not at all.'

The baby, whom they had both apparently forgotten, began to whimper. Lizzie looked at Mr Blackhurst. She was still upset that she had sworn, and now Robert had to start.

He put her at ease straight away, 'Please lift him out of his pram. I only need to get a few details from you and then you can be on your way.'

Lizzie rose, loosened the pram covers, and took the baby up into her arms. Rocking him gently, she soon had him pacified. She liked this bank manager, she liked him very much, but was he going to lend her nine hundred pounds? And if not, why the hell didn't he get it over and done with and say so.

'Now then, Mrs Wilson,' Mr Blackhurst was all at once very businesslike, 'I need a few details from you. Firstly, the name and address of the firm of solicitors who acted for you when you bought number twelve Wilton Road.'

For the next five minutes, he fired questions. Lizzie answered to the best of her ability and he wrote notes on to a pad which lay in front of him.

Finally, he stood up, came around the desk, held the pram still while Lizzie put the baby down again, and then held out his hand.

Lizzle solemnly shook it.

Then Mr Blackhurst did surprise her. He put his arm across her shoulders and looked into her face. 'Now, I don't want you to worry. I am going to make some enquiries on your behalf and I want you to come and see me again on Friday.' He stopped speaking and pondered for a moment. 'If the weather is bad, or for any reason you cannot make the journey, please pick up the telephone. Let me know, and I shall come out to you.'

Jesus! Lizzie thought. Wonders would never cease; she had a bank manager as a friend.

Curiosity was killing Lizzie. She was relieved when Friday came. The bus was late and Lizzie felt flustered as a young fresh-faced boy held open the door of the bank for her.

Graham Blackhurst's greeting was cordial; he

even looked into the pram and asked how the baby was.

Once seated it was down to brass tacks immediately. Professionally, but with a good deal of patience, Mr Blackhurst explained the whole matter.

'It was Mr Wilson who had signed an agreement, undertaking to pay Mr Fleming the balance of twenty per cent of the purchase price of Sea View Guesthouse on the completion of the sale of property known as number twelve Wilton Road, Colliers Wood in Surrey.' Mr Blackhurst had read aloud this information from an official document which lay in front of him.

Now, he raised his head, his eyes met Lizzie's and the smile on his face deepened as he firmly stated, 'Mr Wilson owns no such property.'

What was he saying? Lizzie was no fool, but he would have to be a lot more explicit before she could actually take it in.

'That agreement between your husband and Mr Fleming isn't worth the paper it is written on.' Slowly, Lizzie smiled and Graham Blackhurst smiled with her. She would need a helluva lot of time to clear her thoughts but just at this moment she was cock-a-hoop. She wanted to yelp with joy, grab this bank manager and dance him around his office.

She restrained herself.

It wasn't Charlie she wanted to put one over on. No, never that. It was Mr Frank Fleming.

Graham Blackhurst sat back. Watching Lizzie's face, he saw disbelief turn to glee. He could read her thoughts. He had to chuckle to himself. What he wouldn't give to be a fly on the wall when the next meeting took place between this young woman who had been uprooted from London, and Mr Oh-so-clever Fleming.

'You could go back to London, Mrs Wilson, if you wish to. No one can force you to sell your house.'

'Thank you,' was all Lizzie managed to mutter.

Chapter Seventeen

LIZZIE PUT HER key into the lock, opened the door and let the dog out. 'Come on Bob-Bob, we're going down on the beach,' she declared. The afternoon was still bright since the evenings were drawing out and there were a few people, mainly with their dogs, down on the beach.

She took the zig-zag path down through the dunes and pushed the pram into a secluded recess between the rocks. Turning the baby on to his side, she propped the feeding bottle, half-filled with orange juice, close to his pillow. Baby Robert's chubby, dimpled hands clutched at it eagerly. His eyes began to droop, he blinked a few times, and then he was asleep.

Taking the now empty bottle away, Lizzie tucked the pram covers up around him, then she took off her shoes and stockings placing them into the end of the pram.

'Right, Bob-Bob,' she called out, 'let's go for a run.' The tide was well on the way out and her feet and the dog's paws left clear imprints in the wet sand as they ran. The water was freezing and Lizzie moved swiftly. Up and down at the edge of the sea she ran, kicking water into the air, splashing Bob-

Bob who thought it was a marvellous game in which he heartily joined in.

As she walked towards home, bare footed, for she hadn't brought a towel, Lizzie felt she could easily leap for joy. She had things well and truly in perspective now. But by the time she got home, washed, changed and fed the baby, her feeling of elation had dwindled quite a bit. Whichever choice she made, she knew she would have to bear the consequences.

Did she want to go home to London? All she knew was that she missed Doris pushing open the front door, calling, 'I'm going to the corner shop, Lizzie, is there anything you want?' She missed hearing Lucy's footsteps, as she ran down the side path, coming through the back door panting, 'Auntie Lizzie, Mummy says she's just put the kettle on, are you coming over?' She missed the bus outings, the dart matches and fish 'n' chip suppers in front of Syd's television set. Right now she wished that somebody would tell her what to do.

A sudden thought struck Lizzie – had Charlie known exactly what he was doing all along? Her thoughts flew around in her head. Londoners had a saying, 'Never con a conman'.

Had Charlie done just that? It was inconceivable, or was it?

All along, Lizzie had been thinking that Charlie was a pushover, easy game for Frank Fleming's persuasive tongue. What if she had been wrong?

She tried to see it from Charlie's side. He had

badly wanted a guesthouse and along had come Mr Fleming, doing every mortal thing within his power to get Charlie's signature on the contract.

Just what had it cost Charlie in terms of actual cash. Not one penny! Not even the railway fare to view the house in the first place. Lizzie vowed she wasn't going to think along those lines any further, and she certainly wasn't going to question Charlie.

Should she take the baby and go back to London? No, she told herself, though her decision was very half-hearted.

She thought about Charlie; there had never been anyone else for her from the moment she'd set eyes on him. Just what would it do to Charlie if she packed it all in and walked away? It just didn't bear thinking about.

There was still the mortgage – over three thousand pounds – to be paid. There was the matter of all that new furniture and bedding sitting in the rooms upstairs and not a penny paid on it yet. If she was honest with herself, and she was certainly trying to be, she didn't really have any choice.

Lizzie lowered the gas beneath the boiling kettle and her expression was thoughtful as she spooned tea into the pot. 'Well, Lizzie Wilson,' she said out loud, 'like it or not, I think you're stuck with this guesthouse,' then, as if to boost her morale, she quickly added, 'at least for this season'.

Lizzie looked much the same as she had on his last

visit. She had washed her hair the previous evening and had taken pains with her make-up this morning.

Mr Fleming advanced across the kitchen, hand outstretched, his mouth widening in a broad smile. All animosity apparently forgotten.

'Well, everything sorted out?'

'To the best of my ability,' Lizzie said seriously.

'Good, good. I knew your husband wouldn't let me down.'

'What I have to say hasn't anything to do with Charlie.'

'Carry on then,' Mr Fleming's voice was deceptively quiet.

'I'm afraid you are going to have to wait for the balance of your money.'

His mouth dropped open. With grim determination Lizzie continued, ignoring the fact that if looks could kill she would be dead.

'My husband had no right to sign an agreement stating that when our London house was sold he would pay you the balance.'

Reaching out, Mr Fleming roughly took hold of her arm. Lizzie stiffened instinctively. Her first impulse was to resist forcibly, instead she winced. 'You're hurting me,' she warned. He immediately let go of her arm and stepped backwards.

Leaning forward, Lizzie spoke.

'Our London house belongs to me; to me, Mr Fleming, do you understand? Mr Wilson doesn't own any property, he doesn't have a house to sell.'

Hysteria had made her raise her voice and by the time she had finished she was shouting.

The disbelief on Frank Fleming's face halted Lizzie, but she felt no remorse. 'What the hell are you on about?' he roared.

With a voice that was still shaking, Lizzie answered, 'You understood every word that I said. Now, if you'll excuse me . . .' and she waved a hand in the direction of the back door.

He left and Lizzie heaved a sigh of exhaustion, mingled with relief. She watched him walk the length of the back garden and she couldn't resist a sneer.

Two green-horns, that's what she and Charlie were.

Fancy even considering a twelve-bedroomed guesthouse that was totally devoid of furniture and working equipment, let alone going so far as to buy it. Well, perhaps now Mr Fleming didn't think they were quite as green as he had supposed.

Chapter Eighteen

CHARLIE GAVE UP his job and came to live in Devon two weeks before Easter.

Lizzie was on the station to meet him and spotted his laughing face as he hung out of the carriage window. They hugged each other for a long while and then Charlie lifted Robert from his pram and carried him in his arms.

'Christ, I've missed you,' he told Lizzie.

'Me too,' she agreed.

The house felt more of a home now, with Charlie around.

They only had one booking over Easter, a party of six – four adults and two children, who were due to arrive on Good Friday.

Alan Gregory was tall and thin and his wife, Winnie, was short and a little on the plump side. With them were their two children – a fair-haired girl called Darryl, who was six, and Neil who was four. The two grandmothers, Grandma Gregory and Winnie's mother, Grandma Eaton, completed the party.

No sooner were they inside the house than everyone was on first-name terms. It was more like having friends to stay than having paying guests, and Lizzie liked them all straight away.

Alan had hired a car for the holiday and on Saturday evening after dinner the two grandmothers pressed them to leave the children in their care, so that the two young couples could go out together.

For Lizzie it was a real treat, dressed up and sitting in a country pub, with Charlie sitting close to her side and these new Lancashire friends for company. The weekend was grand.

The following day, Woolacombe looked magnificent in the fine spring sunshine, with its lovely view across the bay and the high green hills stretching down to the vast expanse of golden sands. It was too early for many holidaymakers and the beach was not too crowded. The children threw bread and laughed as the great seagulls swooped low.

On Monday evening everyone was a little downcast, for tomorrow the Gregorys would be leaving. Even baby Robert would miss them, for they had all tended to spoil him.

'When have you got to have the car back?' Charlie asked Alan as he passed him his coffee.

'Oh, not until the end of the week. It wasn't much more money to hire it for the week, rather than just four days,' Alan explained. 'I've still got the rest of the week off from work, so I thought I would take the family on a few day-outings.'

'Why don't you stay here?' Charlie suggested.

'We would love to, but we can't afford it.' Everyone's face dropped.

'Please, be our guests,' Lizzie pleaded.

'Of course,' Charlie echoed. 'It would be our way of repaying you. You've mucked in with the washing-up, helped get picnics ready, taken us out and about in the car, oh, of course, you have to stay.'

'Please, Dad,' Darryl pleaded, and even quiet, shy little Neil added, 'I'd like to stop here.' Everyone laughed and it was decided.

Next morning they all piled on to the bus and went to Ilfracombe. They watched the fishing boats come into the harbour and they bought fish that smelt of the sea for their next day's dinner. It was a wonderful week and when Saturday morning came and the Gregorys finally did have to depart, they promised Lizzie and Charlie that they hadn't seen the last of them.

Several weeks passed before they had any more visitors. Lizzie longed for the season to begin and tried not to worry about their money problems.

During the day, she and Charlie would take the baby for long walks, and each day Charlie would sniff the air appreciatively and say, 'It's so fresh and clean. I love the smell of the sea.'

When summer finally arrived, they were rushed off their feet. Upstairs, doing the bedrooms, Lizzie would look out enviously as the holidaymakers packed the beach and romped in the sea.

Charlie surprised her. Not only was he marvellous at waiting at table, he prepared all the fresh vegetables in the evening, ready for the next day, would bone out a side of bacon, cut up steak and kidney, while she made the pastry for the pies.

In fact, there wasn't one job that he wouldn't tackle.

The height of summer passed all too quickly and then the visitors became far less frequent. Come September and only the odd few bed and breakfast couples came to their door. The situation had to be faced

Carefully and methodically Lizzie and Charlie went through the accounts together. There was little enough money to pay the bills, let alone to keep them during the long winter months. The local traders, the wholesalers from whom they had bought their meat and dry goods, even the hire purchase on the refrigerator, which had been an essential item, would all have to be paid, declared Charlie as he wrote out the various cheques.

Laundry, rates, gas, electricity and telephone were totted up, and thankfully they agreed there was still enough in the bank to cover these items.

'Now, what about the Bideford Furniture Stores?' Charlie asked, not expecting any answer. 'I'll have to go and see Mr Channon,' he insisted.

'I'll come with you,' Lizzie said, and it was obviously what he had wanted her to say, because he gratefully accepted.

'Lizzie,' Charlie's voice was quiet with apprehension as he paused from packing away the account books.

'Yes?' Lizzie was at the door, about to go down-stairs and check on young Robert.

'I'll have to go back to London for the winter,' Charlie blurted the words out. 'I can probably get my job back on the buses.'

Lizzie had been expecting this. She knew it made sense. But in spite of all her resolution the tears came, hot and scalding, running down her cheeks.

'Oh Charlie!' She swayed and he was beside her in two strides. His arms about her, his lips pressed to her hair, he soothed, 'I know, I know, Lizzie. All that hard work, and for what?'

Mr Channon was in his early fifties. A shade shorter than Charlie, he had a mop of hair which was light brown and wavy and his eyes were set wide apart, which gave Lizzie the impression that he was a straightforward kind of man. There would be no pulling wool over his eyes.

Charlie must have had the same impression, for he laid their situation on the line as soon as they were seated in Mr Channon's office.

Silence hung heavily for a few minutes.

'So, you haven't made a fortune during your first season.' Mr Channon's voice was gruff as he con-tinued, 'Too many liabilities. I thought that from the very beginning.'

Lizzie looked at Charlie and her heart ached for him. He was dressed so smartly today in his navy-blue suit, white shirt and paisley tie, now his face was red with embarrassment.

'Can you afford to pay anything now?' the question was shot at Charlie.

He swallowed deeply before answering, 'Only about twenty-five per cent of the total amount.'

Again, the office was quiet and just for a moment Lizzie was gripped by fear. Could they send Charlie to jail for not being able to pay his debts? She couldn't take her eyes off Mr Channon as she waited for him to speak.

'I'm a pretty good judge of character,' Mr Channon said at last. 'Yes, all right, Mr Wilson. I appreciate the fact that you and your wife have come to see me in person. You have been completely honest and that is another factor in your favour. I'll take your cheque for what you can afford and we'll leave the balance in abeyance.'

Despite Mr Channon's generosity, Lizzie couldn't help feeling humiliated as she watched Charlie write the cheque. There and then she made a promise to herself. Once they got out of all this debt she would never owe a penny to anyone, not if she could possibly help it.

A high wind was blowing and the sea was rolling in really rough, bringing with it a heavy rain which lashed against the windows of the house as Lizzie packed socks and underwear into Charlie's case.

'All finished,' she finally said as she straightened up. 'Plenty of time for lunch now before the taxi gets here.'

They sat opposite each other as they ate, each busy

with their own thoughts. Lizzie's blue eyes contemplated her husband thoughtfully. Was it right that they should be separated for weeks on end once again? Right or not, it was a necessary evil, she chided herself. They needed to have money coming in from some source and what other option was there?

'Come with me,' Charlie had urged and she had been sorely tempted. It would be heaven to stay with Doris and Syd, to be part of the family again. Number twelve still hadn't been sold and Lizzie knew that if she went she would never come back to Devon.

Charlie looked at his wife. The weeks of sun and wind had tinged her fair skin to a pale golden tan and brought out the hidden lights in her fair hair. How he hated to leave her, she had never looked more lovely and for the hundredth time he chastized himself. Why on earth had he been so pig-headed? What had made him even think he was capable of running a guesthouse and showing a profit?

The taxi came and Charlie went back to driving a bus around the streets of London while Lizzie faced a long lonely winter.

Chapter Nineteen

JANUARY 1952 HAD been bleak and cold, with snow flurries and bitter gusty winds, but Lizzie still went out whenever the weather allowed, walking miles with the baby in the pram and the dog tagging along by her side. Already it was February and it still hadn't turned much warmer. Lizzie shivered as she walked up the stairs and tugged her dressing gown more tightly around herself. In the kitchen she filled the kettle and put it on to boil, patted Bob-Bob and let him out of the back door into the garden, then switched on the wireless. The King had died. Oh, how sad! He wasn't all that old.

For the rest of the morning the wireless gave out bulletins and played mournful music which did nothing to lift Lizzie's spirits. Like everyone else in Britain that day, Lizzie's thoughts were all of King George VI. It was a funny old world she said to herself; if his brother hadn't fallen in love with a woman who'd been divorced, an American woman at that, he would never have become the King at all. They said he'd died peacefully in his sleep and she was glad about that. She wondered if there would be a lying-in-state. She had to brush away a tear at that point as she remembered Bill taking her up to

London to see King George V's lying-in-state – all those years ago.

As she thought of the past, she remembered a day during the War when she'd been doing a turn on the 88s. As the driver had turned the bus round by the Tate Gallery he had been stopped by the police from driving down the Embankment. The whole of that area had been badly bombed the night before, and Lizzie had watched from the upstairs windows of the bus as the King and Queen had walked amongst the havoc of the demolished buildings talking to the air-raid wardens and consoling men and women who had lost members of their families in the air raids. From the little she knew of him, he had always seemed a quiet, kindly man.

Well, we won't have a King on the throne now, she thought, because King George only had two daughters. That makes Princess Elizabeth Queen of England. Fancy that! She'd been in the ATS during the war, done her bit for the war effort, so at least she knew how the other half lived.

'Oh well! Life has to go on,' Lizzie said to the dog. 'Seeing as how there's no one else here for me to talk to I have to make do with you. Come on, get yer lead, I'll get Robert ready and we'll go up over the cliffs. A good walk and we might all feel a bit better.'

It was the start of their second year at Sea View Guesthouse and Lizzie threw herself whole-heartedly into the preparations.

Bursting with energy, she worked from early morning until lunchtime. The afternoons she spent writing letters. She wrote to town halls, to Darby and Joan clubs, and to every organizer whose name she could glean from magazines in the local library, offering reduced terms for coach parties either at the beginning of the season or towards the end.

She was delighted by the response she received. But one evening, long after she had settled the baby down, she read through several of the letters again and sighed. Most of the groups that were making provisional enquiries had approximately forty to fifty members. Lizzie hadn't got that many bedrooms to offer. Eventually she went to bed still racking her brain as to what she could do.

She hadn't realized that, to make the long journey worthwhile from northern towns, the coaches would have to be either forty-two seaters or fifty-three.

In the post next morning there was a letter from Alan Gregory and, although she was pleased to hear from him, his news only added to her dilemma.

He had been promoted and was now transport manager for a large coach company in Blackburn. Would she like to send a quotation for four parties, two early- and two late-season, full-board?

'Wouldn't I just,' she said aloud, and Bob-Bob put his head on one side, peering at her, wondering what she was on about.

The doorbell rang and Lizzie picked up the baby and kissed him. 'Come and see the postman,' she said, fully expecting it to be the second delivery, maybe even a registered letter with a deposit on a booking.

Lizzie's face reflected her surprise as she stood in the open doorway holding Robert. The man at the door was Ted Armstrong, the manager of the Round House pub just four doors down the hill.

'Wasn't expecting me, was you, Mrs Wilson,' he said with a grin.

'Well, no,' Lizzie stuttered in bewilderment.

'It's just that the wife and me would like to have a talk to you, maybe put a bit of business your way. Would you like to come along to the pub later on, have a bit of lunch with us?'

'Oh, no, I couldn't,' Lizzie hastily told him, 'I couldn't leave the baby.'

'Of course you couldn't, we didn't mean for you to. Bring him along with you, we're not busy, not this time of the year. Push his pram into the saloon bar or into our sitting-room, whatever, we don't mind. Will you come?'

'Are you sure it will be all right?' Lizzie asked anxiously.

'The missus will be right pleased to see you – about half-twelve then?' He nodded his head and gave Lizzie a reassuring smile, 'Don't worry, love, I'll shut your door; you take the baby in the warm.'

There was an expression of doubt on Lizzie's face as she went back to the kitchen. She knew Ted Armstrong to nod to, even to say good morning, but no more than that.

At Christmas time, she and Charlie had popped into the Round House for a quick drink, but it was the only time, for Charlie had only been down for four days.

Visitors spoke very well about the pub, saying that they always got a good welcome there.

'Wonder what it's all about?' she asked herself.

Two hours later Lizzie sat on the wide window-seat and watched Ethel and Ted Armstrong working behind the bar. She was glad she had changed into her red dress, the long full skirt felt good around her legs, and so did the nylons and high-heeled shoes. It made a change to be dressed nicely.

The interior of the Round House was 'oldy-worldy', nice heavy oak tables and chairs, red velvet curtains and horse-brasses everywhere.

Ted Armstrong was a big-built man with a jovial laugh that was infectious: a typical publican, Lizzie thought, as she watched him squeeze past his wife giving her backside a hearty pat as he went.

Ethel Armstrong looked as if she most certainly did her share of the work. Like her husband, she was well into her fifties, her once auburn hair was streaked with grey, her face red and puffy. She served the drinks while Ted leant against the bar chatting to the customers.

Lizzie sipped her milk stout and wondered what she was doing here.

'I'm here. I'll be with you in a minute,' a female voice cried.

'That's Rosie,' Ethel called to Lizzie. 'She'll take over now; nice friendly girl she is, everyone likes our Rosie.'

Rosie appeared, tall and slim and dressed in a tight-fitting black dress.

'Right then, love, we'll go and eat. Bring your drink with you; it's all right, I've got the pram.' Ethel talked baby-talk to the wide-awake Robert as she led the way through to their private quarters.

The living-room was bright and cosy, the table set for three. Ethel nodded to Lizzie, 'Sit down, you don't mind a cold lunch, do you? I don't cook until the evening.'

'This is fine,' Lizzie answered. Before her was a platter on which lay a pork pie, a wedge of Cheddar cheese, plenty of salad and a baked potato.

As Ted Armstrong took a seat next to her, he blurted out, 'This is daft, I'm Ted and my wife's Ethel. What's your first name, love? Can't keep on calling you Mrs Wilson, can I?'

Lizzie laughed; both Ted and Ethel were regarding her with what could only be friendliness and now she felt very much more at ease. 'Please, call me Lizzie.'

'Right, Lizzie it is. Eat up lass, and then we'll talk.'

When they had finished eating, they moved from the table to sit in comfortable chairs by the window. Ethel lit a cigarette, having first offered one to Lizzie, who had declined, and slowly she blew out the match. 'Wish I could give it up,' she said in an undertone, 'but with this life and all the hours we put in I'd go crazy without my cigarettes.'

Still Lizzie was filled with curiosity, she liked these people very much, was actually thrilled at having been asked to lunch. Company was a rare thing to her these days.

Ted leaned forward and looked directly at Lizzie. 'What we want to ask you, lass, is would you like to rent our bedrooms? We've got nine upstairs.'

A few seconds passed before Lizzie had formed a reply. 'I'm not sure I understand what you mean.' She stared at them both in bewilderment.

'Of course, she's new at this lark, Ted. You go at things like a bull in a china shop,' Ethel rebuked her husband.

'It's quite common for folk to rent extra bed-rooms, Lizzie,' Ethel explained. 'Visitors sleep out and come to the guesthouse for their meals.'

'Oh, I see,' Lizzie said very quietly.

'It's like this; I'm not having Ethel doing meals or even bed and breakfast this year. We've quite enough to do in the pub during the summer.' With a grim smile, Ted Armstrong got up and passed an ashtray to his wife.

'While she's showing visitors up to their bed-rooms, especially on a Saturday night, the blasted part-time staff are giving the drinks away left, right and centre to their damn friends. We don't make a profit, all we do is end up well and truly out of pocket. So, now you've got the picture, Lizzie. Like it or lump it, my Ethel can rent you our rooms or they damn well stay empty!'

Ethel lowered her head, winked at Lizzie and stubbed out her cigarette. 'So now you know,' she said. 'But don't worry, love, his bark is worse than his bite.' Lizzie could hardly believe what she had heard. Maybe, just maybe, it could be the answer to her problem.

Ted smirked at them both, 'I'd best be getting back into the bar, I'll leave you two to sort out the details.' Then he stopped short, turned to Lizzie, and in a fatherly manner he told her, 'You take your time, young Lizzie, think it out well. There's the question of where would you seat these extra guests at meal-times, but there again I know a couple of my customers could sort that one out for you. Just come and see us, as often as you like, whether you say yes or no, don't make no difference. You know us now, so don't be a stranger. You'd be doing my Ethel a favour if you let her spoil that youngster of yours.'

He bent over and gave an affectionate tug to Lizzie's swept-back hair. 'Our two are grown up, both married, both settled in Wales, so no excuses – let's be seeing you, eh?'

'Yes, all right,' Lizzie promised in a voice that was husky with emotion.

The whole afternoon Lizzie just sat. She read through the notes that she had made dozens of times, and still all she felt was disbelief.

For the main ten weeks of the season Ethel Armstrong suggested that Lizzie paid her a set fee of £250 plus three shillings and sixpence per person for each night should she use any of the bedrooms at any time other than during those ten weeks.

Christ! Lizzie did her sums again.

Two pages of an exercise book were covered with figures. Whichever way she looked at it, she couldn't go wrong. There were seven double bedrooms and two singles all lovely and clean, nicely furnished and charmingly decorated. Accommodation for sixteen extra guests.

'They can use the lounge-bar, even drink after time, seeing as how they would be residents,' Ethel had cheerfully told Lizzie.

This arrangement, if it came off, would enable Lizzie to accept full coach parties. She scribbled away furiously; the one booking from Alan, for four weeks, fifty people at four guineas a week, would come to over eight hundred pounds.

She'd have to get some staff. A chambermaid for the Round House at least. It was only four doors away – would guests mind walking that far for their meals? Her head was beginning to ache. This pipedream was all very well, but could it become a reality?

That night, Lizzie wrote a long letter to Charlie.

His answer when it came was short and sweet. 'Grab them!'

It was all happening so quickly. Lizzie stood at the

sink, gently squeezing some woollies in the nice hot soapy water. Four workmen were busy in the garden plastering the new extension and in a couple of days' time glass would be in the windows and a large archway was to be knocked through their existing dining-room wall.

Once again, Lizzie had gone cap-in-hand to see Mr Blackhurst. He hadn't hesitated.

'A sound investment,' had been his verdict. 'It could prove to be most profitable, Mrs Wilson, and most certainly will add to the value of your property.' The bank would advance a loan.

As Lizzie thanked him, Graham Blackhurst had pondered on her reasons for staying. He was aware just how disastrous their first season had been in Sea View Guesthouse and his good wishes for the coming season were truly sincere.

The milk boiled over and Lizzie cursed herself for day-dreaming as she mopped up the mess. She made four mugs of coffee, set a plate of her home-made fruit scones and a feeding bottle of warm milk on a tray and walked down the garden path.

'Coffee up!' she called, and the men all grinned and readily stopped what they were doing.

It was the least she could do, Lizzie told herself. Three or four times a day she made hot drinks for the men.

Robert had been as pleased as Punch ever since they had started work. She had to laugh out loud now as he stretched his little hands out for his beaker. Sitting in a mucky wheelbarrow, dressed in dark blue dungarees, a red high-necked jersey and a red woollen hat pulled down over his dark curly hair, he looked the picture of contentment. The bib of his dungarees was smeared with plaster and his face smudged with dirt as he chuckled away to himself. The workmen had been great; even when they had gone off in the van to get supplies, they had taken Robert with them.

He'll miss them when this job is completed, Lizzie said to herself.

Once more, Charlie had left his job and was back in Devon. Everything was ready as they waited for their first coach party to arrive. Unbelievably, Mr Channon had allowed them further credit. Four tables and sixteen chairs, all in a light oak, were set up in the new extension and in the main dining-room there were places laid for a further thirty-eight guests. They were now capable of accommodating fifty-four people in all.

It did not take long for them to get into a steady routine. They had two women who came in every day, plus two extra on Saturdays, all were very reliable and everywhere was kept clean and bright with vases of fresh flowers in the hall and the lounge.

Each meal-time, as the gong sounded, it seemed to Lizzie that people were coming from all directions, down the stairs, from the lounge and through the open front door. She and Charlie would grin at one another, still amazed at their own determination.

Saturdays were a bit hectic ('bloody chaotic' as Charlie put it) as women came from the bedrooms upstairs, arms full of dirty linen, demanding sheets, pillowcases and clean towels. Methodically, Lizzie made out lists and knew exactly what each room needed.

No sooner had the women gone about their tasks than through the front door came the chambermaids from the Round House. Charlie would stop what he was doing and carry the heavy, clean bedlinen down the hill for them.

And then, early in June, Syd got a very good offer for his house, which he accepted. This opened the way for an agreement between Lizzie and Syd which was to solve a great many problems and give Lizzie and Charlie the financial security that they longed for. For Syd and Doris decided to buy number twelve.

It meant that that lovely big old house, where Lizzie had been so happy, would remain in the family and, as Doris assured them, there would always be a bedroom for Lizzie, Charlie and Robert whenever they came 'home'.

When everything was finalized, Charlie went first to Bideford and paid Mr Channon in full.

He came back looking very pleased. 'Mr Channon said to give you his kind regards and to tell you that he hadn't been wrong. He was a good judge of character.'

Lizzie thought of Mr Channon as a compassionate

man. Then, Charlie paid a visit to Mr Fleming.
What took place at his new big hotel was never mentioned.

'Did you have a drink while you were there?'
Lizzie asked him very cautiously.

'Did I hell,' was all the reply she got.

Later she caught Charlie grinning to himself and
she asked, 'What's amusing you?'

'Nothing, really,' he replied; then added, 'eighteen months Frank Fleming waited for his money.'

Lizzie's thoughts flew back; once again she had
her doubts as to just who had conned whom.
Wisely, she kept her thoughts to herself.

The golden weeks of summer slipped by and soon
it was autumn. The early mornings were misty, the
days were no longer so warm, and sharp breezes
blew in across the sea.

Both Lizzie and Charlie heaved a sigh of relief as
they stood on the front steps, waving goodbye to
the last coachload of old-aged pensioners.

'I could sleep for a month,' Lizzie declared.

'Nothing to stop you,' Charlie answered.

'Oh, no, and whose gonna see to Robert and cook
our meals?'

'Well, tonight no one's doing any cooking.' Charlie tenderly took her into his arms. The quietness
was strange and the two of them stood in the
entrance hall, locked in a close embrace for several
minutes.

'We've made it, Lizzie,' Charlie said, his voice

now quite solemn. 'I shan't have to leave you this winter, and tonight I am taking my wife and my son out to dinner.'

A great tenderness filled Lizzie's heart as she realized that this man of hers was saying 'Thank you'.

Christmas came and Syd hired a minibus.

Lizzie was busy for days getting the rooms ready, taking the blankets out of the wardrobes, making up the beds. Charlie declared he would be the chef and wonderful appetizing smells rose up from the kitchen as he prepared many dishes in advance.

Lizzie could hardly contain herself, she was so looking forward to this holiday.

Syd, Doris and Raymond, Polly, Arthur and young Lucy, Aunt Kate and Uncle John, that would be eight from London.

Her sister Connie and Bill, with William, now wearing his first pair of long trousers, or so Connie had written, were coming from Plymouth. Who wouldn't be excited?

There would be fourteen of them in all over Christmas.

Log fires burnt in the lounge and dining-room and a ten-foot tree taken straight off Exmoor, now glittered with baubles and fairy lights in the hall.

The weather the previous week had been very bad, with gale-force winds and massive waves pounding the shoreline. Lizzie had pretended she didn't care, but when Christmas Eve dawned quiet and peaceful, she said a thank-you prayer.

On Christmas morning they all set off for church, Raymond holding Robert's hand, Lucy chatting away to William. They filled two pews and, as they sank to their knees, Doris reached out her hand to Lizzie and they both smiled – each knowing what the other was thinking.

How wonderful it was to all be together again!

Chapter Twenty

THE NEW YEAR got off to a wonderful start. Scores of letters came daily, many containing postal-orders and cheques. Some were from people from the previous year requesting the same dates, many stating a preference for bedrooms in the Round House. Lizzie made her wallcharts and looked forward to another season.

Forgotten were the days when nothing had gone right, when she had envied guests setting out for a day on the moors whilst she and Charlie had to cook lunch – and dinner again in the evening.

Forgotten were the nights when she had practically crawled downstairs to bed because her legs ached so much. When, just as she had snuggled up to Charlie, the front doorbell would ring at one o'clock in the morning and they would have to climb the stairs again to admit an inconsiderate visitor.

Charlie bought a car. 'Come and see,' he called from the front door, and while Lizzie stopped to dry her hands, Robert beat her up the hall.

Utter astonishment showed on Lizzie's face as she gazed at this immense blue car which stood in the street. Charlie laughed out loud as he swung Robert high in the air before opening the rear door and plonking him down on to the leather seat. Robert chuckled with glee as he bounced up and down and slid from side to side.

'It's a Morris Six,' Charlie told her with pride. 'They only made about fifty of them. Isn't she beautiful?' Lizzie had to agree. The interior was sheer luxury and smelled of real leather, and there were mahogany-faced picnic tables set into the back of each front seat. Oh yes, it was lovely.

Owning a car opened up new horizons for them as a family.

As spring came, they often took a day off from the spring-cleaning and set off with no particular destination in mind.

Exmoor was a favourite, with its wild and beautiful scenery, which Lizzie had read about in *Lorna Doone*, but had never in her wildest dreams imagined that she would see. Charlie played hearty, noisy games with Robert until they would both collapse thirsty and hungry on to the rugs where Lizzie had set out their picnic.

On one such day, Charlie stopped eating and his mouth hung open in amazement. Lizzie, too, stared in wonder and Robert let out a shriek of delight. There, not fifty yards away, stood several red deer. 'Majestic,' Charlie said, 'that's the only word I can think of to describe them.'

Friday became a day to look forward to, because it was market day in Barnstaple.

The produce was all fresh from the farms. There was Devonshire cream, thick as butter and as golden as the sun, plus every vegetable imaginable. Lettuce, cucumbers, radishes, tomatoes and mustard and cress, all had been freshly dug or picked that morning.

Home-made pickles and jams, cakes, sponges which were as light as a feather, home-made treacle toffee which was Lizzie's favourite, all were displayed on snow-white tablecloths and served by rosy, apple-faced women.

Large brown eggs lay on straw in huge china bowls, and plump chickens and fleshy ducks, all plucked ready for the oven.

Out in the street on one side of the road was a continuous line of butchers' shops, hence its name, Butchers' Row. No frozen or foreign meat would be seen here. With the abattoir only a few streets away, everything sold was fresh.

Lizzie never went home empty-handed.

Unlike the London markets, the pubs here stayed open all day. One Friday, while Charlie went off to have a pint, Lizzie did something she had been thinking of doing for a long time.

'Christ almighty, you look like an elf!' Charlie declared when they met up later. She had had her hair cut. Now barely shoulder length, it curled under in a page-boy style.

'It will be easier to manage in the summer,' Lizzie told him.

With the coming of May, the weather became more settled, with nice sunny days and long, light evenings. There still weren't that many visitors about, but Lizzie was hoping that they might pick up some more guests if the fine weather continued.

Hopefully, life for Lizzie and Charlie was not going to be quite so hectic this season and, as their debts were now paid off, Charlie had arranged for two local lads to come in every evening from the beginning of June to do the washing-up of the dinner things. It would make quite a difference – it would enable them to sit down and have their own dinner a lot earlier and enjoy longer evenings together.

But there were still times when Lizzie longed for her London life and her friends and family.

As the month ended and June was upon them Lizzie felt disappointed and angry. She knew she had no right to feel so annoyed but she couldn't help herself, for she would have given anything to have been in London this week. It was 1953 and on the 2nd of June the Queen was to be crowned in Westminster Abbey by the Archbishop of Canterbury.

'Thousands will line the route,' she said to Charlie. 'She's gonna ride in a gold coach. Oh, how I wish I could be there!'

'The newspapers will carry colour supplements every day this week, and you'll be able to read all about it and look at the pictures as well,' he said in that maddeningly tantalizing way of his.

'Get out,' she yelled as she threw a tea-cloth at him, 'we don't even have a television set to watch it on.'

The most galling thing of all to Lizzie was not that she wouldn't see the procession, though that was bad enough, but that she wouldn't be there for the street parties – and you could bet your last farthing that there'd be a party in Wilton Road. Syd, Doris, Polly and Arthur would be out there managing things, you could be sure of that. Christ! I'd better stop thinking about it, she thought to herself. For two pins I'd take Robert and get on that train!

Ah well, nobody gets everything in this life. Though that thought didn't make her feel any better.

One lunchtime, towards the end of the month, the phone rang as Lizzie and Charlie were frying fish and boiling new potatoes and peas.

'It's Ethel, wants a word with you.' Charlie came back down the length of the kitchen and took the bowl of creamy batter from Lizzie's hands.

'Hallo, Ethel.' Lizzie smiled into the receiver.

'Sorry to disturb you, won't keep you a minute. What are you doing this afternoon?'

'Taking Robert down on the beach, same as always. Why? Is something wrong?'

'I don't want to go into it over the phone, but I would like to see you.'

'Well, we've only got twenty-two in for lunch,

rest of them took a packed lunch, so we shouldn't be late finishing.'

Charlie had been listening and had got the gist of what Ethel had been saying. 'I'll take Robert down to the beach,' he volunteered. 'You put the deck-chairs out in the garden; have a cuppa with Ethel.'

'Did you hear that?' Lizzie mouthed her thanks to Charlie.

'Yes, so I'll see you about half-past two,' Ethel was saying, and Lizzie wondered why she couldn't have waited until she popped in to check the rooms, but she had sounded pretty flustered.

Ethel often looked tired to death, and no wonder with the hours she had to keep. Wouldn't have her job for the world, thought Lizzie, three hundred and sixty-five days every year; at least in this trade you get the winter to look forward to, though God knows there are enough jobs to do even then.

Charlie watched Lizzie replace the receiver and then smiled at her. 'Trouble?' he asked.

'I dunno. I hope not.' Yet she couldn't shake off the premonition that there might be.

Ethel looked all in, but when she smiled, her eyes still lit up warm and friendly.

'Sit down, luv,' Lizzie pointed to the two deck-chairs. 'I'll just go in and make the tea, I won't be a minute.'

Ethel's eyes were brimming with tears when Lizzie came back and set the tea tray down on the wicker table.

'Oh, love, don't cry. Nothing can be as bad as all

that. It's the season, gets us all, one way or another, bloody working seven days a week is no pushover.' She held out a cup of tea for Ethel to take. 'Come on, drink that up, a cuppa is everyone's answer when trouble is brewing.'

Ethel struggled not to blink but she couldn't help herself and the tears in her eyes brimmed over.

Lizzie settled herself in her own chair with her own cup of tea. 'A trouble shared is a troubled halved,' she ventured.

Ethel sniffed, 'We've got to go and I'm only sorry for how it's going to affect you and Charlie.'

Lizzie looked puzzled. 'I'm not with you. Where have you got to go to?'

'Anywhere, oh, I don't know. God alone knows, really.'

'Ethel,' Lizzie implored, 'start at the beginning and tell me what's happened.'

Ethel nodded her head. 'You're right Lizzie, there's no way of wrapping it up. My Ted's had an awful row with the brewery. Mind you, I can't really blame him, going to treble the rent. I ask you, treble it! They come down here in the summer, see the bar's packed and they think we're making a bloody fortune. Don't bother to think about the winter, do they? Oh no. Don't want to know about the nights when all we serve is a few pints to the local fishermen.'

Lizzie had an awful feeling that she knew exactly where this conversation was leading, but she did not want to believe it. For the moment she wouldn't let

herself think about it. She held out her hand for
Ethel's cup and poured each of them more tea.

Ethel was miles away, lost in thought. Lizzie
leaned forward and put a hand on her knee. 'So what
are you going to do?'

'What are we going to do? I wish I knew, Lizzie.
I wish I knew.' Ethel stared into space as if she had
almost forgotten where she was.

'Ted will sort something out, I'm sure he will,'
Lizzie's voice was full of compassion.

'That's just the trouble. My Ted blew his top,
told them what they could do with their so-and-so
pub.' Ethel's face was blood-red now, as she con-
demned the brewery. 'Took him at his word they
did. He couldn't keep his big mouth shut, could he?
Oh no, played right into their hands. Just what they
wanted. Get us out, new tenants in, agree a new
lease and charge what they like. One month is all
we've got. That's all we are entitled to. One month
either way, it's in our lease, can't get away from
that.'

The truth was out now and Lizzie had to face the
reality. Ethel's voice droned on. 'My Ted says he is
finished working for the brewery. Gonna see if he
can find a small place to buy, somewhere in Wales
probably; be nice to be near the children.'

She was rambling on, half to herself, saying anything that came into her head. Suddenly she seemed
to pull herself together and her eyes were alert again.

'Sorry to worry you, Lizzie, but I thought it best
to tell you myself. Mind you, nothing is definite

yet, no dates set. When Ted calms down, perhaps Charlie will come and have a chat with him; let's hope they can work something out for all our sakes.'

'I don't believe it!' Charlie sat forward in his chair and stared at Lizzie. She had waited until they had finished eating to tell him. 'Bloody hell! You realize what a mess this will leave us in.'

Lizzie took a book down from the shelf and rifled through the pages. She had known Charlie would go mad and who could blame him, it was a dicey situation to be in. There were the peak weeks of the season yet to come and they had accepted bookings on all nine of the bedrooms in the Round House. What if they couldn't fulfil that contract? If Ethel and Ted Armstrong went, who's to say that the new tenants would want to let out their bedrooms. They might have a family of their own and need some of the rooms for themselves. They may even want to take in visitors.

Dear God, the repercussions didn't bear thinking about.

Lizzie found the page she was looking for and pointed a finger to one of the paragraphs as she handed the book over to Charlie. Tension mounted in Lizzie as she watched him reading. 'Damn it, Lizzie, have you read this?' She nodded her head.

'So, if we can't keep our side of the bargain, guests are legally entitled to go to another guesthouse or even an hotel and claim the difference in cost from us!' Charlie's face was red with anger. 'Right bloody mess, ain't it?'

Lizzie wanted to calm him, she was just as worried as he was, but a screaming match wasn't going to help anyone. They were both tired, much better to leave things to quieten down and then sit down and talk about it.

She placed a bowl of fruit on the table. 'You haven't had any sweet yet,' she said eagerly; 'the grapes are nice and juicy, real sweet, or would you like some ice-cream?'

Charlie burst out laughing. 'If you don't take the cake, Lizzie, I'm damned if I know who does. You're talking in deadly earnest about us not having had any pudding, when all the time we're up to our ears in trouble. If it weren't so serious, you know, it would be downright funny.'

Even Lizzie grinned. 'Would it help if I burst into tears? Nothing's for certain yet, we may be jumping the gun.'

'And if we're not?' he asked.

'Well, we could wait until we know for certain before we blow our brains out, we don't have to meet trouble head on, do we?'

Charlie stood up and came to stand in front of her. 'You really do take the biscuit.' He was laughing now, fit to bust, his dark head thrown back, his mouth wide open showing his perfect white teeth. 'You're bloody marvellous,' he said as she stood laughing with him. 'Bloody marvellous!'

*

The following week was filled with anxiety, and
though neither Charlie nor Lizzie broached the subject, each knew that it was uppermost in the other's
mind.

'I've got the bloody jitters,' Lizzie muttered to
herself as she picked up the broken pieces of a cup
she had just dropped.

Ted had phoned and asked Charlie to pop down
about eight o'clock. It was ten minutes past ten now
– he had been gone over two hours.

One minute Lizzie had sunk into the depths of
despair, and the next she'd been telling herself that
Charlie wouldn't have stayed so long if the worst
had happened.

She was baffled and worried, but just when she
felt she would have to pick up the phone, she heard
Charlie coming down the basement steps. The tilt
of his head and the laughter in his bright blue eyes
made Lizzie sigh with relief.

'Everything's all right, love. Put the kettle on;
we've got a reprieve. The Armstrongs are going,
but not until September, somewhere around the
tenth.'

Almost all of their free time was now spent discussing their future. Charlie's ideas were well thought
out and Lizzie listened attentively to all that he had
to say.

'With just twelve letting bedrooms, we would be
back to square one and our income would be greatly

diminished,' he pointed out. 'But I don't care what
happens, even if we sell up and go back to London,
we are never again going to rent rooms from other
people. It's far too precarious. God, we were lucky.
I still break out in a sweat every time I think about
what could have happened.'

It was a lovely afternoon, the sun shone down,
the sky was cloudless and the beach was packed with
holidaymakers.

'Let's go for a swim,' Charlie suggested.

'You know I can't swim,' Lizzie's voice was
sullen, 'besides, I'm too tired and I look a right
mess.'

'Poor old thing,' he teased, as he pushed towels
and a beach ball into the bag. 'Come on, I'm not
taking no for an answer, we'll pick Robert up on
the way; he's only playing in the lane.'

Half an hour later and Lizzie felt a new woman.
They had clambered over the dunes to a fairly
deserted part of the beach, changed into their swimming costumes and romped in the warm sea. Now
Lizzie lay back, resting on her elbows, and watched
her son and his father as they swam quite a way
from the shore.

Charlie was a fantastic swimmer and he had
insisted on Robert being taught. 'I swear that kid
could swim before he could walk,' she said to Bob-
Bob as he came across the sand. 'Oh you horror,'
she yelled as he vigorously shook himself and then
lay down next to her, taking up more than half of
the blanket she had spread out. 'Have they gone and

left you too?' she said to him as she rubbed his wet
sandy fur with his own doggy-towel. 'Well, they've
both got webbed feet, you see, that's the difference
between them and us.'

'I heard that,' Charlie sounded happy as he pushed
the dog out of the way and lay down, all wet from
the sea, beside Lizzie.

'I know what we're going to do,' he said grinning
like a Cheshire cat, 'we're going to buy a big hotel.'

'Oh, no,' was Lizzie's first reaction, 'not again,
not go through all that palaver all over again!'

Chapter Twenty-One

SEPTEMBER CAME, THE Armstrongs departed for Wales, new tenants with three children took over the Round House, and young Robert went to school.

Lizzie dubbed the school 'arsenic and old lace'. Not that she didn't like it, quite the reverse. It was called Adelaide College and it was owned and managed by two middle-aged sisters, both of whom were spinsters, with the help of just six dedicated staff.

The building itself was like a Southern plantation house straight out of a film. Wide wooden verandas, painted white, ran the length of the frontage; large, comfortable rocking-chairs placed at intervals gave one a view of the wonderful grounds. The whole place seemed unaffected by time.

There were only eight pupils to each class; it was an intimate friendly school and Robert loved it from day one.

It was Lizzie who shed a tear as she walked away and left him clutching Miss Warrell-Bowring's hand.

'He's only three years old,' she had reminded the stately lady with the black velvet ribbon encircling her throat.

'All the better, Mrs Wilson, and his classmates

will be of the same age,' she spoke flawlessly as she showed Lizzie to the door.

Just four weeks of coach parties and their third season in Sea View Guesthouse was over.

'Our final one an' all,' Charlie declared as he scanned estate agents' lists.

'Oh, for Christ's sake, let's have a rest before you start dragging me off to view hotels,' Lizzie pleaded.

They had a good rest. They stored all blankets away in mothballs, disinfected all toilets and bathrooms, cleaned the gas cooker, washed out the fridge and threw out all bits and pieces of perishable food. They bagged up piles of linen for the laundry and went back to bed every lunchtime and only got up again when it was time to fetch Robert from school.

Before they knew where they were it was October and Robert had a week's holiday from school for half-term.

Lizzie didn't ask Charlie, she told him. 'I'm going home.' She had all of her arguments ready in case he tried to stop her, but in the end she didn't need any of them. With a straight face Charlie said that he was going to suggest that they did just that. Lizzie wasn't quite sure that she believed him. But this time her face had shown such determination that he had known she really would have up-sticks and gone on her own if he had tried to stand in her way. Far better to go together and travel by car.

'Doris, Doris, Doris,' Lizzie called as they ran towards each other, arms spread wide ready to hug. It was Polly's turn next, as Lizzie broke free from Doris to put her arms around the girl who had been her friend for as long as she could remember. Lucy and Raymond were also claiming her attention and, as she bent and cuddled them both, Raymond whispered to her, 'Auntie Lizzie am I still your superman?' They were all still in a group, on the pavement outside number twelve, chattering away and laughing, when Syd came back out from the house.

'We've taken in all the gear, are you silly cows going to stand there all night?' he called out in a loud voice.

'Ssh, Syd, mind the neighbours,' Doris said in that little girl's voice of hers.

'Sod the neighbours. Charlie, Arthur and me want something to eat if you lot don't, so get in 'ere an' see about getting a meal; just because my daft sister's come 'ome it don't mean we've all got to starve.'

The three girls looked at each other and burst out laughing.

Doris had hold of Robert's hand, Polly had Raymond and Lizzie had Lucy up in her arms as they all went inside what had been Lizzie's first house.

'God, it's great to be home,' she said as her brother gave her a great bear-hug.'

It was after nine o'clock on the Saturday morning when Lizzie came down the wide staircase, through the tiled hall and into the living-room. They'd sat up half the night jabbering away, and when she'd got out of bed this morning she had stood for a long while gazing out of the big bay window at Wilton Road.

My, she'd done right to buy the two houses during the war, especially this one. It really was a beautiful house, so well built. It was all thanks to Gran though; without her legacy none of them would be so well off today.

I must ask Doris about the people that bought hers and Syd's house; being right opposite she must know all about them, Lizzie promised herself as she finally turned away from the window.

'You timed that right,' Doris called from the kitchen as Lizzie sat down. 'The kettle's just coming up ter boil.'

'Where is everyone? It's so quiet, what 'ave yer done with the boys?'

'They've only bin gone about ten minutes. Syd an' Charlie's taken them out; they didn't say where they were going an' I didn't ask.' Doris gave Lizzie one of her slow, mischievous grins before asking, 'Yer don't mind do yer? Got the whole morning ter ourselves.'

Lizzie laughed. 'Still scheming in yer own quiet way?'

'Got to ain't I? Don't do ter let Syd know what I'm doing half the time nor yet what I'm thinking come to that.'

Lizzie shook her head in disbelief as she drank her

tea and watched Doris cook bacon and eggs for each
of them. Doris, so quiet, almost timid at times. I
never thought she'd last, she thought to herself, not
with my Syd and his ducking and diving I never.
She's a proper little dark horse, but she seems to be
holding her own all right.

They had finished eating their breakfast and the
pair of them lapsed into silence, comfortable and
happy to have each other's company, each absorbed
with their own thoughts. The clock on the mantelshelf ticked loudly, a cheerful fire glowed in the
grate and Lizzie remembered when she had sat here
in this same room and nursed and breast-fed her
baby. Automatically she asked herself the question
for which she had no answer. Why did I ever leave
London? How did I come to be living in Devon?
Working seven days a week when the sun was shining and not seeing a soul through the long winter
months.

The door opened and Polly's voice broke the
silence. 'So how are we this morning, an' what are
we doing?'

'Has Arthur gone with the boys?' asked Doris.
'Yes, thank God. Lucy wasn't going to be left
behind either.'

'We're all going ter get our hair done,' declared
Doris.

'Oh, no,' Lizzie groaned. 'You don't want me ter
bleach yer roots, do you?' she asked, remembering
the times she had done them and what a messy job
it was.

'No. I told yer we're all getting our hair done, fer free, at 'alf past eleven.' Seeing the glance that passed between Polly and Lizzie, Doris said, 'Do you remember Vi Dolby? Used ter do women's hair in 'er front room. Well, she bought a sa—lon.' They laughed at Doris's exaggerated use of the word salon. 'Right next door ter Colliers Wood tube station, but it ain't done any good and she wants ter sell it. I met her yesterday and she told me she'd got people coming ter view the place. She hopes they'll buy it. She wants ter make out that the place is always busy an' she said she'd do me hair for nothing if I'd come down there this morning, an' I told her I'd do better than that, I'd bring you two as well.'

'Are you serious?' Lizzie asked in amazement. 'Poor woman going to do all our hairs and not make a penny out of us?'

'We won't be the only ones; she's gonna fill the shop. Got two assistants coming in ter work there as well. It'll be a good laugh and the prospective buyers will think it is a good business, an' Vi will do all right out of it, so yer see it's us what is doing Vi the favour.'

Both Polly and Lizzie fell about laughing. The logic of Doris wanted some beating!

'We've got a good hour yet, so while Lizzie an' I make our faces up you make a fresh pot of tea Polly.'

'Yes, marm,' said Polly giving Doris a mock salute as she went into the kitchen.

They were sitting around the table drinking their

tea when Lizzie remembered she wanted to know about the folk who had bought Syd's house.

'Go on, tell her,' Polly urged Doris with a wide grin on her face.

'Don't laugh then or I won't.' They both agreed and did their best to keep a straight face.

'For a start there's Mr and Mrs Watkins an' they've got a son Tom, an' a daughter Mary. They let two rooms upstairs to an old lady on her own, her name's Thelma, or at least I think it is, though I got told off for calling her that. She said I didn't 'ave to be all lardy-dah with her. She calls herself Felma. Funny old girl, really nice but a bit queer, ain't got much. I took her over a cardigan and a warm dress, she put them on straight away, on top of what she was wearing.'

'Tell Lizzie about Felma's gas meter,' Polly insisted.

Doris shot a look of embarrassment at Polly, before turning to Lizzie and declaring very self-consciously, 'It isn't much. I started putting her money in the meter for her, that's all. Her hands are bad, crippled up with arthritis, and she couldn't get the coins in the slot.'

'That's not the end of it,' Polly took up the story. 'Felma was giving Doris a shilling an' moaning that the gas only lasted a couple of days; said Doris wasn't putting the shillings in right; so what does dozy Doris do now?'

Lizzie had no need to be told. 'She puts two or three of her own two-bob pieces in the meter.'

'You got it,' Polly said.

'Well it don't 'urt me, a couple of bob now an' again, does it?' Doris asked Lizzie with a pleading note in her voice.

'No, 'course it don't,' Lizzie assured her, at the same time thinking what a saint this sister-in-law of hers was turning out to be.

'You were going to tell me about the family themselves,' Lizzie reminded her, and once again Doris looked across at Polly and was obviously embarrassed.

'Don't tell me you're helping them out as well?' Lizzie couldn't help smiling as she spoke.

'I'll tell yer this story,' Polly volunteered. Doris half closed her eyes and gave Lizzie a saucy grin as Polly began.

'The father an' the mother 'ave a fruit stall outside Tooting Baths. Sell good stuff they do, always a queue ain't there, Doris?'

Doris was busy adding more boiling water to the pot so that they could all have another cup of tea, but she looked up and nodded her head in agreement.

Polly took up the tale again and Lizzie wondered when the pair of them were going to get to the point.

'The son an' the daughter work the streets, you know, pushing a barrow; well that Tom does the streets but in the fine weather his sister Mary has been selling from her barrow up on the Common.' Polly paused and giggled at her own thoughts and Doris nearly choked on her tea. 'Syd an' Doris,

Arthur an' me, we'd all been up to Streatham Lacarno for the evening. Well, as we came out it started to rain an' by the time we got to the bus stop it was coming down in torrents. As yer know the bus comes down by St Leonard's Church and runs right along side of the Common. There we were, minding our own business, when at one of the stops on the Common who should get on the bus but this Mary, looked like a drowned rat she did, water was dripping from her 'air and she was soaked ter the skin. Came an' sat on the seat right opposite to Doris an' me an' what do yer think our Doris said to that Mary?' Lizzie shook her head, speechless for once. 'She looked at Mary an' said, "You poor thing, you're soaked, get caught in the downpour did yer and run for it? What yer done with your fruit barrow? Left it under the trees?" I thought my Arthur was going to explode an' as for your Syd, you never heard anyone blow their nose so hard in all yer life. I didn't know where to put me face. I tell yer, Lizzie, we were all damn glad ter get off that bus an' I ain't bin able ter look that Mary in the face since then.'

'I'm not with you,' Lizzie said with a baffled look on her face.

'Oh, not you as well!' Polly screamed, while Doris almost fell off her chair because she was laughing so much.

'You silly cow, Lizzie, ain't yer fell in yet? That Mary's on the game. She weren't up on the Common that time of night selling no fruit!' Then the living-room was ringing with the boisterous laughter of all three of them as they clutched at each other for support.

When they'd wiped the tears from their eyes and settled down again, Doris, never one to mind others having a laugh at her expense, said, 'Here Lizzie I've just got time to tell yer about me taking a lodger, an' then we'll 'ave ter get going if we're gonna 'ave our hair done.'

'I don't know if I can take any more,' Lizzie gasped as she gave her eyes another wipe.

'Oh, you've got ter hear this,' Polly stated as she, too, struggled to stop laughing.

'Well,' (it seemed to Lizzie that all of Doris's stories began with 'Well') 'I thought I might try letting the top flat, like you did ter Wally an' Hilda. We weren't short of money but you know your brother, a millionaire this week, treats the world and his wife ter drinks in the pub, come the next week and he's selling anything he can lay his hands on. Not that me an' Raymond ever go short, far from it, but I thought a bob or two put away for a rainy day wouldn't come amiss. So I wrote out a postcard an' put it in the window of the corner shop. Same day I had a man come ter the door. He was lovely looking; tall and handsome . . .'

'Get on with the story,' Polly begged. 'We'll never get our free hair-do at the rate you're going.'

'He said he was a doctor at the Grove Hospital, went mad about how nice the flat was an' said fifty shillings rent was very fair. I let him move in the

next morning. Syd said at the time that I was mad.
Anyway, at the end of the first week I went up to
clean his rooms an' to change his bed. Young Lucy
was with me. No sooner had we got in the room
than Lucy asked where the clock had gone to from
off the mantelshelf. Then I stripped the eiderdown
and the bedspread from off the bed an' I couldn't
believe me eyes. My two big thick white blankets
were missing an' a blooming old overcoat was lying
on top of the sheet. I'll cut the story short. Syd
nearly throttled the bloke. Made him turn his
pockets out; he hadn't got any money but he had
got two pawn-tickets. Syd put his toe up his arse
an' kicked him out there an' then. It turned out I'd
taken two weeks rent off him in advance, five
pounds, an' it cost Syd a fiver ter get our stuff back
out from the pawn-shop. I won't tell yer what your
brother's threatened ter do ter me if I even think
about taking any more lodgers.'

'Oh, my sides are killing me, I shall ache for a
week,' Lizzie moaned as the tears of laughter were
once more blinding her.

'You 'aven't heard the best bit yet.' Polly was
ready with her two pennyworth.

'We were coming back from Tooting, Doris an'
me, at the beginning of that week, the bloke had
only been in the house for a couple of days. When
we passed him, he said good morning ter us polite
as yer like, but underneath his arm he had this dirty
great big parcel; he even shifted it from one arm to
the other as we watched him. What we didn't know

at the time was that it was Doris's blankets and clock
that the cheeky sod had got wrapped up in there.'

'Pack it in the pair of yer,' Lizzie pleaded with
them as she held her arm to her side, which really
was giving her gip and her laughter was in danger
of becoming hysterical.

'Come on, then,' Doris said, 'get yer coats on an'
I'll take yer ter get this free hair-do, and don't forget
if the woman asks yer, we 'ave a job ter get booked
up in this salon 'cos Vi is always so busy.'

All the way to Colliers Wood Lizzie was chuckling to herself. I knew I was missing a lot by living
down in Devon, but not this much; it's worse than
a Brian Rix farce.

Lizzie's hair had grown during the summer and was
now just beyond shoulder-length. She had had it set
on very large rollers, brushed out and clipped back
with a wide orange hair-slide which Vi had sold her
for one and tuppence. Polly still wore her dark hair
fairly short, with a fringe and the ends curling
upwards. Doris's hairstyle was the most elaborate;
bleached almost white, back-combed until the front
was piled high and sprayed with this new-fangled
lacquer which Vi told her would keep the hair in
place even in the rain, it felt as stiff as a board when
Lizzie touched it. All three of them gave the two
assistants a couple of bob each as a tip, called cheerio
to Vi and walked about twenty yards up the road.
There they fell against the wall and none of them

could move for the next couple of minutes because
they were laughing so much.

'I've never seen anything like it in me life,' gasped
Polly.

'I told yer Vi was going ter do anything she could
to sell that shop, didn't I?' Doris said as she fumbled
in her bag for a handkerchief.

'Yes, you did right enough, but ter go to those
lengths!' complained Lizzie as she tried hard to control her giggling. 'I don't know how those two girls
kept a straight face. There was one of them kept
opening the door to make the bell ring, then saying
in a loud voice, "No sorry can't do anything for you
today, we're fully booked." An' the other poor cow
kept answering the phone that never stopped
ringing, saying that they couldn't fit the customer
in for at least a fortnight. The woman out in the
back room with Vi must 'ave thought the place was
a bloody gold-mine!'

Lizzie's description of events set them all off again
and their uproarious laughing caused two old bidd-
ies who were passing to stop and stare at them.
'Painted molls,' one sniffed to her friend. 'Yeah,
drunk this time in the day, should be bleedin' well
ashamed of 'emselves,' said the other.

'Painted molls!' exclaimed Polly and this time
they really were helpless with laughter.

It took some time for them to compose themselves and to start walking towards home.

'What will we give them to eat now?' asked Doris.

'I've got all the dinner ready for ternight but they'll want something now.'

'How about pie an' mash?' suggested Polly.

'No, can't be bothered ter walk all the way to Tooting now. 'Ere, Lizzie, d'yer, still like faggots an' pease-pudding?'

'Cor, yes, can't remember when I last 'ad them though.'

'Good, 'cos there's a cooked-meat shop opened up at the top of Marlborough Road, we can get some there.'

'What we going ter carry 'em home in?' Polly wanted to know. 'We ain't got a dish with us.'

'I'll buy one at the oil shop. I can do with a new one fer me rice puddings.'

The three of them trooped into the dark, smelly, oil shop and started sorting out the pile of baking tins and pie-dishes that were stacked on the floor.

'They must 'ave been here since the year dot,' Lizzie muttered under her breath as she spat on her handkerchief and rubbed at her fingers.

Doris walked towards the shopkeeper, a biggish man with a round red face, not a hair on his head and a beer-belly that overlapped the top of his trousers. 'Friar Tuck of Tooting,' Polly said in a stage whisper to Lizzie.

'Excuse me,' Doris said in a quiet voice, putting on her little-girl act once again, 'you wouldn't 'appen ter 'ave a kettle boiling out the back would you?'

'As a matter of fact I do, miss,' the bald-headed

man answered her, not in the least put out by Doris's question.

'If I buy one of those enamel pie-dishes, the big eightpenny ones, would you scald it out fer me 'cos we want ter take some faggots and pease-pudding 'ome with us; an' if we get them in paper bags we can't get no gravy, an' we all think the gravy is the best part, don't you?'

'Yes, I most certainly do. Without a load of gravy a faggot just don't taste the same. I'll scald a dish out an' dry it fer yer with pleasure, miss.'

Lizzie couldn't stay and listen to any more; she had to get out of the shop before she started to laugh again. Doris wasn't taking the mickey; she was deadly serious and the shopkeeper was treating her with the utmost respect. Only Doris could act like that and get away with it.

They walked three abreast down the street with their faggots and pease-pudding, Doris carried her pie-dish well out in front of her, very careful not to spill any of the rich thick gravy. As soon as one of them stopped chuckling another one started. 'What a morning,' Lizzie said to herself as she opened the gate and stood back to let Doris go in first.

With their midday meal over, Syd spread the pages of the *Sporting Life* out over the table and, with pencil and betting-slips at the ready, he said to Charlie, 'Come an' see what yer fancy fer the three o'clock. There's racing on the telly all the afternoon.'

Without saying a word, Doris got up from her chair and went to the dresser. From the drawer she took out a tin box that had a picture on the lid of the Changing of the Guard at Buckingham Palace. She spread the contents of the tin all over one end of the table – bottles of different coloured nail varnish, cotton wool, wooden tooth-picks, nail scissors, nail files, and a large bottle of nail-varnish remover.

'Oh blimey! We're not gonna 'ave ter put up with that bloody stink all the afternoon are we?' roared Syd as he got to his feet. With a swipe of his hand he swept the various bottles into a heap. From his pocket he pulled a roll of notes and, with a flash of anger, he pulled a fiver from the roll and threw it towards Doris. 'Here,' he yelled, 'take the kids round the park or something; buy yourselves all the ice-creams an' sweets you can eat but stay out of our way till the racing's finished.'

Doris still didn't say anything as she got the boys' coats out of the cupboard, but as she passed Lizzie a hint of a smile was playing round her lips and she dropped her left eye-lid and winked.

They had a marvellous afternoon, and when they got back Syd was in a really good mood so it was obvious that he had beaten the bookies for once. Polly and Arthur brought Lucy over to number twelve about half-past seven, and Mrs Thompson's daughter from the corner shop came at a quarter to eight to stay with the children while the grown-ups all trooped along to the Horse and Groom.

The pub had a piano and a pianist was always

, it was time to go back to
Devon. But there was one thing that Lizzie vowed
and declared to Charlie as he packed their cases away
in the boot of his car. 'I don't care what yer do or
say; it's not gonna be three years this time before I
come home again.'

Chapter Twenty-Two

THE WEATHER HAD stayed pretty good. There was not much warmth in the sunshine now, and the dark nights were cold, but for October it wasn't at all bad. At least there was no sign of rain.

They had had breakfast with Doris and Syd on the Monday morning and set off from Wilton Road just after ten o'clock. Charlie had made good time, stopping only once in Taunton for them to have some lunch and go to the toilet. He had pulled into their own garage just as the village church clock was striking four. By the time Lizzie had unpacked the cases, put the dirty washing in the sink to soak, cooked the dinner and seen Robert to bed she was whacked. Slouched down now in an armchair in front of the fire, which Charlie had lit in the lounge, she was half-asleep, her mind miles away, when suddenly she was brought up with a jerk as Charlie said, 'I think we'll keep Robert off from school for another week.'

'What the hell for?' she muttered as she struggled to sit up and gather her wits about her.

'Because I want this thing settled one way or the other,' he snapped back.

'Well, there's no need ter be so crabby; just say what's on yer mind an' we'll talk about it.'

Charlie had been in a funny mood from the moment they had arrived back and now Lizzie decided that her best bet would be to tread warily. She knew he had discussed the matter with Syd and she understood why he would like the sale of this guesthouse to go through. If the local agent was to be believed, there wouldn't be any problem finding a purchaser, but what was the point if they had nowhere to go?

Yet to stay on here now would be ridiculous. Without the extra rooms at the pub, there wasn't enough income to give them a good living, unless they had another string to their bow. Lizzie knew exactly what she would like to do – sell up and go back to London. But at this point it wouldn't be fair, she told herself, even to suggest it to Charlie. What would he do for a job? He'd been really good all the time they'd been staying with Syd and Doris. Lizzie chided herself; Charlie deserved a chance to see if he could find an hotel that would be for sale at a price that they could afford.

'I'd like to take a look at Bournemouth,' Charlie's statement broke into her thoughts again. 'What d'yer think? We could take Robert, set out early in the morning, stay a few days in an hotel an' check out the estate agents. By all accounts, Bournemouth has become one of the most popular pleasure resorts in the country.'

Lizzie just stopped herself in time from making an ugly grimace; Bournemouth! Still, if that's what he wanted to do she'd do well to go along with him.

'All right,' she agreed in a happy tone of voice which was far from what she was really feeling. 'Why not? A few days being waited on in someone else's hotel will be a nice change.'

They were in Bournemouth by lunchtime and Charlie booked them into the Royal Exeter Hotel. The large bedroom they were assigned had one double bed and one single bed and looked right out over the sea. By the time Lizzie had freshened up she was feeling much more relaxed, determined to enjoy this unexpected holiday. After they had had lunch, Charlie declared that he was going to visit some of the local estate agents and if possible obtain details of any hotels that might be for sale in the vicinity. Lizzie breathed a sigh of relief when, instead of asking her to accompany him, Charlie suggested that she took Robert on the pier.

Later that night, when Robert was in bed and fast asleep, Charlie persuaded Lizzie to come downstairs into the lounge-bar and have a drink. Settled comfortably at a table near the window, their drinks in front of them, Charlie began to read through the particulars of properties that he had managed to collect.

'Interested in buying an hotel, are you?' A tall, middle-aged man in a well-cut suit held out his hand. 'Martin Fenwick,' he said and, with a grin, added, 'joint owner of this place with the bank.'

Charlie laughed as he got to his feet and shook the fellow's hand. 'Charlie Wilson, and this is my wife. She won't mind you calling her Lizzie, every-one does.'

Martin Fenwick shook hands with Lizzie. 'How do you like Bournemouth? Bit quiet here at this time of the year.' Without giving Lizzie time to reply he went on, 'You're staying a few days, aren't you? You must meet my wife and my two sons. Stephen is just four, the other one, John, has turned six.'

He was a likeable man, Lizzie decided as she went upstairs, leaving Charlie to have one for the road. He hadn't put on any airs and graces, even though he owned this large hotel. Quite the opposite, he had made her feel very welcome and he might turn out to be very useful to Charlie. At that thought Lizzie smiled to herself; she certainly didn't want Charlie getting himself involved in any more com-plicated deals. The buying of Sea View Guesthouse had proved to be enough of a headache for one life-time.

Sunday was a lovely autumn day, not in the least bit cold. There was bright sunshine and the few clouds that there were in the sky were the white fluffy kind like cotton wool.

Lizzie felt a great deal more relaxed as they walked along the seafront in the direction of the hotel they were about to view.

It was Mr Fenwick who, having made several phone calls on their behalf, had finally arranged this appointment.

'Seems a bit odd viewing on a Sunday,' Lizzie had ventured.

'Not at all, quietest day of the week,' he had assured her, 'and, by the way, no need to drag your son along with you. Leave him with us; he'll be happy enough with my two.'

When Robert had been shown the electric train set, he had made no fuss about being left.

Charlie wore a new overcoat, which wasn't really necessary on a day like this, but it made him appear even more broad in the shoulder. His beige cavalry twill trousers were sharply creased and his feet were shod in the very finest brown brogue shoes, for if there was one thing Charlie was particular about it was footwear. Only leather would do, nothing imitation.

Lizzie looked up into his face as they came to a halt outside the hotel. You wouldn't think he had just finished a season; his face glowed with health and his hair was still thick and glossy.

Lizzie herself had lost over a stone in weight since last Easter, and although the brown skirt she wore fitted well, the jacket hung a little loosely.

As if reading her thoughts Charlie said, 'Come on, my Skinny Lizzie, let's go in.' Lizzie was taken aback. No one had called her that for years!

The outside of the building hadn't impressed either of them. Dingy, they thought. The brick-work was dirty and colourless. The entrance hall wasn't much better, gloomy and shabby with arm-chairs that were frayed and faded. No one came, in

spite of the fact that they had rung the bell twice.
Sounds of music and laughter were coming from
below, and they trod the wide staircase that led
downwards. A game of bingo was being played in
a colossal basement lounge that was crowded with
elderly folk.

It was mainly the ribald remarks of the gentleman
seated on the raised platform calling the numbers
that accounted for the amusement of the players.
'Bit near the knuckle!' Charlie said beneath his
breath as the caller's jokes became more and more
indelicate.

They wandered off to one side of the hall and
found themselves in what could only be described
as a casino. Every conceivable type of gambling was
there, plus machines which dispensed hot and cold
drinks, bars of chocolate, packets of sweets and nuts,
even packets of aspirin.

Lizzie thought of the endless hours that she and
Charlie had spent in the evenings making pots of tea
or coffee and boiling milk for Ovaltine or Horlicks.

They retraced their steps and each of them was
embarrassed as a pot-bellied man with a high-col-
oured complexion stared angrily at them.

'Are you Mr Petrock?' Charlie asked in a composed voice.

'Yes, you must be Mr and Mrs Wilson; didn't
expect you this early.' He ignored Charlie's outstretched hand, and merely said, 'I'm the warden.'

'Warden?' Lizzie spoke without thinking.

'Yes,' he replied, giving no further information.

'We'll start with the bedrooms.' He stalked off, leaving Charlie and Lizzie to follow.

'I don't like him,' Lizzie thought, 'miserable old beggar.'

The corridors were forbidding, very narrow, with no windows and badly lit. The decor and colour scheme consisted mainly of fawn paint. At first, Lizzie couldn't grasp the layout at all, as Mr Petrock opened door after door without saying a word.

Suddenly Charlie clutched at Lizzie's arm and held her back for a moment. His voice a harsh whisper, he said, 'I've just fell in. I've got it now. Apart from the main building, this place is a series of terraced houses with connecting doorways.'

There wasn't time for Lizzie to answer. Mr Petrock flung wide yet another door and stood back, though why he is bothering himself, I don't know, Lizzie thought, every room is exactly the same.

Each contained the maximum number of beds it was possible to squeeze in, and the vacant floor space was hardly enough to enable the occupants to walk around the beds. No chairs, no wardrobes, just a hanging space on the back of the door, covered by a dingy curtain.

The rooms were barren even of necessities, let alone any items of comfort. Door handles were broken, dripping taps over wash-basins needed new washers, carpets were frayed, rucked up in some places, light bulbs were burnt out, leaving sections of the corridors in complete darkness.

'Do you have a maintenance man on the staff?'
Charlie asked.

'This is not The Ritz,' was Mr Petrock's ill-tempered reply.

Lizzie was about to say that they had seen enough
when she saw that the room she had just entered
was occupied. 'I'm so sorry,' she murmured, as she
backed away towards the door. She suddenly felt
frightened, although she could not have said what
of. All she knew was that something was very
wrong.

She turned, seeking Charlie, who, seeing the fear
showing in her eyes, hastily pushed Mr Petrock to
one side. Lizzie had to stifle the scream that rose up
in her throat as her glance fell upon a seagull. The
huge, fat, grey and white bird was perched on the
window sill, not outside but *inside* the room.

As she watched, it took off in flight around the
room, its great wings beating and thrashing in frustration. It appeared incredibly menacing at such
close quarters, as it swooped low, squawking and
shrieking, heading straight for Lizzie.

She screamed and covered her face with her arms,
but Charlie shoved her aside. With long strides he
was across the room to where an elderly man lay
wedged between two beds. Kneeling, Charlie raised
the man's head by placing his arm under his neck.
Softly he murmured over and over again, 'It's all
right, old chap, it's all right; you're safe now.' But
the man was in such a state of agitation, rocking

himself frantically from side to side, that he finally collapsed heavily against Charlie.

Quickly enough, Mr Petrock caught the gull and put it out through the window. 'Rough high-tide last night. Must have got in through the window and couldn't find its way out,' he complained – though there was a slight hint of an apology in the tone of his voice.

'Get some brandy, man, don't just stand there,' Charlie was fast losing his temper. Mr Petrock didn't bother to reply, he just went.

Judging from the shocking state of the room, the gull had been imprisoned for some length of time. Its droppings had soiled everything – the counterpanes on the bed and the carpet were liberally spattered, even the curtains were covered.

Charlie wouldn't leave until the man was obviously a lot calmer, and as Lizzie waited in the dingy hallway she asked herself what would have happened if they hadn't gone into that particular room.

The estate agent's list had detailed that this hotel was not an orthodox hotel in the accepted sense, rather a balance between a holiday home and a rest home for elderly people. The owners had contracts with various city councils and civic homes to take old-age pensioners, some on a long-term plan, others for shorter periods of approximately a month.

What had attracted Charlie was the hint that all-the-year-round trade was possible, rather than just a seasonal period.

That was all very well, but elderly people needed constant surveillance. If you took on the responsibility, you should damn well carry it through, Lizzie thought angrily. Like Charlie, she had been appalled at the conditions in which these old folk were roaming about. The whole place was fraught with danger.

'I've made you some tea,' Mr Petrock called from the top of the stairs.

'Have you now,' Lizzie said in a mocking voice, just as Charlie emerged from the bedroom.

'Leave it out, Lizzie,' he ordered. 'Christ, I can do with a cup of tea, the stronger the better, then we'll get out of here.'

A few minutes later they were seated in a private sitting-room. No penny pinching here. There were deep armchairs with plump cushions, thick pile carpet on the floor and full-length velvet curtains hung at the windows. They drank their tea in silence, then, reading each other's thoughts, Charlie and Lizzie stood up.

'Just one question, Mr Petrock,' Charlie said, 'where are the owners of this hotel, is it their day off?'

Mr Petrock was in a cold sweat, the incident upstairs had frightened him. The old man might have died. His hands dropped limply to his sides and he moistened his thick lips before he answered, 'No. They're abroad on holiday.'

'So, you're in sole charge?'

'In a manner of speaking.'

'Oh no, there's no two ways about it. Either you are in charge or someone else is,' Charlie's manner was furious by now. 'For God's sake, man, aren't you at all worried about what happened?'

Mr Petrock looked about him vaguely, then, turning to Lizzie, he murmured, 'I'll show you out through the kitchen, save you going upstairs again.'

The kitchen was the last straw! Both Lizzie and Charlie were horrified. Lizzie couldn't move, she just stood and gawped. Everything was so disorganized, and the smell was dreadful!

The flagstone floor was thick with grease. A complete wall of shelves held vast numbers of cups, saucers, plates and dishes, and even a quick glance showed that the china was far from clean.

Two beautiful, expensive commercial cookers made Lizzie feel sick just to look at them. They were not just messy or mucky, they were plain filthy – absolutely soiled with grease. Unwashed saucepans cluttered the top of each stove.

Neither of them could wait to get out into the fresh air.

Having related the whole experience to Mr Fenwick they sat together quietly, deep in thought until Martin Fenwick made a profound observation. 'You know, Mr Wilson, someone will come along and buy that hotel. They'll have a lucrative business for a few years, then they'll sell it and end up just as rich as the present owners no doubt are.'

Under his breath, Charlie muttered, 'Well, it

won't be us.' Aloud he said, 'I don't understand how
they get away with it. Aren't there regular checks on
establishments that take elderly folk on a permanent
basis? Surely, the local authorities should be
involved.'

'I shall certainly raise the matter at the next meeting of the local hoteliers' association,' Mr Fenwick
said and Charlie knew that his concern was genuine.

Chapter Twenty-Three

CHARLIE HAD TAKEN Robert to school and Lizzie was not yet dressed when the telephone rang.

'Phillips and Ashfield here, Mrs Wilson,' a smooth voice stated as soon as Lizzie picked up the receiver. 'We have a property on our books which may interest you, would you like me to mail you the details?'

'Well, we shall be coming down to the village later on. We'll call in and pick them up.'

'Thank you, Mrs Wilson, goodbye for now.'

Lizzie and Charlie were in Mr Phillips' office by ten-thirty.

'My, you're keen,' John Phillips said as he shook hands with Charlie. 'I've never had the pleasure of meeting you before, Mrs Wilson, though I have downed the odd pint with your husband before now.' Actually, he was quite surprised – Mrs Wilson wasn't at all what he had expected: small-boned, slim, sleek fair hair, a woollen two-piece with shoes, gloves and handbag which all toned in extremely well.

She was no Devon dumpling.

'How does the Manor House Hotel at Milton grab you, Charlie?'

Lizzie watched closely as Charlie scanned the typed sheets of paper. First name terms, these two. Well, well.

This John Phillips was big, and handsome with it, and to be fair, he was the type who would be popular with men as well as women. He turned now and smiled broadly at Lizzie. Yes, he could be a useful friend, she thought approvingly.

That evening, Charlie looked through the motoring guidebooks.

'Yes, here it is,' he pointed out to Lizzie enthusiastically. 'Manor House Hotel, well established, popular with tourists and near a famous beauty spot.'

They were on their way before ten o'clock the next morning. The countryside, though not at its best, still looked fresh and good. The hills were green, the cattle in the fields looked well fed and contented, and the agricultural land was tilled ready for the winter frosts.

Even from the outskirts of the village, the hotel was visible. Perched on a hilltop site, it was very prominent. Clearly sign-posted, Charlie soon drew the car to a halt. Ahead lay a surprisingly lengthy driveway.

Lizzie held her breath for a long time before letting it out in a loud gasp. Formal gardens with low hedges lay each side, and groups of trees and flowering shrubs were still vivid with colour.

They sat in silence as Charlie drove up to the hotel.

Four wide marble steps led up to a huge oak door. 'What do you think of it?' Charlie asked.

'Beautiful,' Lizzie said, 'but we could never afford anything like this.'

The big door opened before they had got out of the car and a slim young woman in a flowered dress walked down the steps to meet them. Lizzie thought her to be about thirty-five. She had a country look about her, rosy cheeks and her cotton dress was stained with earth as if she had been working in the garden.

She came towards them eagerly. 'I'm Phyllis Martin, my parents are expecting you. I'm their youngest daughter. Come in, you're staying for lunch, aren't you?'

Lizzie was amazed at such a welcome.

Mr and Mrs Jeffries were waiting in the entrance hall. Both Charlie and Lizzie soon surmised that Jeffries was not the original surname of this nice couple.

Charlie found holding a conversation with Mr Jeffries heavy going. His birthplace had been Poland and, although he had lived in England for a good many years, his English was not that good. Approaching seventy, he was pleasantly fat, but he had a further handicap, a gammy leg. When seated, it stuck out straight in front of him and, even with the aid of a stick, he couldn't walk without difficulty.

Mrs Jeffries was a homely type of woman; an older version of her daughter, uncomplicated and easy to be with. She ushered them through into a very large kitchen, sympathizing about their long journey, exclaiming over the rawness of the day despite protests from Lizzie that it wasn't at all cold outside. Moving quickly, she drew chairs near to a roaring fire. 'Take your coats off, come along, make yourselves comfortable. Phyllis is just making the coffee. Do you know this area?'

Charlie and Lizzie smiled at each other, Mrs Jeffries didn't seem to expect any answers.

Phyllis came through from what looked like a smaller kitchen, pushing a loaded trolley. The cups and saucers were attractive, white patterned with bold blue stripes, almost matching the gingham curtains which hung at the kitchen windows. The aroma of the coffee was good as Phyllis poured and handed the cups around. Mrs Jeffries handed out matching plates, insisting that everyone must eat a scone, piping hot and served with thick yellow clotted cream and strawberry jam.

While they were eating, Mr Jeffries told them that he had another older daughter. 'Karie . . .' the old man actually stopped smiling as he spoke her name. He took a deep breath and continued, 'Karie, she is on holiday in Jersey with her husband,' and Lizzie felt sure that his expression indicated his relief.

'If you're all set, shall we start the inspection? Are you coming with us, David?'

'Yes, yes, my dear, I'll tag along behind you all.
Slowly it might be, but I'll make it.'

Mr Jeffries smiled apologetically at Lizzie and
Charlie, then nodded gently to his wife and daughter. 'Go ahead, go along,' he shooed them.

The main staircase swept up to a semi-circular
gallery which led to the bedrooms.

On this floor, the rooms were large, light and
airy, not at all like the usual hotel bedroom. Lizzie's
first thought was that they were typical of a country
manor house, then she laughed at herself. How
would she know? She'd never seen the inside of any
manor house. Each room had an enormous, high,
double bed, massive sized furniture and deep,
comfortable armchairs which were drawn invitingly
into the bow-shaped window recess so that any resident could view the grounds through the windows
while relaxing.

The hotel had twenty-five bedrooms and, as they
proceeded, Charlie and Lizzie exchanged glances.
They were able to read each other's thoughts.

To each of them, it was obvious that Mr and Mrs
Jeffries not only had a deep affection for each other,
but also treasured their hotel and were proud of
what they had achieved. Lizzie even felt a little
guilty; the whole place had such a warm atmosphere, much more like a home than an hotel. She
felt that she and Charlie were intruding and even
began to ask herself why this dear couple had
decided to sell up when, without a doubt, they loved
this place.

On the second floor, the rooms were not so spacious but were equally charming. A lot of thought had been given to the furnishing of the bedrooms, although Lizzie got the feeling that most of the furniture had been installed there since the place was built many years ago.

It was the little final touches which added to the attractiveness of this floor. The windows were much smaller, yet the curtains were exactly right; each set was made to be in keeping with the surroundings. Rich, heavy, fully lined fabrics had been hung at the windows of the rooms on the floor below, with bedspreads and chair coverings all co ordinated, but here the accessories were totally different in style and manner. Bright floral, cotton chintz had been the main choice. In parts, the carpets were old, even showing signs of being threadbare, but bright soft rugs had been scattered to compensate for this.

At the far end of this top landing were three rooms set apart up a further short flight of stairs, each so in keeping with the character of the house that Lizzie exclaimed, 'Oh, aren't they marvellous!'

'Not when it comes to working them, they're not,' was Phyllis's quick retort. 'They're very popular with the foreign tourists though.' Everyone laughed. Americans would term them 'quaint'. There was no running water here, only hefty marble-topped wash-stands on top of which stood ornate china jugs and bowls, each elaborately decorated with gilt.

At the base of the staircase, a panel of wood was

fixed to the wall from which hung two rows of brass bells, each suspended loosely by means of a hook-shaped spring. Above each bell, a plaque bore a number which presumably corresponded with a bedroom.

Lizzie's imagination ran riot. Supposing several rang at once, noisy, jangling, ear-splitting sounds – and how many staff would you need to keep running up and down the stairs in answer to their summons?

'It's all right, my dear,' Mr Jeffries chuckled, 'they don't work. The bell push-buttons are still in each bedroom, but they are all disconnected. I fear the days when such service was given are long gone.'

Lizzie and Phyllis exchanged conspiratorial glances.

'Thank God for that,' was their silent answer.

Charlie declared the dining-room to be his favourite.

All the tables were made of oak, and the high-backed chairs had upholstered seats. There was no carpet but the parquet flooring was so highly polished that one could have used it as a mirror.

'We cheat; we use an electric floor polisher,' Mrs Jeffries said proudly.

Next came the lounge. Lizzie unintentionally let out a shriek of amazement. Stepping further into the room, she felt that she had gone back in time – a high, moulded ceiling, an enormous white marble

fireplace, bright wood panelling on the walls and a
view of the sea in the distance from the windows.

Armchairs and settees were arranged into groups,
even a chaise-longue, all covered in uncut moquette
of a deep, rich red colour. The floor-length curtains
were velvet with a deep valance which was decorated with heavy silk tassels. Small side tables and
reading lamps had been placed at strategic points
around the room.

By now, Mr Jeffries was visibly tired and limping
badly.

'Do you mind if we ask to be excused? Phyllis
will finish showing you around; lunch will be ready
soon. David come, rest your leg; leave the youngsters to it.' Mrs Jefferies ushered her husband gently
out of the room.

'You'd better come and see my quarters,' Phyllis
frowned as she spoke.

'You've been marvellous, Phyllis,' Charlie patted
her shoulder, 'we don't want to bother you if you'd
rather not.'

'No, it's all right, really it is.'

Two minutes later, Lizzie understood the reason
for Phyllis's reluctance.

Coming out into a courtyard, Phyllis led them
down a ramp and opened a heavy door which was
set into the brickwork, revealing a flight of steps
leading downwards.

As they hesitated, two bonny little girls, aged
about seven and eight, came running up the steps.

'Mummy, you've been a long time, may we go

over to Grandma's now?' the taller of the two
pleaded.

'Just a minute. Say hallo to Mr and Mrs Wilson,
and then we are all going to have lunch with
Grandma.'

'Hallo,' they chorused, now happily hopping
back down the steps. Lizzie chuckled as she watched
them; they both looked so pretty, shining and spot-
less in identical blue dresses and hand-knitted white
cardigans. Even Charlie was struck by their open
smiling faces.

Phyllis's home was a basement apartment;
nothing would disguise that fact. Clean and
comfortable, but Lizzie concluded that not much
daylight ever penetrated down here.

Soon they were back up in the yard, the two little
girls, now running and skipping ahead of them.
'We've got plenty of garage space,' Phyllis said,
pointing to what could have been a stable block in
years past.

'Are these more sleeping quarters?' Charlie asked,
stopping and raising his eyes to what appeared to be
a recently built apartment over and above the whole
block.

'No, that's where my sister Karie and her husband
Ray live. It was built for them three years ago.' Then
she added, with abruptness, 'They don't have any
children.'

With a sigh, Phyllis led the way up the outside
staircase. 'I don't have a key, you'll have to peer
through the windows.'

It was very modern in appearance, with wide, clear windows, but this one-storey apartment was totally out of keeping with the main building. Noses pressed to the glass, hands cupped around their eyes, they could see that white was the predominant colour – the walls, the furniture, even the carpets were all white.

Lizzie thought it gave a clinical effect, you could tell at a glance no children lived in there. They almost tip-toed back down the iron stairway, acting as if they had been trespassing.

Charlie hung back and, taking hold of Lizzie's arm, he nodded towards Phyllis's back and murmured, 'A sight different to where she has to live.'

Lizzie was still curious and, as she entered the main door held open for her by Phyllis, she asked, 'Where do your mother and father sleep?'

'In one of the main bedrooms during the winter months, but they use a bed-settee in the preparation room when we're busy in the summer.'

At their age! Lizzie almost answered back, for there was something terribly unfair about this set-up.

Charlie quietly asked, 'Why do your parents want to sell this lovely place?'

Phyllis shuddered and, for a moment, Lizzie thought she was about to cry; instead, she changed direction, moving back towards the dining-room.

'Sit down, it's better if we talk in here; I don't want my dad to get upset.'

Slowly, almost reluctantly, she told them, 'When

my father reached the age of sixty-five, which was almost five years ago, in order to be eligible to draw his old-age pension he officially resigned from the business. Legally he made Mum, Karie and me a three-way partnership. We each, from then on, owned one-third of the hotel and all its assets. The trouble started from that very moment, and it was all Karie's fault.' Phyllis sat forward in her chair; her dark eyes were blazing.

'We came close to getting a divorce, my Ron and me. Sorry, Ron is my husband. He's a skilled engineer with a good job in Exeter. That's almost seventy miles and he does the journey every night and morning. Mind you, I freely admit, Ron does his fair share of moaning; he doesn't like living where we do, calls it an underground rat-hole.'

Who could blame him? Lizzie thought. An apt description.in her opinion.

Charlie smiled and shook his head. 'I doubt you're any different to any other family, everyone has their squabbles.'

'Um, well,' Phyllis sighed, 'he doesn't like me to be working when he gets home, says the girls are left too long on their own.'

'What about staff?' Charlie stuck his neck out and asked, 'Couldn't you take on more?'

'There's no bus service that comes up here. Besides, the year before last Karie sacked two girls on the spot – caught them putting tinned stuff into their bags on the way out. She should have turned a blind eye, but no, that's not Karie's way. The people down in the village are a tight-knit community, they only heard those girls' side of the story. Anyway, they have never trusted us. Foreigners we are to them in every sense of the word; you'd think we'd all just got off the boat from Poland only yesterday. My mother and father have been in this country for forty-two years.' Her last sentence was said with bitterness in her voice.

Pulling herself together, Phyllis stood up, 'We'd better go and find Mum and Dad.'

Mrs Jeffries had food ready in the lounge and, in answer to Lizzie's protests, she insisted, 'It is only a light lunch to hold you over until you get home.'

They were each given a tray on their laps in order to eat the crisp cheese salad and hot rolls with butter. Rosie and Linda, Phyllis's two little girls, threw themselves down on to the floor and their grandma lovingly placed a tray in front of each of them. It seemed to Lizzie like a cosy family party.

Later, Phyllis left the room and returned with a glass of milk for each of her daughters and a cup of tea for everyone else.

Soon, Charlie stood up. 'We mustn't intrude any longer,' he said, but Mr Jeffries waved him back into his seat and leaned forward himself.

He was agitated, a fact that did not improve his speech. Mrs Jeffries did her best to calm him down, while Phyllis asked, 'Father wants to know, are you interested in buying our hotel?'

'Yes, we are,' Charlie said without any hesitation. 'Naturally, there's a lot to sort out. We have to sell

our own place and we'll need a loan from the bank.
Depends a lot on the bank, really.'

Mr Jeffries, calmer now, spoke slowly. 'If
additional finance is a problem, I myself would be
prepared to give a second mortgage.'

'Well!' the one word burst from Charlie's mouth.
'I don't know what to say,' he stammered, 'only,
thank you.'

As Charlie drove away, Lizzie felt that their day had
been spent in a completely different world. She sat
day-dreaming, picturing herself cooking in that
pleasant kitchen and reading in the long winter evenings, snug and warm in that wonderful lounge.

Turning his eyes away from the road for a
moment, Charlie looked hard at Lizzie and considered his words carefully. 'Don't build your hopes
too high,' he said, 'there's something wrong with
the set-up there.'

'Oh Charlie, don't put the dampers on it. It was
a lovely day, wasn't it?'

'Yes, it was,' he readily agreed, 'and nicer people
you couldn't wish to meet. I'm just saying . . .'

What he was just saying Lizzie would never
know, and she had the good sense not to ask, yet
for one awful moment she had doubts. She shook
her head hard; she wasn't going to let anything interfere with her dream of living at the Manor House
Hotel.

That same evening, Charlie was on the phone to
John Phillips for quite a long time. 'He feels sure

he's got a cash buyer for this place,' Charlie said, smiling as he sat down, and that was all that was said on the matter that evening.

The following morning, Phyllis Martin rang. 'Would it be asking too much for you to come back again tomorrow?' her voice sounded strained.

'We'd love to,' Lizzie assured her, then her inquisitiveness got the better of her. 'What's happened, are your parents all right?'

Phyllis ignored the latter part of the question. 'Karie's home,' she said, and Lizzie heard her make a cynical sound. 'Father said it's best if we all meet. Mother said lunch would be ready at one o'clock, so we'll see you then, Mrs Wilson,' and the phone line went dead.

'Bit quick, isn't it?' was Charlie's only comment.

He was ready first next morning, wearing a suit, collar and tie, looking every inch a businessman. He scowled as he looked at his watch. Lizzie came through the door, her thin silk dress rustled as she walked.

'Do you think I shall be warm enough in this dress?' she asked and she smiled at him with eyes filled with excitement.

'How the hell should I know? You're taking a big coat, aren't you?'

'Yes,' she said, 'I'm ready.'

'About time, too,' he retorted, still scowling a little.

Lizzie came near and kissed him on the cheek. 'Something worrying you?' she asked.

'I don't know,' he moved quickly towards the door. 'I'll feel a lot better when I find out why the Jeffries have invited us back so soon. At least I hope I shall.'

'Why? Do you think they've changed their minds?'

'Just let's stop supposing things and get going, shall we?' Charlie said abruptly as he opened the door of the car.

When they arrived, it was Phyllis who came down the steps to greet them.

'Come inside first. Mother said we'll have a drink together.' Seeing their puzzled expressions, she quickly explained, 'We're having lunch at Karie's.'

The sherry was good, and the Jeffries seemed exceedingly pleased to see them both again. Phyllis's husband Ron was there, an ordinary, everyday type of fellow, rugged in appearance as if he spent a great deal of his time out of doors. Charlie and Ron Martin hit it off from the moment they shook hands.

Lizzie wasn't prepared for meeting Karie. She gaped almost open-mouthed until Charlie nudged her.

Inches taller than either her sister or her mother, Karie had a fantastic figure. The cream silk dress she was wearing didn't just fit well, it looked as if it had been moulded around her. Most lovely of all was her thick, shiny, auburn hair. Most probably the colour comes out of a bottle, Lizzie thought enviously. Everything about Karie was immaculate, her sheer stockings, elegant court shoes, even her long red fingernails. She was most certainly different to any other member of this family and Lizzie felt sure that this was no accident. One could tell that Karie strove hard to be different. Her husband introduced himself first to Charlie and then to Lizzie.

'Ray Daniels, pleased to meet you,' he spoke quietly.

He was a tall young man in silver-grey trousers and a well-cut black velvet jacket. His eyes were brilliantly blue and shiny, and his smile was warm and friendly. In fact, his whole air was open and boyish, even if his dress was a bit showy.

The lunch was excellent, down to the last detail, but what surprised both Lizzie and Charlie the most was that a dark-haired and dark-skinned young lady in uniform waited on them as they all sat around a glass-topped dining-table.

The mood while they were eating was very different to that of their previous meeting. There were long silences, especially between courses.

Finally, when the last dishes had been removed by the maid, Karie said brightly, 'Shall we have our coffee in the lounge?'

Mrs Jeffries's eyes never left her husband's face as they sat drinking their cups of coffee. The atmosphere felt decidedly strange and Lizzie was beginning to feel uncomfortable. As she repeatedly said to Charlie afterwards, 'I'll never know in God's name what sparked that lot off.'

Until that moment the whole family had been tolerant of each other, then suddenly it was as if a bubble had been burst. Everyone began to talk at once and in seconds the place was in an uproar.

Karie dominated the scene. Staring directly at Charlie, she left him in no doubt as to the frame of mind she was in. 'You are here under false pretences. I don't know why my father contacted an estate agent.'

'Now, dear,' Mrs Jeffries said, seeing her daughter's temper getting out of hand, 'there's no need to be rude to our guests.'

'Well, it can't go on. I won't stand for it. All he thinks about is selling the hotel. An hotel in which he has no legal part.'

'Oh, how can you be so cruel,' Mrs Jeffries uttered a groan while Mr Jeffries took out his handkerchief and wiped the sweat from his face and hands.

Lizzie had never felt so uncomfortable in all her life.

Charlie looked hot under the collar, and, but for the fact that he had just eaten a meal at Karie's table plus the kindness of the old couple, he would have stormed out there and then.

The argument continued in earnest now.

Ron Martin taunted Ray Daniels with the fact that he had no job. 'You live off your wife you do,' he spat out, his face only inches away from his brother-in-law's.

Karie turned on Phyllis. 'You only want money. Sell, sell, sell, is all I hear from you, just so that you can get your hands on a third of the money.'

'Christ! You're the right one to talk about money. You spend it quicker than we can make it. Yes, and I do mean *we*. Mum and Dad and me, we're the general dogs-bodies around her. It's us that does every job imaginable while you swan around playing the lady.'

Mrs Jeffries, her complexion quite flushed by then, placed herself between her two daughters.

And only just in time, thought Lizzie, she'd seen women row, even fight, in London, and this little do was fast getting out of hand.

'Do as your father wants,' Mrs Jeffries pleaded. 'If we sell this place, you can each buy a nice house, and your father and I can have a nice little bungalow; why not be reasonable?'

'It's nothing to do with our father; how many more times do I have to tell you?' Karie shouted.

Mr Jeffries, struggling to stand on his feet, implored his eldest daughter, 'All I ask is that you sign the contract.'

'No. I've told you and I mean it, no.' With a defiant look in Charlie's direction, Karie turned her back and walked out of the room.

Lizzie found that her thoughts were all mixed up. No way did she condone Karie's attitude towards her parents nor yet tolerate the fact that she was ashamed of them, for it was obvious that she was. In spite of all that, Lizzie found a part of herself admiring Karie. Who could blame her for being so stubborn? The business here provided her with a lifestyle she enjoyed, she was well set-up in a home of her own choosing, and she wasn't about to give it all up without a struggle.

She was utterly selfish, of course she was, but Lizzie couldn't help wondering how she might have reacted, given the same set of circumstances. Twice she asked herself the same question and still she honestly didn't know the answer.

To be fair, Ray Daniels did try to ease the situation. He went into the kitchen and made fresh coffee, offering brandy with it as he handed it round. The silence in the room hung heavy and both Lizzie and Charlie were relieved when at last they could say their goodbyes and make their escape.

It was a relief to be out in the fresh air.

Mr Jeffries had been visibly upset and had tried to apologize to Charlie. The women had kissed each other goodbye and all three of them had been close to tears. The journey home promised to be a solemn one indeed. For they now realized that owning the Manor House Hotel had been nothing more than a pipe-dream.

Chapter Twenty-Four

IT WAS GETTING towards the end of October now, and neither Lizzie nor Charlie had much enthusiasm left in them to go searching for another property. And yet the prospect of only having twelve bedrooms to let for the next season was not very encouraging.

John Phillips had twice shown the same couple around the guesthouse, a Mr and Mrs Sadler from Birmingham. They had both expressed an interest in the property. Lizzie had liked them well enough and on each occasion she had cut sandwiches and made coffee for them, but when it came to answering Mrs Sadler's questions as to the running of the guesthouse, Lizzie couldn't be bothered, and even Charlie refused to discuss business details with Mr Sadler.

'What's the point?' Lizzie overheard Charlie saying to John Phillips. 'We can't sell this place until we find an hotel for ourselves, and if we don't do that before Christmas, we might as well forget it.'

That's true, Lizzie agreed with Charlie. Once Christmas was over, there was never much time to spare. The mail had to be the number one priority. Every morning, letters had to be answered and replies back in the post by noon whenever possible.

After all, one could get the place looking like Buckingham Palace, but without any subsequent bookings, you'd be wasting your time.

Lizzie felt sorry for the Sadlers, they wanted an answer; their future was in the balance just as much as Charlie's and hers.

Two weeks slipped by during which nothing of importance took place and Lizzie was quite glad when Friday came round again and they could have their day out in Barnstaple. Having finished the weekly shopping, Charlie asked, 'Where would you like to have lunch?'

'Anywhere that suits you, I'm easy,' Lizzie replied.

'Right, let's make it the Imperial.'

They had almost finished eating when Mr and Mrs Farrant stopped by their table. Mr Farrant was a local solicitor with his own firm in a nearby village. On two occasions, Charlie had taken Lizzie to his office, once when needing advice, and a second time when Mr Farrant had taken care of the legalities when Lizzie's mother had died. Lizzie had also formed a friendship with Margaret Farrant while doing voluntary work for the WVS.

'When are you moving?' Mr Farrant asked.

Charlie's face must have had a blank look, because Mr Farrant immediately said, 'Didn't John Phillips put you in touch with the Jeffries out at Milton, the Manor House? I understood you were going ahead with that.'

Charlie laughed, 'I only wish we were. It all fell
through.'

'Oh, I'm sorry to hear that. Well, finish your meal
and come through to the bar, I may have some
interesting news for you.'

Fifteen minutes later the two couples were settled
with their drinks, on a window-seat in the lounge.
After the usual small-talk, Mr Farrant said, 'Well,
now to business.'

Taking a card from his wallet, he wrote a few
words on the back of it, and then, passing it to Charlie, he spoke quietly.

'Take that to Freddie Clarke and he will arrange
for you to view an hotel. It's a bit hush-hush, not
yet officially on the market, but ideal for you two, I
should think. Anyway, Freddie will fill you in on
the details.'

Today, Charlie thought, it is not *what* you know
but *who* you know that makes the difference.

Freddie Clarke was a well-known local character.
His main occupation was as estate agent but by no
means was it his only method of earning a living.
He had earned the reputation of being a Mr Fix-It.

Not much was said over the telephone when
Charlie rang him, except that he would be in to see
them that same evening.

It was a little after seven o'clock when he arrived
and the first thing Charlie did was offer him a drink,
which he readily accepted. When they were all
settled comfortably in the lounge, the two men with
whisky and soda, Lizzie with whisky and dry

ginger, Freddie opened his case and took out some papers and, nodding grimly, he said, 'These are the only details I have got. This hotel will be going up for sale but with certain drawbacks.'

'Oh, no, here we go again,' Lizzie said beneath her breath.

'Why all the mystery?' Charlie questioned.

'Because the owners don't want to sell,' said the up-to-now serious Freddie Clarke, then he leant forward, picked up his glass and drained it quickly.

'Mind if I smoke my pipe?' he asked, and Lizzie was surprised at just how old this man looked as she waited while he filled the bowl of his briar with tobacco and Charlie refilled his glass. Without his trilby hat, which he always wore when he was out, she could see that he was almost bald and he appeared tired and sluggish. He once more turned his attention to the papers which lay in front of him.

'It's not an unfamiliar story,' Freddie began, 'especially in this trade. Four proprietors, two couples, own one hotel, living in each others' pockets seven days a week, and you end up with friction. Plus the fact this lot has no business sense. Spent more than they earned. It has reached the stage where they have no option. The bank is about to foreclose.'

'Oh, no!' Lizzie muttered to herself. 'Does every family fall out if they work together in an hotel?'

'We can't do anything over the weekend, I'll make an appointment for you for Monday, shall I?'

Charlie agreed and they all got to their feet and shook hands.

'Remember now, just look over the property, don't discuss any business while you're there. It's a Mr and Mrs Fletcher and a Mr and Mrs Kirkland you'll be seeing. Good-night, Mrs Wilson, sorry to hurry off, but I've had a helluva day. Good luck.' He placed his hat on his head, shrugged himself into his raincoat and went with Charlie to the front door.

On Monday morning, if the weather was anything to go by, it was not a good omen.

'As filthy a morning as I ever remember,' Charlie said as he came in from having taken Robert to school; he shook his raincoat before hanging it up and Bob-Bob gave a low growl.

'Who's upset you, old boy?' He patted Bob-Bob on the head.

'You just shook all the rain off your coat on to him,' Lizzie said.

'Has he been out yet?'

'No, not yet,' Lizzie answered.

'Well, it's about time he did. Come on, Bob-Bob.'

Lizzie watched as Charlie opened the back door. The rain was simply lashing down and the high winds blew at gale force.

Bob-Bob took one look, turned tail and went back to lie on his bed in the corner. Charlie stood, and hesitated.

'Leave him be,' Lizzie laughed, 'he'll go out when he's good and ready.'

'Yeah, he's got more sense than we give him credit for,' and Charlie laughed with her as Bob-Bob barked at them both.

They started off on their journey, but with less enthusiasm than before.

Highland Heights was the name of the hotel, situated close to a small harbour just the other side of Ilfracombe, which meant that they hadn't too far to travel.

After about forty minutes they found the place and they looked at each other as they took stock of their bearings. Winding down the window, Charlie exclaimed, 'Look, it's only built about nine foot from the sea!'

The sound of the sea was deafening as great waves rolled in to crash on to the rocks far below.

'Cor blimey,' Lizzie cried, reverting back to her cockney dialect. 'Ain't it rugged here? Look at those cliffs, they look like masses of great boulders.'

Straining her neck, she saw that the building was at least five storeys high. 'The texture and colour of the outside makes it look as if it's built of granite,' Charlie observed. 'Really intimidating on a day like this!'

They both ran from the car to the side entrance, where a man signalled for them to come in.

'Do take those wet coats off,' said a woman standing inside.

They introduced themselves, which wasn't necessary as obviously they had been expected. In turn,
the gentleman said, 'We are Mr and Mrs Kirkland.
Come through to the kitchen, I have the kettle
boiling.'

By now, Lizzie was feeling cold and Charlie
reached for her hand as he said, 'a hot cuppa
wouldn't come amiss, will it, love.'

Their footsteps echoed with a hollow ring as they
crossed a large tiled hall and went into what seemed
to be a small kitchen. Mr Kirkland made the tea and
set the pot down on to a tray that was already laid
out with cups and saucers. Then he excused himself,
saying, 'I'll be back shortly.'

His wife had disappeared already. Gratefully, they
drank their tea and Lizzie poured a second cup for
each of them. Still, no one came. Restlessly, they
began to wander.

There were three kitchens, each one leading
through from the other. It was amazing the amount
of equipment there was, mainly of stainless steel,
each item scrupulously clean. Catering-sized saucepans and steamers, machines for peeling potatoes, a
washing-up machine, three trade-sized washing
machines; 'Perhaps they don't send the linen out to a
laundry,' Lizzie whispered. There were two double-
bowled sinks, each with double drainers, an electric
slicing machine which Charlie switched on and, as
it burred into life, quickly switched off again.

There were two commercial cookers, each with
six burners and a vast oven, beside which stood a

massive cast-iron grill. 'This lot must have cost a fortune,' Charlie said in a hushed tone. 'It's certainly a very professional working area. You could cook for an army with this lot.'

Mr Kirkland reappeared. 'If you're ready, I'll take you up to meet Mr and Mrs Fletcher.'

Going up a narrow flight of carpeted stairs, they found themselves in the main entrance hall, one wall of which was taken up by the reception desk and glass-fronted office. They both now realized that the side door through which they had first entered led only to the kitchens. The hotel was built on steeply sloping ground so that the kitchens, though on basement level at the front of the building, had large windows at the back overlooking the sea.

They were ushered into a small, but comfortably furnished sitting-room where Mrs Kirkland was sitting in an armchair close to a bright log fire. Again Mr Kirkland said, 'I'll be back shortly,' as he closed the door behind Lizzie and Charlie.

Without being asked, they both sat down and in silence Lizzie looked at Mrs Kirkland. She seemed a fragile, timid lady and Lizzie noticed that her thin, fair hair was streaked with white which added to her general appearance of delicacy. Lizzie thought that the poor woman must have been very ill. By comparison, her husband had appeared an active, vigorous man, bursting with good health.

A log moved in the fire, sending sparks up the chimney and at the same moment the door opened;

Mr Kirkland was back and with him were Mr and Mrs Fletcher.

'How d'you do?' said the short man with bloated features. He spoke gruffly as he took Charlie's out-stretched hand and merely nodded in Lizzie's direction.

Funny how opposites attract, Lizzie thought, as she said good morning to Mrs Fletcher. She was a striking-looking woman; her shiny brown hair was brushed into a French pleat at the back, leaving a few curls on the top of her head, but it was the deep suntan, set off by the white jumper she was wearing, that gave the greatest effect.

After the polite greetings were over, Mr Kirkland said, 'I'll show you around.'

The back of the hotel faced the sea. The layout had been so well designed that in the majority of the bedrooms, which were spaced out on three floors, one could lie in bed and watch the sea.

There were twenty-seven bedrooms, not lavishly furnished but adequate. All had wash-basins and hot and cold running water. Landings were spacious. On each floor there were two bathrooms and three separate toilets.

The staircase was grand. 'A work of art,' Charlie remarked as he walked down the wide treads and Lizzie ran her hand over the dark grained wood of the banister rail, noticing how elegantly it curved at each floor.

The public lounge was on the first floor. A plaque over the doorway stated, 'To stay here is to be on board a luxury liner'. Hardly inside the room and Charlie and Lizzie knew that was no exaggeration. An uninterrupted view of the Bristol Channel stretched before them. The size of the room threw Lizzie off balance for a moment.

There were five sets of windows!

Curtain material alone must have cost a fortune, she thought. The windows were gigantic, reaching from the floor almost to the exceptionally high ceiling.

The many deep armchairs all matched, having floral, chintz loose covers, but the dominating feature had to be that view of the sea directly outside.

Lizzie and Charlie held hands as they looked out of one of the bay windows and they were speechless. The huge panes were being lashed by the rain, and the turbulent sea beyond rolled in and crashed on to the huge jagged rocks, sending mighty plumes of foaming spray high into the air.

Reluctantly, Charlie and Lizzie turned away. Reaching the ground floor once more, Lizzie this time noticed port-holes set into the walls of the entrance hall and a board above the reception desk which read, 'The Captain's Cabin'.

On into the dining-room, almost an exact replica in size and shape of the lounge. Here, the nautical look had been maintained. A large anchor entwined with ropes was fixed to an end wall with more port-holes in evidence around the room. Here also, the grey angry sea, with huge waves topped with what

looked like galloping white horses, swept over the
rocks immediately beyond the windows.

Mr Kirkland had hardly spoken a word while they
had been doing the rounds. He had merely opened
doors and stood back.

Returning to the sitting-room, Mr and Mrs Kirkland said a cordial goodbye to Lizzie and Charlie
and left them alone with the Fletchers. There was a
curious hesitation to all of Mr Fletcher's movements. Eventually he asked, 'Would you like to look
over this lot?' and he pointed to a table which was
placed beneath the window.

'Incredible!' Charlie said without thinking. The
whole table was covered with stationery: menu
cards, account forms, booking forms, memo pads,
wage slips, writing paper that looked almost regal
it was so heavily embossed. There were small envelopes and large envelopes all of which were overprin-
ted on the outside in royal blue with the name and
location of the hotel. Not just a few of each, but
boxes and boxes of them.

Again, Charlie spoke aloud, 'God! The printing
bill for this lot must have been colossal.'

Behind them Mrs Fletcher coughed and her husband said indignantly, 'The brochures are in those
boxes on the floor by your feet.'

The brochures were coloured. Views of the
interior and exterior of the hotel were on every page.
The write-up had been done by experts. The coloured plates and blocks were also there and this
time, as he examined them, Charlie kept his

thoughts to himself, for this also must have been a very expensive operation.

Mr Fletcher was pouring himself a stiff drink as his wife led them back downstairs and struggled against the wind to open the side door for them.

'Well, that was over quick enough,' Charlie said as they reached the safety of the car.

Lizzie gave him a sudden quick smile, 'We do get around, don't we? At least we're seeing how the other half live.'

Then, to her astonishment and delight, Charlie leaned across his seat, put his arms around her and very tenderly kissed her. He held her close for a long moment and when he did release her, he said with all seriousness, 'We're going to have that hotel, Lizzie.'

Chapter Twenty-Five

DURING THE DAYS that followed, Charlie walked about the house singing to himself and occasionally grinned from ear to ear.

He had numerous telephone conversations with Freddie Clarke and twice Lizzie got the impression that he was speaking to Mr Farrant. Lizzie had attempted to ask questions, but all she got from Charlie was an instruction to be patient.

Then, one Friday morning, as Lizzie took care with her make-up and hair while deciding what to wear (for she was never quite sure where Charlie would end up taking her for lunch) she heard the telephone ring yet again.

A few minutes later and Charlie almost bounded into their bedroom wearing an open-necked, short-sleeved shirt and still looking very tanned.

'Mr Farrant is sorry for the short notice, but he wants us to be at his office two-thirty this afternoon.'

'What for?' Lizzie asked, squinting into the mirror as she softly pencilled-in her eyebrows.

'How the hell do I know? I'm going to get changed.'

'You don't have to be so irritable,' she muttered and then thought to herself, of course he knows

what it's all about, it has to be concerning Highland
Heights.

Beyond that she would not let herself think, but
if they got a bank loan . . . If – Oh stop it, she told
herself angrily, don't build your hopes up again.

Mr Farrant's office was one of several sited above
the bank, all were occupied by professional men.

A clerk looked up from his work. 'Mr and Mrs
Wilson?' he enquired, then led them through from
the outer office and opened a door on which gold
lettering spelt out 'Farrant, Day and Dalston'.

Mr Farrant himself welcomed them, giving Lizzie
a charming smile which immediately put her at her
ease.

Two other men were sitting comfortably in chairs
placed behind the huge desk. 'Mr Harding you
already know,' Mr Farrant said, as indeed they both
did, for he had acted as their accountant for the past
two years, preparing Sea View's books for the
Inland Revenue, 'and this is Mr Sims. He is here to
take notes. We are only waiting now for Mr Parker.'

Only recently, Graham Blackhurst had been promoted, moved on to a much larger branch of the
bank, and this had made Lizzie sad. He had been a
good friend to both her and Charlie, always available for a chat, ever ready with good, sound advice.
She wondered what this new man, Mr Parker,
would be like.

She didn't have long to wonder.

A sharp tap at the door and he entered, earnestly

shaking hands with Charlie first and then Lizzie, before taking a seat. He was very tall. The tallest of all the men present. At least six foot three inches, he looked every inch a successful bank manager, if a trifle flashily dressed.

An informal meeting began, though Lizzie was conscious of the fact that both she and Charlie were being scrutinized. Weighed up and judged, she thought to herself.

Mr Harding read out facts and figures on their progress since taking over Sea View Guesthouse. Mr Parker had a bulky file in front of him, which he flicked through, pausing now and again to scribble columns of figures on to a pad.

Mr Farrant caught Lizzie's eye, and again he smiled at her, this time in an encouraging way. She thought, not for the first time, how handsome he was.

Mr Parker took off his heavy-rimmed glasses and looked directly at Charlie. 'I understand that, in principle, the bank has agreed to grant you a loan. Well, on your past record and on the recommendations of Mr Blackhurst, you can go ahead now with your purchase of Highland Heights. That is, if you are willing to comply with certain conditions.'

His pause then was so long that Lizzie felt everyone in the room could hear her heart thumping and she saw that tiny beads of perspiration had formed on Charlie's forehead.

'The main condition being that a company be formed, thus allowing the bank to take a debenture

on the hotel.' Maybe Mr Parker sensed Lizzie's confusion. He explained more fully. 'A debenture
would acknowledge the debt to the bank, repayable
with guaranteed interest.'

Mr Farrant and Mr Parker, now with heads close
together, had a quiet exchange of words.

'All right? Are you happy about everything?' Mr
Farrant, with pleasure showing on his own face,
directed this to Charlie.

Apparently, Charlie was more than happy, for he
leaned forward and gravely shook hands, first with
the new bank manager and then with Roger Farrant.

'Providing all the searches and paperwork can be
got through, all loose ends tied up, shall we suggest
January 11th for completion date?'

Charlie's mood could only be described as exuberant
as he drove to Adelaide College to pick up their son,
while all Lizzie felt was utter bewilderment.

Forces behind the scenes must have been working
on their behalf, she told herself, but why did they
warrant such help? They were going to buy Highland Heights. Even a completion date had been set
and yet they had only had a brief look over the hotel.

They had had no real meeting with the owners.
Sadly, Lizzie reflected that if the bank was foreclos-
ing because it was owed money that must effectively
make the bank the owner.

What misery and anguish those two couples must
be going through, the very thought of them having

to leave that lovely place made her feel wretched. I hope to God it never happens to us, she mused.

Minutes later, a smile spread over Lizzie's face as she watched Robert raise his cap to Miss Warrell-Bowring and set off at a trot down the drive.

The run-up to Christmas was spent in cleaning rooms, washing blankets and generally making the place look nice. Charlie did all the repairs that were necessary, including replacing tap washers. They were selling Sea View Guesthouse to Mr and Mrs Sadler, fully furnished as a going concern, goodwill included. Lizzie was more than pleased that she had already taken quite a few bookings for the next season and had quite a tidy sum of money taken as deposits to turn over to the young couple.

The Christmas period was spent very quietly, just Lizzie, Charlie and young Robert alone in the guesthouse.

There were several reasons for this, the main one being that they were short of money. The cash left over from the previous season had been used to place a deposit on their new hotel. The guesthouse deal was not to be completed until 10th of January and even then the profit from the sale would have to go towards the purchase of Highland Heights.

Once again they were getting into very deep waters. Lizzie had worried herself sick when all these negotiations had begun, but now she kept telling herself that Charlie knew exactly what he was doing and that this time he wasn't on his own. He seemed to have professional men not only acting for him but decidedly on his side.

She hoped with all her heart that her assumptions would prove to be right. God help them if they didn't!

Lizzie kept telling herself that she was enjoying Christmas and she was to a certain degree. When she thought back over the years of the war, with their austerity and danger, she realized just how lucky she and her family were – a roaring log fire, plenty of good food to eat and presents and toys spread out beneath a glittering tree. But it was the sight of the Christmas cards standing on the furniture and strung around the walls that brought on the wistful thoughts.

Doris and Syd wouldn't have ordered their turkey from the butcher. They would have waited till it was dark on Christmas Eve before they'd have gone down to Tooting Market and along the Mitcham Road in search of their bargains. She could imagine Syd and Arthur, with a few pints of beer inside them, playing Father Christmas, filling Lucy's and Raymond's stockings, letting the kids put a carrot out for the reindeer, which Syd would probably have a good old gnaw at to show that the reindeer appreciated their kindness.

Boxing day made Lizzie really homesick. The Horse and Groom always put on a party for the kiddies during the afternoon. What wouldn't she give to be there. Whistles, drums, cymbals, trumpets, anything that made a noise would be used; hats, funny masks, streamers and indoor fireworks – the place would be like bedlam!

The men would be making utter fools of themselves, crawling about on all fours. It was the one day of the year when that pub was geared to nothing more than ensuring that every child in the neighbourhood had a good time and received at least one Christmas present. Jack and Dolly Hawkins were publicans of the old type and their customers loved them.

Lizzie didn't voice her thoughts aloud, but she vowed silently to herself that never again would she willingly spend a Christmas away from dear old London – unless, that is, her family came to Devon again for the holiday. For Christmas was a time to be with one's family and to have those that loved you and whom you loved around you.

The Sadlers came and stayed with them as their guests from the 6th of January.

Having their company eased the strain of the last few days. At last, it was the 11th, and Lizzie, Charlie and Robert had breakfast with Mr and Mrs Sadler at seven-thirty in what, legally, was now the Sadler's house.

In the basement bedroom, Lizzie viewed herself in the familiar mirror for the last time. Was she dressed suitably? She had spent ages pressing the grey suit and white blouse she was now wearing. Oh well, she sighed, too bad if she wasn't.

All her other clothes were packed, and already the cases were in the boot of the car. Charlie stood in the doorway, looking spruce and smart. Robert clutched tight at Bob-Bob's lead. Margaret Farrant had offered to have both Robert and the dog for the day, since two of her boys were Robert's school chums.

They kissed the Sadlers goodbye; everyone called out their good wishes. Charlie started the engine and then, with a final wave, moved off.

Assembled in the chambers were five men, Roger Farrant, Gordon Parker, Mr Harding, Mr Sims and one rather young-looking clerk, and now, Charlie made six.

This meeting was vastly different from the previous one, nothing informal about these proceedings. A small table had been positioned against a far wall at which Mr Sims and the young clerk now sat, one on each side. Mr Parker and Mr Farrant sat in their usual position behind the vast leather-topped desk.

Mr Harding sat next to Charlie, facing them, with Lizzie on his right. He agreed to be the company accountant. Mr Farrant used a very authoritative tone of voice to say, 'Charles James Wilson and Elizabeth Ann Wilson as sole directors. Elizabeth as company secretary, Charles to be treasurer. The company to be known henceforth as Highland Heights Hotel Ltd.'

At this point, Mr Harding bent forward and, from

a case which lay at his feet, he took what to Lizzie looked like a heavy press.

'The company seal,' he said, and very formally got up and placed it on the desk. Returning to his seat, he again reached into his case and took out a cheque book which was at least twice the size of an ordinary one. On each cheque, the name of the company was embossed, together with both sets of initials and the surname Wilson. Mr Harding passed the book over to Mr Parker, who immediately began to write out cheques, stating aloud each amount and giving a clarification of the purpose for which it was needed, pushing each one towards Charlie for his signature.

The amounts seemed enormous to Lizzie. She felt queasy. It was all much too complicated. She screwed her eyes up tight and bent her head forward. The next thing that she was aware of was Mr Farrant standing near, a shadow of a smile on his lips.

'All right, Mrs Wilson? I've opened the window, we'll take a break, have some coffee.'

When a young lady, dressed in a severe dark outfit, came into the office bearing a tray on which were several cups and saucers plus a large coffee pot, Lizzie's only thought was, thank God I haven't got to stand up and pour it out, for she felt that her legs would buckle beneath her.

While they were drinking their coffee and Charlie was deep in conversation with Mr Harding, Roger Farrant did his best to put Lizzie at her ease. 'It's not every day one becomes a company director.' His lovely grey eyes sparkled as he teased her.

The cups were cleared away and it was back to business. Try as she might, Lizzie couldn't keep her hands from trembling as first Charlie was asked to sign several legal documents and then herself. During the whole of this time, Mr Sims and his clerk had been busily writing and entering figures into a ledger.

Mr Sims looked up, coughed discreetly and drew the attention of Mr Farrant who left his seat and joined him at the table. The two men had a quiet conversation during which a lot of head nodding and hand gestures took place, resulting in Roger Farrant returning to his desk and turning towards Mr Parker.

'Gordon, how about granting Mr and Mrs Wilson an extra five hundred pounds on their loan? They are on a very tight budget and an extra five hundred would see them in with a lot more ease. In fact, from their point of view, it is almost a necessity.'

It seemed to Lizzie that whole minutes elapsed before the silence was broken. She glanced furtively at Mr Parker; his face was stony, his lips set in a firm line. Lizzie wished she was anywhere but in that room.

Finally, shaking his head, Gordon Parker said, 'No. From bus personnel to company directors in three years is not bad going. As from today, they are on their own.'

Lizzie felt the colour drain from her face. Quickly

she turned to look at Charlie; she was choked. She wanted to put her arms around him, there and then, to tell him to ignore that bank manager. What did he know about them? He'd only just come to the village. Her anger was now getting the better of her. If Mr Parker said just one more word, I'll tell him to shut up, she vowed.

Poor Charlie, he looked so embarrassed; his cheeks were red and his hands clutched together so tightly that the knuckles showed white through the skin. Even Roger Farrant seemed speechless; you could have heard a pin drop, the silence was so great. No answer, not a comment from anyone was made in reply to Mr Parker's judgement.

Finally, it was all over. Everyone in the room, including Mr Parker, shook hands with Charlie and Lizzie and congratulations were offered.

'The keys to the hotel are in the outer office,' Roger Farrant said, insisting that he escort them to the car park.

Although he did not show it, Mr Farrant felt responsible for Lizzie and Charlie. It was he who had set them on this road. From what he had heard, Mr Wilson was a conscientious man, a hard worker, and as to Mrs Wilson, well, Graham Blackhurst had had great admiration for what he had described as a gutsy woman.

He hoped they hadn't gone too deeply into debt.

When they reached the car, Mr Farrant turned to Charlie, saying, 'I'd like you both to listen to what

I have to say. I am convinced that you two, working together, will make a success of Highland Heights. You'll be all right, you're going in at the right time, deposits should be coming in.'

He stopped speaking, looked at them both as if considering something, then, slowly, he continued, 'The forming of the company and preparing of the documents, plus the registration fee has been calculated in your accounts at five hundred and five pounds. That amount is what is owed to my firm. What I am trying to say is that we won't be sending you our statement for at least one year. That will give you a little more time to get on your feet.'

Charlie held out his hand and in silence the two men shook hands.

Lizzie was stunned – such generosity! She swallowed deeply before she was able to say, 'Thank you, Mr Farrant.'

She couldn't get over it. Roger Farrant was everything a woman likes in a man, naturally sophisticated, with a nice sense of humour, but it had always been his jaunty, almost flirtatious manner that had made Lizzie like him. Not a bit stuffy like the usual run-of-the-mill solicitors. Now she was overwhelmed.

Not only was his offer very generous, it was also a face-saving gesture towards Charlie.

It was eleven-thirty when Charlie drove up to Highland Heights. He unlocked the side door, and they smiled at each other, held hands and went in.

Relief! All the waiting, the tension and anxieties were over. They were in their own hotel.

They spent the rest of the morning exploring, in and out of bedrooms, gazing over the banisters from what seemed a great height, staring out of the windows of the lounge, still utterly amazed at the sea that was so close. They lingered in the dining-room watching the seagulls swoop and listening to them screeching. Finally, they went to the kitchens downstairs.

'What's through there, Charlie?' Lizzie called as she watched him disappear.

'My God!' she heard him exclaim.

'It looks like a ballroom. Never been used for years, I shouldn't think.'

'There's three more small bedrooms down here,' Lizzie cried, 'I think they must be staff rooms. Come on, let's put the kettle on. You did put that box with the tea in it in the car, didn't you?'

There was no need for Charlie to go to the car and fetch the box. On one side of the cooker there was a caddy filled with tea, a bowl of sugar, two pints of fresh milk, and further back was a crusty new loaf, a half-pound packet of butter and a wedge of Cheddar cheese.

A hand-written note lay on the cabinet. 'Good luck', was all it said, but it had been signed by M. and T. Fletcher, and H. and D. Kirkland.

'Isn't that kind?' Lizzie murmured.

'Certainly makes a nice beginning,' Charlie answered.

*

The telephone rang, and from then on it never seemed to stop all afternoon. Good wishes from all sides; a florist's van arrived with two bouquets, one from Syd and Doris and one from Arthur and Polly, the postman brought 'Welcome to your new home' cards from Connie and Bill and Aunt Kate and Uncle John.

By the evening they had two adjoining bedrooms on the first floor made up, plus the private sitting-room, now bright with vases of flowers, and their own china ornaments and photographs set out. Though they were thoroughly exhausted, they were both very pleased with the results.

During the rest of the week, apart from taking Robert to school and meeting him, they only went out once. Charlie remarked, 'You'd better come out for a walk, get some fresh air into your lungs.'

It was a very raw, cold morning and, though the sun was shining, there was a keen January wind blowing in from the sea. The surrounding hills were extremely steep and the coves very rugged. Bob-Bob was in his element as he bounded on ahead. Having walked as far as the harbour, they were both glad to turn back. Nevertheless, Lizzie admitted that she felt better for having been out in the open air and their faces were glowing by the time they got back indoors.

At the weekend, the question of insurance arose. Up until now, Charlie had only obtained temporary coverage. Now a more clearly defined policy had to be considered, on this the bank was most insistent.

'Ten o'clock Monday morning, they are all meeting here,' Charlie said as he replaced the telephone receiver.

Promptly on time, Mr Hutchinson, an inspector from the insurance company, arrived. Mr Parker and a colleague from the bank were late.

'Better open the main entrance doors before the bank officials arrive,' Mr Hutchinson whispered to Lizzie. She ignored his advice.

Mr Parker and the official from Head Office came in through the side door. He introduced himself as Mr Thompson, and Lizzie took to him straight away. 'How does it feel to own one's own company?' he asked Lizzie in a friendly, almost jovial kind of way.

'First, we have to assess the building and the contents,' Mr Hutchinson said and Charlie led the way.

Mr Parker hung back. 'I would have appreciated it if you had opened up the main entrance for Mr Thompson,' he said, and his manner was aggressive.

'Why? The side door is good enough for us,' Lizzie answered, and her tone of voice was insolent.

'Careful!' he spat the word out sharply, but before he could say more Lizzie stopped him. Tall as he was, she wasn't about to be intimidated by him, not this time.

'Mr Parker, you have made my husband and myself company directors and this hotel is now the registered office of that company, but it is also our home.' Without pausing for breath, because her courage might have failed her, Lizzie pressed on. 'Please, don't think we're not grateful for all the help and advice the bank has given us, but as I understand it, we shall be paying a large amount of money in interest on the loan and, as you so aptly pointed out the other day, from here on we are on our own. We don't have to kow-tow to anyone.'

To Lizzie's utter astonishment, Mr Parker threw his head back and laughed, a vigorous, strong sound which had Lizzie staring at him open-mouthed.

He took a step towards her and, placing a hand across her shoulders, he said, 'You'll do. You'll make it, Mrs Wilson, without a doubt you'll make it.'

As he turned away to join the other men, Lizzie could still hear him chuckling to himself as he walked down the corridor. Thankfully, she sank down on to a chair. She had made her first impression as a company director.

Talk about being thrown in at the deep end!

Life in an hotel, especially one where the trade was seasonal, was vastly different to living and working in a guesthouse.

They needed staff. Waiters, chambermaids, kitchen boys to prepare the vegetables, work the dishwashers and clean the ovens, girls for the still-room to make endless pots of tea and coffee and wash the silverware, Saturday boys to carry luggage and show guests where the garages were.

They decided not to employ a chef. Charlie boned his own sides of bacon, roasted numerous legs of pork and lamb and huge, succulent pieces of beef. He spent hours preparing chickens, turkeys and cutting up pounds of steak and kidney for pies. Ham cooked on the bone was his speciality. Lizzie made all the pastry, she also made the soups, gravy and sauces and prepared large quantities of fresh fish and side salads.

The sweet trolley, cheese trays, plus the hors d'oeuvres were tasks that they shared. They prided themselves that they could make sixty cold decorative sweets in individual sundae glasses in just fifteen minutes.

All did not go smoothly. Not all the time.

Staff failed to turn up. Guests arrived late, sometimes past midnight. Laundries failed to return the linen on time. The poultry man's van was not the most reliable of vehicles and Lizzie would hold her breath some mornings as she cracked eggs into an oval pan that cooked ten at a time and prayed that some guests would prefer kippers or smoked haddock, because their stock of eggs was running low.

It was no exaggeration when Charlie spoke of an eighteen-hour day, seven days a week. Six in the morning until midnight at least.

From two p.m. until four p.m. was their free time. Maybe! Except on Saturdays, when folk were leaving and arriving all day long. Not Thursdays either because guests' accounts were made up then. Lizzie would write while Charlie would call out names, room numbers and whatever extras, such as early morning tea, had to be added to the bill. On Fridays Charlie would sit at the reception desk while visitors paid their accounts. The money had to be sorted, staff wages made up and then Charlie would dash into town to bank the remaining money, while Lizzie counted the clean laundry, hoping it had all been returned safely.

There was a bright side. Charlie applied for and was granted a licence. Women dressed in their pretty summer dresses, men in flannels and open-necked shirts would sit, making friends, chatting and laughing in the bar at the end of warm, sunny days.

All were exceedingly sociable to Lizzie, whenever she decided to join Charlie for a drink. Everyone complimented her on how well the hotel was run, insisting that she look at the photographs they had taken and would not take no for an answer when requesting Lizzie and Charlie pose for a photograph together.

We shall have enough snaps to fill a dozen albums by the time we retire from here,' was the thought that struck Lizzie.

The first week in July 1954 turned out to be a week that Lizzie would remember for a very long time. The hotel guests were mostly from London, which was unusual, since the majority of bookings, Lizzie had found, came from northerners, and during the wakes weeks every guest in the hotel would be from Lancashire or Yorkshire.

The newspapers had been full of the fact that America had sent two of her special sons to England. One was Billy Graham, a Southern Baptist minister, who had, in May, held a mass meeting in Wembley Stadium. The papers had reported that thousands of people had attended and that hundreds had surged forward pleading to be converted.

The other American to cross the Atlantic was an entirely different kettle of fish. Bill Haley and his Comets were to introduce a new rock beat to country music, an exciting combination which immediately achieved immense popularity. Their first recording, 'Shake, Rattle and Roll' sold thousands of records up and down the whole country.

It was on a warm sunny night in June, that Charlie played this record and, although space in the bar was limited, a couple in their early thirties got to their feet and started to dance to the music. Lizzie had just walked into the bar with a plate of sandwiches and she stood stock-still staring in amazement. 'You couldn't call it dancing,' she remarked to Charlie, as she set the plate down behind the counter. It was all arms and legs as the fellow swung his partner from side to side, twirling her like a top to the beat of the music, finishing by sliding her through his wide-apart legs.

As the record came to an end a spontaneous burst of applause came from almost every guest in the bar.

Whenever Lizzie was to tell this story in the future she always emphasized that not everyone approved. A dear old couple, well turned seventy, rose to their feet and the man, speaking in a very loud voice, said, 'Barbaric! Like a pair of savages. You'd do better to listen to Billy Graham and turn to the Lord.' You could have heard a pin drop as the old folk, quietly and with dignity, made their way through the tables and left the bar. Lizzie hadn't dared to look at Charlie as she beat a hasty retreat muttering as she went, 'Oh well. It takes all sorts to make a world.'

Chapter Twenty-Six

EARLY IN THE new year of 1955, the weather-men on the wireless had forecast that the country was in for a bad winter. That had been putting it mildly! January wasn't even halfway through yet and already the weather was absolutely terrible.

During the last seventy-two hours it had never stopped snowing. Heavy falls meant that most villages in north Devon were already cut off. There was ice everywhere and the roads were treacherous. Lizzie moaned to Charlie that despite all the extra woollens she was wearing she just couldn't seem to keep warm.

'Yer don't wonder at it do yer,' said Charlie, lowering the scarf that he had wrapped round his neck and face so that he could be heard. 'The bloody temperature dropped well below freezing last night and it hasn't risen at all this morning yet. Not likely to either, by the look of that sky.'

The week wore on and they felt like prisoners in the hotel as the weather worsened. The hotel gardens jutted out to the sea, and were reached only by climbing several stone steps. To Lizzie it was madness even to think about climbing up there. Nevertheless that was exactly what Robert and his father insisted on doing every morning. Lizzie watched anxiously from the dining-room windows as the two of them, muffled to the eyeballs, did the precarious climb. Robert had both hands free and was able to clutch at the rocks for support. Charlie had only one free hand, because in the other he carried a shopping-bag filled with soaked bread, dried fruit and dishes of fat. It was the only way that they could think of to keep at least some of the birds alive.

It wasn't too bad for Charlie, his feet were much bigger and he had strong sturdy boots. All Robert had on his feet, other than two pairs of thick socks, was a pair of wellingtons. More than once Lizzie's heart came up into her mouth as she watched Charlie put out his free hand to steady Robert.

Face flushed and excited, Robert would come bursting in again through the back door calling, 'Mum, Mum, you ought to see them all, they were waiting for us to feed them.' But it was a sad little boy who came back a few days later. There had been no let up in the great freeze, in fact the winds had whipped up the snow into drifts, making matters very much worse. Charlie had picked up five dead birds, all frozen stiff.

By the end of the week Charlie declared he had had enough of being indoors. 'Come on, muffle up well an' we'll go for a walk. See how far we get. We can always turn back if the going gets too tough.'

It was slow going as they turned towards the hills, their feet leaving deep imprints in the snow. Already the dog was racing ahead of them. 'He seems to like it even if we don't,' Lizzie said, her voice muffled by her thick scarf.

On the way back, the noise from the sea was deafening, the wind was almost up to gale force and as they no longer had the wind at their backs it was a job for them to get along. Charlie stopped and, much to Robert's delight, swung him up on to his shoulders. As they got near to the hotel Lizzie exclaimed, 'What a welcome sight.' Before they had left, Charlie had switched on every light in the porches and around the building.

Their private sitting-room on the ground floor was cosy and warm, but going up to their bedrooms on the first floor where the wind howled and rattled the huge bay windows was another matter. The kitchens being downstairs didn't help either. The entrance hall became known to them all as No Man's Land.

One night, as Lizzie came up from downstairs carrying a loaded tray, she plonked the tray down, shivered and hugged herself, then held out her hands to the blazing fire.

'I wish we had a smaller cooker,' she said half to herself, 'it takes ages for one of those huge ovens to heat up, and those great big burners are ridiculous when I only need to heat a small saucepan of milk.'

'You're always wishing for something,' Charlie murmured, not really paying any attention to what Lizzie had been saying.

Busy putting the hot pies on to three plates, Lizzie

suddenly exclaimed, 'OK, clever clogs. I've forgotten the teapot. I've only brought the hot-water jug. You cross No Man's Land, go down the stairs and through to the second kitchen and fetch it for me.'

Rather sheepishly, Charlie got to his feet, but had to laugh as Lizzie added, 'If you run quick enough, you won't freeze.'

They were grouped round the fire tucking into their meat pies and jacket potatoes, which Lizzie had split open and lavishly spread with butter, when Charlie asked, 'How about a separate house, or even a bungalow?'

'What?'

'We could live in it in the winter. Be less expensive than to heat this hotel. You and Robert could even live in it during the summer. I could sleep in this room on a divan, and we could then let our two bedrooms.

Lizzie put her hand behind her back, drew out a small cushion and chucked it at Charlie's head. It missed. Robert and his father both chuckled. 'You never could bowl, Mum,' Robert said.

'What's the matter?' Charlie wanted to know. 'Don't you like the idea? I thought you'd be all for it.'

'Oh, I like it all right,' she leant forward and nudged Charlie with her elbow, 'it's you. You've got our bedrooms let to guests before we've even moved out. Besides, talking about another house and buying one is an entirely different matter, and by the way, if, and I said if, this comes about, do you think I might have a choice?'

'Lizzie, my darling,' Charlie bowed his head in mock adoration, 'the choice shall be entirely yours.'

The weather gradually improved and, armed once again with details from estate agents, they were out and about looking at small properties. Nothing suited.

Charlie's arguments were, one, they had to live close enough to the hotel to keep an eye on the place and, two, from Christmas onwards, they would have to pick the mail up every morning. It was essential that all enquiries were answered on the same day, otherwise they would start to lose bookings.

The agents had given details of every property on their books, but Lizzie hadn't seen one that she wanted as a home.

Charlie grew bad tempered. 'You're too critical,' he flung at her.

'Waste of time to look further,' Lizzie decided. The subject wasn't mentioned again for at least a week.

They were sitting in the car outside the gates of Adelaide College waiting for Robert, when Charlie came out with another suggestion. 'How about having a place built?'

'How? Where? How much would it cost?' the questions poured from Lizzie.

'Hold your horses, for Christ's sake, I dunno any

of those answers yet, do I? It was only a thought I had.'

But early next morning, Charlie was off. Curiosity was killing Lizzie as she made the beds and washed her hair to pass away the time.

It was three o'clock in the afternoon before Charlie drove his car up the drive and behind it came the conspicuous car of Freddie Clarke – Mr Fix-It had come to call.

To see Freddie was a tonic, bright and breezy, with his trilby tilted jauntily to the back of his head. The way in which he greeted Lizzie, arm around her shoulders, kiss on both cheeks, made her feel that all was well with his world.

'I've bought a field of Christmas trees,' Charlie blurted out.

Now what? Lizzie had visions of Charlie going to London in December and selling Christmas trees on street corners. Before she could tell him that this time he had gone too far, that he ought to be certified as mentally insane, Freddie calmed her down.

'It's a plot of land. Residential building permits have already been granted. I've got three adjoining plots to sell. I never gave it a thought before. Be just right for you, Lizzie, I promise you'll love it.'

'Where it is?' Lizzie got a question in at last.

'About two miles out on the old road. Get your coat, we've just got time to show you the plot before it gets dark.'

They all piled into Freddie's car.

The surroundings where the plots were situated was truly lovely.

'Makes a change from being right on the sea's edge,' Lizzie said as she stood on the sloping hillside and sniffed deeply at the smell of the pine trees and noticed that there was still a good view of the sea, shimmering away in the distance.

She understood why Charlie hadn't let the grass grow under his feet.

Locally there was only one builder, whose name was Ron Geering, and he was honest enough to admit to Charlie that the job of building a house was too big for him to handle. He admitted he would very much like to be considered for sub-contracted work on the project, but as to being the main builder, definitely no.

Meanwhile, he was prepared to give as much help as he could and Charlie gratefully accepted the benefit of his advice. Discussions began.

'Talk a lot,' he advised, 'before approaching an architect. They charge a helluva lot of money for their time. What type of dwelling do you prefer – house or bungalow? What type of heating – electric or gas?'

No sooner had they settled one thing, than Ron Geering would suggest another point to bear in mind . . . it went on and on. Reluctantly, Lizzie agreed she didn't have the technical knowledge needed for her to join in these discussions. Even Charlie began to wonder whether this time he had bitten off more than he could chew.

Ron advised them to leave it a while. 'The ground won't lose any value,' he assured them. 'You both want to give a great deal of thought to all the matters that I've raised. Don't make any decision in a hurry.'

Charlie thanked him and promised to keep him informed of whatever conclusion they came to.

Lizzie felt defeated.

About ten days had passed during which Charlie had twice driven Lizzie out to visit their plot. Sold notices were now on the two adjoining lots.

It was a quarter-past eleven at night when the shrill ringing of the telephone made Lizzie jump; she had her book in one hand and a hot drink in the other and was on her way up to bed. She left Charlie speaking into the receiver.

'Who was on the phone?' Lizzie raised herself up on one elbow as she spoke.

'Freddie Clarke. He's bringing a chap called Michael Gale to see us in the morning.'

'Who's Michael Gale?'

'I can't rightly say, Freddie said he's known him for years.'

Promptly, at ten o'clock next morning, Freddie was in the hotel introducing Mr Gale, who was a tall, athletic-looking man in his early forties, with blond, almost white hair.

Lizzie made coffee and soon everyone was on friendly terms. Mr Gale certainly had a way with women. While he was speaking to Charlie and Freddie he had Lizzie feeling that she was included, that nothing would be decided without her knowledge or participation. Lizzie liked that.

Having established the fact that Charlie had bought a plot of land and that, yes, it was his intention to have a private dwelling of some kind built there, Mike, as Charlie was by now calling him, stated that he was a member of the Federation of Master Builders.

'How would you feel about a package deal, involving all three owners of those plots?' he tentatively asked.

Charlie looked dubious.

'Have you approached any firms?'

'Only a local builder,' Charlie told him.

'Right,' the self-assured Michael Gale began. 'On such a project as this, insurance is absolutely vital. You must make sure that you don't sign any contract which makes you legally liable for accidents to contractors or workmen. Don't make yourself liable for theft or damage to materials and equipment whilst on your site. Some insurance companies will arrange special temporary cover for building materials and machinery, but would probably charge very heavily for materials that were being left out in the open on your site . . .'

Charlie sighed heavily and Lizzie suggested more coffee.

Freddie Clarke winked at her as she took away his cup to refill it.

'You must also insist on setting a completion date . . .'

Mike Gale was off again with his dire warnings
as he spooned sugar into his cup from the bowl that
Lizzie held. 'Equipment doesn't always arrive on
time. At various stages during the building, inspectors have to attend. Inspectors lead very busy lives,
probably have a long way to travel each time to your
site, Charlie. You'd have to make appointments to
fit in with their schedules, not yours. My firm could
save you all those headaches . . .'

Lizzie could see that Charlie was almost ready to
surrender. She found her courage and spoke up.
'When you say a package deal, exactly what do you
mean? Do we end up with what you want us to
have? Have the other two owners agreed yet? Or
haven't you spoken to them?'

'Whoa, whoa, you're going too fast for me, Mrs
Wilson, let's take your questions one at a time. Package deal first. You allow us to tender for a prototype
external house or bungalow, to be decided at a later
date. All three properties to all extents and purposes
would be very similar, though not exactly the same
from the outside. All your personal preferences and
ideas could and would be incorporated inside. It
could work out very much cheaper, save all three
plot owners a great deal of money. Secondly . . .'
and on, and on.

At last Charlie was able to chip in. 'You still
haven't said whether the other two owners have
agreed.'

Very reluctantly, Michael Gale said, 'No, they
have not. They are still considering the matter.'

Then he played his ace card.

'Come to Bristol. The other two couples have agreed to that. An architect and several members of my firm will be there. We'll show you plans, a film and several colour slides to help you make a final decision as to the type of building you would all choose and decide on. Nothing definite, you don't have to sign anything, just come as our guests. Nice hotel . . .'

'OK, Mike,' Charlie said as they shook hands, 'we'll come to Bristol. Make a nice change for Lizzie if nothing else. Beyond that, I'm promising nothing.'

Turning to Freddie, he grinned, 'Probably cost me a bloody fortune, if I let Lizzie loose in Bristol.'

Freddie hung back and his face became quite serious. 'I didn't pull Michael out of any old hat, you know, Charlie. He *is* trustworthy. His firm is bona fide, honestly.'

'I know,' Charlie told him, equally serious, 'it's just that I need time to think and talk things over with Lizzie.'

When the two men had left, Charlie turned to Lizzie, saying, 'We'll go to the bank in the morning, together. I'll ask Mr Harding to meet us there.'

The meeting at the bank didn't take long. Mr Harding produced copies of the company's returns. Mr Parker approved the idea of a private house as a sound investment and put forward the suggestion that the purchase should be a private one. Outside the company.

'Repayments on the loan can be made from your
own income,' Gordon Parker smiled at Lizzie, 'just
in case.'

He laughed now, and Lizzie turned to Charlie,
'Just in case of what?'

'Just in case the company should flounder,' Charlie told her. 'No creditors would be able to claim on
our home.'

'Oh,' was all she said, but inwardly, Lizzie liked
the sound of that.

'Make a detour, Charlie, please, let's go and look at
the site again,' Lizzie pleaded as they drove home
from the bank.

Charlie just nodded, and before long they were
there. They held hands like a couple of teenagers
and climbed right to the top of the hill. Out of breath
and trying to breathe deeply, Lizzie stood still while
Charlie wandered off on his own.

The view was fantastic. The winter sunshine was
streaming through the green trees and suddenly she
felt a surge of excitement. This spot was going to
be their home. Not the company's property. Not to
be used in any way for business purposes, every
room would be theirs. All of it would be theirs.

All this surrounding natural beauty, it was breath-
taking. She wished she could wave a magic wand,
have the house built now. She hoped that if and
when building did start, as few trees as possible
would be disturbed.

From that vantage-point, so high up, she could

see right across the Channel and, way below, the surf was still booming on to the rocks. Here, please God, they would eventually have stability, an environment of normality, a home where their son could bring his friends.

Charlie made Lizzie jump as he came up behind her and nuzzled his face into her neck. 'You were day-dreaming, miles away, do you know we've been up here for over an hour?'

By lunchtime, a week later, Charlie and Lizzie were in Bristol. Robert was safely away on a school trip, and Mr Gale had arranged everything perfectly.

The Hydro was a nice hotel. Charlie registered at the reception desk, and booked them in for a stay of at least four nights.

They freshened up and then went downstairs into the bar. Michael Gale bought a drink for each of them and introductions were made.

The other two purchasers were a Mr and Mrs Courtney and a Mr and Mrs Marshall. Not local people, in fact, one couple had travelled from Birmingham.

After a very nice informal lunch, during which everyone seemed friendly and at ease, they moved off into a large room which was obviously used for business meetings, and here everyone gathered around a circular table as drawings and plans were laid out. There was talk amongst the men of ground-floor plans, upper-floor plans, south elevation, north elevation. Lizzie heaved a sigh and withdrew to the back a little and so did Mrs Marshall.

'Do you understand the drawings?' Mrs Marshall asked in a quiet voice. Lizzie shook her head and whispered, 'No, I don't.'

'If you will all take a seat now,' Michael Gale gestured to where chairs had been set out in a row, 'we will show photographs of suitable dwellings designed with your situation in mind. If any of you spot anything with which you feel you would be happy, both in size and type, please stop me and I'll be happy to discuss such a property at length and in much greater detail.'

Blinds were drawn down over the windows, the projector started to make a purring sound and the first colour slide appeared on the screen.

The second slide came up, much the same as the first, a dull, long, low type of bungalow.

It was when the third slide came up that Lizzie let out an exclamation of surprise without stopping to think. It wasn't that the house being shown was large or even very impressive. It was different.

'This is a split-level bungalow,' Mr Roberts, the architect, was saying. Lizzie glanced quickly at the other two ladies; both smiled and were very clearly impressed.

Now, having everyone's full attention, Mr Roberts showed more slides of this bungalow from various angles, the interior, lower floor, entrance hall, bedrooms, shower room, bathroom and separate toilet.

'Why bedrooms downstairs?' Mrs Courtney asked.

Mr Roberts grinned, 'I'm coming to that.'

Technical drawings came up on the screen. 'Split-level means that by building the second half high up on and into the hill, one will gain all the benefits of the views. The upper-ground floor, as it is known, would house the kitchen, dining-room and lounge. The lounge would be thirty-five foot long, one wall of which would be mainly glass.'

Suddenly, another slide appeared and even the men gasped. It showed the exterior of the lounge. The glass doors in the photograph were opened on to a huge veranda fenced in by ranch-style white slats and the solid floor was two-toned concrete slabs.

The decision was unanimous, at least amongst the ladies it was. Was all of this real? Lizzie asked herself.

She was bursting with excitement. Had they found the ideal bungalow? Would it eventually be built? Would it look exactly like those colour slides or would it all turn out to be an unachievable dream?

She wanted to laugh, yet she also felt like weeping.

She wanted to throw her arms around Charlie, hug him, kiss him, share all this excitement, but there were too many people around. He must have been having similar feelings, as he tucked his arm through Lizzie's and squeezed so hard it hurt.

That was a very intimate moment.

No one else in the room mattered, just each other.

Chapter Twenty-Seven

THE SECOND SEASON hadn't proved too difficult, the weather had been good most weeks, which must play a great part in any holiday. The guests could get out and about and there were less moans to contend with.

However, with the coming of their third season in Highland Heights, Lizzie felt she was a lot wiser and certainly not so starry-eyed about the job.

They were well into July 1956 when Charlie put the fear of God into her. The pair of them were in the court-yard, which was outside the main kitchen, slumped in deckchairs, having a quiet hour before lighting up all the ovens and getting the evening dinner on the go. Suddenly Charlie lowered the newspaper he was reading, leant forward and touched her knee. 'Do you realize Lizzie, it's quite possible I might get called up?'

Lizzie's heart missed a beat. 'You shouldn't joke about a thing like that,' she quickly rebuked him.

'Who's joking?' he retorted. 'I know you don't get much time to read the papers but even you must be aware of all the trouble there is with Egypt over the Suez Canal.'

Lizzie didn't answer. Of course she had heard rumours, but she took the attitude that she had quite enough of her own problems to contend with without trying to solve matters that were going wrong on the other side of the world.

Charlie continued to read his paper, now and again making a comment out loud. 'Sir Anthony Eden's not very popular with the Americans. Both Eden and France want to send troops in. There's talk of it going to the United Nations.'

'Well, wasn't that why the United Nations was formed? To act as peacemaker?' she asked.

Charlie only mumbled something about her having her head buried in the sand.

Lizzie got up, folded her chair and leant it against the wall. 'Let's 'ope to God that all these men in power see a bit of sense for once,' she flung back over her shoulder at Charlie; 'surely one war in anyone's lifetime is more than enough. Come ter that there's many a person still alive that is still suffering from the First World War.'

The days and weeks of August and September seemed to drag. Life became monotonous, the same old routine day after day, sweltering in the hot kitchens while the guests lay on the beach or swam in the sea, the scorching sun shining down on them.

By the time the season was over once again Lizzie was thoroughly disillusioned. Despite all the promises that she'd made to herself, she had not been back to London since 1953. Doris phoned regularly and she herself would often telephone Doris or Polly. But these conversations only made her feel worse.

Her thoughts would be back in London and it didn't take much for her to conjure up pictures in her mind of what her friends and relations were up to.

This particular Friday seemed endless to Lizzie as she wandered about the hotel. She found herself doing the same job over and over and the silence was becoming eerie; her footsteps sounded loudly each time she crossed the tiled entrance hall and she prayed that the telephone might ring. It could be anyone on the other end, she didn't care who it was as long as it was someone to talk to.

Charlie had gone to Cardiff for the weekend, to see a football match. It was a long-standing arrangement, an outing for the local darts club that Charlie played for. The men had caught The Cardiff Queen at eight o'clock that morning, the last paddle-steamer to leave Ilfracombe harbour this season. Lizzie didn't begrudge Charlie his weekend with his mates but it had coincided with the weekend that Robert was away, staying with a school friend named Stephen Banks, whose father and mother owned holiday flats and a caravan park out at Heale, a very picturesque village on the way to Combe Martin.

Lizzie had found it hard to make friends down here in Devon; she fell between two stools. The largest of the hotels in the vicinity were company owned and run by managers put in for the season only. During the winter months such hotels would be closed up. No one there to get friendly with. She liked some of the women who worked for her and

Charlie, especially the real Devonians and she had tried hard to get one or two of them to go into Barnstaple with her for a day's outing or even into one of the local pubs for a drink. She'd had no luck. They regarded Lizzie as a foreigner from London, their boss and not someone with whom they could socialize.

As the short October day drew to a close and the daylight began to fade, Lizzie could hear the wind howling and the waves crashing on to the rocks. It would probably be a very high-tide tonight and she was thankful that Charlie wasn't making the return crossing until Sunday.

What could she possibly do with herself during the long evening that stretched ahead? 'I know what I would do if it weren't fer you,' she said crossly as she opened the door at the foot of the stairs and let Bob-Bob bound up to the sitting-room. 'I'd be on that first train up ter London. What the 'ell 'ave I got ter keep me 'ere.'

With that thought came the action. None of them had to stay here. Not for another long dreary winter. 'Jesus Christ!' she exclaimed and the sound of her own voice seemed to mock her. People were fond of saying that seasonal hoteliers only worked six months of the year. Well, she now knew for a fact that you did a year's work in that six months. Then what did you get? Maybe October, November and December off, but you had to be here every day from the beginning of January to answer the mail each day and to do all the running repairs that were necessary.

Lizzie dialled the number of her brother's house, but when the phone rang and rang with no one there to answer it Lizzie could have cried with temper. It seemed that everyone else in the world had somewhere to go and more than likely someone they could go with.

It was only after the third attempt that Doris finally answered the phone.

'I can't stay in this bloody place a minute longer. Charlie's took 'imself off to Cardiff, Robert's staying the weekend with his school friend, an I'm stuck in this blasted hotel on me own with no one to talk to but the bloody dog.'

Doris listened to Lizzie's outburst and now in her own placid way she calmly said, 'Why don't yer come up? We've got stew for dinner.'

That was exactly what Lizzie needed. The logic of Doris. She threw back her head and laughed so hard she almost dropped the phone. Stew for dinner!

'Doris, much as I would love a plateful of your stew I don't own an airplane. What I want you ter do for me is ter go to the estate agent's at Wimbledon first thing in the morning, see if they've got a furnished house to rent for three months, tell them it's for me, maybe someone there might remember me.'

'Who's the house for?' Doris's sing-song voice

came down the line and Lizzie was sure she was taking the mick.

'You know damned well it's fer me and Charlie. If we don't get away from 'ere, at least for a while, I shall end up killing him.'

'Anyway, why d'yer want a house, you can all stay 'ere.'

'Doris, if I were near you at this moment I would strangle you!'

Lizzie heard Doris's soft tinkle of a laugh and she relaxed.

'Seriously Doris, it would be better if we rent a house, that way we won't get under one anothers' feet and Charlie won't be able to moan so much if he's in a place of our own.'

Suddenly Doris's voice sounded very serious as she said, 'OK, Lizzie, I'll be round at Wimbledon nine o'clock in the morning. I'll phone you as soon as I've found you something, and Lizzie . . .' Doris hesitated.

'Yes, love?' Lizzie queried.

'Take it easy tonight. Have a drink and go to bed early. I'll ring you before ten in the morning. Night Lizzie. God bless.'

'Good-night Doris. God bless you.'

Lizzie felt a whole lot happier as she replaced the receiver, though she was a little apprehensive when she thought about how she would tell Charlie of her decision.

'Sod him,' she said aloud in an attempt at bravado, 'if he don't want ter come 'ome he can bloody well stay down 'ere in Devon an' see how he likes talking to himself.'

Lizzie spent an awful night, tossing and turning, punching her pillow and moving from side to side in the big double bed. When she did finally fall into a light sleep it was almost day-break and it wasn't long before the noise of the sea and the screech of the gulls had her awake again. She gave it up as a bad job, got out of bed, pulled her dressing-gown tightly around her and made the cold trek down to the kitchens.

'Talk about madness,' she mumbled to herself as she waited for the kettle to come to the boil, 'all in all there must be more than thirty rooms in this hotel an' there's me rolling around the damn place like a bloody pea in a colander.'

It was twenty minutes past ten when the phone rang and Lizzie snatched it up with a sigh of relief.

'I've found you somewhere, Lizzie, only five minutes' walk from us.' Doris sounded excited as she poured her news down the line. 'No houses I'm afraid, but I've put a deposit on a maisonette. Do you remember the big 'ouse on the corner of Longley Road, we used to call it the two-faced 'ouse cos it 'ad windows side and front.'

'But that place is enormous,' protested Lizzie.

'Wait, just let me tell yer, it's bin turned into flats an' they're all being let furnished. Only the bottom one is still vacant and the old boy at the estate agent's said they'd only take a six-month let, nothing less. Well, I told 'im all about you. He said he remem-

bered yer, but I don't know if he did. Anyway, I
said you only wanted somewhere ter stay while you
were looking for another house ter buy, 'cos you
were coming back ter live in London and you 'oped
he'd be able ter find you something nice.'

'And?' Lizzie asked but she knew what was
coming and there was laughter in her voice.

'You got the garden flat, as the old boy called
it, for three months as from a week terday. Next
Monday yer can move in, that's if Charlie don't kill
yer first.'

'Oh Doris, trust you!'

They talked for another few minutes till Doris
said, "Ere this is early morning rate an' if I don't
soon put this phone down Syd will kill ME when
he gets the bill.'

Charlie's reaction surprised Lizzie. He put up no
resistance to the idea, not even any argument. She
had fully expected that they would have a right old
barney, and had been prepared to tell him exactly
what he could do if he didn't want to go with her
to London. Instead, he had smiled in such a way
that would normally have aggravated her, and from
then on had been thoroughly cooperative, going so
far as to offer to go to Adelaide College and make it
right for Robert to be absent until the new year.

It was the end house in a row of terraced houses
with a bay window in the front which looked out
at the houses opposite, and another bay window at

the side of the house which looked out on to the High Street. Situated on the opposite corner was a small shop which seemed to sell every imaginable thing.

The furniture in all the rooms was adequate, but nothing at all to get excited about. Mostly it was 'utility' – furniture that had been available during the war, and then only on dockets issued to newly-weds or people who had been bombed out.

The first thing they set about doing was finding a local school that would take Robert. They were lucky. The headmistress of Colliers Wood Junior School was most understanding and said they would be happy to offer a place to Robert for as long as his parents deemed it necessary.

Their first week in London was progressing nicely. Syd had started his own business, hiring out cars for weddings and such like and had taken a lease on premises in Totterdown Street at the back of Tooting Market. It was Thursday morning, Charlie had gone off with Syd, and Doris and Lizzie had just arrived back at Doris's house from taking Raymond and Robert to school. Raymond was in the junior section, while Robert had settled into the infant department.

'We'll wash up these breakfast things, 'ave a cuppa an' then go down Tooting, shall we?' Doris asked as she put the bung in the sink and poured a kettle of boiling water over the dirty plates.

'Yeah,' Lizzie said, picking up a tea-cloth ready to dry up. 'We can give Polly a knock as we go.'

Doris laughed, 'Polly'll be over 'ere before we're ready ter go. We always go down Tooting on Thursdays.'

At a quarter to eleven the three of them were just going out of the front door when the phone rang. 'I've a good mind ter let it ring,' Doris moaned. 'It's more than likely only Syd wanting me ter do something or other.' The ringing persisted as Doris closed the door, and then something made her change her mind. Putting her key into the lock, she opened the door and ran down the hall. Two minutes later she was back and the colour had drained from her face.

'It's Robert! He's missing! They've rung the bell after playtime an' no one can find 'im.'

'Oh my God!' Lizzie's heart was already beating like a drum inside her chest as she threw down her shopping bag and purse and ran back inside the house. 'I'm gonna phone the police,' she called back to Doris.

'Lizzie! Lizzie! He's 'ere.' Polly was out at the front gate and was pointing a finger up the street.

Lizzie spun round on her heels and was up and out in the road in a few strides, then she stopped, staring in disbelief. Her young son was a few feet away from her, looking very bedraggled, his cap was on crooked, his plimsoles, tied together, were strung round his neck and he was dragging his satchel along the pavement. 'I'm never going to go to school ever again,' he declared as Lizzie swept him up in her arms.

'How did you get home? How did you manage to cross the main road? How did you know to come ter Auntie Doris's house?'

'Lizzie leave him be for now,' Polly put out a restraining hand on to Lizzie's shoulder. 'Come on, let's get him back inside the 'ouse. Doris has gone ter phone the school ter tell them that he is all right.'

'All the boys keep calling me a Devon dumpling,' was the only explanation that they could get from Robert.

They phoned Syd and within twenty minutes Charlie was home. Having found that his son was safe and sound Charlie laughed, which was a great relief to Lizzie. She had fully expected to get the blame.

At one-thirty Charlie took Robert back to the school and once again the headmistress was most kind, promising that she would sort the matter out. Both Lizzie and Charlie were outside the school gates at a quarter to four when Robert came running towards them with three other bigger boys in tow. 'Dad, Dad,' he yelled, 'will you take Jimmy, Sam and Freddie home in our car because they're my friends now, Miss Thompson said they're to look after me.'

From then on Charlie gave all three boys a ride home every afternoon, because, as he said, 'What choice have I got. I've got to look after my son's minders!'

The third weekend that they were 'home' Syd got

tickets for the six of them to go to Chelsea Palace
on the Saturday evening. He couldn't have picked a
worse night.

They got off the tram outside The Weatsheaf at
Trinity Road and walked to the bus stop. It was
almost impossible to see a hand in front of your face
because the damp thin fog, which had swirled round
during most of the day, had now become much
denser. How glad they were when they at last saw
the headlights of the bus penetrating the blackness.
The journey took longer than usual but they were
grateful to the driver of the bus when it pulled up
safely outside the theatre.

'Don't fink we'll be going much ferver, it's turning out ter be a right pea-souper,' the driver called
down to his conductor who had come off the bus
and was standing on the pavement looking up at his
mate in his cab.

'Did yer 'ear that?' Polly called to the men who
had walked on in front of them. 'If the buses stop
running 'ow the 'ell are we gonna get 'ome?'

Arthur, usually the one with the least to say,
turned his head and called, 'You can start walking
now if yer like. Yer silly cow, we've only just got
'ere an' you're worrying about 'ow we're gonna get
'ome. Fer Christ's sake, let's git ourselves inside an'
maybe we'll 'ave time to 'ave a drink before the
show starts.'

''Ark at 'im getting out of his pram,' Polly said
in a whisper to Lizzie, and they were all laughing as

they went inside the warm foyer and made for the bar.

The applause was thunderous as Winifred Atwell seated herself at her Honky-Tonk Piano. 'Ma, she's making eyes at me', 'Bye, Bye, Blackbird', 'California here I come', 'Who were you with last night?', 'Fall in an' follow me', all these great songs were belted out as the audience sang at the tops of their voices and the rafters of the old Chelsea Palace rang as they hadn't done for many a long day. The audience was loath to let her go and for an encore she played a quiet tune, 'Who's sorry now?', which was sung by men and women alike with a great deal of feeling.

When they came out Syd suggested that they walk over Battersea Bridge. A wind had got up and the fog had lifted a little, but as they crossed the bridge the dampness from the river Thames below seemed to Lizzie to spread right over her and she was glad when Syd broke into a run flagging a taxi down.

'I'm on me way 'ome mate, I live at Wimbledon an' I ain't about ter make a detour fer nobody ternight.'

'That's all right. Can yer drop us anywhere between Tooting Broadway and Colliers Wood?' asked Syd, adding ruefully, 'But there's six of us.'

'Must be your lucky night,' the old cabbie said as he put his arm backwards and unlocked the door of his cab. 'Me son's just drawn in behind me, he'll take a coupla yer.'

On the short walk to the house Lizzie huddled up

close to Charlie; the wind might be a good thing, getting rid of that acrid smell of fog, but it was bitterly cold. There was one thing, though, that they were both agreed on; it had been a smashing night out.

Doris and Lizzie were making their way home from the shops, their coat collars turned up against the cold. 'Doris, Doris!' a voice called out as they reached the front gate. ''Ang on a minute, I've got somefink I wanna show yer.'

'Oh hell! Aggie Baggie!' Doris told Lizzie as she put the key in the lock. Half turning she said to the scruffy-looking woman who was by now right on their heels, 'I suppose you'd better come in.'

Lizzie started to take the shopping from the bags while Doris took a poker to the fire. Lifting the banked-down coal, letting a draught through, she soon had bright flames darting up the chimney. Getting up from her knees, Doris spoke to the woman, 'Aggie make it quick, I gotta get the dinner and yer know what my Syd's like.'

Aggie sniffed and, lifting the large patchwork bag from her arm, she emptied the contents on to the table. Lizzie's eyes lit up. There were four or five skirts, real quality, expensively tailored skirts.

'I like the grey one,' Lizzie murmured as she picked it up and fingered the cloth.

As if on cue, the door opened and Syd came into the room. He took everything in at a glance. Thumping his fist down on to the table he shouted at his sister, 'Lizzie, you must be out of yer bleedin' mind, they're Braffman's skirts.' Taking a step towards Aggie, he spoke with menace in his voice, 'You bin up ter yer tricks again? You nicked them, an' all right it ain't nothing ter do with me what you get up to, but I've told yer before keep out of my 'ouse and don't try flogging yer stuff ter my family, 'cos if we get the coppers round 'ere so 'elp me God I'll see you pay for it. As fer you, Lizzie, you might 'ave known she was a tea-leaf. An' you, Doris, what the bloody 'ell did yer let 'er in 'ere for?'

Lizzie put the skirt down on the table and, as she looked up, she saw Charlie was leaning back against the door; she hadn't heard him come in.

Syd wasn't finished by a long chalk. He grabbed the bag from Aggie and shoved the skirts inside it. Charlie moved and Syd shoved Aggie through the door and up the hallway. When he came back he spoke, taking in both Doris and Lizzie, 'If either of you 'ad worn one of those skirts down the market, Wally Braffman would 'ave recognized it an' he'd 'ave the coppers on ter yer as soon as yer put yer foot in the place. Yer pair of silly cows! Ain't yer learnt? Yer never make a mess on yer own door-step.'

The pair of them decided it was safest to keep their mouths shut as they bustled about making a pot of tea and setting the cups out.

'Shall we not bother to cook tonight?' Doris suddenly said as they all sat near to the fire drinking their tea. 'We gotta go over the road ter get the boys from Polly's and we could pop up the road an' get fish 'n' chips fer us all. You might as well stay 'ere for yer dinner, eh Lizzie?'

Lizzie looked across at Charlie and he nodded his agreement.

'It's lovely fish up there, cheap an' all,' Doris said; 'anything yer like as long as yer don't mind waiting while old 'Arry cooks it. Even get a Dover sole if yer fancy it.'

Charlie brought his head up with a jerk, looked at Syd and asked, 'Is she joking?'

'No. 'Arry's brother works at Billingsgate Market; he keeps his brother well supplied with fish that's how come he can do it so reasonable.'

'Gawd blimey! Every bugger up 'ere seems ter be on the fiddle!' Charlie muttered and then, looking at Doris, he spoke in a voice that was very quiet, 'Mind you I could really go a nice thick Dover sole.'

It had become a regular thing for the six of them to go out together on Saturday evenings and the word had got around that the King's Head in Merton was putting on a live show at weekends.

'Come on, we'll give it a go,' said Syd, as he pushed open the swing door and held it back for the girls to go in first.

They had a job to find a free table and were about to walk back and stand against the wall when a thick-set fellow, who was obviously acting as a bouncer, called out, 'Syd, 'ere Syd, over 'ere.' He then spoke to a couple who were sitting alone at a round table and they immediately got to their feet and moved over to join another group where there were two free seats.

'Thanks Mike,' Syd said. 'Ain't much good though, mate, there's six of us.'

''Old yer 'orses, will yer, Syd? Let the girls park their backsides an' I'll git yer another table from out the back an' we'll push 'em together.'

When they were all settled, the men with pints in front of them and the girls with shorts, Doris leant across the table and touched Syd's arm. 'Why did that bloke do that fer us? Do yer know 'im?'

''Course I bloody know 'im, yer daft cow! 'Ow else would he 'ave known me name. I'm doing 'is daughter's wedding next Saturday; booked all three of me cars he 'as. Nice little earner that'll be.'

Part of the show was this new craze for mime. The master of ceremonies stepped to the front of the stage and, with the mike close to his mouth, bawled, 'Ladies an' gentlemen, I give you, JOHNNY RAY.'

Behind the curtains a record was placed on the record-player. A slim, blond young man in his early thirties, flashily dressed in a checked suit and wearing a spotted bow-tie, crossed the stage and took the mike. The music blared out.

The young man's impersonation of Johnny Ray was fantastic; he imitated every action of the well-known singer as he mimed – 'Let your hair down 'n' go on 'n' CR – Y – Y'.

The applause was deafening and as the customers stamped their feet and yelled 'More', Arthur remarked, 'He wouldn't 'ave done 'alf so well if he 'adn't 'ave been 'alf cut.'

'Yeah!' Syd agreed. 'A right piss artist!'

Lizzie fell about laughing. Saturday nights in Devon were nothing like this!

Lizzie loved the trips they made to Tooting Market. There were still some of the old traders left who remembered her from when she had worked there during the war. No matter how many times she went there, they would still call out to her, 'Watcher, Lizzie, 'ow are yer, me old darling?'

There was old Annie, still running her salad stall, lively as ever. She had gazed in wonder at Lizzie when Lizzie had first gone to say hallo to her.

'Cor blimey, you've put some meat on yer bones,' she had cried as she flung her arms around Lizzie. 'I remember you as a skinny bloody urchin; I used ter fink that was why yer mum sent you on the errands, 'cos every bugger felt sorry fer yer, fought yer needed a damn good meal so they always gave yer a good whack fer yer money. Yer mum was a good'n', God rest 'er soul; she was an' all. There's many a one still around 'ere what yer mum helped out of 'n 'ole.'

That had brought a lump to Lizzie's throat and made her smile at the same time as she remembered how, in this very market, she had given her mum rations which they hadn't been entitled too.

And what a fuss there'd been over that!

*

One morning Lizzie was feeling particularly happy. Christmas was only weeks away and, although she was suffering from sheer exhaustion because Doris and Polly had dragged her round so many shops looking for presents to buy for the men and the children, she was really looking forward to the holiday. 'At last!' Lizzie breathed a sigh of relief as they reached the cafe in the centre of the market and they dumped their shopping-bags down and lowered themselves onto chairs.

'Must admit I'm dying for a cuppa,' Polly said as she got straight back up on her feet again. 'I'll go an' get us three large teas while yer make up yer minds what yer want to eat.'

It was about twenty minutes later, as the girls were tucking into hot meat pies and a second steaming mug of tea, when a gruff voice boomed at them, 'Ah! Just the three luvverly girls I was 'oping ter see this morning!'

'Watch out!' Doris said in a stage-whisper. 'When Fred 'Arris pays anyone a compliment it only means one thing. He's after something.'

'Yer right, Dorris me ol' luv,' he said as he took a chair from another table, swung it round and placed it back to front next to Polly. Then he straddled his legs across the seat and rested his arms over the back and faced them all.

'Next Saturday week, ten days before Christmas, we're giving a party in the Central 'All fer the widows, widowers and pensioners. Could do wiv yer 'elp all day if yer ain't got nuffin' better ter do.'

The three looked at each other and all nodded but it was Polly who said, 'We don't mind, glad ter 'elp, but we can't make it all day; what would we do with our kids?'

'That's just it.' There was a beaming smile now on the face of Fred Harris as he licked a stub of pencil and wrote the girls' names down on a long grubby sheet of paper. 'We've told all the 'elpers ter bring their kids along wiv them. Brighten up the place they will an' the old folk'll enjoy watching the antics some of the little sods get up to.'

'Why do yer need us all day? Isn't it just a tea that you're giving them?' questioned Lizzie.

'No it ain't!' declared Fred. 'It's gonna be a proper Christmas dinner wiv all the trimmings. Hemmingway's the bakers are gonna cook the turkeys fer us an' boil the puddings an' all. There's still the soup ter get on early in the morning, all the veg ter do, the tables ter be laid and before yer can do that we 'ave to set up the trestles an' see ter them blasted folding chairs. The bloody china will probably need a good wash, we'll need gallons of custard – there's about an 'undred coming. An then there's the carrier-bags ter fill 'cos every one of 'em is going 'ome wiv a load of goodies, all given free by the stall-'olders of this market.'

The tears of mirth were by now running down their faces as Doris tried to stop laughing and pleaded, 'OK, OK.'

*

The talk now was of nothing else. Arthur, Charlie
and Syd were all for giving their services. Syd
offered his cars to transport any of the old folk who
would have difficulty in getting to and from Central
Hall, Charlie put his own car at the organizers' disposal and also said he would come to the hall with
the girls early in the morning and help with any of
the more heavy type of jobs.

When the day arrived, Charlie made two trips
before nine o'clock in the morning, taking first the
girls down to the hall, where they were pleasantly
surprised to see about twenty other women already
there, about the same number of children and six
men, mostly retired costers. On the second trip,
Charlie brought Lucy, Raymond and Robert with
him, and everyone, kids and grown-ups alike, got
stuck in.

It was a long, hard day for all the helpers; many
more would have gladly been there to give a hand
but being so near to Christmas, trade was brisk in
the market and they had to be on their stalls. Placards
had been displayed for days stating that the market
would be closing at six o'clock that night but would
make up for it by remaining open every other night
until nine o'clock right up to the holiday. Every man
and woman who owned a stall would be coming
straight round to the hall as soon after six as possible
to help with the entertaining of the old folk.

The hall looked marvellous, hung with chains and

bunches of balloons, and holly and mistletoe adorned with tinsel hung in bunches from the walls.

At last dinner was over! Nobody quite knew how they had coped. It had fallen to Charlie to carve the large turkeys and to plate up the meat, while the women strained pots and pots of vegetables into dishes and did their best to keep everything piping hot while the guests had their oxtail soup.

Roars of approval had gone up as the male helpers carried in ten big, round puddings, all ablaze from a liberal soaking of brandy.

It was now seven o'clock and the women all breathed a sigh of relief as they stacked away the washed china and put the saucepans back in the cupboards. The men would take over completely now and they could have a well-earned drink, sit back and watch the fun.

Even the kerb-side barrow boys, who had their pitches outside the rear entrance to the market, had turned up to do their bit. While the band was being set up, two of these young lads came on to the stage with accordions strapped around their chests. They started the ball rolling by playing 'Maybe it's because I'm a Londoner' and there wasn't a silent voice in the hall. As the last notes died away someone shouted, 'It's old Lil's birthday.'

Instantly the men ran, forming a line in front of the raised stage, and with a nod from Fred Harris the music started to play and the men sang at the top of their voices: 'It's 'er blooming birthday, so wake up all the town, Oh, knees up, knees up, knees up, knees up, knees up, Muvver Brown'.

Suddenly all the chairs were vacant. Everyone was on their feet. Kids were in the middle as the old women lifted their skirts and bounced up and down to the music, urged on by the men who were clapping like mad. Not to be out-done, the band took over and within minutes the crowd was shouting 'Oi!' and stabbing the air with their raised thumbs as they sang and danced 'The Lambeth Walk'.

'Take a breather,' Fred told them as he announced that Maureen, who had the flower pitch, would now sing to them. You could have heard a pin drop in that vast hall as she sang 'I'll take you home again Kathleen, to where your heart will feel no pain'.

This was quickly followed by one of the young lads who gave them his version of 'I wanna girl, just like the girl that married dear old Dad'. Lizzie felt a great surge of tenderness fill her heart as she watched Charlie raise a white-haired lady to her feet and stand there, holding her hand. Oblivious of everyone, he sang, in a voice that tugged at every mother's heart, 'To that old-fashioned mother of mine' and as he finished he raised the lady's hand to his lips and gently planted a kiss on her fingers. It became too much for Lizzie, she burst into tears which only made Doris and Polly burst out laughing.

'Come on Syd!' Fred Harris called across the room as he watched Syd toss his head back and drain his pint glass. 'Yer turn ter give us a song.'

'This one's fer the kids,' Syd said into the mike, then, after wiping the back of his hand across his lips, he took a deep breath and began, 'There'll be pennies from heaven fer you an' me'. As he sang the words he tossed handfuls of pennies up into the air and of course the kids were running everywhere, dashing here and there, scrambling to see who could pick up the most. Minutes later, Robert held his hand out and said, 'I got seven, Uncle Syd.' 'I got twelve,' Raymond proudly told them.

'I only got three,' Lucy sadly announced. Doris bent her head and whispered into Raymond's ear. After a moment's hesitation he held out four pennies to Lucy and said, 'You have these, Lucy, then we've all got nearly the same.'

The lights were now turned down low; lanterns were lit, the band quietly played all the old Christmas carols and, as the old folk sang, imitation snow fell gently down on them from the rafters. It was a perfect end to the day.

It took a long while to help the old folks on with their coats and to organize which car or coach was taking them home. As they filed past the table behind which all the women helpers were lined up, each person was given a carrier-bag which contained a gift from every stall-holder in Tooting Market. There was everything from fruit, nuts, oranges and dates, right down to a packet of cocoa, a quarter of tea and packets of dried peas and haricot beans. A bar of chocolate hadn't been forgotten nor had bags of boiled sweets. There was even a two-bob voucher for each of them to change at the butchers.

'Won't buy 'em a turkey but it will buy the saus-age-meat for the stuffing,' Fred Harris had joked as the women had spent more than an hour packing those bags.

'Gawd bless yer,' was said over an over again as the folk accepted their gift and many leant across the table to give a hug and a kiss to the women who had helped to give them all such a happy day.

When Doris turned to Lizzie there were tears in her eyes. 'Did yer see the look on those old folk's faces as they peered into those carrier-bags?'

'Yeah,' said Lizzie.

For Lizzie, Christmas was a time of sheer enjoyment and high hopes. She wasn't lonely, she was sur-rounded by her family, friends and neighbours and to her that meant more than anything.

On Boxing Day they took the children to the pan-tomime, and the biggest thrill for the three sets of parents was to watch the expressions on their children's faces as they cheered the good fairy and booed and hissed the wicked uncle. Muffled up against the cold wind in brightly coloured woollen scarves and gloves, the kiddies faces shone with excitement as they waited at Wimbledon Broadway for the train that would take them home.

Next morning when Lizzie came out into the kitchen she couldn't find Charlie or Robert. She hadn't slept that late, it was only ten minutes to nine;

surely they hadn't gone up to the Common this time of the morning. But even before the kettle had come to the boil she heard the front door being opened and, poking her head out into the hallway, she saw Charlie coming in.

'Where's Robert?' she shot at him as he stood wiping his feet on the doormat. 'He's all right. Give us a chance ter get inside the door an I'll tell yer.'

When Charlie had taken his overcoat off and hung it on a peg in the hall, Lizzie was ready for him. 'Well where is he?' she demanded.

'I've told yer, he's all right. He's round at Syd and Doris's; I've asked them to 'ave him fer a while 'cos I want ter take you out somewhere.'

'Oh yeah? Well, you had me worried,' Lizzie grumbled. 'Why didn't yer wake me?'

'You were sleeping so peacefully. Anyway it's all settled now and I thought we might 'ave a run out ter Epsom, 'ave a bit of lunch out, 'cos I want the two of us ter 'ave a good talk.'

'On our own!' Lizzie laughed. 'What 'ave you got ter say ter me that is so important that you're going to wine an' dine me?'

'Who said anything about wine?' Charlie cut in loudly, putting his arm around her shoulder. 'Look, Lizzie, it's almost time for us ter go back ter Devon an' I don't want us two ter end up 'aving a screaming match. Far better if we clear off this morning, away from everyone, an' discuss our problems sensibly. Then it should be easy fer us ter work things out.'

'Easy!' Lizzie said sarcastically.

*

By the time Charlie had got the car out and they were on their way, they had both calmed down. The weather wasn't at all promising; it was bitterly cold and the dark grey clouds that filled the sky looked full of snow.

When they had left Sutton behind and were approaching Banstead Downs, the scenery was much more interesting. Although most of the trees had shed their leaves and just the long bare branches reached up to the sky, there were still several shrubs wrapped in glory, their foliage shining with rich dark colours made all the more beautiful against the stark background of winter.

At a quarter to one, Charlie drove the car into the forecourt of a hotel at Tattenham Corner. Lizzie excused herself to go to the toilet while Charlie went to the reception desk to request a table for two for lunch. Having combed her hair and refreshed her lipstick, Lizzie came out of the ladies' room to see Charlie standing waiting for her at the entrance to the bar. 'About twenty minutes before they'll 'ave a free table,' he told her, as he put his hand under her elbow and propelled her towards the bar. 'Might as well 'ave a drink while we're waiting.'

Lizzie walked to the other side of the room and stood staring out of the immense plate-glass windows. Even on a dull day like today the view was stunning. Epsom Race Course! Where great horse races such as the Derby and the Oaks were run.

'What yer standing up for?' Charlie's question

broke in on her thoughts. She smiled at him and he smiled back as they both chose a seat near the window. Charlie had finished his pint and Lizzie was just draining the last of her schooner of Bristol Cream when a waiter came to tell Charlie that their table was ready.

The dining-room was elegant, the food superb and they lingered so long over their meal that it was turned half-past two by the time they went into the lounge and found two empty chairs near the enormous fire-place in which a bright log fire was burning.

It was impossible to raise one's voice in such surroundings and in that respect Charlie had the advantage as he put his points to Lizzie.

'Spending three months in London is all very well,' he said softly, 'but coming back to live for good – is that what you really want, Lizzie?'

Lizzie made no answer as she picked up her cup and saucer and sipped her coffee. It seemed that Charlie expected none, for he went straight on talking in low tones. 'Have you given a thought ter Robert's schooling? There's his future to take into consideration. At the moment he's 'aving all the advantages you or I never 'ad.' Charlie paused and picked up his cup of coffee and the silence hung heavy between them for some while.

When, finally, Charlie spoke again he sounded even more serious, if that was possible. 'The prospects of me finding a job in London that will enable me ter provide you and Robert with all the things you've both become used to are pretty slim, wouldn't yer say? I 'aven't got a trade to fall back on.'

'Oh, Charlie,' Lizzie sighed. Her heart ached for him! And at that moment she felt she had been thoroughly selfish.

Again, the silence was long and Lizzie refilled their cups from the silver coffee-pot.

'By the way, it's about time you learned to drive.'

'What?' Lizzie had raised her voice and Charlie laughed at the expression on her face.

'It makes sense yer know. Why don't we give Devon a few more years, at least until Robert is older, see him off to college. As hoteliers we're not doing so bad are we? And if we get you driving you won't feel so isolated; you'll be able ter get out an' about a bit more. Even pop up ter yer brother's on yer own now an' again.' The last statement Charlie had said with a saucy grin on his face.

'Oh, I see! A sprat ter catch a mackerel, is it?' Lizzie asked and there was no smile on her face. 'Don't tempt me too much,' she said beneath her breath. To be honest she did see the benefits of all his arguments. To stay in Devon, at least for the time being, was certainly the wisest choice. Reluctantly, she admitted to herself she didn't have any alternative. They had put up with all the hardships and the rough times of being up to their ears in debt. Charlie was right, damn him, when wasn't he? They would have to be mad to walk away just when all their problems were being ironed out and they were becoming successful.

'All right,' she said grudgingly, 'but it's still the back of beyond and the seasons are bloody 'ard work.'

'Lizzie, if they cut your head off you'd still 'ave the last word!'

Chapter Twenty-Eight

NOW IT WAS time to start thinking seriously about yet another season.

Easter wasn't too far away and the hotel was fully booked for that long weekend. Charlie's time was taken up with repairs and decorating; he reckoned to paint and re-paper between six and eight bedrooms each winter. Lizzie's mornings were spent entirely in the office answering on average forty letters at a time.

Many were from previous guests with cheques enclosed to reserve a particular bedroom for their holiday. These, Lizzie would set aside. They could be answered and receipts sent later in the day; they were definite bookings. Any new mail, either enquiries from the Town Guide or recommendations, she answered straight away and had them back in the post by midday.

They had come to know only too well that hotel life was a highly competitive business. Only by working on the enquiries received, giving each one full personal attention, were they going to achieve the maximum amount of bookings.

To Lizzie, it now seemed a very long time since they had been to Bristol. All the legal formalities had been taken care of, but still she was barely able to contain her impatience.

Week followed week, and nothing seemed to be happening.

'You just have to be patient,' Charlie told her time and time again. 'They can't dig the footings while the ground is still freezing.'

Patience was not Lizzie's strong point.

When the thaw finally did set in and Michael Gale telephoned to say that work could now begin in earnest, Lizzie was up there on the site to see the machinery close in to start on the footings.

With the improvement on the roads, Lizzie was able to take her driving test. The whole village must have known she had passed! Driving back from Barnstaple in the green Austin 1100 that Charlie had bought for her and which Robert had immediately nick-named 'Brussel Sprout', the examiner's words were still loud in her head.

'Congratulations. I wish you many happy years of safe motoring.'

Approaching the hotel, she put her finger on the horn and kept it there until she reached the main entrance.

'Cocky, aren't we!' Charlie said, grinning from ear to ear.

With the season, came the usual problems. One morning, while doing her rounds, Lizzie heard the Hoover going but couldn't see where.

She opened a bedroom door. There, sitting on the bed, reading a magazine, was the young chambermaid who had only recently come to work at Highland Heights. The Hoover was plugged in and switched on, but stood there quite stationary.

'What are you doing?' Lizzie asked firmly.

No answer.

Lizzie looked around the room. Under the washbasin there was sand, the dressing-table was dusty and the towels needed to be changed.

The girl got to her feet and turned on Lizzie, practically screaming, 'The trouble with you is you think this hotel is a ruddy palace!'

Lizzie held her temper in check, but her big blue eyes flashed. In low-pitched, precise tones, she said, 'If it is, then I'm the queen that reigns here and your services are no longer required.'

The older, more conscientious chambermaids, who had worked for Lizzie since she had first taken over, were huddled together on the landing; they hadn't missed a word.

Lizzie heard what they said as she swept by. 'Missus must be in a good mood. Wonder she didn't grab that one by the scruff of the neck.'

Lizzie had to laugh to herself. They didn't know just how near she had come to doing just that.

In what free time they did get, Charlie usually opted to go for a swim, mainly in the sea, using the swimming baths in Ilfracombe only as a last resort if the weather was too foul.

Lizzie would drive out to the site. She was a bit disappointed in the early stages, the area of the footings looked so small.

'Not to worry, mi-dear,' the workmen told her, 'that be everyone's first impression.'

To get up there over the weekends was an impossibility. So, four or even five days might pass without Lizzie being able to pay a visit. Then the progress would be noticeable.

The framework developed at an amazing rate and the buildings began to develop character. At each stage, they were consulted by both Michael Gale and Mr Roberts, who wanted to know their preference for the interior work and design, even down to the smallest detail, such as door design for the garage.

Charlie and Lizzie thought it was great to be actively involved in the building of their house and each trip that Lizzie made out to the site could be guaranteed to bring her back to work in a very happy frame of mind.

Miraculously, by mid-August the house was completed.

Strangely, Lizzie lost the urge to visit it so often. The season was at its peak. Days for them both still had to start very early in the morning and finish very late at night, so, not surprisingly, their energy began to flag and they were often very tired by the end of the day.

But at last another season was over; it was the

second week in October and they were standing in
the grounds seeing the last coach party of guests off
on their homeward journey.

During the next few days, with the help of all
the staff, the hotel was shut down. Bedrooms were
closed up, silver cleaned and packed away, all
kitchen equipment scalded and thoroughly cleaned
and dust sheets thrown over furniture in the first-
floor lounge. The place took on an air of despondency.

Charlie paid off the staff, adding a bonus for each
of them and everyone was well satisfied.

The next few days were grim. Charlie wisely said,
'Don't rush things, breathe out. No one is so resilient that they can spring back to a normal way of life
after working seven days a week since last Easter.'

So they were lazy, sleeping a lot, eating when
they felt hungry, not watching the clock at all. Ten
days later, with batteries recharged, they were both
raring to go.

'Furniture for the house or a holiday?' Charlie
queried.

'What d'you think?' Lizzie asked, giving him a
smug look.

That evening they talked and talked, made lists
and wrote out suggestions as to what they would
like to buy for their new home, and the next morning they set off for Bideford to see Mr Channon.
This time they didn't need credit, they would pay
cash for whatever they purchased.

The memory had never dimmed for either Charlie or Lizzie. Mr Channon had not only treated them fairly, he had been an absolute brick. When all the odds had seemed stacked against the pair of them ever making a go of Sea View Guesthouse, he had shown faith and understanding. Neither of them would have dreamt of going to any other furniture store.

Lizzie had a whale of a time. She quickly chose a bedroom suite and a smaller, slightly more masculine suite for Robert's room. Upstairs in the showrooms, she bounced on beds and divans. Brass headboards? Wooden headboards? She couldn't make up her mind. In the end, she settled on newly imported continental ones, woodgrained to match the suites. One was nine feet wide with bedside tables attached and individual reading lights. Robert's was similar, but half the size.

The dining-room suite was also a relatively easy choice. Charlie liked good wood and traditional styles. Lizzie, in her imagination, was already seeing the oval table with its claw feet, set up and laid. Candles lit, a bowl of flowers set in the centre, she couldn't wait for them to eat their first dinner in their own dining-room.

There was still the question of what to put in that gigantic lounge. They sat on comfortable sofas and easychairs; nothing seemed right. Even with the addition of occasional tables and various lamps the room needed more than an ordinary three-piece suite.

'How about these?' Mr Channon asked, producing three glossy brochures.

This furniture was unique. Expensive for sure, but even Charlie exclaimed that he'd never seen anything like it before.

'It is going on show in London from next week. I've got swatches of colour and fabrics I can show you,' Mr Channon said.

Charlie made a snap decision. 'No, we'll go to London. I'd like to see the actual furniture, wouldn't you, Lizzie?'

'Not half I wouldn't,' she answered, thinking at the same time, a weekend in London, great!

Friday afternoon, with the car well packed, they were outside Adelaide College to meet Robert. Charlie broke their journey in Taunton where they all had a meal in a steak house. Soon they were on their way again and Robert was asleep. Lizzie, lulled by the steady motion of Charlie's driving, also began to doze.

Doris and Syd had the front door open before the car had stopped. Raymond practically dragged Robert out, and there were hugs and kisses for everyone.

At nine o'clock next morning, Charlie and Lizzie set off for the West End. Although it was Saturday, traffic seemed horrific and Charlie had great difficulty in finding somewhere to park.

The three gentlemen in the showrooms, most would say, looked the perfect image of success. To

Lizzie, they looked like tailors' dummies with their pin-striped trousers, cut-away dark grey jackets and starched white shirts.

One man stepped forward and introduced himself, 'Mr Westland, how may I help you?' He shook hands, but his fingers hardly touched Lizzie's. Yet, as he showed them around these expensive showrooms, Lizzie found herself liking this Mr Westland. He wasn't the cold fish she had first taken him for and neither was he stupid. He knew his job; he was intelligent and interesting to listen to.

See! She chided herself, you shouldn't be so quick to form an impression.

The furniture was upholstered in leather. Leather so soft and supple it felt like velvet. The design just as exciting as the brochure had promised. They chose an enormous settee, five-seater open-ended. It had a wide armrest at one end, the other end curved and rounded off to a half circular shape. Also a traditional three-seater settee together with two large, well-cushioned, deep armchairs.

Mr Westland was a little persuasive when it came to pouffes. 'One cannot imagine you would ignore them,' his rather grand voice beseeched as he ran his hand through his mop of blond curls. 'These are the *pièce de résistance.*'

They ordered two. Each three foot square; the top cushion, when removed, revealed a well-polished grained wood table top. 'Great for playing cards on,' Charlie commented.

'You'd have to sit on the floor to do so,' Lizzie retorted.

Import licences and delivery dates were discussed. The actual retailer would be Mr Channon of Bideford. Charlie asked several questions all of which Mr Westland answered with ease. Lizzie, in the end, felt that neither fire nor flood would ruffle that young gentleman's composure.

Saturday afternoon, Syd and Charlie took the two boys to watch Chelsea play an at-home football match, while Doris and Lizzie set off for Croydon and the shops.

At seven-thirty, a taxi came. They were off to the Selkirk Pub for a drink, taking the boys with them. 'Do they still have a children's room?' Lizzie asked Syd.

''Course they do.' Brother and sister grinned at each other, recalling the old days when they themselves had been kids.

Pushing through the swing doors at barely eight o'clock, the place was jam-packed. The band struck up; 'For he's a jolly good fellow' was sung with gusto. Everyone rushed towards Lizzie and Charlie. It was a party in their honour!

All their friends, and what few relatives that were left, were gathered there. Half the street where Lizzie had been born had turned out. Neighbours Lizzie only half remembered. She had forgotten what a cockney welcome could be like.

Lizzie was choked; fancy wanting to cry on such a happy occasion. What an evening! Drink flowed like water. The band never seemed to stop playing and Lizzie told herself over and over again how lucky she was.

On Sunday evening, Polly and Arthur had the two boys while Doris, Syd, Charlie and Lizzie went to Kensington. Flanagan's Restaurant had sawdust on the floor, and a menu chalked on an old blackboard. A pianist sitting at an upright piano belted out all the old songs non-stop.

Lizzie ordered skate and chips.

Charlie was astounded. 'You've never come all the way from Devon to the Royal Borough to eat fish 'n' chips?' he cried.

'It's not fish 'n' chips, it's skate 'n' chips,' Lizzie hurled back, smacking her lips in anticipation.

From Flanagan's, they took a taxi to the Victoria Palace. Tonight's performance was in aid of Jewish Benevolent funds. All the stars were giving their services free. For Lizzie, it was Ann Shelton who stole the show as she sang 'My Yiddisher Mamma' and there wasn't a dry eye in the house.

Monday came and it was back to north Devon.

'That was some weekend!' Charlie said as he shook hands with Syd.

'Yeah, wasn't it?' Doris whispered to Lizzie, as once more they hugged and said, 'See you soon.'

It took nearly a month for the carpets to be delivered and laid. Furniture arrived and was set out in appropriate rooms. A local lady had made the curtains, and Charlie put up curtain tracks and poles and saw to the hanging of them.

Lizzie became a constant visitor to the nearest garden centre. Vans drew up delivering shrubs, small trees, earthenware urns, tubs of all shapes and sizes, colourful hanging baskets, and bag upon bag of peat and John Innes' mixtures.

'Might as well bury money in the earth, the amount you spend,' Charlie grumbled, but Lizzie only smiled sweetly.

The actual day dawned; they were moving their personal belongings from the hotel into their own home.

By evening, the bungalow was filled with familiar, well-loved things and had really begun to feel like home.

Robert's bedroom looked lovely, with his belongings already scattered about and his books all set out on the shelves. The bathroom was a dream, everything co-ordinated, beautiful soft towels – none here with Highland Heights printed in red running through the middle.

Upstairs, the dining-room was to the right, perfect in every detail. Beyond was the kitchen, the only room in the whole house that did not give a view of the sea. It was, however, a cheerful, bright kitchen with large windows looking out over the steep sloping garden where several Christmas trees and other shrubs had been left intact and which Lizzie now thought of as their rural area.

The lounge was open and spacious, the end wall, apart from two foot on either side, was entirely glass, the centre being an enormous set of sliding doors which led on to the upper terrace. Running the whole width of the house, the terrace was so big that Lizzie remarked, 'You could hold a dance out there.'

The concrete paved slabs forming the base were alternately green and white and with the white ranch-style railings all around it looked splendid.

Charlie and Lizzie were very pleased.

Chapter Twenty-Nine

THE NEW YEAR of 1958 was only a few weeks old and every morning Lizzie's first job was to sort and answer the mail.

'Has the postman been yet?' Lizzie called up the stairs to Charlie.

'I haven't heard him but I'm just gonna pick the paper up, I'll bring the mail down if he has.'

Two minutes later Lizzie heard Charlie shout, 'Oh no!' The tone of his voice was so distressed that Lizzie ran to the foot of the basement stairs. 'Charlie,' she called loudly, 'are you all right?'

'Yes, Yes, I'm coming down. I won't be a minute.'

Lizzie was halfway up the stairs before she could see him walking very slowly across the entrance hall with the newspaper opened wide and his head bent low as he read. Lizzie hurried to see the headlines. There had been an air crash in West Germany. The whole of the Manchester United football team had been on board.

They sat facing each other at the kitchen table and listened to the news being relayed over the wireless net-work. The crash had happened because the plane had failed to clear a fence on take-off; the weather was foul and the rescue workers were being ham-pered by driving snow. Charlie looked thoroughly dejected, eight members of the team were among the twenty-one dead. Lizzie got up and went to the gas-stove. 'I'll make us a coffee,' she said as she filled a saucepan with milk and put it on to heat.

'Poor old Matt Busby,' Charlie said half to himself. 'He's a damn good manager, he's become so popular that the team has been nick-named the "Busby Babes". Eight of the boys dead! It's not fair!'

All day Charlie couldn't get it out of his mind and Lizzie let him rattle on about football because it seemed to make him feel better to talk about it. On the six o'clock evening news they heard that Matt Busby had been seriously injured in the crash. 'It's not bloody fair,' was all that Charlie could mutter.

Life went on and Lizzie concentrated on getting as many bookings as possible for what would be their fifth season in Highland Heights Hotel. With the coming of the very busy weeks of July and August the weather was as good as it had been bad at the beginning of the year, which was fine for the visitors but not so good for the hotel workers. A veritable heatwave had the beaches and the surrounding little coves packed with holidaymakers. The hotel kitchens became unbearable as the scorching sun beat down relentlessly.

Lizzie sighed with relief one Monday evening about nine o'clock when Charlie switched off both ovens and the hot plate.

'I think I'll come home with you, love, for an

hour or so, there's plenty of staff on duty.' Charlie
sounded really done in.

They walked in silence to the garage. Lizzie
backed her car out first, then Charlie did the same,
taking to the road first while Lizzie drove home
behind him.

Dawn had hardly come and Lizzie was up again,
after a hot, restless night.

On the upper terrace they kept a set of wrought-
iron garden furniture, four chairs, table with centre
umbrella and two sun-beds. She carried out the
green and white striped mattresses, returning
indoors to fetch the matching seat-cushions for the
chairs.

A breakfast of toast, marmalade and orange juice,
eaten out on the veranda, and Lizzie felt much
better.

The sky was a clear blue; the heat was still there
and it seemed certain to be another hot day. In the
silence all she could hear was the gentle whirring of
a lawnmower and even that seemed miles away.

It was almost ten o'clock and Lizzie stood by the
railings looking down the hill and beyond to the sea.
She saw Doctor Whittaker's car coming along the
lower road; there was no mistaking it – a dark green
MG sports car, roof down. He slowed, tooted his
horn and waved. Lizzie raised her cupped hand to
her mouth and mimed, drink. He tooted his horn
again and gave a thumbs-up sign.

Lizzie had first met Jeffrey Whittaker while

delivering meals on wheels with the WVS. He wasn't their family doctor, he belonged to a panel of three doctors.

The WVS covered a wide area, including many outlying villages. The volunteer women often saved the doctors a journey by delivering a package or even reporting to them how the elderly folk were getting along.

Although quite young in comparison to the other doctors, Jeffrey Whittaker was conscientious about his work. Unmarried, scrupulously clean yet never formally dressed, he mainly wore slacks with sporty-type shirts and, when necessary, a zip-up jacket. He would come bounding into the building where the WVS ladies cooked and packed the dinners, and so invigorating was his attitude that Lizzie always half expected him to call out, 'Anyone for tennis?'

Everyone was on first-name terms with this young doctor. But only being able to do voluntary work during the winter months, it was weeks since Lizzie had had a chance to talk to him.

She heard his car park below, in front of their garage. He used the outside staircase which brought him directly up on to the terrace without going into the house.

'Gee! This is absolutely marvellous, Lizzie,' he exclaimed as he threw himself down on to one of the sun-beds.

'Yeah, fantastic,' Lizzie called back as she went inside to make the coffee.

He must have noticed the weariness in her voice

because, as she came out and put the tray with the coffee cups and saucers on to the table, he gently asked, 'Everything not right with your world?'

'Oh, don't mind me, Jeff, I didn't sleep that well last night, that's all.'

He sat up straight and proceeded to pour out the coffee. 'Milk and sugar? Help yourself,' he stated as he handed a cup to Lizzie.

She had to laugh. Talk about making yourself at home. He certainly was an easy person to be with.

She glanced at her wristwatch, 'What are you doing out so early, Jeff? No surgery this morning?'

'I've been out to Combe Martin. The church camping site. You know the big hut come hall; the scouts use it and the girl guides. Well, they've got a party of young boys staying in there this week. Managing well really, mattresses on the floors. Hotels, guesthouses, cafes all mucking in, helping to give the little lads a free holiday.'

He stopped talking, took out his handkerchief and wiped his forehead. 'It's hot again, isn't it? I can't remember it being as hot as this. When this weather does break we'll have such a storm.'

'Jeff,' Lizzie grasped his arm, 'go on, tell me more about those boys.'

'Well, they probably come from your part of the world or near enough. East End of London, some home, not Doctor Barnardo's, but similar, can't recall the name. You'd have laughed, Lizzie, climbing about the rocks wearing thick, knee-length socks, heavy laced-up shoes, most likely they've never seen the sea before.'

Lizzie winced, 'Thick socks on a day like this? Who's in charge of them?'

'Four men.'

'I might have guessed that.'

'Now hold on, Lizzie, I doubt even you could have got those youngsters to part with their clothing. You should have heard them; they were in their element but still highly suspicious of change or anyone that wanted to do things for them.'

Lizzie's mind took her back in time. Charlie had spent his childhood in an orphanage. When she had first met him, he had been starved of love, yearning for a home to call his own. Look what they had now. She thought of the advantages her son had and then she got cross with herself. Seeing the anger appear on Lizzie's face, Doctor Whittaker wondered whether he had gone too far.

'Have I upset you, Lizzie?'

'Hell, no. There's me wallowing in self-pity all night, worried sick because Charlie was so tired, and there's those unfortunate kids out there glad of a free holiday.'

Jeffrey Whittaker smiled to himself, he had achieved what he wanted to; it had helped to snap Mrs Wilson out of what could have been a nasty spell of depression, had it gone on too long.

Aloud he said, 'You mustn't blame yourself, Lizzie. You and Charlie are both hard workers. You put the maximum effort into every job you tackle.

Now you're both strung up like overwound clock-springs. It'll be September come next Monday, season will soon be over. Book yourselves a holiday; best tonic in the world having something to look forward to.'

Later, when Jeffrey Whittaker left, he tooted the horn of his car and Lizzie stood leaning over the balcony until he was out of sight.

What a kind, caring person he is, she said to herself as she went indoors and picked up the telephone.

'Please, Charlie,' Lizzie pleaded, 'I'll come down to the hotel when we get back. Help get the dinners through. I don't need the evening off.'

'All right. I'll organize it,' his reply came quiet and firm over the line, 'be at the foot of the hill; I'll make it by a quarter to two.'

She had told Charlie everything that Jeffrey Whittaker had told her and really he hadn't hesitated for a second.

The couple of hours that she and Charlie spent out at Combe Martin would remain vivid to Lizzie for a very long time. Charlie had met the organizer of the party, established the name of the children's home and offered a week's holiday to a party of children for the following year at Highland Heights. He had also been to the local haberdashery shop.

'You're too late,' a beaming shop assistant told him. 'Local people have already bought up our entire stock of swimming trunks for the boys. My guvnor has gone to Barnstaple to get some more.'

Lizzie had to smother her sobs as she watched Charlie romp with a couple of five year olds and her heart almost burst with love as she watched him quietly hand some notes over to one of the men in charge.

'See they have a few ice-creams and what nots,' he said in a voice that was barely audible.

Chapter Thirty

'COMING WITH ME tonight?' Charlie asked enthusiastically.

Lizzie was doubtful. Darts matches in Devon were sombre affairs compared with those in London. No food provided, no dancing afterwards, in fact, few wives bothered to accompany their husbands.

On the other hand, this match was being held at The Foxhunter's Inn, a rather lovely road house well out in the country. Young Robert was going to play water polo, they could pick him up on the way back.

'Yes, all right,' she agreed, having weighed up all the pros and cons.

Just as she thought, she was the only woman.

'You don't want to stay in this public bar,' Charlie whispered rather sheepishly. 'Go through to the lounge, I'll bring you a drink.'

She had finished her drink and was sitting, idly looking through the evening paper, when she heard a loud cheer go up in the public bar.

'Is that the first leg over?' Lizzie asked as Charlie came through the archway carrying a fresh drink for her. With him was the captain of the team Charlie played for, Harry Baldwin, well known to Lizzie

because it was he who delivered fresh fruit, salad
stuff and vegetables to their hotel during the season.

'Harry's been telling me there's to be an auction
at Rillage View,' Charlie said as he placed the glass
and a fresh bottle of dry ginger down on to the
brass-topped table.

'Coming up soon it be, Mrs Wilson. Several
properties, contents an' all. Make a nice day out it
will. Shall us be seeing 'ee there?'

'More than likely,' Lizzie smiled as she answered.
She liked Harry, no side with him. A good-natured,
down-to-earth sort of bloke.

Rillage View was a local landmark, a very old type
of hotel standing high up on what was known as
Harbour View Terrace. Difficult to gain access to,
the road being narrow and steeply winding, but
once there, as its address implied, you had a com-
manding view of the harbour.

On the morning of the sale they laughed at each
other, both had opted to wear what they described
as their country outfits. Charlie had on cavalry twill
trousers, a suede-fronted jerkin and a Harris tweed
sports coat.

'You look every inch a squire,' Lizzie scoffed at
him.

'You'd pass at a horse show,' he retaliated.

'Thanks a bunch,' Lizzie said as she half turned to
check herself in the hall mirror. She wasn't too
happy with the low-heeled shoes she was wearing,
but she liked the heather-coloured woven costume.

The pale lavender cashmere jumper with its high neck toned in extremely well, 'At least I think it does,' she muttered, determined not to let Charlie put her off.

'Well,' Charlie made a mocking bow, 'Rillage View, here we come.'

Within minutes of their arrival Lizzie had lost Charlie. She wandered off into the hall and up the staircase. Every item of furniture she passed was marked with a lot number. Looking in through the doorway of each room, Lizzie found it all unbelievable. Everything looked as if it had come out of the Ark.

Having got to the top floor and been really nosey, peeking in all the corners and opening cupboard doors, Lizzie began making her way downstairs. She had to be very careful since the staircase was not only very narrow, it twisted and turned quite sharply at every landing. She reached the first floor and was frightened for a moment; not only was the landing crowded with people, but, looking over the banister rail, she saw that the staircase was also jam-packed.

The auction had started. Lots were being sold from exactly where the various items were situated. Presumably the ground-floor contents had all been disposed of and the auctioneer was moving upstairs to start on the sale of bedroom furniture.

It was like a stampede. Lizzie panicked. There was no way she could possibly get through that crowd. She felt herself being half pushed, half carried into a bedroom. Packed like a sardine, she couldn't move. The auctioneer climbed up on to a wide window sill and the sale carried on. Small objects were held high in the air by men in brown overalls, while large items were pointed to with the aid of a long cane. The auctioneer's gavel fell with monotonous regularity as each article went to the highest bidder.

Lizzie looked around; the room was very large. One double bed, two single beds, each having old-fashioned brass rails at the head and foot. Large cumbersome furniture. A marble-topped wash-stand complete with an ornamental china jug and bowl. God help the chambermaids who had to work in this hotel, Lizzie thought to herself.

Suddenly, Lizzie felt a tug at the hem of her skirt. Moving her feet and knees as much as was possible, she looked down. Charlie's face was peering up at her.

'What the hell are you doing?' she uttered almost under her breath.

He was on his haunches almost underneath the double bed. 'Bid, bid!' he ordered in an undertone.

'What?'

'Don't ask questions, just bid for this carpet,' he hissed.

She glanced at her programme. The carpet was lot number 315. Now she paid attention. 'Lot three one three, a unique pair of vases . . . ' the auctioneer's voice droned on.

Only two lots to go.

'Three one five, ladies and gentlemen, the carpet

on three one three which you are standing.' There was a general shuffling of feet as folk attempted to look down.

'Who will start me off with a fiver?'

Lizzie was too nervous to do anything; three bids had been taken, her skirt was being yanked at again.

She didn't bother to look down, just raised her programme high in the air. Two counterbids were made, each time Lizzie waved her programme.

'Going, going, gone,' the gavel fell. 'Name?'

'Mrs Wilson,' Lizzie said in a voice that didn't sound a bit like her own.

Lot number 315 was hers, whether she wanted it or not.

The crowds moved on and Lizzie made her escape – down the winding stairs and out into the fresh air. Within ten minutes, Charlie had joined her.

'Dirty old carpet,' she shot at him straight away, 'what in the world do we want it for?'

'That's a *real* carpet. One hundred per cent pure wool Wilton. Cost a fortune to buy one that size today. All it needs is cleaning, you'll see. Got our-selves a great bargain there.'

Lizzie gave up. No use arguing about it now, was there!

'Come on, we'll have lunch. Nothing I'm interested in now, not until this afternoon.'

The brightness in Charlie's eyes and the colour in his cheeks as he grinned at her told Lizzie that he was more than pleased with his purchase.

Charlie drove the car down to what was the only

public house on the harbour. Lizzie sat outside on
the quayside while Charlie went into the pub. The
fishing boats were in, unloading basketfuls of shining herrings and pots which held struggling crabs
and lobsters. Huge gulls were screeching overhead,
swooping in low for scraps, and yet the whole harbour had a peaceful air.

They had crusty bread, local cheese and big pickled onions to eat, washed down by cool, sparkling
lager, and were back at Rillage View by a quarter to
two.

The afternoon's sale was to be conducted in the
original dining-room. A makeshift platform had
been set up at one end, with rows of chairs placed
in front, most of which were already taken. Charlie
led Lizzie to where there was a single empty seat on
the end of a row by the middle aisle.

'What about you?' she asked.

'I'll be all right,' Charlie answered, 'I'm just going
to have a word with the auctioneers.'

There were more than a dozen men clustered in
front of the platform. Charlie was soon in their
midst, having quite an animated conversation with
two of them.

'Wonder what he is up to now?' Lizzie asked herself.

To one side of the room, two men were seated at
a table with lots of legal-looking papers spread out
in front of them. One man was quite old, the other,
barely thirty, was writing with his head bent low,
intent upon what he was doing.

'Solicitor and his clerk,' the woman sitting next to Lizzie obligingly said, nodding her head in the direction of the two men.

What are they here for? Lizzie wanted to ask, but merely murmured, 'Thank you.'

Groups of men were standing around the sides of the room, some talking so loudly that Lizzie thought they were having an argument.

Suddenly, the auctioneer rapped loudly with his gavel, and all the men made a general movement to the back of the hall. Lizzie couldn't see where Charlie had got to.

Now there was complete silence in the large room.

'Before the commencement of this sale, I must impress upon you all the legality of these proceedings.' The gentleman conducting this part of the sale was totally different from the previous auctioneer.

His voice was that of a well-educated gentleman, although to look at him, he seemed a typical north Devon farmer. A real open-air type of man, his tweed jacket had leather patches at the elbows, his shirt was open at the neck and he wasn't wearing a tie.

'The highest bidder to whom each property will be sold must be prepared to sign contracts this afternoon and pay to the vendor a deposit of ten per cent of the selling price which will be irretrievable.'

He paused, consulted his programme and went on, 'Mr Button, the gentleman on my right, is acting for each and all of the vendors. We have five properties to be disposed of this afternoon, so if you are all clear in your minds as to the legal points, we will make a start.'

There was a shuffling of feet, a clearing of throats, and the auction began.

'Lot number one. Agricultural land known as Dene's End.'

Lizzie lost interest. She looked around the room. All the furniture had been pushed aside leaving the floor space free. It was all heavy-framed dark wood pieces now bearing 'Sold' labels.

There was an extremely large glass-fronted book-case filled with books which were so dusty they looked as if they hadn't been taken down from the shelves for years, never mind opened and read.

The auctioneer startled Lizzie, his voice got louder, his movements more rapid. 'T'be done, t'be done, t'be done. Sold to Mr Hutchinson,' his gavel fell loud and final.

'Look at your programmes, ladies and gentlemen, lot number two, Hampton Cross Farm.'

Only two serious bidders, same procedure, it was all over.

'Lot number three, known as Ivy Cottage, Larks Lane, and number one, Leigh Lane.' Murmurings came from the audience.

'That's perfectly correct,' the auctioneer said. 'This cottage does in actual fact have two postal addresses. Dilapidated, needs renovating, will take low bid to start.'

Very quiet now, no takers. Lizzie was reading her

programme. The two addresses had intrigued her. She heard the auctioneer plead for someone to start the bidding, but it was slow and she wasn't taking much notice.

'The bidding is against you, Mr Wilson.'

Wilson, did he say Wilson? There was no mistaking this time as she heard the auctioneer say, 'Thank you, Mr Wilson.'

Lizzie jerked her head round so quickly her neck snapped and it hurt. She still couldn't see Charlie. She twisted the other way, still no sign of him. Too many men crushed together at the back of the room.

The gavel fell again with a firm, loud bang.

'Sold to Mr Wilson of Highland Heights.'

Lizzie sat through the rest of the sale in a daze. Charlie had done some daft things in his time, but this beat the lot. Lovely new split-level bungalow built especially for them and he goes and buys a run-down ramshackle old cottage.

The sale was finished and refreshments were being offered. Lizzie pushed her way through and made for the car. She couldn't really analyze her feelings.

She saw Charlie coming and wrenched open the car door. Even before he reached her, she yelled, 'You've just bought a cottage!'

'I know.'

'I know you know. What I want to know is what you are intending to do with it?'

People were looking. She knew she was being stupid.

'Don't be so emotional,' Charlie rebuked her.

Well! That was like showing a red rag to a bull. 'We haven't even seen the place. Come to that, I don't even know where it is, don't suppose you do either. It's got to be derelict, nobody else wanted it. Did you have it surveyed? No, 'course you didn't. You're the great man, Charlie Wilson.'

'Calm down,' Charlie said very quietly, 'trust me. I'll tell you all about it later. Come back inside and countersign the contract.'

'What?' Lizzie was off again. '*You* bought the bloody cottage; *you* sign the bloody contract.'

'God give me patience!' In exasperation, Charlie grabbed her arm and his words to her now were hissed through teeth that were almost clenched. 'This property has been bought by the company. It is an investment. I should have discussed it with you, but I didn't. I'm sorry. None the more for that, it's done. The company has purchased it, and that means you, Lizzie, as well as me. Joint company directors. You and me. Now, will you please sign the contract?'

Lizzie jerked her arm away from his hold; he had said sorry, probably for the first time in his life. Still, that didn't alter things much. He was still an impulsive know-all.

'You haven't left me much option,' Lizzie said, still showing ill-feeling as she walked away.

They each signed the contract, Lizzie wrote out a

cheque for the ten per cent deposit and Charlie signed it.

'You've made a good buy today,' Mr Button said as he took hold of Lizzie's hand. 'I've known Ivy Cottage since I was a lad. Sadly neglected, very sad, but its structure is sound.' Wistfully he turned away to shake Charlie's hand.

'Wise decision, young man, so near to your own hotel. It would have been a mistake to let it go to others.' For the first time, Charlie smiled.

'Thanks, Mr Button, thanks for your help.'

Lizzie watched and waited while Charlie took his leave of several men. 'What now?' she asked as they walked to the car.

It was a foolish question, she knew. Mr Button's comments had aroused her curiosity but her pride would not let her question Charlie outright.

He didn't answer her, but as he held the car door open for her, he said, 'I'm sorry, Lizzie.'

Two apologies in one afternoon, she smiled briefly. 'I am too.'

Before starting up the engine, Charlie placed his hand on Lizzie's knee. She dropped her head a little and clenched her hands together in her lap. She was fed up. Charlie was headstrong and her own temperament wasn't all it should be. That was the whole damn trouble, they clashed.

'Lizzie, look at me.'

She raised her eyes and Charlie chuckled, 'Perhaps you would like to see this cottage?'

They had almost reached the hotel when Lizzie exclaimed, 'I thought you were going to show me this cottage.'

'I am. We'll leave the car in the hotel drive.'

Lizzie was even more confused now.

When the car stopped, Charlie was out and off down the hill like an excited ten year old, his dark hair fluffed up high by the breeze as he ran.

'Come on, run!' he yelled back over his shoulder, and Lizzie found herself doing just that.

She stood there panting, her chest still heaving as she gasped for breath.

Minutes passed and still she could hardly believe it.

Finally, she turned to Charlie, amazement uppermost in her voice. 'I must have passed Leigh Lane hundreds of times. I had no idea that there was a cottage here.'

'Well, you know now,' Charlie said, grinning broadly, 'and what's more, it belongs to us.'

Lizzie stepped back and scrutinized the cottage. It looked as if it hadn't been occupied for years. The windows had odd pieces of wood nailed together covering them. Even the roof was covered with what looked like boards and a waterproof sheet.

Suddenly, she couldn't help herself, she burst out laughing. It was hilarious, it had to be a joke; she laughed so much she had a stitch in her side. Her laughter was infectious.

'You can scoff,' Charlie said as he, too, let out a great belly laugh, 'this place will make us a fortune.'

For once in her life Lizzie kept her mouth shut and listened with deep interest to what Charlie was saying as he sat opposite her at the dinner-table.

'I knew I could buy it for next to nothing and, as Mr Button said, I would have been mad to let it go to somebody else. Staff quarters!'

The sharp and sudden explanation had Lizzie wanting to bombard him with a dozen questions, but no, she still kept silent. Charlie waited for her outburst and grinned when none was forthcoming.

He continued, 'We're losing money in the hotel. Since we've had our bungalow built our private rooms hardly get used. Then there are the three rooms downstairs taken up by staff living in. That's why it is money well spent, that cottage will pay for itself over and over again.'

I must be thick as two planks, Lizzie thought to herself. She couldn't keep quiet any longer.

'So you do that cottage up. Probably cost us a bomb just to make it habitable. Then, you use it as sleeping quarters for the staff? Have I got things right so far?'

'Yes,' Charlie confirmed.

Lizzie smiled at him brightly, then, with a sigh, asked, 'How will the cottage ever make money if we are only going to use it to sleep staff in?' Lizzie put down her knife and fork. 'You are deliberately trying to rile me, Charlie, you know I haven't got the foggiest what you're on about. You just keep throwing out scraps of information, and you sit there watching me get more and more confused.'

'OK, OK,' Charlie threw his hands up in mock surrender. 'Pour me a cup of coffee and I promise I will explain everything, down to the last detail. The huge ground floor dining-room could easily be divided into five bedrooms. All would have sea views and, being on the ground floor, they would be easy to let during the summer and absolutely invaluable for the coach parties of old folk. Do you agree?'

'Yes, of course I do,' Lizzie said but she couldn't keep a hint of sarcasm from her voice as she asked, 'then, just what do we use as a dining-room?'

Charlie thrust out his chest as he delivered his masterpiece. 'All the lower ground-floor rooms beyond the kitchens we turn into a complete new dining-room.'

Excitement now showing on his face, Charlie got up and came round the table, drew Lizzie to her feet and hugged her.

Speechless, absolutely stunned, that's how Lizzie felt. The very idea staggered her. Finally, she did manage to mutter, 'Charlie, you're forever conniving some new scheme.'

Now Charlie held her closer, eagerly as if he would never let her go. 'It will all work out fine, you'll see,' he assured her, and as Lizzie broke free from his arms, she believed him. His eyes were brilliant, he was smiling his loving smile, his whole mood was frank, even boyish, and he was certainly very pleased with himself.

Next morning, Lizzie was awake early. She got out of bed quietly and went upstairs.

The kitchen clock said five minutes to five. She made a pot of tea, drank several cups and was bathed and dressed by the time Charlie came upstairs.

'Seldom seen you ready to go so early in the day,' was Charlie's greeting as he kissed her cheek. 'Can't you wait to get cracking?'

Breakfast was all ready and as they sat eating Charlie seemed so calm and self-assured that Lizzie kept trying to smother her giggles.

They say nothing ventured, nothing gained, but boy, this was some venture even for Charlie!

The kitchen was bright and cheery, the windows were open and, although the breeze was fresh, there was a bite in the air – a sure sign winter was coming again.

Lizzie thought of the hard winter they had experienced the year that they had had this split-level bungalow built, and silently she prayed that this new venture they were about to embark on would turn out just as successfully.

Glancing at his watch, Charlie said, 'Come on, get your coats on, time to go.'

At the first stop they dropped Robert off at school, and at the second stop, the offices of Roger Farrant their now long-term solicitor and friend.

'Success breeds success, eh Mrs Wilson?' Mr Farrant said warmly as he shook hands with them both and offered his congratulations. Lizzie's smile deepened, she liked coming to this office. She sniffed the smell of good leather upholstery as she sat down on a high-backed chair and listened to what the men were saying.

'Mr Harding will present the company accounts to the bank, no problem there,' Roger Farrant confirmed.

Lizzie's thoughts again went back over the past. The bank had been marvellous, helping them at every turn. Without their help, they could never have achieved so much. In the early years, though, it hadn't exactly been easy or without anxiety trying to borrow money. Yet now, it seemed, Charlie had only to ask and further loans would be granted.

Roger Farrant was right, success must breed success.

As always, Lizzie felt the urge to kiss Mr Farrant as they said goodbye.

He still had that flirtatious manner about him as he held her hand longer than was necessary and said in that soft drawl, 'We'll meet again soon.'

Charlie swung the bunch of very odd-looking keys.

'What will it be, coffee or a drink to celebrate?'

'Celebrate what? Our personal disaster?' Lizzie asked, but she smiled as she spoke.

'Pessimist,' Charlie taunted.

They settled for a quick cup of coffee in a nearby restaurant. Lizzie wanted to get to Ivy Cottage as quickly as possible. She fervently hoped it would look better in broad daylight, but her hopes were not fulfilled. If anything, it looked worse!

There was a short rise of steps leading to the front door. Charlie went up these and tried several keys from the bunch, all to no avail. One large key he was able to turn, but even with his shoulder to the door it wouldn't budge.

Looking down over the steps, they saw what they thought was a basement, but which had been detailed in their programme of sale as the ground floor with an address of Ivy Cottage, Larks Lane.

'This door must be bolted from the inside,' Charlie said. 'Now all we have to do is find Larks Lane.'

They walked further down the hill, turned a sharp corner and eventually discovered Larks Lane. Neither of them had been aware of its existence before.

Originally, the pathway must have been coarse cobbles. Now it was covered with a thick growth of moss. The surface was wet and slimy and Lizzie was afraid of slipping. Quite clearly, they heard the sound of water gurgling and bubbling. On one side of the lane, overgrown bushes were forming a fence, even a barrier, and into these Charlie thrust his arm, making a parting. He had discovered a brook. Rushing along, crystal clear, the water flashed and sparkled.

'Oh, it's lovely to watch,' Lizzie declared as Charlie let go of the branches and they fell together again.

It was quite a walk further on before they reached the cottage. Lizzie stood and looked silently at this old dwelling.

'Gran,' she whispered to herself, and then she had to moisten her lips with her tongue. She couldn't have explained her feelings at that moment, not for all the tea in China! It was nothing like Gran's immaculate cottage in Silverdore, and yet it brought memories flooding back. It had the same air of tranquility. Lizzie began to feel optimistic.

It had a front garden, albeit in an extremely overgrown state. They had virtually to fight their way through masses of green foliage and numerous tangled shrubs and bushes.

The front door was almost completely concealed by foliage and Charlie had to clear many branches away before he was able, this time, to turn the key and open the door.

It appeared that this door opened directly into the kitchen. Cobwebs were everywhere.

'It's so gloomy and dusty; put the light on,' Lizzie called to Charlie.

'There isn't electricity in the house, nor gas,' came his answer. 'No water either.'

Dear God! Lizzie didn't believe him.

Taking candles and a box of matches out of his coat pocket, he laughed as he said, 'See? I've come prepared.'

Lizzie was at a loss for words.

Charlie lit several candles. It didn't make much improvement. The guttering sounds from them seemed weird and they sent shadows flickering around the walls. But soon their eyes became accustomed to the gloom.

All the walls appeared to have been painted but

had become so dirty that whatever paint had been used was now an indistinguishable grey.

There was a fair-sized kitchen with an old-fashioned, coal cooking range, on which still stood a large soot-blackened kettle.

Above the range, a high overmantel took up one wall and each side of the range was flanked by two deep cupboards.

'Have them out and you could have two lovely inglenook seats,' Charlie said.

Lizzie wrinkled her nose in disgust and didn't bother to answer.

The centre of the kitchen was taken up by a table. It was a mystery to Lizzie how it had ever got to be in that room. Certainly not through that low, narrow doorway. It must have been there forever. It was thick with dust but she could see that over the years it had been well scrubbed.

Under the small window, which they couldn't see out of because the panes were so dirty, was an old brown china sink, badly cracked and very chipped. Two built-in cupboards underneath the sink didn't look much better.

From the kitchen, a stone-floored corridor led to the only other room on this level, a preparation room of sorts which housed two enormous walk-in larders.

A short flight of steps led up to the ground floor. Charlie's assumption had been right; the front door was bolted and barred from the inside. There were two rooms on this floor, both dirty and bare.

Another short flight of stairs and they came to two bedrooms. These rooms seemed brighter with windows front and back.

'It's because they are on a higher level,' Charlie said, 'they get more daylight.'

One thing Lizzie did like about these two rooms was that each had a small outside balcony, skirted by a wrought-iron trellis, well in keeping with what she was by now thinking of as their rustic cottage.

Coming out into the garden again, having finished their tour of inspection, the daylight was so bright after the gloom inside that, for a few moments, Lizzie had to shield her eyes. Charlie was busy pulling brambles and other prickly hedge plants away from an old garden shed.

Lizzie picked her way cautiously through weeds and stinging nettles to join him as he cleared the door to the shed and, with a tug, opened it.

Inside was a lavatory pan. Spread across the top were wooden planks forming a seat, in the middle of which was a circular hole. They looked at each other and fell about laughing.

A few feet away stood another creeper-covered shed. Charlie hesitated a second before lifting the rusty latch.

Surprise, surprise. It was a wash-house. It had a sink and one tap, which Lizzie couldn't turn but Charlie did. It spluttered into life spitting out filthy rust-coloured water.

'Marvellous,' Lizzie said, 'I had visions of having to draw water up from an underground well.'

'You might have to yet,' Charlie said with a grin. There was a large copper and across the far wall, wooden slats were fitted, like rungs of a ladder.

'Marvellous,' Lizzie said again. 'We could do the hotel washing in here. Hang it all up there to dry and air.'

Charlie swiftly came to where she was standing and grabbed her. 'Any more bright ideas like that and I'll put you in that copper and put the lid on.'

Lizzie tried to wriggle away from his grasp but he held on to her tightly. 'Two kisses before I let you go,' he said.

'I knew you were mad,' she retorted.

It didn't matter one jot that Charlie's suit was covered in dust, that his hair looked as if birds had nested in it and that one of Lizzie's stockings now had a long ladder in it. They had each other and that was enough.

Chapter Thirty-One

WORK COMMENCED ON the cottage first. This would enable the furniture from the staff rooms to be transferred, leaving the entire area clear for the dining-room.

Top two priorities were the roof and electricity. The roofers did a grand job. Two days and they were finished.

It turned out that the roof was structurally quite sound. The steeper upper part needed no attention; the lower part had several slates which had worked loose and quite a few that needed replacing.

The gas company declined to run a supply to such a remote area unless Charlie agreed to bear the whole of the cost. He came to the conclusion it would be far cheaper to rely solely on electricity.

The electricians were very efficient. Lizzie constantly took them hot drinks and certainly didn't envy those men their job. Just taking up all those old floorboards seemed hazardous and dangerous to her. When they had finished the job, Charlie said he was well pleased, although Lizzie thought that the new white power-points looked out of place on the ancient skirting boards.

Next came the plumber – just one local man who had previously done work for Charlie.

As well as running a water supply into the cottage, installing an inside toilet, and turning one of the walk-in larders into a shower cubicle, he also replaced the old cracked sink with a gleaming stainless-steel unit above which the electricians positioned an electric water heater.

Now the job of cleaning the whole place right through could begin.

Three of their regular chambermaids said they were only too willing to help, even though Lizzie stressed how dirty the work would be. So at nine o'clock on a Monday morning, the three of them set off from the hotel with Lizzie.

'A right bunch you look,' Charlie joked and he had to duck to avoid being hit by a brush which Lizzie threw at him.

He was right though, they did look peculiar! All four women had their hair tied up in turbans, and they all wore old slacks. Armed with buckets, scrubbing brushes, numerous cloths and old rags, they made their way down the hill. It was an unanimous decision for each of them to tackle a separate room rather than the four of them working together in a restricted area.

By midday, all the windows of the cottage were flung wide open and the women had worked really hard. Charlie came and was warmly welcomed, for he had brought with him ham and cheese rolls and two large flasks of coffee.

They ate, sitting on upturned boxes in the garden. The weather was kind – a good drying day with a stiff wind and pale sunshine. They didn't feel cold, for the overgrown hedges gave great protection from the wind, and they all agreed that it had been a satisfying day.

'It being so dirty, us is bound to see an improvement,' said Mary with her down-to-earth Devonshire logic.

Over the next few days, they stumbled upon some interesting discoveries.

They came to learn just how good most of the woodwork was beneath the layers of old paint. By continuous use of sugarsoap and Brillo pads, they ended up with lovely surfaces which Charlie decided to varnish, thereby showing the natural grain of the wood.

In the kitchen, they decided to leave the coal fire cooking range intact. Not that there was ever any likelihood of its being used, but it did make a good focal feature.

Lizzie had great difficulty in finding a shop which sold old-fashioned black-lead, finally tracking one down in Barnstaple. After the use of much energy and elbow grease on her part, she declared the end result well worth the effort.

By the end of the second week, the whole place looked different. With the windows open to the morning breeze, the panes now sparkling and clear, the whole place smelt fresh and nice. No more dirt or cobwebs.

Cupboards had been scrubbed out and lined with

fresh paper. Cups and saucers, plates, a milk jug, together with a matching sugarbowl and teapot had been brought over from the hotel.

On the draining board beneath one of the new powerpoints stood an electric kettle. Little things such as these would make their seasonal staff more independent.

Here, during their time off, they would be able to unwind and relax in pleasant surroundings.

Downstairs, there was now a gleaming kitchen, one shining chrome shower unit with sparkling white tiles on the wall and one modern toilet. As they walked through, viewing all that had been accomplished, Charlie leaned forward and pressed the flush lever of the toilet – it was almost a ceremonial act!

Of the other rooms they had made one on the ground floor into a sitting-room, while all the others were now twin-bedded rooms.

The windows were so small that Lizzie had been able to make all the curtains herself. She had chosen cotton material in bright colours. And at last the furniture had been transferred over from the hotel and installed into Ivy Cottage. It was ready for occupation!

Chapter Thirty-Two

To CONVERT THE existing hotel dining-room into five extra bedrooms presented no problems. Mr Roberts, the same architect who had done such a superb job on the bungalow, agreed to draw up and submit the plans to the council, but where on earth could they store all the furniture?

Only one solution. It had to go into various bedrooms up on the first floor. Tradesmen and friends all offered their help. Numerous trips were made up and down the elegant staircase. Soon, all bedrooms were packed with tables, chairs, china and glassware. Cutlery and silverware were packed away in boxes. The overspill of trolleys and two sideboards had to be left on the landing and covered with dustsheets which gave the place a dismal, abandoned look.

Just shut your eyes to the muddle, Lizzie repeatedly told herself, hoping that the end would justify the means.

When drawing his plans, Mr Roberts had been able to utilize all the existing windows, including the two large bays which almost jutted out to sea. They would eventually have three additional double bedrooms and two single bedrooms on what would now be an entirely new corridor.

It was surprising, indeed, how quickly these rooms took shape, and very luxurious they were, too, with coloured hand wash basins, backed by tiled vanity units which housed strip-lighting and shaving points. Because of their size, they were able to make the end of each bedroom into a lounge-type area, thus creating bed-sitting rooms rather than just functional bedrooms. And there were bathrooms and toilets where the old still room had once been.

The construction of the new dining-room on the lower-ground floor, was entirely different. It was a much more arduous and lengthy job.

The workmen had erected sheets of hardboard which sealed off the area and at least partially diminished the amount of dust and dirt which must inevitably rise when the walls were demolished and the floors dug up – for every single interior wall at the rear of the hotel had to come down.

Charlie was totally involved in the project, while Lizzie did her best to keep out of the way. When work was nearing completion, Charlie coaxed her to take a look. She was amazed at how spacious the new dining-room was. The windows, with their immense panes of glass, were truly colossal. In future, when the guests were seated, they would no longer have to look down on the sea, they would henceforth be almost at the same level as the waves.

As much cleaning as possible having been done, the carpet layers arrived. Rolls and rolls of dark red

Wilton, patterned with gold scrolls, had to be laid. The finished effect was rich, bold and regal.

Everyone pitched in to help carry the chairs and tables down the stairs. Every person who was working that day seemed caught up in the excitement of having a dining-room in a completely new setting.

Early spring had arrived once more, and in a few days from now, their first coach party of the season would be arriving.

Lizzie decided to take a tour of the hotel by herself, beginning on the very top floor. Every bedroom was well co-ordinated; bedspreads and cushions matched the curtains; even wastepaper bins Lizzie had covered with remnants of material.

Reaching the first floor, she opened the glass doors of the lounge; they were bright and clear, no finger marks. She stood a while on the threshold. The whole room looked fantastic. The sun was shining through the huge bay windows, a bit weak perhaps, but bringing a promise of summer days to come.

Outside, the sea was calm and way over in the harbour a few gaily painted boats were already bobbing about at their moorings.

Everywhere smelt fresh and clean and the green foliage plants banked up in front of the fireplace looked bright and healthy.

Back then to the ground floor. The reception desk was ready for business, with plenty of writing paper in the pad, pens at the ready in their holders, a vase of fresh spring flowers standing on a ledge.

The new bedrooms still gave Lizzie great pleasure as she checked them once again.

On now to the kitchens, all three were clean and bright, all was shining. The boys had done a good job here.

Last of all she went into the new dining-room. Standing there surveying this magnificent room, Lizzie found it hard to believe that Charlie had brought everything to such a successful end. Had they really accomplished so much that winter? The tablecloths were snowy white, serviettes were folded neatly and everywhere silver was glistening, glasses were sparkling, all in all a picture of elegance.

The following morning Lizzie decided on a visit to Ivy Cottage. Living-in staff would be moving in the next day.

She walked slowly down the hill, approaching the cottage from Larks Lane, which she thought was by far the most attractive entrance. The front garden was neat and tidy by now. It would be a good place to take a deckchair, relax in the sun, read a book or have a snooze.

Going from room to room, the beds had already been made up; Lizzie decided that everything was fine. It felt like a quaint old-fashioned cottage. As she locked the door and walked back down the cobbled path, she looked back at the shining windows and she felt proud of a job well done.

So, they were all set for yet another season.

On her walk back to the hotel, Lizzie began to deliberate in her mind about all the past events. They had achieved so much – their beautiful hotel, a staff cottage and their own lovely bungalow out in the country – it was all a far cry from what they had started out with when leaving London to purchase that first guesthouse.

How lonely she had been in the beginning. God alone knew how much she had missed London. But would she go back now, given the chance?

She wasn't quite sure. She thought back to the years of the war, the humdrum existence, the air raids and the rationing. What of her friends, and Doris and Syd? They still lived there.

She thought of the crowds, so much traffic, travelling perhaps on the stuffy Underground trains. Having to go to the same job day after day. And then she thought of her life here, never far away from the sea.

Lizzie knew better than most that life offers no guarantees, but as far as she could tell Charlie's, hers and their son's future was secure so long as they continued to run an hotel. It was a good living, they had everything they could wish for, and more, but material things weren't everything. People mattered too! At least they did to Lizzie.

She considered, taking everything into account, that she had done very well over the years. She had coped with being dumped in an unfurnished guesthouse in a strange village where she hadn't known a soul, with a young baby to look after, a mountain of debts and a business, which she had known nothing at all about, to get off the ground. If you looked at it that way it had been like taking a small London sparrow, bringing it to north Devon and setting it down amongst the seagulls. And clipping its wings so there was no way it could fly back, she mused with a wry smile on her lips.

If she lived to be a hundred she would never forget the loneliness of those first few months.

Dear daft Charlie! Never happy unless he was thinking up some scheme or other. Well he wasn't the only one who could be a bit foxy. She would let this season get well under way, pick the right moment, and then put her proposition to him, she solemnly vowed. If he could acquire all these properties in north Devon, what was to stop her buying a place in London? Lizzie grinned to herself at the thought, but why not? She was a director of this company, she earned half the money.

Not a big place, she mused wistfully, a flat would do. Just so that she would always have somewhere to go to, even if it were only for weekends and holidays. Charlie loved London just as much as she did, but it was actually getting him there that was so difficult. Perhaps if they had their own place he wouldn't always be so reluctant. A sudden thought came to Lizzie and she stopped in her tracks and laughed out loud. The bugger would more than

likely want to let it when they weren't using it themselves.

'Ready?' Charlie's voice called to her, bringing her
back from her day-dreaming. 'I've done enough fer
today,' he said as she drew level with him.

Lizzie nodded and looked up into his eyes with
love and affection, then, reaching up, she softly
kissed his cheek.

'What brought that on?' he asked as he put his
arm around her waist.

'I just felt you deserved it,' she answered. She was
thinking of that day, long ago, when she had first
glanced across the hall at the sevenpenny dance and
found Charlie, a blue-eyed, wavy-haired young corporal. There had never been anyone else for her. Just
him.

Second Chance

Chapter One

'COR, STONE THE CROWS!' the railway guard groaned to himself as he stared in disbelief at the young lady in the corner seat of the carriage. Still he hesitated, his fingers hooked into the brass handle of the carriage door.

This young lady was something else! And no mistake!

He was used to his female passengers, in the main, being dressed in heavy serge uniforms, dark in colour, sombre in style and worn with thick lisle stockings and brogue shoes to complete the outfit.

The War was over. After nearly six years of austerity, if this young lady was a promise of things to come, then all he could say was that it was a damn pity that he wasn't thirty years younger.

Taking a deep breath, the guard flexed his wrist and slid the carriage door open. 'All right now, Miss? Room to spread yourself out, eh?'

The young lady smiled her thanks as he clipped her ticket and returned it to her. With another appreciative glance at those long legs encased in the sheerest of silk stockings, the guard went on his way, certain of one thing now. And that was that a man's youth were the best years of his life and that he was a fool if he didn't make the most of them.

The London train bound for Plymouth had been packed until it reached Exeter, St David's. Now at Newton Abbot

1

even more passengers had got out and Barbara Hamlin was left as the sole occupant of the carriage.

The engine suddenly let off steam with a roar, the wheels began to turn and the train was on its way once more.

Barbara relaxed in her corner seat, eased off her shoes and stretched her legs out to rest on the opposite seat. She knew from her reflection in the carriage mirror that she looked smart, stylish. For the journey she had chosen to wear a tailored suit, a classic for its simplicity in the ever popular shade of navy-blue, with a white silk blouse. The lacy jabot at her throat gave just the right touch of femininity. It was so hard to obtain new clothes, coupons still being needed, she was glad she had hung on to the basic items in her wardrobe that never seemed to date. Her legs were covered in a pair of the sheerest stockings, not the thick lisle type she had had to endure when on duty with the Red Cross. Her luxuriant dark hair had a sheen on it like a freshly-fallen chestnut and was coiled sleekly upwards, held in place by tortoiseshell combs.

Throughout the whole of this journey she had had misgivings. Was she doing right going off to Plymouth to marry Michael?

Well, it's a bit late now, she mused, still feeling sick at heart as to what the outcome might be.

'For goodness sake, stop being so foolish!' she said aloud.

She would have felt so much easier, she thought wistfully, if only she had told her parents that she was setting off for Plymouth to be married to Michael. Michael loved her, she was sure of that. Sometimes though, for no particular reason, doubts would creep in. The emptiness of Michael's background, the need to belong, to be loved, would overwhelm him, breaking down the easy-going, jaunty barriers which he had painfully built as a front to the world.

Their future together was an obsession with Michael: he wanted her and he wasn't secure enough to allow anyone else to be aware of the fact until they were safely married and she could be known as his wife.

Three weeks ago it had all sounded so marvellous. Barbara found herself smiling. She could not stop the memories from flooding back.

Thanks to a seven day leave Michael had been in London. Nobody, least of all herself, could resist Michael's charm.

'You have only one question to ask yourself,' he had said. 'Do you love me?'

Barbara didn't have to think about this. She answered immediately. 'With all my heart, Michael, but . . .'

He quickly cut her off, 'No buts! Trust me. If you really love me you'll trust me.'

'My parents?' she had hazarded.

Michael had shown anger, just for a moment. 'We've already been over that a dozen times. We'll send them a telegram. Stop being so anxious.' She had given in, but she had never quite got rid of the apprehension.

The anger had gone, the charm was back. 'Please, my darling, everything will be fine. I will make all the necessary arrangements.' His words were spoken with conviction.

In a show of determination that had impressed her and convinced her it was right for them to get married, he had repeated again and again, 'I love you Barbara, I want you for my wife. It has to be like this, there is no other way,' he had told her. Held close in his arms, his lips caressing

3

her, she had done her best to put all her doubts to the back of her mind.

All the same, the thought of her parents' disapproval bothered her still. If only she could have gone to them and asked her father's permission, but on this thought she sighed, knowing full well there would have been little chance.

Her father was an unusual man, a barrister practising in the highest courts of England. His profession had allowed him to provide a protected life for her mother, herself and her two brothers. In the September of 1939 when Neville Chamberlain had spoken on the wireless, telling the nation that a state of war now existed between England and Germany, she had been fifteen-years-old, still at a private school for young ladies, in Brighton. Her brother William, aged twenty-one, had joined the army. Patrick, the eldest at twenty-three, had opted for the Royal Air Force.

The death of William in the early stages of the War, during the evacuation of Dunkirk in 1940, and later the news that Patrick had been shot down whilst on a raid over the Rhineland in June of 1941, had not made her parents bitter, just sad. Always loyal and devoted to each other, the pain and anguish of losing both their sons had made them supportive of each other and as time passed they became even more inseparable.

Their attitude towards Barbara, now their only child, did however become little short of possessive. It was in 1942, having reached the age of eighteen, that Barbara announced her intention of joining the forces. Her father had argued that there really no necessity for his only daughter to participate in the War effort. Her mother had cried.

Penny Rayford and Elizabeth Warren were both friends

of long standing, having been at school with Barbara. They had grown up with each other in the small village of Alfriston in East Sussex, had spent most of their school holidays together and together they had decided to volunteer to work for ambulances throughout the city of London. They shared a rented flat in Parsons Green, which was the north side of Putney Bridge. Most nights, or rather in the early hours of the morning, dog-tired the three girls would be only too glad to drop into bed. Then late in 1943 air raids by the Germans over Britain began to diminish and they were granted leave for ten days. That was when she and Michael had first met.

Barbara twisted restlessly in her corner seat of the train and gazed out of the window. Even the countryside seemed to sense that the War was over: it was a beautiful June day as the train rattled through the West Country. The sky was high and beneath it lay peaceful fields of green with gentle farm buildings intermittently flashing by. All the wild summer flowers were beginning to bloom along the banks. She thought, with amazement, how vastly different this part of the country was to what she had left behind, it was as if it had been isolated by not having participated in the atrocities of the War years. The length and breadth of London had been blasted by bombs, and flowers were a luxury, for long since the Government had decreed that folk should grow vegetables instead of flowers. Seven weeks ago Field Marshal Montgomery had reported to his Supreme Head Quarters that all enemy forces in Holland, Germany and Denmark had surrendered unconditionally and V.E. day, May 8th 1945, would be a day that British people would remember for the rest of their lives. Who could blame them for celebrating?

There was of course the awful knowledge that War was still being raged in the Pacific but the general feeling was the Japanese would capitulate very soon now. The young men would start to be demobbed, come home to their families, the memory of so many dead comrades would never be forgotten but life would have to start afresh. How would they cope? What about herself? Six years ago life had been so different. All youngsters then had been forced, by events over which they had no control, to grow up quickly. Certainly all the youthful innocence had been stripped from her whilst working on the ambulances. Families had been devastated, torn apart, her own included. Was she being fair to her mother and father rushing off to marry Michael, a man they almost certainly wouldn't approve of?

Barbara felt a moment of panic, things had happened so swiftly she had, like most other young folk, been borne along on this feeling of euphoria since V.E. day, and more so the last three weeks since Michael's leave. 'Michael,' she said his name aloud in the empty carriage and that strange, giddy feeling flooded through her veins. When he cupped her chin in his hand and gently put his lips to hers, it was as though he was hypnotising her. Even if she had wanted to she couldn't have pulled away, but then she had never wanted to. No matter where they were, or who they were with, it was as if they were the only two people in the whole world and all that mattered was that Michael should go on kissing her and holding her.

It had been one year and eight months that they had been parted: now he was back in England to stay, as handsome as she remembered with dark brown wavy hair and the clearest blue eyes, and pleading with her to be his wife.

Barbara took her feet down from the opposite seat, stood up, stretched her arms above her head and began to pace the narrow space between the two bench seats. Her thoughts now had flown back to the night she had met Michael for the first time.

The very first evening of their leave, Penny, Elizabeth and herself had done themselves up to the nines determined to have a good night out. To hell with the air raids, they were going to let off steam. Rainbow Corner in Piccadilly was an obvious choice.

The dance hall was full of servicemen and women, Canadians, Australians, Americans and many British. From the other side of the room her eyes had met and been held by this good-looking, able-bodied seaman. It was enough.

Right from that moment love had struck them so suddenly that as he rose and covered the distance between them she had stood up, stepped apart from her friends and stood waiting. No one professes to believe in the possibility of love at first sight, most would say it was a myth, yet it happened to both of them. They were convinced it did.

The tunes the big band played had been fantastic, they had danced the quickstep to *In The Mood*, dreamily moved through slow foxtrots while the big mirrored glass sphere, suspended high above the floor, caught the light as it revolved, showering everyone with multi-coloured prisms of light. Come midnight as the band played the romantic waltz *Who's Taking You Home Tonight*, Michael had become as committed to her as she was to him.

Later Barbara told herself the secret lay in Michael's beautiful blue eyes: they twinkled, sparkled with fire as they gazed at her and spoke volumes. The effect on her had been electrifying.

For the next seven days they had been inseparable. There was no uncertainty. They were madly in love with each other. She was nineteen and he was twenty-six and for that week it was as if the world had been made for them.

Her friends told her she was mad and so she was. 'Mad about Michael,' Penny had grudgingly remarked, adding regretfully, 'In a rough kind of way I suppose one has to admit he's a handsome son-of-a-bitch.'

Much more that that! Barbara had convinced herself.

To her Michael had the masculinity that both men and women respected. He was one inch short of being six foot tall, broad shouldered, clear complexion and those wonderful eyes that continually twinkled with good humour. She had learnt that his pre-War job had been manual labouring and this she felt had given him a wiry toughness. His naval uniform suited him admirably, nipped in at the waist, bell bottoms swishing as he rolled along, he looked robust – as if he had never known a day's illness in his life.

The whole of that week he had treated her as if she was special and she had experienced feelings that were entirely new to her.

Their last night together. Those seven days had been the shortest that Barbara had ever known, they'd seemed to fly by.

'Oh Barbara! You're so beautiful! Say you love me, say you'll wait for me, please darling.'

Her head was still high in the clouds as she clung to him and whispered 'I love you Michael. I'll count every day until you come back.'

Then he was gone. Back to service in submarines. Each and every night she had prayed, 'Please God keep him safe.'

During that long separation of twenty months their love had not diminished, kept alive only by letters, irregular ones at that. Whilst she had continued to write lengthy weekly letters to Michael, his to her would arrive in batches, sometimes with lengthy intervals, not through any fault on Michael's part.

'You're going to drive yourself really mad,' Penny had told her one morning when Barbara came back from standing on the doorstep and watching the postman walk by.

'But it's been weeks.'

'I know, love. It must be just as bad for all sailors' wives and sweethearts. I expect you'll get a whole bundle of letters soon now, he's been writing, you can be sure of that, but how the hell is he supposed to post them?'

She had smiled wryly to herself at this thought. Penny was right, of course! He could hardly have been expected to post letters from the bottom of the sea-bed.

Barbara glanced at her watch. The train was due to arrive in Plymouth in twenty-five minutes at three thirty. Michael would be there to meet her. She felt a warm glow flood over her body as she contemplated their reunion. She still wasn't sure that she was doing the right thing but Michael had become her whole life, he had the ability to have her feeling as if she were walking in air. Taking up her handbag from where it lay on the seat, she slid open the carriage door and went along the corridor to the toilet at the end. Having washed her hands she smeared a little rouge on her cheeks, powdered her nose, then applied the bright red lipstick to her mouth, which Elizabeth had so generously given her, at the same time reflecting how much her mother

would disapprove of her use of make-up. Only Michael
mattered today, for him she wanted to appear beautiful.
She wanted him to exclaim out loud when he caught the
first glimpse of her, and he would.

She made her way back to the carriage, reached her
suitcase down from the luggage rack and was ready waiting
as the train came to a halt in the station. It was a big station,
bigger than she had expected, yet still it had a countryfied
air, not in the least like the grimy smoky London terminals.
There were many more people milling about than she
had assumed there would be. Everyone was talking loudly,
laughing and hugging each other, everyone seemed to be
having a reunion with someone.

Barbara walked down the platform carrying her suitcase,
reached the barrier, gave up her ticket to the collector,
went through to the entrance hall beyond but there was no
sign of Michael.

She stood for several moments straining her eyes for a
glimpse of him, but all she saw were unknown sailors and
ordinary men and women. A young woman went flying
past her, running straight into the wide outstretched arms
of a naval man. Barbara watched with envy as they kissed
and clung to each other. She waited feeling lost and alone.

Five, ten, fifteen minutes dragged by, the platform had
cleared. Slowly she walked the length of the waiting area
and sat down on a wooden bench, placing her case at her
feet. She was thoroughly upset that Michael wasn't there
to meet her and as the time passed she became anxious and
then restless.

Perhaps I've come on the wrong day, or even to the
wrong station, she thought, panic rising up inside her, then

immediately chided herself. Don't be so daft, it's Wednesday.

It was only the night before last, Monday, that she had spoken to Michael on the telephone. From a call box he had rung the flat, his spirits had been as high as a kite as he told her he had obtained the special licence.

Filled with self-pity she felt her eyes smart with tears. Now you're being utterly foolish, she told herself as she angrily brushed them away. Yet was she being foolish? This was a strange part of the world to her, she knew no one, had no idea as to where she could go. The last thing she wanted to do was return to London. To admit she had been fooled would provide a heyday of gossip among her friends, some she could name in particular who wouldn't hesitate to have a laugh at her expense. Both Penny and Elizabeth would be well within their rights to say, 'We told you so!'

Three-quarters of an hour now she had been waiting and she was fast becoming alarmed. As her mind turned over all the possibilities that could have happened to Michael she realised, if she were honest, she knew very little of his family or background. His mother had died when he'd been sixteen, his father had married again when Michael was twenty. As so often happens, his stepmother, who already had three children of her own, hadn't wanted Michael around. He'd walked out of the Blackburn council house in which he had been born and had never to this day gone back. She had had to press Michael to tell her even that much.

The joy of seeing Michael again after twenty months had been marvellous. To *know* that he had come home safely. When there had been long gaps between his letters

11

her nerves had been stretched to breaking point as her mind conjured up pictures of him entombed in that submarine. Even whilst driving through an air raid she had prayed silently, 'Please God keep Michael safe!' From the very first day of his return, nothing had changed. Michael had looked at her with as much love in his eyes as was in her own. He had spent his entire leave pressing her to marry him. He had been so persuasive about his reasons for doing it on the quiet. He wanted her for his wife now, with no delay and no objections from her family.

'I think we should be married just as soon as possible,' he had declared in a voice gruff with passion. 'We've wasted too much of our lives as it is.' In the end she had gone along with his decision: she was convinced it was the right one, at least she prayed that it was.

She had been hoping to get down to Sussex to see her parents before leaving London but there had not been time. Although V.E. day had come and gone and the peace treaty with Germany had been signed it would be a long time yet before things would be back to normal and, like all service personnel and war workers, she was still held to her duties. There would be Red Cross trains arriving regularly, hopefully bringing home the wounded service men and, please God, prisoners of war would also be coming back to these shores. Four days' leave was all that she had been able to wrangle and even that had been a privilege. She had toyed with the idea of asking Michael to wait, to postpone the idea of getting married for a while, but she had recognised immediately that hesitating wasn't part of Michael's nature. Marry him or lose him. She knew there had been no other choice, yet still a small voice in her head had warned her that each of them would need every ounce of courage and all of their love if they were to face the future together.

What a dilemma! Every instinct had told her that her parents would oppose this marriage. She might have been able to tell her mother and father face to face of her feelings for Michael and that they intended to get married, but it wasn't a matter for discussion over the telephone. She had decided to gamble. Once she was Michael's wife she hoped against hope that things would automatically come right. Surely her parents would take to Michael and he to them. Perhaps, in some slight way, Michael might be able to fill the gap that losing her two brothers had left in her parents' lives. Dear God, she hoped so!

'Oh, for Christ's sake,' she said angrily half-aloud, 'sitting here dwelling on all these disturbing thoughts isn't helping one bit. All you're doing is meeting trouble halfway.'

One hour and ten minutes since she had got off the train. Now and again little groups of people stopped to stare at her. Workmen on their way home glanced at her with what she took to be pity in their eyes. The ticket collector was turning the key in the lock of his offices, he too glanced in her direction and she thought she saw a hint of a smile hover on his lips, before he dropped the barrier. She sat rooted to the bench as she watched him turn and walk away. What should she do? Find a hotel for the night? She had just decided when she heard footsteps, her heart leapt with joy, she *knew* Michael would come, he wouldn't leave her sitting here on her own, not on purpose he wouldn't. She was in her feet in an instant, searching for Michael to come into view. It was a sailor, only it wasn't Michael and she had to bite her lip hard to stop herself from crying out loud. She held her breath as the man approached, her vision was blurred by tears of disappointment.

'Are you Miss Barbara Hamlin?' he asked as he drew near.

Barbara swallowed the lump which was stuck in her throat and nodded her head.

The sight of Barbara's tears and her obvious unhappiness embarrassed the young man. 'I'm sorry you've had such a long wait,' he murmured, 'I've brought you a note from Mike, he asked me to wait while you read it and then to see you safely to the hostel where he's booked a room for you.'

Barbara read the short note, gulped and licked her dry lips before saying, 'I see.'

'I don't blame you for being upset,' he said quietly, trying his best to smile.

Barbara just stared at him. The smile vanished. 'It really isn't Mike's fault. By the way, I'm David Patterson.'

He didn't offer his hand to Barbara, as he made the introduction: he gave her no chance to refuse his offer to accompany her, merely picked up her suitcase, turned on his heel and strode off ahead.

Barbara wasn't sure she liked this young man, he acted as if he didn't approve of her. Shaking her head she told herself not to be so unkind, at least he'd come to her rescue, so to speak. Doing Michael's dirty work, she thought, which couldn't be very pleasant for him. He looked quite smart and handsome, the insignia on his naval uniform showed that he also, like Michael, served in submarines and for such service surely they had to be brave men. There must be a host of things he'd rather be doing right now than escorting her to a hostel.

They walked side by side along the road and then not more than five hundred yards from the station David Patterson stopped, placed her suitcase at the bottom of a flight of stone steps, nodded his head upwards and said, 'You'll be fine in there, your room is booked and hopefully Mike will be down to see you in the morning . . .' His words tailed off.

'Wait! Just a minute, please,' Barbara put a hand out to prevent him walking off.

Two things had not only surprised her, they had knocked her for six. One, the sign above the entrance doors stated; YOUNG WOMEN'S CHRISTIAN ASSOCIATION; which meant Michael would not be allowed to join her there, and the second she voiced out loud.

'You said hopefully Michael will see me tomorrow, won't he be able to get out this evening?'

'No, sorry,' was all the answer he gave as he turned to go.

'Why *hopefully?*' Barbara quickly asked. 'Is there some doubt even about tomorrow?'

'Shouldn't think so, can't always tell.' He paused and shrugged, 'Try not to worry, get yourself a good night's sleep.'

Barbara laid her hand on his arm. 'Please, I must know. Why hasn't Michael come to meet me?'

A very embarrassed David Patterson sighed deeply before saying, 'Mike got involved in an argument – he swore at a superior rating. Landed himself five days' stoppage of shore leave and privileges.' With that he turned around and walked smartly away.

There was nothing else she could do. Picking up her suitcase, she walked up the steps and rang the bell.

15

Within seconds the door was opened and Barbara was looking at a grey-haired lady in her early sixties who immediately put out her hands and grabbed the suitcase from Barbara's hand and with a laugh in her voice said, 'You must be Miss Hamlin, we'd almost given you up, come on, come in.'

'Thank you,' Barbara smiled at the woman and knew straight away that she was going to like her. She was the sort of person who had devoted her life to good work and in the process had acquired the particular qualities needed to set folk at their ease. Thankfully Barbara heaved a sigh of relief, she had no time to take in more than a fleeting impression of her surroundings when the woman gave a loud laugh which startled her and she became aware that she was being given the once over.

'My, anyone can see you're from London! Your outfit will be the envy of all the girls – but I'm forgetting my manners, I'm Jean Bailey.' With that she took hold of Barbara's right hand shaking it hard, so hard that Barbara almost squirmed at the firmness of the grip.

'What's your Christian name? We don't stand on ceremony here.'

'Barbara.'

'Well come along Barbara. What's it to be, your bedroom or a cup of tea first in the kitchen?'

'Oh, oh tea please, if it's not too much trouble. I really am gasping.' Barbara followed the short woman down the hall into a room which no one could mistake for other than a kitchen. Beside an enormous gas stove, hanging on the wall were frying pans, saucepans and numerous kitchen utensils. The opposite wall was flanked by a huge dresser displaying row upon row of hanging cups, the shelves holding matching saucers and plates. Four young women were in the kitchen and as Barbara crossed the floor they all turned to gape at her.

Jean Bailey clapped her hands, 'Now, now, she is not a mirage, she's real enough.' Nodding her head at each in turn she named the girls. 'Peggy, Vera, Hilda and Kitty, this is Barbara and she is dying of thirst.'

After only a moment's hesitation they crossed the room and her hand was shaken by each of them.

So thirsty had Barbara been that she had downed her tea in only five gulps. As she put her cup and saucer down onto the wooden table a chorus of voices asked, 'Like another cup?'

Amid all the laughter that followed Jean Bailey pushed Barbara hard against her shoulder, an action that almost overbalanced her onto the floor. Her eyes full of merriment and her face wreathed in smiles, Jean put out a hand to steady her, saying at the same time, 'See, you've made friends already!'

The hostel itself was a surprise. When the bell had rang she had done as she was told and come downstairs for the evening meal. A door on the right from the hallway led into the dining room. Barbara was so surprised at the size of this room she hesitated in the doorway, it was more like a meeting hall, she guessed it to be almost fifty feet long and at least thirty foot wide. At the very far end a table was set out for a meal, as far as she could tell the settings were for approximately thirty people. The outside of the building hadn't been at all pretentious, certainly not suggesting it could house so many people nor boast such large rooms. To the forefront of this dining room stood rows of

17

wooden chairs as if set out in readiness for a meeting. Barbara soon found her assumption to be right.

An evening service was held before the meal was served. Prayers were said but it was during the lusty singing of the hymns that Barbara came to realise that this hostel was affiliated to the Salvation Army.

The dinner turned out to be a simple one, yet very good indeed. Tomato soup, steak and kidney pie, mashed potatoes, carrots and peas, followed by bread and butter pudding. Barbara ate hungrily, enjoying every mouthful. All she had managed to obtain at lunchtime had been two cold sausage rolls from the snack bar on the train.

As she ate, Barbara observed her companions. About twenty girls and young women of different ages and six older types mainly like Jean Bailey, who appeared to be in charge. The conversation was mostly of their Christian work and Barbara reflected how isolated their existence must be within this hostel, but soon realised they wanted nothing different, they were uninterested in the world in general for as far as they were concerned this was their calling. The official seated next to Barbara thanked God continually in her conversation and soon Barbara saw the funny side of the situation and began to wonder idly what would happen if the woman were to be transferred to a larger establishment in London where certainly the pace of life would be quicker and the changeover of guests more rapid and varied.

Dinner over, Barbara excused herself and went to her room. The bedroom was comfortable enough: it held a three foot bed covered by a bright pink candlewick bedspread, one upholstered armchair, a tall wardrobe with a full-length mirror set on the outside and a marble-topped stand holding a white china jug and basin, beside which two pink towels hung from a free standing wooden rack. She removed the jacket of her suit, refreshed herself with a cold wash, took her clothes out of the suitcase and hung them in the wardrobe.

The next few minutes she spent studying herself in the mirror through a blur of tears. Never in the whole of her life had she felt so lonely. What a trip this was turning out to be! She must try to stay calm. At least until she did get to see Michael. She began to wipe away the tears from her cheeks with the back of her hand, sighing heavily as she did so. The silence in the room was deafening. She didn't fancy going downstairs again. 'I'll go for a walk,' she said out loud to her reflection. 'At least that will help to pass the time.'

Barbara couldn't believe it! What was it she had said to herself coming along in the train? The War had bypassed the West Country, leaving it green and tranquil. Well, that certainly did not apply to Plymouth. The whole area was one vast bomb site. The amount of bombing the city must have suffered had to be on par with that of London. Working with the Red Cross she had seen enough sights to last her a lifetime, even helped to drag the injured and dead from beneath piles of rubble, but God help the voluntary services, the police and air raid wardens who had attended this lot. She was standing where the Metropole Hotel had once proudly faced the sea, now reduced to a pile of broken masonry and rubble. The town's older streets, where rows of working class houses had stood, were all eradicated. Even the main thoroughfare and high street shops hadn't escaped entirely. What was amazing was the amount of wild flowers which pierced through the debris, their colours bright, their heads held high, the roots of which were certainly not nurtured in earth or compost – only masses of solid rubble. One thing was for sure, she said to herself, nature is resilient.

On reaching the famous Plymouth Hoe, she found it good to breathe the salty, fresh sea air. She stood a long time leaning over the railings of the esplanade, watching the lights of the small crafts twinkling on the darkening green waters.

There was the statue of Sir Francis Drake, overlooking the Sound and she thought, what an awful lot of history has been made since I was at school learning of The Pilgrim Fathers and how they had sailed from this very city in *The Mayflower*, back in the seventeenth century.

In the far distance, as she retraced her footsteps, she could see the outline of the great naval station, its dockyards and barracks and she whispered aloud, 'Where are you, Michael?'

His note had told her nothing. She didn't know anything of his plans. In her head she could hear his voice as it had come over the telephone. 'I have the special licence, darling. We can be married within three days; come to Plymouth, it will be easier here. You will come, won't you, Barbara? Please. You will be my wife, say again that you will.'

It was rarely that depression ever settled on Barbara, but her feet dragged tonight as she turned back towards the Christian Hostel. She had come to Plymouth, just as Michael had begged her too, but where the hell was Michael?

Breakfast and the morning hymn and prayers were over.

Barbara was just about to leave the dining room when she felt a restraining hand on her arm. With a nod of her head Jean Bailey indicated that Barbara should follow her. Once inside the office, with the door closed, Jean's features assumed a look of pity as she took hold of Barbara's hand.

'I had a telephone call before breakfast, from your young man, Michael Henderson, he asked that I pass a message on to you.'

Barbara looked up quickly. 'Didn't he ask to speak to me personally?'

'Well no, but he did sound as if he were pushed for time,' this kindly woman said soothingly. 'I wrote the message down, wait a minute, I'll find it and read it to you and that way there won't be any mistake.'

Barbara frowned, as she watched Jean shift through an assortment of papers that littered her desk. She felt so humiliated. First Michael didn't turn up to meet her, then he telephoned the hostel leaving a message for her, apparently not even having asked to speak with her.

'Ah! Here it is,' Jean said thankfully, 'I'd written it on the bottom of today's menu. "Am unable to see Barbara today. Everything is all right. Will meet her at the Town Hall registry office tomorrow, Friday, at a quarter to eleven. The ceremony is booked for eleven o'clock. Have found two mates to act as witnesses." '

Jean Bailey came round from behind her desk and patted Barbara's shoulder. 'There now, luv. I expect there's a very good reason why he couldn't get away.'

Barbara was incapable of answering. She just gasped, struck dumb at the starkness of the words.

Once again Jean Bailey's eyes were full of compassion as she looked at Barbara. 'I know you are upset, even lonely, but think about tomorrow, you'll be getting married to your young man.'

Think about it! She had thought of little else.

Barbara was by now consumed by anger, so much so that she had difficulty in stopping herself from pushing this homely woman away from her side. It was so unfair of Michael to treat her like this!

Now as well as the anger there was a sense of shock and loss, a feeling of betrayal was washing over her. Was she a fool? Had Penny and Elizabeth been right all along?

Jean Bailey stooped and brushed a strand of dark hair from Barbara's hot forehead. 'You're not to get yourself upset. Come along, go for a nice walk, it's a lovely day and this time tomorrow you'll be wondering why you got so upset.' Her sympathy was stretched to the limit as she watched Barbara get up and make ready to leave her office. She prayed to God that this nice young lady hadn't come all the way from London on a fool's errand! She couldn't let her go. Not in the state she was in.

'Stay and talk to me if it will help,' she said softly.

Tears welled up in Barbara's eyes. This annoyed her, she wouldn't cry, not in front of this good woman who had been so kind to her. She couldn't help it. 'Two days I've been in Plymouth and I haven't set eyes on Michael,' she sobbed. 'He calmly leaves a message for me to be at the registrar's office. I don't even know how to get there. I can't believe this is happening, not like this.'

Jean held her hand until she was calm again and her sobbing only little hiccups.

'You do want to go ahead with this marriage – that is why you came all this way, isn't it?' Jean Bailey waited for Barbara to answer without taking her eyes from her face.

'You wouldn't rather go back to London today, would you?'

When finally Barbara tried to answer her words were jumbled. 'No! Oh I don't know, I suppose not. Somehow I think I have to go through with it now.'

'Dear me, that's no way to look at marriage.' Jean sounded shocked. 'Marriage has to be a commitment – for life.'

'Yes, yes – I know that.'

Barbara raised her eyes to those of the older woman and the uncertainty in them made Jean stretch out her arms to what she now thought was a very bewildered young lady. Feeling very anxious now, she asked, 'Will your parents be coming?'

Barbara shook her head.

'Do you love this young man?'

Barbara again nodded her head. 'Yes, of course I do.'

'Well wartime has robbed most of us of something, but it's nearly all over now my dear, and when you're settled with your husband I am sure God's love will shine on you both and life will be good to you.'

Barbara couldn't help wishing as she wiped her eyes and blew her nose that she herself felt as sure.

During the rest of the morning Barbara asked herself the same question a hundred times. How come she had let Michael talk her into coming to Plymouth? She had walked about for over an hour, turning matters over in her mind. Had Michael lied to her? Did he really love her? Do *I* really love him? That last question she could answer. Yes, God help me, I do!' Finding herself at the gates of an enclosed park she went in. Her feet were burning, she wasn't wearing the right type of shoes for walking about in, she made towards a bench-seat situated beneath a leafy tree; slowly and thankfully she settled herself down.

Tomorrow she was to be a bride! She had had no engagement, no ring and this wedding, if she turned up, would be nothing like she had always imagined her own would be. She wondered if Michael would have a best man, probably not. He'd got two witnesses, or so he'd told Jean Bailey over the phone. There would be no honeymoon, she only had leave for four days which meant she would have to return to London on Saturday. Naturally no wedding invitations had been sent out. There had been no time. She would write later to her close friends but Christ Almighty alone knew what she would find to say to her parents. Traditionally she should be walking down the aisle holding onto her father's arm, and Penny and Elizabeth should be her bridesmaids. Although clothing coupons were still in use a way would have been found around that and she had to stifle a sob as she thought of the gay old time the three of them would have had touring the shops of London, choosing their dresses and her trousseau.

Feeling utterly forlorn she got to her feet: where could she go now? The rest of the day stretched endlessly ahead.

At one o'clock she was in a side street gazing through the window of a working class café. She could perhaps go in, have a drink and a bite to eat; amongst the occupants seated at the white-topped tables were several young girls and women so she wouldn't be out of place. Inside she pulled a chair from the table and sat down.

'There's no service, luv, you've got to go to the counter ter get served.'

The voice from behind her made her jump. Turning her

head Barbara saw a plump dark haired girl smiling at her and in spite of the abruptness of her statement she felt the girl was trying to be friendly.

'Thank you,' Barbara murmured as she got to her feet again.

As she returned with a cup of coffee, made from Camp Liquid, and a buttered bun, the same girl pointed to a vacant chair and asked, 'D'yer wanna sit with us?'

Barbara swallowed deeply, then again said, 'Thank you.'

The girl and her two companions shifted their seats and made room for her. 'I'm Alice, she's Billy and she's Maggie.' The introductions were made with a prodding thumb and much laughter.

'I'm Barbara, how do you do.'

Great chuckles came from the three girls as Barbara's educated voice came across.

'You're from London aren't yer, midear? Talk about looking lost, from the expression on yer face we'd 'ave to think yer had lost a shilling and found a penny.'

'Or some sailor ain't turned up to meet yer.'

The flush that came to Barbara's cheeks told the oldest girl of the group that she had probably hit the nail on the head.

'Don't take it ter heart love, how did I know? It was only a guess. This is a naval town, what d'yer expect? There ain't one of us it ain't happened to, all of us love a sailor. Some more than others!' she said giving her plump friend such a nudge that she almost fell off her chair. Everyone including Barbara burst out laughing. The awkwardness left her. How could she be anything else than at ease with these friendly souls? It was good to have someone to talk to, to be with.

25

The café filled up and Barbara felt it was a liberty to sit there taking up space with empty mugs in front of them.

'May I buy you all another coffee?' she presently asked.

'No,' they answered in chorus. 'We don't like that muck but the tea's not bad.'

Barbara smiled broadly at all of them, 'Well, shall I make it four large teas?'

'Yeah, thanks very much, for a Londoner you ain't so bad.'

Forty-five minutes later when the three young women said they had to get back to work Barbara felt a sense of loss: they had been good company, telling her about their boyfriends who all worked in Devonport Dockyards and what they got up to at weekends, all with spontaneous good humour. There were smiles on their faces as they wished her good luck and said goodbye. Slowly now Barbara rose from her seat, she couldn't remain in the cafe any longer yet she still had at least three hours to while away on her own before returning to the hostel.

How was it possible to feel so lonely? She sighed heavily.

The eve of her wedding day! There should be so many things she should have to attend to, she should be surrounded by family, relatives and guests. Tomorrow should be the most special day of her life if she were going to marry Michael.

A sudden thought struck her and she bent her head as she walked so that passers-by wouldn't see the tears that were flowing down her cheeks. She hadn't been consulted nor had she had any involvement in any of the arrangements for her own wedding.

At last it was five o'clock, she could return to the hostel.

Barbara had taken off her skirt and blouse, had a good wash and was sitting on the edge of the bed when a tap came on the door.

'Come in,' Barbara called.

'The whole place is thrilled at the thought of your wedding.' The cheery words were spoken by Jean Bailey before she had hardly set foot in the room. 'The staff and the girls have decided to give you a little hen party this evening,' she hesitated, 'and – if you would like us to, myself and Mrs Brackhurst thought we would come with you to the Town Hall in the morning   sort of act as temporary relatives like, seeing as your own parents aren't able to get here. Only if you want us to that is.'

The reply from Barbara came quickly, 'Oh, how kind, I really would appreciate that, it would mean so much, I would not be on my own, well, you do understand what I mean. Thank you. Thank you very much.'

Jean Bailey beamed at her. 'That's settled then. Put your dress on, come along downstairs and after dinner the party will begin.'

Barbara wasn't able to answer for a moment and when she did there was a catch in her voice and tears glistened in her eyes. 'Oh, Jean, all of you here are strangers to me and yet you have all been so kind.'

Jean Bailey dismissed this sentiment with a wave of her hand. Outside of the room she stood at the top of the stairs and asked herself why was this well-bred young lady so far from home and getting married to a sailor with no kith nor kin of her own to be present at the ceremony. Having met the young man when he had called at the hostel to book a room for his fiancée she had thought him pleasant enough, but there was no getting away from the fact that he was only an ordinary A.B. Not an officer. Surely a naval man of some rank would be far more suitable for this young lady, who was obviously very well-educated. Don't be such a snob, she chided herself. The war had broken down many class barriers and the youngsters must grab their chances. Still she was asking herself as she made her way downstairs, do oil and water ever mix!

It wanted only five minutes to eleven o'clock. They were all standing on the pavement outside the Town Hall. Michael had been there when she arrived and the joy of feeling his arms around her and his lips on hers had gone a long way to dispelling her misgivings. Now, as for minutes Michael had kept up a jocular conversation with his two mates, it was as if he was afraid that a silence might settle between them.

'Time to go.' Jean Bailey pressed them forward towards the steps. Shown into an oak-panelled waiting room, Barbara was at last near to Michael. Sitting close to him now, his hand sought hers and their fingers linked tightly. So much she wanted to ask him. So many explanations she needed but this was not the time nor the place.

'You look lovely, Barbara.' His voice was soft and tender. 'I love you.'

She wanted to put her arms around his neck, to be held tightly, she needed reassurances such as this. Their names were being called, there was no time.

Barbara still couldn't take it in: this was her wedding day. A balding man in a dark double-breasted suit was standing behind a long table, reading from an open book held flat on the palm of his hand.

To the right of her stood two motherly-type ladies who

up until three days ago she had never before set eyes on, but dear God, she was grateful that they were there, yet if she had been asked to explain what she felt she would have been unable to give a reason. It was they who had insisted that they visit a florist shop where the young lady assistant had with great skill fashioned two pink carnations into buttonholes and swiftly made the sweetest of posies for herself to carry. With small tea roses and lily of the valley interwoven with maidenhair fern now held in front of her cream silk two piece suit, she at least outwardly looked like a bride.

'Forsaking all others, do you Barbara Catherine Hamlin, take Michael James Henderson for your wedded husband until death do you part?'

Forsaking all others!

The silence hung heavy in the room as Barbara swallowed the huge lump that was in her throat before she was able to answer.

Not until they were again outside in the street did the full realisation hit her. It was all over. Just like that. There was no going back. She had got herself married to Michael.

'It's the privilege of the best man to kiss the bride first.' Barbara heard Michael laugh as David Patterson, looking very slim and smart in his uniform, bent and kissed her gently on the cheek, whispering as he did so, 'Good luck!'

The other shipmate of Michael's, who had been introduced to her merely as Pete, now stepped forward placing his lips also to her cheek and with a broad smile said very loudly, 'Got yerself a good bloke, but you know what they say, change yer name an' not the letter, change fer worse an' not for better.'

Oh for Christ's sake! He's just what I don't need. Barbara

was angry now but was stopped from making a retort by Jean Bailey.

'Ignore him, don't let him get you down. You'll laugh about today in years to come,' she said softly to Barbara, as she held her close for a moment. Then it was Mrs Brackhurst's turn; she put her arms about her saying, All the very best Barbara, dear. Be happy.'

It was too much! She couldn't answer them, her throat was too full. She merely nodded and did her best to smile.

At one moment there had been six of them on the pavement and now suddenly she and Michael were alone.

He took hold of her hands and pulled her close. 'Well Mrs Henderson, how do you like being my wife?'

She nestled closer to him, the lump was back in her throat and tears stung her eyes, she made no answer.

'Oh, Barbara, I know everything didn't go as planned, but I *do* love you. Really I do. I'll spend my whole life making you happy. Say you've no regrets, no doubts, please.'

She looked up at him and smiled. 'No regrets, just a few doubts and a helluva lot of nerves.'

He smiled now and touched her cheek gently. 'I've a few of those myself, but we've got each other now, and our love,' he murmured as he lowered his head and, regardless of people passing by, began to kiss her passionately.

Chapter Two

BARBARA FELT THE anger surge through her veins. She could cheerfully strangle Michael, husband or no husband, with her own bare hands!

She was sitting in the Lord Nelson, a rowdy public house situated just yards from the Town Hall. Michael was leaning on the bar, surrounded by what she supposed were a host of his mates.

As well as the sense of shock that Michael should have brought her straight to such a place, she felt betrayed: How could he do this to me? He must be telling everyone that he's just got married, the way they're all carrying on, laughing and jeering, while I'm sitting here on my own.

'All right, my darling?' is what he had asked as he placed a gin and tonic on the table in front of her. Then without giving her time to reply he had laughed and gone back to prop up the bar. I feel such a fool! she thought. My wedding day! How can he treat me like this?

What would she tell Penny and Elizabeth when she got back? Certainly not the truth.

'What are you fretting about?'

Barbara looked up slowly. Michael set his pint glass down on the table and bent over her. 'What say we go through to the saloon bar, they do meals in there. Get ourselves a bite to eat, eh?'

Barbara brushed a strand of her hair away from her hot forehead. There were too many people around for her to

31

have a showdown with Michael. Maybe he didn't realise that today should be kind of special like, but surely he could have taken her to a restaurant for a meal? Not the fore ale bar of this noisy pub. Stop it. Right now. She chided herself. You've got to make the best of it. Give Michael the benefit of the doubt, don't work yourself into a rage.

'You'll have me all to yourself tonight,' Michael said in an emphatic whisper, suddenly sensing just how upset she was.

In the saloon bar they sat at a table in the corner and, to be fair, Michael was doing his best to make up for his previous lack of attention.

'That's rabbit food,' he teased her as a pretty young girl set a platter of cheese salad down in front of Barbara. 'Ah now, that's a damn sight better!' he said as he ravenously tucked into sausages, baked beans and a huge pile of chips.

There were three empty pint glasses on the table: evidence that they had been sitting there for more than an hour.

'Come on, Michael, please let's get out into the fresh air,' Barbara pleaded as she got to her feet.

The afternoon was warm, the sky cloudless and high and as they walked she slipped her hand into Michael's. A bad start, but she felt happier now. Their slow stroll through the streets inevitably led them to the Hoe, where they sunk down thankfully onto the grass. Michael promptly stretched out on his back but Barbara propped herself up on one elbow and quietly looked lovingly into his face.

She felt like laughing and crying at the same time and her heart felt as if it were ready to burst. This man she was gazing at was her husband. Here in a strange city, far away from her family and friends she had become his wife. She couldn't help herself, she still had this terrible feeling of guilt. She should have told her parents. They deserved that much. Michael just hadn't given her time because, as he said, they loved each other so much that no one else mattered. Now for better or worse her life was linked to his. She still wanted to talk to Michael about so many things but she laughed out loud now, his nose was twitching, his breathing was heavy and suddenly he began to snore. He was fast asleep.

She tried to doze but it was impossible, she couldn't get comfortable, it was too hot. She wished she was dressed differently, more casually.

She sat up, brought her legs up so that she could rest her chin on her knees and gazed at the view. It was fantastic. Wide expanses of grassland and, ahead, the sea stretched for miles before it merged with the line where the sea and sky seemed to meet. Way out, across the shimmering water, she was able to see the outline of several ships and small crafts and in her mind she dwelt on the fact that all must have been engaged in action over the past years. Yet now, with the sun shining and the sea so calm, the whole place seemed so peaceful.

As the sun set lower in the sky her throat was parched and she found herself longing for a cup of tea.

At last Michael woke up, stretched his arms above his head, glanced quickly at his watch, swiftly stood up and gave her his hand and pulled her to her feet saying, 'What ever came over me? Fancy falling asleep on me wedding day, you should have woke me.'

Then tenderly he reached for her, pulling her slender body close to his muscular frame. His arms about her felt strong and virile; all her doubts were swept away as she clung to him, trembling with anticipation at the thought of the night that lay ahead.

It wasn't how Barbara would have chosen to spend the first evening of her married life but she hadn't been given any option. When they had first entered the servicemen's club she had felt apprehensive, especially when Michael left her alone to join other servicemen of all ranks at the licensed bar. The music was nice, albeit only gramophone records. She felt much happier when Michael came and led her onto the dance floor and she thought how festive the organisers had managed to make the place look. They were dancing a dreamy waltz and Michael was holding her in an embrace on the packed floor. 'There's hardly any room to move,' he smiled down at her. 'We'll have another couple of drinks an' then we'll get going.'

She spent the next twenty minutes alone, watching and listening to Michael. He stood surrounded by a group of naval men, the centre of attention; every now and then the men would laugh loudly at something that had been said and all eyes would turn in her direction.

She had had enough!

She got to her feet, gathered up her bag and strode off to the ladies' room. Having been to the toilet she washed her hands then, glancing into the mirror above the wash-hand basin, she got a shock. Her hair was a mess and the two roses she had taken from her bouquet and pinned to her jacket had wilted. What an odd sort of day it had been! If and when she could drag Michael away from the bar they were to spend the night together. A night that would be the only honeymoon she was likely to get!

God, what a mess! She felt awful, lonely; this was supposed to be the happiest day of her life and all she wanted to do was bury her face in her hands and cry her eyes out.

She was prevented from doing so by the opening of the door. The washroom was filled with the echo of the music coming from the hall. The girl that had entered gave Barbara a smile and a nod, went into a cubicle and closed the door. Barbara turned the cold tap on again and cupping the water into her hands she held her face down towards it. That felt better.

She dabbed her eyes and cheeks dry on the roller-towel, then picking up her handbag she walked out to confront Michael.

She pushed her way through the group of men, ignoring the ribald remarks, until she was face to face with her husband.

'Michael, may we go now. I'm awfully tired.'

Of course it was the wrong thing to say.

'Oh, she's tired!'

'Hard luck Mike, all she wants ter do is sleep.'

'You'll get nought ternight Mike, might as well stay and get yourself a skin full.'

This exchange of crude jokes about the wedding night brought the colour flaming up into Barbara's cheeks but she wasn't about to be put down by this bunch of half-drunk mates of Michael's.

'If I were to say goodnight, *gentlemen*, I'd be labouring under a misapprehension wouldn't I?' came the terse reply from Barbara.

'Whoa! Got yerself an uppity one there, Mike!'

'Come on Barbara, we're going,' Michael said firmly, seeing the anger in her eyes. He knew he was in for a right old tirade for having left her on her own but there was no way he was going to allow her to slang him off, not in front of his mates.

Not for the first time today Barbara felt hurt but she shrugged it off. Now was not the time to air her grievances.

'Yes, you go ahead, Michael,' one of the group of men said quickly before Barbara could make further criticisms.

Saying his goodnights Michael began to walk away. With a lot more bravado than she was feeling Barbara held her head high and followed him.

The taxi came to a stop. The district was a poorer residential part of Plymouth well outside of the town. There were rows and rows of three storey terraced houses. The house which they were now standing in front of was numbered eighteen; there was no front garden, only a four foot pavement onto which the front door of the dwellings opened directly. Michael lifted the black knocker and gave it a sharp rat-a-tat-tat. After a moment while they stood together on the pavement without saying a word, the door opened. The woman in the doorway was thin, aged about forty, of medium height with fair hair drawn tightly back from her brow.

'Hallo Mike, me lad, you've made it then,' she said, letting out a great peal of coarse laughter.

The familiarity of the greeting puzzled Barbara but she had no time to ponder on it.

'Come in, come in. Don't just stand there wavering.' She shook her head, still laughing and made a wide sweeping gesture with her hand. Michael went forward first and, carrying her one and only suitcase, Barbara slowly followed him. They walked down a passage, it was far too narrow to be described as a hall, where at the end was a flight of stairs.

Nodding upwards the woman gave a smothered giggle as she said, 'You know which room it is, Mike, you don't need me ter come up with you.'

For answer Michael stretched out his arm and with the flat of his hand patted her buttocks. 'You're all right Daisy, stay where you are.' Then a little selfconsciously he turned to Barbara and said, 'We'll away up then, shall we?'

With no introductions having been made, Barbara felt there was nothing for her to say.

Reaching the first landing Michael stopped, pointed a finger and told her, 'The bathroom and toilet are down there, our room is up here, top of the house.'

With that he preceded her up a further flight of stairs at the top of which there was one door only Flinging it open wide he waited until Barbara had passed him and now as she stood in the centre of the room he kicked the door shut behind himself and with a wide smile on his face came towards her.

Involuntarily she took a step backwards, evading his outstretched arms. Slowly she lifted her eyes and looked into his and what she uttered could have been a cry from a wounded animal.

'What the bloody 'ell's the matter?' he yelled at her.

She couldn't form an answer. The day had taken its toll, everything had become beyond her control, she was shaking with fear.

Michael, watching her, was annoyed and the amount of beer which he had drunk probably made him more insensitive than normal.

'You should be happy, over the moon, it wasn't easy to

wangle it so that we could be together tonight. It's our wedding night for Christ's sake.'

'I know. I know.' Her voice was barely audible.

'What then?'

She did her best to smile at him now as she glanced towards the double iron bedstead that seemed to dominate the entire floor space of this attic room.

'It's just – well, this place, not seeing you before the wedding, the actual wedding, oh *everything*, nothing feels right, nothing is as I always imagined it would be.'

'Oh yeah,' he sneered. 'What did you expect? Westminster Abbey? Organ music, flowers, choirboys?' His voice grew louder, tinted with rage.

Of course she hadn't expected anything like that, but the words he'd flung at her brought home the reality of just how sparse today's proceedings had really been.

Oh wouldn't it have been nice, all of that and a reception, hugs, kisses, congratulations, gifts. That thought brought her up sharply. Not a single wedding present had she received this day!

'Well you'd better get things straight from the beginning.' Michael's tone brought her back to reality as he continued to storm at her, 'I'm an A.B. in the navy, what I'll be when I get demobbed God only knows. I'm not part of the legal profession like your father and his cronies. I've been fighting the bloody War, not like some of the toffee-nosed sods you mix with. Conscientious objectors most of them, I dare say – did anything and everything to get out of being conscripted did they? Well I've got news fer you, my darling, I didn't wait ter get me calling-up papers, I bloody well volunteered I did.'

Barbara couldn't believe it. She couldn't take it in. This

wasn't Michael, she'd had no idea that he felt like this. The acrimony of his words and the temper he was displaying appalled her. She had to grab at the brass knob on the end of the bed to stop herself from falling as she staggered backwards.

Suddenly Michael's arms, which had been flaying the air, came down to dangle loosely at his sides, the anger on his face lessened, he took a step, faltered, then slumped heavily against the wall.

Barbara's heart was thumping away inside her chest. Her hands were clenched into fists and her breath was coming in short gasps. Her throat was dry and she knew that if she tried to speak to him she would begin to cry. The tears were already there, burning and stinging behind her eyes. She bit down so hard on her lip that she tasted blood.

This was a side to Michael she had never seen, never even imagined.

Slowly he crossed the room, wrapped his arms around her and held her gently. She wanted to resist, to tear herself away and run, but where to? Where would she go?

Michael made no apology for his outburst. Releasing her a little he stared into her misty eyes and very quietly asked, 'Do you love me Barbara?' Without giving her a chance to reply he spoke in an emotional whisper, 'Sometimes I'm sure you do. Your letters convinced me you did. Other times, like now, you make me feel I'm not good enough for you – that I won't be able to give you the things that you are used to having.'

Barbara felt a flush come up over her face and neck. 'Michael, of course I love you,' she protested.

'No! There's no of course about it. Either you do or

you don't and if you don't it's not too late, I'll clear out right now.'

But it was too late!

It was she who now made the move. Putting her hands out she cupped his face and said, 'I do love you, Michael, it began the first moment I saw you, it's just that – ' there was a break in her voice and she wasn't able to go on.

He guided her towards the bed and they sat side by side on the very edge. 'Come on, Barbara, finish what you were going to say.' His voice was now soft and caressing.

'Well, today it's as if I didn't know you at all. You're like a stranger. I've been so lonely here in Plymouth, you haven't explained why it was you couldn't meet me before today. Oh – I just don't know.'

Michael's face was very white. His dark, curly hair was damp and his hands were shaking so much it frightened her and suddenly he was the dear, sweet Michael that she had been writing to for so long.

'In plain words, you're having doubts?' He tried to smile at her but it did not quite work.

She leant towards him and gripped his hand. 'Michael, I'm not. Really I'm not, it's just that – '

He didn't let her finish.

'Good. Since you've felt I'm a stranger today we'd better start beginning to know each other. Do you agree?'

'Yes.'

When their long kisses was over, their lips now parted, the magic of this man was back. She knew she wanted him, he was her very own Michael, compelling, strong, irresistible.

Michael stood up and removed his dicky collar, making a great show of folding it properly.

'Oh, Barbara,' he said helplessly. 'I've known a number of girls in my time but, Babs, you are the only one I ever wanted to be my wife.'

It was the first time he had shortened her Christian name, she didn't like it, but let it go.

Having started talking it was as if he couldn't stop. The words came pouring out.

'Socially and in a great many other ways I know you're streets above me, I couldn't believe my luck when we first met and you felt towards me as you did. We didn't have long together, did we? I never expected you to write so often, so regularly, but you did, me mates mocked me about it, every port we put into there was a bundle of letters, never a "Dear John" as so many blokes got. Even me best mate, a married man, got a letter from his wife saying, "Sorry, but!" Separations aren't good, I know that and ours was a long one. Actually just how long have we had together? Add it all up and I don't suppose it amounts to much more than a month.'

Stripped to the waist now, his tunic folded and lying on the one and only chair, he began to pace the floor, still talking almost as if to himself.

'The effect you had on me right from the start hasn't altered, maybe it has for you. I'm not a good catch, not for you I'm not. When I get out of the navy I've no job, nowhere to live, no family to speak of, but I'm sure of one thing, Barbara, I love you.'

He paused in his pacing, turned his head to where she still sat perched on the edge of the bed, the look in his eyes implored her to believe him.

'I will try and be good to you, I promise. I don't blame you if you are having misgivings, I've rushed you along a

41

bit haven't I?' He came to stand in front of her and once more his arms were about her. Now her fear of him was gone and in its place was a loving sensation, a yearning for everything to be all right between them.

'Oh Michael, I *do* love you!' And at that moment she truly meant it.

What followed was inevitable.

To begin with it was wonderful. His lips were covering hers, his hands moving gently backwards and forwards across her body. She was wafted to heaven, Michael did love her. All the pent up frustration of wartime, when the occasional letter had been all she had to remind her of her good-looking, strapping sailor, the uncertainty of the last few days, hesitations over decisions, all were wiped away.

Even this dingy, top back-bedroom of a terraced lodging house, it no longer mattered. Michael was showing his love for her.

Abruptly things changed, it was no longer love. Passion wasn't even the right word. Brutality was. Her body was on fire as he lay on top of her and the fierceness of his movements went on and on. It was more than just physical hurt that he was inflicting on her, he was giving vent to his anger, using violence to show her the urgency of his needs.

His body became still at last, all his resentment had drained away. He rolled off her and within minutes he was fast asleep.

The tears that showed her bewilderment and pain fell silently and she tasted the salty bitterness of them in her mouth, as she lay beside him.

Oh, Michael, she thought, despairingly. Why didn't we

42

give ourselves more time? We've married in haste and I only hope to God that I shan't live to regret it.

Up on the rooftop a cat screeched and somewhere in the distance a dog barked, there was plenty of living things moving about in the night air. Yet as Barbara moved to the edge of the bed and curled herself up into a ball, she was feeling hurt and very much alone.

Tomorrow, she would be catching the train to London. Within six to seven hours she would be back in Parsons Green; would Penny and Elizabeth see a noticeable change in her? They had to, the hurt must show in her eyes if not on her face.

A wave of longing swept over her. If only she could turn the clock back. There had been no time and very little time to feel. Feeling would come later, when the reality of what she had done sank in. If only she hadn't agreed to marry Michael, but she had. It was done. There was no turning back.

Chapter Three

THE PIPS ON the wireless signified the time was just nine o'clock on this mid-January morning in 1947 and Barbara was at her wits' end not knowing what to do or which way to turn.

What the hell can I do? she asked herself.

As the weeks had turned into months and the months now into over a year she wondered whether they would ever get out of this South London area and if they did, would the hell of a life that she and Michael were leading really alter? She was afraid of his violent temper. She hated the jealousy that exploded into vile insults and accusations and, most of all, she hated his foul-mouth and filthy habits. His drinking sessions were having a terrible effect on Michael.

The first four months following her marriage had been fine. She had remained on, sharing the flat with Penny and Elizabeth, whilst Michael was shore-based at Plymouth awaiting his demob. Frequently he had obtained forty-eight hour weekend passes and it was she that booked them into small hotels in and around Chelsea. Only once had she done otherwise, choosing the charming Manor House Hotel set in gentle countryside by the river in Richmond, Surrey. It hadn't suited Michael and for the second time she was given a display of his bad temper. For a start, the hotel held no drinks licence and secondly he objected that the quietness of the countryside was driving him bloody mad.

Finally Michael was discharged from the Royal Navy and they were supposed to settle down and begin to lead a normal life. Like a good many more youngsters who had lived through the War, it wasn't as easy nor as straight forward as they had imagined.

It was Michael himself who had found these rooms to rent, situated above a corner shop in Latchmere Road, Battersea. The first sight of the building had dismayed her, yet even that had not prepared her for the interior. She had shuddered and murmured, 'It's horrible.'

That exclamation had been like a red rag to a bull. 'Why don't you climb down from your bleeding high horse for once,' he had spat at her, and went on at great length about how lucky they were to have found these rooms to rent.

When she had got over the initial shock it was a point she had had to agree was true. Many ex-servicemen, their wives and even their children were being housed in Nissen-huts on open common-land. With whole streets of houses having been demolished during the air raids over London rented accommodation was hard to find. True, the local councils had acted quickly: families wanted and needed to be together after long war years of separation. On wasteland and what space had been cleared of debris, workmen were set to erecting the huts to be used as temporary homes. Being just corrugated-iron sections bolted together to form semi-circular constructions they were ugly, but people still fought to be allocated one. With the rent set at only ten shillings a week they were regarded as a godsend by those fortunate to be assigned such a dwelling and many more would have jumped at the chance.

Whenever Barbara passed such a site something of the same feeling went through her mind, regardless of the fact that they were fast becoming slum dumps. Already the lines of washing, overflowing dustbins and litter were making the locations unsightly. Yet at least these tenants had privacy and each family had their own toilet. Which was a darn sight more than she and Michael had.

Faced with these two box-like rooms and the small kitchenette, finding out that the lavatory on the landing outside her living room had to be shared with the tenants on the top floor, a Mr and Mrs Singleton and their two adult sons, had been the last straw.

Her protests had been cut short by a string of obscenities from Michael. With no other option she had decided to make every effort and had set to with enthusiasm, determined that if that was where they were going to have to live, at least for the time being, she would do what she could to make the place into a decent home for both of them. First off she had cleaned the walls and ceilings, scraping away the grease and grime from the paint work. Michael had been no help at all.

Long since she had come to the conclusion that the two of them were totally incompatible. To be honest, she was like a fish out of water in his world and if the tables were ever turned he would probably be a damn sight worse off in hers. She also decided she had little in common with her neighbours and was now convinced that old Mrs Winters, who owned the shop below, was the only person of her new acquaintances she could consider to be a friend.

Out of sheer habit Barbara began to move about the room straightening things, plumping up the cushions in the two armchairs, emptying the ashtray that Michael had

46

left in the grate. She paused in her moving about to look out of the window down into the street. As early as it was women were lolling in doorways, arms folded across their ample bosoms; each wore a wraparound flowered overall. She often wondered whether these women wore shapeless pinafores as a kind of uniform or more than likely as an announcement of their poverty.

When she'd first come to live in the district several wives had invited her to join them for a cup of tea. She had accepted once. A whole bunch of women crowded into another's stuffy living room to drink endless cups of strong sweet tea was not her idea of a pleasant outing. After the first time her refusal was not due entirely to snobbishness, the longing for company, any company some days, often had her wavering but she clung to her belief, there must be, there had to be, more to life than whiling away time by listening to gossip.

Down on the corner a group of small children were playing hopscotch; the pavement was permanently marked out with chalk into the appropriate squares and only renewed after a downpour of rain. As she watched, a small boy, a great tear in the seat of his trousers, tossed a stone. Instead of landing into a square it rolled away off the pavement into the gutter and as he dashed into the road to retrieve it a van drew to a shuddering stop. Unable to hear from where she stood, Barbara was in no doubt that a stream of foul language was screamed at the child by the driver from his cab. Although many of the children down there were old enough to be at school, their attendance was at best irregular and nobody, least of all their parents, seemed a bit bothered.

Barbara turned away from the window. Was this what she wanted for her children? She heaved a great sigh.

This was the main bone of contention between Michael and herself. He was adamant. He didn't want to start a family. 'I don't care if we never have any kids,' he had roared at her when she had first told him she was pregnant. For the next two days life had been unbearable. He had gone as far as using his fists on her to emphasise that he meant what he said and that he was determined to be master in his own house.

Within six months of living here in Battersea she had had two abortions. Acting on the knowledge she had gained from Mrs Winters the first had been self-induced, having missed only one period the result had not been too drastic. The second time she had delayed telling Michael, clinging to the hope that he might just relent and be as pleased as she was. He wasn't daft! When he had finally challenged her she had no alternative but to admit the truth. Her pleading to be allowed to have the baby had earned her a severe clout round the ear. Michael had been beside himself with rage, even throwing the accusation at her that the baby couldn't possibly be his.

'I can't say I 'old with it,' Mrs Winters had answered sadly, when Barbara had sought her help yet again.

Barbara had flushed with guilt.

'Oh, I know it ain't your fault, bless yer heart. How yer ever come ter get yerself tied up with that sodding lazy bleeder I'll never know. Perhaps it's as well. What kid would want a father what spends two-thirds of his life in the pub an' the other bloody third in the damn betting shop. All right, my luv, leave it with me, though Lord knows I won't sleep till I know it's over an' done with.'

Barbara smiled bleakly at her and once more felt a surge of gratitude towards this cockney woman who had become her friend.

A tall, thin yet big-breasted woman, with a face as wrinkled as a prune, Mrs Winters would have her customers and tenants believe that she was as hard as iron and just as tough. In most circumstances she was. Beneath that craggy exterior, though, there was kindness and compassion for those that she thought warranted her help. Barbara most certainly came top of that list.

For a fat fee a doctor had terminated her pregnancy. The following days of pain and suffering, not to mention the heartbreak, had caused Barbara to vow never again. Besides which, she was tormented by the thought that having numerous abortions might in time cause her to become sterile and a future, despite what Michael said and did, without children didn't bear thinking about, at least for her.

Christ! I've got to snap out of this fit of the blues. Even if by some miracle, and God knows it would take one, Michael did come round to my way of thinking, what future would there be for our children in such surroundings as these? she asked herself, but came up with no answer. If only she could go out to work. How many times had this thought come to her? Perhaps with a job in the city her mind would once more become active, give her a reason to make an effort, dress nicely, wear some make-up – and the money she'd earn wouldn't come amiss.

Taking a duster from the dresser drawer, with a lack of enthusiasm she began to wipe the furniture; coming now to the mirror which hung on the wall she sadly shook her head at her reflection. She looked awful. Tired and dishevelled. The endless nightly arguments between Michael and herself had taken their toll. Why did he always get the better of her? Why had he developed such a degree of possessiveness? The hardest thing to endure was his jealousy, it seemed now that he would do anything and everything within his power to humiliate her.

'You're a spoilt rich bitch,' was his favourite accusation.

Rich! That was a laugh, there was never a week when she had more than a few shillings in her purse.

Most probably she could obtain employment locally, in a shop or a small office, but Michael's threats were no idle matter. 'Men around here support their wives, they don't stand for them dolling themselves up and pissing off each day, so yer needn't delude yerself that you'll ever get to claim that you're the breadwinner. Not while I'm around you won't.' Having made that statement for all the street to hear, he'd been really irritable.

That was another laugh! He'd support his wife! What he really meant was that he'd lose face amongst his drinking mates if they found out that his wife was working.

Well, the way things were heading he'd lose the roof over their heads soon. Even so, he still threatened. 'Get yerself a job, work in a bloody office and I'll make sure they'll be damn sorry you ever set foot in the place. I'll be there to meet you, you needn't worry on that score, an' I'll not only raise hell, I'll rearrange the face of any bloody ponce that thinks for a few bob a week he can have my wife running around after him.' He left her in no doubt. He meant every word.

Nothing she said, none of her reasoning or imploring had been able to shift his bigoted beliefs. Michael was sticking to his guns. A woman's place was in the home, but what was there for her to do all day long in these two poky rooms? And he couldn't bear the thought of their starting a family. Why had they never got around to discussing these matters before they got married? She knew well enough why they hadn't! He hadn't given her the time. Would it have made any difference? She doubted it. Love is blind, so the saying goes, well time had certainly opened her eyes.

She suddenly became impatient with herself. Going over and over all this time and time again is only going to drive you round the bed. So stop it, it's not getting you anywhere, she told herself as she began the task of washing up the breakfast things. Taking the whistling, tin kettle from the gas stove she poured most of the boiling water into the enamel bowl, the single tap above the shallow, brown, stone sink gave only cold water. When drying the dishes and putting them away she left out one cup and saucer in order to make herself a cup of coffee. Michael always preferred to drink tea, on her own she could please herself. First she must go to the toilet, on the way she fervently hoped it would be vacant. It wasn't.

She had to wait ages, with her front door ajar, before she heard the chain being pulled and stout Mrs Singleton's laboured footsteps mount the stairs. Once inside the air made her feel sick, the smell was awful. She climbed up onto the wooden seat and wrestled with the small window, as usual she wasn't able to budge it an inch.

'It's nailed up,' was Michael's retort whenever she complained, but still every now and then she tried to shift it open.

She really did resent having to share this toilet with the tenants upstairs. How many times a week did she thoroughly clean this closet and the pan, only to find it filthy shortly afterwards? As to toilet rolls – they must eat them. No one other than herself seemed to provide them. More often than not the lavatory pan was choked with newspaper. Now she no longer left the roll in there, taking it with her each time and bringing it out when she left. Michael laughed at her, saying she had a fad about toilet rolls, but no, that wasn't it, she wouldn't have minded so much supplying them if others, at least sometimes, would do likewise. On many of the occasions she had been caught out, not only was there no paper left but no evidence that she had ever hung a roll through the string on the back of the door – even the cardboard centre cone was never there, albeit empty of tissue.

Another thing that got up Barbara's nose was the flight of stairs that led down to the street. The carpet (or was it linoleum?) that once had been laid on the stairs was now so well-worn and rotten in places as to be dangerous. When going down or coming up she could never stop herself from wrinkling her nose at the smell that prevailed throughout the building. Inside their own two rooms she had worked wonders, even Michael agreed on that, yet when once she had timidly suggested to Mrs Singleton that they cleaned together the walls, staircase and landing she had been glad when she had at last been able to get away from her. Even now the memory of that clash with Mrs Singleton made her shudder. Petrified she'd been as the bulk of the woman had barred her way.

With a mocking laugh Mrs Singleton had mimicked Barbara's voice, 'So, this place ain't quite good enough for you milady?'

Seeing Barbara cringe only edged Mrs Singleton on and

she reverted to her own guttural tone. 'A bit of sodding dirt never 'urt no one. We've all got ter eat a bushel 'fore we kick the bucket. My old man and me two sons all work on the building and if I did git down on me 'ands an' knees an' scrub them stairs they'd only be just as bad again by termorra what wiv their filfy boots an' all. No, you bloody upstart, you want the stairs scrubbed, get yer lazy sodding old man ter do 'em for yer, I've never seen 'im do a day's work since yer came 'ere. And while we're on the bleedin' subject if yer don't like it 'ere why the bloody 'ell d'yer stay? There's plenty as would be only too glad ter take over your rooms an' I sure as 'ell would be glad ter see the back of yer. You've got yer nose stuck so far up in the air that yer think your own shit don't stink, well let me tell you luv, you smell just as rotten as the rest of us around 'ere.'

Having finished her tirade, she'd waddled off, her breath coming in short ragged gaspings, and over and over again she was muttering, 'I'll kill the stuck-up bitch! I'll kill her! I will! I'll flatten her stone dead!'

The trouble was Barbara knew the old woman spoke the truth; there would be heaps of young couples more than glad to be given the chance to rent these rooms.

For days after that Barbara had gone to great lengths to avoid coming into contact with any member of the Single-ton family, and she had had to quickly cover her mouth with her hand to suppress a giggle when a week later she heard that Michael had got himself a job on the building sites.

He had joined a gang of demolition men. London, and most major cities the length and breadth of the country, needed these gangs to bulldoze the remains of buildings damaged by the bombing and to clear the sites ready for rebuilding.

As Barbara folded her duster and placed it back in the dresser drawer she cursed herself for having listened to Michael's glib tongue. Why, oh why had she allowed herself to be rushed into a marriage that at the moment didn't seem as if it would have a hope in hell of ever working out? But what was done was done. For better or worse, she had saddled herself with Michael Henderson as a husband and she just had to make the best of it .

At that moment she wondered what had happened to the gentle, loving, courteous Michael that she had fallen in love with. Seldom did she ever get a glimpse of him now.

'Michael,' she said aloud. 'Oh, Michael – what's to become of us?' She felt tears of self-pity prickle the backs of her eyes, and she angrily brushed them away.

Oh well, she sighed, better decide what to cook for his dinner tonight. With today being pay-day God knows what time he'll come home. A visit to the pub with his workmates would be of primary importance, none the more for that, whatever the time, Michael would expect his dinner to be ready and waiting for him. And God help her if it wasn't.

Searching through the larder didn't take long. She found two desiccated soup cubes, both oxtail flavoured, some lentils and pearl barley. In the vegetable box, thank God, she had plenty of carrots, onions and potatoes. She'd never have believed that one person could eat as many potatoes as Michael did. Right from the start he had soon made it clear that a dinner was not a dinner unless the plate was piled high with spuds, as he referred to them. One thing, he wasn't fussy about how they were cooked. Roasted, boiled, mashed or in their jackets he always asked for more – as for chips! – she could never get used to watching him eat great mounds of chips liberally smothered in vinegar and that revolting bottled tomato sauce he liked so much.

She laid the pot-herbs out on the wooden draining board and set the potatoes in the enamel bowl filled with cold water, looked around the living room and made certain that Michael could find nothing to complain about.

Going now into the bedroom, she put on her winter coat and wound a long cashmere scarf around her shoulders – it would be bitter-cold outside and the wind seem to bite right through to one's very bones. Not that she would be outdoors for very long, the market was only at the other end of the street.

She had decided to make a casserole and as she slipped her gloves on she gave a wry smile; better not say 'casserole' to Michael, he'd only repeat what he'd told her before. 'Posh name for a stew, that's all it is, so why not come straight out and call it a stew.'

Not that Michael minded having a stew for his dinner. The thicker the better, stand a fork up in it and if it held it must be good. Even cheap scrag of mutton, Michael wouldn't complain, he'd happily suck the meat from the bones while she attempted to use a knife and fork. An apple pie for sweet would be filling. Oh, there she went again, she must try and remember to think of it as a pudding or afters, though how a fruit pie could be known as pudding! Still, anything to keep the peace.

There was many a time now when Barbara had reason to be grateful for the cookery classes her school had insisted upon. She prided herself on her soups. They were excellent and nutritious. There again Michael annoyed her, with one bowl of soup as a start to their evening meal he would polish off half a loaf of bread, dunking great hunks of crust into the hot, rich soup – drawing the dripping bread upwards to his mouth, ignoring the fact that drops were being spilt onto the tablecloth.

She admitted to herself that this was more than likely half of their troubles: to Michael she was much too fastidious, whilst he to her at times was coarse, even uncouth.

Opening the door at the foot of the stairs which led out into the street, Barbara paused a moment and looked into the shop.

'Morning luv, 'ow are yer?' Mrs Winters called cheerfully to her and without waiting for a reply rushed on, 'Talk of the devil, I was just about to call up ter yer, kettle's boiling an' I've only got ter put tea in the pot. Come on – don't just stand there, put wood in the 'ole an' come and sit yerself down.'

'I've just had a coffee,' Barbara protested.

She might just as well have saved her breath. Ma Winters was pulling a heavy armchair nearer to the oil-stove. She plumped up an enormous cushion and placed it against the threadbare, upholstered arm of the chair.

'Plonk yer arse down in there,' she said, with a nod of her head. 'You ain't so busy that yer can't spare a few minutes to gossip with an old woman that'll be right glad of yer company.'

She poured tea into two enamel mugs and came and sat down facing Barbara. When they'd each taken a sip of the scalding tea, she leant forward and said in a low voice, ''Ow are yer managing?'

Barbara was reluctant to answer. This blunt, straightforward type of woman who was her landlady had proved to be a friend – indeed, Barbara was not at all sure that she would have survived these past months without Mrs Winters to talk too. Honest as the day was long, was how Barbara regarded Mrs Winters. Never afraid to speak her mind, offend or please. Affluent compared with most folk around these parts, in as much as she owned a second-hand furniture shop plus the two flats above, which she rented to tenants. Barbara had no idea where Mrs Winters lived; ever ready to listen to Barbara's troubles, she was not one to discuss her own personal life. Life hadn't dealt kindly in other ways with this woman, in spite of the fact that she had prospered. Everyone took her to be elderly, at least in her sixties – her thin frame, pinched wrinkled features and greying light-brown hair made the assumption easy. If the truth were known she was in her late forties.

'Oi! You're miles away.' Mrs Winters' work-worn hand on her knee brought Barbara back from her daydreaming. 'You ain't answered my question yet. You would tell me if there was anything wrong, wouldn't you?'

'Of course I would', Barbara assured her, touched as always by the concern shown to her. 'I'm fine. Really I am, with Michael working now we'll manage a whole lot better.'

It wasn't often that Mrs Winters had a feeling of helplessness, life had taught her to be hard and she could hold her own with any man. When it came to Barbara she was utterly bewildered. Her every instinct told her that Michael Henderson was a right bastard! An arrogant sod! Then again, what on earth had possessed a lovely, gentle girl like Barbara to marry him in the first place? It must have broken her parents' hearts. One could tell just by looking at

Barbara her early life had been good, giving her breeding, education and money. She was totally unfitted for the life she was leading. But Mrs Winters wasn't in a position to interfere. Damn that bloody Michael, she cried to herself, just let him go too far and she'd see he got his just deserts. By hell she would!

'I'd better get going,' Barbara said, setting her empty mug down. 'Is there anything you want me to bring you back from the market?'

'No thanks, luv, an' don't you get 'anging about too long, it's cold enough out there to freeze the brass balls off a monkey.'

Barbara was still laughing to herself as she wound her scarf tightly round her shoulders and set out to do her shopping.

Turning the corner, Barbara was met by a chorus of wolf whistles, she smiled broadly and waved her hand in greeting towards the gang of men who were clearing the site where once had stood the Crown and Anchor Public House. A direct hit from a German bomb had erased it, leaving nothing but a pile of rubble. To the side of the crater a huge bonfire was burning – the acrid smell of rotting timber filled her nostrils, bringing back scenes she had witnessed during the air raids, scenes she would like to have obliterated from her mind. Thick dust covered the men and straight away she thought of Michael, doing exactly the same type of work on a larger scale in the West End of London. Every evening he came home thickly grimed with red brick-dust. It would be in his hair, his eyes, even under his fingernails. It was awful for him. She knew that, but he just wouldn't help himself. Having no bathroom was a disadvantage yet he could so easily have a good wash down. On the ready each evening, she'd have two pans of water boiling, the tin bath placed in front of the gas stove and towels laid out on a chair. Michael could hardly ever be bothered, a quick sluice under the cold tap and he would be demanding his dinner.

Try as she would she couldn't begin to understand Michael.

With the weekend approaching it was a full market day, no empty spaces between the numerous stalls and already the pavement was thronged with many people. Strangely, Barbara loved the hustle and the bustle that greeted her from all sides. Those women, mostly with big families to feed, were bargaining ferociously with the men who owned the stalls, answering their cheeky comments with good humour, giving back as good as they got.

The scrag-end of mutton bought and stowed away in her shopping bag, Barbara now made for the largest of the fruit and vegetable stalls. For a moment she was tempted to ask for two extra-large apples, filled with golden syrup and sultanas they were delicious when baked. Better not. Michael hated stuffed baked apples.

'What can I do yer for, me luverly?' The trader yelled the question at her.

'Two pounds of Bramleys please.'

'They ain't Bramleys darling', he told her with open honesty. 'Wrong time of year, but they're luverly cookers – make a luverly pie and if yer old man don't appreciate it chuck 'im out an' invite me round for a bit.'

The women in the crowd roared with laughter and Barbara joined them. It was impossible to take offence at such cockney wisecracks, even though they were vulgar and loaded with a double meaning.

'There yer go, those five come to a tanner, want me ter take one off?'

'No,' she smiled her thanks at the man, 'they will do nicely.'

'Any fing else?' he asked as he tipped the apples into her shopping basket. She was about to say no when her eyes rested on the high display of grapefruits. It was such a long time since any such-like fruit had been available, quickly she said, 'Yes please, two grapefruits.'

Then the thought came to her if she bought potatoes today it would save her having to carry such a heavy load tomorrow when shopping for the weekend, so now she added, 'And may I have five pounds of potatoes please?'

'King Edwards at fourpence fer five pounds or Whites at threepence?'

'King Edwards please.'

'That the lot then?'

'Yes thank you.'

Barbara handed over a two shilling piece and the young barrow boy gave her sixpence in change, holding on to her hand for a lot longer than was necessary. 'Tat-Ah then luv, take care.' He was grinning at her, his eyes full of admiration.

In response she gave him an open smile. She was fully aware that the hawkers were skilled in the art of bantering with their customers; none the less for that, a little appreciation shown to her by a good-looking young man did an awful lot for her ego.

Snow was in the air: everyone was saying so, the clouds

were low, dark and foreboding as she walked home. The wind had dropped but then so had the temperature. The cold was raw now and the daylight seemed strange, even spookish, which certainly heralded a storm of some sort.

'Christ, I hope we aren't going to get a repeat of last year!'

Last winter had been terrible. Snow had lain in the streets for weeks and most of the country had experienced sub-zero temperatures. If that happened now Michael would be laid off, together with many other building workers and there would be no pay for any of them. Besides, she'd have him home all day cooped up in those two rooms! It didn't bear thinking about. The prospect wouldn't be any better for Michael, he seemed much happier since he had been working and had a few shillings in his pocket to spend.

Tonight I'll make an extra effort, she silently vowed. Have a real good hot dinner ready. I'll be loving to him, put my arms round him before either of us have time to get off on the wrong foot. I'll have the fire banked halfway up the chimney so that the place is really warm for when he comes home. But what time would he come home? Never mind, I won't even comment.

Saturday morning was typical. At nine o'clock she'd gone shopping, leaving Michael in bed. Eleven o'clock she was back and by twelve Michael had gone out. Shortly after three, when the pubs closed, he had come home, eaten an enormous dinner – on Saturdays and Sundays he preferred to have his main meal at this time – then slept the afternoon away slunk down in an armchair drawn close up to the fire.

'Cup of tea, Michael. It's gone six.' Barbara would just as soon let him sleep on but for him to miss a trip to the pub on a Saturday night just wasn't on.

He wriggled himself upwards in the chair, stretched his arms above his head and yawned loudly.

'Thanks Babs,' he said, leaning forward and taking his cup and saucer off of the edge of the table. Three or four gulps and the cup was empty. 'Fill it up, luv.'

He watched as she tipped the slops into the slop-bowl she insisted on using, then removed the quilted cosy from the pot before pouring him out a refill using a tea-strainer. What a bloody rigmarole! Still, with parents like hers and the way she'd been brought up it was a wonder she didn't use a clean cup and saucer every time.

'Gonna doll yerself up an' come with me tonight?' The question had been asked kindly and it surprised Barbara.

'I don't think so,' she answered quietly. 'You'll have your mates at the bar to talk to and I don't know any of the customers. I'd just as soon stay here and read my book.'

He didn't rant and rave or tell her she'd always got her head buried in a book. 'You never will get to know anyone if you stay cooped up in here every night of the week. Besides, I'd really like yer to come with me, it's about time I showed yer off to some of the blokes, I want to see their faces, their wives are proper old has-beens compared to you.' He got to his feet, came to where she sat and put his arm around her shoulders. 'Please Barbara, come with me.'

In the face of such gentle persuasion how could she refuse?

She took pains over her make-up, brushed her long hair

until the glints in it shone, then pinned it into a sophisticated French pleat at the back and piled neat curls on the
top and at the sides. A plain black dress with a wide red
belt and her high-heeled red court shoes and she was ready.

The look of approval in Michael's eyes as he held her coat
for her told her that her efforts had been well worthwhile.

If only he would wear a collar and tie, was what she was
thinking as she watched him wind a white silk muffler
around his neck. This habit favoured by all the local men
seemed as much a badge of poverty to her as did the
wrapround overalls the women constantly wore. She had
the sense not to comment.

Everything was normal for a Saturday evening. The
noise, commotion and smoky atmosphere were all as Barbara had feared. The bench seats set along the wall were
occupied by the older women, grey-haired, with an
unhealthy pallor and dressed in clothes that looked as
though they had been bought at a jumble sale. Pints of
draught Guinness with thick creamy heads were set in front
of each of them. In groups, nearer to the bar, were the
younger females. Peroxide blondes, redheads and brunettes,
all had had the curling-tongs at work on their hair. Rows
and rows of sausage curls enriched by ornaments neatly at
the nape of their necks. Perched on high stools, legs swinging, stocking seams running straight to where their short
skirts barely covered their behinds, now and again showing
bare thigh and a glimpse of a ribboned suspender, they
were – as they intended to be – an eyeful for the men at
the bar.

Having seated Barbara at a small table tucked away in
the corner and bought her a double gin and orange,
Michael had joined his mates at the counter. Centre of this

group of men was Pete Davis. A tall young man with the build of a rugby player, loud-mouthed and flashily dressed, Pete Davis was no stranger to Barbara. Michael had brought him back to their flat quite a few times. Never short of money, very generous – according to Michael – and popular with all the ladies. That was not how Barbara felt about him. She was uneasy whenever he was around. She always felt that she should tread warily where Pete Davis was concerned.

Barbara sighed heavily as she watched Michael pass another ten shilling note over the bar to pay for his round of drinks. He was a big man in every way when among his mates and very popular, yet she found herself wishing that he would get his priorities right. For some reason she suddenly felt very guilty. It was such a pity that they never seemed to want the same things. She did love him and she tried so hard to understand him yet she never seemed able to. At times like this, when he was showing his happy-go-lucky nature and his lovely smile, he was easy to love, just as he had been when they had first met. But the days when he was in a filthy mood and nothing she did was right were becoming far too frequent and it wasn't in her nature to give in to him all the time.

'Funny yer old man leaving yer so much on yer own,' observed the old woman seated nearest to Barbara.

'Not really,' said Barbara faintly. 'He likes to be with his mates.' The woman made a grim face. 'Wouldn't do me. Should 've thought the pair of yer would 've been canoodling up tergether like a pair of doves.'

Well yer thought wrong! was what Barbara wished she had the courage to snap at the old hag. She felt her cheeks flame but was saved from answering by the appearance of Michael.

He bent down until his face was level with hers. His eyes looked at her hungrily as he asked. 'Ready for another drink?'

Before Barbara had time to reply the woman who had been pestering her tugged at Michael's sleeve, ''Ow about buying me an' me friend just one little drink, Michael,' she wheedled.

'My pleasure, me darlin' What's it ter be? Another Guinness or a drop of mother's ruin?'

'Oh, we'll 'ave a little drop of Gordons wiv you, won't we Mabel?'

As Michael made his way back to the bar, the woman who had been referred to as Mabel leant across her friend and poked Barbara in the ribs.

'Got any fags?' she asked.

'No, I don't smoke. Won't your friend give you one?'

'She ain't got no more. That was her last one she's just lit – see – the empty packet is in the ashtray.'

'Mike will buy us some,' said the woman who had asked for the drinks, and without more ado she yelled loudly, 'Mike, be a luv an' get us some fags.'

'Weights or Woodbines?' he called back.

This was carrying things too far. Barbara felt herself stiffen with the sheer audacity of the pair of them. She longed to tell the woman that they hadn't money to spare to be buying casual acquaintances drinks, never mind cigarettes as well, but Michael was enjoying playing the Big I Am and he wouldn't take kindly to her interfering and what would she do if he turned on her here in the pub. Still, it would be nice once in a while if he was as generous as this when it came to handing over the house-keeping money.

When at last the Landlord called 'Time, Gentlemen please', Barbara pulled herself together, squared her shoulders and with some effort pushed through the crowd to where Michael stood. She was determined that they should go straight home. She didn't want Michael sloping off to some late nightclub with Pete Davis, by the sound of his slurred speech he had had more than enough to drink for one night.

As Barbara opened the front door Michael began to sing at the top of his voice. 'Show me the way ter go 'ome, I'm tired an' I wanna go ter bed . . .'

Oh, he was driving her mad, being so contrary. Getting him upstairs was proving very difficult. With her arm around his waist to guide him, it was still case of up two stairs and back down one. Halfway up Michael began to laugh and pushed her flat against the wall. Laughing, tearing at the buttons on her coat, grabbing at her red belt, Barbara was instantly embarrassed. Suppose Mrs Singleton, or even one of her sons should come down to the landing?

'Come on, Michael,' she pleaded. 'Let's get indoors.'

He wouldn't budge and she felt she had to assert herself. With a hefty shove she broke free. 'I'm going on, I'll open up and put the lights on,' she said, doing her best to pacify him.

The heels of her shoes made a tapping sound on the threadbare linoleum as she quickened her pace. She heard him behind her, coming upwards on his hands and knees, whining away in a peevish voice. 'Wait. Oh, Babs please wait. I just wanna show yer 'ow much I luv yer.'

At last. She had him safely inside their living room and she thankfully closed the door.

'I'll boil the kettle, make us some tea. What would you like for your supper?'

'Who the bloody 'ell wants tea?' he roared at her. He made a grab for her, slipped and half fell, just saving himself by tugging at the hem of her dress and almost bringing her down to the floor with him.

She sighed heavily, best get him into the bedroom before he woke up the whole household. Michael tore at his clothing, smiling at her all the while. Much better to give in quietly, she decided, hoping against hope that perhaps, just this once he might treat her gently. Act as if he really did love her and not just want to use her.

She tried. Encouraging him to kiss her softly, showing him affection, hoping for some in return. To begin with he did treat her kindly, fondling her body, caressing slowly, then suddenly it wasn't at all like that. He was biting her. Hard and spitefully. Then he was on top of her, a short sharp blow of lust with no regard for her feelings and he was finished. Heaving a great satisfied sigh he flopped spread-eagled across her and it needed a huge effort on her part to push him off and roll him over to the other side of the bed.

Pulling the bedclothes up over him she felt her throat suddenly tighten. She closed her eyes rather than look at him. He stunk of beer and he was sweating like a pig.

Tears forced themselves from beneath her eyelids and slid down her cheeks. The whole act had been repugnant to her.

Chapter Four

IT HADN'T SNOWED, in fact the weather had improved. This Monday morning Michael had set off for work in a good mood for, according to him, the weekend had been great. Barbara was in a hurry now for she wanted to catch the eight twenty-five train to Eastbourne. She was going to visit her mother. Glancing around the living room she felt everything was neat and tidy, she had banked the fire down with wet slack and placed the guard in front of it. She'd have to hurry for she still had to walk to Clapham Junction railway station. She was excited and there was a spring to her step as she set out, filled with anticipation at the thought of the enjoyable day that lay ahead. She so seldom saw her parents these days.

She looked at her watch in desperation as she queued to buy her day return. She ran half the length of the platform and had just reached a carriage when the guard's whistle pierced the air. Doors banged, voices were raised, a man came running, catching the train by a hair's breadth. A kindly porter bundled her aboard, and slammed the door behind her.

The journey seemed to take forever. The train was icy cold, she couldn't be bothered to go in search of hot coffee. The carriage windows were none too clean and they rattled like mad; Barbara tugged hard on the leather strap in order to tighten it and hopefully stop the draught.

East Croydon was left behind and the view began to

change. Smoke-ridden walls of tenements, litter-filled yards of warehouses and busy suburban streets gave way to green fields and high barns and finally the train drew into Eastbourne.

Good grief! The rain was pouring down and it was still bitterly cold. Barbara's heart sank. She'd have to find a taxi. Then she spied her mother.

'Oh, you poor darling, I thought you must have missed the train. You look frozen.'

Everything was all right now, there were hugs and kisses, and being held close, and both of them talking at the same time, until finally as they reached the car and got into the two front seats there was laughter, because it was such a relief to be out of the cold and going home.

Home was Meads Lodge. A charming house situated just outside the village of Alfriston, surrounded by rolling downs and shaded by numerous huge old trees. No one knew the exact date it was built but her father said it dated back to the Elizabethan period. Tall chimneys and many leaded windows looked out over velvet lawns and flower beds. Two modern bathrooms had been installed while Barbara was only a toddler. The whole family loved the house and despite having one full-time and two part-time gardeners her mother devoted much of her time and energy to the grounds: they were her pride and joy. The stables were her father's dominion.

Her mother swept the car around the circular drive and brought it to a halt outside the main door. Stepping from the car, Barbara let her gaze take in the whole of the house, her bedroom with the pretty chintz curtains, the two rooms that had belonged to William and Patrick and the large room with the big bay windows that was her parents' bedroom, into which she had gone running many a morning to crawl into the warmth and loving arms of her mother for a cuddle. So many memories. Her home now was two rooms above a shop in Battersea. The comparison made her shudder.

'Leave your coat there. Come on straight through to the kitchen.'

The big, familiar room was bright and, oh, so lovely and warm. The fire in the range burnt bright red, a saucepan simmered at the back of the hob, the big kettle sang and a gorgeous smell was coming from the oven. Barbara took off her boots and warmed her hands, while her mother made a pot of tea and set home-made biscuits out on a plate which held a lace doyley. Before long they were sitting at the table, just as they had when she'd been small, drinking their tea and nibbling their biscuits and again both of them talking at once.

'I'm so glad you're here.'

'So am I.'

'You don't come home often enough.'

Barbara made no reply and her mother didn't push her, but she sighed as she looked at this lovely daughter of hers.

She looked the same, much as she had before she'd left home to volunteer for war work. She still had a beautiful figure, bit too thin really, her dark hair still had a sheen to it, still coiled sleekly upwards and held in place by side combs. Beautiful skin, still a few freckles, only her eyes seemed to have changed. Those lovely, deep-brown eyes, shielded by long, thick, dark eyelashes, were sad. There was no getting away from it. Her Barbara wasn't happy.

'It's so lovely to have you home. Are you sure you can't stay for a few days?'

How I wish I could, was what Barbara nearly said, instead she sniffed.

'Something smells good.'

'Beef casserole with mushrooms, tomatoes and baby onions.'

'Mmm, wonderful.'

'Go upstairs, freshen up in your room, and then we'll have a drink before lunch. I'm sure you could use one. I'll set the glasses out ready.'

Barbara picked up her handbag, crossed the kitchen and went up the thickly carpeted stairs, across the wide landing and into what had been her own bedroom for so many years of her life. It still looked exactly the same. The beige, closely fitted carpet, the high wide bed, with its brass-railed head-stand, the pretty bedspread that matched the curtains. The kidney-shaped dressing table and the white Lloyd Loom chairs. Her mother had given it the final touch, a deep-pink potted cyclamen set into a flowered plant pot, stood on the bedside table and Barbara, standing in the doorway, marvelled as she always did, at her mother's ability to create not only her own personality and warmth in a room but real visual pleasure.

Downstairs, Patricia Hamlin was torn with worry, it wasn't just a nasty suspicion that all was not well with Barbara and her marriage – it was stronger than that.

First and foremost Mrs Hamlin was the sort of mother everyone would have loved. She had given her life to the role of motherhood and being a good wife. Sadly that had all changed now, with both her sons having been killed in the War she was left with only Barbara to mother. The turn that events had taken by altering her only daughter's life to such an extent that she was only able to see her on rare occasions, not only saddened her but sickened her. The conditions under which Barbara was living just didn't bear thinking about. Why had she had to be so headstrong? Why had the marriage arrangements been carried out with so much stealth? Not even to have informed her own parents, let alone invite them to be present at the ceremony. That had hurt them badly.

Barbara had had the decency to send a telegram. She knew it off by heart: 'Married Michael this morning. Be happy for me. All my love, Barbara.'

Nothing in this world had ever hurt her husband as much as those words on that flimsy piece of paper.

'She might have given us some warning,' he had stormed angrily. 'To go off like that – and that Michael! – Dear God, what has she done?'

He had sat there, his fingers twisting and fumbling with the telegram. The silence that had followed was so awful she just had to break it.

'Phillip.'

He put out a hand, pulled her close.

'Phillip.'

She looked up him, and he shook his head. She knew that he did not want to discuss the matter, not now. Suddenly he seemed old. He had never seemed so to her before, but now she knew that he felt he had lost Barbara, the last of his children, and it was more than he could bear.

She got to her feet and went out of the room, closing the doors behind her. Upstairs in Barbara's room she had given way to her own tears.

Had Barbara found happiness? She could bear it if she had, but her only daughter! She should have been in church today, the bride's mother, watching her walk the length of the aisle, on her father's arm, a vision in white with a long train trailing behind. Instead nothing but a telegram.

All her children had gone. She had lain down on Barbara's single bed, burying her face in her pillow and cried for the sons that she would never see again and for the little girl who was now a married woman.

'Mother?'

'I'm here.'

Barbara found her in the dining room, not doing anything, just standing staring out of the long windows, deep in thought.

'What are you doing?' Barbara asked her.

'Just waiting for you. I'll dish up lunch now, and then I thought, as it's stopped raining, why don't we wrap up warm and take a tour round the grounds; might even get as far as the village, must be ages since you've been down into Alfriston. What do you think? Shall we eat first and then decide? Plenty of coats, wellies and stout sticks still in the vestibule if you feel that energetic.'

The dishes set out on the table said a lot for Patricia Hamlin's culinary skills, but more than that was the presentation. The fine china, cutlery and table linen were all perfect but the little touches made all the difference. Duchesse potatoes, their piped pyramid shapes coloured beautifully because of the egg yolks she had mixed into the creamed potato, spiced with nutmeg, browned under the grill and garnished with watercress. For added colour she had baked whole tomatoes and arranged these around a dish of asparagus spears. What a difference! Barbara couldn't help her thoughts. Michael would have only wanted a pile of mash and tinned peas with what he would term as stew.

Having done justice to the meal they went through to the back of the house and dressed themselves warmly in the lobby, then let themselves out through the conservatory and into the garden. Side by side they crossed the lawn. The early rain had soaked the turf and they left a trail of footprints on the damp grass. Past the flower borders and through to the rose garden and on into the orchard. Still more memories came flooding back to Barbara. The great chestnut tree way over in the corner which her brothers had been able to shin up like a couple of monkeys. The round patch of grey cinders, the remains of endless bonfires, and she could almost hear the shrieks of delight from long-gone firework nights. Beyond, they came upon the Cuckmere River, flowing deep and narrow between green covered banks. Was their old rowing boat still in the boathouse?

There were sheep on the Downs and away in the distance was Friston Forest. Walking at a steady pace they soon entered the village; the church, raised and built on a circular mound, looked out over the river valley and was, in its seclusion, a symbol of peace and tranquility. A watery sun came out as they crossed the field, making for the cobbled high street with its high pavements and causing steam to rise from the wet grass and give off a sweet smell. It was a lovely smell.

East Sussex, Barbara decided, was all quite beautiful, and she must have been out of her mind when she had rushed into marriage with Michael, thus forgoing the right to live in this lovely village with her parents. Just being with her mother made her view life so differently, here without the hustle and bustle of never-ending traffic she felt calm, safe and secure.

The church clock chimed the half hour, two thirty, oh dear the day was going far too quickly.

By the time they came to The Smugglers Inn set off from Market Square with its huge chestnut tree and market cross, they were both out of breath and warm with exertion.

'Do you remember when Eastbourne Foxhounds, horses and riders, your father amongst them, used to assemble here prior to leading off over the Downs?' Patricia asked her daughter.

'Yes I do,' she smiled, 'and when there were many racing stables in the area and jockeys, trainers and stable lads all lived locally.'

'Times have certainly changed,' her mother sighed sadly.

Seated now in the lounge, in front of a roaring fire, the tea-tray set out on a long low mahogany table in front of where her mother sat, it was Barbara who broke the strained silence which had fallen between them since they had got back from their walk.

'You and Daddy knew my marriage wouldn't work from the start didn't you?'

'Oh, Barbara.'

She met her mother's eyes, and saw that she was right.

'How could we not know, you had been used to so much, though I prayed love would be sufficient for you both to survive the odds.'

Barbara lowered her eyes, unable to meet the grief in those of her mother's.

'The only time you brought Michael here to meet us, he

was coarse, rude to your father and openly contemptuous of our way of life.'

'Oh, Mother, it didn't matter to me then, I loved him so much. Looking back it was more than likely envy which prompted Michael's bad behaviour. He never tires of telling me how spoilt I am.' Tears overcame Barbara for a moment, she hastily brushed them away. 'It didn't matter that Michael had no money, it wouldn't now, if only he would settle down, accept some responsibility. All I wanted was for us to be happy, the two of us together, loving each other, wanting the same things.'

Her mother sat perfectly still, silent for an instant, and then she said his name, 'Michael', as though it summed up every thing that was wrong.

'Yes, Michael. I know now. It was a ghastly mistake. Michael doesn't love me and he won't let me love him. I never dreamed it would be like this.'

'Perhaps things might change for the better if you were to start a family?'

This statement did nothing to comfort Barbara. How could she tell her mother that Michael was adamant about not wanting any children? How could she tell her of the two abortions she had had?

She sat there, in the comfortable lounge of the beautiful house that had been her childhood home, recalling how she had been so willing to give up everything convinced she and Michael were made for each other and would be happy together for the rest of their lives. But of course she had been wrong. Terribly wrong. Now it was too late, she realised to be fair to Michael that she was possibly the worst type of woman that he could have chosen to marry. She felt hot tears prick at the back of her eyes.

'Here,' ever practical, her mother produced a clean handkerchief scented with lavender. 'Wipe your eyes, crying won't help.'

Barbara took the handkerchief and did as she was told.

'Now. Tell me, what is wrong? I don't need to be clairvoyant to know that all is not right between you and Michael.'

'Oh, Mumma,' Barbara reverted to the name she had used for her mother when a child. Indeed she sounded now like a very small child. 'I know now I should never have married Michael.'

It was out. She had admitted it out loud. The relief was great. She looked up and again, met her mother's eyes, and saw them troubled.

'I should have realised that weekend I brought him home. He didn't fit in, did he?'

'I hope your father and I didn't show our disapproval.'

'Oh, of course you didn't,' Barbara hastened to assure her. 'You were very kind to him, both of you. I thought Daddy especially went out of his way to make him feel welcome. It was *him*. He was so insulting, sneering at every suggestion Daddy made. Look how he behaved when we had our meals. He ate like a pig. I think that was what upset you most, Mumma, and there was no need for it. Michael was doing it deliberately.'

'In fairness, darling, I don't think you can blame him too much for that weekend. He was out of his depth. He had obviously been brought up differently. You told me he did apologise afterwards.'

'Yes he did and I made allowances and forgave him.'

'That's hardly surprising, you were sure you truly loved him at the time.'

77

'And you're telling me you know that I'm not in love with Michael now?'

'No, my darling, I'm telling you no such thing. You have just admitted it yourself.'

Barbara sighed. 'What am I to do?'

'Only you can decide that. One thing is for sure, it's no good looking back. Give yourself time, do your best to improve the situation. Perhaps you may even be able to persuade Michael to visit us again, give your father and me another chance, things might turn out different. Michael might feel differently about us now that the War is over. What do you think?

Pigs might fly! is what Barbara was thinking, but what she said was, 'I'll try.'

'Good. Now, please, for my sake, cheer up and let me see you smile.'

Glancing at her watch, Barbara spoke her thoughts aloud, 'I would have loved to have seen Daddy.'

Eagerly her mother leant forward, placing her hand over Barbara's. 'Why don't you stay the night, or better still for a few days, your own bedroom is quite ready.'

Oh mother! Yes, *yes please* was what she wanted to cry out, instead what she said was, 'I must go home Mumma, it wouldn't be fair to Michael if I just stayed away without telling him.'

Patricia watched her daughter's hands twisting restlessly in her lap and she felt dreadful. 'Darling I'm sorry, that was selfish of me, perhaps another time, soon eh? Tell Michael in advance, I'm sure he won't object to you spending a few days with us, oh, I shall so look forward to having you home – and wait till I tell your father.'

Her mother's words sent a shiver through Barbara, she

didn't want to upset her father more than she had already. Such a kind and loving man. He was fifty-eight years old, but the death of his two sons had aged him. Since Barbara could remember, he had been a tall distinguished man, dark suited with bowler hat and rolled umbrella as befitted the legal profession, but only on weekdays. Saturdays, Sundays and holidays his clothes would be sporty and youthful when he took her and the boys walking up over the Downs, out on the river or scrambling over rocks, searching for seaweed when they went to the coast. She vowed to see if she couldn't change Michael's animosity towards her parents.

'Barbara, do you need money?'

The question brought Barbara up with a jerk.

'Your father would be only too pleased to help. You do know that, don't you? If only you could bring Michael round to thinking kindly of us, come and spend some time with your father. He misses you so. He loves you very much.'

'I know, Mother. I'll do my best.'

She knew well enough that her powers of persuasion were not that great. Even if she did screw up enough courage to broach the subject of them having a short holiday with her parents, Michael would cut her short with one solitary word: No. She had taken in what her mother had said about money, and she wondered again, as she frequently did, would money be a solution to all their problems? In her heart she knew it wouldn't really help. A stop gap, that's all it would be until Michael lost it all to the bookmakers or drank it away with his mates in the pub. Money wasn't the only difficulty, if only it were; they needed shared interests, a common ground on which to talk and that they didn't have.

79

Barbara sighed heavily. 'I shall have to be making a move now.'

Patricia put on a brave smile. 'All right, my darling, I'll go and start the car.'

At the station her mother handed her a brown paper parcel. 'A few books I know you will enjoy reading, some tobacco for Michael and some chocolates for you.'

'Oh, mother. Thank you.'

'Goodbye. Ring me when you can.' They kissed and held each other tight.

'Goodbye mother.'

By Wednesday of that week it did snow. Continuous squalls of heavy flakes accompanied by bitterly cold blustery winds. It lay in deep drifts and then it froze. The roads were treacherous. Michael was laid off, outside building work was impossible. With Michael home all day and money scarce the next two weeks were not pleasant but Barbara drew the rest of her savings out from the bank and survived as best she could.

Nevertheless the rot set in and things came to a head one Saturday morning. Michael's chin came out aggressively as he faced Barbara across the kitchen table. 'Are you gonna give me a few bob or shall I start taking this place apart until I find where you keep yer private hoard?'

His features were distorted with rage and Barbara was afraid of him but she didn't have the energy for yet another row. Turning she picked up her handbag from the dresser, opened her purse and checked the coins that were in it.

'Well, it ain't much is it? Hand it over,' he demanded, thrusting out his hand. He looked awful. Two days' stubble on his chin, the inevitable scarf tied in a knot around his neck and now he had taken to wearing a huge checked cap pulled well down over his forehead.

Barbara obeyed. Seventeen shillings and fourpence she tipped into his open palm.

'And the notes.'

Dismay showed in her eyes, He couldn't leave her with nothing, there was hardly any food in the house let alone coal for the fire.

Michael's arm shot out. A hefty push sent her sprawling backwards. He wrenched open the metal stud at the front of her purse and took out the three notes from the wallet section.

'A measly two quid!' He spat the words at her as he folded the one pound note and the two ten shilling notes before pushing them into his back pocket. He sneered at her in triumph. 'I promise it will do me more good than it would you. Honest love, I've got a great tip for the gee gees, I'll be back later on with me winnings and you can go down the market and get the weekend grub then.'

He strode off, banging the door, she heard him clomping down the stairs, whistling as he went and Barbara burst into tears.

Wrapped up warmly, clutching her shopping basket, Barbara nervously pushed open the door to Mrs Winters' shop. Overloaded with second-hand furniture and more knick-knacks than a person would collect in a lifetime, the smoky smelly atmosphere was nevertheless warm and inviting.

'Allo, luv. Bloody cold terday ain't it? Fer Christ's sake put the wood in the 'ole and come over 'ere by me stove. It's great ter see yer.'

Knowing what she had come to ask, Barbara was

embarrassed by the affection. When Barbara remained silent Mrs Winters' smile turned into a suspicious glare.

'That bugger ain't bin knocking you about agin, 'as he?'

'No, nothing like that. Of course he's very moody lately, not being able to work gets him down.'

'Hram,' Mrs Winters sniffed. 'If anyone's got good reason ter be moody, it's you my luv. Tied up ter that no good 'usband. Missing work my arse! All he's missing is his sessions in the boozer with his bloody mates. Wouldn't know a good day's work if it was staring 'im in the face.'

She put her arms across her chest, heaved her bosoms higher and shot a puzzled glance in Barbara's direction. 'You're not sickening fer something are yer?'

'No, no really I'm very well.'

'Then what is it, Barbara? If you can't tell me what's troubling yer after all this time then it's a bloody bad do. I thought we were friends. Good friends, that you could come ter me no matter what the trouble was. Seems I was mistaken.'

'Oh, Mrs Winters, please don't be cross with me. We *are* friends. Without you I never could have survived this winter.'

'Here, sit your bottom down there,' she urged as she pulled forward a well-worn winged-back chair, 'and get to the point of what is the matter, cos I ain't no fool an' if you expect me to believe that all is right wiv your world you must think I was born yesterday.'

'I can't pay the rent,' Barbara murmured, her eyes lowered to the floor.

'So, what's new? No, it ain't the first time you've had to come ter tell me that an' yer know well enough by now that from you it don't bovver me. No, my girl it's more than that and yer better spit it out before I lose me temper.'

'I need some money,' Barbara stammered. Once started she couldn't stop, 'I haven't a penny-piece in cash. I pawned my gold watch two days ago. All the food I bought has gone. I will go and see my parents just as soon as I get the chance and then I could pay you back with interest. I hate to ask but Michael will go berserk if there's no coal for the fire and no dinner ready for him.'

'Bugger Michael. I don't give a sodding toss for him, but you just say how much you need my love and it's yours, and don't you ever let me 'ear no more talk about paying me interest.'

Barbara's eyes were brimming over with unshed tears as she gazed at this skinny scruffy woman who had a heart of gold.

Suddenly Mrs Winters bent down and grabbed hold of Barbara's shoulders. 'Christ orlmighty! You're pregnant again! Oh you silly little cow! Does Michael know?'

Barbara had gone pale and she looked scared as she shook her head. 'Well, one thing's fer certain, you ain't gettin' no more abortions, yer nearly killed yerself last time. I'll take meself off and find out where yer parents live and tell them a few things before I'll stand by and see yer do that ter yerself again. Yer got me? I mean every word I've said.'

Mrs Winters came and squatted beside her. Their eyes came level and she saw that Mrs Winters was quite serious in her threat to visit her parents – not to be in any way unkind, she was merely looking out for her welfare, afraid of what the consequences might be should she plunge into yet another abortion. What a good friend this woman had turned out to be. Her face was deeply lined and very weather-beaten, her clothes were an odd assortment, the top layer being a number of brightly coloured shawls, and on her head she wore the most elegant hat. Purple velour, adorned with artificial flowers of all shapes and sizes, and little wisps of her light-brown hair had escaped and were hanging down over her ears. Crumbs, the colours of some of those flowers! Suddenly Barbara lost all her self-control. Shaking with mirth, she tried in vain to struggle into an upright position in the deep armchair.

After a moment of shocked surprise, Mrs Winters' lips broke into a smile and soon she too was laughing fit to bust.

'Oh stoppit, stoppit!' puffed Mrs Winters. 'You're making me bleeding side ache. Barbara, if you don't take the bloody cake I'm damned if I know who does.'

Clutching her side with one hand and rubbing at her eyes with the other, Mrs Winters got to her feet.

'By Christ, this ain't the life you were meant ter be leading. Yer ain't got a penny piece in yer purse, you've got yerself in the bloody family way yet again, a fact that no-good 'usband of yours ain't gonna be exactly over the moon about an' you're sitting there laughing yer bleedin' head off. Gawd knows what's gonna become of yer!'

The jangle of the shop-door bell saved Barbara from having to answer.

'Here Ma, 'ow much d'yer want fer this brass fender yer got out 'ere?' The question came from a youngish man, well muffled up against the bitter weather; still, his face was pinched with the cold and his nose was bright red.

'Got a load of kids 'ave yer?' The question was flung at him.

'Got me fair share, I suppose, two boys and the new

baby's a girl. Bin looking fer a fender. Keep the kids from playing wiv the fire and 'andy to air the napkins on.'

'Ten bob ter you then son. Fifteen ter any other bugger.'

'Yeah I know. I've 'eard your spiel before. How about seven and a tanner?'

'Cheeky sod! Give us eight bob an' don't argue or I may change me mind.'

'Yer a darling, Missus,' he said holding out the silver coins. 'No need to come out, I'll carry it fine underneath me arm. Ta-tah then.'

'Tat-ah lad, Gawd bless yer.

'Now,' she said, turning back to Barbara. 'I'll make us a brew up and then we'll get you sorted. At least ter see yer over the weekend.'

Barbara watched as she bustled about putting the tin kettle onto the spirit stove, sorting out two enamel mugs and wiping them out on a cloth that was as clean as the driven snow. A mixture of contrasts was this cockney woman.

Barbara was not sure which was worse, Michael when he ranted and raved or this stony silence he had kept up since they had had that awful row.

Michael hadn't got his way, not this time. To begin with he had pleaded, then threatened and would have used violence had not Mrs Winters waylaid him, giving what she chose to call a friendly word of advice. Barbara had turned a deaf ear: not another abortion! Besides she was happy, she longed for a baby, it might just make a difference between Michael and herself; he had to feel love for it when it was born, especially if they were to have a son.

Half of her mind knew that to be a delusion, the other half insisted there was always that possibility.

Meanwhile you could cut the atmosphere with a knife. To look at Michael you would think something terrible had happened and his black mood was making her restless and nervy. He was back at work and still had his bet and spent time in the pub, more so at weekends, though he no longer asked her to accompany him. In fact she hardly ever went out, except to the market, meeting only a few neighbours and dear old Mrs Winters when she went downstairs for a chat.

What she wouldn't have given to be able to go home and stay with her parents for a few days. Their reaction to her news would be so different. The joy on their faces, to be clasped in their arms and told how wonderful it would be to have a baby in the family again. She thought about writing to some of her old friends, meeting up with them again. How could she invite them here? Never mind the state of the place, Michael's reaction would be more than enough to drive them away. She let her imagination run riot when her thoughts dwelt on Penny Rayford and Elizabeth Warren, but the outcome was too depressing. She missed those two girls. The three of them had been such close friends and had shared so many happy memories whilst growing up; together they had also experienced many sad events during the years of the War.

With Michael now treating her with contempt because of her determination to have this baby, she actually began to think that this was the loneliest phase of her life. What Michael was doing now was a deliberate, systematic campaign to break her spirit. His indifference alone was driving her mad. She could be invisible for all the notice he took of her and he could have been struck dumb when you considered the silence he maintained.

As March gave way to April, bringing with it the promise of spring, Michael's attitude softened a bit. He was not so aggressive when making love to her. In other ways there was no improvement. He steadfastly refused to even talk about her parents, let alone visit them. He still remained workshy. He could have found a regular secure job. But no, he preferred the odd few days' casual labouring on various sites, receiving his payment daily in cash. Also, she had found out that in addition to this cash in hand he signed on each week at the Labour Exchange, drawing benefit for her as well as himself she supposed, but what the amount of money was that he was entitled to she had no idea and she daren't ask. He was still convinced that, one day, he was going to make a pile of money by backing three winning horses in a row.

Whenever she attempted to open a discussion on the state of their finances he became hostile. He knew only too well by now that his aggressive temper frightened her and that knowledge gave him even more power to be abusive to her. The trouble was, right from the beginning she had given in to aggression and now had no defence against it.

For the past two weeks Barbara had known there was something wrong; Michael had given her no money and she had been supplementing their income from her own bank account which her father had topped up some months ago. Now there was little left for her to draw on and she would feel both guilty and embarrassed if she had to ask her father for more.

'Can yer let me 'ave fifty quid?'

Michael's blue eyes looked up at Barbara and there was deep malice in them; his voice sounded really strange as he made this request. When Barbara made no answer he dropped his eyes and continued to stare at the pages of the Sunday paper.

'I'm in dead trouble if I don't come up with that amount within the next coupla days. An' I mean *dead* trouble.'

'We're already up to our eyes in debt, you know that – don't you Michael? Where the hell do you think I'm going to be able to find fifty pounds. What do you need it so badly for?' she asked bluntly.

Michael pushed his empty breakfast plate away, tucked the newspaper under his arm and got up from the table.

'Hey, where are you going?' Barbara stood up and caught at his arm. 'We have to talk about this, Michael.'

He tried to pass her but she stood her ground and refused to move.

'I'm not joking. I have to have that fifty quid or I'll end up with a broken arm and maybe a broken leg as well.'

She shook her head blindly in desperation.

'You could get it for me if you wanted to, you callous bitch.' He rounded on her, 'It's a mere flea bite ter you, you've plenty, yer bloody daddy sees to that.' He reached out and grabbed her by the arm and squeezed hard.

'Well?' he hissed at her.

'I did have money in the bank but it's all gone once again. What do you think we've been living on?'

'You could get more if you wanted to, but I've yet ter see the damn day when you'd offer to put yerself out to 'elp me.' He gave her arm a final savage squeeze and then pushed her from him.

Barbara deliberately changed the tone of her voice to

one of pleading, 'Look Michael, let's get out of here, I'm so tired of being cooped up, let's go for a walk, watch the boats on the river; we can talk then, it is such a nice day it seems a pity to waste it indoors.'

He gave her a look of disgust and then to her surprise muttered, 'Okay. Why not?'

They strolled through the streets, across Battersea Bridge and into the park. Finally when she sat down on a seat Michael dropped down onto the grass at her feet. He lay on his back, his hands behind his head.

Presently she asked fearfully. 'What are we going to do, Michael?'

'About what?' The sarcasm was evident in his voice.

'You know very well, we haven't paid Mrs Winters the rent for three weeks, we have only the bare necessities of food indoors, the rental for the wireless is more than a month overdue, we still need coal, it's not yet warm enough to do without a fire but the coalman won't deliver unless he gets paid in cash there and then.'

He made no answer. Just lay looking up at the sky, displaying a pointed lack of interest.

Barbara was suddenly so angry that she became brave. She wasn't going to shoulder all these worries on her own any longer. She levered herself forward into a position where she could stare down at him, before she had got any words out Michael looked up and gruffly said, 'Ask your bloody parents, they're wealthy enough.'

Still angry, she did something she would not normally have done: her arm stretched out, her hand opened flat, she was about to slap his face.

All he did was laugh as he caught at her wrist before her

hand could make contact. Barbara snatched her arm away from his grasp and gave a bitter smile.

'I thought you wanted nothing from my family, you took such painstaking care to tell me it was only me you wanted when you pleaded with me to marry you. Been a very different story since, hasn't it?'

Michael's face went scarlet with rage, he sat up, pushed his face within inches of hers and hissed. 'You were different then.'

If they had been indoors she would have been intimidated by his voice alone, but out here in the open park with people around she wasn't about to let that remark pass without comment. Dropping her usual way of speaking she let her temper rip. 'So were you! By God you were! Now all you want is your working class mates. So long as you have money to go boozing with them and to squander playing the Big I Am with the bookies and at the dog-track you don't give a damn where the money comes from or who has to suffer just so long as you are all right. You accept no responsibility whatsoever. All you think about is yourself, you wouldn't do a day's work if you could get out of it.'

She paused to take a deep breath before sneering at him. 'You get a lot of pleasure out of scorning me for my upbringing; according to you I'm a rich spoilt bitch, but that never seems to stop you when you want something. This fifty quid, as you call it, who's pestering you for that? The bookmaker or the governor at the Falcon Arms? Seems you wouldn't have any objection to being financed by my folks' money in order to pay off this particular debt.'

Michael was astounded. Such hostility. She had retaliated before but never as fiercely as this.

He was up on his feet in seconds. Turning angrily towards her, his head jutting close to her face again, he snarled, 'The pubs are open – I'm going for a drink.'

'Well I'm sure you'll find enough money for that.' Her words were directed at his disappearing back.

Barbara remained sitting where she was for a long time. From her very first meeting with Michael she had been infatuated with him, willing to do almost anything he asked, afraid of losing him. She hadn't minded one bit using her own money to tide them over, but now it had almost run out. She couldn't go to her father yet again. In her heart she knew she would. That fifty pounds had to be paid and quickly, she was well aware of the code of honour that existed between these Londoners when it came to paying their debts. Treatment for welshers was always severe. Oh Michael! All they were doing was leading a day to day existence, forever at each other's throats. Where exactly were they heading? Sadly she knew she had no answer to her own question.

Michael had changed so much, he didn't give one jot now whether she was happy or not. She herself had changed somewhat, there was no disputing that. Would things change for the better if she were to give up fighting? She could so easily fall into slipshod ways. Become as some women were in the district. Would Michael notice if she didn't change the bed sheets so often, or dust the furniture, take pains over her appearance, spend less money on fresh food and use more tinned stuff – as to fresh flowers his opinion had always been voiced loud and harshly, 'Bloody waste of good money!'

Her lips twisted into a bitter smile as she got to her feet and began to walk across the grass. It wasn't only Michael's temperament that had altered since he had been demobbed from the navy; he didn't look anything like the happy strapping sailor she had fallen in love with. No longer was there a jaunty spring in his step or a swagger to his walk, his hair was now long and lank; yet it was his eyes that had taken on the most noticeable change, no more did they twinkle with laughter, more often than not they were veiled with stubborn antagonism. Sometimes, quite unintentionally, she would let slip a slight reference to her childhood or her parents and then God help her!

Why should he be like this? He had known of her background before he asked her to marry him. All the feelings he had for her mother and father and indeed for her most of the time, were bound up with bitterness. Then again, Michael felt bitter about a whole lot of things. The navy had been good for him and the discipline that went with it. He had felt himself a somebody, which indeed he had been, loyal and brave enough to have served in submarines. Now he was a labourer. The years stretching ahead held out no hope to him for betterment. Her father, who would have been able to help, was the one person that Michael would have nothing to do with. Sighing heavily, Barbara decided that she felt very sorry for Michael. Like so many men now out of the forces he was finding civvy street was not so easy. Good jobs not requiring qualifications were elusive. The War might be over but indirectly the repercussions were still being felt.

Glancing to her right, Barbara spied a crowd gathered around a speaker perched high on a box; his voice was loud and carried across to where she stood. The theme of the young man's speech was political. She laughed to herself.

Even Winston Churchill hadn't got the job he wanted or deserved.

People were fickle. In 1940 the Chamberlain Government had come under heavy criticism, had been dissolved and replaced by a coalition led by Churchill. During the succeeding War years Churchill had rallied the nation and led England to victory over Germany and Japan. The whole country owed Winston Churchill a great deal yet the outcome of the first general election since the end of World War Two had seen him become Leader of the Opposition, not Prime Minister. As Barbara walked on she told herself that circumstances did change people, of that she was in no doubt. Yet did all their hopes and dreams have to become stagnant? She stopped dead in her tracks and pondered on what the long term effect this marriage would have on both herself and Michael.

She shivered as if somebody had walked over her grave and she was suddenly afraid.

The weeks dragged by, the weather was fine, but matters between Michael and herself were not: open hostility was how Barbara described it to herself. Now apart from his daily antagonism there were the nights. Nights that were nightmarish. There was no way she could prevent Michael from taking his rights, as he put it. When it came to satisfying his needs he made no pretence of tenderness and his taking of her had become repulsive. It was hellish to have to lie there and allow her body to be used in such a brutal way. It was all too much at times. Her body was heavy with this pregnancy, even her brain was becoming weary; this was not what she had imagined being married to Michael would be like. She had got used to the idea that he was not a good provider, but oh, how she wished that he would show just a little consideration, some kindness once in a while.

He was still his own worst enemy, he wanted to rise above the rut he had got himself into, well there were times when he said he did, yet he made no bones of the fact that he despised the upper classes and in particular her parents.

She turned now and looked around her, it was ten minutes past ten in the morning and still she was sitting on a straight-backed chair at one end of the wooden table. The breakfast things spread out before her were still unwashed, the bed in the only other room remained unmade. What had she come to? How much lower could she sink? For another ten minutes or so she stayed still, when she finally forced herself to stand up her legs felt leaden and she realised she had almost reached the end of her tether.

From the wireless came the sweet sounds of the Inkspots as they sang: '*Into each life some rain must fall, but too much is falling in mine!*' True, how true. Tears slowly trickled down her cheeks.

As Barbara washed herself at the kitchen sink she moaned out loud as she lifted first one leg and then the other up to rest on the seat of a wooden chair, in order to be able to wash her legs and feet. She would readily admit that she still missed the privilege of being waited on, the space to walk about the house that had been her childhood home, her mother's lovely gardens, her father's horses, but if she were to be asked to pinpoint what she missed most there would be no hesitation, the bathrooms would be her answer. The very thought of stepping into a hot bath, perfumed bath salts, unlimited hot water gushing from the taps, large fluffy towels on the heated towel rail. Compared to a tin bath in the middle of the kitchen floor, filled only with water from kettles boiled on the gas rings of the old black enamelled stove, and then the backbreaking job of having to empty the water after she had washed herself down, the contrast didn't bear thinking about.

It had taken her ages but at least she was washed and dressed and felt much more able to cope with the day that stretched ahead.

'Barbara, Bar-hara.' Mrs Winters was yelling at her from the bottom of the stairs.

Opening the living room door, Barbara put her head out and called in answer, 'Yes, Mrs Winters?'

'There's a posh young woman down 'ere in me shop, says she's a friend of yours an' she wants ter see yer. Are yer coming down or shall I send 'er up?'

Barbara panicked. A friend, come here to Battersea?

'I'll be down, give me a couple of minutes. Thank you Mrs Winters.' She ran a comb through her thick hair, straightened her grey maternity skirt, wondered what friend had found out where she was living and slowly went downstairs. At the foot of the stairs stood Penny.

A shrill cry of pleasure, chuckles and then giggles from the pair of them. 'What on earth are you doing here?'

Then they were in each other's arms, hugging tight, touching each other with the familiarity that only comes with long natural friendship.

Upstairs as they entered the living room Barbara felt envious, just for a moment, Penny, she thought proudly, was still a good friend, and so beautiful, with her bright blonde hair and those amazing big blue eyes. No wonder she had always been so popular with the men. Today she looked marvellous. She wore a grey tailored suit, a red silk blouse, her shoes and handbag were red and tied to the handle of the bag was a navy-blue silk scarf. Everything about her was fresh, clean, and shiny, right down to her fingernails which were manicured and varnished.

Barbara swallowed hard to rid herself of the lump in her throat. Maybe I haven't let myself go, well not entirely, but beside Penny I must look decidedly dowdy!

Penny sprawled into one of the two armchairs, her long silk clad legs thrust out, her hands folded in her lap. Barbara sat down opposite with a thump.

'Why didn't you let me know you were coming?'

Penny gave a grin which spread from ear to ear. 'How? You haven't got a telephone, besides, since when did good friends have to make an appointment? By the way, don't get yourself too comfortable – you and I are going to celebrate.'

'Celebrate what?'

'My birthday, it's not actually until tomorrow but I decided to visit you today.'

Barbara raised her deep brown eyes to the ceiling, 'I don't get it, why come here?'

'Why not? To see you, of course, you daft old thing. Your mother told me you were a bit down so I'm taking you out to lunch and maybe on a shopping spree.'

So that was it! Her mother had asked Penny to come and spy out the land. No, maybe that was a little unfair. Her mother did worry about her wellbeing and her concern would have been genuine, her father cared too for that matter, and it was weeks now since she had been able to visit them and to be honest the letters that she dutifully posted each week never told her parents very much. If they had asked Penny to visit her their motives would have been of the best.

'Come on, move yourself Barbara, get changed, let's go.'

Barbara had to laugh. There was no arguing with Penny.

Kensington: it brought back a whole load of memories as together they walked down the busy High Street and Barbara paused for a moment, staring at the passers-by. There was a purpose in their steps, their bodies held straight, no fear in their actions as they strode along showing determination. Most were smartly dressed and self-consciously she looked down at her own suit; it was clean and well-pressed but old, that very fact had her pondering on just how long it had been since she had made up her face, dressed with care and gone out, out that is beyond the limits of Battersea.

Hardly were they through the main doors of John Barker's department store than Penny was exclaiming, 'Oh, I do like these, choose one, Barbara, I'll treat us both.'

Floor walkers paused to give Penny a second glance, she was bubbling with vitality. Through her hands she was trailing Italian pure silk scarves. John Barker's were known for the quality of their merchandise and these scarves were no exception.

Barbara felt her cheeks colour up, it was she that ought to be urging Penny to select a gift as a birthday present from her.

'Certainly not,' said Barbara fondly. 'There is no reason you should be buying anything for me.'

'I don't need a reason, Barbara, love, I just want to.'

Draping a long mauve scarf against the fawn of Barbara's jacket she asked, 'How about this one?' then suddenly changing her mind she selected from the stand a multi-coloured one, the main overtones being copper. 'Now that is you, yes, it picks up the glints in your hair, do you like it?'

Barbara hadn't the heart to dampen her dear friend's enthusiasm. Penny's jovial mood was contagious, Barbara laughed out loud, a laugh such as had not come from her for a very long time.

'Okay, that one for you and this one for me. These two please,' Penny was now saying to the sales assistant. Her own choice was an emerald green, brilliant in colour, exactly right with her fair hair and complexion. By one thirty the pair of them were sitting in the Platter Restaurant, Barbara was by now very much more at ease and thoroughly enjoying herself.

'Pleased I came and dragged you out?' Penny wanted to know as they waited for the waitress to bring their lunch.

'Oh, Penny, you know I am.'

'Good. You know I love doing things on the spur of the moment, they always work out so much better. I phoned Elizabeth and told her I was coming and she was mad at me for not giving her enough notice to arrange to come with me.'

'Really? How is Elizabeth? Do you two see each other often?'

'Elizabeth is fine, sends you buckets of love, and yes, we meet at least once a month.'

'What is Elizabeth doing with herself these days? And come to that, you haven't given me very much gen about yourself.'

'Me? I'm footloose and fancy-free. Well, I am at the moment. Elizabeth is deeply in love, has thrown up the job she had on one of the glossy magazines and gone to live in Windsor in a dear little house that has jasmine growing along the wall, a huge conservatory at the back that is filled with white cane furniture, a fish pond in the garden and she's talking about planting a magnolia tree.'

'Penny, you're making it all up.'

'I swear it's the truth.'

'Has she got married?'

'Don't even suggest such a thing. Elizabeth and Tim Holsworthy are having a trial period to find out if they are capable of living together harmoniously.'

Barbara began to giggle and soon the pair of them were laughing fit to bust.

While they were eating they went back over their memories, recalling the years of the War through which they had lived and worked together, sharing not only the horrors and the fears and the long nights with German planes droning overhead but, as well, the good times such as when the local off-licence had let them have a quart bottle of cider and the effect that it had had on them all, especially Elizabeth. Arms linked, making their way home through the black-out, Elizabeth had stumbled and falling over had dragged the pair of them down with her. At the time it had seemed hysterically funny, that was until an air raid warden had threatened to arrest them if they didn't stop waving their torches about.

'Do you remember what the old boy said as he tried to untangle us?' Before Barbara could make a reply, Penny assumed a stern expression and in a gruff voice stated, 'Aw my Gawd, I've a funny feeling you gals ain't all yer seem to be. Now, Miss, turn off that bleedin' torch or I shall be forced, 'erewith, to take yer all into custody fer signalling to the enemy.'

'How we ever got back to Putney that night, the Lord only knows,' Barbara said, wiping tears of laughter from her cheeks.

Most of the diners had left the restaurant and Penny and Barbara were lingering over their coffee. But now, for some reason, the laughter had gone. A silence fell between them, as though having talked so much, they had all at once run out of things to say. Barbara's felt Penny's eyes on her, and lifted her head to meet that steady gaze.

'You're very pensive all of a sudden, Barbara, is something wrong?' Penny asked the question cautiously and immediately felt a chump. A blind man could tell that Barbara wasn't happy.

'No, no of course not.' Barbara forced a smile and said to herself, How can I tell her, it would take hours to pinpoint everything that is wrong between me and Michael.

Penny's eyes were brimming as she looked at Barbara and said sadly, 'Your marriage isn't working out, is it?'

Barbara's hand shook as she set down her coffee cup and bowed her head.

'Anything you'd like to talk to me about, Barbara? You know it won't go any further and sometimes it helps to get a problem out into the open.' Then stretching out she clasped one of Barbara's hands between her own, adding, 'That's what friends are for.'

Neither of them spoke for a time then without warning Barbara began to cry, silently, the tears running unchecked down her cheeks. She blinked quickly but was unable to control the flow.

Penny had to turn her head away, the lump in her own throat was choking her. It wasn't fair! She couldn't bear to see her dearest friend so upset and as to the way she was living, it was appalling. She motioned for the waitress to bring them a fresh pot of coffee.

The clink of fresh cups and saucers being set out and the aromatic smell of the hot coffee which Penny was pouring from the silver plated pot gave Barbara time to regain her composure.

Penny handed a cup across the table and she deliberately made her voice brisk-sounding as she urged, 'Talk to me. Get it off your chest. You might even feel better if you do, you know a problem shared an' all that.'

'Oh Penny, don't be so kind to me. If the truth be told it's just as much my fault as Michael's, I do try, honestly I do Penny, but nothing ever seems to turn out right.'

After a further moment of silence Barbara began to really talk, the need was there to unburden herself and it was as if the floodgates were now open. Penny listened, her face turned towards Barbara, watching her intently.

'I've had two abortions, only because Michael insists he doesn't want children.'

'But you're having a baby now?'

'Yes, and Michael is making my life hell because of it. Penny, I want this baby, it could make such a difference, surely every baby that comes into the world brings love with it.'

Penny ignored this. She became practical. 'Have you tried to find better living accommodation, maybe in a better class area?'

'And what would we use for money?'

Penny shifted in her seat and sat up straight. Barbara lifted her head and met her friend's eyes, and saw on that beautiful face an expression of disbelief.

'We're in debt, way over our heads.'

Elizabeth Waite

'Is this why you haven't been to see your parents?'

'You think they know?'

'Well, not for certain. Your mother has been so worried. She felt you were unhappy and maybe regretted having married Michael, she knows full well you are in some sort of trouble.'

Barbara sighed deeply. 'Aren't I just!'

'Why didn't you tell your father before? He still makes you an allowance doesn't he?'

'Yes, but it is never enough. I did tell Daddy once, some months ago, and he put an extra two hundred pounds into my account, I can't keep asking him to bail us out.'

'Michael's working, isn't he? Is your rent very high?'

Barbara gave a bitter laugh. 'Oh yes, Michael's working but it's seldom that I get to see his wages. He used to have a bet on the horses now and again and that was bad enough, but suddenly it has become his way of life. He is a compulsive gambler, and what money the bookies don't have off of him goes to the local publicans.'

'Oh, Barbara dear, I had no idea things were as bad as this.'

Barbara stopped talking, closed her eyes and clenched her hands into tight fists. Not even to this dear, well-meaning friend could she bring herself to divulge all the sordid details of her life with Michael. The punches she suffered, the barbaric way he used her sexually. All she could bring herself to tell had been told, it had taken great effort on her part and now her whole body felt listless.

Penny watched Barbara's lips tremble and her heart ached for her. She sensed that she had only been told a fraction of the whole story.

102

'Will you answer me one question truthfully? Do you still love Michael?'

Barbara kept her eyes closed tight. It seemed a very long time since she had been able to answer yes to that question when put to herself. Now she made no attempt to answer. Penny moaned, she was holding Barbara's hand, gently stroking her fingers.

'You've got to do something, come to some decision, you know that don't you? Especially with the baby coming.'

Silently Barbara looked up at Penny, withdrew her hand, brushed at her eyes and began to shake her head from side to side.

In a voice as firm as she could make it, Penny told her, 'You just can't sacrifice the whole of your life because of one disastrous mistake.'

'I know. But just what can I do? There are times when I don't think I can go on much longer, with life I mean.' Barbara's voice had dropped to a mere whisper.

Quickly Penny scolded her, 'Now you are not to to talk like that!'

'I mean it Penny, I've made such a mess of my life, I can't see any future for Michael and me. It's no more his fault than it is mine if you look at it from his point of view; he just doesn't want from life the same things that I do, I mean I did, it doesn't seem to matter one way or the other now.'

Penny sighed deeply. 'You ought to go home to your parents, or at least go and see them, talk to them, tell them the whole story.'

A visible shudder ran through Barbara's body. 'Oh, no, I couldn't, they probably do suspect many things but to confirm their suspicions wouldn't be fair, not to them it wouldn't, they've taken enough knocks losing William and Patrick.'

'But they care about you, you shouldn't shut them out, wouldn't Michael go with you to visit them?'

'I've tried to persuade him. God knows I've tried. My father is probably the one man that could help Michael find a decent job and come to terms with himself. No, there's no budging him, come to that he seldom goes anywhere with me now.'

Penny realised how difficult all this was for Barbara, but the fear that things were far worse than Barbara was telling made her press on. With compassion obvious in her voice she spoke quietly, 'Barbara, you should think seriously about leaving Michael, go home, there would be no recriminations from your mother or your father.'

'No, I can't.' Then under her breath she added, 'If only Michael could bring himself to be pleased about this baby we might still make a go of it, but to be honest I don't think his attitude towards me will ever change.'

'Well then, if you feel you have done your best and I'm sure you have, why not give up, admit defeat, it's not a crime for couples to separate, get out before matters become even worse.'

Barbara's eyes were sad as she raised them to Penny's face. 'There was a time when I thought Michael was a wonderful person.'

Penny half smiled. 'We were all aware of how you felt about him, then Barbara, you left us in no doubt. But it was wartime when you two met, it was a matter of live for the day; now the War is over, we are all having to face reality. Everything about you and Michael is so different. With your background it was an impossibility from the start, only you couldn't see it then and you wouldn't have thanked any of your friends for pointing it out. For you, at that time, Michael was your knight in shining armour, or naval uniform if you like.'

With head bent low Barbara murmured, 'What's going to happen to me, Penny?'

Penny wished she knew, what she said was, 'Well for a start you have to face the situation squarely, neither of you are happy, so stop feeling sorry for yourself and make up your mind to do something about it. It's up to the both of you; can you not try to talk to Michael once more?'

'I've tried. Every day for months. He only sees his side of it, I feel so guilty, that is until his temper flares up – you can't imagine the hostility he feels towards me. He blames me for the whole state of our affairs, I know he does and I suppose I shouldn't blame him for that.'

Penny's eyebrows shot up in disbelief. 'Oh come on Barbara, I'm not going to have that! Most of the responsibility for this disastrous marriage must lie with Michael. Whichever way you look at it, it was Michael who rushed you along, it was him urged you down to Plymouth and what happened? You came back married to him. Not a word to your friends, let alone your parents, not a soul that knew you there to witness the ceremony. Talk about still waters running deep, we all wondered at the time, why all the secrecy? And since now we are down to the nitty gritties, has it never crossed your mind that for him you were an extremely good catch?' A bitter note had come into Penny's voice now as she urged, 'Go on, think about it now if you haven't ever before.'

'I don't think that's true.' Barbara was flustered, her voice faltered, 'I know he loved me, at first if not now. Besides, he hasn't benefited in any way.'

'*No?*' Penny stared long and hard at her friend whom she loved very much – but the time for sympathy was over.

'Have you any of your savings left? Do you still draw your allowance from your father? Doesn't Michael ever plead for you to tap your parents for more money?'

Barbara was shocked. How did Penny know these facts? Her mother must have discussed them. Now she knew for sure that was part of the reason Penny was with her today. She felt *so* humiliated, she didn't want her friends feeling sorry for her. Her mind was in a whirl, she had to remain calm and she did her best to convince herself that she should be grateful. Yes, that was it, she consoled herself, her parents not only worried about her, they loved her deeply and would Penny be sitting here with her now if she didn't care?

'Your resentment is showing, I'm sorry if I upset you.'

'No, really, it's all right. Perhaps we ought to get off the subject. What time does your train go?'

But Penny was not to be hurried. She hadn't finished having her say yet.

'When you talk about feeling guilty, Barbara, you make me mad, I don't feel any sympathy for Michael. What's done is done. As to him feeling hostile towards you – the boot should be on the other foot, it is you who has been deprived. Think about it and remember whatever you decide there is still a lot of living ahead of you.'

There had been moments this day when Penny had wanted to take hold of Barbara and shake her. What had this damned Michael done to her? It was almost as if he had her hypnotised. She shouldn't lie down and accept the kind of treatment Michael was dishing out, she should stand up to him, show some guts. By God she hadn't been gutless during the War. Side by side she had worked with the wardens and police, seeing to the injured, digging with her bare hands to get to someone buried beneath a pile of rubble, ignoring the fact that incendiary bombs were dropping all around her. It wasn't fair. Barbara didn't deserve the way her life had turned out.

Now Penny leant slowly towards Barbara and the look she gave her was one of loving concern. 'We all make mistakes, darling, but that doesn't mean we have to go on paying for them for the rest of our lives, neither does it take away one's right to be happy.'

Barbara leant across the table and kissed Penny on the cheek. 'Thank you.' They both laughed in relief.

'All right, I know when I've made my point.' She began to gather up her purchases, bag and gloves.

Outside in the balmy sunshine their goodbyes were tearful.

'Thank you for today Penny, I hadn't realised just how much I miss you.'

'There are an awful lot of people, including me, who miss you Barbara.'

Their arms about each other they lingered for a moment, then as a taxi drew up to the kerb and as Penny was about to get into it she hesitated, turned her head to look back and speaking very softly she offered a last piece of advice. 'Cut loose now, Barbara.'

Within the next month Barbara was to wish many times that she had acted on it.

Chapter Five

BARBARA STOOD LOOKING out of the window, outside the rain was coming down in sheets, this was no April shower. Being Saturday, she had to go out to shop for the weekend, hesitating as to whether to wait any longer she made her decision; this rain wasn't about to let up, it was set in for the day. As she struggled into her macintosh she realised it was too tight, with this pregnancy she had put on a great deal of weight: it was impossible to do up the centre buttons. Drawing the belt around she knotted it to one side, that would have to do. Giving a final tug to her hat she took up the two shopping bags, closed the living room door before going down the stairs, out into the street.

'Lord, luv us, are you mad?' Mrs Winters had her head stuck around the shop doorway and was yelling after her. 'Come back, come on, come in the shop for a minute.'

Barbara did as she was bid, but asked, 'What am I supposed to do? I need to get a joint from the butchers, vegetables from the market and we haven't a slice of bread left in the house.'

'But it's teeming cats and dogs, you'll get drenched.'

Barbara screwed up her face, 'Can't be helped, I'll be as quick as I can.'

Mrs Winters stared at her and sighed heavily, but her smile was very kind. 'Well take care. I'll have the kettle on an' you come straight in 'ere an' get yer wet things off the minute yer get back.'

'Gawd save us,' gasped Mrs Winters as she watched Barbara struggle up the road, the force of the wind causing her to lower her head into her chest. She moaned aloud. It wasn't right. This beautiful healthy girl from an obviously well-to-do family was fading away, being dragged down more with every day that passed. She couldn't stand by and ignore all the things that worried her about Barbara. Not for much longer she couldn't.

'I'll let things ride over the weekend,' she said, thinking aloud. 'And then, by God, I'm gonna do something!'

Ever since Barbara had moved here she had felt that things weren't right, but these past few months were more than flesh an' blood could stand. There was Barbara, tired out with the cleaning, shopping and waiting on that lazy bastard of an 'usband and what did she get in return? Bugger all. All he dished out was verbal abuse, and that wasn't all. Oh no. It went a lot further than that. Well, it was time to put a stop to it. Let that bleedin' Michael call her a nosy old cow, better that than stand by an' do nothing until the sod went too far an' really did Barbara some harm. If it weren't for the fact that she was pregnant it might well have happened by now. One of these days that sod would come home the worse for drink and then what? Any day it could happen. The very thought made her tremble.

I'll find out the address of Barbara's parents if it's the last thing I do, she thought. I'd bet me last 'alf dollar they ain't got a clue as ter what their daughter 'as ter put up with.

Interference, that's what it would be. 'But the Lord, knows I've got ter do something,' breathed Mrs Winters as she filled her tin kettle and placed it on top of her portable stove.

Despite the rain Northcote Road market was busy, old women as well as young mums with nippers in tow, like herself, had to get food in. Barbara felt sorry for a lot of the old dears. Most wore hats but they still had scarves over them, knotted beneath their chins, to prevent the hats from being blown off. Legs bulging with varicose veins, swollen feet with bunions breaking out of split shoes, they still laughed and bantered with the stall holders who in reply called them all Ma and returned the good-natured teasing back at them.

Normally Barbara would make a couple of journeys but today she wanted to be finished, to get home in the dry. The shelves in the baker's shop were almost empty as she asked for two large split tins.

'Only got one tin left my love, will a cottage do?'

As Barbara hesitated the middle-aged woman took down the cottage loaf from the shelf, 'The nobbies are great, they're me favourite, smothered in butter, a chunk of cheese and a pickled onion, what could be better fer the ol' man's supper?'

Smiling her thanks Barbara took the two wrapped loaves, still warm to the touch, and placed them into her shopping bag. Dodging from one stall to another Barbara hoped she hadn't forgotten anything. It was still raining heavily and she paused in the butcher's shop doorway, mentally going over her purchases. Both shopping bags were full and already her arms were aching like mad. The bag with seven pounds of potatoes and all the vegetables was the worse. 'Oh, to hell with it!' she muttered out loud, 'What we haven't got we must do without. I'm going home.'

It took more than ten minutes to walk the length of the market for now she was battling into the wind which was driving the rain directly into her face. Her chin had been tucked deep into her scarf but she lifted her head as she neared the Falcon Public House and stepped over the brass rim into the shelter of the porch-way. Thankfully she let go of her heavy bags, propping them up against the wall. A thin, wiry man removed his cap, beat it against the wall, sending a shower of rain droplets flying in all directions, before stepping in, arm outstretched to push open the door to the saloon bar. Seeing Barbara he stopped in his tracks.

'Ere, you look all done in, Missus, yer can't go out agin in all this rain, you're drenched to the skin. Is yer ol' man inside? D'yer want me ter go an' fetch 'im for yer?'

'No, no thank you,' Barbara said quickly, 'I'm waiting for him, he'll be along in a minute. Thank you very much, all the same.'

'Yer welcome, lady,' said the man, pushing at the swing doors which when opened let out smoky warm air. Barbara leaned forward but although she saw familiar faces her gaze could not penetrate deep enough into the interior to see if Michael was there. To tell the truth she was half hoping that just maybe he would see her, come home with her – perhaps even relieve her of these heavy shopping bags. Then she remembered, this was the saloon bar. To Michael this pub was his second home, but his favourite haunt would of course be the public bar. She knew just where to find him, propping up the bar with his cronies. Maybe it was as well that this was the wrong bar. If Michael had caught a glimpse of her peering through the door he would have probably flown into a rage, accusing her of spying on him. The very thought of his anger and the way he would have sworn at her, made her shudder as she dragged her shopping bags home.

She said nothing because there was nothing to say when Michael came in soon after three o'clock. Much the worse for drink, he slobbered through his dinner, drew an armchair up to the fire and promptly went to sleep. Only once did Barbara disturb him by lifting his legs gently from the fender in order to replenish the dying embers. Wouldn't do to let the fire go out. If he woke up and the room was cold there would be hell to pay. She usually got severely cursed for her pains.

True to habit, Michael was ready to go out at eight o'clock sharp. Reaching the doorway, he stopped to pull his cap on over his hair that was oily with brilliantine. He gazed back to where Barbara was spreading a dark blanket over the table in preparation for doing some ironing. Something within him must have relented. In a voice that was soft for a change, not at all surly, he said, 'Do yerself a favour, come down the pub an' 'ave a drink.'

For a moment she was tempted, but only for a moment. Gently she declined the invitation knowing no good would come of it.

With the ironing out of the way the evening seemed to drag. Opening the dresser drawer, she took out her needle-work basket and settled in front of the fire to embroider a small pillowcase she was making for the baby's cot. At ten o'clock she put away her work, undressed, gave herself a good wash down before donning her nightdress and dressing-gown. Once again she was sitting before the fire, drinking hot milk and wishing she might go to bed.

112

Michael kicked up such a fuss if he came home and found she wasn't waiting up for him.

It was a quarter past twelve when the side street door banged open and heavy footsteps sounded on the uncarpeted stairs. Michael was not alone. Her first thought was that she must get herself into the bedroom, but having been half asleep in the chair she wasn't quick enough. The minute she saw flashily dressed Pete Davis step into their living room behind Michael, she felt afraid. Good mates these two were, according to Michael but Pete had never made any secret of the fact that he had no time for Barbara. Never had he made any friendly moves toward her, not even the simple courtesies one would expect a man to pay to a friend's wife.

She was under no illusion as to what he thought of her. Once within her hearing he had referred to her as high and mighty, hoity-toity bloody Barbara and since then, whenever possible, she had taken care to avoid him. Barbara felt her face redden. She was so embarrassed, sitting here in her night clothes. Her belly felt swollen and stretched. She spread her hands across her back to help herself to get out of the chair.

It was unbelievable. Michael stood cocky and arrogant beside his mate. Pete Davis stood facing her, tall, heavily built, his long mousy hair lank and greasy, his eyes red-rimmed, bleary with drink. Both of them swayed where they stood, a leering smirk set about their lips. The fear that had already settled in her grew when Michael kicked the door to close it behind them. It seemed a long time before either of them spoke. Michael removed his jacket with great deliberation and unwound his white silk muffler from around his neck, then very quietly he asked, 'You gonna be nice to Pete? You betta be cos he's me mate.' There was a hard-bitten expression on his face that she'd never seen before.

Suddenly it was not fear that Barbara felt but stark terror. 'I'll put the kettle on, make some black coffee. You've obviously had too much to drink.' Even to herself her voice sounded strange.

They both roared with laughter. 'It's not bleedin' coffee I've brought Pete 'ome for, yer daft bloody mare.'

'Too much ter drink,' Pete Davis flung the words at her. 'What would you know about it, yer toffee-nosed bitch. We can never 'ave too much ter drink can we Mike?'

'Don't you dare speak to me like that,' Barbara spoke resentfully without stopping to think, 'I'd like you to leave now or I'll – '

'Or you'll what?' Michael cut her words off short. 'Let me tell you something. Pete didn't wanna come back 'ere with me tonight – but I made 'im. I told 'im what a smashing cook you are – yeah an' I also told 'im you'd give 'im a tasty titbit fer his afters.' Michael was tottering on his feet, his words smeared apart, his hands waving in the air.

By now Barbara was petrified, 'Shut up! Shut up! You're drunk out of your mind, you don't know what you're saying.' She cut off her own words abruptly, looked from Michael's blood shot eyes to Pete's laughing gaping face and the truth hit her. Michael meant what he said. In every sense.

What could she do? What help could she summon? To bang on the floor would be useless: Mrs Winters' shop was only a lock-up premises. The Singletons upstairs might hear if she screamed, but they'd do nothing. Probably be delighted that a row was taking place; so often did that

114

family indulge in screaming matches, that more often than not led to fights, they certainly wouldn't come down and interfere.

Unexpectedly Pete lunged towards her, opened his mouth slurring his words. 'Come on luv, try being nice to me – Mike said he don't mind an' I promise I won't treat yer rough.'

He actually meant it! These awful words, tossed casually at her, made Barbara lose control. She had to get out of here. She had to. Heaven knows what will happen if we all stand around here much longer, she thought. She was terribly afraid. With courage she was far from feeling, Barbara pointed a finger in Pete's direction. 'I think you had better leave, go home and sleep it off.'

Suddenly Michael was shaking with rage, his face scarlet. All the anger that he had been feeling against Barbara ever since she had told him she was pregnant again, and that she intended to have the baby, suddenly came to boiling point. The sting of his hand as he slapped her face sent her reeling. 'So that's it, is it? I bring a friend 'ome an' you think you can tell 'im to bugger off Well, he'll not be leaving. Not till he's had what I invited 'im 'ere for. You're gonna find out what mates are for and get a taste of what mates can do fer each other, an' any more of yer lip an' you'll live ter regret it.'

Poor Barbara was doing her best not to cry but was frozen with fear, her hands and face were clammy, her stomach such a bulge that she knew she couldn't move quickly enough to escape these two drunken louts. The horror of it all was making her feel dizzy, waves of sickness rose into her throat. She had to get to the toilet; if she could get that far onto the landing, who knows but she might be able to get down the stairs and out into the street. *Dear God help me.*

She crossed the room sidestepping Michael, but Pete Davis barred her way. Mocking her, he was. Reaching out, touching her face, stroking her breast. If she had had a gun in her hand she would have shot him.

'Relax darling,' he told her, his face so near to hers she could smell his foul breath. 'Yer wanna know something? I think you're a tasty tart. Don't matter none that you're in the pudden club, all the better really, ain't it? True yer know, what Mike said, a slice orf a cut loaf don't make no difference.'

Barbara was speechless for a second, then anger took over and spurred her on. Reaching behind her she grabbed at a glass vase, swung her arm forwards and upwards and brought it smashing down onto Pete Davis's head. If she had her way it would have been thrust into his lecherous face. Barbara expected him to retaliate savagely and steeled herself against his blows as she flinched and backed away.

The glass of the vase had been thin; it had smashed into fragments doing little damage. A shake of his head sent the pieces of glass showering from Pete's mop of hair onto the floor.

Michael and Pete looked at each other and burst out laughing. They were both so drunk the sight of them made Barbara shudder. She felt the colour drain from her face as she backed away so quickly that she almost toppled over, and the more she trembled the more they laughed.

Michael crossed the room, stood in front of her, his eyes staring into hers, his breath hot on her face. Slowly he pinned her shoulders against the wall with one hand and with the other hand he ripped open the front of her

nightdress. She struggled furiously. Tried in vain to bring
her knee up into his groin, tore at his face with her nails,
all the while yelling at the top of her voice, 'I *hate* you,
Michael! I *hate* you.'

He didn't care that she was frightened or that she was
on the verge of collapsing. All he heard were the angry
cries and the note of revulsion, and so he really lost his
temper.

His arm shot out, swiping her hard across the mouth: it
was enough to stifle her screams. His hands were back on
her shoulders, holding her in a vice-like grip. 'Now you
listen to me.' The words came from between his lips with
a spray of spittle. She was panic-stricken – Michael would
stop at nothing. His look was not just full of hatred, it was
pure loathing.

His voice changed, now it was menacing. 'That's no way
ter treat me best mate. Smashing 'im over the head like
that. Pete's a good bloke. One of the best. He's bin buying
me beer all night. Yer wanna know why? I'll tell yer. Cos
I ain't got no bloody money, not a bleedin' brass farthing.
That's what you've reduced me to, sponging orf me mates.

'Well, now Barbara dear, you're gonna find out I like ter
pay my debts, one way or another, and since you're all I've
got, Gawd 'elp me, you're gonna 'ave ter 'elp me by being
nice to Pete. Got it now 'ave yer?' We can do it all nice
an' friendly or you can treat me an' Pete like we ain't fit
ter lick yer boots, in which case it's gonna be you that's
gonna come off the worse.'

Barbara's heart was thumping, her hands were wet, her
mouth swollen and painful. 'Michael!' she begged. Their
eyes met for a second before he gripped her arm tighter
and although she wriggled and squirmed she could not jerk

it away. Forcing her head to one side he sucked savagely at the flesh of her neck; as he withdrew his lips and brought them together they made a loud plopping sound. His laughter could have been heard half a mile away. 'You, my dear wife, should feel honoured, I have just given you a lovebite.'

'How much bleedin' longer you gonna play around?' Pete Davis's face was flushed with anger as he glared at them both.

Michael put both his hands under Barbara's back and knees, sweeping her up against his chest. 'Open the door Pete, the bedroom's through there. You'll be all right mate – I don't break my promises.'

Barbara gritted her teeth when he threw her down onto the bed. By now she was terror-stricken.

'Michael!' she begged again. 'Think of the baby.'

'Damn the baby,' he yelled.

Then Pete Davis was the other side of the bed, fending Michael off with both hands and shouting.

Michael shouted too, 'Stay still yer silly bitch, that way yer won't get hurt so much.'

'No! Leave me alone! Don't you dare touch me. Go away! Please, both of you, just go away.'

Barbara's heart was beating so rapidly that she thought she might be having a heart attack.

Pete Davis heaved his body onto the bed beside her.

'No, no!' Barbara pleaded yet again. 'Michael, you're never going to stand by and let this happen? Please, please, say something to stop him. You'll regret this when you sober up. I'd rather be dead than let this animal touch me.' Getting no response she screamed. Really screamed.

A whack around the head from Pete's ham-like fist soon put paid to that. There were moments when she was fully conscious when the most dreadful pain and humiliation were such that she hoped death would come. She tried her best to convince herself this was a nightmare. Only it wasn't. It was frightening, horrific reality. It was torture, so much so that her head swam and the blood pounded in her ears.

She wanted to scream and scream and scream, but what was the use, it would most likely bring her another savage blow.

As children in a fit of temper might use a rag doll, they used her. She might have endured the humiliation of being raped by a stranger – just, but this wasn't rape. It had nothing to do with the sex act. This was beastly, savage persecution and even revenge on Michael's part. There were moments when the infliction of pain made her black out, only to be revived by the biting, twisting and pinching of her bare flesh. In their drunken state these two men were vulgar brutes. The soreness of her inner thighs became unbearable as one after the other they used her.

She woke with a start and for a moment she had no idea where she was. The room was quiet. She was alone. Then the nightmare situation that she had been forced to endure returned full force. Looking at the sticky mess of tangled bedclothes, she put her head in her hands and wept. How long had she been asleep? Minutes? Or hours? How could she have slept at all, with all that had happened? What the hell am I going to do? Barbara whimpered to herself. Movement of any kind brought spasms of fire searing through her bruised body. Her legs felt painful, like severe cramp, only worse. What shreds of clothing she still had on were stuck to her body which was running with sweat. Her head hurt like hell. Cautiously she lifted a corner of the bed-sheet and wiped the blood from the side of her forehead. The pain in her stomach was a constant throbbing, attempts at deep breathing only made it worse.

She tried to lie still. There was one thing she clung to: this night had swept away all doubts and uncertainties. She wouldn't spend another day under the same roof as Michael. She wasn't going to be around when he sobered up and made an attempt to express his regret. Forgive him? Never! He had not been a bystander, he had participated. Every blow, every humiliating action had been premeditated. Drink had made him brave and he had sought retaliation on her for everything that had gone wrong since he had been demobbed from the navy. Her social class was like a thorn in his side. Well he wouldn't have to bear with her ever again. Something, a voice, came back to her, much too terrible to remember, yet how would she ever blot it from her mind? Pete Davis growling, 'Some bleedin' wife you've got 'ere, she wouldn't even make a good whore.'

She cried quietly for a long time. She felt no better, only empty, bruised and sick.

When the room began to grow lighter, she got up. What she wouldn't give to be able to lie in a hot bath, but that wasn't possible. Warily she slipped out of the bedroom, then found she need not have bothered. Apart from herself the flat was empty. The air in the living room was foul, the whole place a mess: one chair lay on its side with the back broken away from the seat, and there were cigarette butts ground out on the linoleum everywhere.

Barbara held the tin kettle under the cold water tap until it was half full, then, setting it down on a gas jet, she struck a match, turned on the gas tap and ignited the flame. When the kettle came to the boil she made a pot of tea and immediately refilled the kettle to the brim, placing it once more over the naked flame.

She felt so cold, chilled to the bone, as she sank into the chair and clasped her hands around the cup of tea. Every limb of hers felt numbed and heavy, she ached from head to toe. She looked around the room, stared at the dead ashes in the grate. What did the mess matter? What did anything matter now? Painfully she rose and poured herself a second cup of tea from the brown china teapot.

The sound of the tin lid of the kettle wobbling up and down signified that once more the kettle was boiling. Having poured the water into an enamel bowl and added cold water from the tap, with the bar of soap between her hands she worked up a lather. She couldn't bear to use a flannel: her body was too sore. Gently she washed herself from head to toe, flinching as she cleansed between her thighs, dabbing herself dry on a clean towel. She had to come out of the scullery and go back into the living room in order to sit down.

She felt so ill. The effort of washing herself had been so great. I'm an absolute mess, she thought angrily. It would have been bad enough if Michael had come home drunk out of his mind and used her spitefully, it wouldn't have been the first time; but to have brought that bastard Pete Davis and not only allowed him to rape her but to have actually encouraged him! I hope to God I never set eyes on Michael again, because if I do, so help me I'll murder him, she thought.

It was some time before her anger was spent and she could bring herself to stand up again and get herself into clean clothes. Eventually she was ready. Without even

121

bothering to close the door or with any inclination of where she was going, she went down the stairs and out into the street. Only one thing was she certain of – nothing nor no one would ever induce her to set foot in that place again.

Everywhere was strangely quiet. Despair overwhelmed her: which way should she go? Feeling so unwell, so confused, she didn't rightly know. Just one predominant thought was in her mind; she had to get away. Still being only a little after seven o'clock on this Sunday morning, no one was rushing off to work, no totters toured the streets, no children played in the gutters. Even the permanent chalked games of hopscotch on the pavement had disappeared, washed away by yesterday's torrential rain. She had to stop for a rest, get her breath back. Walking was agony. She leaned against the wall of the working man's café, usually so busy; now its shutters were down, its sign turned to 'closed'. Over the far side of the road scruffy mongrel dogs were rummaging amongst the litter dumped on the disused bomb-site, apparently Sunday made no difference to them. With its three huge brass balls, the pawn shop on the corner was also closed. Come tomorrow morning there would be a queue of women there pawning various articles in order to get a few shillings to see them through the week. There was a gaudy sign above these premises which announced, 'We pay thirty-three shillings and threepence for gold sovereigns.' Who the hell in this neighbourhood possessed a hoard of sovereigns?

It was no good, if she didn't make herself get on the move again she would most likely fall down. With dragging footsteps and interminable stops she finally saw Clapham Junction railway station ahead of her.

In a voice that was little more than a croak, she asked for a single ticket to Victoria.

'Forty minutes to wait, Missus,' the ticket operator told her as he passed over her change. Then pushing his head forward and peering closely at Barbara's swollen mouth and the bruise on the side of her temple, he added kindly, 'Buffet bar is open, pop along there, get yerself a nice hot cuppa an' 'ave a sit down.' Barbara quietly thanked him.

He watched her slowly walk away and, shaking his head, said to himself, 'Another Saturday night family feud. It's always the women what comes off the worse an' by Christ that one's taking a rare old bashing, an' no mistake.'

At the counter of the refreshment bar Barbara passed over a sixpence and took her cup of coffee to a table in the far corner where she thankfully sat down. She tried to take a sip of the coffee but she quickly set the cup back down; she would have to wait for it to cool. Her lips were so swollen the scalding liquid hurt. Time passed, she felt dreadfully ill.

Dear God what am I going to do? she thought. I can't possibly go home to my parents, not in the state that I'm in.

It wouldn't be fair on them and if Michael were to come looking for her that would be most likely the first place that he would try. What was the alternative? Her friends' homes? Both Penny and Elizabeth would be glad to help, they wouldn't turn her away. No, no, of course not, the idea was inconceivable. What could she say to them or they to her? The thing that mattered most to her was that no one should ever know the contemptible things that Michael and his mate had done to her.

Never, never, would she be able to relate those details to anyone. She began to panic, giving in to fear, her insides ached so much; what if she were to have a miscarriage? She had to face the fact that she was entirely on her own, and find somewhere to hide away from prying eyes, at least until she felt better. She had finished her coffee long since and got up now to go outside. She felt a wave of dizziness overtake her and would have fallen if an arm had not gone around her waist and a gentle voice seemingly from far away urged her to sit down again. Two hands lightly pressed her head down until it hung between her knees, soft fingers drew her long hair back and gently stroked her neck.

When her vision cleared Barbara saw that the lady who was befriending her looked a little like a nun, but not completely so. The robe she wore was not floor-length but reached only to her calves and the colour was navy-blue, not black as would be that of a nun from a Holy Order. Around her head and shoulders she wore a veil of the same blue material as that of her robe, held in place by a stiff white band which lay across her forehead encircling a sweet, kind, gentle face. Wisps of golden hair escaped from the sides. She touched Barbara twice on the arm before asking, 'Do you feel any better now?'

Barbara couldn't bring herself to answer, she felt so awful. Suddenly she coughed then made a choking sound as she dropped her head forward onto her chest. It seemed that all the muscles of her face were twitching now. She couldn't control her lips in order to speak. Presently she lifted her head and gazed at the face of the young woman who was obviously affiliated to the Church and in that moment Barbara envied her the quality of peace that shone from her clear blue eyes.

'You need help, my dear. Where were you going?'

For answer Barbara reached into her coat pocket and withdrew her train ticket, holding it out in front of her.

'Victoria. So was I, but we've missed the train now. Were friends meeting you?'

Barbara sadly shook her head.

'Did you have any destination in mind on arrival?'

Again Barbara could only shake her head, evading an answer. There was a long silence. The glass doors opened, two men entered, hoots from shunting trains sounded ominous. The Church lady stood thoughtfully watching Barbara who was having difficulty with her breathing.

Finally she said, 'I'm Sister Francis, I belong to the Church of England Nursing Order. Will you trust me? Will you come with me, if only to rest for a while?'

Then, not waiting for an answer, she softly patted Barbara's arm, 'Wait here, sit quietly. I'll be back in a few minutes.'

Barbara had no idea how long she sat there; no one bothered her and she never raised her glance from the floor until the gentle voice came to her again, saying practically, 'Can you manage to walk? I've a taxi waiting outside.'

They walked together, Sister Francis with her hand placed firmly on Barbara's elbow. They had scarcely covered half the distance when they were forced to stop. Barbara's chest was heaving, the pain in her was everywhere making her feel sick. The taxi driver came to meet them and with his help they finally reached the waiting cab. Barbara got into the back and sank gratefully against the upholstery.

The taxi drove up St John's Hill, turned left into Spencer Park and skirted the row of tall elegant terraced houses which formed a triangle around the lovely green of Spencer Park. They might just as well have been going to the North Pole. Barbara was oblivious as to what direction the driver had taken. Her eyelids had dropped but although she dozed dry sobs shook her even now and then. She did open her eyes as she felt the taxi come to a stop.

The driver was opening the door and got her out with the help of Sister Francis. Panic shot through Barbara, for a fleeting second she thought she had come to her parents' home. As she stood with her hand in the crook of Sister Francis's arm she looked hard at the house. The impression she got was that it was a mansion. Large, dark red bricked, ivy-clad walls and many many tall windows. Beautiful grounds and a long winding drive.

Even with the help of Sister Francis, walking was sheer agony. Barbara kept telling herself to stay calm, take small steps and go slowly, but still she was forced to stop every few yards. Her mouth was dry, her limbs were trembling – she didn't think she could make it, she would have to drop to the ground.

Ahead of them the main door opened and a woman, dressed similarly to Sister Francis, hurried down the stone steps and came towards them. An older woman, quite stout, her face was round and red as any apple. Taking hold of Barbara's other arm she smiled, the smile lit up her homely face and again Barbara saw the same quality of peace and tranquillity that she had first seen in the eyes of Sister Francis. Her voice was soothing as she said, 'Come along my dear, let's get you inside.'

Clustered together, the sisters one each side of Barbara, they moved slowly forward up the flight of steps through the open doorway and into a vast oak panelled entrance hall. The stout sister went ahead and they followed her into what appeared to be a sitting room.

Barbara stood still and breathed a sigh of relief, then

muttered a silent prayer: 'Thank God'. It was a lovely spacious room, but it was the overall feeling of peacefulness that descended upon her as she allowed Sister Francis to press her down onto a chintz-covered settee that she was grateful for. Everything spoke of serenity. In the centre of a round polished table stood a bowl of fresh flowers; at the end of the room French windows stood opened outwards, from which flimsy beige curtains fluttered in the breeze.

Both sisters drew an armchair close and seated themselves facing Barbara. The stout one spoke first and still her voice had such a calming effect that Barbara began to relax.

'I'm Sister Marion, this is Beechgrove House and you will be quite safe here. While we are waiting for some tea to be brought to us by Dorothy, she is one of our helpers, would you like to talk to us?'

Receiving no answer she asked, 'What is your name, my dear? That at least would be a good starting point.'

Barbara bowed her head; tears were trickling down her cheeks. It was their kindness to her. It was too much.

When her head fell lower and sobs began to shake her body Sister Francis rose and came to sit beside her. Slowly she slid her arms across Barbara's shoulders, drawing her head onto her own chest and sat there gently holding her close, her own chin resting on Barbara's bent head. Many minutes passed, the silence only broken by the sound of Barbara's grief, until Sister Marion suggested, 'Let's get her upstairs and into bed, and then I think it would be best if we ask the doctor to come along and have a look at her.'

Compassionate hands had removed her clothes as though she were a baby. A thin cotton nightdress had been slipped over her head and now she was in bed in a room that was small in size, yet she savoured the relief. Everything was so clean and bright. She lay back, propped up against a stack of pillows. The feeling of being between soft clean linen was heavenly but terrible pain still gripped her and the tension was still there. Every thought tormented her.

Where was she? What was going to happen to her? Where would she have gone if Sister Francis hadn't come along? When would these terrible pains go away and when would she stop feeling so sick?

When a knock came on the door Barbara jumped, for it startled her. The door opened, a loud cockney voice announced, 'I've brought yer some tea.' A thin young girl in a skimpy green dress came across the room, setting a tea-tray down on a small cupboard which was placed beside the bed.

She grinned at Barbara and held out her hand to her. 'Me name's Dorothy, Dolly ter me friends. Bin in the wars 'ave yer? Well yer've landed in the right place, like 'eaven on earth this place is. The sisters are bloody angels. Oh, sorry luv, keep forgetting I ain't supposed to swear, but that's wot they are – bloody angels.'

When Barbara made no move Dorothy leant across her and quietly now she said, 'Everyfink will seem better tomorra. After you've 'ad a nice cuppa tea you get yer 'ead down, sleep it orf, yer'll see, a good sleep can work wonders.' Her voice dropped almost to a whisper, 'I've got ter go now, there's twenty of us living 'ere – not counting the staff nor the babies – so there's always plenty ter do. But I'll tell yer one fing, we've all bin frew the mill, one way or another we 'ave, but we've come frew and so my luv will you, you'll see. Ta-tar fer now. Don't let yer tea go cold.'

Left alone, tears were again stinging at the back of Barbara's eyelids. She felt a sense of unreality, none of this was really happening. Last night and how she came to be in this place had to be a dreadful dream. It was so good to feel cleanliness about her, yet she screwed her eyes up tight at the thought of how she had been abused. Her body would never again feel totally clean. Not inside it wouldn't. She felt now that she would like to blot out everything and everyone, even the kind sisters who had suddenly come into her life, and pull the sheets over her head and hide away from the world.

It was all too much. The fragile thread of self-preservation to which she had clung, snapped. She felt a drumming in her ears and it was as though she was falling down into a bottomless pit. And she didn't care. She wanted to go and never come back.

Over the next few days the doctor was worried. Injections had brought about a form of sedation but not entirely so; indeed the sisters reported that Barbara couldn't speak properly or control her movements and she suffered from terrible nightmares. More than once he had wondered whether he should suggest to the sisters that the police be notified, for most surely this young woman had been cruelly used. He was used to being called to Beechgrove House and having battered wives as his patients, but this case was different. The severity of her injuries was appalling. One small wound on her forearm shocked him beyond belief. A small, deep, festering hole that refused to heal caused by, he was in no doubt, a lighted cigarette having been ground into her flesh.

The sisters asked themselves if Barbara had lost her reason. For two days she had tossed and turned, rambling all the time. At one point in the middle of the night she had pushed herself up on her elbow and, staring wide-eyed into space, had yelled, 'I'll kill you, I will, I'll kill you!'

The look in her eyes had been dreadful to see, then her voice had trailed away, her head flopped back down onto the pillow whilst her whole body trembled.

The fourth morning Barbara's breathing was easier. She no longer tossed from side to side but lay still, only occasionally she still moaned. The opinion of the sisters who had nursed her day and night was that she had lived through an horrendous experience.

At the end of the week Barbara got out of bed for the first time since her arrival. She now knew that Beechgrove House was mainly a home for unmarried mothers. Sitting in an armchair by the window, gazing out at the beautiful grounds, her mind pondered on how fate had sent Sister Francis to the railway station on that Sunday morning. Had God sent help to her?

If that were the case, where had God been during the hours she had called in vain for his help? What had she ever done that was so bad that God had deemed fit that she should suffer such perversion?

Chapter Six

DOWNSTAIRS THE GIRLS, almost all from the working classes, were at first cautious of Barbara and she was reserved towards them, even a little shy, but with the help of the friendly Dolly barriers were broken down on both sides as the days wore on. Much time was given by trained members of the staff to Barbara. She no longer had to see the physician daily, for her body was healing. Nothing was physically wrong with her and the kindly old doctor advised her that her pregnancy was safe.

That fact was not accepted by her with any relief. When she had first felt the baby move inside her she had been overwhelmed with an almost unbearable tenderness. Yet she thought, how can I feel like that now, knowing the father is a ruthless sadistic pig? Will I be able to cradle this baby in my arms? More important, will I be able to love this child? What if it should look like Michael, a constant reminder?

It didn't bear thinking about. Should she keep the child, try for an abortion, have it adopted? Despite herself she sighed, heavy-hearted. She had tried. But now, after what she had been put through, whatever she decided she knew full well that the memory of that night would return to haunt her, like some ghastly nightmare, for the rest of her life.

Was she frightened that Michael might come looking for her?

Of course she was frightened. The very thought terrified her. Cowardly, she made a resolution: to push all thoughts of the baby to the back of her mind, at least for the time being.

She had needed little persuasion to accept the offer of the sisters' hospitality to remain as a resident at Beechgrove House until after her baby was born. Where else could she go?

Inevitably there were still signs of what she had been through. She looked nothing like her former self, now she was washed out and pallid, there were still dark circles beneath her eyes. Her lips and the area around her mouth were still swollen and bruised. A bald patch at the side of her head, where the hair had been cut away to enable the wound to be stitched, was a constant reminder whenever she looked into a mirror, of the spiteful way Pete Davis had struck her.

For all the kindly counselling Barbara received no matter how many times the direct question was put to her as to whether she had any parents or relatives living, she never answered. Only the barest facts as to what had happened to her and her married name was all that the sisters could persuade her to tell them.

Soon she settled into a routine. Given the choice, she had opted to work alongside Dolly and four other young women in the kitchens – Sally, Mary, Vera and Peggy.

The girls accepted her and she them. Two were common, even bawdy in their humour, but who was she to criticise? Their friendly gestures to her were unstinting and as such she accepted them and was grateful. Mornings they mostly prepared vegetables which were grown in the grounds, while two of the younger sisters made bread, scones and potato-cakes.

'Are you rich?' Sally, the quietest of their group, asked Barbara as the two of them scraped away at freshly dug carrots, while the others peeled potatoes.

'Of course I'm not rich.'

'Then how is it you speak so posh?'

'Probably because of the school I went to.'

Sally made a face. 'Wish some one had taught me to talk like you do, maybe I wouldn't 'ave ended up in 'ere in the state I'm in.' She patted her own swollen belly.

The group glanced at each other and burst out laughing. Even the dark haired Vera, who was strangely secretive, joined in.

'Yer silly cow!' Mary, the oldest of the kitchen skivvies, as Dolly was wont to refer to them as, playfully pushed Sally's shoulder.

'Her talking different to us ain't stopped 'er from taking a bashing nor from getting 'erself in the pudden club 'as it? She ain't no better off than the rest of us.'

Turning to Barbara, Mary added, 'My old man brought a floosie 'ome with 'im one Saturday night. There was me, in bed, fast asleep, and the two of them climbs in and start their hanky-panky. I split 'is head open, used the brass lamp 'is muvver gave us fer a wedding present. Didn't do me no good. Chased me up the stairs he did, we lived in a basement flat just off the Fulham Road, knife in 'is 'and, blood streaming down 'is face and that's 'ow I come to 'ave this great scar on me neck.'

Dolly sent Barbara a long amused look, and Barbara grinned.

Now it was the turn of Peggy and Sally to explain in

detail as to how they had come to be living at Beechgrove House. It was as if Barbara had been accepted into their club and they had all decided to confide in her in a single burst.

'Booze, that was my Alf's ruination. Nice enough bloke when he was sober, but a bleedin' pig when he'd 'ad a session down the pub.'

Barbara glanced across at Peggy and felt a great deal of sympathy for her.

'Nothing like that about my Jim, good as gold ter me.' Sally came out with the words quickly. 'No. Only thing wrong with Jim, he took a liking to other folk's goods. Been inside a few times before he took up wiv me. Drove a laundry van fer a few months and then one Friday night came 'ome with the takings. Had a smashing weekend down in Brighton we did, 'ad our dinner in a cafe two nights, steak an' chips and we 'ad afters. They was waiting fer 'im on the Monday morning, silly sod went ter work, large as life. He's in Wandsworth jail now. Landlord didn't waste no time kicking me out of our upstairs flat, he knew me an' Jim weren't never properly married. I didn't 'ave a leg ter stand on.'

Vera wasn't about to disclose her life story to anyone. Dolly screwed up her child-like face and winked at Barbara. 'Ain't everyone this lot confides in. Mostly they tell anyone asking questions to eff orf!'

'I don't remember asking for any details,' Barbara murmured.

'All the more honoured then, ain't cher? One day maybe I might get around ter telling yer why I'm still 'ere after two years an' yer won't 'ear none of the sisters asking me ter go. Then agin I might not tell yer.'

134

How sad Dolly sounded, her circumstances must have been pretty grim.

Wisely Barbara kept her thoughts to herself as she sliced the carrots into a saucepan and went to strain the peelings at the sink and throw away the dirty water.

Now, two months later, Barbara had become accustomed to Beechgrove House. She was grateful for the quiet, for peace, for time to rest, read a book, even for the kitchen work of a morning and the jolly company of the girls. It was a gorgeous day, the afternoon sun hot, the sky blue and cloudless. She sat in a deck chair beneath a tall shady tree, her hands lying idle in her lap. Dolly sat near, hemming sides of sheets that had become worn in the middle and were now being made up into cot sheets. George, one of the gardeners, was way over to her right, quietly digging and making the flower beds look fresh with the newly-turned earth. Barbara watched his dry, gnarled old hands and wondered why on such a hot day he still wore a tweed coat and flat cap.

A blackbird came down to drink from the stone bird bath and faintly she could hear the hum of traffic, which at most times was deadened by the great tall leafy trees. She thought of home. Not Battersea and Michael, but her real home: Alfriston, where her mother and father were. Suddenly she wanted to be there, safe and sound, to be a young girl again growing up surrounded by love.

She had written to Mrs Winters, merely saying that she had left Michael and thanking her for all her kindness. The letter to her parents had been harder. Much the same explanation, assuring them that she was well and that she would be home to see them in the not too distant future.

Would she? Even now she was not sure that she would go home, face the love and hurt that she would see in their faces. Well, she had sent the letter, that had to be enough for now, she couldn't face any major decisions at the moment.

She felt mean. She could at least telephone. In the entrance hall there was a pay phone, there was no excuse for not ringing her father. It would be so simple. It wouldn't take a minute. 'Daddy it's me,' she would say, and tell him where she was, outline what had happened, only briefly, but it would be enough and he would be here to fetch her in no time.

One evening she had almost gone into the box. Holding onto the door she had hesitated, trying to pluck up courage. But the telling of the story was beyond her.

She imagined the conversation.

'Daddy?'

'Oh, Barbara! We've been *so* worried about you. Where are you?'

'In a home for battered wives and unmarried mothers.'

She couldn't go on. Not even in fantasy. Her courage failed her and she had crossed the hall with tears in her eyes and shut herself away in her bedroom.

Barbara felt Dolly was watching her and looked up to meet her eye to eye. Dolly was not an attractive person, certainly not pretty. But she had a scrubbed, immaculate look to her. Her hair was short and spiky, cut so that it framed her face, and – Barbara had come to know – discreetly covered a disfigurement that ran down the side of her left ear. Her eyes were brown, her face the sort that one would call an out-of-doors sort of face and she looked and acted much older than Barbara now knew her to be, which was only seventeen.

'Penny for them,' Dolly offered as she laid her needle-work down and gave her full attention to Barbara.

Barbara sighed, half sadly and half relieved to have someone to talk to.

'I was thinking about my parents.'

'Do they know where you are?'

'No.'

'Will they be worried about you?'

'Very much so, I imagine.'

'Then you're very lucky. Wish I 'ad a family that worried about me. By the way, Barbara, yer never mention yer 'usband. Not that yer talk much at all but when yer do it's only ever about yer mum an' dad.'

Barbara saw no reason to comment on that, instead she asked a question. 'Don't you have any family at all, Dolly?'

'No, me mum died when I was eleven. An uncle I'd never even 'eard of before wrote and said me two bruvvers, who were both older than me, could go an' live wiv 'im and his missus in New Zealand. Ain't never 'eard of them from that day ter this.'

'What about your father? Did you live with him?'

'If you're just being nosy an' wanna know 'ow I come ter be living 'ere why don't yer come right out in the open an' damn well ask?'

'You started this conversation,' Barbara pointed out.

'Yeah, I know,' said Dolly shortly. 'All right, don't let me an' you argue. Ter tell yer the truth I get on better wiv you than I 'ave wiv anyone since I bin 'ere.'

Barbara smiled, kept her silence and watched the old gardener pack his tools in a canvas bag which he hung on the handlebars of a bicycle, then fling his leg over the crossbar and wobble off down the pathway.

Dolly straightened her lean frame and took a deep breath, as if to say she had come to a decision.

'Yeah, I lived wiv me father. Lived to regret it an' all. He made use of me most nights as if I was 'is wife.'

Barbara had to stifle her emotions, not let so much as a glimmer of sympathy show on her face.

'Why don't yer ask me why I didn't tell someone, go to the police, or me teacher at school? Yer wouldn't 'ave ter ask if you knew my father. Big an' brutal. He didn't bother to threaten, he just gave me an 'ammering now an' again – just a taste of what I would get if I was ter open me mouth. I was fourteen when me monthlies started, that keep 'im at bay for a while. Then one night he wanted me ter do somefink different and I wasn't 'aving any. I 'ad stood fer all I was going to. Yelled an' screamed, I did. Said this time I was gonna tell the police. He set fire ter the bed. Locked the bedroom door an' buggered off an' left me.'

Barbara felt so inadequate, wanting to hug Dolly and to say something that would ease the memory. She was so angry that men should be able to abuse women, but a little girl of eleven! Her anger was short-lived. Thank God for the wonderful kind sisters and the sanctuary of Beechgrove House.

'Must be about tea-time,' Dolly said matter-of-factly as she folded her work away and got to her feet.

It was decision time. Barbara had an appointment with the gynaecologist and Sister Francis had promised to be there.

Taking out a cotton dress from the cupboard in her

room, she removed her working overall, washed her hands and face at the hand-basin which stood in the corner and pulled the dress over her head. It hung long and loosely over her swollen stomach. Unexpectedly a thought struck her. Every single article of clothing she wore – even her sandals – had been provided by the sisters. Did she have any money of her own? Was her father still paying her monthly allowance into her bank account? With this thought she sat down on the edge of the bed. Guilt filled her mind: she had been so selfish, taking everything that was offered by the sisters without giving a thought as to how Beechgrove House was funded.

There had been plenty of opportunities when she could have gone out, paid a visit to any branch of her bank and checked on her financial position, but she had shrunk from putting a foot outside of these walls. She had never even offered to make a contribution towards her keep, just taking everything for granted.

Well, once she had had this baby and was able to go back and live in the outside world fortunately she would be able to put matters to rights. She would have no qualms about requesting her father to make a donation to this Church nursing order and he would be more than generous, of that she was quite sure.

Down the stairs and into the hall she went. The door leading to the garden stood open, there was no wind, the sun shone, the grass was like an emerald carpet, the trees stood tall and abundant with leaves. What a beautiful place this was, what a haven it had been for her. Not for much longer though.

She turned right, went down the corridor that led to the hospital wing and sat herself down on one of the vacant chairs that were lined up outside of the room which served as a clinic.

'Hi yer Barbara, won't be long now an' you'll be doing this, eh?' Sally sat opposite, unaffected, breast exposed, her three-week-old daughter sucking contentedly at the nipple.

Barbara stood up, went across and smiled tenderly down at the wee mite whose head was covered in blonde hair that was so fine it shone like silk. 'She really is a lovely baby,' Barbara murmured.

'Yeah, ain't she just?' The look of tenderness on Sally's face was unbelievable. With everyone watching, Sally pulled Barbara's head down and, placing her lips near to Barbara's ear, she whispered, 'Her Dad's gonna think the world of 'er. I ain't told no one this, he's a married man, his wife can't 'ave no kids.'

'Then she'll be very precious to the both of you,' said Barbara, kindly but much embarrassed. How will she cope when she leaves here? Barbara wondered. Scarcely more than a child herself, Sally was obviously thrilled to be a mother.

Every patient had been seen in turn and now it only remained for Barbara to be called. The door opened and Sister Francis put her head round the corner. 'Come along in, Barbara, Doctor Osbourne is all ready for you.' The smile and friendliness were as usual a joy to behold and went a long way towards calming Barbara's attack of nerves.

Anita Osbourne was a beautiful woman, tall and slim. What set her apart for Barbara was her striking combination of lightly-tanned skin, dark brown eyes, and copper-coloured hair with more than a hint of red in it which she wore short and cut close to her head like a young lad.

Doctor Osbourne put down the pen with which she

140

had been writing, swivelled round in her chair to face Barbara and let her strong hands with their long fingers and unvarnished nails hang loose between her knees. 'Um, well, have you come to a decision?'

Soothed by the intimate tone of her voice, Barbara felt her spirits rise and told herself to speak up sensibly, not to give way to all of her half-acknowledged doubts but to be firm and stick to her guns. After all, the girls all agreed that Doctor Osbourne was as much a social worker as a doctor when it came to giving advice as to how to solve their problems.

Anita Osbourne would have agreed. She seemed to spend a great deal of her time either filling in forms on behalf of her patients or talking on the telephone to social workers. Barbara Hamlin was to her a case apart. She would have given a great deal to be in possession of the facts that had led to a well-bred young woman such as Barbara seeking shelter in Beechgrove House.

Sister Francis dipped her head in Barbara's direction and before Barbara had a chance to reply to the doctor's question she asked, 'Is anything wrong?'

'Why do you ask that?' Barbara retaliated quickly.

'You look so pale. Are you sure you have come to the right decision?'

'Yes.'

'You weren't so sure yesterday and you weren't very anxious to talk about it.'

'Only because it had to be my own decision. Made entirely off my own bat and with no one else involved.'

'Good girl,' the doctor said pleasantly. 'I'm sure she is absolutely right, don't you agree, Sister?'

'Yes. If she had wanted to ask my advice I am sure she

would have done so by now. Though it is not too late, perhaps I could still help.'

Nobody can help, Barbara said to herself. Nobody can do anything. Barbara thought for the umpteenth time of how much she had wanted this baby, longed for it, but not now. It wouldn't be fair to the child. She would never be able to look at its face without remembering what Michael, yes, and Pete Davis had done to her. It wasn't the child's fault but then neither was it hers. So, if she couldn't bring herself to love this unborn baby, far better that it should go to parents who would love and care for it and, please God, it would never learn the reason why she had signed it away even before it was born.

'I want this baby to be adopted. I don't even want to see it.'

A pin would have been heard had it dropped in the room at that moment. Sister Francis leaned across, took Barbara's hand between both of her own and softly said, 'Oh Barbara.' The sadness in her voice had turned to a sob.

Very briskly Anita Osbourne shuffled and tidied the papers that were scattered across her desk and in a voice free from emotion announced, 'I will set the wheels in motion.'

On the first day of October 1948, Barbara gave birth to a son. Quite naturally her labour had not been without pain, but she had endured it, biting her bottom lip and seldom crying out. She kept telling herself over and over again that childbirth was natural and women the world over went through it daily, besides which she kept reminding herself that this suffering was not being maliciously inflicted.

One final push and with a great whoosh the baby entered the world.

Barbara lay flat, her hair damp with sweat, her eyes shut tight, and she heaved a great sigh.

The last link with Michael was severed.

She never saw the child; indeed she would not have known the sex of it had she not heard a nurse murmur, 'Would you look at the amount of hair he has!'

Anita Osbourne spent the next six weeks fighting her own conscience. She had had Barbara's baby moved to another home, feeling that was in the best interest of everyone concerned.

This child would not be difficult to place. It was a perfect male child. There were very few normal, healthy British babies available for childless couples to adopt. Some authorities had so many potential parents waiting that they were closing their lists.

Anita stood in the doorway of the utility room and watched Barbara, whose back was to her, fold sheets. She would have one more go to try and prevent this young woman from making a decision that she would probably end up regretting for the rest of her life.

'Barbara, when you've finished in here, would you like to come and have a cup of coffee with me? I'll be in my office.' She turned and walked away without waiting for an answer.

Barbara knew what this would be about. More persuasion. She went just the same.

Anita made small talk for the first few minutes, while she poured out the coffee. Then she started to plead. 'Barbara, stop being so ashamed of your feelings. You've never once asked for help. Talking about what you've been through would maybe release all those pent up emotions. Wouldn't you just like to take a look at your baby?' Barbara never lifted her head. It was like talking to a brick wall. 'Is there no one among your friends and family who would be willing to take your baby?'

For one fleeting moment Barbara imagined herself looking over the side of the cot. Lifting the baby out. Taking it home to her parents.

The moment was gone, instantly suppressed by the memory of Michael and his cruelty.

Anita watched with a heavy heart as a single tear escaped and rolled down Barbara's cheek. Oh, dear God, how this girl must have suffered.

'Let me refill your cup,' she said, placing an arm across Barbara's shoulders and wishing like hell that there was more that she could do to help.

The six weeks were up. Barbara signed the adoption papers without giving a second thought as to the untruths she had stated: married, but separated. Father of child unknown.

For herself police action didn't worry her one jot, and should Michael ever surface and want to know about the child that would be a different matter all together. Threaten him she most certainly would.

Two days later, it was time for her to leave. Breakfast was over and everyone trooped out across the hall and through the front door to see her go. It was goodbye to the friendly, peaceful Beechgrove House, to the sanctuary it had given her, to the lovely gardens. Goodbye to the camaraderie that had become so natural between herself and the other girls. Goodbye to the sisters who were indeed angels.

'Thank you for everything.' Barbara held out her arms wide to include each and every person that had helped to save her life. Well, if not her life her reason, for without the care and protection of Beechgrove House what would have been the outcome?

She smiled at them all with sadness lingering in her eyes. They had been there when she needed them, given her a home for as long as she had wanted to stay.

Sister Francis stepped close, enfolding her lovingly within her arms. Gently she kissed Barbara on each cheek, then with her voice full of emotion for she had come to love what she considered this strange lost soul, she murmured, 'Take care, Barbara. Put the past behind you, and may God bless you always.'

Barbara turned blindly away, her eyes brimming with tears, so much of her life was being left here at Beechgrove House. As she walked the path to where a taxicab stood waiting it was the down-to-earth words of Dolly that reached her ears.

'Keep yer chin up luv, there must be some good blokes out there somewhere.'

Oh, Dolly! It was too much. Barbara turned.

Dolly opened her arms wide and Barbara ran back to her. They hugged so tightly they both nearly lost their balance.

'Who knows? We may meet again, one day,' Dolly said in a voice that was husky with emotion. Then she kissed Barbara, hard, and gave her a little push. 'Go on, on yer way, goodbye Barbara.'

Barbara was too choked to reply.

She almost ran to the taxi. The cabby started up the engine and moved off. There was scarcely time for Barbara to turn to the window and wave a last farewell. Just a final glimpse of fat, rosy-faced Sister Marion waving her handkerchief and a group of people, all of whom had become her friends, standing there on the gravel drive in front of that lovely old house.

Then they were gone.

Ahead lay only the busy road and traffic that seemed to be moving much too fast.

Chapter Seven

MRS HAMLIN WAS thrilled to have Barbara back home but at the same time both she and her husband were terribly worried. Although they were both Victorian in their outlook and adhered to a strict sense of moral values, they felt a great deal of compassion towards their daughter. It was so obvious that Barbara had suffered some terrible ordeal. But what?

The happy young girl that had been Barbara had changed so much it actually caused them pain to watch her. She was so secretive. Where had she been these last months? Something dreadful must have happened to cause her to cut herself so completely off from them and indeed from her friends.

Apparently she had left Michael, but under what circumstances and for what reason?

'Can't say I feel any regret about that man no longer being on the scene,' Phillip Hamlin admitted to his wife when they were alone in their bedroom. 'Actually, to be honest I feel relieved. I couldn't bring myself to trust that fellow, right from the start. Think about it.'

'As if I've done anything else but think about it from the very day I heard the name Michael Henderson,' Patricia Hamlin muttered beneath her breath.

'How could our only daughter have taken up with such a man in the first place? Then, without a word to us, take off, marry him and end up living in such appalling conditions. What a mess she has made of her life. It is astounding really!' He laid his silver-backed hairbrushes down on the glass-topped dressing-table, smoothed the sides of his hair flat with his hands, picked up his glasses and a book and walked to his side of the bed. He paused, as though deep in thought, 'Patricia, do you know if Barbara has given a thought to divorce?'

'Probably hasn't, but if you are thinking along those lines then I am entirely with you. I won't be a moment, I'll just wipe this cream off my face and then I will switch the main light off. Be a dear and switch my bedside light on as well as your own. Think I shall read for a while.'

Her husband couldn't settle to reading; like a dog with a bone he couldn't leave the subject alone.

'Best thing that could happen.' He spoke aloud but more than half to himself. 'Obtain a divorce. As speedily and as painlessly as possible.' Some things he couldn't discuss with his wife. His heart racked within him whenever Barbara, unaware that he was observing her, allowed the anguish to show through in her eyes. No doubt about it, his little girl had been to hell and back.

He put down his book, took off his reading glasses and turned to face Patricia. Firmly he said, 'We must at all costs tread warily. Sufficient for the moment that Barbara is safely back home with us.'

Patricia looked at her husband, his hair had turned iron-grey since the loss of their sons. She had loved him as a young law graduate, married him whilst he still served as a pupil to other barristers, sustained him through endless exams and burst with pride the day he had donned his wig and gown, proclaiming himself a barrister. She loved him still. He radiated strength and character. Barbara was withholding dark secrets, there was no doubt about that. She had been made to suffer and if the truth should ever be told, what then? She shuddered. How would her husband react?

'Darling, don't you want to tell me where you have been these last months?'

Barbara and her mother were together in the lounge having afternoon tea.

'No mother, let's change the subject. That was the past, let's talk about the future.'

Her mother laughed and Barbara had not heard her laugh so spontaneously or so happily for a long time.

'I'm so glad to have you home but, Barbara, I do hope you are not going to become a recluse. You haven't been outside this house since you returned.'

Barbara smiled to herself. She was amused that her mother thought she may become a recluse. Quite the reverse were her intentions. When the time was right, she had a lot of living to make up for: the War and the deprivations that had followed were for her at last truly over.

Her mother's voice sounded gentle as she rebuked her. 'You seem to have lost all your feminine ways. If you are going to go around looking as you do now, you can hardly expect to mix with your old friends – let alone attract new ones.'

Barbara had the grace to look away as she felt her cheeks flush up. Seated opposite to her, her mother was a picture of softness, even regal; her grey hair was immaculate as always, her small strong hands were clasped together in the lap of her simple yet elegant blue dress, its severity softened only by the gold cameo brooch on her shoulder. Barbara couldn't help but feel a twinge of guilt. Her own hair was drawn back into an elastic band, her attire anything but neat: black slacks and an old grey jumper hardly suggested that she had dressed with care.

Defiantly Barbara shrugged her shoulders. 'I couldn't care less at the moment,' she declared, 'and if by attract new friends you mean men, don't bother, I never want a permanent relationship ever again.'

'Well my darling, unless you do something about your appearance it's highly unlikely you will ever get the chance. You are so thin, you only pick at your meals, why won't you eat properly? And your hair! It always used to look so attractive.'

'Mother, just give me time, please. I know you and Daddy are worried about me but there's no need, honestly. The important thing at the moment is that I am home, here with you, *safe*.' The last word had been little more than a whisper.

Her mother sighed heavily. If only Barbara would talk to her. Confide in her, it would be such a relief. Ugly thoughts had preyed on her mind for weeks since she had a visit from the kindly Mrs Winters, who herself had been worried sick since Barbara's sudden disappearance. She had learnt enough about Michael to know that anger and alcohol had turned him into a man that Barbara had found impossible to love.

'Why do you say "safe", Barbara? Why not get whatever terrible experiences you have suffered out into the open? If you don't know where to begin then just blurt it all out. It is often the best way to talk about something unpleasant and surely you know by now I really can be a good listener.'

Barbara nodded, choking back tears, her hands were

twitching nervously. What she wouldn't give to tell it all! Deliverance from the guilt of having signed away her baby. She was on the very point of speaking when she saw the look of concern in her mother's eyes. It was after all her grandchild she had given away. Then again she had had no choice. The birth of the baby and the subsequent adoption was the end of that part of her life. If she were to let go and divulge those facts she would have to give her reasons, begin at the beginning as it were, and for that to happen she would have to relive all the horrors and that much she could not bring herself to do. The necessary words wouldn't come from her lips. Not coherently they wouldn't. Her courage deserted her.

Sinking back further into the cushions of the chair, she put her head in her hands, holding back hot, painful tears Still, the bitterness was there but she dare not let it overflow. The tears came then, rolling salty into her mouth. She cried until she felt there were no more tears left in her, and then she felt her mother's arms encircle her, holding her close. Her bitterness had surprised even herself, and she knew she could not bear to go on constantly thinking of the past and whether or not she had made the right decision.

Minutes passed in silence. The tea in their cups now stone cold, the dainty cakes uneaten on the silver cake-stand. Innumerable questions ran through her mother's mind, but she reserved them for later.

'Sorry Mother,' Barbara raised her tear-stained face. 'Please just give me time, let's leave it for now shall we? I promise you quite soon I will be much better, more like my old self.'

'Yes, well, I think it is about time I made a fresh pot of

tea and we both cheered up and put a smile on our faces before your father gets home.'

Patricia looked fondly at her daughter as she poured fresh tea into their cups. 'Shall we have a day out shopping? Eastbourne maybe, or how about doing something really marvellous, like going off to London, stay the night, really scour the shops – after all you do badly need clothes, you've hardly anything here. Could be quite an adventure, what d'you say?'

In spite of herself Barbara sniffed away the remains of her tears and smiled. 'You sound really excited, Mother. All right, give me a few more days then have your cheque book ready and we will go up to town together.'

Her mother grinned. 'Yes, well, just so long as you mean what you say. I don't want you becoming spinsterish.'

Barbara smiled again, the lines of anxiety erased from her forehead. 'You'll have your chance, Mother. Just a little more time and then I'll go the whole hog, hairdo, facial, manicure, new clothes, shoes, the lot. How does that sound?'

Her mother looked at her shrewdly but was prevented from having to think of an answer. To her surprise the door had opened, her husband was home.

'Hallo darling, you're back early,' she said, looking across the room at him. He moved to stand behind her chair and putting his arms around her neck kissed the top of her head. Having done the same to Barbara, he said softly, 'This is a nice surprise, afternoon tea all ready, the pair of you looking so cosy. I thought perhaps you would be out.'

There was such a rush of love welling within Barbara as she gazed at her father. He was a real man, kind and considerate. How could she ever have turned her back on such wonderful parents?

'Come on then, Barbara,' he said. 'How about a cup of tea for a hard working man who has been stuck in the smoky city all day. I'm parched!'

'You!' she pushed him away playfully.

Suddenly the laughter from the pair of them was like manna from heaven to Patricia. 'We were talking about having a couple of days in town, Barbara and I. Your daughter is threatening to bankrupt you and have the whole works – will your bank balance stand it?'

Phillip lifted his eyebrows as he met his wife's gaze. Smiling broadly he shrugged indulgently. Money was not important. Only the return to normality and the future happiness of his daughter mattered. It was on the tip of his tongue to tell them they could have the earth so long as that ruffian Michael Henderson remained well and truly out of their lives, but he had the good sense to remain silent.

Barbara was alone in the room, her mother had taken the tea-tray to the kitchen and her father had gone upstairs to have a bath before dinner. She rose from her chair and went to the window and stood gazing out across the lawns. Though summer had long gone the garden still looked beautiful, the grass so green as to be like a velvet carpet, a few shrubs were still a blaze of colour and those that had ceased to flower were abundant with foliage. Away to the left were the stables. She hadn't realised until now how much she had missed the horses. Oh, to ride again. To feel a horse beneath her once again. Without warning her heart lifted, there was joy to be found in the future, she did not have to spend the rest of her life paying for her mistakes, she had to make a more determined effort to put the past behind her.

To make such an effort, it had taken several days. The nights were the worst because more often than not she would have a brief but vivid dream in which she relived every sordid detail of her night of terror, and she would wake saturated in sweat and with every limb trembling. But she had survived it.

It was shortly after seven o'clock in the morning when Barbara left the house and walked towards the stables. She was glad she had still been able to get into her close-fitting jodhpurs and her riding habit felt good across her shoulders. Amongst others her father had two magnificent thorough-bred horses which a couple of lads from the stables in the village of Jevington came up to exercise daily. She returned the lads' cheerful greetings with a friendly wave. In the stable yard she saw Colin Peterson leading the two bays. He doffed his cap and said, 'Good morning Miss Barbara. We've one of the hacks all ready for you. I'll be with you in a minute, just set the lads off.'

'There's no hurry Colin, take your time,' Barbara told him.

Colin Peterson was a new addition to her father's staff since the end of the War, and Barbara had only made his acquaintance during the few weeks she had been home. Apparently there had been no hesitation on her father's part when engaging this man; indeed he counted himself lucky, for Colin Peterson had served in one of the regiments of the Royal Household Cavalry.

Barbara liked the clean-cut tall man if only for the way

he handled the horses. Minutes later Colin led a grey horse forward, bringing it to a standstill when he came up to her. The horse flung its head up and down and snorted loudly as if in greeting and they both laughed as he handed her up into the saddle.

Barbara soon left the main road, taking the side roads through the Sussex villages that led to the open Downs and gazed about her as she rode.

I never appreciated how beautiful Sussex is, she softly told herself, and clean, oh yes so clean. The trees were dressed in full autumn glory of reds and golds, the rolling Downs appeared as green as ever – while in some fields the earth was newly turned, ready for the winter frosts. Then there was the silence. Not a silence that one longed to be broken, but nature's silence, interrupted only with songs from the birds, or a low moo occasionally from the lazy cattle as they sought shelter beneath the hedges. So utterly peaceful. A fair exchange for the hustle and bustle of street traders, motor vehicles and noisy children with nowhere to play except in the confines of narrow, dusty backstreets.

It was difficult to believe that all this splendour lay less than two hours' travelling from London, or that the small children with whom she had become so familiar had never set eyes on living cattle or frolicking young lambs – let alone climbed trees while playing in the woods. Here one could breathe great lungfuls of fresh air, not air tainted by fumes from the gas works. The tranquillity of it all was as a balm to her soul. Autumn would soon give way to winter, then the ground would become hard and slippery in parts under the horses' feet, while in some parts of countryside the animals would more than likely have to plough through quagmires. This, however, Barbara promised herself would not deter her. From now on she was determined she wouldn't miss a single day, come rain or snow she would ride every morning – for it had been quite a while since she had known such serenity.

After four days spent in London with her mother, Barbara's lifestyle took on a new routine. Her main ambition now was to enjoy life. Her days were spent riding, swimming, playing golf, even indoor-tennis and excessive eating and drinking. The nights were a ceaseless round of parties, society gatherings and visits to West End theatres. Her objective, it seemed now, was to pay back the whole world for the pain she had suffered.

Barbara still found it hard and embarrassing to admit exactly why her marriage had broken up. In time her friends and relatives stopped referring to the fact that she had ever been anyone than Barbara Hamlin and Penny Rayford never once asked what had happened to her baby.

To be fair to her, initially, when Barbara had settled back home with her parents, she had toyed with the idea of registering as a medical student at one of the London hospitals. Unable to do so because of insufficient qualifications, she had rebuked herself severely. What a God-awful mess she'd made of her life. Why, oh why had she spurned education when the chance had been given her? She wasn't unintelligent, she had worked just hard enough to satisfy her teachers. The War and London had called her to what, at the time, she thought of as an exciting life. Even so, when the armistice had been declared she could have gone back to studying, even gone on to university, but no, she had wanted Michael, to be married, and to have a home of her own. Well, she had got all three, plus a great many regrets. All of that was behind her now, so why did she constantly feel this terrible guilt, the feeling that she had abandoned her baby before it was ever born? Why the hell are we all so wise after the event? she angrily asked herself.

Even though Barbara was leading a very different lifestyle, regret still played a large part in her thinking. She had mental scars that wouldn't heal. She had married a working class man and he had rejected her. More than that he had abused her. She had thought loving him would have been enough, she had used charm to bring forth his talents, to stir him to have a purpose, to be ambitious. To no avail. Since being demobbed from the navy Michael had had a chip on his shoulder, the world owed him a living and he was content to lead a shallow life.

Now suddenly, her own behaviour was very different. Outwardly at least. All restraint had gone by the board, at times it would seem that she had no regard for anyone. Her innermost thoughts she kept secret, sometimes telling herself quietly, one day I might even succeed in wiping out the memory of life with Michael Henderson. Even that last ghastly night I might be able to suppress.

But that wasn't enough. She was tired of trying to push it to the back of her mind. If only she were able to erase it completely, for there were still lonesome moments when she felt paralysed with fear, when she couldn't move and she would tremble, her whole body racked with great silent sobs, her cheeks crimson at the recollection of what had been done to her. At such times she would withdraw into herself, giving no one the chance to show sympathy. That was the last thing she wanted. All was now right in her world was the impression she strove to create.

Christmas was only seven days away. In London today, shopping with Penny, Christmas had suddenly lost its appeal for Barbara. She must put on a cheerful face for the sake of her friend, yet her thoughts were filled with regrets. Elizabeth Warren, now happily Mrs Elizabeth Holsworthy, had given birth to twin boys and while she was thrilled for Elizabeth, Barbara could not help comparing her own circumstances. Barbara had been enjoying her day in London – the crowds of Christmas shoppers jostling and pushing, carol-singers at the kerbside and brightly lit shop-windows – but it wasn't over yet, Penny seemed hell-bent on spending more money. They had already pushed their way down Oxford Street, loaded themselves with purchases from Selfridges, bought fabulous gifts from the expensive shops of Bond Street and finally hailed a taxi to take them to Regent Street. As she and Penny alighted from the taxi Penny exclaimed in delight, 'Oh Hamleys, we must go in and see the toys. Besides, we can buy presents for Elizabeth's new twins.'

No sooner had Penny made this declaration than Barbara felt herself being edged towards the revolving doors. Hamleys, always a paradise for children, was filled with nice bright youngsters eagerly pointing out to their parents the gifts they hoped to receive for Christmas. The cold December wind outside was forgotten. Some adults walked the department store briskly, making their purchases without hesitation, whilst others – mainly those accompanied by children – lingered. The queue to visit the plump red-faced Father Christmas caught Penny's eye and she and Barbara stood a while watching the kiddies, their faces wreathed in smiles as each was given a colourful wrapped gift.

Each department looked beautiful with special displays created for the festive season. Little girls' eyes sparkled as they viewed the miniature golden coach complete with occupants in period costume. Small boys tore around the bicycles, the motor cars real in every detail in scaled-down sizes, the aeroplanes that were guaranteed to fly. It was odds on that almost every item would be sold by the time the store closed on Christmas Eve. Grandparents happily clutched their purchases of which each one was tied with a gay red ribbon. Oh yes, Barbara thought to herself, Christmas is a time for children.

But sorrowfully her mind went back to the kiddies in Battersea. Would they fare as well as the children from well-off parents? Probably not, but there again, what they had never had they wouldn't miss and most would feel loved and wanted even without the trappings of lavish presents.

The two of them now stood in the middle of the soft toy region. Barbara couldn't tear her eyes away from the massive arrangement of teddy bears; she picked up a conventional brown one which had a blue bow tied around its neck and hugged it close to her chest. There were innumerable shelves running around the walls and soaring up to the ceiling, holding hundreds of different bears in various colours alongside dogs, bunny-rabbits, tiny kittens and baby lambs – each with a coat of the softest fur. Oh, she liked them all.

Now Penny crossed the floor and called to Barbara, 'Come and see the dolls.'

Barbara's face broke into a surprised but delighted smile. 'Aren't they gorgeous!' she exclaimed. Her eyes caught the display of real china dolls: their wax-like faces appearing so

159

delicate, the finery in which these dolls were clothed was exquisite. She couldn't remember seeing dolls of this quality for sale ever before. Probably because of the War. Dolls such as these were heirlooms, so she had thought, only handed down to children from grandparents and never regarded as toys to be played with.

'Choose one, come on – make your choice,' Penny urged.

Barbara was a little more cautious in her enthusiasm, 'Aren't Elizabeth's twins both boys?'

'Of course you're right. Damn! Can't very well buy them a doll then can we? But there is nothing to stop us having one each for ourselves. Look marvellous laid out on your bed.'

Barbara laughed aloud, 'All right, I am going to have this one, its label says it is one of seven from the story *Little Women*.'

'Then I'm going to have this crinoline lady, her dress will spread wide if I sit her up.'

They had to wait while the lady assistant carefully boxed their choices and neatly wrapped them in decorative paper. 'They're so beautiful, seems a shame to give them to young children,' she remarked as she handed them over the counter.

They looked at each other and burst out laughing. 'They are for us. A Christmas present to ourselves.'

'Nice to be able to afford to indulge one's every whim,' the assistant muttered to herself as she turned towards her next customer.

'Now for these presents,' Penny said.

Barbara laughed, 'I've already decided, one honey-coloured teddy bear and one pale blue one.'

'So what does that leave me?'

'Oh don't be so daft, there's hundreds to choose from.'

Penny made a show of thinking hard and examining several of the cuddly toys before settling on two snow-white baby lambs, each bore a different coloured silk ribbon holding a tinkling silver bell around its neck.

The bedroom in the private nursing home was hung with Christmas decorations. A crystal vase on a side table held long-stemmed red roses. Elizabeth, impeccably attired in a peach silk nightgown and matching bed-jacket, rested back against a mound of pillows, her silky brown hair immaculate above her pale face.

'Hallo darlings,' she eagerly greeted her friends.

Penny and Barbara, in turn, bent low and gave Elizabeth a kiss on each cheek that was the recognised salutation amongst their circle of friends. Penny perched herself on the end of the bed while Barbara settled in a winged armchair beside Elizabeth. Barbara looked around, even knowing it was a private hospital she had not been prepared for the room to be so luxurious. Elizabeth was smiling at them both now.

'It really is good to see you and I don't feel so envious now that you both have such slim figures.'

They all laughed as Elizabeth patted her now flattened stomach.

'You must see the twins. Do you know, Tim told me last night that now we have two sons our life will change radically because of our responsibilities, and I told him it had better be for the better.'

Penny was the one to reply, 'Of course it will be, Elizabeth. Children give shape and meaning to everything.'

What happened to the young light-hearted girls we used to be? Barbara thought wistfully. That profound comment was out of character for Penny but they were both saved from answering by a nurse entering the room. 'You rang, Mrs Holsworthy. Is there something I can get you?'

'Yes please nurse. May we have a tray of tea for three and while we're waiting, would it be possible for my friends to see my babies?'

'Certainly, Mrs Holsworthy.' With a nod in the direction of Penny and Barbara, the slim young nurse asked, 'Would you like to follow me?'

Penny squealed with enchantment as she gazed at the two wee babies. Barbara's hand trembled as she held onto the side of the cots and her eyes misted over. The two little boys were delightful, perfect, their fingers moved nonstop, their eyes were screwed up tight so there was no chance to note the colour, but each tiny head was covered with hair so fine and blond it shone like silk.

Grief welled up in Barbara's chest and her arms ached for the son she had never held; she thought, if only I could put the clock back. Tears were stinging the back of her eyelids but she forced them back. This was Elizabeth's day. She wouldn't spoil it.

Sleety rain was falling when Penny and Barbara left the nursing home. They turned up the collars of their coats and made a dash for the taxi rank.

Their goodbyes were lingering, each wishing the other a Merry Christmas, promising to keep in touch by phone and to meet for New Year's Eve. As Penny's cab set off in the opposite direction she looked back through the rear window, unable to see anything for the rain was now coming down in torrents. Barbara was the centre of her thoughts. While they had been admiring the babies she had studied her, thinking how sad she looked, but what had upset her? Surely she was pleased that Elizabeth had come through her confinement so well and produced two fine healthy sons?

Barbara didn't have a jealous bone in her body, she was too nice a person for that, she had been thrilled when told that Elizabeth and Tim had finally decided to marry. Besides, those babies would bring such a lot of pleasure.

Seeing as how the three of them had been life-long friends it was more than probable Elizabeth would ask Barbara and herself to be godmothers. That would be nice. The christening would be a big social event and, as the babies grew into toddlers and then young lads, she and Barbara would be viewed as aunts with a stake in their future.

Then again, she thought, when I get married and Barbara puts her wretched past behind her and finds a more suitable husband at the second attempt, why, the both of us will have babies of our own and all the children will regard each other as cousins. Penny realised she was laughing to herself. I'm becoming quite broody, she thought, but wouldn't it be nice if things did work out that way for all of us?

Quite abruptly, the vision of Barbara's face as she had gazed down upon those twins burst into Penny's mind, and she remembered, the only emotion revealed in Barbara's eyes had been sadness.

Oh, my God! It came to her in a flash. The day they had spent together, shopping in Kensington, Barbara had been pregnant!

There had been Barbara's disappearance, surfacing only months afterwards, looking nothing like the bright young girl she had been before she had made that disastrous marriage. No mention had been made of her having given birth, not then, nor since. What a dope! What a heartless friend she was! Had Barbara suffered a miscarriage? Barbara's mother and her father had been almost out of their minds with worry, it had been painfully obvious that Barbara had suffered hell and yet they had never talked about it.

She hadn't asked Barbara any questions, just assumed that Michael had been giving her a hard time and that at long last she had had the sense to leave him. Penny chided herself, you haven't pried so far and you mustn't start now, Barbara will tell me if and when she is good and ready.

She was aware from her talks with Mrs Hamlin that Barbara had told her parents very little. 'Oh Christ! Poor Barbara!' she muttered aloud. Fancy, dragging her off to see Elizabeth. She must think me an insensitive bitch. She leant hard into the corner of the seat now and, her face between her hands, she rocked herself and groaned, 'Why the hell didn't I think?' Making such a fuss of Elizabeth and slobbering over the babies and Barbara had never said a word. Oh, God Almighty!

Barbara was drenched by the time she got into the railway carriage and she shrugged out of her wet coat, tossing it careless onto the opposite seat. Taking a handkerchief out of her handbag, she wiped her streaming face before lighting a cigarette. She drew the smoke deep down into her lungs. It wasn't very often that she smoked and never in her mother's presence but, by God, she needed to now. Her hand shook as she replaced her lighter in her bag. It was not surprising she was trembling – she had thought she was going to pass out back there in the nursing home. She had been almost abrupt with Penny, making all that fuss about getting home, refusing to stay in town for a meal. She shouldn't have allowed her emotions to get the better of her. She should be stronger by now.

What had set her off? Well, first off there had been that gleeful celebratory atmosphere in Hamleys, the immaturity of adults as they played with their toddlers, the choosing of cuddly toys for Elizabeth's two boys. Thoughts were in her mind now that never should have been there, thoughts that she had sworn she would never dwell on, thoughts of the past that was over and done with and had no part in her life now whatsoever.

Still she found herself wondering who was having the joy of buying Christmas presents for her son? Someone kind and loving? She prayed then as she had never prayed before. For a moment she wished she knew to whom her child had been given.

No. No I don't, she angrily muttered to herself. That knowledge would be intolerable. I would want to race away to see him, trying to kid myself that all I wanted would be a glimpse of him when all the time I would know that I was lying to myself.

Dear God, help me remember that my decision was the right one and that it is irrevocable.

The house looked wonderful, in the bow-window of the lounge stood a grand fir-tree, rich dark green in colour and its branches were thick and bushy.

'Hallo Barbara. You're back early.'

Barbara turned around as her mother entered the room

and walked towards the open fireplace, holding out her hands to the blaze.

'Hallo Mother. Yes, I decided not to stay in town with Penny. I had finished all my shopping so I thought I would come home and dress the tree.'

'Oh that is nice, your father will be pleased. Would you like a drink before dinner?'

'That's an excellent idea, I'll have a glass of sherry please.'

Despite the fact that her mother knew Barbara was withholding many things from her, a great companionship had developed between the two of them since Barbara had returned home. Essentially different as they were in experience and age, they were now very much at ease with each other, and although this understanding was not spoken of, it was none the less there and both of them were grateful. Barbara was quite aware that her mother knew something of the terrible anguish she had suffered and one day, please God, she might be able to bring herself to confide in her mother, but not all the gory details. No, never that.

Count your blessings, she daily insisted to herself and indeed that was what she was striving to do. She had wonderful parents and friends, a lovely house in which to live and no shortage of money. Painstakingly she decorated the tree, taking her time as to where each glittering bauble should hang, but her own face was a mask.

Patricia Hamlin was not deceived. She handed Barbara a glass of sherry and her thoughts were very much the same as Penny's had been. No matter how or when Barbara smiled, the smile never reached her eyes. Such sadness! What she wouldn't give to be able to ease her daughter's heartache? Now it was her turn to pray and all she asked was that Barbara might be granted peace of mind.

Chapter Eight

ON THE MORNING of the first day of the year 1949, Barbara woke up reluctantly. She had a hangover, her whole body ached – it was too heavy to drag out of bed. The previous night's party with its boisterous activity, too much food and far too much wine had taken its toll on her. She could faintly hear sounds of liveliness coming from downstairs. She squinted towards her bedside clock. It was a quarter past ten, she had promised to go riding with Penny and others of her parents' house guests at half past eight. Still she made no move to get up. She lay staring into space, willing herself to get a move on, draw a bath and get dressed.

New Year's Eve had been great. Off with the old and on with the new, was what her friends had urged. Right after a marvellous dinner the fun had begun, the library floor had been cleared for dancing and games, and the younger members of the party had availed themselves of this with enthusiasm.

Penny's brother Tony, a tall lean handsome young man, had partnered Barbara in a quickstep to the lively beat of a Squadronaires gramophone record. He had swung her around the room and out into the hall, swift and sure footed. She had thoroughly enjoyed the whole dance. Her parents and their friends had withdrawn to the lounge with their preference for bridge, yet even the oldest member had smiled tolerantly at the young ones' antics.

A little before midnight everyone had assembled in the dining room with glasses charged with champagne. Flushed and excited they had waited for the twelve strokes of Big Ben to boom forth from the cabinet wireless set. 'Happy New Year!' voices echoed from all corners of the room. Streamers were unfurled, balloons were popped, everyone was laughing. Patricia Hamlin separated and began to circulate, embracing everyone in the room. Amid all the hugging and kissing going on all around her, Barbara sought out her father. 'Happy New Year, Daddy.'

'And to you, my dearest. The past is well and truly behind you now, eh? Make an effort and you have a new beginning.' He pulled her close to his chest and held her gently, his cheek resting against the top of her head. Minutes passed before he released her and Barbara was able to reach up and kiss him. Softly, in a voice filled with emotion, she whispered, 'You and Mother are two of a rare species.'

The sadness in her voice had wrenched at her father's heart and he was unable to speak and could only cup her face in his hands and kiss her tenderly. He looked past Barbara to Patricia, and, as their eyes met, he saw traces of tears and knew that they had been shed for their lovely wilful daughter, so dearly loved and yet so headstrong. But she was home now, in their care and starting a new life. God grant her this second chance, he prayed silently.

'I'll come with you if you want,' Penny offered. 'But to be honest I'm bushed, I was out on the Downs this morning while you were still in bed.' Lunch was over and Barbara, having drunk several cups of coffee, felt very much better.

'No, you stay and have a yarn with the others.'

'Oh yeah,' Penny answered with a grin. 'If I can find a quiet corner I'm getting my head down, it's me for a snooze.'

Barbara grinned back at her friend, remembering the capers she had got up to last night and wondered how on earth she had managed to rise so early this morning and go riding.

'I'll see you later then. Sleep well.'

Barbara walked into the stable yard just as the hands of the wall clock showed two o'clock. Despite the fact that a weak sun had broken through the clouds, it was a sharp, bitter cold day. Black ice, formed during the night, still persisted in sheltered spots. Colin Peterson led her horse out of the stall; its hooves clattered and it slithered awkwardly on the uneven cobblestones of the yard, its breath condensing in clouds of steam in the cold air.

'I'll be gone when you get back, Miss Barbara. Will you mind rubbing him down yourself?'

'Of course not Colin,' Barbara bent over and patted the horse's neck. 'We're not going far, are we boy? Just a a few lungfuls of fresh air to clear away the effect of last night and we'll be back.'

'That's all right then. It gets dark so quickly now, don't want you out on your own once the light goes, do we?'

'I'll be fine, thanks Colin.'

Barbara gave her horse the signal to trot and in a very short time they were down the lane and out of sight of the house. A rabbit scurried across their path, making for the thick undergrowth. Her horse shied and Barbara tightened the reins and laughed softly. 'Steady boy, he's as entitled to come out for an airing as we are.'

For a long while she trotted him slowly, passing no one.

It was as if she had the whole of the countryside to herself. Reaching high ground she realised the top of the cliffs were invisible, a mist was coming down and far below the sea was grey. She thought to herself it was a long time since she had seen the waves so high and rolling in with such force. A shudder went through her. Fancy being at sea on such a rough night as this was likely to be.

'Time to turn for home, eh boy?' she said, bending forward and giving her horse a soft pat on the side of its neck. 'This damp cold sinks right into one's bones.'

As she dismounted and led her horse into the stable a shadow fell suddenly across her. Since the time when she was raped she had not been able to control her fears. Any unexpected or strange situation caused her heart to start thumping and the blood to rise in her cheeks.

Startled, she peered into the dim interior. Michael was standing a few yards ahead, barring her way. He stood not with the upright bearing and the cheeky grin of the young sailor she had fallen in love with, but with a careless slouch – his face showing nothing but meanness.

'*Oh my God,*' she muttered out loud, the slow words were both an exclamation of sheer terror and an anguished prayer for help.

She felt the icy clutch of dread take over, she stood stock-still shivering with fright.

For that first few seconds he appeared as tongue-tied as she was.

Her eyes, now accustomed to the dimness, saw that his eyes were fixed upon her face and there was no mistaking the hatred he was directing at her.

She made to run. Michael moved quickly, his movements crab-like until he was behind her. She jerked herself around, glancing to the left and to the right. There was no escape. Without warning her horse whinnied as if conscious of danger, the sound echoed loudly, other horses in their stalls raised their heads, stamped their hooves and they too began to neigh. If only the noise had been heard up at the house, would the men come running? It was a vain hope. The horses, having expressed their annoyance, snorted once or twice and turned their attention back to their feed-bags.

'Well, ain't you going to wish me Happy New Year?'

Barbara found she couldn't speak, her voice had deserted her entirely. All she could feel was this dreadful thumping of her heart against her ribs and a breathless feeling of suffocation. She had never, in the whole of her life, felt so frightened. Finally, without looking at him she managed to say, 'Oh, Michael,' and despite all her efforts her voice trembled with fear.

'Sorry I didn't let you know I was coming,' he said with a sneer. 'Got to thinking about you and about the baby, thought it was about time I accepted my responsibilities.' There was no mistaking the sarcasm. 'On the spur of the moment I borrowed a car from one of me mates – see, darling, I've still got some mates – came down on the off chance, like. Don't tell me you ain't thrilled to see me?'

Barbara's agitation was now visible and Michael looked at her with contempt as she let go of the reins of her horse and stepped further back.

'Oh no, you bloody well don't!' He came at her with a rush. 'I wanna talk to you, we've plenty to discuss. Besides, I want you to come back ter me.' He expected her to return to Batterseal To live with him as his wife!

The horse, now free from restraint, stamped on the concrete floor, backed up a little, turned and bolted out

171

into the open. His clattering hooves, resounding at first, gradually lessened until an ominous silence settled once more around them. Michael moved right up close to her and his nearness was like a physical shock. Her knees began to shake and she had to clench her hands into fists to stop them from trembling.

She decided to try and play for time. 'Have you got a job now?'

'I'm surprised you care enough to even ask.'

'Of course I care.'

'Balls! Don't be such a bloody hypocrite. You walked off, back to yer mummy and daddy without so much as a word.'

Some of the fear of him vanished and her voice became much stronger. 'After what you did! What did you expect me to do?'

He reached out and touched her arm, 'I'm sorry, really I am. You never gave me a chance to explain.'

Explain! For Christ's sake! She hated his wheedling almost as much as his anger.

'It wasn't that bad Barbara, things got out of hand, you wouldn't go along with me, I needed help. It all went too far, it was the drink. Honest I'm sorry.'

It wasn't that bad! Barbara was thunderstruck, barely able to believe what she was hearing.

'Wasn't it always too much drink with you?'

'There you go again – always criticising.'

Deliberately she didn't answer: to provoke him was the last thing she wanted. Desperately she racked her brains for a way to pacify him.

'Michael, you really can't be serious – suggesting we start all over again in that awful flat.'

'I don't give a damn where we live just so long as you come back to me. You seem to forget you're still my wife. I only came cos I miss you so much and I wanted to find out 'ow you got on when you had the baby.'

'Oh wonderful, suddenly you care.'

In the eerie quiet she knew she had blown it. Terrified now, her heart was thumping like a sledge hammer. Why hadn't she kept quiet? Her every instinct told her that taunt had been like waving a red rag at a bull.

He lunged at her. She turned her head in disgust at the beery smell of his breath and this seemed to infuriate him further. She flinched even before his hand struck the stinging smack to the side of her face.

He brought his arms up on each side of her and pushed her backwards until he had her pinned against the wall. He lowered his head and brutishly pressed his lips against her mouth. He tore furiously at the buttons of her riding habit and then his fingers were on the silk of her shirt and he was spitefully squeezing her left breast, grunting and dribbling as he assaulted her. 'Jesus, I'd forgotten how good you always smell. I want you Barbara, now, after all I'm only asking for me rights.'

Fortified by alcohol, he had come looking for her and incredibly found her on her own – he wasn't about to pass up a chance such as this. Her struggles only encouraged him, and her tears and entreaties were ignored. She tried to scream but felt she was choking as she had to swallow the bile that had risen in her throat. Despairingly she pushed at his hands and eventually she got the words out from between clenched teeth, 'Michael, let's go somewhere else, I must—' he cut the words off by covering her lips with his open mouth, thrusting his tongue deeply towards the back of her throat.

She couldn't help it – she choked. Michael jerked his head away from her face and with two hands banged her head against the wall. 'That's it – I've stood enough, get those trousers undone. Come on be quick, rip them open down the front.' He gestured with one hand what it was he wanted her to do. She watched his face whilst she attempted to open the thick corded material of her jodhpurs.

'That won't do. Take them off, I'll 'ave a fag while you do a striptease for me, I've waited long enough – a few more minutes won't matter.' He took a packet of Players and a box of matches from his jacket pocket. His eyes never left her as he placed a cigarette between his lips, struck a match and lit it.

Still desperately playing for time, Barbara pleaded, 'Michael, wouldn't you rather we went somewhere more comfortable?'

He blew smoke directly into her face, then raised his fist menacingly, 'Suppose we discuss that later, right now all I want is for you to get those bloody daft trousers off.'

Something snapped in Barbara. Not this time! There was going to be no repetition of that night that still haunted her. She would rather die here and now than endure yet more horrors. She might go down fighting but this hateful beast was not going to use her as a whore.

Michael flicked his cigarette stub out into the open and with a leer on his lips he stepped forward and pressed himself hard against her. She turned her face away but as she did so she brought her knee high and fiercely up between his legs.

Although he instinctively doubled over, his anger erupted. 'You cow!' Pain spurred him on as he retaliated. The blow he struck caught her sharply on her cheekbone, the smarting agony served to make her more determined.

With a rapid movement her hand felt along the wall until her fingers came into contact with what she was seeking. Hatred swamped her, her eyes were burning, her heavy breathing choking her. If she didn't defend herself now she would drown in her own shame, but it wasn't going to be as Michael wanted it — she would fight him off or die in the attempt.

Her trembling hand now held a brush used for grooming the horses, its bristles really sharp. In the second before she struck him Barbara knew that he had guessed what she was about to do, but quick as he was her movement was more speedy. She held her arm high, tightened her hold on the wooden handle of the brush and with vengeance uppermost in her mind, she smashed at Michael's face, raking the pine-like needles deeply from his forehead down to his chin.

'You are a pig, a detestable pig!' she screamed at him, then her voice rising with every word, she added, 'I hate you! Do you hear me — I hate you! Did Pete Davis buy you more beer for what you allowed him to do to me? You're not a man — ' She didn't get to say another word. The next moment his hands were round her throat and he was shaking her violently.

'And you are a stuck-up bloody bitch!' he yelled. His hands tightened viciously around her throat and she could feel herself choking and the blood pounding in her head. She tried to pull feebly at his hands but the pressure seemed to increase. Suddenly he let go of her and she fell to the

175

ground, gasping for breath. Michael wasn't to be beaten, he stood over her, her riding crop held tightly in one hand.

The stinging whip caught her unawares. She pulled her knees up, hunched her shoulders and put her arms about her head for protection. As the blows rained down upon her and heavy kicks connected with her ribs, she asked herself, What have I ever done to deserve this?

Before Barbara thankfully became unconscious all the happy anticipation the first hours of the New Year had given her were gone.

Chapter Nine

LOOKING AT HER daughter, who was unable to move her head and barely able to speak, Patricia Hamlin wanted to cry. Sometimes in these past three days she had ranted at God. She supposed that was wicked of her, but hadn't Barbara been through enough? 'Oh, my darling!' she muttered aloud, her sad eyes never leaving the face of this beloved daughter, now her only child.

At the beginning of the War Barbara had been all youth and freshness, as innocent of life as a baby, with her silky chestnut bright hair, her unblemished skin and a mouth that always seemed to be smiling. With Penny and Elizabeth they had set off for London, so keen to make their own effort to help win the War.

Why, oh why had Barbara been fated to meet Michael? No actual details of the previous ill-treatment Michael had administered to Barbara had ever been brought out into the open. Nevertheless one would have to be blind not to see that the awful effects had become long-term and now just as she was showing signs of becoming more settled, he had reappeared. How could she and her husband have been so careless as to have let his second attack on Barbara take place? Normally she didn't use blasphemous words but now she found herself clenching her fists and saying, 'Damn and blast that man!'

Thank God the men had found the horse still saddled and without a rider. Running to the stables to mount their own horses and begin the search for Barbara, they had found her crumpled body. When at first Barbara had been gently carried into the house Patricia had been convinced that her daughter was going to die. Deep anxiety for Barbara made the next twenty-four hours an absolute nightmare for her parents. She was only twenty-four-years-old and her life lay in ruins.

Her father was so angry, the anger levelled largely at himself. He was overwhelmed with guilt. That this could happen twice to his beloved Barbara and this second time within the bounds of their own home. A damn good whipping was what he would like dealt out to that fellow, and with the mood he was in right now he would have no hesitation in offering to wield the lash himself.

Police enquiries as to Michael's whereabouts had proved fruitless but their investigation had turned up one certainty: Michael Henderson had spent a considerable time in The Smugglers Inn that same lunch-time, consuming pints of bitter with whisky chasers until the landlord had refused to serve him any more. The landlord's statement was that Henderson had been very much the worse for drink and on being asked to leave the premises had hurled curses and threats at all members of the staff.

Phillip Hamlin came quietly into the bedroom where his wife sat at the bedside of their daughter. Looking from one to the other, he asked, 'How is she?'

'She is sleeping but very fitfully.'

'Well now dear, you go and make us a nice pot of tea. I'll stay here for a while.'

Almost reluctantly his wife rose and left the room. Phillip

seated himself in the chair Patricia had vacated and gazed down at Barbara, horrified by what he saw. It was not only her neck covered in bandages which did not entirely conceal the thick ugly weal or the dark bruises that upset him, but also the traces of suffering on Barbara's face.

How could this have happened in a few short years? he thought. It seemed only yesterday that Barbara had volunteered to work for the Red Cross and now she looked so much older than the beautiful girl that had left this house. To think he and his wife had been condemning her for not visiting them more often, and all the time she had been suffering at the hands of that brute!

Suddenly Barbara struggled to sit up, she tried to speak but could only make strange croaking noises as she tried to form the words.

'Barbara, Barbara,' her father kept repeating in a distraught voice. She stared up at him, her eyes wide with fear. 'It's all right,' he soothed her. 'You'll feel better soon, my darling.' Fortunately her mother returned at that moment carrying a laden tea-tray. Placing the tray on top of the chest of drawers, she took from it a feeding cup which she had filled with home-made lemonade and ice-cubes.

She raised Barbara's head and dribbled some of the cold liquid through the spout of the feeding cup into her mouth. 'Try to swallow some, my dear,' her mother urged. The effort brought tears to Barbara's eyes but at last she managed to swallow the liquid and her mother patiently fed the rest of the drink into her mouth, and then gently laid her back down onto her pillows. Barbara touched her mother's hand in gratitude.

While Patricia poured cups of tea for herself and Phillip,

he moved back to sit beside the bed. All the while he was making consoling murmurs, assuring Barbara she was safe now and that they would not leave her alone. Gently he stroked her hair back from her forehead until she finally drifted off into sleep.

Phillip spent the rest of the day in Barbara's bedroom and towards evening he had closed his eyes but opened them again to find Patricia standing beside him. This time she had brought thin creamy soup in the feeding cup, and now Barbara found it a little easier to swallow as her father supported her with his arm. His face wrinkled in fury as he felt the weal that Michael's hands had left around Barbara's neck. The doctor had told them it would fade with time but he knew he would see it to his dying day. His thoughts were tormenting him. He had always felt that the young man Barbara had chosen to marry was most unsuitable but now his strong dislike of him had increased to the point of utter hatred. If Henderson's stance had been more steady that riding crop could have decapitated Barbara! That man should be behind bars – locked away for good.

Phillip had not needed to be told the horrific details of why his daughter had left her husband. In the early days of her home-coming he had spent many sleepless nights listening to Barbara thrash about in agony as she lived through her nightmares, praying to God to ease her suffering and grant her peace of mind. Now he was obsessed by the need to ensure his daughter's mental as much as physical survival. Overruling his wife's protests, he had moved a single bed into Barbara's room and for the past two nights had lain alongside her, soothing her with words, exerting every ounce of his own strong will to give her the wish to pull through. 'Fight back, Barbara! Come on my darling, don't let him win,' he implored her over and over again. There was no responsiveness and that fact only served to make him hate Henderson all the more. He wished him in hell!

Barbara had been depressed when first she had returned home and just when her outlook on life seemed to be so very much brighter this had to happen. Was there to be no end to the unhappiness that man could cause her?

'I'll get Henderson into court if it's the last thing I ever do,' he vowed to himself. On his own ground Phillip knew full well he would be verbally more than a match for the likes of him.

Barbara opened her eyes and saw the look of anger that had spread across her father's face. 'Daddy.' The word came from her lips as a croak forced up from her damaged throat. Her tongue felt enormous and she still fought for breath, but she managed to smile. Her father wept with relief. She put out her hand which he took in between both of his and they stayed like that until Barbara muzzily drifted off to sleep again.

It was ten days later before Barbara came downstairs for the first time. She was having lunch in the dining room with her parents. The doctor had visited her daily, asked numerous questions and suggested she tried to put the whole incident from her mind. Diversion was what she needed now, he had told her father.

Barbara felt she had spent the past days in a long twilight, sick to her soul. Without encouragement from her mother and father she could have so easily have let go. During her conscious spells one or the other of them had always been there. She still shrank away in revulsion whenever her mind slipped back to what Michael had once again tried to do to her.

She loved this house, always had, only now she appreciated it, especially so her own room. It had given her sanctuary. She had lain for hours staring at the walls. The softly shaded lamp beside her bed, in the stillness of the night, had shone on the pastel wallpaper, and on the old polished woodwork of the furniture. The love of her parents and the peacefulness and privacy of that room had saved her reason.

Patricia was worried because Barbara was still eating hardly anything. When the soup plates had been cleared away by Mrs Clarkson, the daily treasure who had been with the family for nearly twenty years, and the main course set on the table, Barbara asked to be excused.

'Barbara, please stay and try to eat a little,' her mother implored.

'Just a few vegetables, mashed with gravy?' her father coaxed, for all the world as if she were a young child.

'I couldn't. Really.'

Her mother gave in. 'All right darling. It's really warm in the lounge, I lit the fire hours ago. Draw an armchair up and perhaps you could do a little of my jigsaw puzzle – it's a very difficult one.'

Barbara smiled in an offhand way at both of them and left the room. She sunk thankfully into the depths of the armchair and stared into the flames of the fire. Outwardly she knew she appeared calm and uncomplicated, but the thoughts within her head were anything but. What was she going to do? Where could she go to be safe? If Michael's visits were going to continue, with him popping up any time the fancy took him, she would never be able to cope.

It wasn't fair! It just wasn't fair. The uncertainty of the situation appalled her. She couldn't take any more of his violence. Michael had become a twisted, perverted bastard. One thing she was quite definite about: never again would he get the chance to practise his abnormalities on her. 'I'll kill him first. I swear I will,' she solemnly promised herself.

She had thought, fleetingly, of filing for divorce but she knew she was not yet emotionally ready to cope with this step. Her father in his wisdom had told her to leave such matters in his hands. 'The future will take care of itself,' he had assured her. But it was the future that worried her.

One week later and still Phillip could not look at his daughter without an ache in his heart. The ticking of the clock on the mantelshelf, the only sound in the room, was hypnotic. The flames in the fire turned blue, showing frost was in the air outside. A log crackled and disintegrated, sending a shower of sparks up the open chimney. Phillip quickly glanced to where Barbara lay on the settee, thankfully she was still fast asleep.

It was early dusk when Patricia kicked gently at the lounge door, pushing it open with her foot. Her husband rose from his chair, crossed the room and held the door open wide. She carried a tea tray on which she had also placed a plate of thinly cut sandwiches which she had decorated with watercress and wedges of tomatoes. She did everything she could think of to tempt Barbara to eat. As Patricia placed the tray on a small mahogany table Barbara opened her eyes, yawned and stretched very much like a contented cat. Her parents smiled at each other: it was a good sign. Spreading a napkin across Barbara's knees and handing her a plate, Patricia said, 'Take one of each, ham and cheese, and I've made a few cakes which – if I do say so myself – look very tempting.'

Barbara laughed as she pulled herself up into a sitting position. 'All right Mother, if it will make you happy I promise to try your fancy cakes.' The three of them ate in companionable silence, though when Barbara sipped from her cup the hot tea was still difficult for her to swallow.

The doorbell rang. Phillip looked questioningly at his wife, 'Not expecting anybody, are we dear?'

She raised her eyebrows and shrugged her shoulders as he rose and crossed the room. Barbara and her mother heard the opening of the front door, then the voices of more than one man. Minutes later her father re-entered the room. There were two men with him, one dressed in police uniform and the other in a long fawn raincoat.

The look of dread on her husband's face and the sight of the policeman caused Patricia's heart to race and the colour to drain from Barbara's cheeks.

'This gentleman is Inspector Watkins,' Phillip stated. The policeman stood back against the wall and was not introduced.

The inspector looked to where Barbara lay propped up against the cushions. 'Mrs Henderson?'

She looked up at him, startled, and the cup which she held rattled as she placed it back down on its saucer. 'Yes.' Her answer was barely audible.

The inspector placed his hand over his mouth, coughed loudly to clear his throat and, in a quiet voice that sounded apologetic, said, 'Ma'am, there is no easy way to tell you this – ' again he hesitated and the pause was ominous. The words now came out rapidly. 'The coastguards have recovered a body from the bottom of the cliffs at Beachy

Head. We have reason to believe it may be that of your husband.'

Barbara said nothing, just held her face between her two hands which were visibly trembling.

Her father walked towards the blazing fire whose flames were illuminating the room on this dark afternoon and with his hands resting on the high mantelshelf he stared into it.

'Are you sure?' Patricia shuddered as she asked the question.

The inspector nodded. The silence was frightening.

Some time passed before the inspector spoke and then it was an utterance filled with compassion, 'We shall need you, Mrs Henderson, to make formal identification.'

Barbara felt her stomach churn. She struggled desperately to stay calm.

'No!' The one word shot at the inspector made Barbara jump. She was not used to hearing her father's voice raised in anger.

'There will be no need for that, my daughter is not well enough. I will identify the body if it is that of my son-in-law.' The words were snapped out by Phillip Hamlin in a manner that surprised even his wife.

Barbara's eyes quickly flashed to the inspector's face. Would he allow that? She didn't think she would be capable of doing it.

'As you wish, Sir. I'm sure that will be quite all right.'

The sigh of relief which came from Barbara was very loud.

The inspector took a pair of gloves from the pocket of his raincoat and drew them onto his hands and with a nod to his constable turned towards the door, pausing only to

say, 'We won't disturb you further just now, but we shall
have to return again tomorrow morning. We need to take
statements.'

While her husband went to show the officers out, Patricia moved across to sit on the end of the settee and sat
holding both of Barbara's hands tightly – as if she could
pump reassurance through them to her daughter.

Barbara never moved but a deep groan came from her
throat. 'Dear God,' she moaned.

Inspector Watkins returned alone next morning.

The raincoat had been replaced by a navy-blue melton
overcoat. This thin, sallow-looking man seemed embarrassed as he stood twirling his trilby hat between his hands.
Endeavouring to put the man at his ease, Patricia smiled,
'Let me take your hat and coat, Inspector. Shall we go into
the dining room?' She led the way, opening the door and
standing back to allow him to enter first.

Seeing Mr Hamlin and Barbara, the inspector's first
words were, 'I'm glad to find you all here.'

When they were all seated around the dining room table
he began to go over the events of the night of Michael's
last visit.

'Who found him?'

The inspector and both of her parents were surprised
when Barbara put the question.

'It was the coastguard who discovered the body, if you
remember,' the inspector said gently.

'Yes.' She must have been told that yesterday. Vaguely
she remembered, but no doubt she had been too shocked
to register anything other than the fact that Michael was
dead.

'You said you struck your husband with a grooming brush, Mrs Henderson. How badly was he hurt?' The inspector's tone was now neutral, neither accusatory nor protective.

'His face was deeply scratched, he was bleeding badly.'

'Did he fall to the ground?'

'Oh no.' How she wished that he had. 'It was then that . . . he . . . became more vicious,' Barbara's chest was heaving and her face was as white as a sheet. 'I'm sorry . . . I don't remember much else.'

'May I be excused for a few moments?' When the inspector nodded, Patricia got up from her seat and left the room.

Some ten minutes passed before she came back with Mrs Clarkson. The two women began offering coffee and small cakes and biscuits which they had set out on doyley-covered plates. Inspector Watkins ate and drank, said 'Thank you,' and went back to writing in his notebook. Now it was the turn of her parents. Mrs Hamlin was confused and her answers were not clearly expressed. Mr Hamlin, however, was in complete control. His version of himself and the three other men finding his daughter, battered and bloody in the stables, was given in precise clipped terms — very much in the same manner as he was accustomed to use in legal battles when in court.

Looking up from his notes the inspector paused, his eyes taking in all three of them.

'The coroner has been notified of the death, he will arrange for a post-mortem to be held; as the death was sudden, probably an accident, your consent is not needed. The coroner will almost certainly decide to hold an inquest, in which case you will be required to attend.'

Patricia felt she couldn't sit still any longer, so she rose from her chair and collected the cups and saucers, stacking them in an orderly manner on the tray.

The inspector began all over again. Endless questions directed at each of them in turn. Phillip, his voice steady as a rock, repeated his version of the events.

Patricia, her voice trembling, told how her daughter had been carried into the house.

The inspector twisted round in his chair to look directly at Barbara, 'Are your husband's parents living?'

Barbara hesitated. It seemed absurd that she knew so little about Michael's background. 'His mother died some years ago, but I think his father is still alive.'

'Can you not give me more details than that?'

'Not really.' This truly was an embarrassment for her. 'His father married again, a lady who already had several children, and Michael being the only one I think felt out of things, perhaps even neglected. He joined the navy as soon as he was old enough and, as far as I know, has not been in contact with his father since.'

Kindly now, the inspector said, 'Don't worry, Mrs Henderson, we'll trace his father through his naval records. He will be notified. One last question – in your opinion was your husband very much the worse for drink when he came to the house?'

Barbara kept her eyes downcast. 'Yes,' she murmured.

'Do you know if he had any bottles about his person?'

She shook her head, 'I'm sorry, I haven't any idea.'

'Nothing else you can remember about that afternoon, no little detail that you have left out?'

Again she shook her head, 'Just what I have told you.'

At last he closed his writing-pad, said, 'Thank you all for bearing with me,' and stood up.

Phillip came forward, 'I'll get your hat and coat and see you to the door.'

Barbara and her mother were both close to tears when the inspector finally left.

Within a week of Michael's death the coroner held a pre-liminary hearing. It had been decided that Phillip Hamlin's presence would be enough. With dragging footsteps he walked along the cold corridor and thankfully sat down on a bench. This past week had been exhausting. He wasn't sure if he was relieved or surprised that neither he nor Barbara had heard from Michael's father. He couldn't fathom how a man could lose touch with his only son. It seemed cruel and hard for no one to express sorrow at Michael's death, but hypocrisy was not in his own nature.

He couldn't erase from his mind the picture of his lovely daughter, with her gentle voice and gentle ways, lying on that cold stone floor of the stable. Abused, bloody and beaten. Barely alive. He had detested the man and the urge to kill him had been strong – at least to have him locked away for a very long time, anything so long as it prevented him from ever again having the opportunity to come near Barbara. Only now Michael was dead, leaving behind him deep shadows and scars.

'This hearing is for purposes of identification only and formal evidence of the identity of the body.' It was all over in minutes. The coroner gave the order for the body to be released and so allow the cremation to take place. 'The inquest proper will take place three weeks from today and will be an inquiry into the cause of death,' the coroner declared, looking somewhat sympathetically at Phillip Hamlin.

Barbara insisted, against all advice, on attending the service at the crematorium. There were a few male mourners in the chapel when Barbara arrived with her parents, but she never raised her eyes to notice who they were. She looked wan and sad, as indeed she felt, in her black suit and hat. It was the way that Michael had died that had hit her hard and she did her best during the short service to think back to the way they had felt about each other when they had first met. Her first mistake had been to go to Plymouth without even telling her parents and her second, and by far the biggest, mistake had been to marry Michael in such haste. From that day things had only gone from bad to worse.

It was midday when they arrived back at the house. Mrs Clarkson had hot refreshments set out ready in the lounge. Three armchairs were grouped close to the fireplace in which a roaring fire burnt halfway up the chimney, looking so cheerful and giving out such comforting warmth.

Her father broke the silence by touching on the subject they had all been avoiding during the past days.

'You must remember, Barbara, Michael had been drinking heavily, he didn't know what he was doing and it is almost certain that they will bring in a verdict of accidental death.'

Barbara made no reply but she thought about it. She wasn't sure if that made it better or worse.

With concern in his voice, her father asked, 'Would you like for your mother and me to take you abroad for a while?'

190

Barbara sipped at her hot coffee before answering, 'No, Daddy, I don't feel the urge to run away.'

'Are you sure? A holiday might do us all good.' His deep-set kindly eyes looked into hers. Had there been a little tinge of longing in the smile with which she had softened her refusal? 'There is nothing you have to prove to anyone, you know that by now, don't you Barbara?'

'I think so.' She replaced her cup and saucer on the table, reached out and covered his large bony hand with her own – it felt warm and reassuring.

'You are intending to stay here, live with your mother and me, at least for the time being? We both want you to stay so much.'

'Hmm! Just what the doctor ordered,' she smiled. 'Who else would love me as you do? And spoil me.' Reaching up, she touched his cheek. 'Oh Daddy!'

Her father breathed out and relaxed. 'Poor Barbara. It's been a hell of a time for you, but you must put it all behind you now. There is a future ahead and I hope it leads you to a happy road.'

'Thank you Daddy.' Barbara's voice was little more than a whisper and he could tell that tears were not far away.

He took her by the shoulders and pulled her close. Watched by her mother he put his arms around her, giving her the protective love that only parents can offer. Phillip looked sadly at his wife.

After a while, Patricia sighed, hauled herself out of her chair, knelt down on the floor and placed her hand on Barbara's head. Very gently, very slowly, she began to stroke her daughter's hair.

'It's all over now, my love. Please, Barbara, please dear,

don't cry. Let's have no more tears. Your father and I will take care of you. Don't be afraid any more.'

Barbara raised her head and brushed her hand over her eyes. 'I'll try not to be,' she whispered, knowing how lucky she was to have parents that not only loved her but were free with their sympathy and understanding. She reached out and took her mother's hand.

Patricia smiled. 'Good girl.' Then clambering to her feet she added, 'I'll see about refilling the coffee pot.'

Barbara felt compelled to attend the inquest.

Her mother and father sat either side of her in the cold corridor. The sound of the heavy rain lashing against the window panes did nothing to lift her spirits.

'Time to go in.' The tall official had a military bearing and an odd expression. He swallowed as if he had a lump in his throat.

'Shouldn't take long. Fairly straight forward.' He made the statement kindly.

The inquiry opened with the doctor who had performed the autopsy stating that Michael's body had contained an excessive amount of alcohol. This was confirmed by the evidence given by the landlord of The Smugglers Inn.

The coroner presiding at the inquest was an elderly but efficient gentleman. He gave his judgement in precise terms. 'Michael James Henderson had been intoxicated at the time of his death and the verdict of this court is accidental death.'

Chapter Ten

BARBARA LIVED THE next few weeks day by day, grateful for the refuge her old home provided, frightened to look back yet refusing to look ahead.

Mornings she walked the grounds a lot, wearing stout shoes and a sheepskin coat, with no other company than her own, and the afternoons she spent in the solitude of her bedroom. There were days when rain turned to sleet at times and pelted against the windows. Then, later, the sleet turned to snow, and her parents gave up trying to encourage her to venture further afield. The wind howled and yet the white snow presented a pretty picture, covering the lawns, mantling the hedgerows, and lying white on the dark boughs of the bare trees.

Friends and relatives visited, asked questions and showed concern for Barbara's health. Their talk flowed over her and she scarcely heard it. She found the time now spent at home alone with her parents strangely soothing. It was like going back into times past, except that her brothers were missing and her mirror told her she was no longer a little girl.

Her mother did her best to get her to talk. The two of them lunching alone one day seemed the ideal opportunity.

'Have you thought what you'll do with the rest of your life?' her mother fearfully asked.

Barbara had. Often. As yet she hadn't come to any decision.

Receiving no reply Patricia pressed on, 'Darling, I know you're not fit enough to do anything too strenuous at the moment, but wouldn't you like to go out a little? See some of your old friends?'

As if speaking to herself, Barbara said in an undertone, 'I hadn't realised how bitter Michael had become.' The comment was uttered in little more than a whisper and her mother had to lean forward to catch the words.

'Stop it! – do you hear me? You cannot go on blaming yourself for what has happened, Barbara, it is about time that you tried facing the truth.' The exasperated tone of her mother's voice caused Barbara to look up sharply. It was totally out of character for her mother to lose her temper.

'The thing is,' her mother insisted, 'if things hadn't happened as they did, God alone knows what the outcome would have been. Your life would never have been free of his threats. Michael was a menace to himself.' She took a deep breath, regretting her outburst, but that damned man had been the ruination of Barbara and it was time she put all thoughts of him from her head and got on with her own life. She forced her voice down to quieter tones.

'Please Barbara, try to look at things in realistic terms. You didn't do anything harmful to Michael. He did it to himself.'

Taking Barbara's hand between her own she sat stroking it. When she spoke again there were tears in her voice. 'Your father and I care about you, Barbara, we just can't stand by and see you fading away. You made a disastrous mistake, fair enough – we all do at some point in our lives – but no one expects you to go on paying for it for the rest of your life. Make an effort. Please. Promise me you will try. How about beginning right now by giving your old mother a smile?'

Penny had said almost the selfsame words to her months ago. What a pity she hadn't heeded them then, left Michael and come home, Barbara was thinking to herself.

'You're not old, Mother, and yes I will try and buck myself up.' There was sorrow still in her voice but she had forced a smile to her lips.

Spring came. Daffodils bloomed in their hundreds, not in neat flower beds, but higgledy-piggledy in clumps around the base of great tree-trunks and tucked away beneath the hedges. Lambs were born in the fields, their plaintive bleating sounding wonderful as they skipped around their mothers. It was all new life. Did it bring new life to Barbara? One evening late in April, dinner over, she asked her mother if she might use her car. 'Of course you may, dear,' her mother readily agreed, smiling happily that at last her daughter was going off somewhere.

In the garage her father's gleaming car looked enormous against the modest black Morris thousand which her mother used. Barbara settled herself in the driver's seat of the small car and was pleased when the engine fired first time. She drove slowly with the window wound down. The air was sweet as wine, fresh and fragrant with the scent from the hedgerows, and as always the smell reminded her of her childhood. Now she was appreciative of all the countryside that surrounded her. In her mind's eye she could see again those two rooms in which she and Michael had lived. The time spent there had been an endless struggle against the dirt and grime. But all that was over. There were times now when she felt cleansed, even renewed, yet other times when the nightmare would still return. Then the filth and sweat of Michael and Pete Davis's actions was so real and horrible that she would panic and feel dirty again.

She drove for twenty minutes, by which time she had left the villages behind and was now approaching the main Brighton road. At the top of the incline she turned the car to the left, taking the winding road which had open fields on each side. Climbing now to higher grounds, Birling Gap with its long low hotel and coastguard cottages was left behind.

When she brought the car to a stop on the cliffs above Beachy Head, she asked herself if it had been her intention from the start to make for this place, and the answer was yes, only she hadn't thought she would have the courage to go through with it. Ever since the thought had come into her mind it had stayed with her, eating away a little more each day. It had to be done or she could not go on living with herself.

'So,' she said aloud, 'I'm here now but why? Exactly why?'

Face the truth, she sternly told herself. This is the place where Michael had died and what she wanted, if she was ever to find peace and start to rebuild her life, was to exonerate herself from Michael's death.

It was ages before she could bring herself to get out of the car, and when she finally did it was dark. She walked up the grass bank, staying well away from the edge of the high precipice. It was a fine starry night. The sea sounded so gentle as it lapped softly against the foot of the cliffs, and the beam from the lighthouse spread out over the water. She felt isolated. Swamped in a cold sweat as she stood there feeling fear and trepidation. For a few seconds she almost lost consciousness. When she recovered she gave a gasp of dismay. This whole area was scary. What the hell was she doing there? Michael was gone, he should be at peace and he should now leave her in peace.

She took a great breath of salt air into her lungs and called out loudly, 'Michael!' The sound reverberated above the quiet night and the small waves which broke and splashed against the shingle far below.

She listened. No human voice answered her. Only the seagulls, disturbed by the sudden burst of sound, wheeled up overhead calling and screeching. Then all at once they ceased, settling again quietly into the crevices of the cliffs. Her eyes stared out into the distance and her innermost thoughts questioned as to whether Michael could hear her wherever he was.

Words. They were so important and she had come here to say so much. With a great effort she thought of all the happy times she and Michael had shared. With the end of the War things had changed. Perhaps, like a good many more, they had been drunk with sudden freedom. With the madness of war behind them came the beginning of reality. A new lifestyle. Poor living accommodation, not enough money, so many responsibilities. Life had become so different.

Shock of having to fend for themselves, in the forces all decisions had been made for them. Quarrels, laying the blame on each other. More sad days than happy days. She thought again of the love there had been between them in the beginning and all the sweet letters they had written to each other. She thought of their son and the thought brought a lump to her throat and the sting of tears to her eyes. Michael had expected her to abort the baby as she had twice previously. She had stuck to her guns and given him birth only to reject him without ever holding him in her arms. Had that gesture been made as a retaliation against Michael? If so, her own action had been wicked. She shuddered – as if someone has just walked over my grave, she thought, as the saying goes. She put both her hands to her head, tugging her fingers through her hair.

She wished they had never rushed into marriage, it had been as unfair to Michael as to herself. With hindsight it had been a crazy thing to do, but then she had been cooped up in London, hedged in by the air raids, seeing sights that were gruesome while Michael had spent endless days and nights submerged in the depth of foreign seas. On first meeting they had been dazzled by each other. Given a different time and different circumstances – who knows? – they might have made it.

She moved, cramped and cold, and started back to the car. This place was thick with shadows but it wasn't haunted. 'There aren't any ghosts,' she softly said, and knew that she was right. Only sky, stars, grassy hills and the sea below. No ghosts.

As she drove her mother's car back along the country roads, Barbara vowed to close her mind to the past. It was over. A strange feeling came over her: she no longer hated Michael.

Chapter Eleven

BARBARA NOW SET about leading her life with a swiftness that surprised all who knew her. Plunging into a kind of desperate routine. Barbara was suddenly no longer the frightened, subdued young lady who had returned to the safe-haven of Alfriston. She filled her time. Life went on. An endless round of parties and social occasions.

That was the Barbara on public view. The other one was known only to herself and only glimpsed briefly by her parents. She saw a lot of Elizabeth and Tim Holsworthy; how quickly the twins were growing. Barbara often looked at them through tears that stung. How different everything might have been! There were days when she thought she had forgotten – well, almost forgotten – how it might have been.

Goodness only knew, she had tried to forget.

Then there were the days when she tormented herself. What did her little boy look like? Did he have kind and loving parents? Did he have wonderful grandparents? Oh, how her mother and father would have loved and spoilt him. She would feel her heart ache inside her. Don't think of such things. Don't think of what can't be helped, she would fiercely scold herself. If only she could bring herself to tell her mother, yes, and her father too. Lose the whole load of guilt and maybe free her conscience.

Never. No, never. She had made the decision and she had to live with it forever. How could she tell the two people she loved most in the world that she had been callous enough to sign away their grandson without even looking at him?

Patricia Hamlin repeatedly asked herself if Barbara was now happy or was it all a sham. Once she had found her sitting looking out of the window, hands idle in her lap. There was such an expression on her face! Something so set, ferocious and sad! When she had softly spoken to her she started, she had to repeat her words and she saw her blink, shaking her head to bring herself back to the room from wherever she had been.

Both she and her husband still worried about Barbara. They recognised the occasional signs of strain in their daughter, perhaps by an unusual sharpness in her normally composed and gentle voice, or a morbid opinion which Barbara would express openly. They made no comment but it worried them.

We've a lot to be grateful for, she often thought to herself. Barbara does love us both very much. We have no great problems, she and I, we can talk to each other about most things. But she's more attached to her father. He adores her, she's the light of his life. But then, that's the way it often is between fathers and daughters. If only Barbara could put Michael and that episode of her life away at the back of her mind. Blot it out. What sense is there in thinking of what might have been? Or in wondering who should take the blame? No sense, and yet I wonder. I'm still not sure that I have been told the full facts, in fact I'm certain it is what has never been brought out in the open that's playing on Barbara's mind.

Patricia sighed, a long quivering sigh, more like a sob. I

mustn't let myself dwell on what has happened either, she thought. All we can hope is that Barbara will confide in us eventually. Given time, everything would work out all right. Time was a great healer, she assured herself — but without much conviction.

Were they happy times in this post-war era? Barbara did her best to convince herself they were. Carefree and fun, bringing new-found opportunities, but she missed Penny Rayford who was away on a cruise. The new look came in. Hemlines were not now acceptable just below the knee — they had to be lengthened, reaching now well below the calf. Some items in one's wardrobe could be extended, but for Barbara and her friends it was justification to indulge in a shopping spree. Chic elegant suits, with skirts that became known as hobble skirts, jackets with velvet collars. The whole bunch of them spent a great deal of money and never turned a hair. Delicate dainty camiknickers and lace-trimmed, long slips to complement new dresses. Outstanding colourful accessories. The price didn't come into it, but all the same money didn't buy happiness.

Barbara arrived home after midnight from a party. Her mother had gone to bed but her father was reading in the lounge. Barbara came in and curled up on the floor beside his chair. 'Good party?' her father asked, not giving her his full attention. Barbara sighed deeply. Her father looked up and quickly put down his book. 'That sounded ominous,' he said lightly. 'What's the matter, Barbara?'

She laid her hand on his knee. 'Oh, I don't know, Daddy. Well, yes I do. I've made such a mess of my life and now I just can't seem to get things together. There doesn't seem to be any purpose. I don't even enjoy these parties I get invited to. Does that sound silly?'

'No, of course not, my dear. This much I know, Michael disappointed you cruelly and because of that you have become very vulnerable. Given time you will work your own destiny out, but you must try and keep things in perspective. There is no way you can alter the past, but you could make the future a whole lot different if you really tried.'

Barbara smiled at him, 'Daddy, how did you ever become such a wise old bird?'

'Takes a lot of living and a whole lot of practice,' he joked. 'But then I have been blessed with two beautiful women who are fully qualified to keep my life running smoothly.'

'No one could say you've lost your persuasive charm, that's for sure. One thing I will tell you though, you don't have to sit up to all hours waiting for your baby girl to come home.' She said the words softly, letting him know that she appreciated and loved him. 'I'm a big girl now, Father,' she added sternly, 'and you should be in your bed.'

His face creased up with laughter. 'Yes, and so should you, my girl.' He held out his hands to help pull her up and they rose to their feet together.

'Good night, Daddy.'

'Good night, my darling.'

Later, when she was in bed, Barbara lay awake for a long time, musing on her father's good advice.

Barbara stood alone in the lounge, trying to decide how to fill her day. Her mother had gone up to town with her father.

202

This room never failed to delight her. Beautiful furniture, huge wide open-hearth to the fireplace with its marble surround, but best of all the high, wide windows that reached from floor to ceiling – giving views over the green lawns and flowering shrubs. She thought again of the shabby rooms she and Michael had shared. The smell! She had never got used to that. Should she have tried harder? Many folk had to live in similar places for the whole of their lives.

Maybe she could have coped better if she had been born into different circumstances. God forbid.

'Hallo! Hallo! Anybody home?'

Surprised, Barbara looked up quickly.

The door had opened and there stood Penny Rayford.

'Good Heavens! I didn't expect to see you, when did you get back? Who let you in?'

'Whoa, hold it, one question at a time,' she laughed. 'I came through the grounds, Mrs Clarkson saw me and let me in through the kitchen.' Penny had a happy-go-lucky air about her and, to Barbara, she seemed considerably pleased with herself. She looked so well. Dressed in a beige linen safari-style suit and a brown, cotton, tailored shirt which contrasted so well. Her make-up was perfect, her mouth outlined in bronze coloured lipstick, her soft brown leather shoes had low heels. I shouldn't be so surprised, Barbara thought to herself as she watched Penny cross the floor, Penny is always elegantly attired no matter what the occasion.

'Barbara – oh, Barbara!' The arms of Penny wrapped Barbara in a tight embrace. She rocked her life-long friend for a moment whilst the two of them shed happy tears at their reunion. It had been more than four months since

Elizabeth Waite

they'd met and though for the life of her Penny would not mention it, she found the change in Barbara, once again, to be shocking.

Penny broke the embrace. 'Enough of this melancholy. I've missed you but now I'm back to remind you life is for the living and life can be wonderful.'

'Yeah, so you say.'

'Yes, I *do* say, so wipe those tears and give me a smile to show you're glad to see me.'

'Penny, you know I am. You are always such an optimist, aren't you? You find the cup half full, you always did.'

'And you find it half empty?'

'Well, often I do.'

Penny gave her a lovely smile, 'Then we must rush to fill it for you, mustn't we?'

The love and vitality of Penny came across strongly to Barbara. She with her air of sophistication, beautiful blue eyes and the bright blonde hair. Undoubtedly she was well-travelled, well-educated, kind and intelligent – despite her devil-may-care attitude – and so loyal to those she loved. When it came down to making an appraisal of Penny, well, she was certainly very different from most people.

'You can't possibly know how glad I am to see you,' Barbara said softly. A tear slid down her cheek, she brushed at it with her hand impatiently. 'Oh, I must stop feeling sorry for myself.'

'Yes you must. Snap out of it. You need company; just as well I decided to invite myself for a few days. I seem to be needed. Now, go upstairs, dress yourself up, meanwhile I'll mix us both a drink. Then, we'll decide where to go for lunch.'

'All right, give me about twenty minutes.' The tone of her voice still sounded strangely subdued.

Penny was thoughtful as she watched Barbara leave the room. It was tragic really. That awful marriage, a sheer disaster. Barbara had certainly had a rough time of it. More so because of the terrible way it had ended.

Anyway, it was over. She would see to it that Barbara now started to live a little. There was still a lot that had happened that Barbara hadn't felt able to talk about, she felt positive about that. All in good time, she rebuked herself, and told herself not to pry.

From that day on both Penny and Barbara had a strange hunger for living. Penny steered Barbara to dinner-parties made up of the eminent and the rich. The wealth had been inherited. That was not an assumption on Barbara's part, just a well known fact. Barbara, having experienced poverty at first hand while living in Battersea, was sometimes embarrassed by the show of riches. In this stream of social waters Barbara was given several opportunities to choose a suitable man to be her second husband. Yes, she cast her eyes over the man allocated to her as an escort, but the bitter truth was she was afraid. She wouldn't allow herself to be interested.

At the insistence of Penny, Barbara was now completely fashion-conscious. Always looking the height of elegance with her expensive dresses and tailored suits. Now her lips and nails were fashionably coloured and her facial make-up included eyeshadow. Her chestnut hair, which had begun to show signs of grey after the last meeting with Michael, was now regularly tinted. The changes in her, however, were only external. Under the veneer of sophistication Barbara was very sensitive. She backed off from forming any lasting new friendships, especially with men.

It was taking far too long for Barbara to come out of the protective shell she had drawn round herself – those were Penny's thoughts on the matter.

Over coffee one morning Penny felt herself become exasperated. The silence between them held faint sadness and she sought for a way to break it. Offend or please – she was going to have to say what was on her mind.

'Honestly Barbara, you're becoming unreal. Half the time beneath all that veneer you look like a ghost. Oh I know you're the life and soul of the party when there's a crowd around you, but let a man come within five yards of you and you run scared. You've got a long time to live yet – a whole life in front of you – you're not being fair to yourself.'

Barbara accepted the telling-off with good grace. Penny only had her well-being at heart. She knew full well that what Penny said was right. She couldn't help it, she preferred not to be left alone with a man, however nice he seemed. She wasn't ready to cope with a compromising situation. Frequently she had been asked out by bachelors and when attending dinner-parties was well aware that her hostess made sure she was seated next to someone supposedly eligible. But always the past came back to taunt her and she reacted against the situation.

Barbara lifted her eyes to the level of her dear friend and in a voice that held a plea asked, 'Why is it so important for me to take up with another man, why can't I just enjoy life?'

'That's just the point,' Penny came quickly back at her. 'You are *not* enjoying life. You're afraid all the time.' More gently now, Penny insisted, 'Barbara, it's easy to see that you're not happy and that makes me unhappy for you.'

'So you think if I took up with one of these chinless wonders you keep producing for me, all my problems would be solved?'

Penny's colour flared up and she made an impatient gesture, 'That's very unfair, Barbara, and you know it.'

'I'm sorry, oh Penny, I wouldn't upset you for the world. I didn't mean to be spiteful, I'm sorry.'

She's still very frightened, Penny thought with a swift burst of sympathy, she's still afraid . . . and yet she tries so hard not to show it.

Barbara's voice cut into her thoughts, 'I've a good mind to give up going to these social functions.'

'You *won't*, you know. You won't do anything of the kind. I won't let you!'

'Well, what do you suggest that I do?'

'You know very well what I think. You should find some suitable man, good family, that sort of thing. Most important though, give yourself a chance, get rid of that deep-seated sense of suspicion. You know, Barbara, there are still some good people left in this world, try trusting your friends.'

Now, in the manner of a woman to whom the past had brought heartache and suffering, Barbara knew the wisdom of Penny's words. It was true. She was distrustful of everyone.

Penny decided to be candid. 'It's still Michael, isn't it? You can't lay him to rest can you?'

Barbara turned her head away.

'To this day I've never been able to fathom out why you

207

stayed with him, let things go so far. Neither of you were happy.'

'Well Penny, there's no easy answer to that.' She drew a deep breath, sighing to herself, trying to find the right words without disclosing awful details that she had vowed she would tell to no one. 'I won't pretend that I'm proud of that period of my life, you know well enough I'm not. You have also made a good guess that when it comes to the truth I have ever only told my parents and you half of what really did take place. Now I'm not sure I could make you understand if I wanted to.'

'Try me,' Penny quietly suggested.

If only she dare! Unleash all her guilt into Penny's sympathetic ear. It would be better than telling her parents. *No*! Even now she couldn't bring herself to tell a living soul that she had not only been raped by her husband but that he had encouraged his mate to take a turn at her as payment for beer which they had drunk together and for which her husband couldn't pay his share. The baby? That was another matter altogether. She couldn't, she wouldn't even think about that. Not in broad daylight. Those thoughts were her own, that only came out of the deep recess of her mind in the darkest hours of the night.

Barbara waved her hands angrily, 'It all went so wrong.'

Again a silence settled between them, Penny had no answer to that. Their half-drunk cups of coffee stood on the table, cold and curdled, unwanted.

It was some time before Penny could bring herself to move. Barbara's face was so sad. She leaned forward, peering at Barbara intently. It was curious the way Barbara's thoughts always reflected in her face. It made one's heart ache just to look at her. Penny leant across the table and grasped Barbara's hand in a gesture of warm affection. 'We both seem to be suffering a fit of the blues. Come on now, buck up. Just promise me one thing, not to shy away from life anymore.'

Barbara nodded. The sad look on Barbara's face made Penny want to put out her arms to her, she wanted to hold her, she wanted her to open up and talk to her, tell her exactly what had happened in those last days before she had finally found the courage to leave Michael. Most of all she wanted Barbara to stop bottling up her secrets – to tell her about the baby. Had she given birth? Had she been driven to having an abortion? So many questions that she knew she'd get no answers to, so what she said was, 'Promise me you will try, please?'

'I'll try, Penny. You shouldn't worry about me so much.'

And the glance they exchanged now was full of understanding and simultaneously they reached for each other.

This friendship between them was very valuable.

Chapter Twelve

THE WHOLE COUNTRY was intoxicated. Everywhere there was a sense of anticipation and excitement, for this was 1953, Coronation Year. The War was long over, men had died in their hundreds and thousands, yet life had continued. The wealthy kept their place in society while the working classes fought for jobs, higher pay and better conditions. For the moment there was no resentment. People had found a common cause in which they were united. Queen Elizabeth II was to be crowned in a ceremony that for the first time millions would be able to see on a television screen.

For the past three years Barbara and Penny had been inseparable. They had taken river boat rides from Tower Bridge, toured museums and Madame Tussaud's – the famous waxwork show in Baker Street. Obtained tickets for every first night West End theatre showing. Been twice to see *Gone with the Wind*; each had come away from the film with the longing to find a real life Rhett Butler for themselves. Afternoon tea was taken either at the Ritz or the Savoy. They were constantly seen wherever it was socially important to be.

The company of these two young ladies provided a challenge to many of the best hostesses in the land. Their time was fully engaged and on the surface Barbara appeared to be enjoying life to the full, though her mother still often thought her frivolous attitude was feigned.

210

The pursuits of the two of them were the talk of Sussex. Not everyone was charitable when voicing their opinions. Awful rumours reached Phillip and Patricia Hamlin about the way Barbara and her friend Penny carried on, drinking to excess, noisy late parties, gambling heavily at race meetings, driving at speeds well above the law. Moving in circles neither set of parents approved of. Many a time Patricia shivered with apprehension. Her own daughter, did she really get up to bad things? She wished often that Barbara would abandon this whirl of self-indulgence.

Phillip Hamlin, still a wealthy man, ignored the rumours. Whatever had happened between Barbara and Michael, he knew the damage inflicted on his daughter was considerable. Her periodically horrific nightmares alone were proof and for that very reason he made great allowances for her behaviour. He denied her nothing.

Now June 2nd would provide the most brilliant social event of their lives. Princess Elizabeth, eldest daughter of King George VI and Queen Elizabeth, was to be crowned Queen of England. Despite the weather being cold and wet, thousands had camped overnight in The Mall. Stands had been erected along most of the route. Tickets for these seats had changed hands on the black market for vast sums of money, while more than a million people stood shoulder to shoulder, most of whom had waited up all night to catch a glimpse of their young Queen.

Thanks to Phillip's influence the Hamlins were asked to join a party in offices which boasted a balcony to the front of the building. A choice site overlooking the route. Inside the premises a television set had been installed in the main office, giving these privileged people the best of both worlds. Included in the party were Penny and her parents. Penny and Barbara were among the young folk who leaned low over the balcony to cheer the royal party on its way to Westminster Abbey. Then, thanks to the television, they were able to see Queen Elizabeth II crowned. The television cameras showed the crowned heads of all Europe looking seemingly impressed as the roar of the crowds outside announced the arrival of the young Queen.

It was a ritual going back centuries but with all the pomp and splendour of the greatest royal occasions. Everyone agreed the television set was marvellous. It enabled them to see in detail the Archbishop of Canterbury place the crown on Elizabeth's head, then watch as she was invested with the robes and emblems of high office.

'Rather her than me,' Barbara sighed as she watched men kneel to pay homage to the new Queen. 'She looks so young and kind of lost.'

'Oh, I don't know,' Penny chirped up, 'I wouldn't mind having a go at it for a while. Imagine the power one would have.'

'That's just it,' Elizabeth Holsworthy laughed. 'It's like getting married, isn't it Tim? You can't have a go at it just for a while, especially not if you find yourself with twin boys. Being Queen is like becoming a mother, it's a job for life. More so in the Queen's case. She has the whole British Empire as her family.'

This statement caught Barbara on the raw, even more so as she watched Tim Holsworthy look tenderly at his wife and say, 'Well, if Prince Philip is blessed with as much good fortune as we have been, he won't have gone far wrong, will he?'

'Whoa! Serious, serious!' This exclamation came from

one of the young lawyers who had helped swell their numbers today, and all the young folk laughed.

Back outside, crushed together on the balcony, the older men opened bottles of champagne. 'Long live the Queen!' was the toast they drank to and this was echoed around the street parties in the suburbs and towns of all England, while the crowds who had poured into London roared their approval as their newly invested Queen rode in the golden coach back to the Palace.

Afterwards the Hamlins and several mutual friends had been invited to a party given by Jane and Stephen Mortimer in their lovely old house in Hampstead. Stephen was a judge and most of the male guests were members of the legal profession. Champagne flowed, food was plentiful and delicious. Talk was mainly of the glittering pageantry that they had witnessed in London today. Every man present was of the opinion that no other country in the world could accomplish such a magnificent show as well as the British.

Barbara was surrounded by women, all talking loudly. She looked away to where her father stood and wondered – with so many brilliant young men in the company today, was he thinking of her two brothers? He never deliberately avoided talking about them, yet on the other hand he never entered into a conversation should her brothers be the topic under discussion. Surely he must have so many regrets, she thought now, this room is filled with men who have pursued their education to such lengths in order to be qualified to plead cases in the high courts and Daddy has no one to follow in his footsteps – no one he can encourage and pass on his knowledge to. What she saw was a vigorous man in a well-cut grey suit, a kind and loving man where she was

213

concerned. He was in good shape. Didn't look his age. He hadn't run to fat like a good many of his older colleagues had.

He must have felt Barbara's eyes on him for he turned his head, caught her glance and immediately smiled and beckoned her to come over, 'Barbara, dear, I would like to introduce you to James Ferguson, an up-and-coming young man – unless I am very much mistaken. James, this is my daughter Barbara.'

The colour flooded into Barbara's cheeks and what she wanted to cry out was, Oh no, not you Daddy! With everyone else having a go at match making, doing their best to see that I'm always paired off with a suitable young man, I don't need you to start.

Instead she held out her hand and raised her eyes to meet the clearest blue eyes she had ever seen. James Ferguson was not handsome, more the rugged type, with fair hair and a fair complexion. He was in his early thirties, with the assurance of wealthy parents and position charmingly concealed by an attractive good nature and perfect manners.

'I really am very pleased to meet you, Barbara,' he said and taking her hand between the both of his, he raised it to his lips and kissed her fingers. There was to be no standing on ceremony with this man! Her pulse in her wrist was beating hard, hastily she withdrew her hand hoping James hadn't had a chance to notice this.

Placing an arm around Barbara's shoulders, her father bent his head and, speaking softly, he said to her, 'I'm going to mingle a bit. Should really go and have a chat with Stephen, it was awfully good of him to lay all of this on.'

'Your father is a great man,' James stated as he bent towards her. 'Feared by many when he has them at his mercy in a court room. Can't say I've ever felt the wrong side of his tongue, quite the reverse – he has been very valuable to me as I've slogged to climb the slippery slope. Unstinting in both help and advice.'

Barbara felt he was only talking so fast to put her at ease and she appreciated his efforts.

'If you want to go and join the men, please don't feel you have to stay.' Her words sounded stilted even to her own ears, 'I should go and find my mother.'

He threw back his head and laughed. 'Oh dear, have we got off on the wrong foot or are you usually this hostile – or perhaps it is only us legal beadles that ruffle your feathers?'

Barbara had the good grace to murmur, 'I'm sorry.'

'Not at all. I was rather foisted on you, but it is a day for celebrations so what say I fetch us both something to drink and we'll see how we go from there. Yes?'

Despite her attempt to be aloof Barbara found herself smiling. And her answer to this was simply, 'Thank you.'

'There! See! It isn't so difficult to be friendly with the natives, is it?' Without waiting for her reply he moved away and Barbara was left to ponder on this lively young man, who seemed so determined to be friendly.

From across the room Penny had been watching. She found the situation easy to read. James was smitten and Barbara now seemed sufficiently at ease to allow her to hope that something good might come from their meeting.

They talked as they sipped their drinks and Barbara was surprised to find that she really was enjoying his company. How could she put it to herself? Well, James was easy to be with and, yes, if she was honest, she didn't want him to go away.

215

They became aware of talk and movement in the room. People began saying their goodbyes, hugs and kisses, promises to phone one another, meet again soon. The day was coming to an end.

'My folks live at Eastbourne, quite near you isn't it?'

'Yes it is,' Barbara agreed.

'I shall be coming down at the weekend. Do you ride?'

'Yes I do,' she was studying his face as she answered.

'Then we'll meet on the bridle path, foot of the Downs, Sunday morning, eight a.m. sharp.'

There was no sign of nervousness in Barbara now as she smiled with pleasure.

Walking to their car her father grinned to himself, her mother kissed her warmly, hugging her with affection, and Barbara found herself looking forward to the weekend and wondering how a stranger could so quickly become a friend.

It was three weeks before Barbara really let herself think about how happy she was. Life as a whole had suddenly become good. People were good – especially James. There was a longing inside her for this relationship to be a lasting one. Whether it would turn out to be, well, that was another question. It was a quarter to eleven on this Tuesday morning and she was alone in the house. Seated on her low stool, knees tucked under her kidney-shaped dressing table, she had her elbows resting on the glass top and her chin cupped in her hands.

She stared at her reflection in the mirror and sighed. She was twenty-nine-years-old. Old enough to know her own mind. But did she? Her love for Michael had been instantaneous, or so she had thought at the time, and how quickly that love had turned to hate, even fear. Did she know the difference between love and infatuation?

Here in the safety and comfort of this lovely house, the serenity of not having to worry about money, the caring love of both her parents, and the sweet smelling air of Sussex, yes, she had to admit that there were times when she could completely blot out the episode of life lived in two rooms in Battersea. She didn't hate Michael any more. Hate was a useless emotion, more so when directed at a person who was no longer alive. But he had sent her to hell and back. Twice. That fact would be with her for as long as she lived. Reaching out she picked up her silver-backed hairbrush and began slowly to brush her hair. Nodding at her mirror image she felt the anger rise in her.

'You're too hard on yourself,' she said aloud. 'You put up with everything that Michael dared to dish out for so long because you hadn't the guts to admit you'd made a mistake and walk out. Michael treated you in a manner that no man should – many a man has been sent to prison for less. So let me remind you that you stood enough from that marriage to make you bitter, but by now you have found out that being bitter doesn't get you anywhere. Nor does putting on a brave front and letting the world think that you don't give a damn for anyone but yourself.

'You've been offered a second chance, well maybe not quite that yet, but at least a friendship with a decent man, a man from a good family, so what are you going to do about it?' She laid down her hairbrush, stood up and went to stand at the window, to stare out over the beautiful grounds. She thought for a moment with sadness, how different her life might have been if she had never met Michael. When the War was over she would have come home, lived a privileged life, mixed with all the right people, fallen in love with a suitable man, and perhaps had two or three children by now. Instead, what had happened to her?

'Oh, enough of this talking to yourself, what is the good of keeping harping on the past and what might have been. It isn't going to do you any good, surely you've learnt that by now?' She knew that, if she allowed it, love for James could easily grow. But would it turn sour with time, be as savagely painful as it had been with Michael?

Did anyone really have a say in their own lives? Or was it God that ordered and set the pattern? She didn't know, but whoever it was it seemed one had no choice but to go through with it. But that didn't alter the fact that sometimes you were given more than you could bear, and when good times cropped up why was it that one felt so frightened, fearful that this was not for real, that it wouldn't last? Should one grab an opportunity to be happy, to form a relationship – knowing full well that there were no guarantees to be had? Already, in James she half-believed she'd found the man who could bring her happiness. One who could wipe out the nightmares from her mind. To be honest, she admitted, she felt the physical pull whenever she was near to James. In these few short weeks she had only met him at weekends and yet she was fascinated with this sophisticated man who led an exciting busy life and promised her a wonderful future – if only she had the courage to reach out and take hold of it.

Chapter Thirteen

AT THE LAST minute her parents remembered that they had a previous engagement and Barbara would have to be hostess alone to James Ferguson. It was a thinly veiled excuse. They might have been more open about it, Barbara smiled to herself. As if it would make any difference! It was just one more try to throw them together. Her father was always praising his brilliance, indeed he had prayed that such a man might come into her life. She knew that. She only hoped that James wasn't offended: he was by no means stupid, he would surely know what they were doing.

She was afraid. They had been together, but never exactly alone, except when riding and that was slightly different. What would they talk about during the meal and then there would be the long evening . . .

Mrs Clarkson put her head around the door, 'I've seen to the melon; soup only needs heating; salad, ham and chicken already in the fridge.'

'Thanks, Mrs Clarkson, but I'm not looking forward to this dinner one bit.'

'Good heavens, why ever not? You should be over the moon. He's a real nice man, your Mr Ferguson. I took a liking to him the first time he came to this house. It were when you were so ill, he was a great comfort to your father. Apparently he took on a lot of your father's cases. I'm telling you, you've got a good one there.'

'I didn't know about that. I like him, too. I just feel,

219

awkward, as if Daddy is thrusting me onto him. It was him that invited James here for tonight, wasn't it?'

'Never mind about who invited him, he's coming an' like I've told you he likes you, I could tell he did. I bet he'll be ever so glad to have you all to himself. You'll see.'

'I hope you're right.'

'Course I am. Well, I'm off now. Relax, enjoy yourself, I'll see you tomorrow,' and as she closed the door Mrs Clarkson muttered to herself, 'God above knows you deserve a bit of happiness, my love. If anybody does, you do.'

Barbara didn't know why she felt so nervous. It might be rather nice to have dinner alone with James. So why did such a simple thing seem so difficult?

'What's that scent I can smell?' James asked when she opened the front door in answer to his ring.

'It's pinks. My mother planted a whole heap of them under that hedge.' Barbara turned on the outside light though it was not yet quite dark: the pink, white and deep red of these heavily-scented flowers made a pretty show. 'They smell very much like cloves, I always think. My mother loves the old-fashioned cottage type of flowers.'

James said quietly, 'It seems so peaceful out here, even Eastbourne seems miles away. Do you really know how wonderful this home of yours is?'

'Oh, yes.' She answered too quickly. There was no way in which she could explain to him exactly how and why she appreciated her home and parents as much as she did. 'It is a lovely house, isn't it?'

'I didn't mean the house. I meant your wonderful parents. Warm, good people. Gentle, caring people. Losing two sons would have turned many a soul bitter, but not them.'

'I think they comfort each other, kind of anticipating the needs of each other. It's not only that, of course. But that's part of it and the main thing is that they love each other.' Now she felt embarrassed as she looked into those clear blue eyes, but he wasn't talking for the sake of talking: he really did have a great admiration for her father and her mother, and she felt herself drawn to him.

'Will you pour us both a drink?' she asked as they walked into the lounge, 'I'll have a sherry but there is plenty of whisky there so, please, do help yourself.'

With his drink in his hand, James walked to the end of the room, picked up a book from a side-table, glanced at it and replaced it. 'Are you happy now Barbara?' The question was out of the blue and caught her entirely unawares. She was astonished, unable to form an answer.

'Forgive me. That was out of order. I feel a great deal of distress when I think how very ill you were only a short time ago and, since I have come to know you, your happiness and well being do mean a great deal to me. I wasn't meaning to pry, you do know that don't you?'

Barbara was suddenly aware that he knew a good deal more about her than she did about him.

'I don't mind answering your question,' she said shyly. 'Yes, I am very much happier now that I live at home.'

'So? What are you interested in? What do you aim to do with the rest of your life?'

'Well, one thing's for sure — I can't continue on this perpetual round of gaiety. Every day wasted, frittered away, there has to be more to life than an endless round of parties and race-meetings. I think I would like to work with children. Children that aren't very well cared for. Children that need help. I don't know exactly what I could do – offer my services to some organisation, perhaps one that deals with handicapped children . . .' She was talking too much, and she finished abruptly, 'I guess I really want to do something useful, only I don't know what.'

'You can be very solemn at times,' James said thoughtfully. 'I know a lot about your childhood, how you grew up here, in this house and where you went to school, but very little else. Tell me about your Red Cross work during the War.'

'I was a driver. At times it was dangerous and dirty, often very sad. But then again we had our moments and a good many laughs. Did you know there were the three of us? Elizabeth, Penny and myself. We thought we were so grown-up. We knew it all. Had our own flat in Putney.'

Why was she talking so much? This man drew the words from her.

'Since my father went to such lengths to contrive that we should be alone, I think we had better go and eat this meal.'

They looked at each other and burst out laughing, and then James's laughter broke off. He stared at her. 'You're the most extraordinary girl!'

'I'm not. I happen to be able to see through my Dad's schemes, that's all.'

He stood up and came to where she was sitting. He took her hands and pulled her lightly to her feet, 'Barbara, I'm going to say this right out while I have the courage. I want to see a great deal more of you. I want us to become close. Can you think of a good reason why we shouldn't be?'

She didn't answer. She hung her head.

'Because I think we get on so well together. I don't know about you, but I haven't felt so happy to be with someone, or so much at ease like this for a long time.'

Was it possible? Could it be she was to have a second chance? Would things work out between them or — like before — would it all go so terribly wrong? Still she didn't answer.

He put his hand beneath her chin, forcing her face up. She looked into his eyes, which were gentle and kind. She saw he meant every word he had said.

Her eyes filled with tears.

He pulled her closer and kissed her forehead. 'I don't know what that means,' he whispered. 'Does it mean yes or no?'

'I think . . . I think it means yes,' she murmured, doing her best to keep back the tears.

'Barbara, that's great. I hoped so much you felt the same way but I had to be so careful not to rush you.' He pulled out his handkerchief and dried her eyes, 'No need for tears, we'll have a terrific time, I promise we will.'

She nodded, laughed, and still a tear rolled down her cheek. She wanted to explain why she was crying, because she had half hoped this might happen and yet feared that it never would. Because she was almost thirty years old, because she had made such a mess of her life. Because she and Michael had been so wrong for each other. Because he had died so tragically. Because she had a son somewhere, a son she would never see, never hold in her arms. And now James was offering her a new start, maybe a happy future. With him.

The meal was a success. They were comfortable with

each other and their laughter rang all through the house as they talked away nineteen to the dozen.

'Black or white?' Barbara asked, as she came back from the kitchen carrying a tray on which she had set out the coffee things.

'Is it milk or cream?'

'Only milk I'm afraid, there didn't seem to be any cream in the fridge.'

'That's good. I like my coffee half an' half, made with boiling milk.'

'That's funny, that's the way I prefer it and I did boil the milk – it's in that separate jug.'

'We shall get to know all these little preferences. We have a lot to learn about each other, don't we Barbara? And, by the way, I think a very good time to start finding out such things would be at Henley.'

'Henley?' She raised her eyebrows in question.

'Yes, Henley Regatta, it's the principal rowing event in England. The best oarsmen from all over the world come to Henley-on-Thames for this event every July. You *must* have heard of it.'

'Of course I've heard of it – I was even there on one occasion – but when you said "Henley", just like that out of the blue, I didn't catch your meaning.'

'My meaning, Barbara dear, is to have you to myself for a whole weekend. Well, not exactly to myself, my whole family will be there but I'm sure we'll be able to give them the slip at some point or other. Say you'll come, please.'

Barbara was almost ashamed of the joy she felt as she listened to his enthusiasm. She hadn't been this happy for so long.

'The weekend will be very informal,' he was saying, with

laughter in his voice. 'It will be a great chance to get to know each other better. My mother arranges marvellous picnics. My sister Chloe told me a long time ago I should pay more attention to you. You want to know something? I think she was right.'

'Barbara, relax,' James scolded as he negotiated a round-about on the outskirts of Henley. 'We're going to have a great weekend.'

'Do your parents know you're bringing me?' she asked for the third time.

'They know,' he said patiently. 'They're all looking forward to meeting you. They will love you.' He took one hand from the steering wheel and squeezed Barbara's hand in reassurance.

'James, I want them to like me. Do they know anything about me?'

'Only that you were married a long time ago, your husband died and for a while you were very ill. No more than that.'

He drove slowly now along the road that ran parallel with the Thames. It had been a lovely hot day. Too hot. The breeze coming from off the river felt marvellous and the sun, not yet set, still glimmered on the water.

'I'll have to park up at the back of the house,' James told her as he slowed the car down. 'You won't see the beauty of the house until we are inside. Its frontage runs right down to the river's edge. It belongs to my grandfather, much too big for him now, more so since my grandmother died, but he'll die before he thinks of parting with it and I can't say that I blame him. See what you think.'

The door stood wide open and as they crossed the

grass they heard the sound of laughter inside. 'Seems we've arrived in time for dinner,' James grinned as he sniffed the savoury aromas of roasting meat and fresh baking which filtered out into the hallway.

Waiting to greet them was a small, fair-haired lady. Barbara knew instantly it was James's mother.

'Mother, this is Barbara, Barbara Hamlin.'

'We're all so pleased that you accepted our invitation to spend the weekend with us and even the weather is set fine for you.'

In minutes Barbara was surrounded by James's father, his sister Ann, and her five-year-old twins Harry and Lucy. 'Are you Uncle James's girlfriend?' Harry asked, giving her a cheeky grin.

'It's rude to ask things like that, isn't it, Mummy?' And without waiting for an answer Lucy added, 'I think you're very pretty.'

Everyone laughed.

'Thank you, Lucy.' Impulsively Barbara bent down and hugged her.

'Where's Chloe and Roddy?' James looked around.

'I'm here, have you got a kiss for your baby sister?' James moved forward to kiss a taller, younger edition of his mother.

Chloe came towards Barbara when James released her, arms outstretched. 'I really am pleased you're here,' she said, giving Barbara a hug. 'I know your father. Well, perhaps I shouldn't say *know*, rather know *of*, but I do admire him. I made a point of going to the Old Bailey every day for two weeks when your father was acting for the defence. The whole trial fascinated me. Your father is an absolute wizard.'

'Are we going to stand in this entrance hall for the whole night? I'm starving.'

Lucy, a bundle of energy, darted to the side of a grey-haired, tall, broad-shouldered man, took hold of his large hand and announced, 'This is our Great-Grandfather Ferguson.'

'And this is Uncle James's girlfriend,' piped up Harry.

Lucy giggled as her grandfather scooped her up in his arms.

In a few minutes James's brother Rodney and his wife Elaine appeared. There was no mistaking that James and Rodney were brothers; alike as two peas in a pod, Barbara thought as she watched them slap each other on the back. His wife, Elaine, was taller than the Ferguson women and had very dark hair swept up at the back and fixed with a comb. The welcome they gave to Barbara was spontaneous and she liked them both, sensing that they would be fun to be with. After introductions had been made, Mrs Ferguson ordered everyone to the table.

To Barbara the sense of affection that surrounded the dining room was incredible. Under the table James reached for her hand. From that moment she had a feeling of belonging.

'So, Dad, tell us what you're doing with yourself these days?' James asked. 'Are you enjoying retirement?'

Mr Ferguson's eyes met his wife's. 'Forget about retiring,' he chuckled. 'That's like saying you've finished with life and are waiting to die. With a wife like I've got I will never be idle.' He spoke directly to Barbara. 'What with all the committee and charity work, the children, whom she still thinks aren't able to fend for themselves, and the grand-children, I'm never allowed a moment's peace – never mind a day on the golf course. No other man would put up with it, I'm telling you!'

Barbara looked to where Mrs Ferguson was sitting, a sweet smile hovering around her lips, and she decided that James's mother came into the same category as her own mother. They were two of life's real ladies.

'I'm one of Grandad's children, aren't I, Dad?' Young Harry shot the question to a thickset man who had just entered the room.

'Sorry I'm so late, bit hectic in Fleet Street today,' he said. Making towards Ann, he bent over her shoulder and kissed her cheek.

'My son-in-law, Jack Tully,' Mr Ferguson nodded towards Barbara. 'You'll have gathered he's my daughter's husband and, for his sins, a newspaper editor.'

'Pleased to meet you,' Jack put out a hand to Barbara. 'Have my nippers been driving you mad?'

'That lady is Uncle James's girlfriend!' Harry had no intention of being ignored.

'You are a precocious brat, Harry, an' I'll deal with you later,' Ann said loudly her cheeks turning red. 'I do apologise, Barbara.'

'No need,' Barbara quickly assured her and then she laughed. Her laughter was contagious and soon everyone was chuckling.

By the time dinner was over, Barbara felt exhilarated. She had been accepted by James's loving family.

'I want to take you to a party,' James said, as they left the dining room. 'You have just one hour in which to tog yourself up, then I'm going to show you off. The party is being held on board a boat that belongs to a colleague of mine, Peter Bradley. You'll like him.'

Fifty minutes later Barbara came down the stairs. She was wearing a loose shift dress of pale green, with two long strands of coral beads. As she moved, the necklace caught the lights and glittered in multicolour. The events of the day seemed to have released the tension within her. James couldn't take his eyes off her. How nice to see Barbara so happy, he thought, and then what he exclaimed was, 'Barbara, you look stunning!'

'Why, thank you,' she answered, flashing him a sudden, radiant smile that instantly transformed her normal sad-looking face.

They strolled along the tow-path, James's hand at her elbow. The boats looked marvellous, gleaming and sparkling against the grassy banks. Their woodwork glowed and the brass shone.

Barbara looked flushed and excited as she climbed aboard the long sleek craft whose name on the side showed it to be *Special Lady.*

James led her down a narrow corridor that was rich with the smell of polish. At the end was the saloon. The room was crowded and alive with a medley of raised voices. Almost everyone held a glass.

'Jamie!' A tall broad-shouldered man with the kind of astounding good looks one normally associated with sportsmen, was striding towards them, shouldering aside groups of guests who were in his way.

'Jamie,' he repeated as he drew level, 'you made it, I was beginning to think you weren't going to.'

'Wouldn't miss a bout of your hospitality for the world, Peter, you know that. And in any case I wanted to introduce you to Barbara, Barbara Hamlin; this is my work-shy companion, Peter Bradley.'

His teeth flashed as he smiled at her and took her hand between both of his, holding onto it for far too long.

She heard James laugh once, a burst of amusement. As for herself, she took in his immaculate white trousers, shirtsleeves rolled high revealing strong suntanned arms, and she thought this friend of James was almost too good to be true. A steward offered a glass of champagne to each of them, then, out of the blue Peter asked, 'And are you two thinking of living happily ever after?'

'Ah!' James pondered. 'That remains to be seen, time will tell. This is damn fine champagne – drink up Barbara, Peter can well afford it!'

Barbara shot a glance towards James, he winked and she laughed.

'I get the message,' Peter said, flickering his eyes to take in the two of them. 'Taboo subject at the moment, is it? Well, my topper and morning suit are available when you decide to tie the knot. Meanwhile, enjoy yourselves, only just make sure you're both sober enough to watch me row to victory tomorrow.'

Enjoy themselves they did. Much more than Barbara would have thought possible. To dance with James was like moving in a dream. His arms about her, his footsteps light, she was happier tonight than she had ever thought she would be again.

James was unsure of himself. He stood very close to Barbara as they leaned against the rail and looked out over the water. To date he had never found anyone who met his criterion of an ideal wife: that was the only reason he had never married. He hadn't led a celibate life. He'd enjoyed several affairs, which had been accepted by both parties as temporary and without obligation. That was not what he wanted now. He wanted Barbara. Something in the past had frightened her, he would give a lot to know the details. She was like a young fawn, go too close and she would cringe away. He would have to tread very carefully.

An inky blackness had settled over the river, but on either bank small boats and large yachts bobbed at their moorings. Threads of light from the portholes wove a pattern of ribbons in the fast flowing water.

'Fascinating, isn't it?' James asked as he slid his arm around her waist.

'Yes,' she murmured. 'Absolutely beautiful.'

'Time we made tracks,' he whispered. 'Should be a good day tomorrow.'

Barbara felt sure that it would be.

James stowed the oars, letting the boat dance of its own will. There was something different about him today and it disturbed Barbara. The weekend had been glorious, brilliant sunshine, blue skies and wonderful company. The weather had been ideal for the Regatta. The chief races had drawn the crowds and the Ferguson family had had the advantage of being able to watch from their upstairs balcony which looked directly down onto the river.

The loudest cheers, in Barbara's opinion, had been for the Ladies Challenge Cup. The fashions displayed by the young women and men alike had amused her and at the same time fascinated her. Everywhere there had been bright colours. With the dreary War years not so far behind, it had made an unusual, and sometimes comical, spectacular show.

The boat bobbed. James leaned forward in his seat and took hold of Barbara's hand. A funny look came to James's

231

face. Barbara thought he looked as if something had upset him. 'Barbara, have you been happy being here with my family?'

She knew that if she were to answer her voice would come out very strange. There was a pain in her throat and her eyes were stinging like mad. She didn't want to cry. She was too happy for that, but how could she convey that to James?

For a while James didn't say anything. Then he began to talk in that way he had which was so gentle, as if he were almost talking to himself and not expecting any answers. 'I realise I know very little of what happened to you. This much I do know, if I could erase those bad memories, which seem to haunt you, from your mind I would. For what seems to me a very long time I have loved you. You don't have to say anything, I've seen you on the edge of tears whenever anyone speaks kindly to you. If you should ever, at any time, feel you are able to talk to me I want you to know that I will always be there. You don't have to tell me that your first marriage was a nightmare, that much I've worked out for myself. You've had more trouble than most. More than your fair share. It's about time there was a little happiness in your life. I hope I can be the one to help you find it.'

It was too much. Suddenly she was crying like a child, sobbing, her breath coming in gasps. James was so kind. So good. She didn't deserve him, she could never bring herself to tell him that she had given up her own son for adoption. Could she?

In a little while she felt a handkerchief being thrust into her hand. She wiped her nose and eyes, and looked up. 'If I could talk to anyone it would be you.'

James didn't answer right away. Instead, he took the oars and the boat sprang ahead. They had to bow their heads under a low sweep of willows, and in this hidden cool dark place at the water's edge he put the oars down again. The boat gently rocked.

Suddenly Barbara began to speak and in seconds the words came rushing out, 'James, if there is to be any chance for us you should know the truth. I don't know any other way to tell you but like this. I was pregnant. Michael abused me and stood by watching while his mate raped me.

'It was the end. I couldn't take any more aggression. I left him. I was in a home for unmarried mothers and women with problems until the birth. I never saw the baby, I couldn't bring myself to look at him. I only know it was a boy because I heard a nurse say so.' Never once had she raised her eyes to look at him, and her words were spoken so softly James had to strain to hear them.

Minutes ticked by as James watched her struggle to speak further. Tears burnt at the back of his eyes but he knew he had to stay still, say nothing, until Barbara had finished.

With what seemed a great effort, Barbara took a deep breath and began to talk again. 'At the time I thought any life would be better than the one I could give him. I thought I would never be able to love him, every time I looked at him I would have been reminded of his father. I couldn't stand the thought of what that would do to a small child. I signed adoption papers.'

There! She had done what she had sworn she never would. She had told someone. But James wasn't just someone. Would he understand? Or would he now despise her? Loathe the sight of her?

She covered her face with her hands. Unable to look at

James. There were no tears now, she doubted that there were any left inside of her. She gave a long shudder and then sat perfectly still.

'Oh, Barbara!' His voice was so sad it tore at her heart-strings. 'You went through all of that on your own! You've never told a soul?'

She shook her head without looking up.

There was a long silence until he leant forward, putting his face on a level with hers. 'Barbara, you have to come to terms with the fact that you made the right decision. At the time no other choice was open to you. You are the one that was sinned against. If you don't believe that, you'll drive yourself crazy.'

'I suppose you think I should have told you before now?' Now Barbara was thinking out loud, 'I wouldn't blame you if you decided to have nothing more to do with me.'

Beyond the screen of foliage a motorboat shot by, rocking the quiet water. Still neither of them spoke. James was searching his mind for the right words to use to break the silence and to tell Barbara he loved her to such lengths that at that moment he would gladly kill for her. The bastard! What if her father had known this! It was better that he didn't!

'Barbara, I want to say just one thing and I want you to remember that it is the truth. Will you do that, no matter what?'

She nodded.

James still had tears in his eyes as he said, 'I love you, Barbara and I always will.'

Minutes passed, then James bent to the oars and began to row, parting the green-coloured curtain of leaves. They came out into the sunlight that still sparkled on the water.

The boat drew up at the dock with a soft bump and James stepped ashore and tied the rope. They walked hand-in-hand across the lawn towards the house.

'You will remember what I said, Barbara? I mean it. From now on I shall devote my life to making you happy and perhaps one day you will feel able to put the past behind you.'

They had reached the house. Barbara forced herself to smile. James straightened up, and with one hand resting on Barbara's shoulder, they walked towards where the family were sitting.

Chapter Fourteen

IT WAS FOUR o'clock on a Tuesday afternoon in the first week of August, hot and sticky, the pavements burning the bottom of their feet through the soles of their shoes.

'I think we must have been in and out of every shop in the West End,' Penny sighed. 'Please, girls, let's call it a day and find somewhere to park our behinds before I fall to the ground in a dead faint.'

Elizabeth looked at Barbara, and they both laughed. 'Aren't you the cheeky one?' Elizabeth complained. 'Barbara and I were for stopping for lunch hours ago, but no, you had to try on one more outfit and then one more pair of shoes and now you're the one that's moaning about being dead beat.'

'Okay, it's too damned hot to argue. Here – grab some of these bags, stay where you are and I'll try and flag down a taxi for us.'

Elizabeth and Barbara had no option but to stay put. Despite the hot weather the pavements around Regent Street were thronged with shoppers and now the pair of them were surrounded by parcels.

'I've told the driver we're going to The Wayfarers, is that all right?' Penny asked as she picked up some of their purchases and herded them to the waiting taxi.

'I wouldn't care if it was Joe's café, as long as they serve long cold drinks,' Barbara muttered as she sank back gratefully into the cushioned seat.

The coolness of the restaurant and the camaraderie of the ladies in their summer-suits and dresses was infinitely preferable to tramping through any more stores. A plump, amiable waitress in her forties led them to a long table set in the recess of a bay window. 'Salads?' queried Elizabeth.

'Yes,' they all agreed. 'And long, cold fruit juices with loads of ice, please.'

'Are you sure you're all right, Elizabeth?' Penny asked, suddenly showing concern.

'Of course I am. Being pregnant isn't an illness, though I will admit this hot weather does tend to sap my energy.'

'Well, I haven't noticed you dropping behind,' Barbara said kindly.

'No, and I think I've spent an absolute fortune, nearly as much as Penny has.'

'Why pick on me,' Penny laughed loudly. 'Neither of you needed any encouragement to spend. Anyway, how long since the three of us had such a binge?'

'Elizabeth certainly looks well, doesn't she, Penny?' Barbara asked as she smiled at her friend.

'She most certainly does. Be quite the little mother with a brood of three, bet you are hoping for a girl this time?'

'I am, but Tim wouldn't mind another boy, I just hope he hasn't any ideas of forming his own rugby club.'

They all three giggled. It was true: pregnancy did suit Elizabeth. She was blooming, her freckled face was faintly tanned by the recent good weather but pregnancy had also given her skin a fine glow of health.

'What about you two?' Elizabeth asked briskly. 'Leaving it a bit late to start a family, aren't you? No sound of wedding bells in either direction from what I can make out, lost all those feminine wiles in your old age?'

They were prevented from answering by their waitress, who, having cleared away their plates, was now setting glass bowls filled with fresh fruit salad and topped with thick clotted cream in front of each of them.

'Umm, lovely,' they chorused.

Some minutes passed before Barbara took up the conversation again, but not before she had heaved a great sigh, 'You're right, Elizabeth. I hear what you say and I'm scared.

'Be fair Penny,' she said, turning her gaze towards Penny, 'we lead a useless frivolous life. To be honest, when do we ever give a thought to anyone but ourselves? I don't know about you, but I feel I'm getting older and parties and dinners are becoming less important. The day will come when I'll be regarded as a maiden aunt. I'll be trailing around looking for a good time, a headache to any hostess who will be hard pushed to find an escort for me.'

Penny was staring at her in disbelief. Then she put down her dessertspoon, threw back her head, and burst out laughing, 'Oh, for God's sake, Barbara, don't paint such a depressing picture, you'll have yourself believing you're edging onto fifty instead of thirty. And what's all this nonsense about nobody wanting you? James is crazy about you – if only you'd open your eyes! So you've been married once and it didn't work out. Stop being such a coward and be grateful that you are being offered a second chance. James is a good man and anyone a mile off can see he's in love with you, willing to give up his freedom. He's told you he's not interested in having an affair – he wants marriage and it's you he wants as his wife. What more do you want, men don't come with a guarantee.'

Elizabeth put out a hand to console Barbara. 'Penny means well,' she assured her.

Barbara took a deep breath. 'I'll admit all you say is true. I think James *is* in love with me, but I wish he would be more cautious. How can I know that it would work out any better this time? I think maybe I do love James, but is that because of the security he can offer me? As a companion he's marvellous and, to be truthful, I'm afraid of loneliness.'

'There are worse reasons for getting married than being good comrades,' Elizabeth said gently, directing her words at both of her companions. 'A husband still has to be a good friend'

'Right!' Penny exclaimed. 'Since we have to dispel all this gloom and doom that had settled on us, I may as well drop my bombshell and then we'll order a pot of tea. I've a feeling you two are going to need it,' she ended on a laugh.

Barbara and Elizabeth exchanged amused glances but stayed silent.

'I'm going to marry Neil Chapman!'

'What!' Both girls doubted they had heard right.

Elizabeth was the first to recover, 'Penny, is this some kind of a joke? You've always referred to Neil as a wet blanket.'

'You're so offhand with him,' Barbara murmured. 'Sometimes I've even felt sorry for the man.'

'I know, but that was then, now I've learnt to sort the wheat from the chaff. As you so rightly said, Barbara, age is creeping up and I suppose you could say I've gained experience and with it has come this terrible kind of wisdom. I want you both to know that Neil loves me. And God help me, I find I love him.'

'Heavens!' Barbara marvelled. 'This is not the Penny we

all love and fear.' While she silently rejoiced that at long last her friend was going to settle down, she also wondered why she had not seen the signs. Neil was a good man. He did not have the height and breadth she herself liked in a man, but he was handsome in a way, with his sandy hair, blue eyes and clear skin. And his speaking voice was so attractive. Thinking back Neil and Penny had been practically inseparable for months now. Unexpectedly Barbara began to chuckle, Elizabeth couldn't help herself either and soon they were both laughing fit to bust.

'Oh, blow the pair of you, I knew you wouldn't take my news seriously. Is it so hard to believe Neil knows all about me and still wants me for his wife? Warts an' all.'

Barbara wiped at her eyes, conscience-stricken, 'Of course not Penny. Oh please don't be mad, I'm happy for you, really I am, it's smashing news – it's just that you've hoodwinked everyone, most especially me.'

'By gosh, some bombshell!' Elizabeth exclaimed. 'There's me rattling on about you two becoming old maids and all the time each of you have charming eligible men tucked away. I can see it's true, Penny; you do love him and, thinking back, Neil has adored you for years. It's not just puppy love with you two is it?'

Penny looked at her with some surprise. 'For an old married woman you're a lot wiser than you ever let on, aren't you?' She drew herself upright in her chair, 'Come on let's order that tea, I don't know why I allow you two to be so much trouble to me.'

They linked arms, their faces wreathed in smiles. 'Here's to births, engagements, marriages, friendships and a happy future for us all,' Penny said quietly.

'We'll settle for that.'

'Yes, one hundred per cent.' Barbara and Elizabeth responded.

Chapter Fifteen

IN EARLY OCTOBER Barbara gave in to James's urging and agreed to join him at his father's holiday cottage in the Lake District for a few days. It was not high season, there would not be crowds of holiday-makers about, but even so the weather was delightful, promising an Indian summer.

The house was quite small, set into a hillside, approached only by a narrow track just wide enough for one car to negotiate.

As Barbara stepped from the car, she stretched her arms above her head and gazed at her surroundings. The garden gave a sweeping view of the countryside. Autumn, she decided, was lovely.

The interior of the cottage was divided into two. The front door opened into a large room that held two lounge chairs, two high-backed wooden chairs, a settee which folded down to serve as a double bed, a pine-wood topped table for eating at and a small desk set back against the wall. The main attraction was the open fireplace, flanked by a stone surround and wide hearth. To the rear, a section had been made into a kitchen. Upstairs there was one large bedroom with a double bed and its own washbasin. Next door a tiled bathroom with a shower unit fixed to the wall and a lavatory with a wooden seat.

They had stopped for lunch, breaking the journey, and it was still too early to start to think about dinner. With the cases brought in from the car, James said, 'You know what I'd like to do? Have a swim.'

Half an hour later she and James walked from the house across the lawn to the swimming pool. 'I much prefer the sea,' James told her, 'to walk beside it or to romp in the waves. Still, Father is rather proud of owning his own pool.'

In swimming trunks, James looked like a young lad. His shoulders were broad, his waist slim, his stomach firm and flat. She thought how fit he looked. 'Come on!' he yelled as he made ready to dive. 'Let's see how cold the water is.'

It was very cold but exhilarating. Barbara came up for air and with swift strong strokes made for the side, pulled herself up and out, grabbed for a towel which she quickly wrapped around herself and then pushed her arms into the sleeves of a white towelling robe, one of many that had been stored in the cupboard under the stairs. The air was different, she could smell the faint dampness from the trees and grass and hear horses neighing in a nearby field. Oh, she was going to like it here.

James stood up, laughed and waved to her. 'Had enough?' he called.

'Yes, I'm shivering.'

Within minutes they were racing across the grass. Wood sticks, rolled newspapers and logs were set ready in the iron fire-basket. One match set the flames crackling and soon the room was glowing and warm.

Barbara appreciated James's attention whilst they were having dinner, which she had cooked using the provisions her mother had thoughtfully packed and insisted that she bring with her. He praised every dish she set on the table, though Barbara suspected that he was playing the gentleman. A role he played to perfection.

After dinner, James suggested that they go for a walk. 'But pull a heavy jersey on,' he instructed. 'It can get very cold up here at night.'

They walked hand-in-hand in comfortable silence. She never felt out of place with James, nor forced to make conversation. Suddenly her mind went back and she wondered had she ever really relaxed with Michael? Stop it! she immediately scolded herself. That was all a long time ago.

The light began to fade, the sky darkened and soon the stars would be out.

'Barbara, I don't want you to give me an answer yet, I don't expect one,' James said softly, 'but you must know how I feel about you. I'm in love with you, have loved your dearly almost from the moment we met. Will you marry me? Please?'

She stopped dead, her heart pounding.

'James, I – I don't know . . .'

'Take your time, my love. I've told you I don't need an answer now, just your promise that you will think about it.'

Think about it! She had thought about nothing else for weeks. The prospect of life without James was fearful. And yet the prospect of living with him . . . could she? She floundered.

'James,' she uttered his name and it came out on a sob. 'I keep telling myself that life with you would be wonderful, it would be different. Yet there is this awful unreasonable conflict that goes on in my head. Yes, I want to be with you, all the time, but I can't seem to blot out the memory of how wrong it was with Michael, no matter how hard I try. I still have nightmares, all the abuse, the terror, it still looms up vividly sometimes. It wouldn't be fair to you.'

'Nonsense.'

'Is it?' she quietly asked.

'Barbara, the past has gone. I have to find some way of proving to you that there is no life for me without you. The one thing I long for is for you to say that you'll be my wife. For the moment there is no problem, I shan't rush you. It has to be your decision. The best thing I can promise you is that I shall go on loving you and each day I shall not only tell you so, but do my utmost to prove it to you. All right?'

She gazed at him, tears welling in her eyes. How kind and gentle James could be — despite his sophistication, his powerful position with the law firm of Bradley and Summerford. Tonight he seemed like a boy, a boy that was truly in love, earnest in every word he said.

When he lifted her face to kiss her, she prayed. Should she take this second chance? If only it were possible.

That night James slept downstairs on the bed-settee. He made no effort to come into the double room which she was occupying. Barbara told herself that she was relieved: James was a gentleman, he was giving her time to think. But she was more disappointed than she would have cared to admit.

But did she want to have sex with James? With any man? Wouldn't sleeping with James bring back all the terror and humiliation of the night when Michael and Pete Davis had forcibly raped her. Then again, maybe, just maybe, making love with someone as loving as James would wipe out forever that horrific memory. If only she could be sure.

Each day was more wonderful than the previous one. The weather continued to be kind to them. They hired bicycles and toured the pretty village of Coniston, with its white-washed cottages sheltering in the shadow of the mountains, had a cream tea in Grasmere, took a steamer cruise on Lake Windermere, had dinner at Bowness in a restaurant that looked out across the lake. The fact that the trees and shrubs grew right down to the edge of the lakes, their autumn colours rich and glowing, where the calm water gently lapped against the dark earth, held Barbara spell-bound. She caught her breath at the beauty of it all and felt so happy and contented. At peace with the world. These days had meant such a great deal to her.

Friday dawned bleak and chilly. 'Let's go walking before it rains,' James suggested as they cleared their breakfast things from the table. 'You'll need a scarf around your head because the wind seems pretty fierce.'

The view was obscured today by a curtain of mist, which swirled around the hilltops. Every now and then a listless sun did its best to shine before sliding back behind the clouds. The wind tore at Barbara's scarf. It drowned their voices so that they had to shout at one another to be heard, and so they walked on without speaking. They passed no one and there was no one in sight. A few birds left the shelter of the trees and took flight as they approached. At the edge of the lake ducks quacked and squabbled for the bread that Barbara crumbled and threw to them. The water wasn't calm today.

'Let's go back,' James shouted. 'The house should have warmed up by now.'

Back at the cottage James threw more logs onto the fire and they rubbed their hands in the welcome warmth. In a few minutes the extra logs had caught, flames spread, fluttering, the bark crackling. Barbara watched while James, on his knees, fanned and used the poker.

'You're really quite domesticated,' she said slowly. 'I feel as if I never really knew you until we came here.'

James rose from his knees and straightened up. 'This place has done us both good. Do you feel better for the break?'

So much better than he would ever know, but she was too embarrassed to put her feelings into words. 'Yes, oh yes,' she said hurriedly. 'I'll see about making us some coffee.' She moved towards the kitchen.

He waved her back. 'No, you take that jersey off and stretch out in front of the fire.'

When James came back with the coffee things on the tray they both sat down on the rug in front of the fire. Barbara poured the coffee and as she handed a cup to James their fingers touched. She felt a stirring, a tenseness. They glanced at each other and then quickly looked away. It felt as if this was the first time they had ever been alone together. She was puzzled and thrilled at the same time. Her eyes filled with tears and she turned her head away. But he had seen.

James stroked her hair. 'You've suffered too much. You were too young.' Lifting her face, he kissed away a few tears on her eyelashes, kissed her cheeks, until finally his lips found her mouth.

It was tender, soft and gentle. He clasped her closer and her doubts were swept away. For a while they lay back in the firelight, she quite content to have his arms hold her, while he revelled in the fact that she no longer seemed afraid of him. What happened then seemed so natural. She

247

was not aware of anything at all but that James was making love to her. Pure sweet unselfish love. .

A long time later came a deep calm while his arms were still holding her close. Perhaps, Barbara thought as they lay quietly side by side, perhaps there is more hope for James and me to have a happy marriage than I'd ever have believed possible.

'We are going to be very happy together, you and I, Barbara. Do you believe that now?' James asked, anxiously scanning her face.

She swallowed deeply before answering. She wouldn't be able to lie to James, he was sharp, neither would she get away with trying to hide anything from him. 'I'm still trying to convince myself that I haven't imagined it. Can love between two people really be that good?'

He laughed. 'If they each have love, one for the other, then the answer is yes. Always!'

The sight of his triumphant pleasure brought a smile to Barbara's lips, and then a laugh. It was a laugh such as she had not brought forth for months. She would try her damnedest to put all the sorrow of the past behind her. Even when this holiday was over and gone she wouldn't allow thoughts of Michael to surge again; she would remember this cottage, this hour and the tender yet passionate way that James had showed her how fantastic lovemaking could really be, for the rest of her days.

As if he were able to read her mind, James said, 'I knew it would be like that between you and me. It is the most wondrous thing two people in love can do.'

Later, when they were dressed, they came back to the fire. The logs were burning down, and the afternoon outside was darkening.

248

'I'll start the car up and we'll go out for dinner,' he said. 'But first will you tell me something? If it can be like this when you and I are together for the first time, how can you still have doubts as to whether you would be happy with me?'

Barbara considered and answered slowly. 'How do we know it would last? Maybe you would stop loving me.'

'Oh Barbara! What do I have to do to convince you? I know I said earlier in the week that there was no hurry and that I wouldn't press you for an answer but . . . please, Barbara, marry me.'

She shook her head. 'I still can't be sure, perhaps – '

He interrupted, 'You can't blame yourself forever for what happened in the past. As to your baby, you have to forgive yourself even for that. It was the right decision at the time. It's over. Gone. You can't live for a hope that is never going to come true.'

Barbara gave a cry. It was a sobbing sound from deep inside.

'You think I've been brutal, that I should never have mentioned the baby. Don't you see, my darling, he's not dead, he has other parents now – two, a mother and a father, you can be sure of that. And sure that they love him. People don't adopt babies unless they are longing to have a child, a child they can love and take care of. You did me the honour of confiding in me, therefore it is not a taboo subject between us, it never will be. We can be happy for him, talk openly about him, remember him with love. Between us it is not a secret and as to other folk, they just don't matter. You trusted me when you told me what had happened, it made no difference as to how I felt about you. Please, trust me now.'

Barbara sighed. It was still a sorrowful sound. 'You are a good man, James, just give me a little more time.'

James stood up, he gave her his hands to pull her to her feet. 'All right, my darling, sufficient unto the day, and today you have been mine, I can afford to be patient.'

Barbara began to weep. James pulled her close and stood there holding her, very gently and without saying a word. When Barbara made to break away James only held her closer against his strong body, her head tucked beneath his chin.

'I meant this to happen, though you never did,' he admitted.

'I dare say I'll survive.' She was doing her best to sound flippant.

'No, we'll survive *together*, Barbara. I had to prove to you that making love with the person you are in love with can and will be a marvellous thing. You no longer need to be frightened. No more doubts, eh?'

Foolishly all she could think of to say was, 'We'll see.'

James still held her tightly and she knew he was smiling. 'We shall indeed, my love.'

Chapter Sixteen

THE BANNS HAD been called for Penny and Neil and the wedding fixed for the first Saturday in December, to take place in Alfriston. Besides all the relatives, it seemed almost everyone in the village would attend. Penny's mother had made three cakes of different sizes and Barbara's mother had been roped in to ice and decorate each tier. After the ceremony there would be a sit-down dinner in The Smuggler's Inn for the main guests and in the evening a buffet set up with a dance band to play in the village hall, to which everyone would be invited.

It seemed to Barbara that everything in Alfriston revolved around plans for Penny's wedding. No one seemed to talk of anything else.

Boys had been selected to sing in the choir, the vicar had agreed to the request that the bells should be rung.

Elizabeth declined the offer to be matron of honour, merely because her pregnancy was showing, and Barbara shuddered at the thought of being a bridesmaid. Neil had no relatives other than two aunts and his elderly mother and father, so in the end Penny asked James's sister Chloe if she would be a bridesmaid and settled on having Elizabeth's twin boys, William and John, as pageboys.

After three days of torrential rain the wedding day dawned bright and clear, the sky deep-blue and cloudless. Barbara was woken early by her father. 'I've brought you a

251

cup of tea,' he said and Barbara squinted as he pulled open the curtains.

'Thank God, it's stopped raining,' she muttered.

'Amen to that,' her father replied. 'But it is still very cold. Tim and the boys went out about an hour ago, I think Tim was afraid that they would have the whole house in a turmoil if he didn't keep them occupied. Your mother has just gone in to wake Elizabeth. You know, love, she is so pleased to have Elizabeth and Tim staying here.'

'I know she is, Daddy, and it's so much better for Elizabeth. Are you going to fetch her father here or take him straight to the church?'

'I'm off to pick him up now. He always seems happy enough to be in that residential home – suppose it was the best thing when his wife died – but he must look forward to having a break, see fresh faces.' He was about to add that it was a pity that Mr and Mrs Warren had only had the one child, Elizabeth, but he caught his breath and checked himself. He and Patricia had had three children, and now because of the War they only had Barbara. Thank God for her.

He himself was the third generation of Hamlins to practise law. There would not now be a fourth. Who knew what fate had in store for anyone? He sometimes thought when he looked at his wife, whom he loved even more with the passing of time, that if God were good he would take couples together, not leave one partner to flounder along on their own after a lifetime of loving companionship.

'Penny for them, Daddy,' Barbara said as she replaced her cup and saucer down on her bedside table.

Phillip shook his head. 'Just dreaming, pet. Weddings

have a way of making us look back. Anyway, time I was off and you got yourself moving.'

By eleven-thirty everyone in the Hamlin household was ready. Tim had gone some time ago, for he was to be one of the ushers and was also picking his parents up from the hotel where they were staying, having travelled down from Yorkshire. Elizabeth had confided to Barbara that the only reason Tim's parents had accepted the invitation was the fact that their grandsons had been chosen to be pageboys. And who could blame them?

'Are you sure being a pageboy is important?' William asked.

'Really and truly,' Elizabeth promised.

'Auntie Penny told us it was' John said solemnly.

Barbara felt a lump rise up in her throat at the sight of the twins. She had vowed she wouldn't get upset today but it was going to be hard. The boys looked a picture. Dark-blue velvet suits, white shirts with ruffles at the neck and cuffs. Elizabeth had brushed their fine golden hair, which fell over their foreheads, until it shone. It was coming up to their fifth birthday. They were ten weeks younger than the son who was lost to her because she had let him go on the day he had been born. Michael had wronged her and she had wronged her baby. Oh, but it had been right to agree to that, she assured herself, at the same time offering up the prayer that she did so often: 'Please let his adoptive parents love him.'

Was there ever a more beautiful setting for a wedding than that of the parish church of St Andrew, Alfriston? Set alone on a huge grassy circular mound at the far side of a green field, which boasted huge leafy trees, and numerous wooden seats mostly set in the shade. A typical peaceful village scene. The church was surrounded by a splendid, low, flint stone wall, behind which lay the carefully tended family graves of local residents, watched over by the single spire of the church which rose high towards the sky. Inside, the winter sun shone through the stained glass windows, the eight wooden pews each side of the aisle were full, the small Lady chapel to the right of the high altar also had every seat occupied.

Penny looked radiant in her wedding gown. How different, so handsome, Neil looked in his cut-away jacket, pearl-grey waistcoat and dark trousers.

James reached for Barbara's hand as they listened to their friends take their vows. The vicar was pronouncing them man and wife when Barbara glanced up at Penny and Neil there at the chancel steps. Neil's eyes were on Penny, his gaze held hers, and it was as if they were the only two people in the whole world. Then Penny took Neil's arm, and he and his bride began to move towards the vestry.

Barbara sunk to her knees. They had some time to wait until the bridal pair would reappear and everyone would surge out into the daylight. The truth was, she wanted to pray. She needed to pray. If in the near future she was to become a bride herself, wife to James, then she needed guidance and reassurance. How could she deserve the wonderful happiness that James was offering her when she had made such a mess of her previous marriage? Most of all she prayed that James would often look at her with as much love in his eyes as Neil had when he looked at Penny.

The taking of the photographs, the kisses and the hugs, the good wishes and congratulations, the wedding breakfast and the speeches were all over. The evening festivities could begin. The scene in the village hall was superb. Children, including William and John, were running around like it was a school playground. 'Leave them be,' Mrs Rayford beamed at Elizabeth. 'Childish high spirits – nothing more. Everything went well, don't you think?'

'Oh, yes,' Barbara and Elizabeth both agreed.

'Began to think our Penny was going to play fast and loose forever. Still, she's settled well with Neil. You'll remember this day when your children get married,' she smiled as she nodded towards Elizabeth's bulge. 'Well, I'd better circulate. I'll send the men over with drinks for you.'

'Hi, you two, why are you hiding away in the corner?' Chloe came up on them from behind. For the wedding Chloe had worn an Edwardian-styled cream-coloured dress with a shoulder cloak made from the same blue velvet as that of the pageboy suits. Now she had changed into a slinky pale-blue dress that looked as if she had been poured into it. She looked fantastic, her fair hair swept up into a pile of curls, her cheeks glowing with excitement. At that moment, James, and Tim appeared bringing a tray of beverages.

'Sis, Anthony has been looking for you; we told him the vicar had made off with you to have his wicked way,' her brother told her, a wide grin which spread from one ear to the other on his face.

'Don't be so irreverent,' Chloe scolded her brother. 'I'll go and find Anthony and bring him back and introduce you to him,' she told the girls, but as she turned away she did a half-turn backwards. 'He's gorgeous, you'll see.'

They all laughed. 'She's well an' truly smitten,' James stated. 'She could do a whole lot worse, though. Tony does happen to be a very nice chap – don't you agree, Tim?'

'Yes I do,' Tim answered without hesitation, 'and from what I hear he does a heck of a good job.'

No one would ever call Anthony Holt good looking, Barbara thought as introductions were made. He was far too serious for that. Three to four inches taller than Chloe, only twenty-nine-years-old and already his light-brown hair was receding, his high forehead shone as if it had been polished and his gold-rimmed glasses added to the dedicated look of the medical profession.

'How d'you do, Mrs Holdsworthy,' he said, smiling at Elizabeth. 'How d'you do, Miss Hamlin.'

'Surely we are not going to be formal?' murmured Barbara, as she took his hand, immediately thinking how soft it was and how long his fingers were. 'I'm going to call you Anthony, so that you may call me Barbara.'

'Anthony and I work in the same hospital,' Chloe added eagerly, by way of explanation.

'Chloe, you work in the dispensary, yes?' Elizabeth queried.

'That's right,' Chloe agreed. 'And Anthony is a paediatrician,' she added, while all the time she gazed lovingly up into his face.

The band struck up and everyone stopped talking and watched as Penny and Neil took to the floor for the first waltz.

Having circled the floor once, other couples joined them. 'May I?' James asked, holding out his arms to Barbara. The lights dimmed, the music was dreamy and Barbara felt she was floating on a cloud as James expertly twirled her across the floor.

All too soon the married couple were saying their goodbyes. Penny, now dressed in a going-away, beige-coloured

costume with coffee-coloured accessories, the very simplicity of which belied the enormous sum she had paid for
it, bent low to embrace Elizabeth, 'Now, make sure you
take care, I'll see you in the New Year.' Having left Barbara
until last, Penny threw her arms around her and whispered
in her ear, 'When I get home I want to hear that you've
said yes to James.'

Barbara felt her cheeks flush and playfully she pushed at
Penny, 'Get on with you, have a good time, I'll miss you.'

Neil, having shaken hands with Anthony and James,
turned his attention to Tim, 'Keep your nose to the grind-
stone, buddy,' he said, punching at Tim's shoulder. 'I don't
want to come back and find my desk loaded with ledgers,
be kind to me, eh?'

Tim threw back his head and laughed loudly, 'That'll be
the day when you tackle more than one set of books at
any one time. Besides, you'll probably need a rest, having
been on your honeymoon.'

Tim and Neil both worked for the same firm of account-
ants, the only difference being that Neil's father owned the
firm — hence the four weeks off to go cruising with his
new wife.

A lull settled over the hall when the bride and groom
finally left and the caterers began to hand out refreshments.

James had steered Barbara into a corner and, with plates
balanced on their knees, he grinned, 'Got you to myself at
last. Keep next weekend free, Barbara, there's a house I
want to take you to see, I'd appreciate your opinion.'

Barbara lifted her head and looked directly at him, 'Are
you telling me you've bought a house?'

'No, no,' he stuttered, his mouth full of smoked salmon,
'I've owned it a long time.'

Elizabeth Waite

'You mean someone died and left it to you?'

'That's exactly it,' he grinned. 'I'm not joking. Two of my mother's maiden aunts lived in it for years. It was left to me by my mother's parents, I shouldn't think any other members of the family would have wanted it.'

Barbara was curious by now and it showed on her face. 'Where is this house – is one allowed to ask?'

'Of course.' He made a mocking bow. 'The other side of Jevington. Not a million miles from here, eh?'

'But I go through Jevington almost every time I go out riding. I don't know any empty properties in the village.'

'Who said it was empty? And I didn't say it was in the village.'

'Oh, now you're teasing me. Tell me about it.'

'It isn't all that grand, you know. Actually the large stables and the three acres of land are its best features. Say you'll come with me next weekend and give it the once over?'

Wild horses weren't going to keep her away, was what she was thinking but what she actually said was, 'I shall be looking forward to it, honestly I shall.'

Later as Barbara undressed and made herself ready for bed she decided it had been quite a day, one way and another.

Saturday was dull and cloudy but the weather did nothing to dampen Barbara's spirits. 'I thought we'd have lunch in the Eight-Bells,' James told her as he drove away from Alfriston. 'You look marvellous. You know that don't you? That silly hat becomes you.'

'I still like to hear you say that I do, and my hat is not in the least bit silly.'

It was true she had taken a heck of a long time to decide

258

what she would wear today, but she was pleased with the finished result. A dark-brown wool dress topped with a heavy camel coat; the cloche hat made gay by the small feather that was stuck in the band, covered her ears and would be warm; a stout pair of shoes in case they had to go tramping across fields, she looked quite the countryfied lady.

James was lucky to find a parking space in the small car park. The bar was inviting, warm and cosy with great logs burning in the open fireplace, giving off that wonderful smoky smell of winter. Having taken Barbara's coat and settled her at a round table just big enough for two, he asked, 'What'll it be?'

Without any hesitation she replied, 'A whisky-mac and a ploughman's, please.'

They chattered as they ate, James laughing to himself at the enthusiasm Barbara was showing for this outing and he only hoped she wouldn't be terribly disappointed.

It still was not one o'clock when they came out from the Eight-bells. James had meant for them to have an early lunch so as to give them the benefit of the daylight. It got dark so early these December days. About a mile after having left the car park, James took a turning to the left, driving now down a lane that was flanked with gigantic hedges to protect the fields from excessive winds. Further along he swung the car between high wrought-iron gates which were wide open, secured back against the stout flint walls. The drive was long and winding but suddenly Barbara caught a glimpse of a long, low, very old house with a deep-eaved roof and very small windows. She couldn't wait for the car to stop.

259

'It's absolutely charming!' she cried, breaking into a run and heading for the porchway that sheltered the front door.

With quick strides, James caught up with her. 'Hey, steady on,' he ordered as he pushed open the wicker gate and they walked up the weed-covered path. Clematis, which must have looked beautiful when in bloom, still struggled to cling to the porchway.

The oak door opened easily enough to the key James used. The smell of musty damp came to them at once. What a shame, was Barbara's first thought; everything looked so dusty and neglected. The huge inglenook fireplace still held dead ashes from long-forgotten log fires. Barbara ignored the doors that led off from the wide hall and made straight for the staircase.

'There'll be much more of a view from up here,' she called down.

Laughing happily, James took the stairs two at a time.

Barbara was right. From the upstairs bedroom windows, the garden view was breathtaking. A neglected garden, almost a wilderness, lay close to the house and an apple orchard behind, which had also been left to run wild. Beyond, she looked out over rolling fields, sheltered by the high hills of the South Downs. The ceilings in the bedrooms showed damp patches, window frames needed refitting but the deep window-seats were her favourites. The floor boards creaked as they walked and would need replacing, nevertheless by the time they came to the bathroom, Barbara was in love with this house. It was, she felt, like stepping back into a time warp.

'That Victorian bath is something else, don't you agree?' James could hardly contain his mirth as he watched Barbara gaze in wonderment at the size of it.

'Magnificent,' she muttered. 'The weight of it must be colossal, look at those great claw feet.' She turned her attention to the huge washbasin and the toilet with its rusty cistern and wooden seat.

Reading her thoughts, James said, 'There would be an awful lot of work to be done, if I even think of keeping this place.'

'James! You wouldn't part with it, would you?'

'I've given it some thought. My father's advice is to sell.'

Barbara's face fell.

'On the other hand, knowing from the start the work that would be entailed, it could be great fun. We could use local workmen. Replace that rickety staircase for a start, making sure it was fashioned authentically. The reward could be a very nice home.'

'Oh, you tease! You've no intention of parting with this lovely old house, have you?'

'Not if you like it, I haven't; but to be honest you have seen the worst part first. Come on, we'll do a tour of the stables and I'll introduce you to the man that keeps that part of the estate running efficiently and economically. Besides, I'm sure you want to come an' see the horses.'

'Horses? You have horses stabled here?' asked Barbara with the enthusiasm he had expected.

'No, unfortunately. The stables are leased out to owners and trainers, but we do have our own manager, my father was adamant about that. He does a damn fine job too.'

The stables were well away from the house, purpose-built and well maintained. Gallops, sprints and hurdles were set out on fine flat grassland which looked rich and well cared for to Barbara's keen eye.

A wonderful sight met them. Jockeys were bringing in

a stream of horses from a canter that had presumably gone well.

'Afternoon, Mr Ferguson. You're earlier than I expected.'

'Never mind us,' James replied. 'Let me introduce you to my fiancée, then we'll get out of your way. Miss Barbara Hamlin, meet Clement Tompson, known to his friends and acquaintances as Clem, an' to employees as Mr Clem.'

Barbara smiled as he shook her hand. She already liked this man for the way he had greeted each horse in turn before he was aware that either James or herself had arrived. She was also secretly smiling to herself: James had introduced her as his fiancée!

Clem Tompson was a small, compact man, with a ruddy complexion and rather unusual features. A different sort of face that was utterly transformed when he smiled. He wore tweeds, leggings and brogues, a yellow scarf around his neck and a brown corduroy flat cap. He looked what he was: a man that had been around horses for the whole of his life.

'Do you ride, Miss Hamlin?' Clem asked.

'Whenever I can,' she replied.

'We'll always find you a mount, be our pleasure.'

'Miss Hamlin might just take you up on that in the not-too-distant future, Clem, when she's out this way – or better still, she can ride over and let you give her own horse the once over.'

Clem regarded Barbara for a few seconds before he said, 'Miss Barbara, that rings a bell.' Then, slapping his forehead with the palm of his hand, he asked, 'Phillip Hamlin! He is your father, yes?'

Barbara smiled as she nodded.

'Sorry, Miss. Should have made the connection sooner.

262

Had a lot of dealings with Phillip, one way an' another. I went with him, after the War, to look some horses over. We've become great mates over the years.'

'Does your father have horses here?' Barbara asked James.

'No, this is really not our territory. We own the stables and the land, or I suppose *I* do, strictly speaking, but as I told you it is all leased out and we leave it all in the capable hands of Clem here.' He added, 'It's time we were going.'

'Goodbye, Miss, Remember me to your parents and I hope to see you here again soon.' Clem Tomson gave Barbara a smiling nod of farewell, then shook hands with James before he hustled away, his heavy shoes clacking on the flagstones of the yard.

Back in the car James was suddenly very calm, and his voice sounded very intense. 'Barbara, why do we have to wait any longer?'

With restless fingers she twisted at her handkerchief, she could hear cattle lowing in the distance. The silence between them lengthened.

'Well?' James asked a little sharply.

Barbara turned her head away. 'I suppose it's no good pretending, James. I do want to spend the rest of my life with you, but marriage, it still frightens me.'

This time the quiet was fraught with question.

'I thought . . .' she said at last, 'that you would realise what that commitment would mean to me.' She turned her head back, gave a brave smile and looked directly into his eyes.

'Couldn't we just live together . . . for a while . . . kind of see how it works out?'

He was staring sharply at her, Barbara felt her cheeks flush up.

Abruptly he shook his head. 'No! That's *not* what I want. I love you, I want you to be my wife. I want to go to sleep at night with you in my arms and I want to wake up in the morning knowing that I'll find you lying beside me. I want us to have children, a family of our own. Barbara, if you really love me, surely that is what you want too?'

'But what if –'

He stopped her words by reaching for her, hugging her close.

She leaned against him, her hat now lopsided, wisps of hair dangling across her forehead. 'If only we could see into the future,' she sighed.

'Oh Barbara, darling, why won't you trust me? Don't you know by now I would never hurt you?'

The misery of the past, the quarrelling, the awful things Michael had said and done to her, were still imprinted in her mind; yet she knew with sudden awful clearness that should James go out of her life, if she were to lose him now she stood no chance of ever finding real happiness ever again.

She shivered a little, though it wasn't cold in the car. Silently she prayed: This time, dear God, let it be right for both of us. Then she told James that she would marry him.

'Oh, my darling,' she heard him say. 'Oh Barbara!' Slowly he moved, his lips came gently down over hers, then he was whispering, 'I love you, Barbara. I love you *so* much.'

She stayed leaning against him, his arms holding her close, and now she felt blissfully warm. She thought, This is so right. How could she have ever thought that she didn't really want to marry James?

Now it was her turn to tell him how much she loved him, 'Oh James! I can't believe how happy I suddenly feel!

It's like my life has all at once become peaceful, no more fears or doubts, I really do love you.'

'For us life will only get better from now on, you'll see,' he promised her. 'Now, the question is, *when* will you marry me? Please, Barbara, make it soon. I can't wait.'

'Nor I,' she answered. 'I'll marry you as soon as you like.' In each other's arms the minutes ticked away in silence.

In the end it was Barbara who spoke. 'Are we going to go and tell your parents first, or mine?' she asked.

'Neither,' James said. 'We'll tell no one today. Today is just for you and me. Nobody else matters.'

Chapter Seventeen

'MOTHER, I'M GLAD you asked Tim and Elizabeth here for Christmas,' Barbara said. 'It means Mr Warren will be able to be with them on Christmas Day and Boxing Day, whereas I doubt very much that he would have wanted to travel to Windsor. It will be so nice to spend it all together here, in Alfriston, especially having the twins.'

She was trimming the Christmas tree which stood in the bay window of the lounge; it had become her task each year since she had returned home.

'You seem to have a great deal more enthusiasm for Christmas this year,' her mother remarked. 'Are you happier now?'

'Yes Mother, I am. Does it show?'

'Of course it does. It wouldn't have anything to do with James being around, would it?'

Barbara smiled, like a satisfied cat, 'You'll have to wait until tomorrow morning before I give you the answer to that question.'

'Well, I'll not try to guess then.' Her mother turned away in order to hide her knowing smile; she was hoping against hope that James and her daughter were going to announce that they were to be married. Oh, wouldn't that be the perfect gift that she and her husband could receive – to know that after everything that Barbara had suffered she had at last found happiness. James was such a kind man, it would be an ideal match.

Barbara stepped back to view her work. She was really pleased with it. 'And when all the presents are placed around the base this evening it will look even better!' she said. 'We've had all these baubles for years, haven't we, Mother?'

'Most of them. In any case I prefer familiar things, they bring back such happy memories. That one there, the sleigh, and the one of Father Christmas with his sack, your brothers chose them; I remember them taking so long to decide which ones they were going to buy. That was a long time ago now,' her mother said sadly, 'so they're rather precious.'

'I know they are. I'll move them, hang them near the top of the tree so they won't get knocked off by the twins.'

'Hallo, you two. Hard at it, I see.'

They both looked around in surprise. 'Daddy! How nice you are home early,' his daughter greeted him.

Patricia kissed her husband and said, 'I'd better pour you a drink, dinner will be some time yet.'

'Have Elizabeth and Tim arrived yet?' he asked.

'Yes, ages ago. They've taken William and John off to see their grandfather; apparently Gildredge Grange put on some kind of a tea party for the residents to invite their grandchildren to. All the boys wanted to know was whether Father Christmas was going to be there and would they be getting a present from him.'

Phillip threw back his head and laughed. 'What it is to be young! Must say, it will be nice to have the house full for a change and real nice to have the boys around.'

Patricia laid her hand lightly on her husband's shoulder. She knew what was behind his last remark, knew he too was thinking of when they had had two small sons of their own. Sons that they had loved deeply.

'Did James travel down from town with you, Daddy?' Barbara asked, aware of her parents' feelings and wanting to steer the conversation onto happier topics.

'No. James was still tied up with paperwork.'

'Any idea of what time he'll be home?'

'Who knows? The trains will be at sixes and sevens with it being Christmas Eve. But knowing James, he'll ring you before he leaves the office.'

Barbara's smile said it all: James was so thoughtful.

'He'll be tired,' her father said. 'Last week was a blinder for him. Acting for the defence in a fraud case at the Old Bailey is never an easy task.'

'Hmm,' Barbara murmured. 'Will you tell me something, Daddy, does James practise almost exclusively in the criminal courts?'

'No, I wouldn't say exclusively,' he grinned to himself before adding, 'but I would agree that James shows a certain amount of skill when it comes to crime.'

'Really, Phillip!' Patricia protested. 'You make it sound as if law was some kind of a game.'

'Well, put it this way, all the time London has industrious criminals there will always be work for men of James's calibre.'

Before either of them could take this discussion further there was a commotion at the front door.

'That means Elizabeth is back with the boys,' Patricia said. The twins never moved quietly, but wherever they went they brought sunshine with them; as they did now, coming into the lounge on this drab December day. Elizabeth's appearance was also lovely. Very much pregnant, her skin glowing from the cold, her light hair escaping from each side of her felt hat.

'It's freezing out there!' she exclaimed. 'Wouldn't it be wonderful if it snowed for Christmas! Tim won't be back for dinner, he's staying to have a meal with my father.'

'Oh, that is nice. Did you tell your father we are picking him up early in the morning?'

'Yes, I did. And he is very grateful and so am I, Auntie Pat, it really is good of you an' Uncle Phillip to allow us to descend on you like this.'

'Nonsense, we're thrilled to have you here. Will make our holiday,' Phillip assured her.

'We *did* get presents,' William said, including everyone in his statement, 'an' a jolly good tea!'

'True,' John stated. 'But tell Auntie Barbara what we decided.'

'Oh yes, there are too many old people living in that house where Grandad's staying; they ought to invite some younger people as well.'

'I don't suppose you two are offering to go and live there?' she teased.

'No, we've got Mummy and Daddy to look after us,' he protested.

'Yes, of course you have – silly old me,' Barbara said.

'Would you two like to stay up for dinner?' Patricia asked. 'I have asked your mother's permission and she said as it is Christmas Eve you may if you want to.'

'Yes please,' they chorused eagerly.

When they sat down at the long table in the dining room both Barbara's mother and father looked at the laden table and thought how lucky they were. Their daughter looked so different. She had come a long way, hopefully put the past behind her and with James, please God, she would have a happy future.

'Why aren't we having Christmas pudding?' John asked.

'Christmas pudding is for tomorrow,' his mother said.

'Will there be sixpences hidden in it?' William wanted to know.

'You'll have to wait and see,' Aunt Patricia told him patiently.

'Why?'

They were all saved from giving an answer by the ringing of the telephone in the hall.

'I'll answer it,' Barbara said. 'It'll be James.'

She rushed out of the room. Everyone at the table smiled at each other. It seemed ages before they heard the faint click as Barbara replaced the receiver and came back into the room.

'It was James,' she said. 'He's leaving the office now. He wont' be coming here tonight. He said he'll spend the evening with his family, help fill stockings for Harry and Lucy. They're his sister Ann's children,' Barbara explained to Elizabeth. 'Like you she was lucky, had twins. Two babies at one go must be very nice,' she added wistfully.

'He'll be here about eleven in the morning.' It was as if she was floating on a cloud, everything about her shone, she couldn't conceal her happiness.

'May I be excused, please? Time I saw my two sons into bed. It's very late for them,' Elizabeth said, rising from the table.

'Mother, would you mind if I went with Elizabeth?'

'Of course not, darling, you go up with the children,' her mother told her. 'Your father will help me to clear the table.'

270

When Elizabeth and Barbara came downstairs, Tim was back and everyone had moved into the lounge.

'The tree looks splendid!' Tim said. 'You did a good job there, Barbara.'

'Yes, you did,' her father agreed. 'And now we're all going to have a glass of hot toddy.' He handed the glasses around, wondering if he had guessed right and that tomorrow they would be toasting Barbara and James as a happy couple.

It was well after midnight when everyone went to bed.

Patricia was brushing her hair. Phillip came up behind her and looked at her reflection in the mirror.

'I love it when you let your hair down, it's like silk and it always smells so fresh.' He leant over, buried his face in her hair. She turned around and drew his head down to hers, her lips finding his.

'Come to bed,' Phillip said.

After all the years their lovemaking was still satisfying to both of them.

'We've got a lot to still be grateful for,' she murmured later, as he drew her head into the hollow of his shoulder, put his arms around her and they settled down to sleep.

In her bedroom across the hall, their daughter was thinking very much the same thoughts.

When Barbara went downstairs next morning Tim was up and dressed, making tea in the kitchen.

'Hope the boys didn't wake you,' he said. 'They were up before the birds this morning, came bursting into our room like a tornado. Forgot – I haven't wished you a Merry Christmas yet.' He leaned forward and planted a kiss on her cheek. 'Merry Christmas, Barbara; Merry Christmas, Patricia,' he added as Mrs Hamlin came into the kitchen behind Barbara. 'I was about to bring tea in bed for everyone.'

'That was a nice thought, Tim. You take a tray up for your father and Elizabeth, Barbara. Tim and I will have ours down here.'

Upstairs, Barbara knocked then entered her father's room, 'Happy Christmas, Daddy. I've brought you some tea.'

'Happy Christmas, my darling. The boys sound excited.' He raised himself to a sitting position and Barbara planted a kiss on his forehead.

'Yes, I'm about to go in an' see them.'

Elizabeth put out a welcoming hand to Barbara as she entered the room, 'Come an' sit on the bed, love. Have they woken the whole household?'

The two boys had toys spread out all over the floor.

'There was a sugar mouse in the toe of my stocking,' John told Barbara.

'Really?'

'Yes, look,' he said, holding up the white mouse by a length of string that was supposedly its tail.

Not to be outdone, William cried, 'Look at this, Auntie Barbara! A fire engine and the bell does work.' His face was beaming as he pulled the short rope which set the bell clanging.

John wasn't going to lose his aunt's attention that quickly. 'I've got a racing car, its lights flash. They didn't till Daddy put the batteries in. Good job Father Christmas remembered to bring me some batteries, wasn't it?'

272

'Yes, it was very thoughtful of him,' Barbara said, doing her best to keep a straight face.

'Come on now, back to your own room and get washed and dressed,' their mother urged them. 'There'll be a whole lot more presents once breakfast is over.' It was all the encouragement they needed. Both Elizabeth and Barbara were grinning broadly as they watched the pair of them scarper.

Barbara was on edge all through breakfast.

Everyone was thrilled by the presents that were exchanged when the meal was over. Screams of delight turned into shouts as the twins tore the gaily-coloured paper from the frames of their new bicycles.

'Daddy!' Barbara exclaimed with glee as she unpacked new riding boots, but all the time she had one eye on the clock.

She heard the motor and was out in the hall before the wheels had stopped turning. She opened the door, stepped out and ran to meet James. He caught her in his arms.

'Happy Christmas, Barbara.'

'Oh, it will be. Happy Christmas, James.'

Barbara was dressed for the seasonal holiday. She wore a grey silk skirt which flared out at the knees, a soft bolero to match, beneath which she wore a red silk blouse. Two silver chains fastened around her neck added a festive touch.

James thought she had never looked more appealing. He took her face between his hands and kissed her lightly on the lips. When he broke away she was smiling, then her smile turned into a laugh, not a loud laugh but a soft laugh of true contentment.

273

He reached into his pocket and pulled out a small leather box.

'I've waited a long time for this,' he said.

She opened it. She gazed at the ring resting between dark-blue velvet and she gasped, tears welling up in her eyes.

'James, it's so beautiful.'

'Let me put it on.' He lifted the diamond cluster set on a band of platinum and slipped it onto the third finger of her left hand.

Then he tilted her face and really kissed her.

Her mother and father had stood well back from the bay window but they had missed nothing. Silently Phillip held his arms out to his wife, they stood close for several seconds before he whispered to her, 'See, prayers *are* answered.'

'Well, sometimes they are,' she whispered back.

Chapter Eighteen

JANUARY BEGAN MILD and everyone said it would shorten the winter. Come the last week, though, and it was a different story; it blew itself out with a gale which tore branches from the trees and dislodged roof-tiles all over the village. February came in bitterly cold, with dark skies and a warning that snow was on the way.

It was Thursday of the third week in February and only seven-forty-five in the morning when Barbara heard her mother calling her from the hall downstairs.

'Barbara, come down, James is on the telephone.'

Barbara didn't wait to put on her dressing-gown, just pushed her feet into her slippers and, clad only in her nightdress, ran down the stairs.

'James?'

'Yes, darling, sorry to get you up. How do you fancy a trip to Jersey?'

'Very much so, but why call about it now?'

'Because I have to leave for Jersey tonight. Long story! You know I've been in Kingston all week at the Surrey assizes; well the lawyers acting for the Crown have sprung a surprise on us. Offshore investments. I'll explain more fully later. Thing is, if I'm there ready first thing in the morning, I can deal with what I have to and we'll have the whole weekend to ourselves.'

'That's lovely, James. Where do you want me to meet

you? Shall I phone for an hotel reservation? What about flights?'

'No, calm down; I can get all that dealt with by one of the office secretaries, but it would help if you could be at my parents' home say about four? Depends on how the hearing goes today as to what time I get away, should be home by five. I've asked my mother to pack me a bag. There's a flight from Gatwick about eight-forty-five.'

Barbara was beaming. 'Sounds as if you've planned things well. I'll be in Eastbourne when you get there. Oh, there is one thing, the weather forecast last night was not so good; did you hear it?'

'Yes. Forecast snow. All the more reason we should escape to sunny Jersey. Must go. See you this evening. Love you.'

'I love you too.'

Very much, she added to herself as she replaced the receiver.

By the time Barbara had bathed and dressed, Mrs Ferguson was on the telephone. 'James rang me, Barbara. Don't wait till this evening, can you come for lunch? Lovely as this old house is, it seems very lonely when there is no one but me rattling around in it. Everyone is about their own business today. You'd be doing me a kindness.'

'Of course I'll come – love to. I'll be there by one.'

'That will be nice,' her mother exclaimed when Barbara had told her the gist of the conversation. 'Can I help with your packing?'

'Mother, don't start fussing! I'm only going to Eastbourne for lunch and to Jersey for the weekend. I'm not taking a trunk!'

'Don't be so cheeky,' her mother retaliated. But in spite

of herself she couldn't hide her smiles. Oh, it was good to see Barbara so happy. She blessed the day that Phillip had introduced their daughter to James Ferguson.

Home to the Fergusons was a five-storey house in the Meads, one of the highest points in Eastbourne. Almost at the foot of the South Downs, Meads Village was sheltered and yet only a short walk from the seashore. It was also a place unaltered by time. Only a few shops, but shops where courtesy and service was given without question. The village boasted two pubs, The Ship and The Pilot; neither were ordinary public houses but were places where folk met to enjoy conversation, a nice drink in congenial surroundings.

When the houses in Darley Road were built no expense had been spared. High, wide and grand was what sprang to Barbara's mind each time she visited. From the flight of steps leading to the heavy front door, the pillars which supported the porch, the tall bay windows and the long wide hall: everything was huge. Even the wainscoting throughout was at least eighteen inches high and the cost of the curtains in the main rooms didn't bear thinking about.

It was a house built for a family. A family who in years gone by would have employed many servants. It didn't seem to bother the Fergusons, apparently they got by with a couple of cleaning ladies. At get-togethers, when the whole family, including in-laws and children, would turn up, Barbara had been amazed at how smoothly things were planned. Everyone mucked in, children and adults alike, each had their allotted tasks and performed them without any resentment. Above all it was a happy house, and Barbara always looked forward to going there.

It had started to snow as Barbara drove out of Alfriston and by the time she reached Eastbourne it was snowing heavily. She received a very warm welcome from Mrs Ferguson and the two of them enjoyed a most companionable lunch, eaten in the vast, but somehow cosy, basement kitchen.

It was dark by four o'clock, still snowing and Barbara was starting to worry. At a quarter past five Chloe and her father arrived home together.

'Damned hazardous weather, is this,' Mr Ferguson grumbled to his wife as he shook the snow from his overcoat. 'Look at it and I've only walked across the drive from the garage.' Turning, he saw Barbara, 'Hallo my dear, fancy you being out in this weather. Not that I'm not delighted to see you,' he hastened to add.

'Hallo Barbara!' Chloe came into the lounge, rubbing her hands to get some warmth back into them. 'Nice to see you; rotten weather though, bet you'll have to stay here tonight.'

Explanations were left to Mrs Ferguson. 'She's meant to be flying to Jersey with James this evening. They have to be at Gatwick by eight.'

'No sign of James, eh?' Mr Ferguson tut-tutted.

Chloe put a reassuring arm across Barbara's shoulders. 'He'll ring soon, I shouldn't wonder. The roads were very slippery in places. I was driving, it was awful trying to see, wipers couldn't cope. More like a blizzard than a snowfall and trouble is there are patches of ice forming where you least expect them.'

'Stop frightening the girl,' her father rebuked Chloe. He

took hold of Barbara by the elbow and led her to an armchair close to the fire. 'Sit you down my dear, stop worrying. How about some coffee? Know I could do with a cup. Come along, stretch your legs out, James will make it home. Relax.'

'Dinner's ready, move yourselves. I've set it downstairs in the kitchen, it's lovely an' warm down there.' Mrs Ferguson had opened the door to the lounge and popped her head in, disappearing again before they had time to answer.

The scene was certainly cosy. She had pulled the big square table close to the fire and set the four chairs to be facing the range.

Muriel Ferguson was doing her best to hide the fact that she was worried about her son, she had drawn her husband aside and in a low voice asked him, 'Robert, isn't there anyone we can telephone? It isn't like James not to call.'

'If James is on the road there is no way I have to contact him,' he quietly told her. 'Serve the dinner, my dear, and try not to let Barbara see that we are worried.'

Muriel put the food on the table and the four of them sat doing their best to do justice to the meal, hardly speaking, except that once Chloe said, 'I expect James has holed up somewhere, we would have heard – ' but at a look from her father she didn't finish the sentence. Barbara helped Chloe to wash-up while Mrs Ferguson made coffee, which they carried back up to the lounge. Robert Ferguson sat in his armchair with the evening paper, not really reading it. The wind coming from off the sea rattled the windows. This February night was turning out to be a very long one.

It was almost nine o'clock when the doorbell rang. Mr Ferguson rose to answer it. Hearing male voices, the three women were sure it was bad news. It was a few minutes

279

before he returned to the lounge, walking slowly, followed by a policeman who must have removed his overcoat or macintosh in the hall because his uniform was dry.

'There's been . . . I have to tell you,' the young man began. He stopped – obviously he hadn't had much experience with this sort of thing.

Robert Ferguson took over. 'James has been involved in an accident,' he said softly.

Barbara was impatient to know the details: 'Hurry up, tell us if James is badly hurt. Where is he? In which hospital? was what she wanted to yell; instead she remained quiet.

The policeman took a deep breath, 'The roads are really treacherous with icy patches. Seems the car skidded on a curve.'

'You're not telling us he is *dead*?' Muriel, her voice rising to a high pitch, flung the question at the policeman.

'*No!* Sorry – no, nothing as bad as that. In fact, from what I've been told, the ambulance was called by another motorist and they got your son out and away to hospital pretty quickly.'

The sigh of relief hung in the air.

Mr Ferguson took down details and telephone numbers obligingly offered by the constable, and then went to the door with him to see him out.

The three women, now alone, held out a hand to each other. That brought the tears.

'I'm going into my study to make a few calls,' Mr Ferguson told them. 'I'll be as quick as I can an' then I'll come back and let you know exactly what I have been able to find out.' At the doorway he hesitated, half-turned and said to Barbara, 'My dear, I think you should call your parents, tell them what has happened and let them know you'll be stopping here tonight. Use the phone that's down in the kitchen.'

'We'll come with you,' Chloe said, speaking for her mother as well as herself. 'I'll make some tea. Be glad of something to do.'

The telephone lines were fine: You wouldn't know there was a blizzard raging outside, Barbara thought as she listened to her mother say how sorry she was. 'Please, darling, phone us again as soon as you have any news.'

'I will, Mother. For the moment at least James has been taken to Kingston General Hospital. Just pray that the roads are not going to be too bad; anyway, even if we have to come by train, Mr Ferguson has promised to get us there as soon as he can. Goodnight, Mummy. Say goodnight to Daddy for me. God bless you.'

'Don't hang up for a minute, Barbara.' Her mother's voice sounded tense. 'Tim rang soon after you left this morning: Elizabeth has had her baby, a little girl, six pounds six ounces, born in the early hours of this morning.'

'Is she all right?'

'Yes. Tim is over the moon. Said mother an' baby are both doing well.'

'Thank God for that.'

Barbara couldn't help herself: as she turned to tell Chloe and Mrs Ferguson about Elizabeth she was feeling downright envious.

Why did everything go so right for some in this life and so terribly wrong for others?

In the past three weeks everything that could be done for James had been done. He had been taken from Kingston

Hospital to the London Clinic and put into the care of Mr Brooks, a Harley Street specialist. James's family had shown Barbara nothing but kindness, but somehow she often felt shut out. All decisions and information came to her second-hand through his father. Only right, she would tell herself: she wasn't James's wife. James had undergone surgery for a broken pelvis, that much was certain, but there was so much more that she hadn't been told. For one thing – why was James unconscious for such long periods and why did he seem to be in constant pain?

Dry-eyed, Barbara had kept a watch by him through long lonely days, taking her turn with his family. Most times he drifted in the half-world of delirium. As she listened to his all but unintelligible mutterings, the one name she did hear over and over again was her own.

Today she had cause to be joyful: James was awake and clear-headed.

As she entered his room he tried in vain to raise his head from the pillow. His kind gentle eyes and her own tear-filled ones met, then his own brand of humour saved the moment, 'Tied me down good an' proper, have you darling?'

She took his hand between her own. 'Yes,' she said, simply. 'You, my love, will have great difficulty in ever getting away from me again.'

She kissed his forehead, his cheeks and then his lips and was thrilled to see the wide smile which came to his face before he once more drifted off to sleep.

She hoped against hope the worst was over. Those awful days she had lived through asking time and time again, dear Jesus, how bad is he? Is he going to die? Then quickly rebuking herself: Don't think of that. Don't even think it. Instead she would try her best to think of Henley, a boat on the river, James telling her to let go of the past and love him, of riding their horses across the Downs, of their stay in the Lake District and their wonderful lovemaking.

She would go and get some exercise while James slept.

It was still bitterly cold. The snow hadn't really cleared, it lay in dirty piles of slush along the kerbstones and gutters. A cold wetness touched her cheek, and then another. In the glow of the embankment lights, small white flakes drifted down. More snow? The tow-path was dry, but already the white flakes were drifting into layers along the wall. Flakes fastened onto her eyelashes as she walked. Others landed on her uncovered head, making her hair wet. She had walked a lot further than she had intended.

A taxi appeared and she hailed it, and soon she was back in the warmth of the hospital.

With some relief she found no medical staff in James's room, but Barbara had barely removed her coat, thinking how lovely and warm it was in here, before a nurse entered bringing coffee with her. 'I saw you come back, Miss Hamlin. You must be frozen, I knew you'd be ready for a hot drink.

'Mr Brooks left a message for you, would you go along to his office before you leave?'

Barbara smiled her thanks. The coffee was delicious, unexpectedly so.

The summons to the specialist's office had her worried. Her pulse began to race as she heard him bid her come in in answer to her knock.

'Ah, Miss Hamlin,' Mr Brooks rose from behind his desk

as she slowly walked across the carpet. He was a large, broad-shouldered man, immaculate in his dark suit and white shirt.

'Come and sit down. Mr Ferguson senior has asked me to have this little chat with you. Only fair in the circumstances. I understand you and James are engaged to be married?'

Barbara felt he was an instantly likeable man with a relaxed, comfortable manner, but who nevertheless looked and sounded like the serious doctor he was.

Mr Brooks got right down to business and Barbara was grateful for his forthrightness, and that he wasn't trying to raise false hopes in her. He watched her as she let out a long shuddering sigh and, used as he was to delivering sad news, he felt compassion for this elegant young woman who was so obviously in love with James Ferguson.

Barbara had heard right. James was paralysed, yet she had this weird idea that this strong capable doctor was talking to the wrong person. It couldn't be James he was speaking about. No, of course it couldn't be, James was so much better today, alert – even humorous.

'I am so sorry, Miss Hamlin. James will in all other aspects be healthy. Unfortunately his spinal cord was snapped, it is irrevocably damaged. With the best will in the world, there is nothing more anyone can do for him. Short of a miracle the nerve-ends will not mend.'

He stood up again and came around his desk to where Barbara sat. He took hold of her hand and very gently told her, 'There is no damage to his brain. That must be a lot to be thankful for. The top half of his body will quite soon be strong and healthy. He'll need a wheelchair to get about in, but you'll see, he'll cope. James will even be able to continue with his profession, if he so chooses. With time things will improve.'

'Yes, yes.' She managed to nod her head. 'Thank you,' she stammered. Her brown eyes were shining with unshed tears as she raised her head and looked at him.

She'll cope, Mr Brooks said to himself, she won't desert the man, she will remain steadfast and loyal – of that he felt certain.

The experience of the past weeks was over. James was coming home. They say that money smooths all paths. In James's case that was true. His father had had two rooms, on the ground floor of their Eastbourne home, turned into a suite for James. A special bed had been ordered and delivered. At a touch of a button the bed could be raised or lowered. A backrest worked in a similar way, allowing the patient to sit or lie in several positions. A pulley swung over head, a chain ran through a grooved rim attached to which was a wooden handle: by pulling on this, James would be able to raise himself to a sitting position.

'Thank God his arms are strong,' his mother had remarked as she watched it being fitted.

Paul Soames had been engaged to take care of James; he would sleep in the room adjacent to that occupied by James.

Barbara had finally come to terms with the fact that up until now she had never been willing to admit, even to herself: James would never walk again. Barbara felt she loved James even more since the accident, if that were possible, but she was only human and she did sometimes harbour a deep resentment. Why James? Why him? She had been given this second chance, they were so happy together. All their plans! It wasn't fair!

But then, as she had discovered to her cost, only a fool thought life was fair. Life was cruel, unjust.

James was aware of his dependence on Paul Soames, but rather this than on others. Paul not only acted as his male nurse but as a good companion; at thirty-two years of age he had performed his war service in the RAF as a ground engineer. James and his father had agreed to employ Paul not for his medical knowledge, but rather for his brawny physique. His powerful, strong arms and massive shoulders made simple work of preparing James to face the day. When it came to lifting him from his bed and into the specially installed bathroom there was no exertion. Paul would carry him as a baby, James's useless legs dangling over his forearms.

They talked together discussing many subjects, the biggest bonus being that Paul did not regard him as a helpless invalid.

Doubtless James had his bad days, when he longed for the clock to be turned back to when he had been a whole man – a man with a good life stretching before him. On a good day he counted his blessings. His mind had not been impaired, he could carry on his work with Bradley and Summerford. In that quarter he had been very lucky – every member of the firm had visited him, assured him they were expecting him to return to the practice and to pull his weight in full.

Even without working money would be no problem, for since his grandfather's death ten years ago he had been a wealthy young man. Besides the house near Jevington he owned several acres of land there about. But that wasn't the point: he could never lead an idle life. The profession he had chosen to follow was one that intrigued him, it was never dull, it stimulated his brain and kept his mind active. Yet he was only human. There were times when he wanted to bawl his eyes out, so overwhelmed was he by his love for Barbara. She had suffered so much in her life and he had promised her such a rosy future. What could he offer her now?

What girl in her right mind would want to saddle herself with a man who was paralysed from the waist down?

Heavy-hearted, for it had been one of James's bad days, Barbara returned early one evening from Eastbourne to find Penny keeping her mother company.

'God, am I glad to see you!' she told Penny, holding her at arm's-length after they had embraced. 'You look marvellous, Neil must be treating you right.'

'Oh he's doing that all right, but he's away to Scotland till the end of the week, some important account that had to be dealt with in person. Still, ill wind an' all that. I rang, and your mother said I was welcome to stay here, so here I am.'

'Thank you, Mummy. I can make a guess at what you thought.'

'And you'd be right too. Penny will be a tonic for you, and for me come to that.'

During dinner the two girls never stopped chatting for a moment. Penny prattled on about the cruise, 'Service was fantastic! Wish for something an' somehow it appeared.'

Mrs Hamlin was well aware that all the idle gossip between the pair of them was only to put off the awkward moment when the matter of James would have to come

287

under discussion. She was relieved when, at the coffee stage, Phillip announced he had a lot of papers to go through and would take his coffee into his study.

'You are never going to go through with the wedding!' Penny cried in dismay when Barbara at last let it be known how she felt.

Even her mother let out a gasp, too upset to comment.

'Listen, both of you,' Barbara began, 'I'm not quite sure how to explain my feelings and I don't expect you to understand.'

'Understand!' Penny roughly interrupted. 'Darling, you can't have thought things through. As I understand it, James will need professional nursing.'

'Have you *really* thought about it, Barbara?' her mother gently asked.

'Yes, for hours on end, if you really want to know, Mother, and I am still going to go through with it. That's if James will have me.'

'You mean the two of you haven't discussed it?' Penny asked.

'No, not yet. But look at it like this, if James hadn't had the accident he would have taken care of me. I love him, very much,' she had to pause there and swallow the sob that rose in her throat. 'I hope he loves me, I'm sure he does, nothing between us has altered.'

'*Please*, Barbara,' Penny was pleading with her now. 'Don't commit yourself, not for the second time. You're fooling yourself. What kind of a marriage can it possibly be? You told me yourself James will never again be an able-bodied man.'

Barbara gave an impatient shrug to her shoulders. 'Don't

you think I've said all these things, and more, to myself over and over again?'

Emotions were running high and Patricia groped for words, 'Darling, it's early days yet. Your father was saying the same thing to me this morning, be patient, let things take their course. We both of us want your happiness more than anything on earth. But at the moment what you are contemplating would test the love of *any* two people.'

She paused and sighed heavily and, when neither of the girls uttered a word, she went on speaking in a very soft voice, 'I don't know a finer man than James, and your father has great admiration for him and for what he has accomplished. We do know how much you care for each other. But there are so many things I am sure you have not given a thought to. What about children? You're not getting any younger, won't it break your heart to know you can never have a family?'

Oh Mother! Barbara was on the point of screaming. Children! She had to bring that up, didn't she? I've thought of nothing else. Regrets, all her life seemed to be made up of regrets. Being sorry didn't alter the facts though, did it? She took a deep breath, she wouldn't cry – she couldn't anyway, she hadn't any tears left to shed.

'What else can I say to you, Barbara, dear?'

Barbara forced herself to answer very quietly, 'Nothing, Mother, that I haven't said to myself.'

Somehow, Barbara's quiet words touched Penny. She rose to her feet, went across to where Barbara sat and put her arms around her, gently kissing her on her cheek.

'You really are determined, aren't you? Well if that's the case, darling, you had better sort things out with the groom and we'd better get on with the preparations, don't you think, Auntie Pat?'

Patricia was sadly telling herself that, as parents, she and her husband couldn't protect Barbara from all the bad times, even those she didn't deserve. We just have to continue to love her, to be here when she needs us, she vowed as she held her hands out to her daughter.

'If you've made up your mind, if this is *truly* what you want, then, my darling, what can I say but God give you strength.'

Thank you, Mummy,' Barbara answered, throwing herself into her mother's arms. 'It won't be all doom an' gloom, you'll see. James will get stronger. I know he'll never be one hundred per cent but we shall be happy.'

Barbara looked from her mother to her friend; she managed a smile, yet for all that it was a solemn smile that still held a trace of sadness. Now, she thought to herself, all I have to do is bring James round to my way of thinking.

Patricia decided she could offer no more advice or make any further comment. She bent her head to receive a good-night kiss from the girls, put her head round the study door and said, 'I'm going up, darling, I'll read for a while.'

Phillip raised his head and smiled at his wife, 'All right, my love, I won't be too long myself, just winding up here and I'll follow you up.'

In her room, however, Patricia was unable to read let alone sleep, but lay there fretting for hours with worry that her dear daughter was about to be hurt again.

It had become a custom of Paul Soames to nip out of the house and go tramping across the fields towards the village when Barbara arrived to sit with James. Usually he was back within the hour. On this particular day, however, James was wide awake, had all his wits about him and when Barbara arrived seemingly full of the joys of spring, it was immediately obvious to Paul that something was afoot. He wasn't wrong.

'I'll walk to the door with you,' Barbara said cheerfully, as Paul took his leave from James.

She hesitated, then screwed up courage, 'Paul,' she began, 'Would you . . . do you think . . .'

'Walk a bit further today, give you and James a little more time on your own?' Paul quietly suggested.

'Yes, would you mind?' Barbara asked half-heartedly.

'Not at all, I'm sure James will be fine,' said Paul and a moment later was gone out of the hall, leaving it strangely empty and Barbara's mood dropped. Now she felt forlorn. How would James react to her proposal?

Only one thing for it, she vowed: jump in feet first.

Seated by the side of the bed, James's hand held between both of hers, she could contain herself no longer.

'How would you like to discuss our wedding plans, James? I can't see any reason why we should wait,' Barbara continued.

With a sober sincerity that almost broke her heart, James said 'Is it a matter worth discussing?'

After a moment's hesitation, Barbara answered. 'Yes, it is.'

James sighed. 'I can see so many problems – for both of us.'

Barbara paused and then, with a touch of sorrow in her voice, admitted, 'Frankly, James, so can I. But we shouldn't let anything stand in our way. You're going to advise me to wait, aren't you? I don't want to wait, James. I want us to be married as soon as possible.'

James managed a trace of a smile and didn't try to avoid Barbara's eyes.

'I don't deserve you,' he whispered.

And I don't deserve you, was what she said to herself; instead she said aloud, 'Shall we talk about wedding plans?'

'Hey! Not so fast,' he pleaded.

'Why? Are you going to tell me that you aren't in love with me any more?'

'Oh, Barbara! Nothing could be further from the truth.'

'Well then?'

The look on James's face softened. 'Barbara, let's talk sensibly about this. To have you for my wife is what I've dreamed about. I've told you over and over again, I love you. I wanted nothing more from life then to spend every-day with you. But now . . .'

'But *now,* what? You are still you, and I am still me. Let's be grateful you weren't killed.'

'That's all very well, Barbara, but life wouldn't be a bed of roses, for you or for me. We would both us feel utterly frustrated at times, remorseful for what might have been. No, my darling, I love you too much to let you sacrifice the rest of your life tied to a cripple.'

He turned his face to the wall and his body shook. Barbara's heart ached for him, but if she let the matter rest there she might just as well get up now and walk away. He deserved better than that.

'A cripple, you said! T'hell with that! Is *that* what you see yourself as?'

'The paralysis of my legs is permanent.' He rubbed at his eyes with the corner of the sheet. 'I can't be the same as I was. I never will be. How can I be your husband, Barbara?'

'There are thousands worse than you. Men who lost limbs, even their sight, during the War. Did their wives desert them? If you haven't got the courage to tell me to my face that you don't want to marry me, well, that would be a different story. But I need to know right now.'

'Don't be so bloody daft.'

She didn't touch him, didn't comfort him. She let him cry, watching the tears roll slowly down his cheeks.

After what seemed an eternity she got up from her chair, went into the bathroom and came back with a wet face-flannel and a dry towel. Without a word she handed them to James and stood by while he washed his face. From the bureau which stood against the wall she fetched a silver-backed hairbrush and again waited while he brushed his tousled fair hair.

'Now I'm going to tell you one more thing and then I shall go in search of some tea for us.'

'Is there any way I could stop you?' he asked with a touch of his old humour.

The laugh Barbara gave almost bordered on hysteria but she pressed on, 'When Mr Brooks spoke to me he didn't pull any punches. He told me everything that was negative about your condition but he also pointed out all that was positive. Mostly he emphasised there was no damage to your brain. I've clung to that, and James, you should too. You are not a vegetable, your mind is *not* crippled, it is still as brilliant and active as ever. You have been told by your firm that in time they expect you to go back, to continue to practise law, even Daddy says there is no reason why you shouldn't . . .' Her eyes were full, her throat choking; she couldn't go on pleading for much longer. 'You see . . . if only you would marry me you'd still be able to keep me

293

in the type of luxury you promised.' She was making an attempt to be flippant now, before adding, 'I'm not trying to be a martyr, honestly, James, I'm not. I love you *so* much. I can't think of what my life would be like without you.'

It happened naturally. Their arms automatically went round each other, their faces touched and their tears mingled. Outside the cold dry day grew darker, but in that room nothing and no one mattered but the two of them.

'If you're quite sure?' James softly queried, much later. 'It won't be easy.'

With much more brightness than she was feeling, Barbara said, 'Nobody's suggesting it will be easy, we'll learn to cross each bridge as we come to it. Together. Now may we talk of wedding plans? Set a date!'

What was going through her mind was the fact that nothing worth having ever seemed to come easily. At least, not to her!

Chapter Nineteen

TIME NO LONGER hung heavy on Barbara's hands and she was never short of a topic of conversation or a funny incident to relay to James. Their decision to make the house in Jevington their home after they were married was a unanimous one. James's father entered into the spirit of the operation and proved himself invaluable when it came to finding the exact workman for each and every job that needed to be done. On all points he consulted Barbara, asking not only for her views but demanding that she voiced her preference wherever there was a choice to be had. They were in complete agreement that, by and large, the house should retain its character.

On one point only did she dig her heels in: the huge bath with its iron claw feet was to stay. Workmen argued, plumbers pleaded. James laughed his head off, Barbara didn't give a damn.

'Work around it,' she implored. 'Paint the feet, install mirrors on the wall, put up a new ceiling, new washbasins, a modern toilet – anything you like, but leave the bath in the centre of the room. It looks majestic.' The workmen smiled behind her back. Mr Ferguson aired his views, all to no avail. The bath stayed put.

Barbara would now burst into James's room, armed with wallpaper-pattern books, carpet samples, catalogues showing pictures of kitchen units and cooking stoves. His mother

Elizabeth Waite

would put her head around the door to ask if they were ready for tea.

On more than one occasion, Paul, who would be involved in all the discussions, would say, 'You come and sit here, Mrs Ferguson. See what you think about this paper for the hall. I'll go an' make the tea.'

Muriel Ferguson's heart was a whole lot lighter these days. Since Barbara and James had decided that their wedding would go ahead, it was as if James had taken on a whole new lease of life. She thanked God each night that James had come to terms with his disability and she prayed that her son and Barbara would indeed find happiness. She did her best not to let her thoughts dwell on the limitations there would be to this marriage. Sufficient unto the day, please God.

Barbara and James had both been determined James wouldn't be confined upstairs and out of touch with what was going on. So plans had been drawn up, agreed on and passed by the local council for an extension to be built onto the end of the house. A door was cut through the main wall and James would be able to wheel himself through the hallway, from which led off the main lounge, dining room, and the kitchen. In the new building would be James's large bedroom, another bed-sitting-room for Paul Soames and a big bathroom with special fittings to help with James's disablement, also a smaller room which would in time serve as his office.

It had been James himself who had held meetings with the architect, and his influence and preference that had determined the outcome of the finished plans.

Most days would find Barbara down there, walking the grounds, thinking it was a marvellous old house of great

character and charm. The thick natural stone walls that surrounded the garden gave it security and privacy. It had all the eccentricities and the beauty of an old village house. Long, low, leaded windows downstairs, small ones upstairs. Low doorways and arches that led to the fields beyond and, further afield, the stables.

It was a house that should happily ring with the sound of children's laughter.

When such thoughts came into Barbara's mind she would do her best to banish them. Nobody has everything in this life!

James wasn't bright and cheerful every day. Who could expect him to be?

On such days when she didn't know how to comfort him and his dark mood would peeve her, she would make the effort to drive to Jevington and trudge off to the stables. She'd liked Clem Tompson since the first day she'd set foot on the place and he always seemed so pleased to see her.

She would change her clothes and shoes in the locker-room and wait in the yard for one of the lads to bring her a mount. Clem usually made sure it was the same one, Lady, a grey filly with a sweet, passive temperament that suited her mood.

Barbara would mount up and let Lady amble down the track that led to the Downs, giving the horse her head only when they were beyond the bridle paths. Born and bred around horses, the weather held no fear for Barbara. Should it be raining she would accept the offer of an oilskin cape and ride out to find the smell of fresh horse manure, wet grass and dripping trees truly exhilarating. Later she would return to the yard to share a mug of steaming coffee with Clem. Always able to judge Barbara's moods, Clem would talk of what was happening in the racing game and, more often than not, had a message for her to relate to James from several trainers, most of whom had a considerable reputation in the world of racing.

The day came when Barbara was in a relaxed mood.

'James getting stronger?' Clem Tompson asked, handing Barbara a mug and warning her that the coffee was scalding.

'Improving every day,' she beamed in delight. 'Honestly, Clem, you should see him manipulate that electric wheelchair. He can turn it on a sixpence, wonder he doesn't give his poor mother a heart attack. She cringes when he comes flying across the room – fearful for her beautiful furniture – still, as yet he has managed to avoid bashing into it.'

'So, shall we be hearing wedding bells before too long? Or am I not allowed to ask?'

Barbara slid her arm across Clem's shoulder, and tilted her head in a saucy gesture. 'Clem, it won't be long now, you'll know in good time to tog yourself up!' Then her face became serious. 'Thanks isn't enough, Clem, for what you've done for me. Many a day you've saved my reason.'

'Get on with you, love, all I've done is see you've had a mount. Not much to that.'

He turned his head away. He didn't want her to see how much her words had meant to him. His heart had ached for the pair of them. All these months James had been laid up, knowing he'd never walk again – and them with everything in the world to live for. Didn't seem but yesterday that the two of them had stood in this yard, fit an' able the both of them; telling him of their plans to do the old house up and live in it. Man and wife. God this lass was plucky! She'd stood by James. But then James deserved no less. He'd known the lad since he was a nipper, never did a wrong turn to anyone, nice lad was James. Never seems to be those that deserve it that get the bottom knocked out of their world, he was thinking to himself as he watched Barbara walk back across the yard.

The year had gone by; Elizabeth had had her baby daughter christened Hannah. Barbara hadn't gone down to Windsor for the event, she wouldn't leave James for that length of time. Both her parents had attended, so had Penny and Neil and Penny's parents also. The reports brought back to Barbara was that the baby was gorgeous and had behaved very well, only crying when the vicar had sprinkled her forehead with the holy water.

The house was almost ready. Christmas had come and gone again and Barbara and James were all set to have an Easter wedding. The awareness that soon they would be man and wife lent a special intensity to their relationship. Each day Barbara would arrive in Eastbourne not knowing what to expect. If James was perky, full of good humour and so loving towards her, she thanked God. If he was withdrawn she would be choked with emotion, sad for him and even more so for herself, knowing that there was no way she could reach him. All she could do was talk to him and wait.

Some days seemed to drag on interminably until suddenly James suggested that he taught her how to play chess. For that she was eternally grateful. She learnt quickly and from then on she never had to coax him into a game, it was something they both enjoyed.

Poor James! Paul Soames knew more than anyone what he was going through. His bride-to-be was beautiful. Tall, slim, long dark hair that glistened with chestnut glints whenever the sun caught it, skin that was as fresh and clear as porcelain and a personality that would charm the birds out of the trees. Of course James felt frustrated! What man wouldn't!

Paul had become extremely fond of both Barbara and James; he knew by now that they had a special kind of love, a love for each other that seemed to him to be very rare, and there wasn't anything he wouldn't do to help either one of them. What he asked himself was, how were the two of them going to survive in a marriage that could never be fully fulfilled? Could they survive?

Easter Saturday, Patricia Hamlin watched as her husband donned his jacket, then carefully she placed the white carnation into his buttonhole. The expression on her face showed sadness.

'If only James hadn't had that accident,' she spoke half to herself. 'It hurts that Barbara will not really have a normal married life.'

'I know it does, dear. But then, the decision is Barbara's after all. James is a good fellow – you know that for yourself. He will certainly care for her. He will be still be able to work. His mind is active enough, even without his earnings he can offer our Barbara security, a lovely home and above all else, Patricia, they love each other. Come on now, no tears today, powder your nose and be happy for them.' Dropping his head he softly added, 'Things could have been worse you know, much worse.'

In the pretty bedroom that had been hers as a child, Barbara pulled her wedding dress over her head, carefully so as not to disarrange her hair. The dress was a simple one: a delicate shade of yellow, cut straight across the bodice with two thin shoulder-straps, over which she wore a loose bolero that fell to be gathered into a band at the waist. Heavy Belgian lace formed cuffs for the sleeves.

Her dark hair had been teased into an up-swept hairdo. A few wisps escaped at the nape of her neck and in front of her ears to show below the soft cream-coloured, straw, wide-brimmed hat that she wore. A narrow band of the same Belgian lace was the only adornment on the hat.

Her flowers were a small posy of pale yellow roses, interwoven with maidenhair fern.

'Ready, darling?' her father's voice crackled with emotion. 'Turn around and let me look at you,' he ordered. Barbara did as he asked. 'You look beautiful,' her father said softly. Coming forward he bent to kiss her. A gentle kiss that said it all.

No motorcars for Barbara today, or for the main wedding guests. Colin Peterson, who still had charge of her father's small stables, and Clem Tompson were driving open carriages each drawn by a pair of well-matched horses.

Folk had gathered to line the long narrow High Street of Alfriston. Perched insecurely on the cramped high pavements they were a jolly lot. Some waving balloons, others calling their good wishes. The quaint shops with bottle-glass bow windows that overhung the pavement carried placards: 'Good luck to Barbara and James!' The story of this wedding and all that had gone before had touched the hearts of local people and they had turned out to show their goodwill.

There was no shortage of ushers. Neil Chapman, Peter Bradley, who had made them so welcome on his boat at

Henley, Anthony Holt, now engaged to James's sister Chloe, and Mark Bradley, son of one of the senior partners of the law firm that employed James. All were dressed for the occasion.

Barbara and her father descended from the carriage at the end of the lane and walked the path through the well-mown grass to the entrance of St Andrew's Church.

Barbara had no bridesmaids, only Penny to stand behind her to take her flowers when the time came.

It was not until Barbara entered the church, saw the sun shining through the high stained glass windows that rose high above the altar and heard the organ notes that she faltered.

Her arm was through the crook of her father's elbow and he used his free hand to tighten his grip on her. 'Brave girl,' he whispered.

She was vaguely aware of seeing people she knew: Mrs Clarkson, who had been a gem this last few weeks, and – wonder of wonders – sitting beside her was Mrs Winters! Oh, that was nice of her mother to have invited her.

'God bless you,' Mrs Winters whispered softly.

Barbara smiled her thanks.

Without the help and kindness of Mrs Winters she would never have survived all that time she had lived in Battersea. But she wasn't going to dwell on the past. Not today.

Her heart lurched as her eyes met those of James. There was nothing pathetic about James, so elegantly attired in his morning suit as he sat bolt upright in his wheelchair. His brother Rodney, acting as his best man, looked tall and stately standing on the right-hand side of James.

As Barbara and her father neared the front pews she was aware that these seats were occupied by those for whom

302

she cared and who cared for her. Tim and Elizabeth with their three children. James's parents, his sister Ann and her husband Jack Tully with their twins, Lucy and Harry. Rodney's wife Elaine sat on the other side of little Lucy and was obviously amused at some remark the child had made, for she was dipping her head to hide her smiles.

Barbara felt the tension ease. This was such a happy day. She would have two families now. Brothers and sisters, nieces and nephews, she and James wouldn't have to face the uncertainty on their own in the years that lay ahead.

The vicar, splendid in his robes, gave a smile of encouragement to Barbara as she took her place besides James.

The ceremony began.

When it came to Barbara's responses she turned her head, gazed directly into James's eyes and with all the love that was in her heart she vowed, 'I will.'

James made his responses in a strong voice, smiled up at her, took her left hand in his and, gently but firmly, slipped onto her outstretched finger the gold band that signified they were man and wife.

Behind her, both their mothers were weeping, others too perhaps, but Barbara was filled with joy. No more misgivings, she and James would face the future together.

Chapter Twenty

ON THE SURFACE of things life in the new Ferguson household had settled into an even pace.

Modernised now, to a great extent the charm of the house remained unchanged. Beautiful wood had been restored and polished, the staircase with its carved banister rails set to rights by craftmen who loved their work. Some of the most beautiful pieces of furniture had been left to James by his grandparents. A tall rosewood bureau, mahogany desk, two high-backed hall chairs with ivory inlaid decoration and two beautiful lounge chairs carved with graceful lines.

She was happy for James, when soon after their marriage, with Paul driving the car, he took off for London four days a week to resume business with his law firm. The silent emptiness they left behind them in the house was terrible and, for Barbara, depressing. She needed to divert herself by doing something useful.

Barbara sat alone in the kitchen, lingering over a third cup of tea. James and Paul had left for London more than an hour ago. She looked out the window at the persistent rain that had been falling since early yesterday evening. A right old dreary day this was going to be!

'Right – make a move,' she ordered herself. 'Don't sit here moping.'

Darting upstairs she made sure all the windows were

closed. With speed she changed her dress for a suit, found shoes and a handbag that matched, and went to phone her mother-in-law.

'Could you do with a visitor?' she grinned when Muriel Ferguson answered her call.

'Anything wrong?'

'No. No, everything is fine; I'm just feeling bored. James is in town for the day.'

A sigh of relief came down the line. 'You're more than welcome, love to see you. Chloe is home for the day. Bring a pair of stout shoes, if this rain lets up we can go tramping over the Downs – or along the beach, come to that.'

Twenty minutes later, Barbara sprinted through the rain to the garage, settled herself comfortably in the driving seat of her car and within minutes was on her way to Eastbourne, pleased at the prospect of having Chloe's company.

It stopped raining, the sky became brighter and Barbara's mood lifted as she drove through the fresh countryside.

Her mother-in-law opened the front door, her face shining with pleasure as she hugged Barbara.

Appetising smells were rising up from the kitchen.

'Coffee an' home-made gingerbread is all ready and I've put a casserole in the oven which won't spoil, no matter what time we decide to eat.'

'You're an angel,' Barbara said and meant it. 'If I'd have stayed on my own today I would have wallowed in self-pity.'

'Well, you're here now and Chloe is so pleased.'

Cake and coffee were consumed quickly.

Two Thermos flasks were filled with boiling water, packed into a wicker basket that already held jars of tea, coffee and sugar. Another flask was filled with cold milk, spoons were held secure by a box of the still-warm gingerbread and a packet of biscuits.

'Make sure there are three walking sticks in the boot, and wellingtons, just in case,' Muriel called up the stairs to Chloe, who had been given the job of taking the hamper to the car.

The wet May morning had given way to a sunny, warm afternoon. Twenty minutes later, Muriel Ferguson turned the car left and drove beneath the wide canopy that displayed the name: 'BUTCHER'S WHOLE BOTTOM, OWNED AND PROTECTED BY THE FORESTRY COMMISSION'.

Along a tree-lined path and she brought the car to a halt beside several other cars, all parked in order on the shingle-covered ground. Dogs of every shape, colour and form romped across the grass and set off for the woods, their owners in tow.

'Difficult to know who takes who for a walk up here,' Chloe laughed.

'When I was at school we had two dogs and my father used to bring us all up here at weekends,' Barbara reflected aloud. 'No matter what the weather, snow, ice, torrential rain, we never ever arrived here and found no other cars. Such a popular place isn't it?'

Chloe laughed, 'Beats me why the locals always refer to this place as Butcher's Bottom Hole.'

'Me too,' said her mother. 'Suppose it's easier to say quickly than Butcher's Whole Bottom. Whatever, it has always been a very popular place and one has to admit a truly marvellous place. Your father always states that one could come here every day for a month and take a different route.'

She twisted her body around to look at the two girls seated still in the back of the car and asked, 'Well, are we going for a walk or not?'

Shoes off and wellington boots now on, each armed with a stout crook-handled walking stick, they set off. The beginning of the woods had a well-trodden track running through thinly-spaced, tall trees along which people walked in both directions. Not one person passed another without a greeting. 'Afternoon. Lovely now isn't it?'

'Yes, cleared up nicely.'

'Oh, look at that dog! Isn't he lovely?'

'Spoilt rotten, that what he is, all this petting, he laps it up.'

How could one have a black mood in a place like this? Barbara mused to herself, as she stood by while Muriel bent and patted an Old English sheepdog. Half a mile further on, tracks branched off to the right and to the left of where they were walking.

'Let's take the right side,' Chloe insisted. 'The roads on this side wind up higher and the views are magnificent.'

Making good use of their sticks, they began to climb. It was very quiet now. Warm like a summer's afternoon. The trees were taller, the bracken dense, the breeze soft against their cheeks. It took some time to reach the top. Thankfully they sank down among the rough grass and bracken fronds. There was no need for conversation. The view was magnificent!

Old farmhouses with their great barns and outbuildings were strung out at intervals in the distance. Fields of gold, green and brown covered the earth like a patchwork quilt, so that there was no way of knowing where one farm started or another finished. The only sound was the distant hum of farm machinery.

'Up you get,' Chloe broke into their thoughts. 'We've a long way to go yet.'

Another mile along a pathway bordered by bushes of yellow gorse and wild flowers and they came to a path that led downwards.

'I'm going to make my way slowly back to the car,' Muriel decided. 'I'll set the chairs out, have a snooze and I'll make you a drink when you get back.'

'Are you sure you'll be all right?' Chloe questioned her mother.

'Quite sure. You two young ones go are far as you like. I'll see you later.'

They watched as Muriel followed the road which led right down to where they had set off from, then they turned off the track and took a narrow, high-hedged lane that wound up and over even higher.

'I wish I'd never worn these wellingtons, my feet are burning,' Chloe complained as they came to a white-barred gate and a rough path that had been hewn out of the hillside.

'I remember this path, it's a short cut; rough going but eventually one does come out near to where the car is parked,' Barbara said, having first taken several minutes to get her breath back.

'Not yet,' pleaded Chloe, walking beneath a great, leafy tree and thinking how nice it was to be in the shade. 'Park your bottom down here for a while. I've got some chewy fruit-sweets in my pocket, they'll refresh your mouth, do till we get back an' can have a drink.'

'Oh smashing! Barbara ripped at the paper of the sweet with her teeth, the sweets were a bit sticky from having been in Chloe's pocket for so long.

With her back resting against the tree, and her bottom wriggled comfortably into the dry growth of ferns, she tossed a handful of pine cones into the air and sighed contentedly.

'Gosh, I'm glad I came over today and even more glad that you were home, Chloe. I feel a different person for having walked up here. It feels as if we're sitting on top of the world.'

'Mother said you were down in the dumps when she came off the phone this morning. Anything you want to talk about? I can be quite a good listener you know.'

Chloe truly liked her sister-in-law. Now she was worried that Barbara might be regretting her decision to marry her brother. More so when Barbara made no answer.

'Bit of a strain, is it, coping with James?' Chloe sighed, sympathy had been in her voice.

'Not at all!' Barbara rushed quickly to dispel any thoughts that things weren't going right between herself and James. 'James is every inch his own man. One hundred per cent. More so now that he is back in the city, practising law, doing work that he trained for years to be able to do. No, Chloe, it's me. I just don't know what to do to fill my time.'

'I'm sorry,' Chloe softly told her. 'I didn't mean to pry. As long as you and James are happy, that's all the whole family prays for.'

Barbara reached over and took Chloe's hand in hers. 'I know, dear.' Then on impulse she sat up straight and said, 'Chloe, James and I love each other. Probably it isn't natural

309

that either of us can live without full sex. I can't pretend that it doesn't matter all the time. Mostly it doesn't. We get by. We do really love each other and we make love. In our own way. I had such a bad time in my first marriage I sometimes think I am grateful not to have to cope with that side of things.'

Chloe hung her head and murmured. 'Poor Barbara.'

'Chloe, you won't tell anybody about this?'

'Barbara, you know I won't,' Chloe scolded.

Colour had flushed up into Barbara's cheeks. It embarrassed her to talk to anybody of what went on between her and James. It was personal and wonderful for them both. Not enough at times. But then it had to be.

Not every night did she take the stairs to her own bedroom to lie alone in the double bed. She would lie in James's bed, in his arms, and relish in the fact that he adored her and she him. He was tender, attentive, ever conscientious of her needs. Sometimes they would talk into the early hours of the morning. James making sure that she knew of what work he was doing, of cases in which he was involved and relating to her any interesting gossip that often came from the Old Bailey.

The fact that Barbara had blushed had brought an awkward silence between them, a silence that Chloe sought to break but didn't know how.

Barbara was still struggling to hide the intensity of her feelings, but determination showed in her dark eyes.

'What I'd really like to do, Chloe, is get a job. Voluntary work of some kind. I'd like to help others. Especially children,' Barbara added wistfully.

'Well I'll be blowed!' Chloe exclaimed, pushing boisterously at Barbara's shoulder. 'The person you want to talk to is my Anthony,' she said proudly.

'Why Anthony?'

'Just listen and I'll explain. For ages a group of doctors that Anthony works with have wanted to set up a clinic in London to help children. Children that are not classed as hospital cases but need help never the less. Young mothers that can't cope, babies that have disabilities, unwanted babies that are found to have been neglected, that sort of child.'

Barbara's eyes glowed with enthusiasm.

'Go on,' she urged Chloe.

'Well, three months ago a clinic was set up in Vauxhall.'

'How wonderful,' Barbara showed her approval. 'Has it turned out to be a success?'

'It certainly has. The clinic had only been in operation a month when money began to pour in. From sources one would never expect, Anthony said.'

'I want to help,' Barbara declared. 'And don't say James won't let me.'

'As I said, the best person to talk to about this is Anthony. He's been involved with this project long before the clinic was opened.'

'Will you ask him? Tell him I'd like to offer my services. Once or twice a week at least, I don't mind what job he finds for me to do.'

'I'll ask him,' Chloe agreed. 'But make sure you discuss it with James.'

'Oh I will. I promise.'

'Good. You sound a whole lot brighter now. Ready for the traipse back? You do realise that on this path we have to climb even higher before we start to descend down to where the car is parked?'

'Let's get started then. That cup of tea your mother promised would be ready will go down a treat, eh?'

The dark panelling of the walls gleamed in the light from two standard lamps and the log fire that burned in the huge fireplace. Soon they wouldn't need a fire in the evenings; with summer well and truly on the way they would be able to spend more time outdoors in the garden.

James smiled at Barbara as she looked around the room. The hearth held a basket piled high with logs, the vases on the side-tables held masses of spring flowers. There was age and tradition here in this house, yet it did not lack a sense of comfort nor yet the homely touches of books, magazines and board-games scattered around the room.

'Would you like a drink, darling?' James asked as he propelled his wheelchair to the cabinet.

'Yes please,' Barbara answered enthusiastically.

James mixed the drinks, whisky and dry-ginger for each of them, while Barbara moved towards the windows.

'Going to be a nice day tomorrow, look at that red sky.'

James came up behind her, handed her the drink, then sat back and studied her. She was thirty-one, small-boned and slender, quite beautiful with her dark colouring and dark-brown eyes. He still couldn't fathom why she had agreed to marry him. He knew everything now of her life with Michael, she had held nothing back in the telling except perhaps the most intimate details. God – what she must have been through. It was no wonder at first he had thought her bubbly personality to be somehow tensed, even forced.

Tonight she seemed relaxed, different somehow, very happy. Oh, he hoped so. They had both known the limitations they faced when they had taken the vow, until death us do part. He silently prayed that he would always be able to make her happy.

As if she had caught his thoughts Barbara raised her glass and said, 'To us, James.'

It wasn't until after they had eaten their evening dinner that Barbara broached the subject.

'James, have you heard about this clinic that doctors in London have set up to help children?'

'Yes, actually it was your father who was telling me. A voluntary group, I understand. Working under very limited conditions. Three portable buildings set up on a disused bomb-site. Must be very dedicated men.'

'Chloe was telling me today that Anthony is very much involved in the project. James, I'd like to offer my services, as an unpaid volunteer. Would you mind?'

She saw his eyes widen in amazement. 'The children they are trying to help will be poor desperate mites.'

'All the more reason why I should do this. Or don't you think I could be of any help?' she challenged.

'If I agree, will you promise not to do too many hours?'

'I promise, James. It's just that the days are so long when you are away in town and my life has no meaning. This is something useful I really would like to do. Please.'

'It won't be nice work, not all the time,' he warned.

Barbara gazed intently at him. 'Are you saying I may offer my services?'

'Could I stop you?' he smiled broadly.

'You intended to agree all along,' she accused.

313

'Whatever makes you happy. All right,' James capitulated. 'But remember, two days a week at most.'

Barbara's face radiated pleasure. 'Oh, James, thank you!'

He held out his arms. Barbara knelt on the carpet and he brought her to his chest as though she were a tiny child, herself in need of comfort and help.

Would working with children be good for her? Or would the sights she was bound to see break her heart?

It was four weeks now since Barbara had worked her first day at the London clinic. This Tuesday she had arrived earlier than usual. Anthony, too, came in ahead of his schedule. They sat together in the partitioned-off reception room, before the staff came on duty and the mothers with their babies began to arrive.

'I feel so guilty,' Barbara confessed. 'So many of these small children are suffering badly and their wretched mothers don't seem able to cope, those that could haven't enough money to get by on.'

'Barbara, you're doing a great job here,' Anthony said. 'You mustn't try to take everyone's troubles so seriously. But somehow I feel there is more to this conversation than you have so far told me. Something in particular is worrying you. I am right, aren't I?'

'Maybe, I could be wrong.'

'Wrong about what?'

'Well, I suppose it's best someone else is aware that we have a thief working here. I've fretted about it long enough.'

'Barbara, tell me, make me understand what has been going on,' Anthony commanded.

'The first week I was here, half-a-crown disappeared from my purse. I put it down to the fact that I must have been mistaken, though I was almost sure that I wasn't. The second week it was a ten-shilling note. The week after, nothing; so I let the matter drop, but last week I brought with me chocolate buttons, dolly-mixtures and some jelly babies. I thought it would calm the kiddies, make them less frightened if we gave them a few sweeties.'

'That was a nice idea,' Anthony smiled.

'It would have been,' said Barbara. 'When I went to my bag there wasn't a sign of any sweets. I thought I must have been imagining things, perhaps have left them at home. I hadn't. They had been taken, all right Silly isn't it? Such paltry little things.'

'You've no real evidence, I suppose?'

'Only that the two cleaning women were going at it hammer and tongs when I went in to the cloakroom last week. Mary, the quiet one, was saying it wasn't right, while Joan, the loud-mouthed one, was telling her she should mind her own business.'

'Morning,' several voices chorused and the sound of the metal doors clanging shut could be heard. The nurses were arriving.

'We'll talk about this later on,' said Anthony, his eyes serious as they watched Barbara leave the room.

During the whole of the shift Barbara felt troubled. Should she just have left the matter alone, be more careful where she left her bag in future? But then again, she couldn't walk around clutching it all the time, and the area given over to the staff was very small. To tell the truth she felt sorry for Joan. Convinced that it was her that had taken the items, she could bring herself to imagine why. Also, that loud domineering attitude that the woman adopted could be a brazen front she presented to the world to cover up her own short-comings. Working in this clinic had certainly opened Barbara's eyes to just how privileged a life she herself led. It also summoned up memories of the time when she had lived in Battersea. Memories she would far rather forget.

She had once thought that the area where she and Michael had lived together could have been described as reaching the bottom of the barrel.

How little she had known.

The tenant buildings around this area where the clinic had been set up were ten times worse. Dirt-encrusted, old blocks of flats where no sunlight seemed able to penetrate, surrounded by bomb-sites now cleared of most the debris, they had become unsightly rubbish tips. A place where the fight against dirt must be a losing battle and disease an ever-frightening threat.

The clinic closed at two. The cleaning women came for only two hours, twelve until two. From the narrow corridor Barbara watched as Mary donned her coat and Joan lingered checking items in her straw shopping bag.

'Goodbye, Mary, I will see you next Tuesday,' Barbara said quietly.

'Cheerio, Mrs Ferguson,' Mary answered.

'Can you hang on a minute, Joan, please,' asked Barbara, her heart beating very fast.

'No, I can't, I've got me kids to pick up,' came the sullen reply, from this skinny woman with thin, mousy-coloured hair.

Barbara blocked her way. 'May I have a look in your shopping bag, Joan?'

'What yer gonna look for? These packets of sweets an' bloody chocolate biscuits? Is this what you're after?' Joan

316

asked, pulling several items from her shopping bag and holding them high almost in triumph.

Barbara was taken back by the woman's matter-of-fact acceptance that she had stolen the articles.

'They don't belong to you,' Barbara warned. 'Would you like to tell me why you took them and all the other things, including money.'

"Old on there, missus 'igh an' bloody mighty. You ain't got no proof that I took anything other than what I've got 'ere in me bag, an' seeing as 'ow I ain't left the premises yet, 'ow d'yer know that I'm gonna pinch 'em, eh? Go on answer me that.'

Barbara stared at her, but she held her ground. 'All I'm asking is that you come back into the room and tell me why you thought you were more entitled to a few sweets than some of the poor little mites that come here for treatment.'

Joan pointed a finger at Barbara, 'You fink these are fer me? Well let me tell yer one fing: while you're 'ere playing the bloody lady bountiful, 'anding out sweets an' making out yer some kind of Florence Nightingale, I've got four kids at 'ome who ain't 'ardly ever seen sweets, let alone chocolate biscuits. My kids deserve a treat now an' again just as much as anybody else's kids do, only I ain't the type what goes round pleading in yer so-called clinics. I've always bin taught, God 'elps those what 'elp themselves.' Her rage had to dry up, at least for the moment, she was out of breath.

Barbara seized her chance. 'If you don't come and sit down and talk this through rationally I shall call the police.'

'Fer a few bloody sweets!' A worried look had appeared

317

Elizabeth Waite

on Joan's face. 'What d'yer want me ter do?' she asked in a rush of anxiety.

'Just sit down and talk.'

'What about?'

'Oh, come on, Joan, you're not that stupid, and it wasn't only sweets, you have had twelve and six out of my purse.'

Joan sagged in shock. 'I never fought yer would miss it.' But she had the grace to turn on her heel and go back into the staff room.

Joan's mouth was working but no words came, she crumpled down onto a chair, pulling her threadbare cardigan tightly across her flat chest.

Barbara wanted to weep for the woman. She'd known the time when she had had to go begging to Mrs Winters for a loan in order to buy food.

'Is your husband out of work?' Barbara asked.

'Ain't got no 'usband.'

'I'm so sorry, but you don't have to cope on your own. If only you had spoken to one of the doctors when you applied for the job, I'm sure some help would have been offered you. How long have you been a widow?'

'I never said I was a bloody widow.'

'Sorry, I assumed – '

'Well, I was married at the beginning of the War, got meself pregnant on 'is first leave. After the second time, when I was swollen up like a balloon, he never came 'ome no more.'

'What about the father of the other children?'

'Mind yer own damn business. I don't ask yer about what you do, do I?' She had a point, Barbara conceded to herself.

'All right, Joan. We'll forget the whole thing. I expect

318

your kiddies look forward to you bringing them home something, but will you promise me one thing?' Barbara was being gentle now.

Joan looked pathetically relieved. 'What is it I'm supposed to promise?'

Barbara swallowed. 'Will you let me arrange for a social worker to visit you?'

'No! No interfering bloody busy-bodies. I've 'ad some of them ter put up wiv in the past. None of 'em ain't coming over my doorstep. I mean it.'

'All right. If I leave it until I'm here again next Tuesday, would you agree to talk to someone if I offered to be there to help? I promise it would only be for your good and for the good of your children. There are many allowances that I am sure you would be entitled to, and many people only too pleased to help.'

'Yeah,' Joan sneered. 'And the rest! What about the things?'

'If you mean the things you've already taken, as you so rightly pointed out I have no proof. As to what you have in your bag, I am more than happy for you to take them home as a little gift for your kiddies.'

'Ruddy good of yer, I must say. Bet it makes yer feel bleedin' good, don't it?'

Oh dear, Joan wasn't going to give in gracefully. Compared to all the robbing and killings that went on, what Joan had done had been nothing. In a crazy sort of way Barbara even admired her. She was fighting for her children in what was possibly the only way she knew how. A little laugh escaped her. 'I'll see you next week then.' Barbara bent and picked up the straw shopping bag and handed it to Joan with a smile.

Joan took it from her without voicing any more objections.

Barbara woke up next day with a sore throat and what promised to be a heavy cold. Numerous hot drinks and large amounts of aspirin did nothing to help. By the weekend she was worse and James insisted on calling the doctor.

'You've picked up a virus, my dear,' he announced, having taken Barbara's temperature and listened to her chest with his stethoscope.

'Stay in bed, keep warm, drink plenty and see that you take the tablets I've prescribed for you.'

It got worse, not better. A dry hacking cough, every bone in her body ached, a hammer continually beating in her head, Barbara was only too glad to stay in bed.

Her mother came over daily and one morning she made a declaration that had both James and Barbara sighing with relief.

'I've found a daily treasure for you, and I do mean a treasure.' Patricia gave a self-satisfied grin before saying, 'Her name is Mrs Margaret Harvey, youngest sister of our Mrs Clarkson. Extremely fortunate to get her,' she said proudly. 'She lives at Wannock. For years she's been a daily up at Ratton Manor, but the old gentleman died three months ago. We've Mrs Clarkson to thank: she put the word in for you, been on for ages that you two needed someone to take care of you. There was a time your father and I thought Mrs Clarkson was considering deserting us to come to you herself.'

'Oh bless her,' Barbara grinned. 'She always has had a soft spot for me and I know she adores James.'

'Well, you will be set up now.'

'I'm sure we shall,' Barbara readily agreed. 'Please thank her for me, Mummy. I have felt so guilty, all the extra work has fallen on Paul's shoulders, he's been bringing me up trays and goodness knows what else he has been having to do downstairs.'

'Well lie back now and concentrate on getting better. Maggie, as she insists on being called, is well and truly installed. Ironing sheets when I got here this morning.'

'Such a relief,' sighed Barbara. 'Mother, will you ring Anthony for me, please? And if you can't get hold of him, ring Chloe.'

'Darling, you aren't still worried about not being able to go to that clinic, are you?'

'Not really . . . well yes, Anthony will understanad. There is a matter that I must get sorted. The sooner the better.'

'All right, dear, I'll go downstairs now and make us all some coffee and while the kettle is boiling I'll phone Anthony'

Barbara was downstairs, a travelling-rug wrapped around her knees. She sat in the lounge with the bottom half of the sash-window open to the garden. It was a lovely June evening, the weather had turned warmer, she felt very much better but as weak as a kitten.

Today she and James were giving their first dinner-party. There would be ten people sitting down to the meal: both hers and James's parents, Penny and Neil, Chloe and Anthony, James and herself.

James had insisted that a local couple who specialised in outside catering be allowed to do the cooking.

Maggie Harvey was to be here also — at her own insist-

321

ence. Plump, rosy-faced, friendly Maggie had already endeared herself to both Barbara and James, and even Paul wasn't adverse to a bit of spoiling when it came to Maggie's cooking.

Barbara watched the first car turn into the drive, and smiled with pleasure when she saw it was Anthony. It wasn't hard to guess why he had deliberately showed up early.

He walked across the lawn. 'How's the invalid?' he called.

'Anything but!' she called back.

He put a leg over the windowsill and climbed into the room.

'Total fraud then, are you?' he asked, bending his head to plant a kiss on her cheek.

'I'm fine now, raring to go, though I must admit whatever that damned virus was it certainly knocked the stuffing out of me. But Anthony, please, before the others get here, tell me about Joan. Did she turn up for work the day after our little rumpus? I've been so worried as to what kind of hornet's nest I might have stirred up there.'

'Hey, hang on. Not so fast. That's the reason I'm here so early, to put your mind at rest. It's amazing really, Barbara, as things have turned out you did Joan Crosbie an enormous favour and, more to the point, she is grateful.'

Seeing the look of astonishment on Barbara's face, Anthony laughed, 'True! Honestly. She even made a point of asking me to thank you. Quite a climb down, eh?'

'I'm still not with you,' Barbara exclaimed in exasperation.

'We've managed to straighten her affairs out; not as well as we would have wished, but at least we have got some help for her. God alone knows she needed it! Too proud, that's half her trouble. Do you know, one of the children that she is struggling to bring up isn't her own?'

Barbara raised her eyebrows and Anthony answered her unspoken question, 'The little lad had been abandoned. Seems his mother ran off with another man, father managed for a while then he left the boy with a neighbour — the neighbour being Joan. She's never seen hair nor hide of the father since. That was eighteen months ago. Poorly fed and clothed but clean, oh yes, very clean was our social worker's report. Children happy. All of them quite bright. Joan was scraping by, doing three part-time cleaning jobs. Fifty shillings a week at most to pay the rent and feed and clothe all of them.'

'In what way are matters better for her now?' Barbara was anxious to know.

'Every way. I promise you. She's accepted the fact that she does need help and I'm told she is on quite a friendly footing with her social worker. Hard to believe isn't it?'

'Oh, Anthony, I'm *so* pleased, I really have worried about that woman and her children. I can't wait to come back to the clinic.'

'Ah! . . . That's another thing I wanted to talk to you about.'

'What? You aren't softening the blow? Saying you don't want me to return?'

'Not exactly.'

'That means yes, doesn't it? I know what you're going to say, I've given it a lot of thought. Me being different, well-dressed, having money, has annoyed those woman. I don't fit in, do I?'

'It's not that, well, to be honest, more or less that's true,

323

but please, Barbara, hear me out; I have a proposition I want to put to you, a very worthwhile project.'

He spoke with such sincerity that Barbara decided to reserve her judgement. At that moment James propelled himself into the room, followed by Paul carrying a tray of drinks.

Quickly Anthony said, 'Barbara, it's not a private matter, we can all discuss it after dinner. I promise you will be interested.' With that she had to be content.

'Anthony, good to see you, how are you?'

'Fine, James, and you? Plenty of work in your line of business, I hear.'

'Criminals never take holidays,' was James's quick retort.

They all laughed.

'I'll put the tray down here,' Paul said. 'Mr Ferguson's car is just turning in the gate, I'll let them in.'

'Is Chloe with her parents?' James asked.

'Yes, she rang to tell me not to pick her up. She'd decided to come with her mother and father,' Anthony told them as he moved towards the door to greet his fiancée.

The caterers had done them proud. Seafood platter as a starter, followed by buttered asparagus tips, roast leg of English lamb, baby onions in creamy sauce with several dishes of fresh young vegetables, tiny new potatoes and crispy roast ones, almond-topped open apple tart with thick clotted cream. Petits fours and coffee now being served, Barbara's father and Robert Ferguson asked permission to smoke. With the grand smell of rich Havana cigars now pervading the room, they settled down to serious conversation.

'So,' Barbara said, turning her head towards Anthony,

'are you going to keep me in suspense all the evening or are you going to tell me about this new scheme of yours?'

'Anthony been having a go at you, has he?' Muriel Ferguson had butted in before Anthony had a chance to answer.

Barbara laughed at her mother-in-law, saying, 'I'm a glutton for punishment.'

'Well you're certainly asking for it this time. If this is about what I think it is, then there'll be no stopping him. It's Anthony's pet subject.'

'Mother!' cried Chloe. 'Give Anthony a chance to plead his own case.'

James, seated at the other end of the table, caught Barbara's eye and they both grinned.

'Isn't it just?' Penny murmured. 'I've heard him go on about this before now.'

'Isn't it just *what*?' Neil asked. 'You've lost me.'

Everyone laughed.

'Isn't it just Anthony's pet subject,' Chloe's father explained. 'We'd do better if we all kept quiet and gave the poor fellow a chance to say what he is obviously dying to tell us.'

Anthony drained his coffee cup, his eyes glittered with assurance as he turned to face them all.

'I suppose I do go on about this subject, I make no apology; that's because it is very serious. I don't have to convince Chloe. She's seen it first hand.

'It all began for me when I came up against the atrocious way mentally-retarded children and those who are handicapped were written off. There always has been, and probably always will be, much speculation amongst the medical profession as to the rights and wrongs of various treatments.'

Elizabeth Waite

Anthony paused and when everyone remained silent he continued, 'My own opinion in respect of specific children, is that their condition is often made worse by cruelty and neglect. More attention and a lot more love would benefit so many of our small patients.'

Anthony now had the attention of them all – especially Barbara, who found herself following his every word with interest. She had known he was totally dedicated to his work, but just how deeply he cared came as a surprise. She wanted him to continue, to hear everything he had to say on this subject.

'I became acquainted with Ivy Pearson through the out-patients department at the hospital. She is Matron of Coombe Haven, which is a residential home in Surrey, quite near South Croydon station, well known for the remarkable work it does for under-privileged children. It is a home for any child up to the age of twelve who is in need of specialist care for several reasons. Some of the children have been abused, beaten, you wouldn't believe the cruelty. Others are deformed and therefore unwanted and a few are mentally impaired. The home depends largely for funds on voluntary contributions. I felt very privileged when, some time ago, I was asked to become a member of the committee.'

Anthony stopped speaking and smiled his thanks to Barbara as she refilled his coffee cup.

James was the first to break the silence, 'Organisations, such as you are describing, Anthony, already exist for children of the Church of England faith, Roman Catholics and those from Jewish families. What makes this home different?'

'Because it is of no special religious denomination and

the children are not what one would term "ill". They are classed as backward or deformed and for that reason society as a whole doesn't want to know them. Left to the system they would be written off. Hidden from the world.'

'Is this what you had in mind for me to be part of?' Barbara asked timidly.

'Well, yes. There are never enough money or helpers,' Anthony was saying now. 'We have to give a lot of thought to just how best to help each child.'

He raised his head, gazed at everyone seated further down the table, making sure he wasn't boring anyone.

'Some think our methods are unconventional, we have to take things slowly. We set up meetings, argue until everyone is agreeable, prepare our notes and hopefully we have enough volunteers to press ahead. Perhaps Chloe would like to tell you more about how they work one-to-one with a patient.'

Barbara looked at Chloe in surprise. 'Do you work there?' she asked.

'Unfortunately no. I would have told you before this if I did; I just don't have the time. I do visit sometimes – so does Mother, more often than I do.'

'What I do mostly is rattle the begging bowl,' Chloe's mother answered. 'I organise fetes, coffee mornings, bring-and-buy sales, things like that. Barbara, your mother held a coffee morning for us not so long ago and we have in mind to rope the men in soon: we're setting up a mock auction when Penny has persuaded Neil to be our auctioneer.'

Neil Chapman groaned. Penny tapped the back of his hand with her teaspoon: 'You know very well you're anticipating the event with glee. You'll wring loads of money out of your friends without turning a hair. Won't you, darling?'

Neil smiled his answer, laying it on thick, 'For you my angel, *anything*.'

'Come for a day, Barbara,' Anthony suddenly urged. 'See one of the volunteers working with a child who has never walked, yet whose legs are not withered. She or he will massage for an hour at a time. Others may read a story to a child who just will not speak, there being no apparent reason why he or she can't. The helpers will ask questions, show the pictures in the book, pressing and probing for answers. Sometimes it can turn out to be a very rewarding experience.'

Barbara glanced across the table to where her father sat. He had kept quiet all this time.

She raised her eyebrows in question.

He smiled his encouragement and, turning her head to face James, she was heartened to see that he too was silently applauding what he knew was to be her decision.

'Anthony, I'd very much like to be involved,' Barbara quietly said. 'You've more than convinced all of us that it is indeed a worthy cause.'

Chapter Twenty-one

MAY HAD GIVEN way to June and June into July before Barbara was really fit enough to make her first visit to Coombe Haven. She had travelled by train from Eastbourne to South Croydon station, where Anthony had promised to meet her. He had stressed that he would only have time to make the necessary introductions as this was not the day that he did his stint of voluntary work at the home.

Barbara felt a little apprehensive as she stepped down from the carriage. This soon vanished as she spotted Anthony waving and smiling at her from the end of the platform; the sunlight sparkling off his gold-rimmed glasses, he looked quite boyish, even eager – as if he were considering this outing to be a great adventure.

His arm around her shoulders, he said, 'The car is parked almost outside the station, we'll be there in ten minutes. Am sorry, Barbara, I can't stay, pressure of work an' all that. Still, I'm sure you'll enjoy your visit and Paul rang me to say James will be finished in court about four, so he said they will pick you up and you can all travel home together.'

Barbara gave an audible sigh of relief. 'Oh, that's nice, better than travelling back on the train in the rush hour.'

Everybody expects the Matron of a home to be stiff and starchy. Ivy Pearson didn't fit that description in the least.

Barbara liked her instantly. Ivy exuded competence, humour and kindness to such a degree that she instantly

329

put Barbara at her ease. A large woman, gaunt and long-necked, though her eyes were kindly and lit up her whole face, as she explained to Barbara the progress some of the children had made since having been admitted to Coombe Haven. Continuing on their tour of the building, Barbara noticed that in spite of her size Ivy's every gesture was graceful and when handling the children she was always so gentle.

In the kitchen four women were gathered.

'These young ladies attend to the morning cleaning, breakfast and lunch,' Ivy Pearson explained. 'Working until two o'clock. Two other married women take over for the afternoon until the night-workers come on duty. We also employ three full-time workers in our own laundry which is housed in a separate building in the grounds.'

'Maisie, Shirley, Ethel and Rose,' Matron introduced the women to Barbara. 'They are indispensable when it comes to the running of this place and the children trust them. This, ladies, is Mrs Barbara Ferguson, hopefully we shall be seeing her on a regular basis after today.'

Four pairs of eyes were sizing Barbara up, making her wait while they formed their opinion of her.

Three had the appearance of the working classes, sallow complexion, drawn-in cheeks and hair dragged back from their faces. The fourth woman, Rose, tended to be plump, yet she was pretty and round-faced like a country bred girl. She seemed to have decided that Barbara was a friend, for she held out her hand, saying, 'Hallo, Miss, you'll find it's a nice place 'ere.'

The others gave in. 'Ow d'yer do, Miss,' they chorused.

Barbara nodded, smiled, and said, 'Nice to meet you all.'

Down a long corridor and Ivy opened a door into what

appeared to be a large play room. 'Listen everyone, I want you to meet Barbara Ferguson,' she called loudly. 'She's our new volunteer.'

Three young women simultaneously called a cheery, 'Hallo Barbara,' while a dozen or so pairs of children's eyes surveyed her cautiously.

Against the wall were chintz-covered chairs, and an old upright piano, its lid being raised showed its keys had turned yellow. The room was bathed in sunlight and heavy with the smell of fresh flowers.

A very much lived-in room, books and toys were strewn over the floor, a furry teddy bear, muddled wooden blocks, a gaily painted pedal-motorcar. Liveliness was the word that sprang to Barbara's mind.

'Right, apart from upstairs, and the treatment room, which we will leave for the moment, that's the end of the grand tour. We'll go back to my office and have a cup of tea.'

Following Matron without question, Barbara decided that she was a fast talker who looked one squarely in the eye and made an instant judgement. She had already formed the opinion, from listening to her non-stop account of the work that was carried out at Coombe Haven, that it was her energetic enthusiasm for the home and its patients that in turn gave her the wholehearted devotion of the staff.

With the tea brewed and a cup now set in front of Barbara, they were entirely at ease with each other.

'I don't mean to make us sound like angels of mercy,' Matron began, 'all the same, we can't operate on a nine-to-five basis. Once the kids here touch your heart, and some will, there is nothing more rewarding than having one of them respond to you. Now if we are to have you with us, shall I call you Barbara? And you call me Ivy. We all tend to use Christian names here.'

Barbara opened her mouth to reply, but Ivy was already racing on, 'I know you don't have any experience, but all you need for now is common sense and a caring attitude. Now when can you start and how many days will you be available?'

Barbara hesitated. She badly wanted to become involved with this well worthwhile project, but at the same time was frightened of being seen to be a failure. It hadn't occurred to her that she would be asked to plunge right in without some period of training.

'Would you like me to stay now? Well, until about four o'clock?' she fearfully asked.

'Good girl,' Ivy smiled approvingly. 'Hang your jacket through there and I'll take you to meet some of the children. There's one little boy in particular that I want you to see.'

Striding purposefully through corridors, Ivy turned her head and called, 'Not going too fast for you, am I? I want you to see what is known as the treatment room.'

There was no need for Barbara to form a reply. Ivy came to a halt in front of an open doorway, proudly she said, 'You've no idea of the amount of effort and time that some of our ladies put in here.'

Barbara's heart warmed towards her, she so obviously loved her work and believed in it.

'I can imagine. What a lovely well laid-out room this is.'

The room was large, bright and sunny, its tall windows looking out across lawns and flower beds. Around the wall there were three medical couches on which small children lay, each with a lady assistant in charge for safekeeping. On the floor two little girls were playing a game, using coloured counters and plastic cups.

Ivy approached the nearest couch and smiling at Barbara, she said, 'This is Hilda Whitely: she handles the physical exercises of the youngest children.'

Hilda was a short, attractive fair-haired girl about Barbara's own age.

She smiled, warmly acknowledging the introduction, but all she said was, ''Allo.'

Ivy grinned. 'Hilda is a true Londoner, as you will soon find out.' They moved on and Ivy, lowering her head, whispered, 'Heart of gold, that one.'

At the next group, Ivy said, 'This is Barbara Ferguson, from today she will be joining us. Brenda Smith I think you already know, you worked with her for a short while in the clinic at Vauxhall.'

'Yes, hallo Barbara. Welcome, it will be nice having you helping out here.'

'Thank you, Brenda, I'm looking forward to it.'

'Next to Brenda, is Catherine Bateman, she is everyone's dogsbody.' Catherine was a stout dark-haired girl of thirty-five or so.

'Hallo, Barbara, yeah I get every thankless task,' she said humorously.

'And last but by no means least our youngest member of staff, Julie Stevenson, she is always willing and able.'

A pretty youngster, no more than nineteen, smiled brightly at Barbara.

'Hallo,' they greeted each other.

At the far end of the room a white-coated man sat at a leather-topped desk, his back to the windows.

'Come and meet a dedicated man,' Ivy said softly to

Barbara. 'One of two full-time doctors that are employed here.'

As they walked towards him, the doctor rose to his feet, his hand outstretched in welcome.

'Our new recruit, eh? I'm Richard Turner.'

'Barbara Ferguson.' They both smiled, and shook hands.

Barbara guessed he was about forty, but somehow he appeared much older. A thin, worried face and grey, serious eyes that seemed to change as he smiled.

He seems nice, Barbara thought, with some satisfaction; it won't be hard to work with him.

Ivy said, 'We haven't fed Barbara yet. How about you, Richard, have you eaten?'

'It doesn't matter. About lunch, I mean. Please don't worry.' Barbara felt awkward.

Doctor Turner had sat down, leaning forward with his elbows on the edge of the desk. 'Aren't you hungry?' he asked Barbara.

Barbara didn't answer.

'I'm starving,' Ivy declared. 'So come along, let's all go and eat.'

To tell the truth Barbara had had a very long morning. Leaving home so early, having only had a bowl of cereal for her breakfast, she was feeling hungry, so she gratefully took her cue from both of them.

Having a meal together would break the ice, help Barbara to settle in, was what Matron was thinking and she made sure that it was in an entirely natural and easy fashion that the three of them went to the kitchen.

There was a smell of steak-and-kidney pies, mouth-watering.

'Are you eating here, or in the dining room?' Rose cheerfully asked.

'As it's so late we'll have it here, at the big table. Don't you worry, Rose; we'll see to ourselves,' Ivy Pearson assured her.

Leaving Barbara and the doctor to sit themselves down, Ivy went to the huge stove, took a pair of oven-gloves from a hook on the wall, and crouching down she opened the oven and took out a tray of individual meat-pies.

'They aren't dried up, are they?' Rose asked anxiously.

'No, just right,' Ivy said, setting the tray down onto the table.

Rose placed a tureen beside it. 'I put all the veg that was over in the one dish to keep it warm,' she said, taking the lid off of the dish and allowing steamy smells to rise. 'There's plenty of lovely gravy in the copper pan on the stove. If you're all right then I'm gonna go an' finish clearing up in the dining room.'

Some time later, Ivy asked, 'Have you two had enough to eat?'

Richard nodded.

Barbara said, 'Oh, yes thank you, it was a lovely meal. Did Rose make the pies?'

'Rose? No. We have a cook. She's here by six every morning, goes home at lunchtime. Marvellous, you'll see, she's been with us some years now. Would you like tea or coffee?'

'You know I don't like tea,' Richard shot in.

'I wasn't asking you,' Ivy laughed.

'Coffee is fine for me,' Barbara quickly told them, watching Ivy open a huge fridge to take a bottle of milk from the shelf on the door.

335

When the coffee had been made and a cup set in front of each of them, Richard leant towards Ivy and asked, 'Have you considered Barbara to work with the Rowlings boy?'

Barbara turned and stared, wondering who the Rowlings boy could be.

'Yes, I have. It was my intention to introduce young Sammy to Barbara when we set out on our tour. Somehow we got sidetracked. Perhaps you would like to fill her in on some of the boy's background?'

Richard had insisted that he too wished for Barbara to address him by his Christian name and now, smiling at him, she queried, 'Richard?'

He straightened up, folded his arms across his chest.

'Begin at the beginning,' Ivy prompted gently.

'I get a bit embarrassed when speaking of this boy. His name is Samuel Rowlings, he's two-years-old, and I'm sorry to have to tell you, one of our failures – not that we've given up hope, not by any means. Both myself and David Bennett, that's my colleague, have racked our brains for a solution for this child.'

Barbara was impressed by the sincerity that showed in Richard's whole manner.

Abruptly now, he took up the story, 'Samuel Rowlings was born with a harelip. Other than that we have found no physical deformities whatsoever. The mother was pregnant when she got married . . . far too young, hard on the father as well as herself. A trying time. Six months after the baby was born the father upped and left the pair of them. Disappeared. To give the young girl her due, after the initial shock had worn off, she did her best for nearly a year. Not in the happiest of circumstances. She had no family and the father's family openly showed their disapproval of his choice.

'The girl committed suicide. Baby was found in an upstairs bedroom. The mother had not turned up at the welfare clinic for two weeks and staff became worried.

'The welfare officer almost fell over Samuel – the body of Samuel she had thought at the time. As it was, he was filthy but alive. His mother's body was in the next room. Empty drink bottles were strewn everywhere. Dark-brown coloured, empty tablet bottles lay beside her.

'Samuel's legs and bottom were raw with sores from his stinking napkin. He was in a shocking state.

'He was given a series of injections against the germs. Even his eyes were almost closed, filled with yellow pus.

'His mother had been dead four days. She hadn't ill treated him. We are quite sure about that, she had reached the end of her tether. Couldn't cope any longer. Not on her own.

'If only she had sought more help, or had a family she could turn to.' Richard reached in his pocket and brought out a packet of cigarettes, 'D'you mind?'

Both women shook their heads.

He took one from the packet and struck a match. When it was alight, Barbara asked, 'Had she no one?'

'No. She grew up in a home. Later was farmed out to several different foster families. Married at eighteen, had Samuel six months later. Too young!'

'*Yes*! Far too young,' Ivy Pearson muttered almost to herself. 'It would be nice if – ' she broke off mid-sentence.

'If what?' Barbara asked.

'If that child could relate to someone, if someone could show him some love.'

337

'The boy has to learn to trust a person first,' Richard said quietly and then added, 'and learn to speak.'

'*What?*'

'That's right,' Ivy told a shocked Barbara. 'Sammy has never uttered a word to anyone from the day he was found. He has had an operation to repair the roof of his mouth and later perhaps he will have surgery to his top lip. There is no reason why he doesn't talk, he just doesn't.'

In the shiny, sunny kitchen, you could have heard a pin drop. Each person was deep in thought, until Richard spoke, 'Are you going to take Barbara along to meet Sammy?'

It was a sort of dismissal, but a kindly one. Ivy sighed, 'I think I'd better. Let her see him for herself.'

There seemed to be so little of him. His skin was creamy-smooth, his face unblemished except for the red, sore-looking patch on his top lip. His tousled hair was a mass of tight, fair curls which clung to his head. He sat in the centre of a playpen, surrounded by soft toys. As they approached, he lifted his head and stared at Barbara, only to drop it almost immediately.

Ivy smiled at Barbara over Samuel's head, 'He's shy. He's pretending you aren't here, he doesn't want to look at you.' She bent her head to say to the little boy, 'Come on you silly-billy, this is a nice lady who has come to see you.'

The poor little mite grunted angrily under his breath and crouched down slightly as if to hide.

Barbara quietly said, 'Hallo.'

'Say hallo, Sammy,' Ivy prompted. Then said, 'Don't be lazy, Sammy. You could say hallo Barbara, if you wanted to, Bar-bar-a, that's this lady's name. It's easy, listen, Bar-bar-a, you try.'

Ivy rose to her feet. Softly, sadly, she said, 'As usual he isn't going to utter a word.'

'What does he do all day?'

'Barbara, he does all the normal things the other children do. He eats well, though he won't feed himself. We still aren't sure if there is any permanent damage to his right arm, he doesn't use it much; his right leg is very weak too, though there again, doctors can find no reason why it should be. He plays, he sleeps, and in the afternoon he goes out in the grounds. When we have outings, we have our own special bus, he comes along, always seems to enjoy the ride.'

'I see he has plenty of toys, does he like picture books?'

'Mostly he tries to tear the pages out. He does seem to pay attention if someone is reading to him, or explaining a picture.'

'You're fond of him, Ivy, aren't you?'

'Yes, I just wish he would respond.'

'Does he make friends with the other children?'

'Some. He gets very annoyed if they touch him. Probably he'll be better when he's older. If he has a preference for anyone it's Hilda, and she seems able to cope with him better than most.'

Sadness swept through Barbara. Tears welled up in her eyes.

Ivy said quietly, 'Are . . . you all right?'

'Yes,' Barbara, answered. But she wasn't.

Her first thoughts had been, how could a young mother take her own life, abandon a tiny mite, not giving a thought as to how or where he might be brought up. Then suddenly she was reproaching herself.

Who am I to level such an accusation! If I'm such a kind and caring person, how come I signed my own baby away without even having set eyes on him? Did I know to whom he was going? I still only have Sister Francis's word that he would be adopted by a very good family.

A guilty conscience was something she thought she had put behind her. But it had caught up with her. God pays his debts, she tortured herself.

Barbara looked so sad that Ivy asked, 'Would you like to help get some of the children ready for their walk?'

Barbara didn't trust herself to answer. She was so near to tears, she just nodded.

Ivy felt she had to say something. This new volunteer was so obviously upset. 'Don't be disapproving or try to pass judgement will you, Barbara? It's not nice that these kiddies get rejected, cast aside; we all know that, but people have a thing about handicapped or disfigured children. They look away most times. It's hard enough if there are two parents. One on their own . . . Well.'

Barbara asked herself, what could she possibly say to that?

Sounds of adults talking and laughing drifted in from the corridor.

'Ah! That will be the Red Cross ladies. You'll like them, Barbara. Their headquarters are only a short distance away and they have a rota of helpers who come in and feed the children, and others who come in the afternoon and help our own staff to take the kiddies out. For walks or outings we only put one child into the care of one volunteer. Safer that way.'

'Come on, cocker!'

The loud voice made Barbara jump. She turned to see Hilda Whitely bending over the side of the playpen.

'Time t'get yer outdoor clothes on, Sammy. We're gonna go out in the gardens, might even see the dogs. Yer like the doggies don't you, luv, they bark at yer. One of these fine days yer might even 'ave something t'say t'them, eh?'

Hilda lifted him over the side and set him down. Sammy, eyes downcast, began to totter unsteadily towards the corner of the room. There he stood, face to the wall, his little head slumped forward onto his chest.

'No, no, yer fat-'ead,' Hilda ran to him. ''Ere, put yer arm in this sleeve. All the others will be gone if we don't 'urry up and then yer won't like that, now will yer?'

Within seconds, Hilda had Sammy dressed in a bright-red linen coat and a small peaked cap with a badge on it. She hesitated, looking at Ivy, and if Barbara had turned around she would have seen the direct look each gave the other and the little wink that was exchanged between them.

Then Hilda said, 'I 'ave t'go an' get one of the pushchairs out of the cloakroom. Will you 'old Samuel for a minute?'

Barbara dithered, 'Will he come to me?'

'Course 'ee will.'

Hilda lifted the boy up, hoisting him towards Barbara.

'I shan't be a tick, Sammy,' Hilda assured him, and she turned and went out of the room.

Sammy looked right into Barbara's eyes as she put her arms around him and drew him close. Near to, his harelip looked very red, and sore. He smelt of talcum powder and fresh soap. Lovely. Suddenly she felt his fingers grip her shoulders and then she felt pain, such pain that it made her eyes water and her nose hurt.

341

Sammy had brought his head back and butted Barbara straight in the face. Now he wriggled and twisted, using his knees to give himself leverage against her chest, yet he never uttered a sound. Barbara almost dropped him, probably would have if Ivy had not intervened.

'Ready then, my old son,' Hilda was back with the pushchair.

She took one look at Barbara, dabbing her nose with a white handkerchief and mouthed the word, 'Sorry.' When she had Samuel safely strapped in the chair, she raised her eyebrows at Barbara and said, 'Bit determined, ain't he? Wriggles like an eel, but 'ee'll get used t'yer, yer'll see.'

Ivy was worried. Had she pushed things too fast?

'Had enough?' she asked. 'Or shall we go out into the grounds and watch what goes on?'

Barbara found herself chuckling, imagining what she was going to say to James when he saw her battered face.

'Was a bit unexpected, wasn't it?' Ivy couldn't help herself – she burst out laughing.

'I'll live,' a smiling Barbara assured her. 'Lead on.'

Barbara was amazed at both the size and the beauty of the gardens. Huge rhododendron bushes flanked the high stone walls, and azaleas in such colours as Barbara had never seen before. Across wide, green lawns a play area had been set up. Small, low swings, gaily painted roundabouts, helter-skelter slides and a sandpit. There were a dozen or so children there, each with an adult to keep a watchful eye on them. Cries of delight and chuckles of pleasure could clearly be heard.

It wasn't hard for Barbara to pick out Sammy, her eyes soon focused on his bright-red blazer.

342

Hilda had him chained in a swing that had a box-like seat with safety rails at each side. She was gently pushing him back and forth, not from behind, but from in front, so that he could see her at all times. 'One a penny, two a penny, three four five,' she crooned as she bent almost double in order to be able to see Sammy's face.

Ivy and Barbara watched in silence for a few minutes until Hilda slowed the swing down and lifted Sammy to the ground. They couldn't hear what she was saying to him, but there was no mistaking that she planted a kiss on his cheek before patting his bottom and pushing him in the direction of the sandpit.

He wobbled off, reeling to the right, followed closely by Hilda.

Barbara turned to face Ivy. 'He drags that right leg, doesn't he?'

'Afraid so.'

'Do you do anything about it?'

'Yes. He gets daily massage and exercise. Not for as long as we would like, but we only have so many volunteers that can spare that amount of time.'

'Is that what you would like me to do?'

'Is it what you would want to do?'

'Very much so, if you think it comes within my capabilities.'

'I certainly do, and naturally we wouldn't leave you on your own, not to begin with. Could you manage a whole day every week?'

'I could manage two days if you're sure that I would be of some help.'

Ivy Pearson smiled broadly, 'I'm positive, Barbara. A

343

willing volunteer is almost always worth two of every paid employee.'

'Would I be working with Samuel?'

'You've no idea of how much I was hoping you would want to. It wouldn't be solely with Sammy,' she laughed aloud. 'He has to sleep sometime. The doctors will do something about repairing his lip when he is a little older but there is no guarantee that he will ever walk really well.'

Barbara glanced at her watch. 'It's just on four,' Ivy confirmed. 'You'd better see about getting yourself ready, your husband will be here soon.'

Several thoughts were racing through Barbara's mind as they walked back to the house.

Never ever walk properly! *Oh yes he will!* Barbara vowed to herself. If I have to help him exercise for the rest of my life I swear to God, he'll walk properly one day.

Chapter Twenty-two

BARBARA GAVE AN unconscious sigh as she drew a writing-pad and pen from her desk. Her thoughts were so tangled that she had decided she would put her feelings down on paper in a letter to Elizabeth.

Her visits to Coombe Haven had become very important, or so Ivy Pearson assured her. Barbara was not so confident. Of one thing she was certain – each visit had come to mean a great deal to her. Not that she had made a lot of progress with young Sammy, he still hadn't uttered a single word in all the weeks she had been going there. Signs of recognition, yes, even going so far as to climb onto her lap.

Occasionally even that could go wrong. Seated with his back to her chest, Sammy would bounce up and down, demanding silently that Barbara gave him a ride on her knees. Fearing that he might fall she would tighten her arms around his waist, holding him close. Twice he had resisted this action. His little head had gone forward, only to be thrust up and backwards, quickly slamming hard into Barbara's face. One such tantrum had resulted in Barbara having a black eye.

Both Paul and James had been highly amused, a fact that neither of them tried to hide, as they travelled home to Jevington.

'Quite the little boxer!' Paul had exclaimed.

'I'd put our Samuel down as a heavy-weight, don't you

345

agree?' James had replied, tears of laughter showing in his eyes.

The fact that the two men had met Sammy, on more than one occasion, had to be accredited to Brenda Smith. Having met each other at the clinic in Vauxhall, Brenda knew that their interest in what Barbara was doing was vital. And so it had come about.

Seeing Paul turn the car into the drive early one afternoon, she had approached Matron, 'Would you mind if I offered Barbara's husband and his male nurse a cup of tea?'

'By all means, Brenda. By the way, where is Barbara?'

'Still over at the sandpit.'

The two women looked knowingly at each other.

The result had been that Paul and James arrived at the sandpit, in the nick of time.

'I want another chocolate biscuit!' a little girl named Jill was screaming, but Julie Stevenson, her carer, said, 'No, you've already eaten yours. There was only enough for one each.'

Sammy hadn't started on his biscuit; he was watching Steven, a bigger boy, pat the end of an upturned bucket which he had helped to fill with sand, plop it over, and then carefully lift the bucket away, to produce a perfect shaped turret for the edge of the sand castle they were making.

The little girl saw her chance. She reached out and snatched the biscuit from Sammy's hand.

Sammy's face turned red and he hit Jill with his shovel.

'No, no!' Barbara cried.

Steven, the big boy, pushed Sammy. He fell and hit his head on the bucket. Paul jumped into the pit, looked at

Sammy's head, 'He's not hurt,' he told Barbara, amazed that the small boy hadn't screamed.

'He hit me with his shovel!'

'That's true,' Julie told her little charge, 'But, Jill, you have got to learn that you can't have everything you want and you certainly mustn't take things away from other children.'

James groaned in mock despair, 'Good God! How often do you have to settle clashes like this?'

'Just lively kids,' Barbara explained. 'More often than not a pain in the neck, but all perfectly normal.'

'Come on,' Paul said to the still screaming little girl, swinging her up in the air. 'How would you like a ride in my friend's carriage?'

The child eyed the wheelchair with mistrust.

With a broad grin Paul dumped her onto James's knees and turned back to the group of by now wide-eyed children.

'Shall I help you to make sand-pies?' Paul smiled the question at Sammy and was rewarded with a nod of his head.

When it was time for the children to return to the house they made comical procession. Jill still sat on James's lap, queening it over the other little girls, showing she was enjoying the ride. Sammy, legs wide apart, was being carried on the shoulders of Paul and to compensate the other children, Hilda Whitely walked backwards, facing the group, beating time and singing loudly, "Umpty Dumpty sat on a wall, 'Umpty Dumpty 'ad a big fall . . .'

Ivy Pearson had rushed to the window on hearing the noise.

'Well, I'll be sugared!' she exclaimed, hardly able to believe her eyes.

A city gentlemen, wearing a dark pinstriped suit, in a wheelchair, with Jill, their most cantankerous little girl, riding on his knees. And to top that a huge fellow had Sammy astride his shoulders. Sammy, who normally shied away from men! As for Hilda, she had thought that nothing that one could do would surprise her, but she'd come up tops today. Talk about leading the band!

'You think Sammy is a nice little boy?' Barbara had asked anxiously, as Paul had driven them home.

Being quite used to the conversation being solely about Samuel Rowlings on these journeys, James wasn't put out; indeed he was thrilled to know that his wife had taken up such a worthwhile occupation. Now he smiled as he answered her truthfully.

'Yes, yes, he's a really likeable little lad and very brave into the bargain.'

Barbara nodded happily, 'I know. I'm so glad you've seen him for yourself. I've wanted to hear your opinion for ages.'

'I had a word with Ivy Pearson while you were getting yourself ready.'

'Oh! What did she say?'

'She said that although Samuel still doesn't speak, he has come a long way since you have been helping at Coombe Haven. She also said for Paul and myself to drop in whenever we were able.'

'Ivy's so patient with the children,' Barbara remarked. 'She really loves them, you know.'

James observed, 'Because in one way or another they are all orphans of the storm.'

'Probably. I feel grateful to Anthony, and to your sister

348

Chloe, for having introduced me to Coombe Haven in the first place.'

So a pattern was formed and James had never found cause to complain, or to regret his decision to become personally involved.

'Barbara?'

Her husband's voice behind her in the doorway broke into Barbara's thoughts.

'Barbara . . . what are you doing in here on such a lovely autumn afternoon? We won't get many more opportunities like this. It will soon be winter. You said you were coming out into the garden and were going to write a letter to Elizabeth.'

'I am, darling. Here – you can take my pad and pen and I'll carry this tray; I've squeezed some lemons and made a jug of squash.'

It was Sunday. Paul Soames had taken his lady-friend, Maureen O'Connor, to Brighton for the day. With time, James had become a little more independent. He had learnt to do some things himself but it did worry Barbara: what would happen if Paul decided to marry his lady-friend and leave James? Time enough to meet trouble when it comes knocking on the door, she told herself.

With two chairs set out on the lawn, a table between them and a glass of lemonade within easy reach, James became absorbed in the Sunday papers and Barbara settled to writing her letter.

October 29th

My dear Elizabeth,

Well here I am, having stayed the course at Coombe
Haven for four months. Am writing, because I feel I can
say so much more, express my feelings better, than I'm
able to when we have our weekly natter on the
telephone.

My feelings have been mixed, thrilled with Samuel's
progress one day, down in the dumps the next because
he sometimes reacts so violently towards me. Such a sad
little boy. And lonely. Though he is never alone, children
and adults around him all the time. It's as if he has a shell
around him and no one seems to be able to make the
break through.

Elizabeth, with three kiddies of your own you must
be wise as to how they act and think. Tell me, please,
do you think that Sammy realises that he has no one?
No family of his own? It would make your heart bleed
to see his little face when I say goodbye to him. I always
make a point of assuring him that I am coming back.

As you know, I go to Coombe Haven Tuesdays and
Thursdays. It's a long break between Thursday and the
following Tuesday. Samuel is quite hostile when I do
return. How I wish to God that boy would speak. If it
were only to rant and rave at me.

Penny has visited Coombe Haven a couple of times,
she was quite taken up with Sammy. 'Nice enough to
eat!' she declared.

Funny enough, he didn't object to Penny picking him
up. Maybe because she isn't hesitant, goes for it, laughs
a lot and is always in command. Do you think that is
possible?

350

The biggest thrill I get is when, perhaps, I put my hand out and brush the hair away from Sammy's eyes, he'll make a grab for my forefinger, rolling his own chubby little fingers around it like a sausage. He'll hold on to it for ages. It's the nearest I ever get to a cuddle from him.

Elizabeth, I meant this to be a cheerful letter and here I am writing of all my misgivings when I should be asking after you and Tim. What of William and John? Growing fast I expect. Are they doing well at school? And baby Hannah? We don't see enough of each other, do we? I must get James to agree to come to Windsor for a weekend.

Which brings me to another point. I'm a coward or I would have started off with this.

James wants to attend a do being given by the Law Society. Thing is, it is being held in Scotland, over three days. James wants for us both to go and then for us to stay on at the hotel for a further ten days or so. I know he's right to insist – we haven't had a holiday and this would be the ideal break. Paul has offered to accompany us, bring his lady-friend as well, so it would be great for them.

But oh Elizabeth, the thought of leaving Sammy without a visit for maybe more than two weeks fills me with dread. Be like deserting a sinking ship. Worse! He would be entitled to believe I had abandoned him. Another rejection.

I have made some headway with him. I'm sure I have. There are times when I could shout out loud with pleasure because of a fleeting moment when I catch an expression on his little face, and for the briefest instant a smile will transform his solemn features.

I know I must put James first, yet I feel the next few weeks with Samuel will probably be more important than all the rest put together.

Why can't we all be as wise as King Solomon?

Ah Elizabeth, I suppose I shall go to Scotland, or rather I should say WE shall go to Scotland. Will ring you before we leave.

Our love to you all,

Barbara.

She sat back, thinking of Tim and Elizabeth, their children growing up in that uncomplicated family, with security and so much love.

She looked across at James. He was still young, only thirty-eight. Life wasn't fair. Still, he hadn't let the accident ruin his life. He wasn't bitter, never regarded himself as a cripple. He worked hard at keeping himself fit. His pale-blue, short-sleeved shirt hung loosely over lightweight cream linen trousers. He felt her gaze and looked up directly at her, and she felt a glow spread over her. His arms were brown, his face tanned from the good summer weather they had had, and his belly was as flat as a pancake.

He leaned over and reached for his glass, his forearm brushing across her lower thigh. She watched the muscles in his forearm flex when he pulled the table nearer.

She touched his hand, felt the warmth and the springy hairs which covered the back of it. Oh James! she breathed to herself. I love you so.

They didn't have everything in life, but then who does? Life could be a whole lot worse. They had their moments when some nights she lay in his arms and he proved beyond doubt that she was the only woman for him and she certainly needed no convincing that marrying James had been the absolutely right thing for her to have done.

As if knowing something of what Barbara was thinking, James leaned across, his lips seeking hers.

Oliver, their big Labrador retriever, wriggled to his feet, cross at being disturbed, then moved to the shade of a tree and flopped down again.

James laughed, 'That dog has a wonderful life.'

Barbara smiled warmly. 'And so my darling, do we, and please God, the best is yet to come.'

Barbara couldn't help herself. The tears were spilling over, falling warmly on to the back of her hand before she had time to brush them away.

'*Please*, Sammy,' she begged. On her knees beside him on the carpet, she tried to swing his body round to face her. He would have none of it.

'Leave 'im be, Barbara,' Hilda advised. 'Most likely 'ee will pine, but that might just do 'im a bit of good. Yer never can tell. Good Lord, you're entitled t'have a break, same as the rest of us. I'll see ter 'im. That's a promise, cross me 'eart. I won't let 'im forget that you're gonna come back. Now do us both a favour an' sling yer 'ook, go on, while the going's good, else you'll 'ave us all in bloody tears before you're finished.'

Apparently the seminar had been a great success. Certainly James was in a good mood as he asked Paul and Maureen to join them for a drink before they set out for their evening walk.

353

There weren't many guests left in the hotel now, the four of them had enjoyed a lovely dinner, taking their time over it, and were now sitting in the comfortable lounge with coffee set out in front of them.

'Brandy, Paul?' James asked and when Paul nodded, he added, 'And liqueurs, is it? For you two lovely ladies?'

The waiter brought their drinks and just as Barbara was about to raise her glass, Paul said, 'Maureen and I have something to tell you both.'

Barbara's heart sank down into her boots.

Taking hold of Maureen's hand, Paul smiled as he said, 'We've decided to get married.'

Barbara tried her best to smile and Paul, watching her, knew exactly what she was thinking. He spoke quickly.

'I have a proposition to put to you both, if you don't think I am being too presumptuous.'

'Paul!' James cut him off quickly. 'I thought you regarded Barbara and myself as friends?'

'Oh, I do,' Paul hastened to assure him. 'The last thing I want to do is to leave you. Working for you, James, suits me very well.'

'So, spit out what you were about to say.'

'The cottage in your grounds – with some renovations it would be a grand place for Maureen and myself to set up house. Don't think you're aware of it, but Maureen is a barmaid-cum-waitress at The Smugglers in Alfriston. She has a room there. Lives in. All her family are still in Ireland. We have been having lengthy discussions about this for ages. She'll be over the moon if you agree.'

Barbara looked first at Maureen, who by now was blushing. Then she turned to James, their eyes met and they both smiled.

'Congratulations!' James and Barbara said simultaneously. James was shaking hands with Paul, Barbara was kissing Maureen, then found she was being hugged by Paul while Maureen rose and bent to plant a kiss on James's cheek.

His eyes wide with happiness, Paul sat back. 'What a relief,' he murmured. Maureen, who had always appeared self-conscious when around Barbara, now smiled happily. 'Oh thank you both. 'Tis such a lovely cottage, we'll be able to fix it up fine. I'll keep on with me job for a while, but the joy of it, to come home to me own place instead of just having me own room.'

James became serious, turned to Paul first and then to Maureen, 'I would like to pay all expenses for your wedding – Barbara's and my wedding gift to you both.'

'We'll not be having a grand wedding, Mister James,' Maureen hastened to say.

'We'll go into all of that when we get home. I dare say Barbara and some of her friends will relish the idea of going shopping with you and doing all the things you girls do in preparation for a wedding. Meanwhile, will you please drop the Mister. Maureen and Paul, you are to us, and Barbara and James we are to you. All right?'

It was a happy pair of lovers that set off for their walk, and a relieved married pair that remained behind in the hotel to toast them once again with fresh drinks that James had quickly asked the barman to bring to their table.

This hotel, in Dunoon, had been selected by the Law Society. First off, both Barbara and James had been disappointed that it wasn't on the edge of a loch or set amongst Scotland's mountains. Now it suited them to stay in Dunoon for their extra days, one of the main reasons being

355

that the resort had a long level promenade, not far from the hotel, which enabled Barbara and James to take a leisurely walk of an evening. Besides which, the hotel was of the older type, not plush, giving excellent food and service. Barbara especially liked the fact that log-fires were lit in all the public rooms early in the afternoon.

They hired a car, dressed casually, and the four of them toured the spectacular Western Highlands, making sure they spent one day on the shore of the lovely Loch Lomond. The only fly in the ointment being Barbara's remorse at having left young Sammy.

James, well aware of how his wife felt, did his best to reassure her.

Early one afternoon, they arrived at a particularly lovely spot.

Having made sure that Barbara and James were quite comfortably settled in a cottage that served cream teas, Maureen and Paul set off to stride away across heather-covered hills.

The cottage had tremendous views, made all the better by the glowing autumn foliage.

Barbara was looking out of the windows, quite happily watching several squirrels scampering up and down the trees, when James put a hand on her knee, making her jump, intruding on her thoughts.

'Tell you what, Barbara,' he said. 'When we get back to London, we don't need to go straight home, we could book ourselves into Brown's Hotel in Dover Street for the night and go pay a visit to Coombe Haven.'

'Oh James, I *do* love you,' she squeezed his arm. 'You're sure you don't mind? You won't be too tired?'

'Well,' he paused, as if he were giving thought to the

question. 'We aren't exactly slumming it on the train, are we? Gourmet food, excellent sleeping berths, we'll arrive fresh as daisies.'

'Oh, you!' She pushed his arm this time, a scone that was halfway to his mouth got there faster, cream, squashed from the filling, now spread along his top and bottom lip.

Barbara roared out laughing.

James bought Scotch whisky for his colleagues, and a bottle for each of their fathers. Barbara bought lots of tins of butter-shortbread for the children at Coombe Haven, a teddy bear dressed in a kilt for Sammy, and a warm tartan shawl for Mrs Clarkson and Maggie Harvey. For her mother and also for James's mother, she couldn't resist silver brooches, fashioned in the shape of a twig of heather.

They had been back in London for less than two hours. Washed and refreshed, they stood beneath the canopy on the top step of the entrance to Brown's Hotel, watching as the doorman raised his hat and whistled up a taxi for them. There was no shortage of offers of help from the staff when it came to manoeuvring James's wheelchair down the steps and into the cab. Paul saw that everything went smoothly, waiting until Barbara was seated up front with the driver before getting into the back seat to sit beside James. Maureen had travelled straight on to Eastbourne: she was due to start work the next morning.

There was no mistaking the warmth in the welcome Ivy Pearson gave them. In the doorway to the playroom, Barbara stood still for a moment, uncertain, the thumping of her heart loud in her ears, nervousness making her legs tremble.

357

Hilda Whitely sensed her presence, looked up, put a finger to her lips and mouthed the word, 'Shush.' Hilda than quietly got up from the chair on which she had been sitting and backed herself out of the room.

Smiling broadly at Barbara, she gave her a gentle push, sending her forwards.

The sight that met her eyes brought her almost to tears. Sammy was snugly dressed in a pale-blue jersey, sitting on the floor actually looking at the pages of a picture book. Oh, he is a handsome child, was her first thought: his tight, fair curls still clung to his head, falling down over his forehead as he bent forward. With his chubby face and rosy cheeks, the scar on his lip didn't matter. Strong dimpled little hands held the book. 'I can't help it,' she muttered beneath her breath, 'I adore him.'

Further down the room children were rattling tins, piles of bricks were being knocked over and carers were helping others to do their exercises. Sammy was oblivious to everything that was going on around him.

'Sammy,' Barbara's voice was scarcely more than a whisper.

He turned, he stared. His lips didn't move but he made a noise. Not words but sounds, just sounds. He stood up, tottered towards her, then stopped a few feet away.

'Ba . . . ba . . . bar . . . bar . . . a,' his voice was low and hoarse.

Barbara was unaware that James had wheeled himself up close, that Hilda and Ivy were halfway into the room, silently applauding.

Her heart was filled with so much love for this little mite she didn't know what to do first.

358

'You said it! Yes you did, my lovely, you said it. My name. Barbara, you said it!'

The little boy stared at her a few seconds longer and then he began to cry. The first tears Barbara had ever seen him shed.

'Slowly,' James urged. 'Don't frighten him.'

There was no stopping her.

Arms out wide she ran, swooping him up, holding him close, wrapping him in safety, smothering him with love.

She didn't dare let herself believe it. He didn't resist, instead he nestled his head into her neck: he was crying softly, rubbing his wet face against her bare skin.

Heavenly! She was finally cuddling him.

'Don't cry, my pet, please, don't cry,' she crooned to him. 'See, I *did* come back.'

Keeping Sammy in her arms she turned towards James, there were tears in his eyes.

'Did you hear him? Did you? He said my name. After all this time he said my name!'

'Yes darling, I heard,' James smiled. He was more moved than he would have cared to admit. Watching Barbara, and Sammy, who was still clinging to her, he had this protective feeling towards the little lad, that as the weeks had gone by had got ever stronger and was by now becoming so familiar.

Behind her, Barbara heard footsteps coming down the room. She turned her head and saw Hilda, who, when she reached her side, stood looking at the pair of them.

'Fank the good Lord f'that!' Hilda let out a great sigh of relief. 'I've bin saying Bar-bar-a over an' over again, till I'm blue in the face. Even bin saying it in me sleep, so me 'ole man tells me. 'Ee finks I've gone a bit funny like, found meself a woman friend, if yer know what I mean.

359

Elizabeth Waite

Yer got t'laugh at my Bill, he's bin going all round our council estate asking ''oo the 'ell is Barbara?'

Even James couldn't control his mirth!

Barbara, still rocking Sammy back and forth, was laughing fit to bust.

'I think you'd all better come along to the dining room,' Ivy instructed them, putting on her stern matron's voice.

Barbara lowered Sammy to the floor. He wouldn't let go his hold, grasping a handful of her dress, his eyes never leaving her face.

'Come on, a little bird told me it's shepherd's pie today. Your favourite. If you give me a smile, just one, I'll come and sit beside you.'

He managed a smile all right. It lit up his whole face.

Ivy Pearson, severely dressed, still very much the matron, waited until they were round the bend in the corridor, out of sight, and then she leant against the wall and fumbled in the pocket of her dress for a handkerchief. Her sight kept blurring with tears.

360

Chapter Twenty-three

JAMES HAD BROKEN with his routine and taken a day off from the City to attend an open-day at Coombe Haven. Invitations to the press and local dignitaries had also been sent out. The weather had been kind: for November it was a grand day, clear and dry even if it was a little cold. They had managed to set up several stalls in the grounds besides the various activities that were going on in the house.

The day had not originally been organised as a fund-raising event but the results, judging by the number of people that had turned up, must be good.

'Ladies and Gentlemen!'

Doctor Richard Turner and his colleague Doctor David Bennett were both standing on chairs, near to the sale-of-work table, looking out at the crowds that had gathered on the lawn.

Voices were hushed and heads turned expectantly in their direction.

'Thank you.' Having got everyone's attention, Richard held up a sheet of paper.

'Just before we all go into the house for a hot cup of tea, the committee of this children's home have asked us to thank you all for your generosity. The results of today's gathering will, I'm sure, gladden the hearts of all who are involved with Coombe Haven. As most of you are aware, many of our workers are volunteers and the few that are paid a wage are dedicated to the children far beyond the call of their duties. Serving and giving as they all do, they are inspired by and grateful for the money which has been donated today. Such has been the success of this operation, so we have already been told, that it has resulted not only in donations of cash, many of which are from unexpected quarters, but offers have been made of equipment from various firms in the district. Equipment that the home so badly needs and which will be very much appreciated. I speak for us all and on behalf of the children, when I say, we are truly grateful. If you would like to know more of the workings of Coombe Haven, my friend, David, here, will be only too happy to give you one of our brochures.'

Sounds of gladness and goodwill rippled around the grounds.

Sammy, whose little legs wouldn't carry him any further, was riding piggyback on Barbara as they made their way back to the house.

'James and Paul were looking for you two.'

At the sound of Richard's voice behind her, Barbara stood still, turned around and waited for him to catch up with her.

'They said to tell you they would see you inside.'

'Oh, right. We were just making tracks, getting chilly now.'

Barbara bent down and let Sammy slip to the ground.

'Had a good time, haven't we?' she said to the little boy. 'Tell Doctor Richard you had a ride on a pony.'

Sammy looked up at the doctor, smiled, nodded, but never answered.

'Still hasn't much to say for himself,' Richard's tone reflected concern.

'Oh, he's still very wary of folk. Chatters away to me sometimes now, nineteen to the dozen.'

Sammy must have felt he was being ignored.

With a lot of force he flung his arms around Richard's knees and butted the doctor's legs with his head.

Neither Richard nor Barbara took any notice. They stood there, still carrying on their conversation.

Sammy slammed his whole body against Richard's legs again, this time causing him to take a step backwards.

'He doesn't relish sharing you, Barbara, does he? He wants the whole of your attention. Not that anyone can blame him for that,' he added with a grin. 'He's an amusing little character on the days you're here, withdraws back into his shell other times. Pity. He will eventually have to learn to trust others.'

Barbara was still pondering on Richard's words when she entered the dining room and saw Paul waving her to a table where he and James were already seated.

'Here, take my cup,' Paul offered. 'I've only just fetched it, it is still hot.'

'No, I'll go, you stay where you are. I'll get Sammy some squash at the same time.'

'Hallo Sammy, old chap, have you had a great time?' Paul, doing as he was told, had bent down to take charge of the small boy, lifting him up onto a chair.

James stretched his arm across the table, took a chocolate cake from the plate of assorted fancy cakes and offered it to Sammy.

The boy's lips twitched into half a smile but he made no sound.

With the cake half-eaten, Sammy slipped down from his

363

chair, put one foot on to the platform of James's wheelchair and climbed up into his lap.

'Ride,' he demanded.

'Say please,' James told him without thinking.

'Please,' Sammy obediently said.

Paul laughed to himself.

James let off the brake and let the chair roll back and forth.

Barbara, arriving back with a tea-tray, couldn't believe her eyes. It was such a happy scene. Paul Soames nodded his head, let his eyelid drop in a saucy wink, as if to say: see, even James is taken up with the little toddler.

Her thoughts were still troubling her. What if Richard had been trying to warn her that soon Sammy might have to leave Coombe Haven? Foster-parents would be found for him.

It didn't bear thinking about!

Yet that very idea had been there all the time. She mustn't brood on it. Lose Sammy! She was so strongly opposed to the idea that it made her feel sick.

Sammy banged her with his fist and said, 'Look!'

Barbara looked, and saw his sticky fingers, his beaming, chocolate-smeared face, and she pulled him from James's lap into her arms and hugged him.

James watched and heard her say, 'You little monkey. I love you. D'you know that?'

Sammy didn't answer.

She tickled him, he wriggled, laughing loudly.

His laughter eased her tension.

Visitors were leaving, only the part-time volunteers and a few employees such as Hilda had remained to help with the clearing-up.

'Isn't it time you were going home, Hilda?' Barbara asked, as she helped Hilda to stack dirty cups and saucers onto a tray.

'It's all right, Barbara; me 'ole man is on two till ten t'day, he won't be there now anyway.'

'Have you got any children? I've never thought to ask you before now.'

'Bless yer 'eart, course I 'ave. Two boys, ten an' twelve. Me mum will see t'them, give 'em their tea. 'Sides, they take more notice of 'er than they ever do of me or their father. Do anything fer their Gran they will.'

'Oh, you're lucky, having your mother nearby. That's how you manage to be able to work. Peace of mind, eh, knowing someone is there when they come home from school?'

Hilda laughed as she passed an empty tray to Barbara, and lifted the loaded one to take to the kitchen.

'Me mum lives wiv us. Me dad died eight years ago, couldn't leave me poor 'ole mum t'get by on 'er own, could I?'

Barbara was thoughtful as she regarded Hilda setting off, most likely to give a hand with the washing-up. Happy soul was Hilda, ever ready to give help where it was needed. So, there was a family of five living in the Whitelys' council house. She knew about this estate, where Hilda lived: very unusual type of houses they were. Built years ago, more as country cottages, when Croydon was still very much part of Surrey. The front doors opened straight onto the pavement. They were very small dwellings, without bathrooms and yet to hear Hilda, she was quite sure that the Whitelys were a very happy, contented family.

Life was a puzzle at times.

There was James and herself living in the country, plenty of room in a beautiful house, horses to ride whenever the fancy took her, lovely walks and not very far from the sea. What more could a woman want from life than this? She had comfort, security, love and tenderness. The one vital thing that was missing was children. Whatever else she might possess that was what she didn't have. And never could have.

'Ladies.'

Ivy Pearson waved her arms in the air to silence the talking that was going on in the dining room.

'May I have your attention for a moment, please?'

There was a sudden hush amongst the adults, but not the children, who merely glanced up at Matron and then went on with their chattering.

'Just before you all go home, may I raise the question of Christmas? We have been most generously offered toys and even entertainment, spread over the holiday. We shall as usual be having agency nurses to come in to supplement our live-in staff. The children will want for nothing. If, however, some of you volunteers could manage some form of involvement, no matter how small, it would be greatly appreciated. Thank you all for the effort you have put into making a success of today.'

Matron gave a friendly wave, signifying the end of her little talk, and turned to descend from the platform.

The swell of voices broke out afresh.

Barbara was stunned. Christmas!

Couldn't she just imagine it, without being able to see Sammy?

Yes! was her own answer. Vividly!

Her gaze took in the fact that Paul was busy stacking

chairs against the wall, but James was lounging back in his chair studying her intently.

It was on the tip of her tongue to demand to know what they were going to do about Samuel during the Christmas holiday, but knowing such a question at this moment would only hurt James's feelings, she gave a little shrug of her shoulders and went back to stacking dirty crockery onto trays.

''Ave a look at Sammy, e's more than 'alf asleep,' Hilda nudged Barbara with her elbow.

'Oh bless him.' He was curled up on the carpet, one leg tucked underneath his bottom, his head resting on his arm.

Barbara bent to pick up a wooden brick that was jammed beneath his elbow, and speaking softly she said, 'Come on, my darling, you mustn't go to sleep on the floor, someone will tread on you if I leave you lying here.'

Without a word Sammy held out his arms to her and when she had him curled up in her arms he stuck his thumb in his mouth and, sucking contentedly, closed his eyes again and drifted off to sleep.

'There's a good boy,' she murmured, not really knowing what to do with him now, but not wishing to part from him. Very soon Paul would be telling them it was time to set off for home.

'I'll take him, Barbara,' Hilda said. 'The nurses are taking most of the little ones up to their cots.'

Barbara stroked his silky, soft, curly hair and whispered, 'Bye-bye, Sammy. I'll see you on Tuesday.'

She was relieved that as she passed him over to Hilda's outstretched arms, he didn't stir, nor did he open his eyes.

She paused before going to join James.

All children need parents. A child shouldn't be shifted

from pillar to post. It would be a poor, lonely life if that was all that Sammy would have to look forward to.

'Let's go,' Barbara said to Paul as she buttoned up her coat.

James sensed the effort this was costing her, and he felt extraordinarily moved. He recalled the time at Henley, when Barbara had first told him of the rough treatment she had received at the hands of Michael and his mate, and how subsequently she had refused to even look at her own baby. He had clung to the hope that his love for her would eventually wipe out all the nightmares of her past. It might have, had not fate intervened. His accident had banished all hope that they would ever have children of their own.

'I'm ready,' Barbara looked into his face, saw his blue eyes, full of love and understanding, and the sweetness of a soft smile came to her lips.

She said faintly, 'We can't leave him here. Not for Christmas.'

'No. I'll see what can be done. We'll sort something out.'

She breathed out. Thank God for James. She closed her eyes and tried to say a prayer, but somehow the right words wouldn't come.

She wasn't asking to have Sammy for good. Just for Christmas. Was that too much to ask?

Apparently it was. The answer was No.

Barbara could see the reasoning of the doctors and the members of the committee, but that didn't make it any easier to bear.

James had dreaded having to tell her of their decision.

'They are right, you know, Barbara; we just didn't take

the time to consider what we were asking. As Anthony pointed out, normally home visits are encouraged, at least for the older children, but under strict supervision and in calm, quiet circumstances.'

'Christmas time being the wrong time,' Barbara said thoughtfully.

'Well, yes. Lots of people in and out. Festivities and presents, could be bewildering for a small child in strange surroundings, don't you agree?'

Barbara found herself saying, 'Yes', when all she wanted to do was scream in frustration.

James manoeuvred his wheelchair nearer to where Barbara stood looking through the lounge windows. He felt self-conscious about what he was going to say to her. Would he be touching a raw nerve?

'Barbara, would you . . . well, could you . . . bring yourself to think about adoption?'

It hadn't been easy to say. Would she reproach him because that was exactly what she had done to her own son?

'I've spoken to my partners,' he plunged on, as she remained silent. 'The firm would handle all the legal aspects for us, and I only ventured to ask because the panel of doctors at Coombe Haven said that was one of the possibilities they were considering in Samuel's case. They would, of course, have to trace his father. No one envisaged trouble from that quarter.'

Barbara was agitated. She found it was much easier not to cry if she screwed her eyes up tight and refused to open them.

'I don't mind if you want to cry,' James told her, endeavouring to show her just how much he did understand.

'I'm doing my best not to.'

'Sammy will be fine. Matron will see to him and she won't be the only one.'

Barbara knew he spoke the truth, yet none the more for that Christmas would seem a never-ending holiday this year.

Chapter Twenty-four

WITH THE COMING of the New Year, endless discussions were under way as to the suitability of James and Barbara Ferguson to become adoptive parents of two-year-old Samuel Rowlings.

On two weekends, a fortnight apart, they had been allowed to have Sammy home for two days. The first time had been a strain. He had clung to Barbara, wouldn't let her out of his sight, and had withdrawn back into his shell, scarcely uttering more than one word at a time during the whole of his stay. The second time had seen an improvement. Paul and Maureen O'Connor had spent the Saturday with them, helping to amuse Sammy and making him laugh.

Sunday, Penny and Neil had arrived, and as James had been quick to remark, 'Who on this earth could resist the charms of the beautiful Penny?' She not only had Sammy talking, she had him yelling with joy at the tricks she got up to for his benefit.

James was a hundred per cent certain that this was what he wanted. Given the chance he had vowed to himself that he would love and care for Samuel, never treating him any less than if he had been his son by birth.

For Barbara it was different.

God alone knew just how much she longed to bring Sammy home to their house and never have to take him back to Coombe Haven.

To wash and undress him and put him to bed. To read him stories. To wake up in the morning and go into his bedroom, find him all warm and still smelling of sleep. To bathe his knees when he fell over, to try and understand when he had a fit of bad temper, to be there for him. Always!

She was, however, faced with one of the most painful decisions she had ever had to make. She had to give herself definite answers to certain questions and on no account must she lie to herself. Could she agree with James, that they take Sammy and make him their son for the right reasons – or was she striving to atone for having given up her own child for adoption?

Whichever way she looked at it, Barbara decided she would be firm in her mind by the time it came to making the ultimate resolution. It was in a much happier frame of mind that she took Sammy back to Coombe Haven on the Monday after his second visit and stayed the day with him.

Paul and James picked her up from Croydon soon after three and they were back at the house by five o'clock.

Getting out of the car, Barbara noticed Maggie Harvey was watching her from the lounge window. Why was Maggie still here? She usually set their evening meal ready and went home about half past three.

Maggie had the door open before Barbara could set her key in the lock. 'Mr Holsworthy rang you, twice,' she reported, trying to hide her anxiety. 'He said to tell you Elizabeth has been taken into hospital and would you or James ring him at this number as soon as you got home.'

'Did he say what was wrong with Elizabeth?' Barbara took the slip of paper.

'No, only that she had been involved in an accident, but

372

Mr Warren phoned from the nursing home, he sounded very upset.'

Barbara turned to Paul and James in anguish. 'Something has happened to Elizabeth.'

James held his hand out to her, 'Paul will get the number for us. Thank you for staying, Maggie.'

'I'll see you all in the morning.' Maggie wanted to get away home, before she started crying.

They gathered around the phone in the hall.

'You're through to the General Hospital,' Paul said, handing the telephone to James.

Barbara couldn't bear the suspense. Neither could she interrupt the only side of the conversation that she could hear.

'Tim, don't worry yourself about Mr Warren, Paul will go straight over to the home and fetch him here. Yes, I know we have to face that possibility,' James was speaking so gently. 'We'll be here all night if you feel like ringing again later. It won't do any good if we go to pieces, Tim. We'll be with you first thing in the morning, but we'll speak again as soon as I've told Barbara what has happened.'

'Three days ago Elizabeth had a nasty fall. She was riding her bicycle, on her way to a meeting of the Women's Institute at the local village hall. Gashed her face and arm rather badly.' James's matter-of-fact tone heartened Barbara for an instant.

'The bad news is, during the examination the doctor discovered a lump in her left breast. They have admitted Elizabeth to hospital and today she has undergone a series of tests. We shall know the results in the morning.'

Barbara looked at him in dismay, her face white with shock.

'Come on now,' he said gently, 'let's not panic. It might not even be a tumour.'

'Have they taken X-rays?'

'Apparently an X-ray doesn't tell the doctors what they need to know.'

This wasn't real – it was a nightmare. Suppose it was breast cancer? The thought of sweet, gentle, Elizabeth being exposed to that kind of surgery!

'Did Tim say if there was any way of knowing yet?'

'If there was the doctors weren't saying,' James told them both. 'Tim said they had done their best to reassure him.'

'I wish we could go to Windsor right now.' Barbara was struggling to keep her voice calm.

'We'll go in the morning, get a real early start. Most important thing now is to comfort her father. Poor old chap. Tim felt he had to ring the home and the warden kindly offered to notify Mr Warren. He must be worried sick.'

Elizabeth sighed, 'I'll go up and make the bed in one of the spare rooms, he'll stay here with us, of course. Do you think, James, that he will be up to making the journey to Windsor?'

'I really don't know. Let's cross that bridge when we come to it. At worst we could leave him here with Maggie. For tonight the old man will feel much better knowing that he is with friends who really care about him and his daughter. Now go upstairs and see to his bed. Paul will be back shortly and we'll all have dinner together.'

It was a struggle for Barbara to swallow her food. She was grateful that Paul was there and that he and James kept the conversation going, making sure that Mr Warren didn't dwell too much on what had happened to Elizabeth.

In bed with James — she couldn't bear to be alone — Barbara lay awake, going over and over in her mind what might happen if things turned out badly. Why, oh why should this happen to Elizabeth, of all people?

There was no justice!

Staring into the darkness, she prayed as she had never done before.

'Barbara,' James reached for her, taking her into his arms. 'Elizabeth will be all right. Don't torment yourself, it won't help.'

'I keep thinking of the children. Did Tim say who was looking after them?'

'No, but we'll find all that out in the morning. Now go to sleep, my darling,' his voice was soothing.

'I'll try,' she whispered.

It was close to dawn before she fell into a troubled sleep. Maggie opening the bedroom door woke her and James.

Glancing at their alarm clock James saw it was only six thirty. 'I came early to make you all some breakfast. I presume you are going to Windsor.'

Barbara lay still, trying to prepare herself to face whatever this day was going to bring. Her eyes followed Maggie as she poured out the tea and took a cup round to James's side of the bed.

'I've taken a tray into Mr Warren and Paul was up and about when I got here,' Maggie said.

James made several phone calls but when Paul drove the car up to the front door, he, Barbara and Elizabeth's father were in the porchway, dressed and waiting. Barbara held the door open as James propelled his chair out in to the cold, sunlit morning. She turned and looked back, Maggie came at her with a rush, her strong arms going round Barbara's waist.

'I'll be praying you find things all right. Now don't take on so, ring me if you get a chance and if you're not back by the time I go home I'll take Oliver with me. I'll give him a bit of a run anyway, seeing as how Paul hasn't taken him out this morning.'

'You're a treasure. You know that, don't you?' Barbara said, brushing angrily at her eyes to wipe away the tears.

'Hope the traffic's light this morning,' Paul muttered, a hand at her elbow as he helped her into the car. 'We should be at the hospital in about two and a half hours.'

Barbara went into Elizabeth's room on her own. Tim was sitting beside the bed. Elizabeth looked as if she had been in a fight!

Dressed in a stiff, white, hospital gown rather than one of her own pretty nightdresses, her silky brown hair looked in need of a good brush. There was an angry looking bruise on her left cheek and a gash that ran the length of her chin, this wound had been stitched with black thread which served to make it look raw and ugly.

'Barbara!' Elizabeth pulled herself up on her elbows. 'Oh, it is lovely to see you but you shouldn't have come all this way. There isn't any need.'

'No need! Don't talk daft. Since when didn't we come running when one or the other of us was in trouble?'

'Well, now you are here, don't look so worried, darling. I'm going to be fine. You'll see.'

'Fine! You can't even ride a bike now, so I hear, without

falling off,' Barbara was doing her best to keep her tone light. Inside her heart was pounding.

'Thank you for coming, Barbara,' Tim rose to his feet and kissed her on both cheeks. He looked ghastly.

Before she could tell him that his father-in-law was outside with James and Paul, a nurse came into the room.

With a cheerfulness obviously meant to reassure them, she explained, 'I shall have to ask you to leave for a little while. Doctor Wimbourne will be here shortly with Mr Shard, and you, Mr Holsworthy, really should get some rest. We don't want to end up with you as a patient, now do we?'

Turning to Barbara, she urged, 'Take him along to the cafeteria, see that he drinks a good hot cup of tea and has something to eat.'

Paul queued up at the self-service counter, coming back to the table where they were sitting with a loaded tray.

'You've got to eat,' James told Tim, brushing aside his protests.

Tim did his best, only to please them, but all he could think about was Elizabeth. 'We had no hint of it,' he told them. '*Nothing.*'

'It'll probably turn out to be nothing,' James said.

No one answered him.

Two men in white coats approached. Tim obviously knew one of them, he rose to his feet. 'Hallo, Doctor Wimbourne. These are family friends.' He made the introductions. 'I'd like them to hear what you have to say.'

The doctor smiled and nodded, 'This is Mr Shard, he will

377

be the surgeon looking after your wife. We've scheduled for her surgery at nine o'clock tomorrow morning.'

'Then it is a tumour?' Barbara interrupted, the colour draining from her face.

'We have to face that possibility,' Mr Shard said gently. 'We have just discussed this with Mrs Holsworthy. If the biopsy shows that the growth is malignant, we'll go ahead and do a mastectomy immediately.'

Barbara flinched.

'But,' Mr Shard quickly added, 'we don't even know that it's malignant yet, so let's not fear the worse. Most tumours prove to be benign.'

'Does my wife really understand what might happen?'

'She understands, Tim,' Doctor Wimbourne said softly.

'Will I be able to go back in and see her before we leave?' Barbara struggled to keep the fear out of her voice.

'You'll all be able to see her as soon as the nurses have tidied her up. Please only two at a time, and don't stay too long.'

'Thank you, Doctor Wimbourne.'

James went in to the side ward with Barbara, he did his best to keep the conversation cheerful.

Barbara was choked right up when she came out of the room, having said an emotional goodbye to Elizabeth.

'She'll be all right,' James held out his hand to her, though to tell the truth he was feeling utterly helpless. 'Tim will phone us as soon as there is any news. We will all pray and you'll see, Elizabeth will come through with flying colours.'

In bed, Barbara lay awake. Staring into the darkness, wishing morning would come.

378

It was the longest day of their lives. Penny came and the two friends hugged each other. Lost for words.

Maggie made endless pots of tea and coffee.

It was three o'clock before the phone rang. On the second ring James picked up the receiver.

'It was malignant! Elizabeth hasn't come round yet, but the doctors are optimistic.'

Tim sounded whacked out but he insisted to James that he was spending the night in the hospital, 'I'll ring you again first thing in the morning. Goodnight James.'

Two days and there wasn't much change. On the third day Paul drove them back to Windsor.

They took it in turns to sit with Elizabeth. When the sun had set and dusk was settling outside the windows, they all feared the worse.

'I wish to God she'd wake up,' Barbara couldn't keep the tears from falling.

Paul patted Barbara's shoulder. 'I'm going with James to the bathroom and I'll get some tea for us on the way back. I won't be long.'

Barbara got to her feet, stretched and crossed to the open doorway. Nurses and doctors were going about their duties. Patients in wheelchairs and on crutches, others walking dressed in slippers and dressing-gowns, were talking to each other in the corridor. Visitors were arriving, clutching bunches of flowers. It was hard to believe.

She tried to focus on the fact that miracles did happen. She closed her eyes: Dear God, she has three little children, they need her.

'Barbara . . .' James's voice came to her from a room across the hall. She looked, his face was serious. Doctor

Wimbourne was talking to Elizabeth's father, Paul and James.

Barbara hesitated, took a deep breath and covered the distance between them.

'I am so sorry,' Doctor Wimbourne placed his hand on her arm. 'We did everything possible.'

'Thank you,' she had to force herself to say it.

Doctor Wimbourne turned to face the men, 'Your son-in-law is in Mr Shard's office, Mr Warren. If you and your friends would like to go and join him . . . he will be able to explain matters far better than I.'

Barbara felt she was sleep walking as Mr Warren took her arm, guiding her along behind Paul and James.

Mr Shard's voice droned on, 'In any surgical operation there is always an element of risk.'

'Mr Shard,' Barbara interrupted, 'we were told earlier that Elizabeth came through the operation well.'

'And so she did, my dear,' his voice held not only a note of sympathy but sincerity also.

'What happened after the operation is in medical terms, a pulmonary embolus. Unfortunately it is a complication that can occur after major surgery.'

Barbara shuddered.

Elizabeth's father must have asked a question. Mr Shard had swivelled his chair around to face the old gentleman.

'You are quite right, Mr Warren. A blood clot detached from the wall of a deep vein is swept into the bloodstream through the heart and along the pulmonary artery to the lung.'

Mr Warren tried hard to choke off a sob. Although his voice was only a whisper, they all heard him say, 'You never expect your children to die before you do yourself.' There was nothing more anyone could say.

Mr Shard rose to his feet, 'Please.' Tim had made to rise. 'Stay where you are. My office is at your disposal.' He hesitated, 'I am so sorry, words fail me.' With that he left the room, closing the door quietly behind him.

Oh Elizabeth! Elizabeth, kind, generous friend. Why? Why? She never did an unkind thing to anyone in her life.

Oh God, her poor children. How sad these little ones would grow up without a mother.

Scalding tears were running unchecked down Barbara's face. She was choking. Her nose was running and she felt so mad she wanted to smash anything that she could lay her hands on.

They left the office and waited in the reception room while Tim and his father-in-law went in to stay a while longer with Elizabeth, only now it wasn't Elizabeth. Only her body.

Tim and Mr Warren came out from the side ward. They both looked as if they had aged ten years.

Now it was the turn of Barbara and James to say their goodbyes to their dear friend and when they came back to join the men Barbara managed to a weak smile. 'Come on, you're coming home with us,' she said to Tim.

Elizabeth's body was being brought home to Alfriston to lie beside her mother in the small churchyard of St Andrew's, the parish church. Tim had gone to pieces, not caring whether he lived or died. James had made all the arrangements, urging Tim to sign all the necessary documents. William, John and Hannah were still in Yorkshire with Tim's parents, who weren't going to be able to attend the funeral. Both of them were elderly and Mr Holsworthy had confided to James, on the telephone, that he feared his wife was suffering the early states of senility. When Barbara had learnt of this she wondered briefly if she should insist that Tim bring the children home for the funeral and then decided against it.

The church was packed. Folk who had seen Elizabeth grow up in this peaceful village questioned the ways of a God of love that would take the life of a young wife and mother and leave her father – an old man and widower – to grieve and her husband to be driven half out of his mind.

Even before the flowers had died on the freshly-dug pile earth on Elizabeth's grave, Tim had left them.

Without hint or warning he had gone. Not back to work, Neil Chapman had been on the telephone daily to report that no one at the office had seen hide nor hair of him.

Letters and telephone calls from Tim's father in Yorkshire had then worried everyone as to how the old gentleman was coping with three children.

'What about the boys' schooling, James? Someone has to start considering things like that.' The children being so far away in Yorkshire was worrying Barbara more than she would admit.

James swung his chair away from the table and drew up close to her. 'You're right of course. In the long term there are loads of problems that need to be sorted; meanwhile, as soon as I get to the office tomorrow I will get my secretary to telephone the welfare people, they'll contact Yorkshire and make sure that help is at hand.'

Barbara wiped her mouth with her serviette, they'd finished dinner and sweet and coffee could wait a while.

'James, there's another matter I want to talk to you about: Sammy! I'm longing to see him and yet I dread to think what his reaction will be. It's been ten days since I've been near Coombe Haven.'

'That's hardly been your fault, my darling. Matron will have done her best to explain your absence to Samuel.'

'That's all very well,' she moaned. 'How do you go about telling a two-year-old little boy that you hadn't been near nor by him because one of your best friends had died.'

'Now stop blaming yourself,' James said sternly. 'It has been a trying time for all of us. Unfortunately, as in many things, innocent people get caught up in the repercussions; in this case, sadly it is a little boy. All you can do is have patience, show him that you *do* love him and hope for the best.'

Hope for the best was right, but she feared the worst!

Barbara had arrived at Coombe Haven so early that the children hadn't quite finished their breakfast. She stood in the doorway of the dining room watching, unable to control the trembling of her legs.

Hilda put the last spoonful of boiled egg into Sammy's mouth, wiped his lips clean and lifted him down from his chair. Today he was dressed in blue dungarees and a canary-yellow shirt. He looked gorgeous! His hair was still unruly, a mass of tight curls. She wanted to rush in, to swing him up in her arms, hug him tight, but decided not to.

'Sammy,' she called, opening her arms wide, praying he would come to her. He didn't move.

'Yer daft 'apeth,' said Hilda briskly and gave him a push

with her hand. 'Go and give Barbara a kiss, I kept telling yer, didn't I, that she would be back? Well, she's come back – so go on, be quick.'

Sammy walked slowly. 'No, no, no,' he muttered to himself. Suddenly his pace quickened, he flew across the room, his right leg dragging badly in such motion.

Barbara let go of her handbag and bent her knees to receive the little arms that she hoped would lock around her neck. That wasn't what happened. Fists flying, feet kicking, his cheeks turning a flaming red with sheer temper, Sammy laid into Barbara, so unexpectedly that she lost her balance and reeled over backwards to lie on the floor.

Hilda ran to her assistance. Barbara waved her away. She sat up but remained on the floor. Sammy was crying now, not softly as he used to, but great yells and screams, letting out all his resentment until the yells turned to hiccups, his breathing became tight and his face was a bleary mess. Still Barbara sat on the floor and waited.

Reluctantly, at last, he leaned against her. Lifted his head and examined her face long and hard. 'You didn't come.'

The words broke her heart.

'Oh Sammy. I couldn't come. I wasn't well.' It was a bad lie, but the best she could think of.

Slowly the red-rimmed blue eyes melted in forgiveness and his arms crept up to cling around her neck.

Barbara let out a long sigh of relief. Calmly, gently, she put her arms around his wriggling, warm, sweet-smelling little body; he shuddered and the movement frightened her. Carefully she got to her feet, still clasping him in her arms.

If only she could shield this small boy from all the knocks

of this world. Surely he had had more than his fair share already in his young life?

She made a promise to herself: in future she would do everything that she possibly could to see that he never had reason to cry like that ever again.

In a very short space of time, Samuel Rowlings became very much part of Barbara's and James's life. They had him home for two days on alternate weekends, gaining so much pleasure from his visits that life without him now was unthinkable.

'Let's take him to the seaside, next time he's here,' Maureen O'Connor sounded as excited as a child herself.

'Well,' she said, seeing that not only Paul but Barbara and James were also laughing at her. 'That wee mite would creep his way into the hearts of the saints, so he would. Tell me now, be honest, which one of you could refuse him the moon, if that's what he was yearning for? Sure an' away that angelic look he turns on would melt the heart of our Blessed Lady, never mind us poor mortals.'

It was true, Barbara thought to herself. That lively, lovely boy had everyone he came into contact with eating out of his hand. Her own parents adored him. James's entire family had taken him to their hearts. Even Colin Peterson and Clem Tompson were talking about teaching the lad to ride.

It was still only the first week in May, not yet exactly summer, but that didn't deter Maureen, she was determined to have her way. Cold as the weather was, Sammy's next visit was enlivened by a visit to Norman's Bay. A mile further on than Eastbourne, Norman's Bay boasted a silver, sandy beach at low tide. Wrapped up well in jerseys, woolly hats and scarves, they made a colourful picture as they set off down the almost deserted beach. Leaving Paul and James to watch from the open doors of the car, Maureen and Barbara held tightly to Sammy's hands, swinging him back and forth as they ran. Sometimes his little feet left the shingle to swish through the air, much to Sammy's delight as he yelled, 'Again, again!'

The little boy had never seen the sea before and was, at first, terrified of the noise it made and of its bouncing waves. Barbara stood one side of him and Maureen on the other, right at the edge of the water, pulling him backwards as the waves rolled in to lap at their wellington boots. Sammy tore off his gloves, and once or twice bent to trail his hand in the foam that was left behind as the waves receded with the tide.

'Come back,' he called out, his eyes wide with wonder, his cheeks rosy with the excitement of it all.

'Brrr, it's too cold to stay here,' Barbara declared loudly. 'We'll look amongst the stones on the way back up to the car, see if we can find some pretty shells, shall we?'

Maureen dried Samuel's hands on the towel she had brought with her, Barbara brushed the sand from the seat of his damp dungarees because twice he had decided to sit himself down.

'Come along – ' she stooped and hoisted Sammy up into her arms, and led the way back up the beach.

'I see the sea!' Sammy yelled, throwing himself at Paul's legs.

'We know – we've been watching you.'

Sammy wriggled free and Paul helped him to clamber up onto the back seat of the car, landing with a thump into James's lap.

'I see the sea,' he repeated. 'Look.' He unclenched his

little fists and held out a collection of shiny shells. 'Mine,' he declared as James went to touch them.

'May I see them? *Please*,' James pretended to plead.

Sammy considered for a moment, opened one fist and said, 'Yes.'

'Was the sea nice?' James asked.

'Wet,' he shouted, then chuckled as he took back the two shells that James had been inspecting.

Slowly, one at a time, Sammy laid the shells out in a circle on the seat of the car. He was totally absorbed in this occupation. His dimpled fingers were red with the cold. He persevered in laying them right side up.

Watching him, filled with fondness, James wondered about Sammy's vulnerability. He felt so protective of this child that seemed to have found his way into his heart, not to mention that of Barbara and the rest of their friends and family. Let's hope the matter would be resolved to the satisfaction of all concerned, it was certainly taking a long time, he thought.

The whole situation was tricky, to say the least of it. When he had first suggested to Barbara that they might consider adopting Samuel, she had, at first, appeared to be frightened, then overcome with joy. He was well aware that for the two of them to take this extraordinary step was somehow a marvellous opportunity. But not one to be taken lightly.

Once his firm had agreed to set the wheels in motion the subject had been avoided. With no questions from Barbara, no answers had to be found by him. Which was just as well, for he had none to give.

Everything hinged on gaining the consent of Samuel's

father and as to yet, despite great efforts, he had not been traced.

Barbara climbed into the car and lifted Sammy from James's lap to sit on the seat between them. She looked across and saw the expression on her husband's face. He was not looking at her, he was looking at Sammy. He was looking really proud, as proud as if the little boy was their own flesh and blood.

Chapter Twenty-five

THE WEEKEND THEY would long remember with regret began with the arrival of Penny and Neil Chapman. Conversation was light and friendly until dinner was over.

Barbara passed the mints round. Penny put a restraining hand on her arm, 'How long is it since you or James have seen Tim?'

'I can't put my finger on the exact date,' Barbara answered. 'Tim has only stayed here with us once since Elizabeth's funeral. I've written to him, he doesn't answer and his telephone appears to have been disconnected.'

Neil sighed, sat down close to James. 'Sorry,' he said. 'There's no way of wrapping this up.'

'You're going to tell us that Tim has gone to pieces, hasn't been to work?' James muttered. 'He was in a pretty bad way when we last saw him. We tried, so did Paul, weren't able to get through to him. Letting himself go, if you want the truth. Barbara tried to persuade him to go up to Yorkshire, see something of the twins and Hannah. It can't have been easy on those children, can it?'

'He's fast becoming an alcoholic,' Neil's voice was low as he made the statement.

'What?'

'That's right, James, no other word for it. He hasn't been home to Windsor in weeks, he's taken a flat in London. I think the drinking started as a little something to help him get over Elizabeth's death. Who could blame him for that? Poor sod.'

Neil stood up and began to pace the carpet.

'How did you find out?' Barbara wanted to know.

Neil shook his head. 'You don't want to hear all the details. Believe me – you don't. In fact I would much rather you girls took yourselves upstairs, or wherever, and left me to tell James the facts.'

'Wait a minute, Neil. This is a rotten shame and if there is anything we can do – ' Barbara's voice trembled.

'It's not a shame, Barbara, it's a illness.'

'Well if Tim is so ill, shouldn't we be taking him to see a doctor?'

'You think we haven't tried?' Penny cut in. 'He won't go.'

'Perhaps we ought to make sure that a doctor pays a visit to this flat of his, don't you think so Neil?' By now James was the only one who was speaking softly.

'My father has already done that. He values Tim, not only as a friend but as a good employee. Tim handled some of our largest accounts. He's missed in the firm.'

'What happened?' James asked.

With a half-smile on his lips, Neil reluctantly told them, 'Tim laid one on the doctor. He was stoned out of his mind. Punched the doctor straight in the face.'

Both the girls sighed.

Barbara spoke first, 'Such a pity! We'll have to find a way to help him.'

Penny cleared her throat, 'There's more. Worse in a way.'

'Worse?' James frowned. 'How?'

'Neil and I went up to Yorkshire. We thought his parents

might be able to help. Poor souls, they need help themselves.'

Neil took up the story. 'We couldn't bring ourselves to
tell his father about Tim's alcoholism. They certainly have
enough troubles of their own without us adding to them.'

'Yes,' Penny chipped in. 'That visit was a ghastly nightmare. I've never felt so helpless in the whole of my life.'

'I won't wrap it up. I'll give it to you straight.' Even to
himself Neil's voice sounded angry. 'Tim's father was not
strong enough to cope with the situation. His loyalties were
torn between the grandchildren and his wife. He has sent
the twins to a boarding school, and the social workers have
found a place for Hannah with foster-parents. It would
have been madness for him to have done otherwise. There
are so many complications with Mrs Holsworthy now. Her
husband clings to the hope that she will recover, but of
course she never will. It isn't safe to leave her alone for a
minute. Poor woman has lost so much weight and her
mind, well, eventually I suppose she will have to be admitted to a home.'

'But why did the children have to stay in Yorkshire?'
Barbara asked. 'Why couldn't Tim have made arrangements
for them to be looked after in their own home?'

'I've asked myself that same question time without
number, and I haven't been able to come up with any
sensible answer,' Penny sounded resentful.

'I know how you must be feeling,' Barbara reassured her.
'Bad enough that the children lost their mother, surely the
one person they need to be with is their father, not an
elderly grandfather and a grandmother who is desperately
ill.'

'Stop getting so hot under the collar, you two, it won't

help to solve anything,' James brought himself back into the discussion. 'I think we are all agreed that something will have to be done. With the long summer holidays coming up it would be wrong to leave those children up there in school, and the baby with strangers. They are used to us and with the nice weather they can play in the fields and run wild down by the sea. There are enough of us, with our families to help, to surely see to three children. We owe it to Elizabeth.'

'That's exactly what Penny and I agreed,' Paul smiled now. 'And this seems the right time to tell you: we have rented a cottage down here for three months, we intend to look for a place to buy, we've had enough of London, besides – ' he paused, turning to Penny. 'You want to tell them?'

'I'm going to have a baby.'

The words weren't out of Penny's mouth before Barbara was by her side. 'Oh, congratulations! That's wonderful, how long?'

'Three months, a Christmas baby if all goes well.'

'It will, of course it will. James, isn't it marvellous! We'll have them as neighbours again and a new baby into the bargain.'

'Hold your horses,' Neil laughed. 'We haven't found anything to buy yet. Besides, to get back to the serious question, what are we going to do about Tim?'

It was James who answered for them all, 'Enjoy the weekend, the weather is set to be fine and warm, and first thing Monday morning we'll all travel up to town together and pay a visit to Tim in this new flat of his. Between us we should be able to talk some sense into him.'

'Or get some help for him. It's very possible that he is

going to resent our interfering in what he will regard as his own business.'

James stared at Neil as he finished speaking. He realised with some astonishment that he was angry about the way Tim had palmed his children off onto his parents.

'Well,' he said aloud. 'All of us turning up out of the blue should take the wind out of his sails.'

The flat that Tim had rented was part of a Victorian mansion in Gloucester Road, Kensington. By good chance they found two parking places in the carpark quite close to Gloucester Road station. As a group they arrived at the foot of the wide marble steps that led up to the front door.

'Stay there,' Neil said to the girls and turned to Paul who was standing beside James's wheelchair. 'I'll go up and ring the bell. Looks as if there is a list of occupants' names on that wall there.' He ran up the steps, before he had reached the top step the massive door was flung open wide, and a slim tall man in a well-fitting suit, wearing a trilby hat, made to push past Neil.

'Who the hell are you?' the man rudely asked.

Neil was silenced by astonishment; he stared, opened-mouthed.

'Well? I asked you a question.'

Recovering quickly Neil said, 'I'm looking for a Timothy Holsworthy.'

Before he could say another word the man began to pull at his arm. 'I say, I do apologise, it's been a heck of a night for me, and now this. I'm Detective Sergeant Whicker, Kensington Police.'

Neil turned and glanced at Penny and the others still waiting anxiously on the pavement.

'I think you had all better come in,' the detective indicated with a nod of his head.

Minutes later, they were assembled in a very large, well-furnished room, which lay on the right hand side of the wide hallway, overlooking the busy Gloucester Road. Detective Whicker kicked the door shut, flung a bunch of keys and two white envelopes onto a table, looked at each of them in turn, then in a very quiet voice said, 'Before I ask you to identify yourselves, I'm very sorry but I have to tell you that Mr Holsworthy is dead.'

Penny said, 'Oh no, I'm sorry, but I think you're making a terrible mistake.'

Neil reached for her hand and held it between both of his.

Barbara moved to stand between James and Paul.

The silence in the room now was disturbing. The awareness of the truth of what the man said, hit them all. To Barbara it was really frightening. She flinched from the stare of this stranger. She had a feeling she had been along this road before, when Michael died.

James spoke first. 'I'm a partner in a law firm, Bradley and Summerford. If you will outline to us what has happened, I will take it from there.'

The detective recognised the voice of authority.

'Tenant in the flat opposite spoke to an officer early this morning. The lady was worried, no sign of Mr Holsworthy. The constable knocked, got no reply, contacted the station for permission to enter. The gentleman was dead. Two letters beside him, one addressed to the coroner, the second – ' he broke off, went to the table and picked up the two letters, peering closely at the writing, 'is addressed to James Ferguson.'

Somewhere in the house a telephone rang, a motorhorn sounded out in the street and a dog could be heard barking. No one in the room moved or spoke. Suddenly everything came together. Shock, pity for Tim, regret that they hadn't acted more quickly, impatience and anger that Tim should take the easy way out, dumping the whole mess on his elderly father. Everything.

But mainly, what Barbara was feeling was panic, and at the same time she was so afraid.

Detective Whicker cleared his throat. 'I'm sorry. Always a nasty business. I must be on my way.'

'I take it we can get all the information, identification, date of inquest, and such like, from the station; is that right, Detective Whicker?' James asked.

Reluctant to confirm too much, the policeman took a card from his wallet, handed it to James, before he formed an answer. 'Telephone number is on there, sir. My superior will give you all the assistance you need. If you don't mind though, sir, I shall have to see you all off the premises. I have to lock up, keep the place tight until our boys have finished all the paper work.'

They came out of the house into brilliant sunshine and a clear blue sky. James reached for Barbara's hand and together they looked upwards, the sun felt warm and bright on their faces.

'James, tell me,' Barbara whispered, 'tell me, between us haven't we had enough trouble to last a lifetime? I don't think I can take much more.'

'Listen to me! We weren't to know that things had got to such a pitch with Tim. Blaming ourselves isn't going to help anyone, least of all his three children. You think because Tim couldn't face the thought of living without

395

Elizabeth, he didn't give one iota for the twins and Hannah? Do you?'

'Yes,' Barbara said cruelly.

'My feelings exactly,' said Penny, as she covered her face with her hands. 'We might feel differently later, but at the moment I can't help it. I don't think he gave a thought as to what would happen to his kids. He hasn't been near them in months.'

'Hey, steady on, old girl,' Neil put his arms around his wife's shoulders. 'We none of us know how we would react in the same circumstances. God forbid we ever have to find out.'

'I think perhaps we had better make a move,' Paul said. 'You girls stay there with James. Neil and I will fetch the cars.'

Barbara's and Penny's mood had shifted, the anger had subsided, absolute shock had taken over.

'If only,' Barbara muttered to no one in particular.

Penny knew exactly what she meant.

If only they had come up to town on Saturday morning, straight after their discussion on Friday evening. The weather had been lovely, the sunshine hot, they had spent a relaxed happy weekend together.

Tim had been on his own.

Everything had been left in order. A valid will. Everything he owned, was left in trust, equally shared, between his three children.

The letter to the coroner stated that Tim had decided that William, John and Hannah should go to live with James and Barbara Ferguson, if they were willing, and that he wished for the Court to appoint James Ferguson as their legal guardian.

The letter, written to James, had been very brief: 'Try to forgive me. There is no life without Elizabeth.'

'A sad business,' James said, his eyes shining with tears as he passed the note to Barbara.

She read it, looked away. Too choked to answer.

James waited. 'Do you want us to take the children?'

Barbara nodded her head, 'Why is it we never realise how much we love a person, until that person dies? Those children are orphans. Why? Why?'

There was no answer.

'Only the children matter now,' James remarked. 'The kindest thing we can do is bring them home, care for them, show them we really love them, want them, let them know that this is their home.'

'I'll do my best,' Barbara declared.

'I know. I know you will. Once they, and we, get over the blinding pain of loss and the terrible shock of it all, together we'll both do our best to make sure that they feel secure and that they have a happy life.'

It was agreed that the three children should stay in Yorkshire until the end of July when the boys' term at the boarding school would end.

A nagging thought was hammering away in Barbara's head. She could cope. She was determined to cope. Finding a school for the twins would be no problem. Hannah was a different matter, she was not yet two-and-a-half-years-old.

Maureen had offered to give up her job at The Smuggler's in order to help Barbara. James had immediately offered her full-time employment, which she had gladly accepted.

What a blessing in disguise Maureen O'Connor had turned out to be. Now Maureen Soames. She and Paul had slipped away quietly to Eastbourne one weekend and had been married in Eastbourne Town Hall.

Deprived of the opportunity to pay for a reception, James had bought them several beautiful pieces of furniture to go into the cottage which had been renovated so well.

With Maggie Harvey coming in daily Monday to Friday and now Maureen on hand to do whatever needed doing, which would include driving the boys to school and meeting them in the afternoons, Barbara counted herself very lucky indeed. The main problem now being, how would she fit in her visits to Coombe Haven? So far she hadn't missed any, and she had no intention of doing so.

For once fate intervened in a kindly way.

It was the second Thursday in July. Barbara was at Coombe Haven, out in the garden with most of the other helpers and almost all of the children. With Sammy contented enough in the sandpit, Barbara leant back on her elbows and turned her face to the sun.

'You're looking much better, in fact you look bright-eyed and bushy-tailed. Something good must have happened to you for a change. About time, I'd say.' Brenda Smith was smiling across at Barbara from the swing-chairs.

'Not really, Brenda,' Barbara called. 'It's just that it's such a lovely morning, everything's all bright and colourful. To tell you the truth I could use some good news.'

'Oh, about young Sam, you mean? Officialdom never was noted for their speedy results, we all know that. Besides in Samuel's case, he still has a father somewhere, must be taking time to get a trace of him. Out of the blue, you'll see, the conclusion will be a happy ending.'

Her enthusiasm was endearing. 'You really think so?'

'Yes I do.' She looked at her watch. 'It's lunchtime.'

Barbara sat up and called to Sammy, stretching out her arms to lift him up onto the grass.

Brenda said again, only loudly this time, 'It's time for lunch.'

In a group, ladies and children, they moved towards the house.

'I'll take 'im,' Hilda said as Barbara reached the dining room. 'Matron wants a word wiv you.'

Ivy's expression, as she waved Barbara to a chair, had Barbara's spirits soaring.

'You've had some news?'

'Yes. They've traced the father.'

'And?'

'He's living in New Zealand, he's married again. Apparently he had no objection to his son being put up for adoption.'

'Why didn't someone tell me? Why didn't they discuss it with me.'

'I don't know. It's just their way I suppose.'

'And when will it all go through? Become legal?'

Seeing Ivy frown and the straight set of her mouth was suddenly frightening to Barbara, and she was pleased when Ivy spoke again.

'It isn't that I want to dampen your hopes but I can't stand by and watch you be disappointed.'

'How can I be disappointed when you've just said that Samuel's father has agreed for him to be adopted?'

'It's not as simple as that, Barbara, and you know it.

399

Adoption is a lengthy business, the courts have to be thoroughly satisfied before their final consent is given.'

Lengthy business! Barbara felt sick at the thought of it.

'There is one ray of hope. With the approval of the committee of this home there is always a chance that the Court would allow you and James to have custodianship of Samuel. As the child has already been made a ward of court that would not be an unusual step for them to take.'

Barbara stared at her. Then suddenly, she shook her head and laughed, 'I should pay more attention to what my husband tells me. He spoke of this some weeks ago. It appears that you are now telling me exactly what James said his partners were aiming for. Custody, under supervision, while an adoption order is considered.'

Ivy Pearson bent and picked up a piece of paper from the floor, folded it neatly and stared out of the window and prayed, 'Don't let this nice couple be turned down. They can give a good home to a little boy that nobody else wanted because he was disfigured. And most of all they will give him love and he will love them in return. When a child from this home is offered a fresh start it makes this job so worthwhile.'

The house rang with laughter. There had never been a better summer and James was convinced that he had never before seen Barbara looking so happy. It had taken a while for William and John to settle in, but with James taking a month off from the office and Paul around at all times, not to mention Clem down in the stables, the boys had never once been left to their own devices. Hannah had taken to living in Jevington like a duck takes to water. The little girl had attached herself to Sammy straight off; he still being scared of strangers, and a little bit jealous if the truth be known, refused to speak to her at first.

'Perseverance must be little Hannah's middle name,' James remarked as he sat beside Barbara beneath the tree, listening to her repeat nursery rhymes.

'Jack an' Jill went up the . . .' Hannah paused, and waited. Sammy jerked his head forward, took a deep breath and yelled: 'Hill!' Hannah put her two dimpled little hands together and clapped.

Sam chuckled at his own cleverness.

James swallowed hard. He still found it unbelievable that they had four children living under their roof.

Barbara smiled. She had established a great rapport with Helen Brown, the social worker who dropped in unannounced from time to time to see how Samuel was faring. None the more for that, she would feel a whole lot more at peace with the world once the court had made the order permitting James and herself to become the legal parents of Samuel Rowlings.

She chided herself to have more patience. The day would come, she had to believe that much, when Sammy's name would be entered in the Adopted Children's Register. All the new information could be recorded and then Samuel would be issued a new full birth certificate.

From that day forth she would sleep more soundly. When that day dawned he would become, legally, Samuel Ferguson. Son of James and Barbara Ferguson.

Chapter Twenty-six

WEEKENDS WERE ALWAYS special and this one was going to be marvellous. Tomorrow would be Easter Sunday 1965. Barbara and James were about to celebrate their tenth wedding anniversary. Everyone would be here. The house would come alive, resounding with boisterous laughter.

Barbara looked out into the garden to where James and Paul were preparing everything for tomorrow.

'The marquee has gone up a treat,' James told her as he wheeled himself into the kitchen.

'That's great, a safeguard in case it rains, though the forecast is good. Would you like a cup of tea?'

'That's what I've come in for,' he smiled.

'And there's me thinking it was because you love to look at me!'

'Pour the tea out, woman, and don't be getting ideas like that into your head!'

Barbara, feeling a glow as she always did when James was around, took the cosy from the pot and filled a cup for him.

'Boys arriving home tonight?' he asked idly.

'I'm not sure. Expect they will ring later. If not tonight, you can bet your boots they'll be home by the crack of dawn.'

'Fill one of those big mugs with tea and I'll take it out to Paul when I've drunk mine.'

With the kitchen to herself again, Barbara poured herself

a second cup of tea and sat slowly sipping it, letting her mind wander back over these past ten years. She couldn't believe how quickly they had flown, nor how happy they had been.

Before she had wed James, she had been through hell. Having told the details of her first marriage to James, details she had never told another living person, it had made no difference to him; he had insisted that his love for her was so great that he would settle for nothing short of marriage. How could she not love him with all of her heart?

Even then disaster had struck. James had almost lost his life in that car crash. When finally they had started their married life she had felt herself to be worthless. James, with sheer guts and determination, had gone back to practising law, while all she had to do was keep the house clean and tidy. James's sister, Chloe, and her husband Anthony, had come to her rescue – only Anthony wasn't her husband then, she reminded herself.

The clinic in Vauxhall had been her first try at voluntary work. At this memory, Barbara felt herself shudder: the poverty and the shameful way some little children were made to suffer. Then had come Coombe Haven and Sammy. It was as if a lifeline had been thrown to her. A chance to redress some of the wrongs of her earlier life.

Next there had been the death of Elizabeth. To this day she had never been able to come to terms with that, and James and she had been devastated when Tim had taken his own life.

'The lights are not working properly.'

Paul had thrust his head through the open kitchen window and the sound of his voice brought her back to the present with a start.

'What?'

Paul laughed. 'You were miles away, weren't you? I said I can't get the lights to work; the first lot we've put up amongst the trees are fine, the ones we are trying to string nearer to the house need some new bulbs. I'm taking the car down to the village, just thought I'd let you know.'

'Fine. I'm glad the marquee is up, ready for the caterers. I couldn't face organising all the food that we shall need.'

The telephone rang, Paul waved a hand, calling, 'I won't be long,' and Barbara went to take the call.

'Mum!'

Her heart leapt with joy.

'It's me, John. Wills has gone to take some of his books back to the research lab, but we'll both be getting a lift; should be home by seven.'

'All right my darling, we'll keep dinner for you.'

'Good-oh, hope it's a roast. See you later.'

She heard the click of the phone as it went dead. She held the receiver against her cheek for a second before she replaced it.

Mum! It always thrilled her to hear the twins call her and James 'Mum and Dad'. James had never officially adopted Elizabeth and Tim's three children, he hadn't thought it right to take away their surname. Legal Guardian had served well. Neither had they asked to be called anything other than Barbara and James. It had come about when the boys had been attending Eastbourne College; always encouraged to bring their friends home, the twins had soon fallen into the habit of saying 'This is our Mother and Father,' when making the introductions. The habit had never altered. Incredible. They were both in their first term at Sussex University now. Her mind went wandering off again. How well she remembered the Christmas that they had been born.

She had come home to her parents, battered and bruised in both mind and body. She had also given birth to a son. And without giving a thought to the consequences or to the heartbreak she would have to endure, she had agreed to have him adopted.

Only weeks later she and Penny had been Christmas shopping in London, touring stores like Hamleys where they had bought soft toys as presents for Elizabeth's new-born babies. Without knowing the tragic truth, Penny had dragged her off to visit Elizabeth in the nursing home where she had had to hide her own feelings as she watched Penny drool over those two tiny boys.

Envious, that's how she had felt. Guilty too. Oh yes, very guilty. With her mind so much in the past today, Barbara found herself hoping and praying that, whoever the couple were, and wherever they lived, that had adopted her child, they might love him and care for him as much as she and James cared for the four children that had come to be the light of their lives. She felt that must be so, they wouldn't have adopted a child if they weren't intending to be loving parents. They would be repaid ten-fold if her experience was anything to go by.

Toot-toot. That was the mini. Maureen was back from the school run. Barbara quicken her steps and she had the front door open as Maureen pulled the car to a halt.

Oh, just look at Sam! How *did* he manage to look so grubby when he came out of school, whereas Hannah, with books held under her arm and a satchel slung over one shoulder, still looked as if she had stepped out of a bandbox.

Amazing the bond that still existed between these two. Oh, they had their squabbles like any other normal brother and sister, but harm one and you had the other one to deal with. Barbara felt her heart swell with love as she watched them come flying towards her.

Hannah reached her first. Everything was dropped onto the porch step, arms were flung around her mother's waist and her cheek was being given a warm wet kiss.

'Hallo Mum, may I go down to the stables as soon as I've changed?'

'Give yourself time to get into the house,' Barbara laughed as she hugged Hannah.

Wham! not much altered with Sam. He got his mother's attention one way or another, Barbara thought to herself as he too planted a kiss on her cheek.

'Mum, I'm starving.' He could still look so pitiful when he chose.

'You always are,' she teased.

There was just a year between these two. Hannah being eleven was the spitting image of her mother; she also had the same kind, gentle nature that Elizabeth had had. She was truly a lovely child and being the only girl around the place, men and boys alike were very protective of her.

With Sammy it was uncanny. At the age of twelve he hadn't lost his fair complexion, not yet his head of tight fair curls – much to his annoyance. He hated being teased about his curls and would spend a great deal of time in the bathroom trying to flatten them straight with a wet comb. His colouring being so very much the same as James's made him a natural Ferguson, and no one needed telling twice how proud both she and James were to have him as their legal son.

406

Twice Sam had been into hospital, each time to have an operation on his top lip and to the roof of his mouth. The ugly red gash, which had been so prominent on his top lip, had long since disappeared. All that remained of his harelip now was a thin white scar. William and John were forever telling him that nobody noticed it, but if it worried him they reassured him he could always grow a moustache when he grew older.

Once he had come to the dinner-table with a black pencil line drawn over the scar and extended to form a moustache. Barbara had been terrified as to what his reaction would be if anyone laughed.

It had been Sammy himself who had broken the silence, laughing out loud as he had said, 'Now you know what I shall look like when I am old!'

His words had had them all in hysterics, more so when his father had said he needn't wash it off until after dinner.

Buttering tea-cakes and filling glasses with milk to keep these two going until dinnertime, Barbara laughed to herself. There had been no shortage of joy and laughter since the four children had come into this house.

Barbara woke early, she had spent the night downstairs in James's bed, as she did so much more often as time had gone by. The sun was already shining through an opening in the curtains: it was going to be a lovely day. She turned in his arms, and buried her face in his chest.

'Happy anniversary, my darling,' he whispered against her hair.

Barbara thought for one awful moment that she was going to start the day by crying. Don't be so ridiculous, she told herself, what in heaven's name have you got to cry about? 'I love you, James, very very much.'

'I love you too,' he answered, 'I don't think you can possibly know just how much.'

Now she did cry.

James laughed and held her close.

They lay there, making plans for the day. 'So many people are going to be here.'

'Yes,' James agreed. 'And if we don't get a move on they will start arriving before we are even dressed.'

It was not only a lovely day. It was wonderful.

Barbara sat at a table just inside the marquee. James was seated in his chair across from her. 'Just look at them all,' she murmured.

Most of the adults had come inside for their lunch which was being served superbly by the caterers.

There were grandparents, parents, god-parents and friends. Outside a great mass of children were enjoying themselves.

James's brother Rodney and his wife Elaine waved. Over to the right stood Jack Tully who was married to James's sister Ann.

'Good God!' Barbara suddenly said to James. 'Just goes to show that we don't see enough of our families. Look at the size of Ann's children: Harry and Lucy must be turned eighteen by now.'

'Here's to many more happy years.' A head came over Barbara's shoulder and she twisted round to kiss Chloe. Anthony was shaking hands with James.

'I've just rescued Oliver from the clutches of a gang of youngsters: they were trying to have rides on his back, but that dog wasn't standing for that,' Anthony told them, fighting to keep the laughter out of his voice. 'It's a job to know to whom all these children belong to on a day like this.'

'Well I expect your two were in the fray somewhere,' Barbara replied.

'Our two weren't.' Penny came round the back of James's wheelchair and flopped down onto a seat beside Barbara.

'Hannah has taken our Jane off to the stables. I begged them to keep themselves clean but I've a feeling I was talking to myself. Clive is all right, he and Sam have got the grandfathers to organise a three-legged race when we've all finished eating.'

Barbara covered Penny's hand with one of her own, feeling enormous pleasure that her dear friend was here today. Not that she didn't see a great deal of Penny. Neil had bought 'Walled in House', a mile or so up the road: a rambling old farm house that, in the last eight years, had come alive, restored by skilful workmen to its former glory and enhanced by the birth of their son, Clive, and two years later their daughter Jane.

The daylight was almost gone.

Paul and Neil, like two pied-pipers, led the way through the garden to the field beyond; children followed, a straggling laden procession.

Between the wall and the orchard, far away from the stables, wooden frames had been set up to hold the fireworks and here everyone set down their boxes and formed a circle.

Whoosh, the first rocket made for the sky, sending a

shower of coloured sparks shooting outwards. Young voices were raised in glee as the firework display got underway.

Only the youngest members of the families had accompanied the children, the older ones preferring the warmth of the house and a well-earned drink.

Barbara and James were out on the porch alone.

'Have you enjoyed today, Barbara?' James's voice was unusually soft.

'More than I can put into words,' she answered.

'So you don't mind spending another ten years with me then?'

'Oh James! More than that! Another *fifty*, please God.'

'We'll both be very old by then, maybe we'll be grand-parents, or even great-grandparents, who knows?'

'Who knows indeed!' They both laughed and James took hold of her hand, and together they waited for their children to come back up to the house. A house that had become a family home for all of them.